Mrs. Leith-Adams

**Robert Ord's Atonement**

A Novel

Mrs. Leith-Adams

**Robert Ord's Atonement**
*A Novel*

ISBN/EAN: 9783337007546

Printed in Europe, USA, Canada, Australia, Japan

Cover: Foto ©Andreas Hilbeck / pixelio.de

More available books at **www.hansebooks.com**

# ROBERT ORD

## A Novel

BY

## ROSA NOUCHETTE CAREY

AUTHOR OF 'NELLIE'S MEMORIES,' 'BARBARA HEATHCOTE'S TRIAL,'
'NOT LIKE OTHER GIRLS,' ETC.

*POPULAR EDITION*

LONDON

RICHARD BENTLEY & SON, NEW BURLINGTON STREET

Publishers in Ordinary to Her Majesty the Queen

1892

TO

MY BROTHERS

# CONTENTS.

*CONTENTS.*

# ROBERT ORD'S ATONEMENT.

## CHAPTER I.

### THE KING'S HEAD.

" The sultry summer day is done,
The western hills have hid the sun,
But mountain peak and village spire
Retain reflection of his fire.
Old Barnard's towers are purple still,
To those that gaze from Toller's hill ;
Distant and high, the tower of Bowes
Like steel upon the anvil glows,
And Stainemore's ridge, behind that lay
Rich with the spoils of parting day,
In crimson and in gold array'd."

Scott's Rokeby.

" I used him for a friend,
Before I ever knew him for a friend.
'Twas better, 'twas worse also, afterwards
We came so close, we saw our differences
Too intimately."

Aurora Leigh.

" BARNARD CASTLE."

"All right for Barnard Castle. Any luggage, sir ?" was the
civil inquiry addressed to the solitary occupant of a second-class
compartment who was leisurely folding his paper and shaking off
a liberal allowance of dust as he did so. "Any luggage in the
van, sir ?" ·

A shake of the head was the somewhat curt rejoinder as the
gentleman gave *The Leeds Mercury* a final fold, and shouldering
his shabby black bag stepped on the platform, looking about him
with the air of a man who was treading new ground, and who
seemed to deduce a certain amount of pleasure from that fact,
judging from the curious glances he cast around him as he threaded
the little knot of passengers and porters who blocked up the narrow
doorway.

Out into the broad sunny road beyond, where there was a cloud

1

of gray dust and a cheeping and twittering of brown sparrows, and
where one homely country equipage was lumbering along by the
side of a farmer's red-wheeled gig and a donkey-cart.

"King's Arms?" persuasively suggested the conductor, a dark
saturnine man with a straw in his mouth.    "King's Arms?—take
you up there in three minutes, sir; best beds and best accommodation in the whole of Barnard Castle."

"Which are your other inns?" asked the stranger, as three
unmistakable commercial gentlemen pushed past him to secure the
best places, and two more clambered up to the top to the tune of
jingling seals and chains.    "This seems to be a quiet place, but I
suppose there is competition even at Barnard Castle."

"Law bless you, yes, sir !" replied the man rubbing his head,
"especially in the season.   Why, let me see, there's the Commercial, the Rose and Crown, the Hangel, the Turk's Head, and
the Bay Horse, but there's nobody but will say the King's Head
will beat 'em hollow.   Come, we're filling up, jump in, sir," but
the offer was declined.    An old blind woman with a bundle, a
basket of vegetables, and some sunflowers tied up in a blue-spotted
handkerchief, had followed the commercial gentlemen, and after
her came two servant-girls out for a holiday ; the interior looked
hot and fusty, and the best outside places were taken.

"I have no fancy for old women and onions," muttered the
stranger.   Then louder, "Don't wait for me, my man, I shall walk
on."   And so saying he strode off at a pace which would have
suited few men on a hot June day, especially as the sun was almost
vertical, and poured down its rays on the long shadowless road
with a steady glare that made the heaped-up dust feel like heated
blankets to the feet.

He had soon left the road behind him and was halfway up the
long straggling street that leads to the market-place, a drowsy
grass-grown old place, where the old-fashioned inns blinked sleepily
at each other across the wide empty street, where a few antique
shops displayed fewer and still more antique wares, where the green
weeds grew up between the stones, and the stones were rutty and
uneven from age and not from traffic ; where for six days of the
week there was an almost sabbath-like stillness, and only a sem-
blance of life on market-days ; where the grating of wheels was the
exception and not the rule, and the children trundled hoops and
upset their little go-carts fearless of horses' hoofs ; and where a
few factory lads and lasses were wont to congregate on a summer's
evening,—a place which, in its sunny drowsiness, reminded Robert
Ord of some quaint old Continental town he had once seen many
years ago.

The host of the King's Arms was indulging in a siesta under the shade of his own portico, perhaps seduced thereto by the general sleepiness of things animate and inanimate. Some fantail pigeons were strutting about in the dust almost at his feet. He woke up rather startled at being suddenly addressed, and seemed bent on vindicating himself.

"I beg your pardon, sir; I believe—that is—I think I was asleep."

"A very sensible proceeding on such a hot morning," assented the stranger politely. "I am sorry to have disturbed you. I only asked if you were the proprietor of the King's Arms?"

"Yes, sir; Samuel Morison, at your service. Here comes our bus with some of our commercial gentlemen; perhaps you will walk in, sir, it is piping hot outside. Do you wish for a private room, sir?"

"I should like a place where I could speak to you alone for a few minutes," was the somewhat impatient reply. "Look here, Mr. Morison, my name is Ord. Now you know my business with you and the King's Arms, and that I have a question or two to put to you that I shall want answered without delay."

"Mr. Ord; certainly, sir, a dozen if you wish. I had no idea, none whatever, to whom I had the honour of speaking. Come in pray, sir." And so saying he led the way through a long dark old hall, with a far-off glimpse of a cool stone yard, where a gray-haired ostler was rubbing down a horse, up a narrow and still darker staircase into a small room looking over the market-place, with a sweet stuffy smell in it—the scent of fresh roses and dried lavender together.

There was some needlework neatly folded on the table, which made Mr. Ord hesitate and look inquiringly at his conductor.

"This room is engaged, is it not?"

"Yes, sir, but Miss Maturin won't mind—and I have no other room unoccupied at present; she's lying down now with a sick headache, the chambermaid told us, and so it is quite at your service."

"Who is Miss Maturin?" was on Mr. Ord's lips, but he checked himself on remembering that it was no business of his, and, declining refreshments somewhat shortly, took possession of the wide old-fashioned window-seat, and throwing down his black bag turned round to his host and begged him also to be seated.

"Now, Mr. Morison, I want to know how it came about that my aunt—Mrs. Ord, that is—died at your house."

"Mrs. Ord, sir?"

"You see I know all about it, bad news travels fast; I was

quite aware of what happened before I started. I got Mr. Tracy's two letters together—by the bye, I never thought of asking if he be here."

"Yes, sir; léastways he was here this morning, but he's gone on to Deepdale with a party, and we don't expect them back till latish; but perhaps you will prefer to speak to Miss Maturin."

"Who in the world is this Miss Maturin?" broke out from Mr. Ord, this time impatiently enough. "I cannot understand what Miss Maturin has to do with my business."

The landlord coughed.

"Why, Miss Maturin is the young woman—the young lady, I should say—who served as companion to the deceased lady. She's lived with her nigh upon four years I've heard tell, and some of us do say that hers has not been a bed of roses; leastways there must have been a power of thorns in it too, judging from the poor lady's ways and words with her. But still for all that she's taking on and pining that way after her that it makes one quite sorry to see her, poor young creature." And the compassionate landlord wiped his eyes with the feeling of a man who had daughters of his own.

"I suppose she is friendless and has lost a comfortable home; but I think we are wandering a little from the subject, Mr. Morison. I am rather anxious to know what brought my aunt to the King's Arms, Barnard Castle, of all places."

"Yes, sir; and I brought in Miss Maturin's name because I thought she might give you more information than I could; not but what I will willingly tell you all I know about the poor lady."

"Well, sir, the first time I ever set eyes on her was last July, when she and Miss Maturin arrived late one evening. They were on their way from the Cumberland Lakes, and there was some break-down or stoppage on the line. It is not the first time, sir, by a great many that folk come for one night and end by staying some days; and to make a long story short, your aunt, Mrs. Ord, sir, took a fancy to the place, as she told me in that free pleasant way of hers that she had sometimes, and she and Miss Maturin and her maid and their bag and baggage were with us I should say nigh upon five weeks."

"Hum, capricious as usual," muttered Mr. Ord, under his breath. "Well, Mr. Morison, I don't suppose you often have such a good customer as my aunt?"

"Well, sir, the King's Arms has had better and it has had worse in its days, though I say it that shouldn't; not but what the poor lady dealt fairly enough with us, and it is not for the likes of us to judge them that have gone before. But not to detain you, sir, about three weeks ago comes a letter from Miss Maturin, post-mark Clifton, engaging rooms for Mrs. Ord and herself, with just a word at the end saying that she hoped the house was quiet, for her lady was a sad invalid.   It seems that she had been off and on ailing all the winter, and when the fine weather came she was sort of restless and kept moving from place to place, which the doctors told Miss Maturin was a symptom of the disease. Nothing would do but she must have her old rooms at the King's Arms, and see a little more of her favourite place, and not all they could say or do to dissuade her had the least effect.   And as I said before, to make a long story short, she just came in one fine summer's evening, as I was sitting behind the bar with a commercial gentleman of my acquaintance."

" Did she look very ill ? " asked his listener, with the first sign of interest he had shown yet.

" Mr. Ord, sir, there was death in her face," said the landlord solemnly.   " She had that look of breaking up that isn't to be misunderstood in any case, least of all in a lady of her age.   Some of us who were following her minded how she clutched at Miss Maturin's arm to steady herself from falling ; but all the same she said in a cheery sort of a voice, 'Mr. Morison,' she said, ' I hope you have given me my old rooms, for I am going to disappoint my doctors, and get well here as fast as I can,' and those were the last words I ever heard her say."

A brief sigh from Mr. Ord was his sole comment.   He had put his elbow on the window-sill now, and was looking down into the market-place.   Perhaps the landlord's discourse wearied him, but he offered no interruption.   Mr. Morison cleared his throat, for he was getting a little husky, and proceeded — evidently his story was after his own heart, and he thought he was telling it well :

" Man disposes, sir, but the Almighty has the making up of it all in the end ; and the best of us makes a sad mess of the little we do.   Well, when we had got the poor lady upstairs, Miss Maturin and the maid helped her to bed, which some of us knew she would never leave again ; not Miss Maturin though, for she told our chambermaid that she really thought Mrs. Ord had taken a turn for the better, she was so sprightly like ; but when the morning came she was too weak to rise, and the next day and the next, and so it went on.

" Well, it might have been a week or it might be more, I was down in the Castle garden which belongs to the King's Arms, and is so called because it is laid out partly in the ruins, which is one of the sights of Barnard Castle, that strangers come to see—I was down in the Castle garden, I say, getting in our peas, when who should I see but Miss Maturin coming down the centre walk, and looking as white as her gown. And when she gets up to me she says :

" ' Mr. Morison, will you send one of your people with this to the station immediately ? Mrs. Ord is much worse, and I am afraid she is dying. You must not lose a minute—not one minute, please, for,' says she, clasping her hands, ' there's wrong may be done that will be past undoing.' You may not believe me, sir, but what with the sunshine, her white dress, and the scared look on her face, I was sort of dazed ; you might have knocked me over with a feather. For the life of me I could not think what man I had to send, through it not being the full season, and our single-handed waiter being laid up with lumbago, and the boots having gone up to the station already with a commercial's luggage ; and all the time I was considering, she stood twirling the paper round in her long fingers in a way that made me giddy.

" ' I think if it's a telegram I had better take it myself, Miss Maturin,' I said at last.

" And then she began thanking me and telling me how it was to the lawyer, who lived in London, and how he would have to travel perhaps all night.

" ' I pray God he may be in time,' she finished ; and I noticed how she sort of wrung her hands as she spoke."

" And was he in time ? " asked Robert Ord in a voice that startled the worthy landlord, it was so quick and intense in its eagerness.

" Why no, sir ; leastways she never roused to full conscious-ness again. They did all they could. Mr. Tracy waited on and on, but it was no manner of use. They used to give out that she was reviving sometimes, and Miss Maturin would come flying down the garden for Mr. Tracy, and take him up to the poor lady ; but as soon as ever they spoke to her she was back again in the stupor, and so it went on to the last."

" Has Mr. Tracy been here ever since ? "

" Oh no, sir ; he went up to London directly afterwards, and only returned in time for the funeral. I think he had some idea of finding you here."

" True ; but I was away from home, and received his letters too late. Thank you very much, Mr. Morison, for all you have told me. I will not trouble you with any more questions. I can wait for any further particulars till Mr. Tracy returns." The landlord rose at the hint. " And you do not wish to see Miss Maturin, sir ? "

" I have no objection if she wishes it; perhaps I may be of some use to her. She is placed in very unfortunate circumstances. Any lady would feel such a position keenly, especially as I am afraid from what you tell me that she is without friends."

" Not a creature belonging to her in the world, sir."

" And she is young, you say ? "

" About one-and-twenty, sir."

" Hum, hardly old enough to take care of herself. Well, Mr. Morison, I think I shall be glad of those refreshments you offered me before."

" You shall have them at once, sir. I will just give the chambermaid a message for Miss Maturin; and maybe she will come and speak to you herself."

Robert Ord nodded, and the door closed on his host. He gave a genuine sigh of relief when he was left alone, and walked once or twice across the room with the air of one who had shaken off a burden. But his freedom was of short duration, for the door again opened, and a respectable-looking young woman entered.

" Miss Maturin desires her compliments, sir, and thanks you for your kind message. But she is very sorry to say that she cannot possibly see you till the evening, as she is suffering from a bad sick headache."

" I have no wish to disturb Miss Maturin, I assure you," replied Mr. Ord drily, as though he were slightly annoyed. " I only offered my services, hearing from the landlord that the lady was without friends in a strange place."

" Yes, sir ; Miss Maturin understood that, and she is extremely obliged to you ; she desired me also to say that she hopes you will make use of your aunt's sitting-room, as the inn is very full, and it is quite at your disposal."

" Thank you ; I may take advantage of her kindness for a few hours," he replied a little less stiffly, but half disposed to refuse the thoughtful offer ; it was curious how this continual mention of his aunt's companion ruffled him. " I wish people would not drag in other people's affairs in the middle of one's private business," he said, fuming to himself as soon as he was left alone. " What in the world is Miss Maturin to me, or I to Miss Maturin ? That's the worst of talking to a garrulous landlord. I declare I am quite sick of the name."

The coldness and hauteur of his manners had not been lost on the chambermaid, who was as quick to observe as the rest of her class ; for in retailing the short interview afterwards to Miss Maturin, she described Robert Ord as the proudest as well as the handsomest gentleman she had ever set eyes on — a double ex-

aggeration, seeing that there were many men handsomer and
prouder even than he. But he was a good-looking man enough,
possessing those elements of manly beauty which are sufficiently
attractive to the feminine eye. He was tall, and well though
rather slenderly built, and his face was decidedly prepossessing,
though a physiognomist might have found fault with his mouth—
the lips were too thin, and closed over each other so firmly as to
give an expression almost of hardness to his otherwise pleasant
features. One seemed to feel in looking at him that his firmness
was a fault, that he could be a loving friend but a bitter enemy,
and no one's enemy more than his own. And yet there was something about the man that must, in either character, win your
respect. He was so honest and so terribly in earnest. Women
always liked Robert Ord, though they feared him a little; and
good men valued his opinions. But perhaps the best criterion of
all, little children loved and clung to him, and even dumb animals
followed him about, and with unerring instinct seemed to know he
was their friend.

He was sorely in need of refreshments by the time they arrived,
and did ample justice to the excellent fare set before him, but as
soon as his repast was over, he strolled to the window-seat again,
more in the hope of enjoying a little fresh air than of seeing any
special objects of interest.

"I always thought Blackscar the dreariest place imaginable,"
he said half-aloud, as he leant his elbows on the sill and looked
over the sunny market-place, "but one has the sea there, with its
perpetual changes, but this Barnard Castle looks as though it has
gone to sleep for a score of years and has not begun to wake up
yet. A nice little nest for an idle man perhaps—nay, even as the
landlord of the King's Arms, existence might be endurable here—
but not to a restless Ord, unless it be Austin." And here he
broke off, as though too indolent this hot summer's afternoon to
carry on any consecutive train of thought, and stared instead at an
enormous placard opposite him, containing the astounding information that on that very evening might be seen one of the most
remarkable wonders of the world—the Blue and Hairless Horse,
at the ridiculous sum of one penny, children half-price.

"I suppose he has fallen into some lime-pit by accident and
then got painted, but, all the same, those louts of lads will go and
believe in him, so much for the innocent credulity of the Barnard
Castlers;" and then he leant out farther, as a little equipage
rattled over the stones and stopped at a neighbouring tin-shop; it
was rather an odd-looking turn-out—a low carriage drawn by a pair
of fat sleepy mules, with a huge tawny St. Bernard dog keeping

them company. There was a jingle of little bells about it too. A lady in a large straw hat was driving a tall gentleman; there was quite a small crowd round them, and the tin-man looked obsequious. Robert Ord found out afterwards that it was the owner of Rokeby. After that came a cream-coloured performing pony, led by a foreigner and escorted by small boys; they disappeared down a dark entry however, and the small boys dispersed with a general whoop of disappointment to reassemble presently in hot pursuit of a Punch and Judy show; the place was quiet enough after that; the pigeons strutted again in the sunshine, and only a solitary factory girl, with the usual shawl over her head, passed listlessly along.

"I think I've had enough of this," said Robert Ord, suddenly rousing himself. "It is cooler now; I will go and have a peep at the Castle gardens, and perhaps at the Castle itself; it is better to ventilate one's thoughts when they are as heavy as mine."

And being a man of energy, Robert Ord was as good or better than his word, for he not only saw the ruined Castle, with its hermit's chamber, and the cell where through the slit in the wall the unhappy prisoner could view the enchanting landscape with its noble river below, but he perambulated the town itself, and after having counted the inns and alehouses in the High Street, which reached the shady side of twenty, and explored the factory quarters, with its bridges and grimy river, he returned to the King's Arms, and having made friends with the apoplectic-looking waiter, was conducted by him across a stone yard and through a side gate into the far-famed Castle garden.

"Mr. Morison is very proud of his garden, sir," the waiter had assured him; and as he strolled on after thanking him, he was fain to acknowledge that Mr. Morison had something of which he might justly be proud.

Beautiful old-fashioned gardens they were, lying within the ruins, homely enough, but brimful of sunshine and sweet-smelling old-fashioned flowers, none the less lovely that they bloomed in the same plot of ground with apple-trees, cabbages, and gooseberry bushes.

He had never seen such a profusion of flowers anywhere; they might be counted by hundreds; there was a perfect blaze of colour in the sunshine, and great brown bees were humming about them and filling their honey-bags as though rejoicing in the bounteous harvest.

Flowers, flowers everywhere; great clumps of golden-hearted lilies, looking, as they are, the white queens of the garden, and behind them, like ranks of sentinels, tall dazzling hollyhocks;

roses, delicious creamy tea-roses, and rich crimson ones, some of
them deeply, darkly purple ; pale pinky roses hanging in clusters
like tinted cups, blush and white roses—there was no end to them
anywhere ; they festooned the walls in company with the fruit
trees and throve in every border, bushes of them bloomed on the
ruined walls themselves, or made inroads on the gravel paths.

There were great orange beds of eschscholtzias, and lupins,
blue, rose, and yellow, climbing convolvuli and marigolds of all
sorts, double daisies and stocks, and trails of rich dark nasturtiums,
with homely sweet-peas running to seed ; flowers that brought back
the garden of one's childhood, when a bush of southern-wood was
one's delight, and monkshood, sweet-william, and yellow-eyed
pansies were the rarest flowers in the world.

Robert Ord dearly loved old associations, and flowers were his
especial delight, and as he strolled down the wide gravel-paths and
under the sunny walls he felt brighter than he had done for many
a day ; for Robert Ord was a disappointed man, he had missed his
share of this world's good things somehow, and the world had in
consequence turned rather a cold shoulder on him.   The star of
the Ords was not just now in the ascendant ; people had begun
to say of them that they were poor and proud, and might have
managed better if they had only bent those obstinate wills of
theirs a little and learned to be humble.   But it was a lesson no
Ord had ever yet learned, and so they had gone on their ways chew-
ing the bitter cud of experience with a sorry face or a cheerful one
according to their several natures ; and a little hardness had crept
into Robert's heart, the good things of this world had been promised him and then had been suddenly withdrawn, and he had
grown sore with longing for them ; but none the less did he feel
some stirrings of hope within him that brighter days might be in
store for him and his.   He had felt it as he alighted from his hurried
journey and stepped into the dust and sunshine, and he felt it still
more as he walked between the gay coloured bushes, and looked
across at the blue-black ruins of Barnard Castle with a pile of
amethyst and scarlet clouds behind them.

He had stopped for a moment to lean on the little gate that
connects the upper and lower gardens, when the slow rustle of a
dress attracted his attention ; and looking up he saw a lady coming
round the angle of the wall, evidently towards him.   She did not
see him till he had opened the gate for her to pass ; then she
bowed slightly with a quiet well-bred air, but without raising her
eyes.   He had just time to notice that she was tall, very young,
and dressed in rather deep mourning, before a sudden and most
unaccountable impulse made him lift his hat and say :

"I beg your pardon, but am I not addressing Miss Maturin?"

She was passing him as he spoke; perhaps the abruptness of the question startled her, for she hesitated, seemed painfully confused, and at last stammered out in the lowest voice he had ever heard:

"Yes; I am Miss Maturin. I suppose—that is—I believe I am speaking to Mr. Ord."

"Certainly."

"I thought so; I was sorry I could not meet you as you wished, in the earlier part of the day. I only came out now to see if the air would do my head good;" she spoke quickly, with a flurry and indistinctness in her words, which made them nearly inaudible; and the nervous trembling of her hands spoke volumes.

"She is very young, and is afraid of me," thought he; and he answered her in his pleasantest tones, as though to reassure her.

"Yes, there is nothing so painful and depressing as a bad sick headache. I have had several in my time, and know how trying they are to bear. This cool evening air will do you good, Miss Maturin; now as we have met one another so opportunely we may as well have our little interview out here in this lovely old garden, it will be ten times better than 'that stuffy little room upstairs, and I have so many questions to ask about my poor aunt."

"Have you? Yes, we will stop out here if you like," she returned, looking round her in a helpless sort of way, that made Mr. Ord think she was meditating an escape. He could not help scrutinising her narrowly as she stood there under the low apple trees—a tall slim creature, in her black dress, with a lace kerchief tied over her brown hair, and a face so young and so surprisingly pale that it moved him to pity in spite of himself. He had just made up his mind that she was not at all good-looking, and that she was very unhappy, when she looked up at him with a pair of soft troubled eyes and said:

"If you have questions to ask, of course I will stay and answer them; but I thought, perhaps, you would wait for Mr. Tracy."

"Mr. Tracy cannot tell me all I want, Miss Maturin. Forgive me if I am too cruel in keeping you when you are evidently in need of quiet; but my time is short. A few hours is all I can spare from my business, and my talk with Mr. Tracy must be of a far different character."

"Yes, I know," she answered with a little shiver, and turning paler than ever, "it must be all so sad for you. Ah, why have you come so late? We did what we could, Mr. Ord; indeed we did, but it was all too late."

"I could not come before," he returned, anxious to defend himself, and wondering at her exceeding agitation. "I was travelling for our firm, and Mr. Tracy's letter never reached me; and as ill luck would have it neither of my brothers could come either, for Garton had hurt his foot, and Austin could find no one to take his duty. Then the funeral took place yesterday. Was the will opened then, Miss Maturin?"

"Yes," pressing her lips together.

"Who was present?"

"Only Mr. Tracy, Mr. Compton the clergyman, and myself; the other executor could not come."

"Who is the other executor?" he asked anxiously; but she interrupted him, almost in distress.

"It is Mr. Morrell or Murrell—I don't know which; but please don't ask me any more about that, Mr. Tracy will tell you;" and putting her hand to her head, "I am so confused—oh, so dreadfully confused with it all."

"Tell me something about my aunt's illness," he said kindly, and putting aside his evident desire to know more; for Robert Ord was very tender over weakness, and very chivalrous and courteous to all womenkind, and this shy, timid girl excited his compassion. His soothing tone seemed to give her confidence, for she brightened up a little; and by means of frequent questioning and an encouraging word or two he was soon put into possession of all the facts connected with his aunt's long mental illness—an illness aggravated by restlessness, and resulting in the break-up of all her vital powers.

"It seems so dreadful for her to have died at an inn, with only hirelings round her," finished Miss Maturin; "if her old friend Mr. Tracy had not been near her, I should have said it was almost too sad."

"I should think you must have been an old friend yourself by this time, Miss Maturin; you have been three or four years with her."

"Nearly four. I know I tried to do my duty to her. I wish now that I had not tried quite so hard; no, you will not understand me, Mr. Ord, but she seemed so lonely, poor thing, and so bitter with some secret trouble, that one could not help pitying her, and trying to make her life a little less unbearable to herself and others. I did not mean to say that, God knows; she was my only friend, and I miss her"—and Miss Maturin wiped away a few quiet tears in a way that touched the young man to the heart.

"Are you so wholly without friends then?" he asked gently.

"I have not any one belonging to me in the world," was the sad answer.

" Pardon me ; not a sister, not a brother ? "

" No ; I was an only child."

" Tell me some more about yourself; that is, if you do not mind," he said, with quite an elder brotherly feeling towards this young girl, thrown so suddenly and so unprotected on the world ; " not that we Ords have much interest; but I know some good women who would go very far out of their way to assist one of their own sex."

She smiled gratefully at that; and then, as though his kindness had won her from her timidity, she told him in a few simple words, all the more pathetic that they were so few and simple, the particulars of her poor little story.

She told him how she had been the only child of an Indian officer, who had died while on his voyage home on sick leave, and how in two or three short years her mother had followed him, leaving her a lonely child, only ten years old ; how they had left a little sum of money for her maintenance and education ; and when that was exhausted, she had become a pupil-teacher in the same school where she had been educated, from which drudgery Mrs. Ord had rescued her.

" I was only seventeen then," concluded Miss Maturin, " but I was doing the work of two people. When I look back I do not know which was worse, that school life or the years that came after. I don't think "—clasping her hands with a movement that seemed habitual to her—" I don't think I ever had a friend in the world except the music-mistress, Mrs. Carruthers, and she was good to me. I see now that Mrs. Ord liked me, and meant to be kind ; but how could I have guessed it—how could I—how could I ? "

The nervous flurry of manner had returned, and as she spoke these last words she looked so white that Robert Ord at once proposed they should return to the inn.

" I will see you again to-morrow," he said, holding out his hand with a friendly look as they parted in the hall. " I shall not leave very early in the morning after all, and I shall expect you to tell me what I can do to help you."

" Thank you, thank you gratefully for all your kindness," she answered ; but either she did not or would not see his hand.

Robert Ord watched her gliding up the staircase like a black shadow, and then he turned the handle of his door with a brief sigh and went in.

# CHAPTER II.

"O false my friend !
False, false, a random charge, a blame undue ;
Wrest not fair reasoning to a crooked end :
False, false, as you are true !"       JEAN INGELOW.

ROBERT ORD had expected to find the little room as empty as when he left it ; he was greatly surprised therefore to see a gray-haired gentleman with a florid face busily writing at the centre table; in the dim light he had some difficulty in recognising him till he pushed back his chair and came forward with outstretched hand.

"Good evening, Mr. Ord."

"Good evening, Mr. Tracy ; you have taken me quite by surprise. I had no idea that you had returned."

"My dear sir, a thousand apologies for keeping you so long waiting; here I have been all day with a party at Deepdale—ought to have known better at my age—time is money to a business man. Never expected you for a moment—why did not you telegraph ?"

"True, so I might," returned Robert Ord.

"Might ! I should think so. 'If he means to come he'll send a telegram,' thought I ; 'and if not, I shall be off to London to-morrow.' What were you doing at Glasgow ?"

"Something wrong with our machinery, and they sent on my letter instead of opening it—that's Gar all over—and so, of course, there was no way of being present yesterday."

"I supposed business had kept you ; couldn't the parson come either ?"

"Who—Austin ? No, just at the last minute he couldn't find any one to take his duty. I believe there was a wedding and a funeral on for that day."

"Humph ! just as well, perhaps, as things have turned out," returned the lawyer, taking out his snuff-box and tapping it nervously. "Of course we were obliged to open the will."

"So Miss Maturin informed me."

"What! have you seen Miss Maturin?" asked Mr. Tracy in a tone of unfeigned astonishment. "I thought she told me that nothing would induce her to see you. Well, women are queer creatures to manage—they tell you one thing and do the other. So she told you about the will, eh?"

"No, indeed; she referred me to you."

"I am sorry for it; I thought she was going to save me an awkward piece of business," said Mr. Tracy, ruffling up his gray hair in a way peculiar to himself—it was coarse hair, and made a grating sort of sound. "Crump took down all the particulars of the will—she was our oldest client—I never understood why she sent for my partner instead of myself, but I understand it now; rather a hard customer she was to manage—confoundedly hard, I should say;" and he rapped his snuff-box thoughtfully on the table before he took a pinch. "Pray, Mr. Ord, if it be not asking too downright a question, was your aunt on such very bad terms with you and the rest of your family?"

"I am sorry to hear you asking that question, Mr. Tracy; it sounds ominous. She was on the worst possible terms with us all, sir."

"Humph! thought so," taking another pinch. "Couldn't comprehend it otherwise—had always heard she had educated and made so much of her three nephews—brought them up, in fact, as though they were her own sons."

"So she did till the last four years. But, look here, Mr. Tracy, doesn't it strike you that we are beating about the bush a good deal? It does not require much penetration to see that you have no very good news to give me. What is the good of all this preamble? Of course my aunt has left all her money to a charitable institution."

He spoke quietly, but there was an anxious, almost an eager look about his face; he had told himself coming along that he had little or no hope, and that whatever disappointment might await him he would bear it like a man; but he knew now that hope had been strong within him, that he had coveted that money as earnestly as he knew how to covet anything—all the more that it had once been within his lawful grasp before misunderstandings had arisen, and the Ord pride had estranged them; and now his heart was growing heavy and sore within him, for Mr. Tracy's jovial face looked graver and longer than he had ever seen it.

"I suppose she has endowed some orphanage or hospital, or left funds for building another church; she was largely given to such good works," he continued, trying to speak lightly, but failing utterly.

"I wish to heaven Miss Maturin had told you herself," said the lawyer, rubbing his hands fretfully.

"My good sir, what has Miss Maturin to do with the subject?"

"Unfortunately, Mr. Ord, she has everything to do with it. Your aunt has left her the whole of her property." Robert Ord started from his seat, with an exclamation rather strong than polite.

"Now do be calm, my dear sir—pray be calm;" and the lawyer took three pinches in succession as he watched him nervously. "I can't tell you how heartily grieved I am for your disappointment, but pray be calm."

"The whole of her property, Mr. Tracy!—impossible."

"Every penny, I give you my word; every stick and straw, except a large donation to the fishermen and a munificent bequest to the Convalescent Hospital. Of course there are minor legacies to servants and executors, and she has not forgotten two or three old pensioners; but the bulk of her property, in houses and funded property, with Bryn and all its furniture, plate, etc., amounting to about five thousand a year, goes solely and entirely to Miss Maturin."

"Miss Maturin—good heavens! Miss Maturin!" And Robert Ord's expression was not pleasant to see.

"Mr. Tracy, on my word of honour as a gentleman, I will never believe my aunt intended to do us this deadly wrong."

"Tush, my dear sir. I have the exact copy of the will before me now; you may read it for yourself in black and white," and he pushed the papers towards Robert Ord. "Look it over; you will find the instrument correct and valid enough. Crump knew what he was about when he drew up that document—and a rascally document it is," muttered the lawyer, as he turned towards the window. He was a good-natured man, softer-hearted than many of his class, and the sight of the young man's pale face moved him to pity. "He has played his cards as badly as a man could play them," he said to himself; "those Ords are all alike—they never know what is good for them; there's not one of the three could manage a cantankerous old woman; but all the more, it is a grievous pity this fine young man should be the loser. Humph! I should like to know the rights of it." And he was still turning the matter over in his mind when Robert Ord threw the paper from him with a gesture of anger and disgust.

"Mr. Tracy, I shall dispute that will. As sure as I am standing here I shall do it."

"On what grounds, Mr. Ord?"

"On the grounds of insanity—imbecility, if you like. My aunt was not in her sane mind when she dictated that will."

"Fudge, my dear sir."

"Mr. Tracy!"

"Come, come, this is going too far; do let us be reasonable. Of course I agree with you that it is a confounded shame—that, morally speaking, the young woman has no more right to the money than I have, and a more unjust will was never executed; but when you talk of disputing the validity of the document you are simply flying in the face of reason."

"Never mind, I will go to law; I will have the thing properly sifted. What right had she to disinherit her lawful nephews with-out cause, for the sake of a designing stranger?"

"Mr. Ord, my good sir——"

"It is no use dissuading me, Mr. Tracy. I have made up my mind. I will talk the matter over with Austin, and he will agree with me."

"I think better of the parson than that."

"What! you think he will not fight the thing out with me? You are mistaken."

"No, no, Mr. Ord; I think better of him and of you than that. Go to law, indeed! Why, you have not a leg to stand upon."

"How so?" asked Robert Ord. His excitement was cooling a little before the lawyer's phlegm.

"Why, in the first place, the costs would ruin you; and, in the next place, you would gain nothing. Ask any lawyer, he would tell you the same. Granted that it is a most unjust will; but, after all, I suppose the deceased lady had a right to do what she liked with her own."

"I deny that my aunt was in her reasonable senses when she dictated that document."

"Will you undertake to prove that, Mr. Ord? No, no, let us glance at the main facts of the case. Here is a lady with— with——" Here the lawyer hesitated for a word. "Well, let us say a decidedly unpleasant temper, variable and capricious as the winds, and full of all sorts of jealous fancies. Well, this lady brings up her nephews, treats them in a way like her own sons, and finally adopts one and makes him her heir. By and by misunderstand-ings arise; there's coolness, first with one and then with another of the brothers—all on account of this touchy temper and the Ord pride —no insanity, mind you, ever having been known in the family; presently there's ill blood between her and the heir, and she there and then refuses to have any more to do with him—that's some years ago—they don't meet again; and when the will is opened,

2

he finds she has only left him her forgiveness and a blessing. Isn't that the long and the short of it, Mr. Ord?"

"I believe you have stated it pretty correctly."

"Well, how can you make out your case for presuming the deceased was of unsound mind? Crump will tell you she was never clearer and better than when she dictated the points of that will, looked as hale and hearty as though she would live till eighty— was terribly irascible with him to be sure, and rapped on the table with her gold-headed cane every time he ventured on a remonstrance. Never had such an interview in his life; it quite aged him."

"You really think I cannot contest the will?" asked Robert Ord hopelessly.

"My dear sir, it would be the maddest thing you ever did in your life, even to attempt such a thing. 'Pon my word your aunt was a most unaccountable creature though—here she led that poor girl a sad life of it, every one says so, and then goes and leaves her all her money as though to make up for it."

"Poor girl indeed! Who ever would have thought my aunt could have been so duped, and she such an acute woman, too?"

"What do you mean by that, may I ask?"

"Now, Mr. Tracy, is it possible that you can be so simple as not to see there must have been some undue influence at work? I could not have believed that any one so young and so seemingly simple could have been so designing."

"There, she said you would say so—she said you would take it like this;" and the lawyer rubbed up his hair with vexation till it stood on end all round like a gray halo. "I can well understand you feel inclined to play at fisticuffs with the world in general for having used you so badly, but when it comes to speaking ill of that poor young woman because she has innocently defrauded you of your aunt's property, I must say, Mr. Ord, I hardly expected it of you."

"I suppose she has talked you over, sir," sneered Robert Ord. "Ah, I can see it all now. No wonder she dreaded to meet me; no wonder she could not look me in the face and answer my questions; fool that I was, to be gulled by all that seeming simplicity."

"Mr. Ord, you are cruelly misjudging that poor girl."

"Of course, Mr. Tracy, if you are going to take up cudgels in her defence, I have no more to say; but I should have thought a lawyer the last man to be deceived by fair specious words. Miss Maturin is nothing to me, but I should have certainly liked a different sort of neighbour at Bryn; it is rather too close to the Vicarage to be pleasant."

"Upon my word I pity that young creature coming into the

midst of you," returned the lawyer warmly; "that was a cruel
provision of the will obliging her to live at Bryn. When we read
it out to her she turned as white as that table-cloth." 'What!
shall I have to face them day after day and week after week?'
she said, turning to me. 'Mr. Tracy, it is too dreadful, I cannot
do it. I shall feel as though I have robbed them of their money. I
have no right to it, none at all; and they are all so poor, you tell me.'"

"We are much obliged to Miss Maturin for her commiseration,"
returned Robert Ord haughtily, stung by the concluding words.

"My dear sir, do let me proceed; it is my duty to remove
this suspicion if I can. We had some trouble to make her understand that she was sole legatee; she kept interrupting us by telling
us that she was sure Mrs. Ord had repented of her injustice, and
that she had meant to make another will in favour of her nephew
Robert; and at last she got so urgent that we were obliged to ask
her reasons for what she said."

"Well?" asked Mr. Ord eagerly, as the lawyer paused.

"Well, it seems about a week before her death Mrs. Ord let
fall some words about the final disposition of her property which
excited Miss Maturin's suspicion, and she begged her to tell her
more, but she would not. She only asked her jestingly how she
would feel if she woke up one morning and found herself a rich
woman; and when she said that, it came upon her all of a sudden
that some injustice was going to be done, and then and there she
begged and prayed Mrs. Ord not to leave her any money, or not
more than would keep her from drudgery all her life; and she
implored her by all she held sacred not to leave the world bearing
a grudge against any one, and least of all her own flesh and blood.
I don't know what more she said, but she told us that Mrs. Ord
seemed much shaken by her words, and not a little touched. She
patted her kindly on the head—she was kneeling by her at the
time—and promised she would think over it; and she was not to
fear for herself, for she would see that she was remembered; and
later on in the night, just as she was dropping off to sleep, Mrs.
Ord woke her and said she was a good girl, and that she might
send for Mr. Tracy if she liked, for she had made up her mind
now, for she knew she had committed a great mistake, and she
would see that everything was put right."

"Go on," murmured Mr. Ord hoarsely, as soon as Mr. Tracy
leant forward to refresh himself with another pinch.

"All right, my dear sir; I thought you would be interested.
Well, when the morning came there was a change for the worse—
a sort of lethargy or stupor seemed creeping over her—and when
the doctor came it was his opinion that she was not far from her

end. Then it was that Miss Maturin sent for me, stating that she had reasons for believing that the poor lady wished to alter her will. She was rather incoherent in her expressions. I was a stranger to her, you see; but I gathered from her excitement that there was some great interest at stake. Well, I did what I could; and, what with Mrs. Ord being our oldest client and having large dealings with our firm, and my not having much work on hand, and being rather disposed to loiter in a strange place, I just stayed on a day or two hoping for a lucid interval, but none came. She would revive a minute or two, and then the death-like stupor would return, and so it was all of no use."

"She never rallied?"

"Not for more than a few minutes at a time. Miss Maturin used to fetch me up to her room, but it was fighting against fate; and so we found when we came to open the will and saw how things were left. Good heavens!" continued the lawyer still more vehemently, "I thought Miss Maturin would have been beside herself when I read it. She would hardly listen to us when we congratulated her. She hated money, she said, and this great millstone should not be hung about her neck. She was for delivering up the whole to you; and when we proved to her that that was impossible, she insisted on a fair division. But you see for yourself, Mr. Ord, how such an arrangement is guarded against in a special clause of the will, and how the executors are bound over to see that the property, without division, is for the sole use of Rotha Maturin and her heirs for ever."

"A monstrous injustice! Mr. Crump ought to have refused to have drawn up such a will."

"Why? She would only have employed the nearest lawyer; and Crump saw no good in offending a rich client. She might have had a harder customer to deal with in me. I am rather given to plain speaking in such matters. I have known the Ords off and on for a score of years, and I would not have seen them so cruelly wronged if I could have helped it."

"Thank you, Mr. Tracy; I am sure of your sympathy."

"Why, you may be sure of that, my dear sir, and welcome; and if there be anything I can do for you at any time—short of contesting the will—I will gladly do it. One thing I must confess, that I am rather curious to know what led to this final breach, if it be not trenching too much on private matters."

"My aunt never enlightened you, then?"

"No, she got to be rather close with me during the last few years of her life. I suppose, as I just hinted, I was too plain-spoken for her. I know the parson put his foot in it by marrying

a young lady without any fortune; that was just after Mrs. Ord
had endowed the church, and so he never got his new Vicarage."

"There, that was just one of my aunt's inconsistencies; she
was lavish of her money, always giving it away in large sums,
which impoverished her property, and then she insisted on our
marrying rich wives to repair the breaches, as it were. Who ever
heard of such despotism? Austin was the first to rebel, and so it
was all up with him."

"But the parson was never the prime favourite, Mr. Robert?"

"No, he was too downright and outspoken. She could not
bear his sermons, as she called them. Did you ever see his wife,
Mr. Tracy?"

"To be sure I have, when I called at the Vicarage one day;
a pretty bright-coloured girl, very pleasant spoken, and every inch
a gentlewoman."

"Oh, that's many years ago; she looks worn now, and no wonder, with four boys and a small income to manage. You were asking
me just now how I fell into disgrace. Well, that was all her fault."

"Mrs. Austin's fault?"

"Yes; the vicaress, as we call her. Her mother, Mrs. Clinton,
died, and she and Austin, not being poor enough already, must
needs have her sister to live with them."

"Humph! I begin to see light."

"To be sure you do. Of course we fell in love with each
other, and, as she is ten times prettier than her sister, that's only
natural. I think you might travel half the world over before you
find two such women anywhere."

"No doubt, no doubt, Mr. Robert, but all the same it was a
crazy move of yours."

"Of course it was suicidal, but I was almost as blind as men
in my position usually are. I daresay if I had foreseen everything
I should have acted just the same. I could not have helped
myself; but I certainly had no idea at the time that my aunt
had already chosen a wife for me. You have heard of Mr.
Ramsay of Stretton, the great ironmaster. He was worth, I
should be afraid to say how many thousands, and he had an only
daughter. This young lady was destined by my aunt to be the
future mistress of Bryn. And if my affections had not been already
engaged, she would not have chosen ill for me, for Emma Ramsay
was a sweet-looking creature, and most amiable and accomplished;
but as I had already proposed to Miss Clinton, I was not specially
thankful when this paragon was offered for my acceptance. I
suspect her father rather wished the match, as well as my aunt.
Well, I believe you know my aunt's peculiarities, and I will leave

to your imagination the scene that followed when I told her that Miss Clinton and I were engaged. You spoke just now of the Ord pride in not very complimentary terms, if I remember rightly; it was well up then, I assure you, and there were bitter words spoken on both sides—not quite pleasant to remember now. It ended in my refusing to give up Miss Clinton, or to take Miss Ramsay on any terms, and that night I shook off the dust of Bryn with no very enviable feelings."

" Did Mrs. Ord disinherit you then ?"

" Virtually, I suppose she did, for she vowed that if I married Miss Clinton I should never touch a penny of her money. Of course Austin tried to patch up the matter and make peace between us, but that only widened the breach, for she told him it was all his own and his wife's fault—they had tried to get up the match to spite her, and that she never wished to see an Ord face again."

" Poor lady! that was when she came up to London. I thought she looked ten years older when I saw her."

" Yes, she shut up Bryn at once, and before any of us knew what she was about she had taken a house in London. Austin wanted me to go after her, but I declined ; Garton went, but they never had got on well together, and she would not have anything to say to him. He came back looking rather the worse for London air, I can tell you."

" And you never attempted a personal reconciliation, Mr. Ord ?"

" No, indeed ! What was the good of bringing flint and steel together ? I tried writing once, but the answer I received did not encourage me to proceed with the correspondence. She would only make peace on her own terms, and as that involved my giving up Miss Clinton, of course I would not listen to them ; and so it went on from bad to worse. But I don't think we any of us quite thought that she would carry her animosity beyond death." And Robert Ord's face darkened as he remembered that bitter will.

" How is it she never got on with your brother Garton ?"

" Oh, that is easily accounted for. Garton never would put up with her queer speeches. He was always letting her see that he despised her vagaries, and saying some blunt thing or other that hurt her feelings. Gar always was under a cloud, as it were. She had not any patience with his wish to be a clergyman—one was quite enough in any family, she said ; and so there was never any sympathy between them. It was a pity, because Garton would have suited her best in the end. Good heavens, what a miserable world it is for general crookedness and misunderstandings !"

" I daresay you feel it so now. It is very hard for an idle man, brought up in luxury, to have to put his hand suddenly to the plough."

"Yes, a managing clerk's place at two hundred a year is not a very lively prospect after four years' work, especially when one has to partially keep one's brother."

"You see no chance of maintaining a wife just now, I am afraid?"

"No, indeed! it is that that makes me feel so badly about it all," and Robert Ord's voice took a hard bitter tone. "It is hard lines for us. We have been engaged four years, and shall probably remain so for four more. No hope of a rise just now—when there are two sons coming into the business—unless by a lucky chance. It is wearing us both out, I believe; for of course a man cannot bear such a heap of troubles quite patiently. Well, Mr. Tracy, I think I have bothered you enough with our family history. We are sitting in total darkness; shall we ring for lights and a cup of coffee?"

"With all my heart, my dear sir," returned Mr. Tracy, pulling the bell. "Thank you, thank you for all your confidence. I confess I was curious to learn the rights of this painful case, and in return I trust that I have removed your unhappy suspicion of poor Miss Maturin."

Mr. Ord remained silent.

"Come, sir; acknowledge that you have been rather too hard upon her."

"I don't think a man can be expected to be otherwise than hard when he sees all the good things of this world snatched suddenly away from him."

"Of course not, of course not; but I do hope, Mr. Ord, that you will make things a little less unbearable for her when she comes among you."

"I hope always to remember that she is a lady," returned Robert Ord in his most high and mighty manner.

"There, that's an Ord all over. Why, bless my soul, however do you manage to get on in the world at all, Mr. Robert? There, forgive an old man's pertinacity, for the girl interests me somehow. Do not let her see that you harbour this unjust suspicion of her. Mark my words, my dear sir, it will just break her down."

"I am afraid she must put up with a general coolness. I am very sorry, Mr. Tracy, as she is a pet *protégée* of yours, but I cannot help it. I cannot feel that my aunt would have left her all that money if she had not been toadying for it more or less. She may be quite innocent, as you say, but a man is bound to have his own opinion, and I have mine. There, let us change the subject; my head aches so confoundedly that I think I will go out for a stroll to get a little fresh air."

# CHAPTER III.

What prospects, from his watch-tower high
Gleam gradual on the warder's eye !—
Far sweeping to the east, he sees
Down his deep woods the course of Tees,
And tracks his wanderings by the steam
Of summer vapours from the stream.

. . . . .

Then in broad lustre shall be shown
That mighty trench of living stone,
And each huge trunk that from the side,
Reclines him o'er the darksome tide,
Where Tees, full many a fathom low,
Wears with his rage no common foe ;
For pebbly bank, nor sand-bed here,
Nor clay-mound, checks his fierce career,
Condemned to mine a channell'd way
O'er solid sheets of marble gray."            SCOTT'S *Rokeby.*

ROBERT ORD was in no very placable mood the next morning; his
long solitary walk in the darkness had been followed by a wakeful
miserable night; anxious thoughts had stared him in the face and
kept him company, and he had failed to combat them with his
usual courage.   Bitter feelings such as he had never experienced
before filled his veins with fever and stirred him to impotent
anger; courage and hope were at their lowest ebb.   And when he
had succeeded in obtaining momentary oblivion, it was dearly
purchased at the expense of harassing nightmares.

He arose with the morning light jaded and unrefreshed, to find
a new source of annoyance awaiting him.

"Things always go by contraries in this world, at least they
do with me," he observed, as he and Mr. Tracy sat down to breakfast together in the coffee-room.   "There's a pleasant sort of letter
for a man to receive just as he is longing to shake off the dust of
a place from him."

"What's the matter now ?  Hum, letters of advice to Darlington. Darlington? Why, that's not much of a distance. Only a matter of sixteen miles from here—is it?"

"I should not mind if it were sixty," was the grumbling answer. "It is not the distance to which I object; but just now I am not exactly in the humour to have a few idle hours on my hands."

"Why not deliver the letters at once then, and take an early train to Blackscar or Thornborough?"

"Impossible. You see I have to confer with our junior partner, Mr. Clayton. Well, he was in Lancashire last night. He cannot be in Darlington, I should judge, till about nine this evening."

"Humph, I begin to understand; and it is not the sort of place where you would care to spend a solitary day."

"Well, not exactly; Mr. Broughton thinks it probable that Mr. Clayton may bring us up news which may oblige me to return to Glasgow at a moment's notice. Anyhow my orders are stringent. We shall telegraph from Darlington and await their reply. Of course I shall pass the night there."

"And you will have your day to yourself. I wish I could keep you company, but I must be off by the eleven o'clock train."

"To London?"

Mr. Tracy nodded.

"Are you going to leave your *protégée* behind you, sir?" The sarcastic tone suited Robert Ord ill. Mr. Tracy rubbed up his hair as he heard it.

"If you mean by my *protégée* Miss Maturin, she will follow me to London in a day or two. I don't mind telling you that I have invited her to take up her residence for a little while in Manchester Square."

"At your house, Mr. Tracy?" and Robert Ord knitted his brow in surprise.

"Yes, at my house, sir; have you any objection, Mr. Ord? I don't think she will quite contaminate my wife and daughters."

"Probably not," was the curt answer. But Robert Ord winced a little nevertheless at the lawyer's irony.

"She has to hunt out a friend of hers in London. That's her present purpose, I believe. For, as you may be aware, sir, a young creature can't live quite alone, and she wishes this Mrs. Carruthers to come and live with her. You may not do the poor young woman justice yourself, Mr. Robert, but I think even you must confess that she has a pretty clear notion of what is fitting in her position." To which piece of intelligence Robert Ord vouchsafed no manner of answer.

The conversation languished after this. Mr. Tracy took up

his paper and was soon absorbed in the leading article, and Robert Ord, after wandering listlessly from the table to the windows, and observing that there were sullen-looking clouds about, and that he would as soon be suffocated as take a walk on such a sultry morning, took up his hat and went out, after bidding him good-bye rather stiffly.

The day was before him. But though in his hard-working life holidays had been scarce with him, and idleness a thing unknown, he made no sort of plan for himself ; he had taken a distaste to the whole place ; he was in no mood to be charmed by natural beauty —nature in her sweetest aspect would have failed to soothe him. But as his restlessness goaded him to some sort of action, he went out, not caring whither he went.

He had gone down by the river the previous evening, and he remembered a little weir which had pleased him with its cool splash and endless movement. Perhaps farther on he might find shade and repose. And so he crossed the bridge again, and leaving the factories behind him, struck into a little footway across the green fields, which seemed to track the course of the river. But as he walked, the dense thundery air added to his oppression, and served to increase his brooding sadness. Two or three anglers looked up from their pleasant work in surprise at the tall handsome man striding so quickly under the trees, looking neither to the right nor the left. Business was alien to them just now, the humming gnats and great leaping trouts were more in unison with their holiday mood. Robert Ord glanced at them half in envy and half in contempt, and marvelled how the world had dealt with them that they could stand so happily on those smooth white boulders, looking down into the deep sunny pools for the silvery plash, which was just now the object of their thoughts.

One of them was a poor artisan, with a disabled arm—a thin sickly-looking man ; he was humming a Methodist hymn-tune as he mended his rod—a sturdy white dog was barking savagely at his own shadow in the water at his feet. Robert Ord noticed that his elbows were ragged, and by a queer transition of mood tossed him a silver coin. The man took it up languidly and thanked him in a subdued sort of way.

" There's a storm coming up, maister ; there's a taint of thunder in the air," he said in a rough Yorkshire dialect, and then he went on with his tune. Robert Ord stood and envied him before he turned away. What a bad bitter mood was on him ! As the old lawyer quaintly expressed it, he was just in the humour to play at fisticuffs with the world at large.

A great blow had just been dealt him, and he was by no means a man disposed at any time to turn the other cheek to his enemy; all such smitings were odious to him, and he was much given to show a very muscular sort of Christianity on such occasions. Mr. Tracy's generous defence of Miss Maturin had secretly exasperated him, and he had had some difficulty the previous night in concealing the fact that the whole tenor of the conversation had been insupportable to him. In his own mind he called him a fool for his credulity, and mocked at the old-fashioned chivalry that prompted him to go down into the lists. And being very slow at all times to yield up a preconceived idea, however erroneous, he was not likely to be won over even by the lawyer's eloquence, and least of all by his generous hospitality.

He chose to believe that Miss Maturin had gained influence over his aunt for her own purposes, and nothing short of a miracle would be ever likely to alter his opinion, and of course, so judging, he was not disposed to hold out the sceptre of his favour to so hardened a sinner because she had eloquent eyes and a soft voice.

No, that was not probable, and as he walked along he strengthened himself in his indignation all the more that the smart of his injuries was fresh upon him. She had coveted that money; all those rich belongings had seemed desirable to her poverty. Very young women could be designing sometimes, and scheme for their own benefit. Doubtless she had so schemed; doubtless during those four years she had so ingratiated herself into her protectress' favour with her smooth subtle ways, that it was no wonder that she had forgotten her own flesh and blood, seeing that her own flesh and blood had so sinned against her. Her hands were not clean, so he told himself—not clean, that is, with an honest whiteness, and as he suffered no degrees of comparison in his mind, he soon grew to believe that they were of absolute blackness, that her deceit was odious, and that any forgiveness on his part would be a reprehensible act of weakness.

It never occurred to him that he might be drawing a wrong conclusion, that it was possible that even his opinion might be mistaken, and that he was unjustly condemning the innocent.

There are few gems without a flaw, comparatively few, that is to say, and so it is with human nature. The time came when Robert Ord owned that he was more sinning than sinned against; when the scales of his own self-sufficiency fell from his eyes; when he saw clearly and judged righteously; when he owned that his pride and his uncharitableness had wrought his troubles and marred so long the beauty of his life; that he had himself to thank, and no other; and when, in the subdued wisdom of his riper years, he confessed "that it was good for him that he had been afflicted," and that he had gained his knowledge through the bitterness of experience.

He had reached the Abbey Bridge by this time; about three-quarters of a mile beyond lay Rokeby, as he well knew, but he felt no sort of desire to see it. Already he had passed " Eglistone's gray ruins " unnoticed, and now he stood leaning his elbows on the stone battlements of the bridge, and looking moodily down into the bubbling river with eyes that saw nothing.

And yet the scene that lay before him was fair enough for a poet's dream: behind him was Eglistone, or, as the guide-books have it, Athelstone or Egglestone Abbey, built on the angle formed by the little dell called Thorsgill with the Tees.

In this Abbey Sir Walter Scott laid the closing scene of his *Rokeby.*

From the Abbey Bridge one looks down the magnificent valley of the Tees, with its richly-wooded banks; the river itself flowing in a deep trench of solid rock, chiefly limestone and marble; and from where Robert Ord stood the view was exquisitely beautiful, the whole course of the river was broken up by huge boulders of snowy whiteness, over which the water bubbled and frothed in the sunshine with an endless fret.

By and by the noonday glare disturbed him, and he left the bridge and climbed down amongst the underwood to the very edge of the water; the smell of the cool dark vegetation refreshed him, and then he seated himself astride a low bough that hung over the water. He had set himself a task: he was looking things in the face, as he called it—reviewing his past, present, and future, all the time that he was dropping the loose pebbles into the current and watching the tiny eddies in which they disappeared. The shiver of leaves and the wet splash of large drops on his face recalled him from this dreamy introspection, and the low growling of suppressed thunder warned him that a storm was impending. The air was close to suffocation, and the clouds looked electric. He always keenly enjoyed a storm, and as he scrambled up the banks it came into his head that he would seek shelter in the Abbey ruins that towered a little way above him; it would be better than having to exchange civilities with the toll-gate keeper on the bridge.

The drops were coming down faster now, with an ominous pattering and splutter, and he was obliged to hasten his steps; but as he ran up the green slopes and was about to vault over the low palings, he saw to his chagrin that some one else, a female, had taken shelter in the same refuge.

For a moment he had half a mind to retrace his steps, and was

turning round for the purpose, but on second thoughts he restrained
his impulse. The rain was coming down now with a steady down-
pour that would have drenched him to the skin, and he saw that
the person, or lady, whichever it might be, was standing vainly
trying to shelter herself under a broken buttress : mere humanity
prompted him to go to her assistance ; Robert Ord was a gentleman
both by instinct and education ; in another minute he was beside
her.

"You will get very wet if you stand under the ruined window,"
he said courteously, as though to a perfect stranger, but at his
first word she turned round and looked at him.

It was Miss Maturin.

She had evidently seen him coming up from the road, for his
sudden appearance did not seem to surprise her. She looked up
at him half timidly, half wistfully, as though she hoped that he
would greet her ; she even made a movement as though she would
put out her hand to him, but something of sternness in his face
forbade this.

"You here, of all places in the world, Miss Maturin !" And
now it was impossible for her to mistake the surprised displeasure
of his voice.

"Yes, I was down on the river-bank, and the rain overtook
me," she faltered.

"You have chosen a very poor refuge then," he returned ;
"there is a better shelter over there," and he pointed to a low
range of out-buildings that skirted the Abbey.

But she hesitated a moment.

"Pray do not lose time or we shall have the storm upon us,"
he continued impatiently. "You do not mind the wet grass, I
suppose."

She shook her head, and mutely pointed to her dripping dress,
which was clinging round her in lank folds, and in another moment
he had hurried her across the wide green, and they were standing
together under the doorway of a ruined dwelling-house.

"What a desolate place," he muttered, as he relieved her of
her wet cloak, and bade her shake out her dress, after which he
proceeded to eject a coal-black heifer, evidently an occupant of the
tenement. Several horned heads appeared from time to time, and
seemed greatly astonished at being refused admittance.

"They have turned it into a cattle-shed, I suppose," he continued, looking round at the crumbling walls and grateless fireplace
of their undesirable refuge ; and then, without waiting a reply, he
picked his way among the mouldering bricks, and leant against the
empty framework of the window.

It was not an exhilarating scene, and one can forgive Robert Ord if, in his present mood, he looked at it with lowering brows and wished himself a hundred miles away.

The whole place was misty with driving rain, the sky sullen and lurid; every now and then there was the glare and dazzle of sudden lightning, the tree-tops looked gray and indistinct, the river ran molten, the cattle herded together under the projecting eaves, lowing their discontent with their sweet breath full on Robert Ord's face. Across the green space rose the gray old ruins; some birds had taken refuge in the great bare east window, and twittered and trimmed their wet plumage. Loose stones and mortar crackled down the yawning chimney where Miss Maturin stood shaking out the folds of her dress and looking wistfully at him.

She had on a little straw hat, and she had tied it in gipsy fashion over her face, with a broad black ribbon; her face was paler, if possible, and there was a red swollen look about her eyes as though she had been weeping. He thought her even plainer than he had yesterday; but he could not deny that her expression was very sweet.

She eyed him timidly for a few minutes before she could summon up courage for her simple question.

"Do you think we shall have to wait long, Mr. Ord? I mean is the rain nearly over?"

"Over? Well, no. I am afraid there is no chance of our leaving here for another three-quarters of an hour or so," he returned, moving his arm for a moment from the dripping window-sill.

"Three-quarters of an hour!" she exclaimed, in a tone of such genuine dismay that he smiled grimly in spite of his own discomfiture.

"I am sorry that you are so uncomfortable; but the fact is we cannot help ourselves."

"Mr. Tracy told me that he thought it would not rain, or I would never have ventured so far," she continued, as though distressed at the awkwardness of her position.

"Mr. Tracy was a bad prophet, then," he replied coldly; and then he turned himself again as though to study the prospect. He had nothing to say to her; between them there was a gulf which he had determined nothing should induce him to bridge over. If they were to remain there an hour he would only address a curt observation or two. She had come between him and his lawful rights, and he was not likely to forget that for a moment; and, as he remembered his wrongs, the frown gathered darkly to his brow. No wonder her heart sank within her as she watched him.

"I was right, and he hates me," she said to herself mournfully;

"and he was so gentle with me yesterday before he knew all ;" and then, with the courage of sudden impulse which comes sometimes to the weakest and the most timid women, she determined that at all cost she must speak to him. She had had a final interview with Mr. Tracy that morning, and had gathered much in spite of the lawyer's guarded speech. She knew that Robert Ord had been bitterly disappointed, that there had been hard words said, and harder things thought than were ever likely to come to her knowledge. And as she looked at the rigid lines of the handsome face before her, and remembered the few icy words with which he had addressed her, she felt that her task would not be a pleasant one ; but none the less did she resolve that she would ask his forgiveness for being the innocent cause of his wrong. "I must meet him again and again, as I must meet all of them," she thought. "Oh ! if I could only soften him, if but one of them would look kindly on me and be my friend, I think I could bear it better," and then in her impulse she moved a little closer to him.

"Mr. Ord, I must speak to you," she began ; but as he turned round she stopped, scared by the very sternness of his face.

"I am quite at your service," he returned ; but not looking at her nevertheless.

"Yes, I know ; but then there are some things so hard in the telling."

"Some things—— Well—yes."

"But none so hard as this. Do you know, Mr. Ord, when you spoke to me last night I was almost dumb before you."

"I remember it well, Miss Maturin."

"You questioned me then, but I could not answer you ; I felt almost desperate when I thought of all that there was to tell. Mr. Ord, shall I ever be able to tell you how grieved I am for what has happened ?"

Then the blackest frown that had ever been seen on Robert Ord's brow gathered there again. She had dared to speak on that subject to him—to him !

"Oh, Mr. Ord !"

"Well, what now ?" he asked haughtily.

"Because I can see it in your face, because I can feel it here," putting her hand on her heart ; "because I know, as well as though I had heard them, all the bitter things you have said and felt. Do you think I blame you ? Not I. You have been cruelly wronged, you and all of them ; but your suffering is nothing compared to mine."

She spoke passionately, but without any idea of defending herself ; for the anger of his look stung her beyond endurance. Her spirit was fairly roused now.

"You know that if it had been in my power this thing should never have happened to you."

Then he remained absolutely silent.

"Oh, Mr. Ord, this is too cruel, when you know how wretched, how utterly wretched, all this terrible money has made me." And then she broke down, and for a moment wept before him as though she were heart-broken. "Do you not think that if I could undo it I would? God knows that it is not my fault that all this trouble and wrong have come upon you."

"I accuse you of nothing, Miss Maturin."

"No; but your silence does; it accuses me terribly. Do you think I was to blame in anything? that I might have sent for you before?"

"No, I do not think that."

"Then in what have I failed?" she continued, her face growing paler; for it was impossible to mistake his manner. But again he hesitated.

He was wishing himself most earnestly away by this time. No appearance of innocence on her part could alter his opinion, so he told himself; but something of the hard bitter humour was oozing away. In reality he was gentle at heart, and he could not bear to treat her churlishly. She might be what he thought her, but he could not bring himself to tell her his suspicions. Not at least unless she should drive him to it; but his silence was betraying him.

"Miss Maturin," he said, not unkindly, "this is a very unfortunate subject you have chosen; pray let us change it."

But she shook her head.

"Not till you have answered my question, Mr. Ord."

"I must decline to answer it."

"What! you decline to tell me wherein I have deserved blame; is that generous, is that fair?"

"You forget. I accuse you of nothing. The time for all such accusation is past. Let us consider the matter at an end. I may hold my own opinion, but I do not care to allude to it again."

"Allude to what?" she returned, looking bewildered. "What is at an end? Do you not see how hard all this is for me? You will not speak to me because I am the innocent cause of all this trouble."

"Pardon me, I do not regard you as the innocent cause, Miss Maturin. There, it is your own fault. I would have spared you this. You are compelling the truth from me."

"Yes, yes; I know."

Thus driven in a corner, he continued steadily:

" I cannot regard you as innocent. In my own mind I think there must have been undue influence at work, or my aunt would never have left you all her money. Ah, you shrink from me. Why did you make me tell you this ?"

" You believe this—you believe this of me, Mr. Ord ?"

" I have thought so, and I think so still ; but I am grieved that you oblige me to speak so plainly. I do not wish to be churlish to a lady. I think that you were young and friendless and needed help, and the position was one of great temptation. We were strangers to you, and under a cloud ; you were hardly aware of the moral wrong you were doing ; you might only have coveted a small portion of my aunt's wealth. I can quite believe you are sorry now for what has happened, but how can such sorrow avail us ?"

" You believe this of me ?" she repeated in the same tone, but he never forgot the look with which she said it ; it haunted him long afterwards—there was no anger, but the incredulous sorrow in her eyes moved even him to compassion.

" Miss Maturin, do let us say no more."

" There is nothing more to be said," she answered wearily, and her hands dropped to her side as she spoke. " I must bear it, I suppose. I cannot defend myself, for you would not believe my word ; you have not believed all that Mr. Tracy has told you, of how I have worked and watched for you." Nothing could exceed the hopelessness with which she said this.

" I am sorry all this has occurred."

Then for a moment the colour came into her pale face.

" Are you sorry, Mr. Ord ? Well, that is something. No, I will not let this imputation crush me ; I will not, I will not. I don't think you quite know what you have done, being a stranger, but I forgive you ; you have almost broken my heart, but you have given me an object in life."

" How so, Miss Maturin ?"

" Ah ! you do not know me ; I am a poor creature, but I can be very patient. I will not call Heaven to witness my innocence, for you would not believe my words ; but I will never rest, I will never cease from striving day after day, and year after year, till I remove this suspicion. Mr. Ord, it will be my one, my only thought."

" You heap coals of fire on my head," he returned, but the sarcasm somehow failed him.

Once more she looked at him with that mild reproach in her eyes.

" Yes, the time will come when you will own that you have

3

wronged me; it may be years hence, but I know it will come, when you will surely own it."

"Be assured that I shall not delay coming to you if any such taking back of words be necessary."

"No, I know you will not; I can see that you are true, though you are so terribly hard;" and then she moved away from him, and he saw a look in her face as though she was heart-broken.

"I hope I am having a very pleasant day, on the whole," thought Robert Ord bitterly, as he walked up and down among the brick-heaps: he had done his work—she had forced him to do it; but the result did not satisfy him. What good was it to him that he had convicted her of her sin if she would not own that she had so sinned? He had grappled with her, and she had glided from him with a look of reproach which haunted him against his will; do what he would, he could not banish a certain feeling of remorse as he thought of it. He had accused her of virtual dishonesty, or at least of obtaining an undue influence over his aunt, and she had not defended herself by so much as one word. Surely he had been gentle enough with her. He had been betrayed into anger once or twice, and had then repented and refrained himself. With all his wrath he had not said anything specially bitter, though the sternness of his look or tone might have rebuked her. But of what avail was all this mildness and refraining, since she would insist on assuming the airs of heart-broken innocence? It made him feel as though his magnanimity had been thrown away; and yet a few hours ago he had sworn that on no account could he bring himself to forgive her.

These were not pleasant thoughts, as he stumbled over the brick-heaps, among the mouldering passages. How he loathed the whole place with an impatient loathing that recurred to him in future days! He could always recall that scene, it was so vivid in his memory—that desolate dwelling, with the strips of plaster clinging to the damp mouldering walls; the gaping window-frame, the broad green level, and gray ruins misty with driving rain; the dull thud of horned heads striking impatiently against the doorway; and always motionless, always the central figure in that picture, the tall figure in the clinging black draperies: he could see the curve of the long neck, the small head bent slightly forward, the fluttering of the thin hands; could almost hear the monotonous tones of the low murmuring voice, "Yes, the time will come when you will own that you have wronged me." When and how did that time come to Robert Ord?

The rain was ceasing now; he had just become aware of the fact, and wondering how he was to break the silence and open his lips to speak to her, when she relieved him of his embarrassment.

"The rain is over now, I believe," she said, turning round to him. There was not a trace of colour in her face, but her calmness was wonderful: all the tremor, the nervous agitation that had so disturbed him yesterday, had left her; she looked like one who had unexpectedly received a deadly blow, but who was rallying from it. Her perfect self-possession astonished him.

"The storm has not turned its back upon us yet," he returned, trying to speak with equal sangfroid, "but, if you are willing, we will take advantage of this lull;" to which she briefly assented, and in another minute they were walking side by side along the high road and under the dripping trees, greatly to his surprise, for he had expected her to decline his escort; but he did not know her.

There was another awkward silence, which neither attempted to break, and then he took courage and relieved himself of a perplexity.

"Miss Maturin, after what has passed there can hardly be very cordial feelings between us, as it is impossible for me to consider myself otherwise than injured; but still, as I said before, you may not have anticipated all these consequences. I do not wish to judge you harshly. I feel sorry that you compelled me to speak."

A dim smile flitted across her face, more mournful than any tears.

"Do you mean there can be peace between us? I certainly do not wish it otherwise, Mr. Ord."

"Neither do I," he returned hastily. "What is done, is done. I have no wish to make your position wholly unbearable. I suppose we can always exchange the civilities of strangers?"

"I have no intention whatever of avoiding you, Mr. Ord."

"You could not if you wished," he returned, piqued by her perfect indifference. "Bryn and Kirkby Vicarage are too close together."

"Yes, I know," she answered, with a shiver. "Do you think I forget what lies before me? If you will let me come amongst you, I will come; if not, I will bide my time. I do not mean to shun any of you. Why should I? I have done nothing of which to be ashamed—all such shunning will be on your side."

"I cannot answer for it that we shall be very cordial, Miss Maturin."

"Of course not. Do you think I expect it? Of course you will make my life bitter amongst you. But then I do not mean to blame you. You are very unjust. You do not know how to be merciful. But I can wait my time." And after that he had nothing to say.

It was a strange dreary walk, and one which they were not likely to forget. It was a relief when they had left the river behind them, and were treading the well-worn pavement of the High Street; and still more a relief when they had reached the portico of the King's Arms.

And then they parted.

"I suppose I may not offer you my hand, Miss Maturin?" he said, with some slight feeling of compunction, as she turned her white wistful face to him.

"No, Mr. Ord, you may not; you must never offer it to me again till you have taken back all you have said—till you have cleared me from this terrible imputation." And then, when she had said this, she left him and went in.

# CHAPTER IV.

## MEG.

" Oh, what makes woman lovely ?   Virtue, faith,
And gentleness in suffering.   An endurance
Through scorn or trial : these call beauty forth,
Give it the stamp celestial, and admit it
To sisterhood with angels !"                    BRENT.

IN a well-known suburb of London—a suburb so widely known
that its very name will bring a flood of reminiscences to many of
us—there is a retired and pleasant thoroughfare called Chatham
Place.

The glory of Hackney is departed.   The traces of past grandeur
are fast fading away from its sunny old streets.   The monster
tide of fashion that has set in during late years has swept family
after family westward.   The wealthy citizens who lived in these
great brick mansions, dwelling not figuratively but in reality under
their fig-trees, pleasant old places set in the midst of shady gardens,
have long ago migrated, each man according to his several degrees
of consequence and ambition—some to the sun-baked pavements
of West-End squares and streets ; a few to the humbler precincts
of Russell Square ; while others, less ambitious, and pining for
green fields and country lanes, have sought out dwelling-places for
themselves at Hampstead or Highgate, never dreaming that those
fields would soon lie low, and those leafy lanes be trodden under
foot, under the ever-advancing needs of increasing population.
Alas ! for those brick-and-mortar paradises ; those long winding
streets, modernised and uninteresting, where not so many years
ago the children loitered in the narrow lanes to gather hawthorn
and sweetbrier roses, or dabbled knee-deep in fields of golden
buttercups ; where the blackbirds and the thrushes used to sing
in the early mornings, and in summer the air was full of the sweetness of new-mown hay.   Now one walks as a stranger through the
old spots, remembering as in a dream some favourite clump of
trees or well-worn stile where a glittering gin-palace now flanks

the path, or a labyrinth of intersecting roads branch into endless lines and divisions of undeviating and hopeless uniformity.

But though such glory as it once possessed is departed from Hackney, there is still a pleasant air of repose and quiet about its old familiar streets. Here and there some of the old families still linger, clinging fondly to bygone associations, and despising the tyrannies of fashion. The whole place is a little oppressive and heavy in its respectability. There is monotony in its aspect—one day resembles another—but one feels a dim sort of tenderness for it nevertheless: one is haunted by a desire to linger long in the shady churchyard, where the old church-tower and the church are so strangely dissevered, and where one walks down the flagged path under the trees, with the dead lying on either hand, and the children plucking daisies out of the rank grass, or playing on the gray discoloured gravestones.

Branching off from the churchyard, and passing under the railway bridge, one finds oneself in Chatham Place. Here quiet would become dreariness save for the hum of voices proceeding at set hours from the great schoolhouse. It is impossible to connect life and activity with Chatham Place. The houses are dull and obscure, standing back in long narrow gardens, with great gates that swing solemnly backward and forward. The windows are long and narrow, and scarcely require the adjuncts of wire blinds. But they look pleasantly on a long strip of triangular green, where a few sheep and cows are always browsing, and beyond which lies Homerton Terrace. There are few trees, but plenty of dust and sunshine. There is no deafening traffic to jar one's nerves. All the knockers are bright as gold, and the one stone step is conspicuous for its whiteness. Few footsteps crunch in the long gravel-path. Here again respectability and monotony go hand in hand.

In one of these houses, many years before the events we have recorded took place, lived Mrs. Carruthers, Rotha Maturin's friend —or Meg Browning, as she was then.

Meg, as she was always called—for never in all her days had any one been known to call her by her baptismal name of Margaret —Meg lived with her father and mother in one of these shady old houses in Chatham Place.

Meg's father was a clerk in some mercantile house—a hardworking industrious man, going forth to his business in the early morning and never returning till late at night. And her mother had failing sight and delicate health. Never was any youth less gay and exciting than Meg's, but never was any richer in dutiful unselfish happiness.

Meg helped her father. She treasured and made much of her one talent—rising early and taking rest late, that she might bring it to fruition. By and by came the reward to her industry, when she gave music lessons in the same school where she had learned as a girl. But Meg did more than this: besides her daily drudgery at Miss Binks', and her trudgings backwards and forwards across the churchyard, she had her household duties to transact. She had her simple cookeries, and fine ironings, and plaitings of her mother's caps, and hemming of her mother's snowy handkerchiefs. She had shirt-fronts to stitch, and to unpick and rectify her mother's knitting, always ragged with dropped stitches. She had to read the paper, or make conversation when her father came home tired at night; sometimes to play cribbage with one or the other, or to take a hand at whist when her father chose to play dummy.

Then on Sunday morning she would go across the churchyard hanging on her father's arm. She would sit with him under the sunny west window in the old pew, and look out his places in the Psalm-book—they sang Tait and Brady then. She must remember all the heads of the sermon for her mother's benefit, and retail them in the hot drowsy afternoon, when her father was having his after-dinner nap. And in the evening she read long pages to them both out of Blair's *Sermons* and Harvey's *Meditations*, with sometimes a spell of Doddridge's *Rise and Progress*. In the twilight she would play to them the old-fashioned tunes they loved— Luther's grand old hymn, "How cheerful along the gay mead," with a spice of the Old Hundredth; while the parents would sit hand in hand, listening with tears in their eyes: the father joining in now and then with odd trills and roulades of the old style.

Then for pleasures: did they not go once or twice in the summer to the grand London parks, and listen to the band in Kensington Gardens, and feed the ducks in St. James', or go over to Battersea, or take the steamer to Greenwich? And in the winter did not Meg's father take her twice to hear Shakespeare's plays, *Hamlet* and *Henry V.*, regaling her all the way there and back with glorious tales of Mrs. Siddons and the Kembles?—dissipations which made her lie a whole half-hour longer in bed the next morning.

Meg had no young friends, but she never missed them; she had an odd sturdy character of her own—individuality that would have marked her in a crowd. She had very little in common with girls of her own age. She worked while they played; she was old-fashioned, reserved, a trifle repellent—and then she was no beauty.

To tell the truth, one could not conceive a woman more unattractive. She had just the sort of face and figure about which

there could be no doubt.    Positive ugliness is difficult to redeem.
Meg's defects were lamentable.    A husband would be the last
thing one could prophesy for her.    And, to tell the truth, Meg
was so sensible as to know her shortcomings.    In her own person
she never dreamt of love.

Meg had a tall bony figure ; she had broad high shoulders and
angularities innumerable, added to which she was short-sighted and
stooped ; she had a strong Scotch face, hard-featured and freckled,
with high cheek-bones, with large light eyes rather grave than
mirthful, and flaxen hair without glint or gloss, which she combed
up regardless of ornament into a knot behind.

Meg knew her plainness, and wore sad-coloured gowns, like a
Quakeress.    Her mother bought her sometimes knots of ribbons
and pinned them on with her own hands ; but they hardly looked
well against her complexion.    Meg's colours were all muddled and
ran into each other, faint thick reds and browns ; her forehead was
sallow ; and, worst of all, in speech her voice was rather too deep
and unmusical, somewhat masculine in fact.

Meg's one beauty was her passionate love of music.    Those
strong large hands of hers could draw sweetest tones from the
cracked old piano, purchased second-hand on Meg's one-and-twen-
tieth birthday, to replace a spinnet nearly dumb with age.    As she
played, a grave solemn light would shine in her eyes, her voice
would give out rich deep notes ; there was something grand about
Meg then.    "Oh, Day of Wrath ! oh, Day of Mourning !"—Meg
would sing the "Dies Iræ" in a way that would have thrilled
you to hear her.

When Meg was almost seven-and-twenty her father died.    He
had worked as man and boy for more than fifty years, and had
laid by a few thrifty savings for his widow ; besides which, a
maternal aunt had left a few hundreds to Meg.    With a little
prudence they might still continue to live in the old way ; nay
more, Meg was able to relinquish a few of her labours, and to
minister more fully to her mother's needs, who had become totally
blind.    Meg played oftener now for her own pleasure, and picked
up stitches with a vigorous hand as she listened patiently to the
long list of ailments which constituted her mother's chief topic of
conversation, interlarded with stories of her dearly remembered
youth.

Meg used to look up and nod by way of parenthesis.    She was
never a great talker, even in her most confidential moments ; but
her face would be a marvel of content.    She would glance out at
the long narrow garden with its cabbages and sunflowers, where
some fine linen would generally be bleaching on the lawn, and then

back at the horsehair chair, at her mother's placid wrinkled face, with its gray hair and snowy closely-crimped cap, at the drab silk shawl and net kerchief, and great strip of yellowish soiled knitting, and the pins which moved so feebly in and out. "Another stitch dropped, mother; it will be Jacob's ladder soon," she would say, with a little laugh; and she would run off row after row with her nimble fingers, humming a low soft tune as she did so. She thought her mother's conversation the most delightful in the world; the old lady's prose never seemed to weary her. She would listen to a story she had heard a dozen times over, with never-varying interest; her nods would be brisk and regular, and she would even look disappointed when a brief nap interrupted the narrative in the most graphic part.

Perhaps there is a serpent in every paradise; even the humble household in Chatham Place was not to be exempt from its tempter in human shape.

Meg was nine-and-twenty when she met Jack Carruthers for the first time—handsome Jack Carruthers, as his fellow-clerks called him. It was at a birthday party at one of her pupil's houses, and Meg was to go and play for them while they danced —at least, that is how she interpreted the invitation. One may be sure Jack thought little about the tall angular woman in black, who played polkas and schottisches, bringing rare music out of rather a wooden instrument. When she was not wanted, Meg hunched her shoulders, and peered curiously at some engravings at a side table. No one noticed or spoke to her. Jack quizzed her a little as he flirted with handsome Susan Smithers. After supper, when she sang some Scotch songs to them in that deep rich voice of hers, he condescended to ask who that woman was; and was told in sneering whispers by a friend of his that she was "the daughter of old Dick Browning. One of our fellows, Jack, and a precious old skinflint—so I've heard. Worked hard all his life. Plenty of money. Must have saved no end of tin. Made his daughter drudge, though, as a music teacher. Plays well, doesn't she? Not much of a beauty to look at, though. Daughter has some cool hundreds of her own, I'm told. Lives with an old blind mother in Chatham Place. Eh? what? want an introduction? That's right, my boy; wide awake, as usual. Think I'll try and cut you out myself; only it would not be friendly. Mind you pay me the money you owe me on your wedding-day;" and so on, with many claps on the shoulders.

Jack makes a grimace and haw-haws a little, but finally walks up as bold as brass, and begs to thank Miss Browning for her charming music, Jack adores music, and so on. Meg reddens rather; perhaps she is not accustomed to be addressed. She drops her eye-glasses nervously. She says very little, but stammers a great deal. She looks up at him shyly once or twice, and thinks she has never seen so personable a man. Jack is very handsome, certainly; he has a fine brown complexion and bold black eyes, and his whiskers curl most delightfully; perhaps his lips are thick, and his face rather coarse, but to Meg he seemed a stalwart Adonis. Something in her frame seemed to beat most strangely, as he stood by her chair, pulling his whiskers and speaking quick determined sentences; he made her sing some more Scotch songs, and chanted a sonorous bass by way of chorus. And when she rose to go, his friend and he walked with her all the way home to Chatham Place, Jock carrying her music-roll.

Where there is a will there is a way. How it fell out Meg never knew; but, before many weeks had elapsed, Jack Carruthers had made good his footing in the little house at Chatham Place, and was well received by both mother and daughter. At first he brought his friend, but afterwards he came alone. By and by Meg would stand regularly at the window of an evening, watching until she saw him striding from under the dark railway bridge. When he reached the row of posts she would turn from the window with a blush on her sallow face, and pick up her mother's stitches nervously, with her heart beating so loudly that she could hardly breathe.

Jack would bring her new music and flowers, little bunches of narcissus and jonquils, or fragrant clove-pinks, which he would buy in the city for a few pence. Sometimes, as he sat on the top of the omnibus, he would employ himself in picking off the dead leaves. Meg thought them the most beautiful bouquets in the, world, and would redden more than ever as she put them in water. She would sit quite silent in her great happiness, while Jack played with her ball of darning cotton, and discoursed on politics in his bluff quick way. By and by he would ask her to play or sing, and then nothing could exceed her bliss.

They say love can beautify even a plain woman. Meg became almost brave in her attire; her hands got white and soft by magic, and her hair grew smooth and almost glossy; she still wore her sad-coloured gowns, but she brightened them up with knots of pink ribbons—a faint drowsy pink being the only colour that blended with her faded tints—and girded herself with wonderful aprons worked in floss silks. Jack used to note these changes with a satirical eye as he stood in the dark corner by the piano. He was sure of the cool hundreds now. Sometimes he would sigh or swear softly to himself as he walked home across the churchyard, and through Clapton Square, and past the five houses, and so on, on his way to Stamford Hill, where he lived— "things must be at a pretty pass indeed with Jack Carruthers when he took it into his head to marry Meg Browning."

Things were at a pretty pass indeed!

I do not know in what language Jack couched that villainous proposal of his. He was a tolerably hardened reprobate—most likely he did it coolly enough. Meg's head drooped over her hands, and great tears splashed on the keys—Jack could almost hear them; the deep passionate nature which lay beneath all her reserve and shyness awoke to life at his first words with a suddenness that frightened herself. Oh, the power of love in such women—the pure unselfish worship, the profound adoration, the blindness, the credulity! Meg, raining tears of unalloyed happiness, placed her hand in Jack's, and felt as though Heaven had no more to offer her.

Jack was an ardent wooer: he was all impatience—perhaps his creditors were pressing. Meg was nearly thirty now; even her mother agreed that there was no reason for them to wait.

The little household in Chatham Place was to go on much as usual. Jack was to be received there as an inmate—Meg could not leave her mother. Jack entreated her, almost with tears in his eyes, not to go to any needless expense on his account: Meg was for refurnishing; the shabby horsehair chairs and sofa were insupportable to her now. With tender reluctance she renounced her ambitious projects and contented herself with a little painting and papering and a gay-coloured chintz.

Poor Meg! she wove one blissful dream after another as she sewed those chair-covers; the great sprawling lilies and roses were not brighter or more preposterous than some of those dreams.

The wedding was a very humble one. Meg had few friends, and Jack had potent reasons why he would ask none of his; so one sunny May morning Meg, dressed in her new gray silk, took Jack's arm and walked with him under the dark railway arch, and between the long rows of grassy hillocks, where the children looked up from their daisy-wreaths, to the old parish church, and there signed her name for the first time as Meg Carruthers.

Meg's passionate happiness did not last long; before many weeks were over she was a broken-hearted woman.

Meg knew she was the dupe of a heartless profligate; she knew that he had married her to save himself from a debtor's prison, that he loathed his bondage, and could not conceal his scorn of the woman who had linked her fate with his; but she had more than this to bear. Jack, gross in his vices, came home night after night to the affrighted women with curses on his lips, and speaking in the thick voice of the drunkard, terrifying those pure souls immeasurably, and filling Meg's cup of woe to the brim.

Alas, what she suffered! Scorned, despised, and often hardly used, she yet clave, as only a woman can, to the reprobate she called husband : when he cursed she held her peace ; in his rare moments of sullen half-contemptuous amity she played and sang to him, striving to win him a little from his indifference ; many a rude blow she averted by hiding her head in his breast, or, if he flung her from thence, she would crush down the sobs that almost strangled her, and look up in his face and try to smile with the black bruise from his grip still smarting on her poor arm.

She denied him nothing ; every penny of her little hoard was wrung from her, and when all was gone, she made no complaint, but took up her old drudgery again, and went out in the sleet and snow morning after morning that her mother might want for nothing.

Oh, what he made her endure for her mother's sake! Meg's filial love was a passion. Day after day she saw the tears roll down the wrinkled cheeks from those sightless eyes, as she left her beside her lonely hearth. No more picking up of stitches and sweet endless gossips in the sunshine. One by one Meg saw her mother's little comforts disappear, saw how gradually but surely the miseries of their daily life preyed on her tender heart.

"Meg, I shall never hold your baby in my arms," she would say, as her daughter led her upstairs of a night and undressed her like a child, "but I pray God that it may be a girl." And Meg felt that her words would come true, for two days after she closed those blind eyes, and kissed them in the coffin, she lay down on her bed of pain, and knew that the baby that never nestled in her breast was dead also.

There is not much to tell after this. Meg was never a demonstrative woman in her happiness, and she was not confidential in her misery. She was a strong-minded woman—she bore her troubles in a strong-minded way, making small ado and shedding few tears ; she never reproached her husband for her mother's and baby's death, though in an indirect way he was the cause of both ; there was nothing melodramatic about Meg ; in their most terrible scenes the woman kept silence.

Jack got everything he could ; then he went into debt, the furniture was seized—not a stick or straw was left in the old house in Chatham Place. Meg, tearless still, locked the door with her own hands and asked her husband whither they should go.

One cannot repeat his answer, but Meg knew then that her husband had resolved to rid himself of a hated incumbrance. A year and a half, only eighteen months ago, she had passed under that dark archway, a bride leaning on her lover's arm ; now she stood looking again towards the archway, knowing that she was worse than widowed.

"I have never reproached you, Jack, and I never will ; but I did not think you would leave me," was her sole answer, as she looked at the bloated handsome face, still so cruelly handsome to her ; perhaps, reprobate as he was, that tender forgiveness abashed him, for he hung his head.

"I don't think we were made to pull together, Madge," he said rather huskily. "It is not your fault — you are a good woman, I know, and I have been your curse ; but, anyhow, you won't see the face of Jack Carruthers again."

And Meg believed him.

She went to her desolate lodgings that night, just in sight of the old house ; she could not wear mourning, but no widow ever lamented as she did over the grave of her lost love. There was something grand in her exceeding silence ; from morning to night she worked uncomplainingly at her old drudgery, sitting by her lonely fire through the long evening, with only grievous thoughts for company ; and every night and morning she prayed for Jack as only the loving and heavy-laden can pray.

How many such prayers shall be written in letters of gold by the Recording Angel ! How many and how great the sum of them !

# CHAPTER V.

" A little by his act perhaps, yet more
    By something in me, surely not my will,
    I did not die.   But slowly, as one in swoon,
    To whom life creeps back in the form of death,
    With a sense of separation, a blind pain
    Of blank obstruction, and a roar i' the ears
    Of visionary chariots which retreat
    As earth grows clearer . . . slowly, by degrees,
    I woke, rose up . . . Where was I ?—in the world ;
    For uses therefore I must count worth while."

*Aurora Leigh.*

IT was a drowsy hot afternoon, and the small patch of green, which was generally an object of rejoicing to the inhabitants of Chatham Place, an oasis in their desert, was all burnt and barren, offering but poor pasturage to a few forlorn-looking sheep that had long ago discontinued cropping the dry herbage, and were now herded together for shade.   Sunshine and dust were the order of the day ; the pavements were bleached and glaring, the trees distilled gray dust on the passenger's head, the roads were ruled into tiny furrows of the same, the paint on the doors was blistered and peeled in long brown flakes, and the bright knockers were like molten lead. The very windows gaped wide open, as though striving for more air ; wire blinds were withdrawn ; and there was a flutter of white curtains.   Sometimes through the half-open doors one caught a glimpse of green leaves ; here and there a canary piped loudly in its gilded cage ; some brown sparrows twittered on the hot ledges. The children had betaken themselves to the shelter of the railway arches, and were hooting amongst them like so many owls ; the chiming of many voices from the National School rose and fell in one drowsy hum ; there was pent-up animal life there—a discontented hive of busy workers longing for the sunshine, sturdy urchins yearning to join their vagrant companions among the dark railway arches, restless fingers counting marbles to the tune of the

multiplication-table ; outside, a sky intensely blue, plenty of yellow
sunshine, but the glare and glitter almost oppressive.

Meg, sitting in her little back parlour, all shade and coolness,
could hear the droning; the mixed indistinguishable hum in the
clear summer air soothed and lulled her; those crescendoes and
falls of shrill young voices softened by distance had a music of
their own. Meg used to listen to it as she plodded through her
darning. She could picture the great bare rooms with the rows of
rosy faces and sunburnt white heads; she used to nod and smile
at the little ones as they came trooping past her windows; some
of them would drop a shy curtsey. The solitary woman, in spite
of her grimness, had ways with her that could touch children. In
the churchyard she would stop and speak to them ; once she found
a boy who had strayed all the way from Bethnal Green with a
baby sister. Meg found them both asleep on her mother's grave,
with a tattered handkerchief full of chickweed and dandelion beside them. Meg took them all the way home, carrying them in
her arms by turn ; the youngest child cried at parting with her.

Those summer days were very lonely with Meg; it was holiday time now at Miss Binks', and the large preparatory school
where she gave lessons ; her two or three private pupils had
betaken themselves to the seaside, and Meg patched and mended,
turned her old gowns, and thought weary thoughts through the
long hot hours ; in the evening she took slow aimless walks over
the downs—there were downs then—coming back jaded and
unrefreshed in the twilight to her patching again. She had no
piano now, and the few books her pupils lent her were soon exhausted ; her only pleasure was to water her geraniums and feed
her linnet. When this was over she knew that nothing more
would occur to break the monotony of these endless days. No
wonder that before a week was over she would have given anything to resume her old drudgery ; the hot walks through the
churchyard, the long hours in a close schoolroom, the din, the
ceaseless headache, the thankless labour, all appeared enviable by
the side of this enforced idleness. Sometimes she felt as though
she must give it all up, as though she could not bear the solitude
a day longer ; she must go into the world, learn nursing, visit the
hospitals, do anything or everything, so that she might be brought
face to face with her kind, and be of use to some one ; she was
wearing her heart out only just to gain her daily bread, and what
would that avail her, seeing that her bread was only bitter to her?

To be of use, to be necessary to some one, not to be loved, that
was all her thought now. Meg had awakened from that pitiful
dream of hers, self-degraded, perhaps a little hardened, but with a

fearful thirst and misery of love aroused within her that nothing
could allay; like many another fond worshipper, she had fallen
down before a stock and a stone; nay, worse, she had suffered
such usage that any other woman would have found it hard to
forgive; she knew there were bruises that she would carry about
with her to her dying day, and yet she had only clung to the hand
that inflicted them.   If he had come back to her would she not
forgive him?—ay, unto seventy times seven.   But he would never
come back.

Poor Meg! she was resolving all sorts of weary fancies in her
mind on this afternoon; while she was piecing the old faded
mantle that must last her through the summer, she was chiding
herself for her cowardice.   Why are some women so slow to plan
or rather carry out any self-conceived line of action for themselves?
had her secluded life checked all spirit of enterprise? why should
she be so afraid to risk her little all and venture on an untrodden
path?   What if she should fail?—she was the only sufferer.   Her
solitude, the harass of these cruel and incessant memories, were
killing her by inches; she was a woman of iron nerve, but this
was beyond even her endurance, and yet she shrank from taking
the first step into the new life.

If only some one would help her!   And then the pieces of silk
fell apart in her hands as a low tap at her door startled her from
her reverie.   Visitors were so rare with Mrs. Carruthers that she
scarcely raised her head as she uttered the mechanical "Come in."
It was only her landlady or the maid with her tea equipage, she
thought; it was therefore no slight surprise to her when the door
was pushed briskly open, and a tall slight girl in mourning came
forward with outstretched hands.

"Meg, my dear old Meg!"

"Rotha!   Good heavens!"   And then they embraced each
other after the fashion of women; Rotha, with a little flurry of
demonstration that seemed habitual to her, clinging to her friend
with quick earnest kisses in an almost childish way.

"Are you glad to see me, Meg?"

"Not more glad than surprised."   But Meg, in spite of her
characteristic abruptness, looked more than her words.   There was
a pleasant light of welcome in her eyes as she cleared the litter of
work from the one arm-chair, and brought out the little round
footstool.   She did not sit down and talk to her, as most women
would, but after her first greeting moved quietly about the room,
letting down the blind and arranging the table, bestirring herself
for her comfort in her quick short-sighted way; the hard muscles
of her face relaxing visibly as she untied Rotha's bonnet and shook

out the dust from her mantle. Those large strong hands were very gentle in their touch, as Rotha well knew; they had an odd knack with them that made you comfortable in spite of yourself. Rotha knew Mrs. Carruthers' ways by this time; she was well aware that she must bide her time for talking. Her dusty walk had wearied her, she looked even paler than usual. The room was deliciously cool and shady. She lay back contentedly in her arm-chair, while Meg squared her high shoulders and peered into corners. It was five o'clock. The little tea-table must be spread and garnished. There were mysterious whispers; the red-armed maid-of-all-work appeared and disappeared continually. All at once there was a delicious fragrance of mignonette and hot bread together; tiny curls of blue smoke wreathed the little black teapot. Meg would not talk to her visitor, but she was compounding a cup of tea for her, such as her soul loved, and Rotha, who knew her quaint ways, and was wearied past weariness, sat meekly sipping it, taking in everything with quick womanly instinct—the dull room, Meg's worn face and shabby dress, the wedding-ring hanging so loosely on the thin wasted finger, everything down to the faded patches that were being turned and pieced. That quiet observation was telling her more than hours of talk. "She's dying of *ennui* and dullness, and feeding on her own thoughts," said Rotha to herself. "Why should we not be the happier for each other's company? Things will not be quite so hopeless if I can infuse a little sunshine into her life;" and then she leant forward with a little colour and eagerness.

"Ah, there is the netting. I suppose I may talk now?" for Mrs. Carruthers had brought forth a long strip of netting, yellow with age, and was weaving her shuttle to and fro as though her life depended on it. Meg nodded as she pulled and knotted vigorously, but made no other answer.

"I am glad I may talk now," she repeated; "I have been watching you for such a long time. Do you know your face has been telling me tales?"

Mrs. Carruthers shook her head.

"Oh, but it has; you are so changed, my poor Meg. You look so thin and worn; and there are positively gray streaks in your hair. You were not gray when I saw you last, dear Meg."

Again that mournful shake of the head.

"And then you are so silent; you will not talk to me now. I am treading on forbidden ground, I suppose. Do you think that I do not know what your life has been?"

"Oh, Rotha; hush!" and Meg's voice was almost grating in its harshness.

4

"No, I shall not 'hush!'—you are always trying to silence me. You would not write to me, and now you will not speak. I know he has left you, that you are deserted and broken-hearted; but I never knew how broken-hearted till I saw your face, Meg."

"Rotha, if you have any pity for me——"

"Pity! I wonder if any one ever felt such pity as I have! When I heard your child was dead I thought and almost hoped that you might die too. I so trusted and prayed that your baby might comfort you."

A quick catch of the breath, a quivering of those harsh muscles, and Meg covered her face with her hands.

"If you only knew how I longed to come to you! You have been so good to me. Do you think I shall ever forget those old days? No one ever understood and loved you as I did. Try and speak to me, dear."

Meg raised her head from her hands. She so rarely wept that her face was quite burnt and blistered with her tears. Nothing but the mention of her child ever caused them to flow: ill usage she could bear, contempt, drudging labour; but the thought of the little coffined body—flesh of her flesh—which her eyes had never looked upon and her arms had never cradled, touched the spring of her womanhood.

"Rotha, I cannot bear it; you must not speak to me of my child."

"Why not, dear Meg?"

"Why not? Do you not know they took him away and buried him? They never brought him to me and laid him in my arms; no, not for one moment; though he was beautiful as the day—that was his father's doing."

"He did it for the best."

"Perhaps so. They tell me that I was delirious. My mother had only been dead a few days then. It was all trouble and misery together. But I did so pray that my child might win me his love, Rotha."

"It was not worth the winning, my poor Meg."

"Not to others, perhaps; but to me it was everything. You should not have said that, Rotha. Though he were black beyond all blackness, he is my husband."

"There, I have made you angry."

"I should think any wife might be angry at such a speech; but you are only a child, Rotha. I don't expect Jack will ever come back to me. Why should he, unless he be in trouble? But somehow I feel I shall see him again."

"I trust not, for your own sake. No, you must not be

vexed with me—it is the honest truth, only I did not mean it to escape me."

"Ah, there again ; you have never loved, or you would not say such things.  Child, I cannot die till I have seen him again."

"Meg !"

"How frightened you look !  I am not mad ; indeed, I am speaking in sober earnestness.  But now you know why it is best for me to keep silence.  The heart knoweth its own bitterness, Rotha."

"Its own bitterness ?  Well, yes."

"You know me best, but you cannot understand my feeling. You think me daft for hinting at such things.  When you have lived a little longer you will know that still waters run deepest."

"I always knew you were very deep and still, Meg ; but—but——"

"But you did not expect that I could love quite so fervently— that is what you were going to say.  Well, I am not offended. What has a grim woman such as I am to do with such things ? Why did I ever love ?  But he made me.  Oh, Jack ! Jack !" And Meg rocked herself to and fro in infinite distress.

"Ah, I must hush you now."

"Yes, you must hush me ; I deserve it.  I am forgetting my-self.  But it is all your fault.  Why did you come and speak to me of my trouble ?  You harass and excite me ; you know I never talk of such things.  You have stirred me up dangerously to-night, Rotha."

"If I have, I must calm you.  Don't shake your head, Meg, and think it beyond my power.  I shall throw no oil on the troubled waters ; instead of that there must be a mingling of salt tears—a general brackishness.  Since I have seen you I have been in the deep waters myself."

"Do you mean you have been in trouble ?"

"Trouble ?  Well, yes, I suppose so.  I have sounded and found it forty fathoms ; there is no anchoring anywhere."

Meg gave a faint smile.

"There, I knew I could quiet you.  You always had a fancy for my quaint similes.  How many years is it since we last met ?"

"Three, is it not ?"

"Three, or thirty—I forget which.  I don't like mentioning my troubles in the same breath with yours—it seems too much like weighing iron and feathers together ; but I don't think I would willingly live those years over again."

"Probably not."

"No, indeed ; there were days and months when I thought of Miss Binks' as though it were paradise itself.  You used to pity me and tell me that I was always tired. Oh, Meg, how I used to long even for the headaches and cramped fingers again!"

"Poor child! you look utterly worn out now."

"Worn? I should think so; they have crushed all my youth out of me between them; and yet it will not quite die, poor thing. Sometimes I feel so old. There, take up your netting again; I have a long story to tell you, and I mean to tell it in my old place." And Rotha brought her footstool and laid her head against Meg's shabby gown.

How she talked; how she poured it all out as one woman will to another; with what utter abandon, relief, and passion of words! No stammering, no painful suppression of pent-up pain, no fear of being misunderstood here. She made Meg see it all as though she had been present. That interview in the Castle garden, with the sunset and the apple-trees and the ruins, the almost guilty terror with which she met Robert Ord, and the miserable cowardice that kept her tongue-tied in his presence, and the crumbling walls of Eglistone Abbey; how graphically she described it all! No wonder Meg's netting fell from her hands, and that she scarcely stirred or breathed in her profound interest.

"My poor child!" That was all she said when Rotha had finished, but the tones conveyed a world of pity, and once again, very tenderly, "My poor child!"

"You may very well call me that." And then there was a long silence between them; only Meg gently stroked the hand that lay so listlessly on her lap. It was not a pretty hand, not specially small or well shaped, but very thin and white, and, as Meg touched it, it felt to her in its soft helplessness like the hand of a sick child.

"I shall never be happy again, Meg."

"No, you must not say that."

"Why must I not say it? I could have borne anything but that; but his accusation has crushed all the spirit out of me."

"It was very hard, certainly."

"Was it not terribly hard, and so cruel! But I must not think of that now."

"I must say that I think you acted very nobly."

"Oh Meg!"

"Yes, nobly. I always thought that you were so proud, Rotha, and yet you could bear yourself as though you were not angry with the man."

"No more I was. I quite wonder at myself now for my want of anger; but then his wrongs were so great, he looked so wan and sad with all his harshness, that, though I was utterly wretched, I could not find it in my heart to speak bitterly."

"Of course I think that you were right, but yet——"

"Well, Meg?"

"I hardly like to finish my sentence; it sounds unsympathetic after what you have told me; but it does strike me that you are just a little morbid about it all."

"Now you are going to be unkind."

"No, you must not say that—you must not think for a moment that I do not pity you. I am sure it is all miserably hard. Your position for the present must be cruel. But, Rotha, don't make it quite unbearable by taking too morbid a view of it —that was always your danger."

"But not in this instance," she interposed eagerly.

"Yes, in this instance. Surely it is no fault of yours that the man cannot get his rights."

"No, certainly not."

"Neither are you to blame for being the innocent cause of his suspicion. It is true he has it in his power to injure you and make you miserable, and yet it seems to me as though you could avoid such misery."

"How so?"

"By accepting it as your cross. You have already by your Christian forgiveness robbed your pain of its chief sting. I would have you bear yourself now as though you were indeed guiltless."

"And do I not so bear myself?" she returned, somewhat proudly.

"No, you are failing utterly. You are letting the pain and misery of it all wear you to the heart; there is a look on your face, Rotha, that I cannot bear to see. I say again that you are taking too morbid a view of it all."

"I cannot help it if you fail to understand my feelings."

"I know them well, Rotha."

"No, you do not, or you would not accuse me of being morbid, Meg. I told you that I wondered at myself for my forbearance; but I shall always feel as though I have wronged Robert Ord."

"And why him only—why not the others?"

"The others of course. But do you not see he was her favourite, the child of her adoption, whom she loved and forgave at the last. Meg, you may call me over-scrupulous, unreasonable, anything you like; but I know, and she knows that the money is his."

"Absurd! it is yours by will. Have you not told me so yourself?"

"Of course I am mistress of Bryn; but that does not alter my words. Meg, Mrs. Ord was going to destroy that will."

"Yes, I know."

"Every time she roused from that dreadful stupor she was trying to collect her faculties for the effort. She used to look at me so piteously, as though to ask me to help her; but it was all no use: before she could say a word to us she was floating away again."

"True, but was that your fault, Rotha?"

"Just before she died she beckoned me to her; I could see her hands groping over her chest as though she wanted to write. She made me put my ear quite close to her lips, and as clearly as I hear you now, I heard her say, 'Rotha, mind it is all for Robert;' and then the death-rattle stopped her. Meg, she was thinking of him then."

"I daresay, poor woman! It was very sad."

"Yes, but saddest for him. I have heard so much of him, of them all—not from his aunt, she never mentioned them, but from Mr. Tracy and the maid. They are all very good, but so poor and proud, and full of strange crotchets. They say that Robert Ord has been engaged for years, and now that they can never marry. How they must hate me, the very sound of my name! and yet you tell me that I am morbid."

"I say so still. I cannot take back my words."

"Perhaps not. You were always an obstinate woman."

"My dear, no; but simply straightforward and matter of fact, thank God, or how should I have got through my own troubles? You are too gentle and imaginative, Rotha. You are a brave creature, you have plenty of endurance, but you are so unselfish and scrupulous that you will wear yourself out."

"Scruples are not specially heinous sins, Meg."

"Are they not? I don't know. It seems to me that all this business is not in your hands at all; that this wealth has come to you by a direct interposition of Providence—whether for good or ill the future and your own conduct must decide; but one thing I am sure of, that, being yours, you will have to give an account of your stewardship."

Rotha dropped her head.

"My darling, I do feel as though I am very hard on you."

"No, not hard; but you are always so dreadfully sensible."

"I wish I were; I wish I were half as brave and forgiving as you, Rotha. Do you really mean that you will have the courage to face all those Ords now he has set them against you?"

"Of course if they will open their doors to me I shall go amongst them; but there is not much fear of that."

"They will not ask you to the Vicarage."

"Then assuredly we shall not meet, for they will never come to Bryn. Oh dear! oh dear! I wonder how the same village can

hold us. I suppose once a week we shall all own we are miserable
sinners together."

" You mean you will meet at church ? "

" Well, I suppose so. I wonder if the Vicar will consider it
his special mission to convert so hardened a reprobate. Meg, I
declare I am so sick at heart I would as soon joke about it as not."

" I would rather have your woebegone look than that."

" You shall have both. I have not forgotten all my dry
humour in spite of my misery. Anyhow, we shall have time to
get tired of each other, for no one else will come to us. I wonder
if I shall dare to visit the cottages ; perhaps I shall if you will
mount guard at the door."

" Are you joking ? "

" No, indeed ; I was in sober earnest."

" I thought you spoke as though I should be with you."

" Yes, of course ; but still I am not joking. One thing I can
certainly assure you—that I shall never go to Bryn without you."

" Rotha, you cannot be serious ? "

" And why not ? Do you suppose that I can live by myself ?
I should have thought Chatham Place and Miss Binks would have
taught you propriety by this time."

" My dear, you must not allow yourself to be influenced by
merely generous feeling. You think I am poor and lonely, and
that is why you think of it."

" Perhaps so ; and because I am rather fond of you in spite of
your queer ways."

" As you would be fond of any other broken-down creature
whom you could benefit. I know your goodness of old, Rotha."

" Goodness, eh ? Now, you are going to make me angry. I
have given you three reasons why I want you, but I have still
another remaining."

" And what is that ? "

" That you are my only friend, and what I cannot demand as
a right I must ask as a favour."

" And do you really want me—really, Rotha ? " The harsh
face was wonderfully softened now.

" Yes, really and truly. Can anything be more natural ? I
have known you half my life. When I was a lonely schoolgirl,
and a still more lonely teacher, you were kind to me. It will give
you more interest in life to know you are useful to some one. If
we shall not be happy, at least we can make each other less
miserable. Meg, will you come ? "

" Yes, I will. God bless you, Rotha ! " And the warm hand
clasp set the seal to her words,

# CHAPTER VI.

> " It was a village built in a green rent
> Between two cliffs that skirt the dangerous bay."
>
> JEAN INGELOW.

> " For contemplation he, and valour form'd ;
> For softness she, and sweet attractive face :
> He for God only, she for God in him."
>
> MILTON.

SOMEWHERE in the north of England there is a small seaport town called Blackscar. On the whole it is not a prepossessing place. Its chief attractions are its fine bay and extensive sands, but the town itself is tasteless, not being yet seasoned with the salt of fashion. It consists mainly of two long streets, running as nearly as possible parallel with each other—the wide old-fashioned High Street, and the other looking seaward, embracing the small harbourage, always full of fishing-smacks and such small gear, and the handsome sea-wall running directly on to Kirkby, a small suburb of Blackscar, which looked as though it led to the end of everything.

Kirkby is nothing more nor less than a village, and its most enthusiastic admirer can find little to say in its praise. The first impression generally left on the visitor is a sense of meagreness and desolation. One looks over a narrow row of kitchen-gardens and grass hillocks to the grand sweep of sands beyond. There to the left is the low range of rabbit-warrens belonging to Bryn, and beyond a small slip of land stretching out into the sea like a one-pronged fork, called Welburn. At low tide one can discern the black shining edges of some dangerous-looking rocks, which tell a tale of their own. Shipwrecks are plentiful at Kirkby and Welburn, as their inhabitants know to their cost.

Kirkby itself is not conspicuous for beauty of architecture, except as concerns its church. It has its grammar-school, its rows of low bay-windowed lodging-houses, but those fronting the sea are principally cottages, to which the kitchen-gardens appertain.

Walking along the sandy road from Blackscar, and passing the schoolhouse, one sees first a patch of whitewashed or yellow walls, with blinks of diamond-paned lattices, then a brown narrow house, with a window on each side of the door and a scanty plot of ground in front; next a low gray house with old-fashioned bay-windows, and at the bend of the road, before the fence shuts off stubbly-looking land and distant furnaces, a substantial stone building, with its pleasant windows looking seaward, and this is Bryn.

Bryn, from its many windows, looks straight down the Kirkby street and full at the gray old Vicarage, with Robert Ord's house adjoining it. The three gardens run parallel together, though they do not positively join. From the back they look over the purple range of the Leatham Hills. There is a certain weird look in that view by night. The church stands out finely with its old lich-gate. The graves are sparse and scattered. From the church porch one can catch a glimpse of the dark sea-line; sometimes there is the fret of endless splashing; the sand comes swirling up the long road. At night the blue blackness of the sky is illumined by the lurid fires from the distant furnaces. One comes out of the warm lighted church into the darkness, into the salt cool air under the star-lit heavens, to the silent sleeping village; and the distant lights from the town.

The Vicarage itself had a pleasant homely look; in reality it was once two houses. One rarely understood at first the multiplicity of small rooms and passages. There were enough and to spare : every one seemed to have his or her sitting-room, christened after its owner. There was the Vicar's study, and the mother's room; Garton's den, which the boys shared; and the little outer study, in reality the Vicar's also, where they did their lessons. The dining-room was a mere passage-room, and was only used at meal-times. There was a continual cloth spread—a perpetual clatter of knives and forks. Upstairs was the gathering-place of the whole family, especially of an evening, and this was Belle's room—drawing-room being a title abhorred at the Vicarage.

The mother's room was suited for *tête-à-têtes*, for quiet droppings-in of two or three; a place for the Vicar to sit before the fire, with his long coat tucked over his knees, and read his letters. It had a great crimson couch appropriated by invalids. Here sick bodies and sick hearts were nursed by the mother herself. Every one loved the room; it was always so full of sunshine and sweet welcomes. The great window opened wide on the pleasant lawn, with its beds of scarlet geraniums and roses. Two great ducks waddled and straddled all day among the flower-beds, in company with a white kitten and Jock and Jasper, the Vicar's two dogs. Here the mother sat in her low chair, with her work-baskets, repairing dilapidated garments, and minding her youngest born ; but, dear as the room was, the family reunions were always, by mutual consent, held in Belle's room.

There, there was more space and less cosiness ; then its windows were so delightful, the front bay looking over the sands and the rabbit-warren, and the back, with its view of the Leatham Hills, though one could not see the church itself.

Here there was everything for the needs and requirements of a family. A sweet-toned piano and a harmonium, a large round table, plenty of easy-chairs, writing-desks, and drawing-boards, and much wholesome litter ; everything a little shabby, perhaps ; the chintz, a pretty Chinese blue, pieced and faded; but, as Guy somewhat vaguely expressed it, "a lump of comfort."

Robert Ord, walking along the sea-wall and looking across at the sunset, has a pretty tolerable picture of it, and the party sure to be assembled in it at this hour. For it is just after tea, and before the bell rings out for the evening service ; the day's work is over, and the Vicar and his boys are sure not to be far apart.

Yes ; sure enough there is the Vicar in his usual place before the fireless grate, haranguing his boys and his women-folk to his heart's content, and possibly to theirs too, to judge from their faces.

The Rev. Austin Ord and his wife are a goodly pair. Perhaps the Vicar is a little ponderous—not that he need pray just yet to be delivered from the burden of his flesh—but he is a large grand-looking man, with everything large about him.

Not that he is specially well favoured—Robert is the only hand-some Ord amongst them ; but he has a face that is pleasant to look upon. The mouth may be a little querulous or obstinate ; but the forehead is so massive, and the large gray eyes open so widely and honestly, and yet so keenly ; there is such strength and such goodwill in his expression ; there is something so boyish too in the crisp curly hair, that never can be straightened, and which one sees reproduced on the curly heads of his growing lads.

The time has gone past for calling Mary Ord beautiful : cares and the harass of daily life have sharpened the round cheek, and taken away its bloom ; the cheek is very thin now, the Vicar thinks sometimes, with a sigh ; but still she has never been fairer in his eyes, and in truth there is still much comeliness left.

The mother, or Mother Mary, as her brothers-in-law persist in calling her, was just one of those soft-looking women whom it was impossible not to love. She was not very young, but as yet no gray had touched her pretty wavy hair. She had just the same wide-open gray eyes as her husband, only perhaps they opened more softly than his, and her laugh had the same happy clear ring in it. She was one of those mothers whose arms and laps are never quite empty. Her great boys liked to rest there still sometimes. Mother's shoulder always rested their aching heads; to them it was their natural pillow. Garton, in spite of his three-and-twenty years, liked to crouch at her footstool in company with Jock and Jasper, and it was Arty's favourite place. No one could have been with her an hour and not have opened his or her heart to her. It was not that she was so clever, but that her sympathy was always ready.

Belle, who had double her attractions, was not half so lovable; not that she ever failed in gentleness, but she was always so preoccupied. It was rather sad at times to watch the younger sister. There was a grave anxious expression about her face that marred its beauty. At such times she would look like a faded queen. Mary Ord was often tired, painfully overwrought, perhaps a trifle querulous, but there was no such look in her face, though mind and body were often sorely overtaxed; and only she and her husband knew with what difficulty they made ends meet and provided for their growing boys. No anxiety ever seemed to rob her for long of her sweet content. She was one of those women who take a man for better and for worse, and who, when the worst comes, make no ado, but work on cheerfully as long as strength lasts.

Belle was equally courageous, but she failed in the cheerfulness. She was quiet, but it was not the quiet of repose; perhaps her long engagement was trying her; perhaps Robert Ord, in spite of his fondness, was not a very patient lover. Some men are apt to be a little peremptory and domineering with the woman they love. In spite of their mutual affection they were not perfectly suited to each other.

Unfortunately, Belle was of a shy reserved nature. She was not one to talk much of her own feelings at any time. Robert, who was quick and ardent, felt himself sometimes almost repulsed by her silence. At such times he would reproach her in no measured words. But I don't think she ever fully answered him. He would come round presently, touched by the gentleness and sorrow in her face, and try and atone for his anger, and she would not reject such atonement; but, as she sat with her hand in his, she would be longing to tell him that he was dearer to her than anything in the world—that, if needs be, she could die for him, but that she could not open her lips to answer his reproaches. Those who did not know Belle Clinton called her cold; but they were wrong. There was no coldness about her; she would have worked her fingers to the bone for Mary and her boys. When they were ill she nursed them night and day. But not even to her sister could she fully open her heart. She would sit at her side for hours, working silently, or letting her chat about her boys and parish; but when the conversation turned to her own affairs, either evading her questions or answering them with grave reserve, till Mary was obliged to quit the subject.

The Vicar used to quiz Belle rather mercilessly for this failing of hers. In his heart he thought her rather tame and spiritless. His own wife had a brisk tongue of her own, and was much given to state her opinions on all subjects rather freely; but I think he loved such briskness. Belle's reticence was rather a fault in his eyes. In his opinion she was too much given to occupy her own corner, though it must be owned that she was seldom quite alone in it. Belle's special nook was by the window that looked over the Kirkby sands: here she could see down the village street. She knew the exact time that Robert would come from his daily work at Thornborough, and would be at the window watching for him as he went into his own gate. He and Garton would sit down every evening to their solitary meal. By and by, when the Vicarage folk were gathering round their more social board, the brothers would come in—Robert having freed himself from the dust and smoke of the day—and take their special places—Robert by Belle, and Garton under his sister-in-law's wing; but they would rarely join in the meal itself. Austin had too many mouths to feed already, Robert always said. He would let both Austin and Mary know sometimes how it galled his pride to see his future wife dependent on their hands. He used to tell Belle so over and over again. It did not make her position more comfortable. Belle was working quietly in her corner now, while the Vicar was holding out on the subject of church decorations, Mary and the boys making their comments. The lads always joined freely in their parents' conversation, sometimes interrupting—after the manner of boys—

"I say, father," exclaimed Guy, the eldest, a big broad-shouldered lad, with his father's curly head caricatured to a nicety, "Garton will turn rusty if you say anything to him about it." For by a sort of tacit understanding the boys never called Garton uncle, though they were profoundly respectful to Robert, and, strange to say, their parents never disapproved of this freemasonry. "They can't help seeing that he's half a boy himself," as the Vicar said, who was rather more indulgent to his younger brother than Robert was ever likely to be.

"Garton will not like your interfering, Austin," observed

Mary; "the decorations are quite in his province." And then she took mental measurements, to judge from the way in which she was eyeing a piece of black serge.

"Gar should choose a more efficient staff of workers, then," retorted the Vicar; "his designs are very good—rather elaborate, perhaps—but then he's such a capital hand himself: all I complain about is, that there is no such thing as satisfying the womenkind —they are always taking offence: if you appoint one to wreathe the font she is sure to turn sulky because she is not chosen to do the chancel. Why, there was quite a mutiny last harvest festival amongst the Misses Travers, and all because Miss Knowles had the pulpit and lectern, and they only the reading-desk. It is no good Garton having the management if they are to come and bother me for weeks beforehand."

"But there can be no talk about a harvest festival for months to come, Austin: why, this is only the end of June." And Mary put down her black serge with a sigh which the Misses Travers' wrongs had certainly not evoked.

"Can't you make that do?" interrupted the Vicar, with some appearance of interest.

"No, it will want another breadth. Arty grows so. I wish I could afford a suit for him. He does look so shabby at church on Sunday morning."

"I never see anything but his clean collar," replied the Vicar, leaning forward to pat the head of a very small boy curled up on his mother's footstool. "Never mind; Arty must wait, that's all. No, of course there's no question of another festival till the harvest is in, you silly woman. What put it in my head was, I was walking down towards Leatham with Farmer Dykes, and he was showing mo his crops. 'I hope I shall have some sheaves, as usual, this autumn,' I observed; and he promised me I should have some oats and barley, as well as wheat, and then I remembered that you always get them from another man."

"Never mind; we shall only have a double supply," returned Mary. She was rather absent, for a wonder: her mind was still running on the serge. "I can't help wishing I could have done without that new dress, Austin; but my old one was too shabby, I am afraid."

"I don't know how you could have avoided putting on mourning for my aunt, Mary, if that is what you mean." The Vicar's voice was a little displeased.

"My dear Austin, what an idea! I should have worn my old black gown, of course; but I daresay you are right, and new mourning is more respectful. There, I will not say any more

about it.   Arty must go shabby this summer, poor little fellow !"
and Mary put away the serge resolutely, and consoled herself with
kissing the yellow glossy curls.

"I do wonder," she continued presently, looking up at her husband cheerfully, "what has prevented Robert from writing to us?"

"Writing?—nonsense !   Belle has a letter, I believe."

"Yes, just a line to say why he was detained.   But he must
know how anxious we all are."

"No news is good news, mother," observed Guy.

"I don't know," she repeated doubtfully; "it does seem to
me that if he had any good news to impart he would not have kept
us in such suspense—it is not like him."

"No, it is not," returned the Vicar slowly.

"If it were Garton, he would delight in keeping us all in the
dark, and startling us by a sudden burst of good news when we
had ceased to expect it.   But Robert is different—and then he
has Belle to consider."   And she looked across significantly at her
sister ; but Belle did not raise her head.

"There's Garton himself !   Talk of the—et cetera, you know,"
began Guy, laughing ; but his father shook his head warningly.
He never preached long sermons to his boys, but he was quick in
rebuking them.   In a minute there was a rush of all four lads to
the window, Arty scrambling up on the window-seat in the greatest
hurry of all.

The two younger boys were great contrasts to each other.
Rupert was a long loose-limbed fellow, rather plain in face, and
somewhat freckled ; Laurence, or, as he was generally called, Laurie,
was a slight fair boy, very tall and slender, and carrying himself
with a slow sleepy grace of movement which won for him the
name of Lazy Laurie.   All three boys sang in the choir, but
Laurie's voice was the sweetest of all.

"Halloa, Garton, where's the Shadow?" shouted saucy Guy,
as he leant over his brother's head.   A tall dark young man, in a
flapping wideawake and a long and rather singularly-cut coat, looked
up as he swung back the little brown gate, and nodded to the boys.

"All right ; I am coming in directly.   Robert's up at Blackscar."

"You don't mean it !"

Belle put down her work and listened breathlessly.   The interjection came from the Vicar.

"Yes, he is : he has a little business detaining him, but he
asked me to come on and let you know he was here."

"There's the church bell, Gar !"

"So there is.   Never mind.   I must come up a moment.   I
want to speak to Mother Mary."

Two of the boys ran down to open the door directly, with Arty trotting after them, sure of a ride upstairs again on his uncle's shoulder; and true enough there he was a minute afterwards, his small face completely hoodwinked by Garton's wideawake, and shouting lustily.

Most people would have considered Garton Ord a plain man— at least, not exactly a handsome one; but his individuality would have distinguished him among a thousand; and yet it was a singular face too, almost an ascetic one, with its brown irregular features, and dark closely-cropped hair. When at rest there was something a little stern and sad about it; but then it was seldom in repose. With every change of thought or feeling the irregular features worked powerfully. Never was there such a face for betraying emotion of any kind. At any sally from the boys there would be a display of white teeth; the muscles would relax, there would be wonderful puckers and lines; and at the least provocation the strong frame rocked to and fro with suppressed merriment.

Never was there such restlessness, such continued movement, in any man—never such quick transition from one extreme to another. People could not make out Garton Ord, the boyish ascetic baffled them; there was too great a mingling of the ridiculous and the sublime in his nature; no one seemed quite to understand which predominated, any more than they could understand the cause of his variable temperament. Robert called him weak, and vowed that he wanted ballast. But Austin, more accustomed to read human nature, was wont to speak highly of his purity and singleness of aim; and no one regretted more than he when a stubborn fit of illness prevented Garton from obtaining his degree. He had always set his heart on securing him as his curate, and he was consequently grievously disappointed when his brother failed to pass.

"It is just like my bad luck, Austin," he groaned, when the Vicar came in to comfort him; "but I don't think I should take it to heart so much if it were not for Robert."

"Robert is just as sorry as I am, Gar."

"Yes, but not for the same reasons. He is thinking about how he is to give me bread-and-butter, I suppose. He will have it that if I had read more I should not have failed in obtaining my degree."

"I think with him that you do not read enough."

"But I suppose that you will allow that I could not help my illness?"

"No, indeed—that was very unfortunate."

"Everything is unfortunate; but if Robert means to make

himself disagreeable because I have failed, I may just as well get quit of the whole business."

"I thought you had set your heart on entering the Church;" and then, as he noticed Garton's face work in an agitated manner, he put his hand kindly on his shoulder.

"Well, never mind; don't be downhearted, Gar. I don't think you are to blame in this instance. You know Robert's special grievance is that you waste half your time with boys. Perhaps it would be as well to check that a little; a curate can't have half a dozen village lads perpetually at his heels."

"Do you mean to class Guy and Laurie among village lads?" demanded his brother sulkily.

"Well, no; I had some one else in my mind just then. Well, we will not talk any more about that. The lad's a nice lad, though you are taking him out of his proper place. What Robert and I have to consider now is how we are to contrive to give you another chance."

"I suppose it is no good applying to Aunt Charlotte again?"

"No, I will not have that. We must wait a little, and see how things turn out. I suppose by a little contrivance we might manage it,—that is, if Robert gets a rise. But it is rather hard that you should be a drag on him, poor fellow!"

"I think I had better give it up, Austin."

"No, no; not till we have thought over it a little. In the meantime you can do the part of a lay curate and help me with the boys, and we will read together when I have time." And then the Vicar took up his felt hat and went out.

And so Garton was eating his brother's bread and grumbling terribly over it; but he did what he could in return. He taught the Vicar's boys, and was his right hand in the parish. He was sacristan and leader of the choir, and sometimes bell-ringer too; he turned those thews and sinews of his to account. Often at five o'clock in the morning he was digging in the Vicar's garden, or in their own adjoining; though he was not always punctual in his readings with his brother, he was always in his place at the two daily services. People used to marvel to see the brown ascetic face always in the choir-stall. Ten minutes after he would be striding away to the schoolhouse, still in his cassock, with a troop of boys after him, laughing as heartily as any.

"Well, Garton, what is it you want with me?" asked Mrs. Ord, when Arty had been rescued from his perilous position and deposited on her lap.

"Oh, it is only a lot of surplices I want you and Belle to mend; can't stop to explain now; facts speak for themselves."

And he pointed breathlessly to Laurie, whose arms were closely packed with rather dingy-looking linen.

"All those for me, Garton?" and Mary looked rather alarmed.

"Yes; one or two are slit down, and some of the sleeves must be curtailed in length; and Symond's is too long for him, and—and——"

"Oh, go away," returned Mrs. Ord good-humouredly, packing him off; "you can leave them on the table till you have time to explain. How long did Robert say that he would be?"

"Half an hour or so; couldn't get a word out of him. It is my opinion he looks rather——" And then Garton stopped, and looked hesitatingly at Belle.

"Rather what? No; she is not listening, Gar."

"Oh, I don't know; let us wait and hear what he has to say for himself. Come along, boys;" and he was out of the room in a moment.

"What did Garton mean by his unfinished sentence, Mary?" asked Belle, when they were left alone.

"I don't know; you heard as much as I did. I am afraid he thinks that Robert has not very good news to communicate."

"I never expected any very good news."

"No; nor I."

"But still I am afraid Robert does. And after all, Mary, she may have left him a little."

"Oh, a little would be something."

"Of course it would. They want Garton to make up for the time he has lost during his illness. As far as that goes, I think his reading with Austin is a failure."

"I don't think Austin will ever make much of him."

"Robert says he is too much a Jack-of-all-trades in the village. He has too much and too little to do; in his opinion he wants to be regularly coached, as he calls it,—he is so lax and desultory. But I don't think he ought to look to Robert or to Austin either for any further help."

"Austin is too rash and generous, considering he has four boys of his own," replied Mary, who in her secret mind was still hankering after the serge frock for Arty; "and yet I think we must all allow that it would be a pity for Garton to waste his college education. Austin is so sure that his heart is quite set upon entering the Church."

"Yes; if we could only depend on his health and application. But if Robert could have his way, I am sure he would be in a situation at Thornborough by this time."

"Oh, we all know Robert's opinion," returned Mary, rather hastily; and then the conversation dropped.

# CHAPTER VII.

" But when the heart is full of din,
  And doubt beside the portals waits,
  They can but listen at the gates
And hear the household jar within."
*In Memoriam.*
" Over proud of course,
Even so ! But not so stupid . . blind . . that I,
Whom thus the great Taskmaster of the world
Has set to meditate mistaken work,
My dreary face against a dim blank wall,
Throughout man's natural lifetime could pretend
Or wish." *Aurora Leigh.*

IN spite of Garton's prophesied half-hour Robert Ord did not make his appearance until the elder branches of the family were gathered round the supper-table. Belle, who had stayed away from the evening service in the secret hope of securing a quiet talk with him before the others came in, was much chagrined at the failure of her little scheme, but as usual she kept her disappointment to herself. But the Vicar was not quite so reticent.

" I cannot think what possesses Robert to absent himself like this !" he said, rather irritably, as he cut the thick slices of bread with no very sparing hand. " He is certainly treating us rather badly." And then they heard the door-bell ring, and a moment after Robert Ord was amongst them. He went the round of greetings in his ordinary manner. Nevertheless the Vicar and his wife exchanged meaning glances as he took his seat silently at the table. The Ord look—as Mary called it—was strong on him this evening, and already they augured no good news from his face. Belle, as she made room for him, could not conceal her anxiety.

" How tired you look, Robert ! Are you sure you are not ill ?" she asked in a low voice—not willing, however, that her question should be overheard. But Robert was in no mood for such soft questioning.

" Tired? Well, I suppose I am; but I do not see how the failure of one night's rest is to make me ill." Then Belle knew that things were not going well with him.

" I think you might have written and explained matters a little," began the Vicar in a slightly aggrieved tone. " You might have understood that it was impossible for us not to feel anxious."

" I should certainly have written if I had had any good tidings to communicate."

" Ah! that was just what Mary said. Some of us were flattering ourselves that no news was good news; but she would have nothing to say to such lying prophets."

" Mary was perfectly right."

Then the Vicar remained silent.

" I thought you would understand how it was, Austin."

" Well, perhaps I did; but one cannot help being like Pandora's box, and having a little bit of hope at the bottom."

" Ah, that was just my case."

" Do you mean to say;" began the Vicar again after a pause, and letting his knife fall heavily from his hand,—" do you mean to say that she has willed away all that property?"

" Every penny."

" That she has left you literally nothing?"

" Nothing at all, Austin."

" Good heavens! What injustice! Not to any of us—not even to Garton?"

" Certainly not to Garton. I was not aware that you expected a reversal in your own favour."

" To tell you the truth, Robert, I have got quite as much as I expected. I knew her better than any of you. Perhaps, as I said before, I had a lurking hope that it might be found that she had remembered one of us at the last; but I was never so sanguine as you were."

" I always told myself that I had no hope at all."

" Oh, but you had—one could see it in your face. You were too much excited; you looked a different man that morning when you started. I took myself to task afterwards that I had not given you a word of warning."

" I do not think I needed the warning, Austin."

" But I should have given it to you all the same; and I feel now as though some such word of consolation is due from me, but for the life of me I hardly know how to say it."

" I think you may reserve it, as we are all fellow-sufferers."

" Yes, but then the cases differ. My injuries are the same,

certainly; but then I did not permit myself to hope. I knew that there would be no absolving of such an offence as I had committed; but with you it was otherwise."

"I suppose I may be considered the chief mourner?" But the Vicar was too much in earnest to comprehend the bitter joke.

"Oh, as to that, there was not much love lost on either side; but I must say that I think you have been shamefully used, Robert." Then Mary got up and came round to her husband.

"Mary thinks that you deserve equal pity," observed Robert, on whom this little by-play was not lost.

"No, she cannot think that."

"Oh, but I do, Austin! I think you made quite as great a sacrifice for me as ever Robert did for Belle. And there is something else that I think——"

"What is that, dear?"

"I think you are both so good and noble that all this loss will be made up to you. I am not a bit afraid of poverty for you, Austin; and were you ten times poorer I would not change my opinion, that I am the happiest woman in the world." No wonder that the Vicar felt himself comforted.

"You forget, Mary, that Belle is not equally fortunate," said Robert, still more bitterly. "Remember she has not the comfort of feeling that she is bearing poverty for my sake."

"Ah! I see what you mean."

"I think Austin is lucky in having such a wife; in my opinion he is scarcely to be pitied at all."

"That is just what I think," interrupted the Vicar, with a proud look at his Mary.

"Of course he has been injured; but then it is the duty of his cloth to forgive all such injury. He has certainly many mouths to feed, but as yet there has been no difficulty in feeding them."

"Mary and I know better than that," replied Austin. "But you are right, Robert; somehow, in one's needs, one always finds 'the stone rolled away' at the right moment."

"Yes, and then you have the happiness of doing the day's work together. I think you will allow that our case is somewhat different."

"Belle is not a bit afraid of poverty either, take my word for it," exclaimed Mrs. Ord. Then Belle looked up and made a sign for her sister to be silent.

"I am not going to try her courage just yet, Mary. We have been engaged for more than four years now; and, as far as I can see, we shall have four more to wait."

"Oh, I hope not."

"What is to prevent it? Sometimes I think we shall never be married." Then Mary saw that Belle gave a long shiver.

"I declare that I am getting quite desperate; Austin knows that I am. And to think that only a designing girl stands between me and my happiness!" And Robert Ord's face darkened as he remembered that interview in Eglistone Abbey.

"My dear Robert, I do not understand you. I thought all the money had gone to some hospital or other?"

"No; I have kept back that part to the last. Don't go away, Garton; the story is too good to be lost. I think you ought all to know what sort of a neighbour we are going to have at Bryn." And then, as they pressed round him, he told them of his talk with Mr. Tracy.

"A designing woman, indeed!" exclaimed Mary, who was rather given to be a little rash in her judgment.

"What do you think of that, Austin?" asked Garton. He had never ceased for one moment to rock himself slowly during the conversation, and as he asked the question his teeth quite gleamed from under his slight moustache. But the Vicar made no answer.

"Did you accuse her to her face?" asked Belle, whose indignation was stronger even than Mary's.

"Well, not at first." And then he went on to tell them about the thunderstorm and the strange meeting in the ruined abbey, and how the accusation had been drawn from him; and after that Mary again gave it as her opinion that Miss Maturin must be a very designing person.

"No wonder she was afraid when she met you in the Castle garden, Robert."

"Yes, and to think that I was fool enough to pity her; and then there was that want of anger on her part that was enough to excite any man's suspicion."

"She would certainly have defended herself if she had been innocent—do you not think so, Austin?" But the Vicar was again silent; he had left his chair and was walking up and down the room with heavy footsteps; it seemed as though he hardly dared trust himself to speak.

"Yes, of course she would, Robert. I cannot think how you could have been so forbearing."

"Well, I do not know myself, Mary. There was something about her that, in spite of her sin, almost disarmed anger; she looked so wretchedly unhappy."

"I am glad of it; she will find that her ill-gotten riches will only bring misery to her after all. I declare I can hardly believe in such duplicity and double-dealing."

"My dear!"    The rebuke came from her husband.

"Let me speak, Austin.    I don't wonder at all now that Robert should have felt it so bitterly ; it makes it almost unbearable for him and Belle."

"What has Belle got to do with it?   It is all the same to her whether the money goes to a hospital or to Miss Maturin."

"No, not quite, Austin."

"Isn't it, Belle?   Well, I should have thought so."   And then the Vicar resumed his walk.

"And what makes it worse for us all is that she is coming to Bryn."    And Mary, who had been rather chilled by her husband's last words, roused herself again to renewed anger.    "I cannot imagine how she can have the boldness to show her face among us."

"That is just my feeling," argued Belle.

"She will be visiting the cottages, and putting down her name in the list of charities.    Those sort of people always do."

"Very probably, my dear."

"And she will waylay you and pretend to be interested in the schools, and play at being Lady Bountiful; and perhaps even she will come to you for advice, Austin!"    And Mrs. Ord opened her eyes very widely.

"Perhaps she will, Mary ; and then certainly I shall give it her.    I think I can promise you that it will be sound wholesome advice."

"Oh, Austin, you are not joking?"

"No, indeed ; I was never more serious in my life."

"Austin has some crotchet in his head.    I should not be surprised if he is going to prove to us that we are all wrong in our judgment."

"Well, I must say that I do think you are all a little too hard on Miss Maturin."

"There!—I told you so," returned Garton triumphantly.

"No, no, Gar ; don't misunderstand me.    Robert looks quite troubled enough without that.    I am not at all disposed to be too charitable in my estimate of this young lady.    I think it is quite possible that Robert's opinion may be right."

"Of course it is right."

"Yes, it is quite possible ; he is generally tolerably correct in his surmises about people ; but it is not fair to condemn wholly on circumstantial evidence.    I do not think you need treat her as though she were quite a Pariah, Mary."

"Now, Austin!"

"Robert may be mistaken, you know."

"Oh, I don't think that at all likely."

"Well, I do not know. Mr. Tracy is as shrewd an observer of human nature as Robert, and you see he defended her."

"Mr. Tracy is an old fool, who is talked over by any soft-spoken woman who likes to take the trouble," interrupted Robert wrathfully.

"Well, he may be, but still he is a clever lawyer, and he was loath to cast the first stone, you see. I say again that we ought not to condemn her entirely on circumstantial evidence."

"I shall hold my own opinion, Austin."

"Well, so shall I, and you see I am disposed to agree with you; but here is Mary talking as though she cannot say her prayers in the same church with her."

"That is because she takes my view of the subject."

"I do not believe any of us differ from you, Robert; but I can't say I am much struck by either your or Mary's Christian feeling."

"Please don't get up in the pulpit, Austin."

"Oh, but I must;" and the Vicar made himself look very big as he spoke. "I think both Mary and you deserve a sermon, and I am going to deliver one." Then Mary looked up in his face with soft appealing eyes.

"I daresay you are right, Robert, and that Miss Maturin did obtain an undesirable influence over Aunt Charlotte during those four years; but then I do not think that we ought to shut our eyes to her youth and temptation. In her case, perhaps, we might have done likewise."

"Well, I do not see that."

"Nay, Robert; it was a position of awful temptation for any girl, especially if she were poor and homeless."

"That is what I told her. Remember I was the first to excuse her. I was not half so hard upon her as she deserved."

"No, you were tolerably merciful; it is only women who use nothing but superlatives in their anger Don't shake your head, Mary; I am ashamed of you."

"Never mind what he says, Mary."

"You are not a bit fit to be a clergyman's wife. Robert is quite fiery enough without your stirring him to fresh anger ; and it seems to me that, as long as we are deprived of it, it cannot matter to us who has Aunt Charlotte's money."

"Austin, how can you be so absurd ?"

"Absurd, am I ? Never mind, Robert, there is method in my madness. I assure you that it does not make the slightest difference to me who has the property, providing the hands that hold it are clean."

"I am glad you have added that proviso."

" Yes, indeed—that is of the greatest moment to me.  Think of the influence over the parish."

" Oh, I am not thinking about that."

" But I am, and that is why Mary made me tremble.  Think how terrible it would be to have a person of that sort up at Bryn. I do not look at it quite with Mary's eyes, but nevertheless I think my position will be an awkward one."

" That's your own look-out, Austin.  I know what I should do in your case."

" So do I.  You would have me follow her advice and send Miss Maturin to Coventry."

" Austin, I do think you are very naughty."

" Was not that what you wished me to do, Mary?  There will be no possibility of crossing over to the other side, unfortunately, unless we land ourselves among the cabbages ; but I will promise to draw down my felt hat over my eyes whenever I see Miss Maturin approaching ; but I must be sure first that it is Miss Maturin."

" Austin, you ought not to joke, for Robert's sake."

" I don't think there's much joking left in me to-night, but then you will keep interrupting my sermon.  What I really meant was that I wish to reserve my opinion ; in anything so grave as this I must certainly judge for myself."

" Well, that is reasonable."

" I think we are all too interested to be quite unbiassed in our judgment.  Mary and Belle will of course follow Robert blindly. Women are always like sheep jumping through a gap in a hedge— one takes the first leap and then the others follow.  I don't know quite what Garton thinks."

" I have not the vestige of a doubt.  Of course we all condemn Miss Maturin."

" Ah, then indeed she will go to Coventry.  I think I see a flaw here and there in your arguments, and Mary especially is not charitable , but I do not mean to compromise myself : six months hence you shall have my verdict."

" Guilty or Not Guilty, I wonder ?"

" Oh, that is impossible for me to say ; at present it is decidedly Not Proven.  There, I have finished my sermon.  I think you can find out the text for yourselves."

" The best part about it is its brevity," observed Robert drily, as he rose.  " Come, Belle, I want to say a word to you before I go.  Good-night, Austin."

The Vicar looked at the timepiece.

" Why, it is getting very late, I declare.  Garton, you had better be off too, as you have to be up so early in the morning."

"And, Robert, don't keep Belle up," said Mary, as the door closed upon the three, and she and her husband were left alone. Mary, as usual, had her work in her hands, but the Vicar sat doing nothing.

"Have you any letters to write to-night, Austin?"

"Yes, several; but I do not feel as though I could write them now, Mary. I do feel all this terribly."

"I am sure you do."

"I did not want Robert to know how sorry I was for him. Did you ever see a man so changed in a few days?"

"He looks very haggard, certainly."

"For the matter of that, so does Belle. I am beginning to think that this engagement will do neither of them any good. Belle's beauty is not a bit what it was, and she is losing flesh visibly."

"I think Robert tries her a little."

"I am sure he does. He is not the man to bear all this waiting patiently. Upon my word I can see very little hope for them both."

"Don't you think he might ask for an increase of salary, Austin?"

"No, I am certain that would not answer. It will not make their case better for us all to sit down and bemoan ourselves in sackcloth and ashes, but I almost feel as though it would be comfortable."

Then Mary put down her work and came a little closer.

"Austin, I can see how grieved you are."

"I am horribly grieved, Mary. I do not say that I expected otherwise, but still it is such a cruel thing for him."

"Oh, I can't give him all my pity."

"Nay, there you are wrong. It is so many years since I lost Aunt Charlotte's good graces that I have almost forgotten my special grievance. I was never such a favourite as he was, remember."

"Perhaps not."

"I will not deny that I have my private disappointment. Of course, if Robert had had Bryn we should all have been in a better position. Belle would have been off our hands, and Garton also, and there's no knowing what he would have done for the boys."

"No, indeed; Robert is always so generous."

"But it is no good thinking of that. To tell you the truth, Mary, I am half afraid to look into this year's expenses; Garton's illness and then Laurie's have used up all my surplus money."

"You ought not to have paid Garton's doctor's bill."

" What could I do ?  I could not leave it on Robert's shoulders. Affairs seem so complicated just now.  I wanted to tell you this evening that you might have bought that frock for Arty, but upon my word I could not reconcile it with my conscience."

" Oh, Austin, how could you think of such a thing ?"

" But I did.  I did so hate to see you look so disappointed, Mary, and to hear you begrudging that common stuff gown of yours.  I wonder who deserves to wear a silk one more than you do ?"

" Silk for me ?  No, thank you.  I am happier in my old stuff one, though I am not fit to be a clergyman's wife ;" and Mary smiled playfully in his face.

" Oh, but I was not serious, you know."

" I was half afraid you were.  I certainly did feel very angry."

" Did you ?"

" Yes, of course I did ; and Belle got quite white with anger."

" I do not think Belle's anger was so fierce as mine, though ; when I walked up and down it was because I dared not trust myself to speak.  If I had spoken I should have terrified you, and yet Robert thinks I am cool."

" I am afraid he does."

" Let him think so ; it is no good heaping fuel on a furnace.  I think my wrath would have matched his.  And then it occurred to me that we were all condemning Miss Maturin merely on his evidence."

" And then you scolded me."

" You were the sheep that was foremost in leaping, Mary. Robert's gap was a tolerably wide one.  My dear, I must positively see this young woman and judge for myself before I can accept his opinion."

" Oh, of course, Austin.  Well, perhaps I was a little hasty."

" We are all prejudiced against Miss Maturin ; we must therefore be careful to form our estimate all the more slowly.  As the Vicar of this parish, I shall not be able to avoid coming into very close contact with so influential a member of my congregation."

" But, Austin, she may be a Baptist."

" I never thought of that."

" Or a Unitarian."

" Oh, I hope not."

" Or a Plymouth sister, or something of that sort."

" Very well, Mary, then you will not have quite so much trouble with your prayers on Sunday ; but of course I shall be very strenuous in my efforts to bring her over to the Church."

Then Mrs. Ord had nothing to say.

" I suppose, if you really become convinced that Robert is right, we need have nothing at all to do with her ?" she began again after a pause.

" Robert did not say so. After ·all, Mary, he is more forbearing than you."

" No, but seriously, Austin."

" Seriously, then, we shall not be able to avoid it, I am afraid ; but at least I can promise you this—that we will do as little as we can." And after that the Vicar betook himself to his study, and Mary went up to her sister.

It was her motherly custom to see all her sons tucked up safely in their beds before she retired to her own, and, however weary she might be, she never omitted this duty. Often a restless sleeper stirred at the light kiss and whispered blessing. When Belle first came to the Vicarage Mrs. Ord included her in her rounds as a matter of course, but it must be confessed that Belle derived no special delectation from her sister's visits. She was unsociable by nature, and at such times she preferred the solace of her own thoughts.

Mary found her sitting by the open window with her head on her hand.

" What ! up and dressed still, Belle ? Have you any idea how late it is ? "

" Yes ; I expect it is very late."

" Ah, that is just what makes you so thin. Do you know Austin has been making some uncomplimentary remarks about your looks to-night ? I wonder what he would say now if he saw you ? "

" Austin is never complimentary to me, Mary."

" Now, Belle, that is too bad."

" No, indeed he is not ; he is always drawing comparisons between us. Of course a man must think well of his own wife. But sometimes I wish he would leave me alone altogether."

" You would not say so if you knew how sorry he was for you both to-night. I have hardly ever seen him more grieved about anything."

" I don't think he was particularly kind to Robert."

" You mean that he did not talk to him much. But that was because he would not trust himself to speak. You know Austin is sometimes afraid to say all he thinks."

" But, all the same, he need not hurt Robert with that half-joking manner of his. I don't believe he understands it."

" Oh, Belle, that is only his way."

" It is not a pleasant way, Mary ; it makes him seem as though he did not feel for people in their trouble. Robert always says it shuts him up so; he has gone away quite hurt to-night."

"Then it is very foolish of Robert. Never mind; Austin means to have a talk with him to-morrow. The fact is, Belle, he thinks we are all a little premature in our judgment about Miss Maturin."

"Oh! if he has talked you over, Mary, I have nothing more to say."

"I don't know what you mean by talking me over, but I am not going to get vexed with you, Belle. I can see that you are dreadfully unhappy." Then Belle turned her head away without speaking.

"Robert has no right to make you so wretched. If he goes on much longer in this way, I shall speak to him myself."

"Oh, Mary! you must not think of such a thing."

"But I shall. Here Austin says you are losing flesh visibly. Every one notices how pale and thin you are getting."

"I wish every one would mind their own business."

"Oh, Belle!"

"I do, indeed. How can I help his making me wretched? I cannot alter his nature."

"There, you have found it out at last."

"I don't see what there was to find. Of course he is miserable, poor fellow; and of course his misery makes him impatient. Any one but Austin would see what he suffers."

"I don't envy you the first three months that Miss Maturin is at Bryn."

"I don't envy myself, Mary. But at least I can understand and share his feelings. He said to-night that he knew where to come for sympathy." Then Belle got up and made some little demonstration as though she would prepare herself for her couch; on seeing which, Mrs. Ord kissed and bade her good-night. But as she tucked up Arty, she told herself that she had not done much to comfort her sister. But, in truth, Belle was not one that could be easily comforted.

# CHAPTER VIII.

" And now be patient with me ; do not think
I'm speaking from a false humility.
The truth is, I am grown so proud with grief,
And He has said so often through His nights
And through His mornings, ' Weep a little still.'

    .        .        .        .        .        .

                        I gave you love ?
I think I did not give you anything ;
I was but yours only. . . ."     *Aurora Leigh.*

BELLE had got up from her chair, and had made some little demonstration of preparing herself for the night. She had moved across the room and wound up her watch in a decided sort of way, and her sister had understood her and taken the hint; but when the door had closed upon Mrs. Ord, all Belle's briskness of movement had ceased, and she had dropped down again into the seat by the window, propping her cheek upon her hand, and staring moodily across the dark road to the darker sea-line beyond. Mary had complained to her of the lateness of the hour, and she had accepted the fact without questioning ; but, in truth, she was so utterly wretched that the lateness was of small moment to her. She was much given at all times to trim her midnight lamp in solitude, and in consequence sleep had become rather a rare visitant to her, beguiling her only by fits and starts. She never complained to any one of her wakefulness ; she bore it quietly, as she did most other ills that befell her. Lately the shadow of a fresh trouble had oppressed her, and was making her nights dreary ; in spite of her efforts she had not been able to shake it off, but it never occurred to her to seek relief by imparting her fears. And so her burden had grown heavier day by day, and the strain on her harassed nerves had been aggravated by want of sleep and mental distress.

Nor was it a mere shadowy foreboding of evil that was robbing her cheek of its bloom and depriving her of flesh. The thing, whatever it might be, was assuming tangible shape and reality. In the daytime she would rate herself for her cowardice, and would succeed in regarding it as purely imaginary, as altogether baseless and puerile. But at night she had no such relief; she would cower away from it with a real terror and a real belief that made her nights dreadful to her. Then it almost seemed to her as though she must make her sister her confidante. But when the morning came she shrank from the avowal of her weakness; all the more that she saw that in spite of her sister's solicitude she noticed nothing.

But to-night her oppression was such that she could make no pretence of sleeping. Mary had been kind, and had striven to say a word of comfort, looking upon her affliction as one that words might have some power to alleviate, and she had repulsed her with a decision that had somewhat of abruptness in it. But how could Mary know that she was too sore for such words?

Even her interview with her lover had brought her no consolation; it had been brief and unsatisfactory.

"Well, Belle," he had said directly they were left alone, and putting his two hands on her shoulders, "I shall have to come to you for sympathy. I wonder what you will say to comfort me?" And then she had looked up at him rather pitifully, and had made no sort of answer.

"Things have come to a sorry pass with us," he went on. "It is all very well for Austin to joke, but I look upon our game as a lost one." Then again that long shiver had passed over her frame, thrilling her like ice, but no words of comfort had occurred to her.

"Austin did not mean to be unsympathetic," she ventured at last.

"No, I know he did not, nor Mary either, but it is very galling to a man in my position." And then he had gone on to say a few things decidedly bitter about his brother, and Belle had not dared to contradict him; and after that he had spoken a sentence or two as though he had felt himself assured of her sympathy.

"I wish I did know how to comfort you, Robert," she said, and her tone had been very soft and pleasant to him; "but it seems beyond my power."

"Yes, it is beyond your power, Belle; I don't think any one on earth can make my position endurable to me now." Then he had taken down his hands from her shoulders, and had bidden her good-night.

It was this last speech of his that had tormented her; she was revolving it now as she looked out at the sea-bound horizon;

she had borne a great deal for his sake : the four years of her engagement had not been, on the whole, happy years—she had had her secret burdens, her sorrows, and her regrets ; but, had they been doubled, she could never have brought herself to have told him that her position was unendurable, and yet it was owing to her that such was the case with him. It was not that he was unkind, for even then he had said a lover-like word or two that at another time must have given her comfort ; but he was proving to her as plainly as words could prove it that she was failing in yielding him happiness. If it were so—if his position were indeed unendurable, and the thraldom of this hopeless engagement were fretting him, might it not be her duty, seeing that she loved him better than herself, to set him at liberty ; at least, might she not clearly make him understand that she was so willing ?

True, he might be angry with her, and refuse to take her at her word ; indeed, she rather suspected that such would be the case. But would it not be as well to brave his anger, so that she did her duty ? She did not suppose that he would misunderstand her ; undemonstrative and silent as she was, she had given him plain proofs that she loved him, though even he had no idea of the extent of her powers of loving. , Already she yielded him loyal obedience in all things that concerned herself and him ; for his sake she had renounced a project she had secretly cherished for securing her own independence, and, at his expressed wish, consented reluctantly to be a burthen on her brother-in-law.

Nor was this the only instance in which she had moulded her will to his ; and so Robert had no conception of the courage and strength which lay beneath her quiet manners. It was not that he intended to domineer, but he grew so accustomed to her yielding that he forgot at last to question her opinion : had he been able to marry her during the first months of their engagement he would have made her a model husband, but his was a nature that grew harsh with opposition ; no wonder, as Mr. Ord said, that he tried her a little.

But, after all, there was nothing abject in Belle's submission— no placing the neck in the dust, after the fashion of some women ; it was rather the yielding of a strong proud will to a stronger and a prouder one, and that out of pure love. There were times when Belle could almost have prayed to have loved Robert Ord less, that his troubles should not have so darkened her life to the exclusion of her own, but she never told him so.

Well, it was no good looking back : she would give him this one chance, and risk his anger, though it was the only thing on earth she dreaded ; she would tell him, if he would give her the opportunity for such speech, that he had better give up this losing game of his, that she knew that they would never be married—that it would be far wiser for him to teach himself to look upon her as his friend ; and at this point she laid her head down on the window-sill in the darkness, and cried till her arms and hair were wet with her tears, till from very weariness she could cry no more. But not for that was her resolve shaken.

One thing she deliberated upon long as she dragged herself to her bed, feeling conscious at last of her cramped aching limbs—should she tell him of the haunting fear that had lately beset her and robbed her cup of its small portion of sweetness ? She turned this over long in her mind, but at last she resolved that she would not tell him. Unselfish herself, she was keenly alive to the generosity of Robert's real nature ; such telling, she thought, would undo at once all the purpose of her words, and so, with the asceticism which was in reality as much a part of hers as of Garton's nature, she replaced her moral hair-shirt. It would be discovered some day, she knew, and then he would thank her for her reticence. Like many another fond enthusiast, it never struck her that Robert might perhaps hold a different opinion.

Her first waking thoughts were very sad ; she was physically exhausted, too, from her lengthened vigil. For a few minutes she hesitated whether she might abstain from appearing at the family meal, but she had never excused herself yet on plea of illness, disliking all fuss and softness, and she would not spare herself now. Once or twice her strength failed her in the process of dressing, but she made head at last against her weakness, and was in her place by the time the Vicar had returned from service.

She had a little difficulty in eluding Mary's inquiries as to her rest last night, and was very short with Arty when he told her she had black spectacles round her eyes ; but after breakfast she went out to her district, and got through her duties in a mechanical sort of way, and came home at dinner-time feeling as though her feet were weighted with lead, and with no voice ; but nevertheless she was down at the school all the afternoon. She was always very zealous in performing her duties, and took a great deal of her sister's work on her shoulders ; but, in spite of her patience and gentleness with them, the poor people liked Mary's cheerful face best.

But all the time she was looking at the girls' long seams, or setting them their tasks, she was thinking how she could best contrive to see Robert alone ; she must stay away from the evening service again, she thought ; at such times Robert would often be busy gardening. Mary sometimes stayed away too, to finish her work or mind Arty; she could easily tell her sister that she wanted a word alone with him. Robert always managed these things in an off-hand manner; she had seen him turn all the boys out of the room if he had anything particular to say to her; perhaps she might not find it difficult after all. Robert would probably be busy gardening, and she could go out and speak to him. Anyhow, she was determined that she would not let him go till she had so spoken to him.

As they sat down to tea she did manage to say a word to him, but he noticed that her voice trembled.

"You have been tiring yourself at the school again," he said rebukingly; and she had hastened to assure him that such was not the case.

"At any rate you are right to stay at home. I think Mary and you have quite enough to do without attending all Austin's services." By which it may be seen that the Vicar's innovations were not altogether pleasing to his brother.

"I am thinking of making Belle my assistant organist again," observed Austin, who had overheard the heretical speech; "Lambert is going away on sick leave."

"I shall be very glad to help you, Austin," returned Belle pleasantly; "I managed it very well before."

"Yes, but you will not be able to play the truant for two evenings then, remember." And then Belle knew that the Vicar was aware of her little shortcomings.

Mary was still hard at work upon Arty's old suit, and she looked up rather imploringly as Belle went to fetch her hat. Belle noticed the look in a moment.

"I am sorry that I cannot stay to help you this evening, Mary; but I am going out with Robert."

"With Robert! Why, you have been out all day!" And Mrs. Ord's tone was slightly aggrieved.

"Yes, but only in the district and at the school. I have been working with the girls all the afternoon."

"I had ten times rather you had helped me with all this work. I don't see how I am to finish it by Sunday. It is quite dreadful to see how I stay away from church now."

"Never mind; Austin will not scold you: he reserves his rebukes for me."

"I suppose he thinks that it will never do to encourage Robert in his dislike to week-day services."

"Do I encourage him, Mary?"

"Of course not. How you take me up, Belle!" and Mrs. Ord looked for once decidedly ruffled. "I think I should have asked you anyhow to have remained at home to-night; but, if you are going out with Robert, of course it does not matter." But Belle, as she went out, looked as though it mattered very much indeed.

She found Robert walking up and down the Vicarage lawn, rather impatient at her delay.

"I thought you had changed your mind, and were not coming," he said, when she had got up to him.

"Oh, that was not likely."

"Nothing would be more likely with some women. What kept you?"

"Mary; she was in a fuss over the surplices, and wanted me to help her. I am afraid she has a headache coming on; nothing else ever seems to put her out."

"I don't think I feel much in the humour for a walk after all, Belle. I was up at five digging with Garton, and I am as stiff as possible this evening."

"If you are tired we will certainly not go."

"You are sure you do not mind remaining in the garden?"

"Why should I mind it, Robert?"

Then she put her hand on his arm and walked slowly on.

"Austin went with me to Thornborough this morning," he began, for Belle had relapsed into silence. "It was his day at the Cottage Hospital. We had a long talk together."

"Well?"

"He was very kind."

"I am glad of it, Robert."

"He reserves all that joking manner of his for public. I don't think we ever understood each other so well as we did this morning. I am sure I ought to feel very much obliged to him for his kindness."

"I told you that he meant to be kind."

"Yes, but his manners mislead one so. Of course I held my own opinion, and of course he twitted me with my obstinacy; but I can see what he thinks about it."

"Do you mean about Miss Maturin?"

"Yes; he has just as strong a prejudice against her as any of us, only he does not mean us to see it. Austin ought to have been a lawyer, he is so chary of committing himself."

"Please don't let us talk about Miss Maturin to-night, Robert."

"What! you are getting tired of the subject already? Oh, by the bye, you wanted to talk to me about something, Belle."

"Yes, I did want to speak to you;" and then for a moment her voice literally failed her.

"Well, let me hear it," he replied impatiently. "I hate mysteries. I suppose you and Mary have been putting your heads together over all this business, and have come to some impossible result."

"Mary has nothing at all to do with it."

"Well, that is right. I would rather have your own words and your own ideas than a hundred women's." And in spite of her soreness the little compliment soothed her.

"I never care somehow for Mary to talk to me about our difficulties; but I know that both she and Austin look upon our engagement as pretty nearly hopeless."

"That is our affair, Belle."

"Yes, it is our affair; but it is very hard, nevertheless, to have other people always discussing it. One is never left alone in this world. They say it is well to belong to a large family; but I think it has its trials."

"Well, I don't know; few people are so unsociable as you, Belle;" and then he smiled at her as though her reticence were a beauty in his eyes. There was something specially soft in his manner to her this evening; no wonder she found it difficult to go on.

"One gets to believe what is constantly affirmed," she continued after a pause. "Mary and Austin too are continually letting fall some word which shows what they think about it; and, Robert, you said yourself yesterday that the chances were all against us."

"Of course they are against us."

"Yes, and then you went on to say that your position was unendurable."

"I do not think I quite made use of that term, Belle."

"Yes, you did: you said that it was quite beyond my power to comfort you; and then you added that no one on earth could make your position endurable."

"What makes you remember my words so correctly?" he asked; but he had the grace to look a little ashamed of himself.

"They were not words that I could well forget, Robert; I know I tried, but they would keep recurring to me. I was awake all night thinking about them—and—and some other things."

"That was very childish of you. No wonder Arty said you had black spectacles on;"—a speech which the Vicar had duly reported, as he did most speeches of his youngest-born—"you might have known that I was not accountable for my words last night."

"I quite understand that, Robert."

"Then I think it was very childish of you. What were the other things? Come, I mean to hear them all."

Poor Belle! He was certainly making her task a hard one.

"I don't think you were particularly consolatory yourself last night : if you are going to reproach me in this way, it is only fair that I should tell you that," he observed, while she was considering how she could best bring it out ; but to this she made no response.

" Come, Belle, you are making me believe it is something very important."

" And so it is—very, very important, Robert. I think it is of the utmost consequence that you should not waste your life as you are wasting it—that you should not remain any longer in a position that you feel to be unendurable."

" Now, Belle, I did not think it was in your nature to knag——"

" Robert !"

" Well, is it not knagging to be for ever repeating one word over and over again ? I would sooner do my penance and have it well over—if you will only let me know what penance I have to perform."

Then she took her hand from his arm and walked on in silence ; but as he was about to replace it he saw that she was very pale, and that her eyes were full of tears.

" Why, Belle ! What is it ? You are not angry with me in earnest ?" And then, as he saw that she scarcely knew how to support herself, he made her pass through the open window into the mother's room, which was always deserted at this time, and put her in the Vicar's big arm-chair. " Belle," he said, taking her hand as he stood before her, " I insist on knowing what all this is about !" And as she brushed her tears away, " I see I must be careful of my words in future ; but I never knew you to be fanciful before. I certainly do not wish to rob you of your night's rest again."

" Oh, Robert ! it was not only that."

" Well, what was it, then ? I was always glad that you were one of the quiet sort, Belle ; but I am not so sure just now that it is a virtue."

" I did not mean to be so foolish."

" Oh, you need not mind about your crying, if that is what you mean. I will not be hard upon you for that ; but I wish you would not try my patience."

" No, I will not. Robert, you must forgive me ; but I am not quite myself to-night. I want you to understand that I love you well enough to give you up, if it be for your happiness."

Then he looked at her, too much astonished to speak.

" Indeed I mean it. I have been thinking all night over what I had to say to you, and I have made up my mind that it was my duty to speak. Of course it is very difficult—of course you will misunderstand me; but still I feel bound to tell you that, if you wish it, I will set you free."

" But why should you set me free?" And his tone was very loud and angry as he asked her the question.

" Because, as I said before, you are wasting your life and wearing your heart out with this hopeless engagement. Every one owns it is hopeless—Mary and Austin. Why, you said yourself last night that we should never be married."

" Did I say a word about giving you up?"

" No, of course not; but still it is my duty to give you the opportunity. Long engagements do not matter to women. Some would wait ten or fifteen years for the man they love; but I think it is otherwise with men. I cannot bear the thought that I should spoil your life, Robert—that all your best years should be spent in this tedious waiting. If you were free and unfettered you would go away from here, and perhaps make a fortune for yourself."

" Have I ever coveted a fortune except for your sake, Belle?"

" No; but I cannot forget that I have robbed you of one. I am just as much to blame in that as Miss Maturin, though we are so bitter against her."

" Pshaw!"

" Yes, indeed I am. All last night I was accusing myself and calling myself your curse. I do not think it will ever be in my power to make you quite happy, Robert. In spite of my love Mary is always telling me that I fail in cheerfulness."

" I wish you were more like Mary."

" Of course I know she is superior to me in everything."

" Oh, it is not that. I used to think that she was not to be compared with you, but I am not so sure of my opinion now. At any rate I cannot fancy Mary telling Austin what you have told me."

" Oh, Robert, you must not say that!"

" No, indeed! Fancy her separating herself from Austin in his trouble, and offering to set him free. Why, the thing would be impossible. I do not think it ever came into her head to imagine that he could do without her. I declare I am beginning to envy Austin such a wife."

" Robert, I don't think you ought to be so angry with me."

" Well, perhaps not. I ought not to have expected that you would have put up with me so long. Mary has often told me she wonders at your patience. I am very trying, I know; but still I did not think that you would come and offer to set me free like this."

"It is because I love you better than myself," she returned in a choked voice; but he hardly heard her in his wrath.

"And to say it so quietly, too. But then you had a whole night in which to plan your speech." And then, as she looked up at him with her face full of reproachful misery, he checked himself; for, as we have before said, Robert Ord was in spite of his faults really gentle at heart.

"Why, Bella," he said, putting his arm round her, "whatever is the matter with you to-night? You are not a bit like my own Bella." And as he said this he compelled her, as it were, to support herself against him, and indeed she was in sore need of such support by this time.

"I do not know myself," she returned, now speaking through her tears. "I have been trying all day and all night to force myself to say all this, but I cannot bear your being so angry with me."

"Then I will promise not to be so angry again; but you must never repeat your offence;" and his tone was a little triumphant, as though the sense of his power over her were sweet to him. "Of course I shall never give you up. I wonder what you would have done without me, Bella, if I had taken you at your word?"

"I never thought of myself at all in it. What seemed to me of most consequence was that your life should not be wasted."

"And so you were willing to be sacrificed. I always said that you were too ready to make yourself a martyr. Some women carry about with them a flavour of the stake and the faggots. I don't think men are quite so lamb-like."

"But, Robert, I thought you knew I would do anything for your sake."

"I have had such a notion, certainly. But, all the same, I should dislike to see you tie yourself to the stake. I am quite sure you would crumble into ashes with becoming fortitude, but I would never be the consenting party to such a sacrifice."

"I can't think how you can care for such a poor thing as I am, Bertie."

"Well, it is strange, certainly; but do not think I am going to make any lover-like speeches to-night. You don't deserve them. I wonder if every evening when I come home oppressed and out of spirits you will offer to set me free?"

"I will never offer it again." But as she said this, and pressed closer to him, feeling how dear he was to her, it suddenly came into her mind that she had not been thoroughly honest with him —that at any rate she had kept a part back. Last night she had worried herself to death, doubting whether she should tell him of her trouble, and had come at last to the conclusion that she was weak and nervous, and that possibly there was no foundation for her fears. He would only laugh at them, as she did herself sometimes; but now, as the thought recurred to her, she felt as though she were hardly honest.

" I shall never offer it again," she repeated. " Your anger has been too dreadful to me. But, all the same, it may come to pass that you may wish you had accepted it."

" I shall never wish that," he returned decidedly. " I would rather wait ten years for you than six months for another woman." And as he said this, and she felt the strength and vigour of his arm, the shadow of the nameless evil passed from her, and she felt for the time almost happy.

# CHAPTER IX.

## NETTIE UNDERWOOD

"Women, so amiable in themselves, are never so amiable as when they are useful; and as for beauty, though men may fall in love with girls at play, there is nothing to make them stand to their love like seeing them at work."
—ABBETT.

AT this time there was a young lady dwelling in the parish of Kirkby who went by the name of Nettie Underwood, although, if the truth be told, there was a certain entry in the baptismal register of St. Barnabas, the old parish church of Blackscar, to the effect that one Eliza Ann Underwood was duly christened on a particular day one November, about a quarter of a century before the date of our present story.

There is no law to prevent people from exchanging a hideous name for one less lacerating. But many are slow to achieve such successes; therefore when Eliza Ann Underwood, on leaving boarding-school, turned her back upon the register of St. Barnabas, and, eschewing the bondage of fashion, had her cards printed as plain Nettie Underwood, it was thought by some to be too daring an experiment, and she lost three female friends on the spot.

But Nettie Underwood, being a young person of great courage, did not waste much time in mourning over one such small defeat. The loss of three bosom companions would certainly have harassed most girls, but it did not disturb Nettie's equanimity for a moment. She was always performing unexpected actions, and shocking the nerves of the female population of Blackscar and Kirkby. She had already obtained a reputation for doing extraordinary things, though no one exactly knew what they were; such reputations are very easily acquired, and scarcely need much trouble to keep up. But whether appreciated or not, the Nettie Underwoods of society furnish a sweetness of gossip which makes them invaluable in a small place such as Kirkby, where every one knows his or her neighbour's business better than their own.

But in spite of one or two failings, a dreadful love of gossip, and a knack of doing odd things at odd times, Nettie was a good little girl. She thought a great deal of herself, as most small persons do, and some people were far too ready to take her at her own estimate. But indeed Dame Nature had endowed her with not a few of her good gifts, though she had counterbalanced them with an equal number of defects. Thus, though she had pink cheeks, a saucy little *nez retroussé*, and a pair of bright eyes, these beauties were marred to a certain extent by a wide mouth, and a square solidity of figure which no French dressmaker, however great an artiste she might be, could ever fashion into any degree of elegance.

Nettie lived with her aunt, also Eliza Ann Underwood, spinster, in a little low-windowed house fronting the church, and hardly a stone's throw from the schools just round the corner. The house, which was very small but pleasant-looking, adjoined a still smaller shop, where they sold carvings, hymn-books, and other ecclesiastical matters, together with stonemasonry. The sexton kept this shop. From the upper bow-window, which was Nettie's drawing-room, the view was over the lich-gate and the churchyard. No wonder, as the old lady was much given to remark, they were always reminded of their end.

Miss Underwood the elder was rather a masculine-looking lady. She wore a brown front, had a moustache, and more than an indication of beard, and talked in a loud deep voice. She was the sort of woman who would grasp one's hand until one was obliged to cry out with pain, who was very loud and decided at all maternity and clothing meetings, and learned in respect of school tea-drinkings—a big hearty woman, who called very young men by their Christian names, and patted them on the shoulder, and whom strangers feared to contradict, but who was perfectly lamb-like and docile to her own niece.

People wondered how Aunt Eliza could be domineered over by a chit like Nettie, but presently the truth leaked out. The little bow-windowed house in reality belonged to Miss Underwood the younger, and not only that but a good substantial six hundred a year besides, received in half-yearly dividends. Miss Underwood was only a pensioner on her niece's bounty, and wore handsome silk dresses on sufferance. Nettie could do odd things with impunity now, and not one of her three-and-twenty intimate friends would have deserted her. All the scandal of Kirkby and Blackscar was talked round Nettie's cosy little tea-table, which was the rallying-place for all the spinsters of the neighbourhood.

Nettie was not without her ambition. She would have agreed with Cæsar that it was better "to be first in a village than second in Rome;" and as Bryn was without its representative, she was in some degree the leading lady in the parish.    Mrs. Blake, the widow of Colonel Blake, was *par excellence* the lady of the place— the Vicar's wife excluded.    But she was of a retiring nature, and disposed to plead bad health and many troubles as excuses for so retiring.    Then there was Miss Brookes, who was first cousin to a baronet, and who led the van of all the spinsterhood of Kirkby. She was an irascible sort of person, with a high Roman nose, and her irascibility was such that it was not always easy for Nettie to rout her on every occasion.    It is very nice certainly to be first cousin to a baronet, and there is something to be said in favour of a Roman nose; but Nettie's energy and good nature were better for everyday use, even though her name was plebeian and her *nez retroussé*.

The Vicar was often heard to declare, with much inward groanings of spirit, that the female, or rather the unmarried portion of his congregation were wont to give him most trouble.    On the last harvest festival he had been much exercised in spirit.    The Misses Travers had been thorns in his side, and thorns of forty years' growth are apt to be prickly.    In his masculine ignorance he had chosen the most skilful hands for the nicest work, and what aspiring spinster will bear that?    Miss Brookes' feebleness and irascibility had caused her to be put aside altogether, and Mrs. Blake's good works had been wholly vicarious, but nevertheless the Vicar had had much soreness mixed up with his harvest thanksgiving, and even Mrs. Blake's prickly pears and hothouse grapes had given him no pleasure.

But whomsoever he blamed, he certainly exonerated Nettie Underwood; in spite of her follies and affectations the little girl was somewhat of a favourite with our Vicar.    If he had had the management, the prettiest pieces of work should have fallen to her share; but Garton and Belle were not always so gracious.    He always bore most good-humouredly with her chattering, though, when he had had enough of it, he would silence her with a word. Through his instrumentality she had become almost domesticated in the Vicarage, where she was perpetually "buzzing in and out," as Mary called it.

When Nettie had nothing better to do, she would drop in for a moment and stop for hours.    Mary, who did not altogether share her husband's partiality, and who secretly felt these morning visits unnecessary inflictions on her time and patience, was wont to remonstrate gently with her better half.

"Austin, I wish you would not encourage Nettie in such idleness," she would say when her nerves had been severely tried by a whole morning of dawdling and gossip. "She used to be rather nice, but since you have taken so much notice of her she is getting perfectly spoiled."

"Well, I don't know," the Vicar would answer slowly. "After all, Mary, Nettie is a good little girl."

"So she may be, but that is no reason why the Vicarage should be a refuge for all the good little girls of the parish; we might as well have Lydia Beckworth, or Miss Brand, or Kitty Merton continually running in and out, as far as that goes; they are all good little girls enough, and Lydia particularly would be of some use to me."

"There is no reason why you should not have Miss Beckworth if you wish it, my dear;" but the Vicar made a wry face, for Lydia Beckworth was one of his special thorns. "I certainly have no wish to dictate on the choice of your friends."

"That means that you do not admire poor Lydia. Well, neither do I, but I have always found her very good-natured; she would not see me, for instance, with all this pile of mending beside me and never offer to do a stitch, as Nettie has been doing all this morning."

"Perhaps she had forgotten her thimble," suggested the Vicar charitably; he was well used to these thrusts at his favourite. "Of course that is always her excuse, but it is my private opinion that she could not darn a sock if she tried." Then the Vicar smiled as he took his paper and went out on the lawn. He was well aware of Nettie's misdemeanours and little failings; he used to store them up in his memory and tell her of them in his own way. Nettie would tingle down to her fingers' ends at some well-merited rebuke, uttered half in pleasantry; at such times her feelings for the Vicar were not unmixed with awe, but in general they were the best of friends.

Nettie's visits had been more than usually trying to Mrs. Ord of late. She was in constant dread that Nettie would question her about the new owner of Bryn. "If she gets hold of all this business about Miss Maturin she may make it terribly unpleasant for us all," she said once to her husband.

"Don't let her get hold of it," was his only answer.

"Oh, but, Austin, we shall not be able to help it; you don't half know how curious Nettie is; she will ask questions and worm everything out. It is all very well for you to keep her at a distance, she is in wholesome dread of you as her spiritual pastor and master, but it will not be quite so easy for us."

"Very well, then, I will give Garton a hint to keep his tongue quiet."

"And then she will come to me."

"I hope you will refuse to answer her questions, Mary. Nettie is a good little girl, but of course she has her weak points, and love of gossip is one of them; it does not matter to me personally how much is known or not known, but I think we owe it to Robert to be cautious."

"Yes, and Robert is always so hard upon Nettie."

"That is because she is such a chatterbox. Well, we must all do the best we can; but of course the truth will leak out by degrees. People will soon find out that we have no friendly relations with Bryn."

"We are certainly in a most painful position," sighed Mary, who had felt herself much oppressed during the last few days at the prospect of her new neighbour; "it is doubly trying for us, because the clergyman's family is always expected to show kindness to strangers."

"The clergyman—but not his family, my dear, if the stranger prove a doubtful one; and then for every cup of cold water there will be Robert's wrath to face. Yes, we are not in an enviable position; the difficulty is to decide between such conflicting duties, and to be sure we are judging and not misjudging—if one were not so prejudiced to begin with. Heigho! it is a contradictory sort of world." And then Belle entered the room, and the conversation dropped.

Mary's prediction about Nettie's curiosity and love of gossip was soon to be verified. The very next morning, as the Vicar and his brother were doing some hard digging among the strawberry beds, they heard the well-known click of the lock proceeding from the green door in the wall.

"Here's Nettie Underwood again," exclaimed Garton, as he rested his foot on the spade a moment. "I declare that girl lives here; she bores Mary terribly."

"Mary cannot understand why idle people are suffered to live at all," observed the Vicar, with grim humour, as Nettie came up to them rustling in her crisp muslins and looking wonderfully fresh and bright; it was Garton's standing joke that Nettie always crackled as she walked. She was fond of starched cambrics and muslins, and was very great in ruffles and frills. In this she differed from Belle, who loved all soft and clinging materials. Nettie decked her little person with bright-coloured ribbons, a bow here and a bow there; she wore toy aprons, and little high-heeled shoes that creaked with newness. Garton in his satire sometimes called her the "Dresden Shepherdess," though he generally added, under his breath, that she was rather too

Dutch - built for Arcadia and would require a substantial crook.

"Mrs. Ord is always finding fault with my idleness," returned Nettie, pouting, as the Vicar threw aside another shovelful of earth. "I don't think it is any merit for people who like work to be industrious. I am sure you are handling that spade with as much delight as I should a croquet-mallet."

"Perhaps so, Miss Nettie; but I do not think Mary is quite so fond of mending as I am of digging."

"Don't you think she is, Mr. Ord?" very incredulously.

"Well, I don't know; you ought to be a better judge than I am. I observe she frowns dreadfully when she sews on buttons."

"Why are buttons always coming off, I wonder?" asked Nettie innocently.

"To give occupation to idle young ladies, I suppose. By the bye, Miss Nettie, I hope you have your thimble with you this morning."

"I—I have left it at home," returned Nettie, much discomposed at this unexpected attack.

"Left it at home! Dear mé! Thimbles are not very heavy to carry, are they? and Mary wants you to help her this morning. Never mind, I daresay Belle's will fit you."

"I don't think I shall have time to sit with Mrs. Ord this morning. Aunt Eliza wants me." And, as Nettie uttered this fib, she glanced uneasily at Mary's work-basket in the distance.

"Oh, indeed; then I suppose your visit is to Garton and me? Gar, you uncivil fellow, why don't you say something entertaining to our visitor?"

"Of course I shall go in to Mrs. Ord directly; I am going now." And Nettie turned very red as she detected the slight vein of irony in the Vicar's speech. "I only came up for a moment to see if she and you had heard the news; but as you are so busy"—and so disagreeable, she was going to add—"I will not interrupt you." And so saying, she rustled off, rather piqued by the coolness of her reception.

"So ho, my little lady! that is why you have come; and Mary is right, as usual," muttered the Vicar; and his lip curled with an amused smile as he fell to his work with an energy that surprised his brother.

"There, I have finished my bit of ground, Garton," he said, looking admiringly at the result of his labours; "and my arms are pretty stiff by this time, I can tell you. Don't forget we have a funeral at a quarter to twelve, and there is no one to toll the bell.   Now I must go in ; for Nettie is up to mischief, and I must settle her, and then I have some letters to write."

Nettie's tongue was in full swing as he approached the window, and Mary's face looked sorely perplexed.   She seemed quite relieved at the sight of her husband.

"Austin, do come here a moment," for the Vicar was feigning to pass the window ; "is it not strange, Nettie has heard all about Bryn ?"

"Well, I don't see anything strange about that, Mary.   I suppose Hannah Farebrothers will tell everybody that she is expecting a new mistress.   She was brimful of it to me ten days ago, and so was Peter.   I think they were rather disappointed at my want of interest."

"Do you mean that you were not really interested, Mr. Ord ?" exclaimed Nettie.   She had forgotten her pique already in her eagerness.   "Why, it seems such a wonderful event to us all at Kirkby."

"Little things please little minds, Miss Nettie."

"Yes, but this is not a little thing ; the owner of Bryn will take a leading influence in the parish."

"Mary suggested that she might be a Plymouth Sister," observed the Vicar slyly.

"A Plymouth Sister ?" returned Nettie, opening her eyes rather widely.   "Oh, that must have been Mrs. Ord's nonsense. Of course she must be a Churchwoman."

"I don't see any 'of course,' Miss Nettie."

"But the Plymouth Sisters have everything in common, have they not—wear each other's gowns, and say their prayers in white-washed rooms ?   No, I don't think the owner of Bryn is likely to be that."

"You see that was only a theory of Mary's.   Mary is rather clever at such things.   You have a theory yourself about work, have you not ?"

"Hannah Farebrothers told me," interposed Nettie hurriedly, " that the young lady had come quite unexpectedly into this fortune. The story was quite a romantic one.   She had been a governess and then a companion, and all at once she woke up one morning and found herself an heiress."

"That is very romantic indeed.   I never knew that you were such friends with Mrs. Farebrothers."

"One of our servants knows her—and—and Harriet is a great talker——"   And Nettie broke off at this point, rather confused.

"Most servants are talkers," returned the Vicar quietly ; "I

suppose she found a good listener. Ah, well! Hannah Farebrothers is a sad gossip, as Miss Maturin will find to her cost."

"Isn't Miss Maturin a strange name?—Rotha Maturin—it
sounds nice somehow. I suppose you will leave your card within
the week, Mrs. Ord?"

"I? I don't know. I have not made up my mind," stammered Mary; but her husband came to her assistance.

"What do you mean to do, Miss Nettie? That is more to the
purpose."

"Of course I shall wait till the Vicar's wife sets us the
example," returned Nettie sententiously. "Aunt Eliza says the
clergyman's family always call first."

"Mary, did you hear that? I hope you will make a memo-
randum of Aunt Eliza's advice. Miss Underwood ought to understand the proper etiquette in such cases. The clergyman's family
always call first."

"Did you not know that before?" asked Nettie, very much
puzzled.

"My dear Miss Nettie, you cannot expect us to be all Aunt
Elizas. What can a poor country parson know about fashion and
etiquette? I suppose Mary ought to send a round-robin through
the parish, stating the exact day on which she leaves her card. If
so, I had better have a form printed at once."

"Mr. Ord, I do believe you are laughing at me."

"Laughing? Not at all! It is quite pleasant to hear a little
gossip, for a change. One does not often have the opportunity of
hearing a good racy servant's tale. Mary has a prejudice against
them—that is another of her theories. Have you tried on Belle's
thimble yet, Miss Nettie?"

"I see clearly that you are trying to tease me," said Nettie,
looking very much injured. "I don't see why I am to be scolded
and laughed at because I choose to be idle, and because I have
brought you a piece of news, and I did so want to know if it were
true," she continued piteously.

"Which? the idleness or the news?"

"Oh, Mr. Ord, it is no good trying to get anything out of
you."

"Try Mary, then."

"No; she will not answer me either. I only wanted to know
if it were true that Miss Maturin had been a companion, and
whether you meant to forget bygones, and call upon her as you
would on any ordinary newcomer; because, of course, it was not
her fault, poor thing! as Mrs. Farebrothers says——" And here
Nettie stopped, confused under the Vicar's eye.

"What did Hannah Farebrothers say was not her fault?" he demanded quickly.

"That the property came to her, and not to Mr. Robert; and she was hoping that he would not bear malice, and—and——"

"Really, Mrs. Farebrothers seems a very interfering woman," said the Vicar, now really displeased. "I shall take care to inform Miss Maturin what sort of person she has in her service. She was not so presuming in my aunt's time, but I suppose she has been too long her own mistress. Well, as Hannah Farebrothers' tales never had any interest for me, I may as well betake myself to my letters; it is only idle people who can afford to gossip."

Then Nettie got up and shook out her ruffles, looking very much as though she had got the worst of it, and said some meaningless little word or two to Mary about Aunt Eliza expecting her.

"What! are you going too?" said the Vicar, holding out his hand with a relenting smile. "Well, good-bye; give my kind regards to Miss Underwood, and tell her I shall hope to meet her this afternoon at the district meeting. We are always very glad to see you at the Vicarage, Miss Nettie; but next time you come I hope you will not forget your thimble."

# CHAPTER X.

''I will not shut me from my kind,
And, lest I stiffen into stone,
I will not eat my heart alone,
Nor feed with sighs a passing wind:

.        .        .        .        .        .

''I'll rather take what fruit may be
Of sorrow under human skies:
'Tis held that sorrow makes us wise,
Whatever wisdom sleep with thee.''

*In Memoriam.*

ROTHA MATURIN spent some three weeks under the lawyer's hospitable roof, and both she and her kind entertainers were unfeignedly sorry when the visit came to an end.

Mr. Tracy had become sincerely attached to his young *protégée*; his good opinion of her had increased rather than otherwise, and he never ceased to lament Robert Ord's unfortunate prejudice against her. His hearty sympathy did much to re-establish Rotha in her own self-esteem. She began to look upon her misfortune from a less morbid point of view; something of the old courage and spirit returned to her, and though she was still painfully subdued, and the languor of an unnatural oppression was still heavy on her, there was a quiet vigour and self-reliance discernible now in her actions which strangers were not slow to appreciate.

On the whole those weeks had done much for her; the very atmosphere of the house in Manchester Square was restful and pleasant to the sorely tried girl. Mr. Tracy's quaint old-fashioned politeness—a little out of date perhaps, but perfectly kind-hearted —the good-natured chatter of his homely wife, and the prim ways of his two daughters with their old-maidish notions of the fitness of things, and their kind womanly hearts at the bottom, the endless gossips over trifles and shreds of events, the little tea-parties with the never-failing rubber of whist to follow, all the ins and outs of a quiet old-fashioned household, interested Rotha Maturin, and soothed her at the same time.

7

Sore from her lifelong experience of a cold and unsympathetic world, and yearning, as only a woman can yearn, for the pure sweet atmosphere of home, for sympathy, for contact with congenial natures, for the bare crust of mere human kindness, no wonder if Mrs. Tracy's motherliness and the harmless garrulity of her gentle fussy daughters were pleasant to the lonely girl. In a few days she had roused out of the dangerous apathy that had been creeping over her ever since that unfortunate interview in Eglistone Abbey; in very gratitude she strove to interest herself in their pursuits, in Mrs. Tracy's silk patchwork, and Miss Harriet's missionary basket, prolific of woollen jugs and gaudy striped cuffs, and even in Miss Louisa's innocent penchant for the consumptive young curate who stammered. She listened patiently while Miss Louisa, with many faded blushes, expounded a receipt for black-currant jelly which would cure any incipient pulmonary complaint. She won golden opinions from the placid women; her patchwork was a marvel of neatness, her silk stars and diamonds miracles of needlework, and her woollen jugs the tastiest in the basket; and though she did not actually assist in the concoction of the black-currant jelly, she was careful to taste it, and won Miss Louisa's heart for ever by her judicious praises of the useful introduction of cayenne pepper, which was secretly to work such results. And in all this there was no unnecessary and weak pandering to the fancies and whims of strangers; it was only the readiness of a simple affectionate nature to adapt itself to the pleasure of others. It was not that Rotha Maturin cared to knit woollen jugs or snip old pieces of brocade into grotesque shapes; it was simply that she wished to please the kind Samaritans who had taken her under their roof. She was glad that they considered her such a capital partner at whist, and though she secretly disliked the game, she was never too busy or too tired to take a hand; and then she was so quick to replenish the silver snuff-box, whose contents travelled so endlessly down Mr. Tracy's nankeen waistcoat. Rotha used to marvel at first at the brown stream that effected lodgments in every crease and fold; by and by she got used to it—as she did to Mrs. Tracy's frilled caps, and to Miss Harriet's false front and velvet band; it was a little odd, but then they were old-fashioned people.

Yes, those weeks had done much for Rotha Maturin; it was a new thing for the poor pupil-teacher and the still more lonely companion to be treated as though she were a person of some consideration; in her humility she had forgotten the prestige which the world attaches to an heiress: when her opinions were listened to and treated with deference she felt abashed and almost ashamed: she could not understand it at all.

Rotha shed tears when she parted from her kind friends and took her place beside Mrs. Carruthers in the railway carriage. To her this was a dark day's journey. As she leant back upon the cushions and closed her eyes a feeling almost amounting to agony took possession of her as she thought how the fierce speed was already lessening the distance between her and that hated home; she felt almost like a criminal whose reprieve was drawing to an end, and who had not yet attained to the sullen indifference which is to blunt his fear. What a nightmare of oppression was on her —a blank of suspense and unreality! She could have envied Mrs. Carruthers looking out on the prospect with such thorough appreciation of its beauties; the green fields and flying hedges and rolls of brown uplands were nothing to her now; sometimes they passed sweeps of pasture-land scarlet with poppies, and Meg would wonder and exclaim. The whole country was gay with these flaming weeds; they blazed on hill-tops, or dipped into knolls and valleys; now they stood flaunting by the roadside like beggars in gay-coloured rags, and now they hung out from the stony rocks in scores and hundreds, like tattered banners streaming with blood; now and then there was a glory and a waste of colour when the yellow sunshine flooded some distant height. Meg held her breath and checked herself when she saw Rotha's tired face; she was almost vexed with herself that the fresh air and beautiful scenery gave her such pleasure. Rotha strove to rouse herself into something like interest when she saw this. But, in spite of her own and Meg's efforts, it was a long weary journey, and it was almost a relief when they reached Blackscar at last.

Mr. Tracy had made every possible arrangement for his young friend's comfort; and the old factotum and house-servant, Peter, had orders to meet his new mistress at the station and escort her to her future home. Mrs. Ord's carriage and horses had followed her to London, and had been sold after her death; for Rotha was determined that no idle pomp and ceremony should be hers. She and Mr. Tracy had already regulated the extent of the modest household. The old servants, Hannah and Peter Farebrothers, were to be kept on, and a couple of young maids under them—so much was absolutely necessary. But when Mr. Tracy proposed a phaeton or pony-carriage, he was almost surprised at the haste and decision with which his proposal was negatived. It was in vain that he assured her over and over again that such a convenience was thought nothing in the country; that it was indispensable, respectable, and only becoming her station. Miss Maturin shook her head; she would never ride or drive when she could walk. She could not help it if people looked down on her and called her stingy. She must learn to live without her neighbours' good opinion, she supposed. And her lips trembled and set themselves as she said this.

"But, my dear, how will you manage to spend your money?" Mr. Tracy had persisted, "with no house-rent, and handsome annuities secured to the servants? Recollect, you owe it to your benefactress to make a good use of the wealth left you. I would rather see you squander it than hoard it up like this."

"Indeed I do not intend to hoard it up in the way you mean, dear Mr. Tracy," she answered, smiling a little, but very sadly. "I am going to live well and comfortably, and to want for nothing; but you must not ask me to spend one farthing that is not absolutely necessary."

"But why, my dear?" asked the old lawyer, now thoroughly bewildered by what he chose to consider an obstinate whim, and yet somewhat shaken by her seriousness.

"Because I am keeping it all for him. No, my dear old friend, you must not be angry with me. Of course I know how I am fettered by that unjust will. I ought to know something about wills now. I have made my own. I may never have the opportunity—of course I never shall—of giving it to him in my lifetime. But I am not very strong. Young people die sometimes. He may have it all sooner than he thinks. Oh, Mr. Tracy, how I wish he might! how I wish he might!"

"And a very wicked wish, my dear. As though your Maker did not know what was best for you and him too. That comes of having a lot of morbid fancies in your head, and not listening to the opinions of those who are older and wiser than yourself. It was bad enough your making that will; and very weak of me to give in to such folly when there was plenty of time. Only, of course, there was nothing to say against it; but when it comes to your wishing yourself dead because an ill-tempered young man chooses to think a lot of lies against you—there—there, we won't talk any more about it." And Mr. Tracy pushed away his snuff-box and rubbed his head irritably.

Rotha gave one of her soft little laughs as she saw him.

"And I need not have the carriage?"

"Of course not. If you choose to be miserly."

"Oh, I don't mind being called that at all. Other people may think me stingy. I suppose Mrs. Farebrothers will. I cannot tell everybody that I am keeping it for him. But the thought that I am—that I am only a steward of her money for him will keep me brave and patient. I know it will, Mr. Tracy. And in God's good time all this miserable mistake will be rectified."

" There; go along with you," finished Mr. Tracy testily. " I am glad you are no daughter of mine." And the lawyer helped himself to a liberal pinch of his favourite mixture. " And that fool of a fellow can't see what a woman he is persecuting ! " he muttered, as Rotha walked away. " And she has made me promise to keep her counsel, too. A steward of his money, indeed ! A conceited young stone-flint. My daughter ? No ! no ! She is far too near the angels. Now I have it why she wears those black stuff gowns, and would not look at the silk one my wife chose for her. If there is one thing I hate it is senti- mental rubbish." And here Mr. Tracy shut up his snuff-box with a click that woke up his wife from her afternoon nap.

Rotha had one or two more conversations with her guardian, as she persisted in calling him — she was very ignorant on the subject of executors and trustees — but they always ended in this manner. She got plenty of scolding and grumbling, but not a few valuable hints. Among other things he advised her to make the vicar her confidant in all matters relating to parish matters and charities.

" He is a good sensible man, and not much stuck-up, though he is an Ord, and you may rely safely on his judgment. They say he is a rare one for making the women work, though. What's that you are saying ? Not come to Bryn ? Why, of course he'll come to Bryn. What's the use of a parson if he can't shirk his feelings when they interfere with his duty ? "

" But if his brother poison his mind against me ? " put in Rotha timidly.

" Why, he'll come all the same. Isn't it a parson's duty to look after his flock ? What's the good of wearing a long coat, and being down on his knees half the day, as they say he is, with his open church and his daily services, and all that nonsense, if he does not know his duty better than that ? If he doesn't come he ought ; and I hope you'll send for him. I suppose you have got a soul to be saved as well as the rest of the women ; though such as yours must be safe, I should think. Poison his mind ! Nonsense ! Isn't this a free country ? Why, we should be ashamed to convict a criminal on circumstantial evidence, not to speak of an unoffending young woman." And Mr. Tracy frowned angrily as he dismissed the subject with a wrathful wave of the hand.

" And you think I must not ask Mrs. Farebrothers to do all the cooking ? " asked Rotha, returning to the principal subject of her thoughts.

" Why, Hannah is not so young as she was, nor Peter either.

They've had a hard life of it. One cannot ask old servants to slave at their age. Better have the two young women and finish with it. It will make your mind easier, and do better in the long-run."

" But two people don't want four servants, Mr. Tracy."

"Two people want twenty sometimes. It is no use asking my advice and then flying in the face of it. But young people will have their own opinions."

"And you really think I must not ask Mrs. Farebrothers to do more ? "

" That depends on the toughness of your conscience," replied the lawyer grimly. And Rotha, seeing the contest would be a stubborn one, and rather mistrusting her own inexperience, gave in somewhat hastily to her friend's judgment ; and so one point was gained.

It was Mr. Tracy's thought that Peter should be at the station. If Rotha could have had her wish, she would have slipped into her new home after dark, like a thief ; but Mr. Tracy had determined otherwise. And as the train steamed into the station there was the gray-haired old servant peering anxiously at every well-dressed lady who alighted, in the hope of recognising his unknown mistress. His countenance fell a little when Rotha quietly accosted him ; the two dowdily-dressed women standing by their boxes had not once attracted Peter's notice, whose ideas of mistresses were chiefly founded on Mrs. Ord's satins and sables. The tall thin girl in black might have passed for her own maid, only a lady's-maid would have been smarter. The quiet tone of authority, however, left him no room for doubt.

" Peter, will you help Mrs. Carruthers to count the boxes ? She is at the luggage-van. I suppose you have a cab for us out-side ? Thank you. I will wait here till you have seen to the luggage." And, as the bewildered servant obeyed his orders, she leant wearily against a truck till Mrs. Carruthers summoned her.

Blackscar and Kirkby were looking their best that evening. Such season as appertained even to Blackscar was rapidly filling the scanty measure of lodging-houses and hotels. The old-fashioned shops were dressed more gaily than usual, the jewellers especially. The carvers of jet might have hanged themselves by hundreds on the long pendants and chains of curious workmanship that de-corated their shop-fronts. The endless festoons filled the lookers-on with incipient feelings of strangulation. Nobs and blocks of funereal-looking jet resolved themselves everywhere into earrings and other instruments of torture. To judge from their mul-tiplicity, every female in Blackscar might have been condemned by some fury of fashion to carry black weights protruding from the lobes of their ears in the shape of rings, startling-looking butterflies and daisies, pinnacles and oblongs, cruciform monstrosities, and other relics of barbarism.

The haberdashers were not nearly so prolific of goods : a meagre supply of blue draperies festooned the windows of the principal depôt of fashion, to be relieved on the morrow by a still more scanty supply of green ; every day of the week had its appropriate colour, its faint pinks, and its dingy browns. The shell-shops looked brighter, and drove a brisk trade with the young members of the community ; but then Blackscar was a little out of date.

Still, it was looking its best this evening. There was plenty of sunshine. Some church-bells were pealing. The air was blowing freshly from the sea. An itinerant band of music had struck up. Knots of gaily-dressed people lingered on the sea-wall or at breezy corners. Now and then, down some side street, Rotha could catch a glimpse of yellow sands—of a sea intensely blue ; now and then there was a sudden sense of salt freshness, faint sea-weedy smells, a slow ripple, and a pause, and then the low musical rush of a breaking wave—some restless pulse of Rotha's heart beat more quickly when she heard that. Down past the Grammar School and the rows of low bow-windowed houses ; past the church, with its lich-gate, with the Leatham Hills, and the flickering fires smoking luridly in the distance ; behind it, down past the schoolhouse and the sexton's ; and there were the grass hillocks and the long sandy sweep, the whole grand curve of the bay, with Welburn lying westward.

Rotha uttered a little cry of pleasure at that sight. How still and calm it all looked ! What blue distances, what masses of black uncovered rocks ; how lurid those tongues of murky flame looked from those distant furnaces, and how softly the purple line of hills cut against the sunset sky. They had passed a few white-washed cottages and a gray-looking house or two. By and by they came to a bridge over a disused little railroad, and nearly opposite, another gray house, a little larger and more substantial than the others ; beyond this were some stubble-fields, a suspicion of distant factories, a tract of barren land, intersecting railroads, sandy hillocks in profusion, with a range of rabbit-warrens below.

Rotha knew this was Bryn almost before they stopped. As she walked across the strip of green lawn she was almost relieved at the want of pretentiousness about the whole place.

Bryn was an old-fashioned two-storied house, built of greystone, which gave it a weather-beaten aspect. Just now its many cracks and stains were hidden under a wealth of greenery and climbing roses, which festooned the bay-windows and crept in luxuriant confusion over the stone porch ; long trails of Virginia creeper covered up the gray baldness and made old age beautiful.

The front door stood open. Rotha had just time to catch a glimpse of a long dusky hall, with a wide shallow staircase, and glass doors opening on to a pleasant lawn, before a woman with a shrewd sensible face came from behind some swing doors with two comely-looking country lasses behind her.

" Now Prudence, now Emma, here's the new mistress. Come, look alive, girls ! Where's your manners ? I am sure, Miss Maturin, we all bid you welcome kindly to your new home," continued Mrs. Farebrothers, as she dropped one hurried curtsey after another, in dire perplexity as to which the new mistress really was. She was fixing on Mrs. Carruthers in her mind when Miss Maturin quietly stepped forward.

" This is my friend Mrs. Carruthers, Hannah, who is to come and live with me. I am Miss Maturin. I am sure you mean to welcome us very kindly. I have heard so much of you and of Peter," continued the young girl, holding out her hand to each ; " you have been such faithful servants and friends to my bene- factress—I have heard her so often talk of you both—that I feel as though I know you already." And then, as Hannah held her apron to her eyes, she turned round with a kind word and a smile to the two shy damsels behind.

" I'll never think that silks and satins make a lady again," said Peter, when he sat down beside the hearth that evening, when all the bustle of the arrival was over. " I was thinking to myself at the station how that young-looking creature in the black stuff gown can't be our Miss Maturin—why, our Betsy was a sight smarter than her !—when she up and spoke to me. ' Peter,' says she, quite clip-like, and like a Londoner,—' Peter,' says she, ' just look after them boxes while I stay here.' Why, you might have knocked me all of a heap all the time the porter was loading his truck. I kept saying, ' That young woman in the black gown our Miss Maturin ?' over and over again, like a blockhead as I was ; but law ! when she put those long fingers of hers in my hand, with never a ring on them—did you mind that Hannah ?—and spoke so prettily, not a bit pert or proud for all her grand fortune, I just said to myself, ' That there young woman is the right sort after all.' "

" Yes, she is the right sort," returned Mrs. Farebrothers, thoughtfully regarding a tin she was polishing, and which was already bright enough to reflect her hard-featured Scotch face. " I am not for denying that, Peter ; but all this evening I can't get it out of my mind that the poor lassie has a sore heart of it. Her eyes have too sorrowful a look in them to be quite natural to such a young creature. It made me dour to look at her."

"The other one is a widow, I've heard say," suggested Peter.

"A widow or not, she's no beauty to look at," returned Mrs. Farebrothers, with whom Meg's homely face and ways had found no favour. "If Miss Maturin wanted a dragon to keep her, she needn't have gone farther and fared worse. She is a Welshwoman by her looks, if ever I have seen one. Well, as I was saying, Peter, I am sure there is something lying heavy on that young creature. When I had given her the keys, and said something suitable of course, I was for showing them the house directly. She wanted to put it off a bit; but Mrs. Carruthers said, very sensible, 'Better get it over; you will feel more settled like,' says she. And so after that she made no more ado. Well, the rooms are good rooms and handsome ones. But law! what was the use of Prue and me beeswaxing and polishing and fretting ourselves for the last three weeks? She only just looked round them in a tired sort of way, as much as to say, 'I've seen you all before; and I don't want to look at you again.' The Welshwoman kept nudging her: 'What a pretty room, Rotha,' she kept saying. 'What nice feather-beds, Mrs. Farebrothers. Look here, my dear, what a view from your dressing-room window.' But, bless you, she wouldn't take the hint. But when I threw open the missis' wardrobe, and showed her that pile of yellow lace, and the plate and jewel case, 'Don't show me all that, Hannah,' she says very quick and sharp, and with a kind of shudder, 'I don't like to see it. So this is where she slept, poor thing;' and she went up to the bed and patted the pillow in such a pitiful way. 'I think she would have liked to have laid her poor head again there, Meg,' she said so soft and sad. Well, I didn't like to hear her go on like that; so I said without thinking, 'Yes, this was her favourite room, poor lady. That one next to it was Mr. Robert's. Yes, she was that fond of him that she could not bear him to be far from her.' Bless your heart, I could have bitten my tongue out before I'd have made such a speech. She seems to be a poor sickly-looking body at the best. But she just went that sort of colour like waxwork. 'So that was his room?' she said, with such a sigh. 'See, it was just within her own; she always treated him as though he were her own son. You are very right, Hannah, to have left it just as it was,' she went on. 'It must never be touched—never. Some day, when he comes to see it, or to hear of it, it will please him to think we have left his old room just as it was.' And as she closed the door gently I could see her eyes were full of tears. Was it not odd, Peter, and they such strangers to each other ?"

"Odd ? Not a bit. We shall see stranger things than that before we've done, missis. What's more natural than that a young woman, kindhearted, with not a bit of pride about her, should take on and pity the poor fellow ? Of course it would be against nature not to be pleased with her fine fortune. But, all the same, she won't forget them that's lost it." And Peter administered a brisk kick to the coals with an energy that made his wife jump.

"Miss Nettie says that there is some ill-blood in Mr. Robert's mind about her. She couldn't get a word out of the parson nor his wife neither. I don't think they ought to make things difficult for her because the old missis chose to leave her her money. Every one knows how badly Mr. Robert behaved ; ' but the stubborn neck shall have a fall,' as Solomon says."

But how much farther Hannah would have got in her quotation was not evident, as at that moment the upstairs bell rung.

# CHAPTER XI.

BRYN.

" *I* know that this was Life,—the track
     Whereon with equal feet we fared ;
     And then, as now, the day prepared
The daily burden for the back."

                                        *In Memoriam.*

" All day within the dreamy house,
     The doors upon their hinges creak'd ;
The blue fly sung in the pane ; the mouse
     Behind the mouldering wainscot shriek'd,
     Or from the crevice peer'd about.
     Old faces glimmer'd thro' the doors,
     Old footsteps trod the upper floors,
Old voices called her from without.
     She only said, ' My life is dreary,
     He cometh not,' she said ;
     She said, ' I am aweary, aweary,
     I would that I were dead ! ' "          TENNYSON.

MRS. FAREBROTHERS' homely account had not been exaggerated.
Meg had been deeply pained for the good woman's disappointment
when she saw the weary indifference with which Rotha viewed her
new possessions ; her simple praises and hints had all been thrown
away. Rotha could see nothing but the shadowy Nemesis of her
fate lurking in the corners of the rooms. The jingling of the
household keys filled her with a sharp pain and dread. While
Hannah opened the presses of sweet-smelling linen, or pointed out
the three-cornered cupboard, where the best purple and gold china
was kept, or showed her stores of delicate preserves, Rotha's
thoughts were far away in the darkened inn-chamber. Again she
was wiping the death-sweat from the wrinkled brow. She could
feel the touch of the clammy fingers clutching hers so desperately,
yet powerless to keep their hold. She could see the livid lips
parting slowly as the words dropped from them one by one,
" Robert, remember it is all for Robert." Good heavens ! Who
was she that she should be enriched with another man's goods ?

Mechanically she followed the other two from room to room. It might have been that she was dazed from her long journey; it was strange how dream-like and misty were her first impressions of her new home; but in a vague unreal way she saw it all.

She noticed that the passages were dark and narrow, and full of curious sweet smells; she found out afterwards from the great jars of dried rose-leaves that flanked every doorway and blocked up the staircase. And she remembered how the oaken carving of the balustrades attracted her notice, and how broad, and low, and slippery the staircase was. In a dim sort of way she recalled too that the dining-room was low and dark, and had heavy brown wainscoting; that there were marble pillars in the long drawing-room, and a great Chinese cabinet; and that there was a close damp odour about the room, as though it had never been used. By and by they had come to a little room full of evening sunshine, with glass doors opening on the lawn, with a low couch, and book-cases, and a tea-table spread with all manner of good things. And Meg had said, "How bright and pleasant! This must be your room, Rotha." There were tall white lilies peeping in at the window, and there was a great spray of red roses overhead. The church-bells were still ringing out. Rotha stood looking at the smooth green lawn, with some carrier-pigeons strutting across it. "Now, we will go upstairs, and Miss Maturin can rest and refresh herself," she heard Hannah say, and she had turned herself round to follow them.

They had gone into Mrs. Carruthers' room first, a trifle faded and old-fashioned, but very comfortable, quite a nest of luxury to Meg. The humble creature could have sat down and cried with gratitude at the pleasant lines at last vouchsafed to her. But the strange fixed look on Rotha's face forbade all such demonstration. Rotha was glad that her friend should be made happier by all this comfort. She was glad, too, with a sort of relief, that her own room looked seaward, and was full of soft green colour. She felt unconsciously that even such trifles might influence her moods more healthfully, but nothing had really roused her till Hannah had opened her late mistress' wardrobe to show the hidden treasures —in the shape of jewels and lace, and then there had been a sharp sound in Rotha's voice, never heard before, as though the action displeased her, and after that they had shown her his room.

Meg was very sorry when she saw Rotha's face at that moment. She understood in a moment the quick revulsion, the heart-sickness, the sudden failure of courage: when Mrs. Farebrothers had left them at last and gone down, she sought Rotha in her own apart-ment and found it empty. She had gone at once with unerring instinct into Mrs. Ord's chamber. She knew she should find her there. Rotha turned round when she saw her and held out her hand, and the two women passed over the threshold of Robert Ord's chamber and into the chamber beyond with bated breath, as though they were in the presence of the dead.

It was only an ordinary room, fitted up for a young man's accommodation, with a door leading into his aunt's dressing-room. Most of the rooms opened one into another. When he had been a boy this door had been kept open that she might pass in and out to him more freely. But of late years this mode of entrance had been closed up. Rotha noted all those particulars. The other boys had slept across the passages, anywhere; but this one, the favourite, had always kept his boyish room, where she had first placed him when he was a delicate child, that she might minister to him more entirely. Rotha remembered she had heard all this from Mrs. Ord's maid.

There was a little inner sanctum, which had evidently been a playroom once, and had been furbished up in late years into a kind of rough study. Every article of furniture, every picture on the wall, belonged to the boy or the man. There was the bow and arrows side by side with the case of pistols and the formidable gun. A fully-rigged boat under a glass shade shared the top of the bookcase in company with a rusty toy sword and a couple of foils, besides boxing-gloves and a life-preserver. The very books in the well-stored bookcase told the same progressive tale. For, while the top shelf boasted of such volumes as *Robinson Crusoe*, the *Arabian Nights*, and the *Last of the Mohicans*, with a sprinkling of battered old school-books, the lower shelves held handsomely-bound volumes of Sir Walter Scott, Ruskin, Carlyle, and other standard authors. Rotha wondered a little that their owner had left them to such useless repose; but when she had opened one or two her wonder subsided. In every one there was the same clear bold handwriting—"Robert Baldwin Ord, from his loving Aunt Charlotte." Somehow that little token of Robert's pride and resentment seemed to send a chill through her heart.

She dropped the books with a sigh and turned to the pictures. Over the mantelpiece was a wretched daub, representing a curly-headed child in a velvet frock tearing some red poppies and a few cabbage roses to pieces. Rotha puzzled a little over the unnaturally red cheeks and staring blue eyes till she saw R. O. in the corner. Some itinerant artist had painted the picture, but it had been thought a striking likeness at the time, and judged worthy of the massive gold frame. On the other side there were crude water-colour sketches done by some boyish hand—a mastiff's head in crayons, with "Keeper" written in faded ink under it. The others were prints of a sporting character.

Slowly and softly, as one manipulates the relics of the dead, Rotha looked and lingered, and touched softly the several objects that attracted her notice: the ebony inkstand with the faded violet ink at the bottom, the well-used blotting-case, and the carved book-rest; there was the empty bird-cage which had successively held a sickly generation of linnets, sparrows, and finches; a mouse-trap and a box fitted up for dormice still littered the window-seat; a number of the *Quarterly* lay on the cushion of a great easy-chair as though just flung down. "None of us were allowed to touch a thing in the young master's room," Mrs. Farebrothers had said as she dusted down the table with her apron, and Rotha stood and marvelled at the strange inconsistency of a love that could retain every relic of his boyhood, and yet had never once flinched from its stern purpose till it was too late.

After a while Meg had drawn her gently away, and it was an evidence of the strong but silent sympathy that existed between these two that, although no word had been spoken, Rotha was conscious that she was understood, and was grateful for Meg's forbearance.

She made no opposition, therefore, when Mrs. Carruthers proposed that they should go downstairs. She went back to the sunset and the lilies. The pigeons fluttered up to her as she took the low seat by the window and tried to do justice to the various dainties that were pressed on her notice, but it was a miserable pretence and failure.

What a quiet meal it was! neither spoke much, but now and then Rotha dropped some restless word or two. The red evening light fell full on Meg's rugged face and figure; the large light eyes looked solemn and plaintive beyond their wont; to the elder woman it seemed as though the quiet breadths of sky were meet emblems of the long interval of rest that stretched before her. Active suffering had subsided into passive with Meg; the long habits of submission and a certain sturdy endurance went far to reconcile her to the inevitable. It was not that she ever forgot the fact that there was any actual negation of pain, but it was as though she were some wrecked vessel that had been towed safely into still waters where the cruel storms would cease to buffet her maimed sides, and where there was no fear that she should be torn roughly from her anchorage, where, for a little while at least, she might be left to float idly and at peace.

Meg could have chanted the "Nunc Dimittis" as she sat there. Afterwards, as she unpacked Rotha's things and put away her own poor little store of clothes and books, she broke into fragments of it; Prue could hear the grave deep voice chanting brief snatches as she put away the things in the sweet-smelling drawers: all sorts of lavender bags and sprigs of rosemary were strewn there. "The green pastures and the still waters"—she was thankful for them all. Here she thought she would dwell safely, doing daily duty and praying loving prayers for her stray sheep—her poor prodigal: she always thought of Jack as she read the story of the Prodigal Son; he was afar off even now feeding on the husks; not till he was a-hungered, till the measure of his degradation was filled up, and want and misery impelled that feeble repentance, should she ever see him again. But she always knew that she would see him.

She had never spoken to any one of this belief of hers till that strange conversation she had had with Rotha in Chatham Place, but such was her natural reticence that not even to her did she again refer to it; she shrank from averring it in open words even to herself. It was an article of her woman's creed, tacitly acknowledged and religiously held. She guarded that simple faith of hers as jealously as though she feared it would not bear the test of human experience. Credo—I believe: how many a woman, disdaining the hard clear light of réason, holds to some such shred of self-made evidence, clinging to it with instinctive trust, seeing God's image in the bleared and miserable wreck of manhood she calls husband: mothers hoping against hope, and leaning all their purer faith on some spendthrift of a man—sisters weeping angel tears over some fallen brother, shuddering away from the sin, yet loving the sinner.

Meg never questioned how this thing could be—never asked herself what should bring her guilty husband to her side again; she only knew that one day he would come: that thought was always uppermost; in her waking and her sleeping dreams she always saw him coming, sometimes by land, sometimes by sea, but always the same, always ragged, weather-beaten—a wreck of himself. Latterly these dreams had become more frequent; she knew now when she closed her eyes that she would be sure to see him: he was always in beggar's guise, sometimes so changed that even her loving eyes could not recognise him. Now and then he would draw near and hold out his arms to her, and then some unseen power would keep her rooted to the place, and he would go away covering up his face with his hands. Once, when the vision had been terribly real, the thought had come to her to follow him. Meg never thought of that dream without a shudder: she had followed him down long endless roads, each one longer and darker than the last; sometimes she had nearly overtaken him, when a sudden turning hid him from her sight. She tried to cry out to him, to utter his name, but her tongue was powerless, her step grew heavier and more lagging—she would lose him altogether now, but presently she found out that she had a child in her arms, and that this was impeding her progress. With the subtle reasoning of a dream she thought that if she could only lay the child down by the roadside he must really turn round; but when she tried to free herself it only clung the closer; she could feel the little cold hands creeping over her breast and round her neck. Those baby hands held her fast with their mysterious hold, and then all at once she knew he was behind her with his face still covered up in his mantle, and, with the child on her bosom, she was trying to draw it away. The cloak felt to her like black velvet, and then it hardened in her touch and broke into splinters as though it were wood; but still she tore and grappled with it, when all at once it rent asunder and there was the grinning face of a skeleton behind it.

Meg had woke from that dream with a loud cry, but she never told any one of her terror. For a few days she went about almost silently, and something of strained pallor in her looks; her faith had received a shock. What if he were already dead and this was her warning! But after a time her strong good sense returned to her, and though she still trembled at times with the remembrance of the ghastly vision, she soon grew to believe that it was only an exaggeration of her excited fancy, and to strengthen herself still more in the thought that she should see him again.

It was strange how this expectation deepened; day by day it harassed her daily walks; she would start and change colour if a beggar suddenly accosted her; often she would turn round to look at some maudlin shrinking wretch that would follow them whining for alms. Rotha would hurry on or speak sharply; but Meg always dropped a furtive coin, with a "God bless you," into the shaking hand. Once, when a gipsy beggar with bold eyes stopped their path with an impudent request for money, and Rotha would have dragged her on quickly in the dusk, she had gone a little way and then had made an excuse and left her. When she found him again there was a thin haggard-looking woman sitting beside him on the roadside with a baby at her breast. The fellow eyed Meg in sullen surprise when he saw her come back and drop a silver piece in his hand. Meg asked to look at the child, and drew the ragged shawl aside with her own hand; the man was brutal and sodden with gin, but the woman was a sickly-looking patient creature.

"The parish has buried four," she said in a subdued voice

that had the pathos of hunger and ill-usage in it, "and I reckon they'll have this one too." Meg burst into tears as she put back the fluttering rag over the baby's pinched face. There was an ugly-looking wound in its foot which the mother had tried to bind up with a strip of coarse stuff. "The master was in one of his tantrums last night," she whispered, as Meg knelt down to inspect it. "I had the child in my arms and couldn't ward his blow off." Then the man got up and slunk off in search of fresh alms.

Meg tore up her own handkerchief and bound up the child's foot with tender skill, and then put some silver hurriedly into the woman's hand. "You mustn't let him hurt it again," she said; "when it's dead you'll be so sorry—so very sorry." And as the woman rocked herself, crying, but very softly, lest he should hear her, Meg bade "God bless her, God bless her!" and went hurriedly away.

Rotha saw the tear-stains on her cheeks when she came up; she was waiting at the gate for her—not over-pleased at her defection. "I don't think it well to encourage beggars," she said, somewhat sternly, in answer to Meg's excuse; "and that man was such a repulsive villainous-looking fellow, and quite drunk besides."

"Yes, I know," Mrs. Carruthers had answered. "But oh, Rotha!"—and Meg hung her head—"he was so like Jack." And then Rotha had put her arms round her and kissed her.

Meg was thinking about Jack now, as she arranged Rotha's things. There was a great china bowl full of carnations standing on a little round table beside her—dusky-red carnations and fragrant clove pinks. Meg never could bear the smell of those flowers now: they brought back so vividly those days in Chatham Place when Jack was courting her; when she stood of an evening looking at the dark railway arch till he came striding through the posts and down past the triangular green, with the drowsy sheep huddled together. He used to bring her bunches of roses and carnations— nay, often she would put a few of them in her dress, in the vain hope that their rich crimson might become her. Jack always said they did, but that was one of his lies. Meg's simple chants died away on her lips now, and she made haste to finish her business. She was glad when Prue came in and carried them away. When all was done she went downstairs and played softly to herself in the twilight. Rotha was out or about somewhere, and Meg knew better than to follow her. As the grand old hymn-tunes floated through the empty room, the bitter-sweet memories faded. "Angels ever bright and fair;" "Let the bright Seraphim." Meg's courage grew steadfast and strong now, "Up above the thoughts that know not anguish." Meg could almost see the radiance on her parents' dead faces as she wove in the rhythm with the notes, and sang them softly in the darkness :—

> " Up above the thoughts that know not anguish,
>     Tender care ; sweet love for us below,
> Noble pity free from anxious terror,
>     Larger love without a touch of woe."

Rotha could hear her singing as she came through the long garden. Meg's voice, so noble in its earnestness, always sent thrills through her ; she could have envied her the power of such utterance, it would have healed half her restlessness to have sat down and sung like that.

Rotha had been terribly restless when Meg had left her to unpack. She had grown weary of the sunset and lilies, and had wandered aimlessly to and fro. Prue and Emma had come upon her gliding through the rooms with her black dress and pale face ; to escape their notice she had betaken herself to the garden.

It was a pretty sunny garden, and well kept, and for a little while Rotha found it pleasant ; but after a time even this seemed too confined, there was a restless oppression on her. By and by she would grow used to her position. She thought now she would go down by the seashore a little, and let the soft breezes blow away her pain. There was a green door opening into the lane ; as she came out she could see other green doors a little lower down, and it came across her that one of those must belong to the Vicarage.

The only way to the sands was over the little bridge that was directly opposite Bryn. Rotha was afraid Meg might see her as she hurried across, and, in order to avoid her notice and because she would be perfectly alone, she directed her steps to the ridge of low grassy hillocks that formed the warren. Here she found herself in complete solitude ; as far as she could see were green undulations, or hills and valleys of soft yellow sand, spread in a connecting chain ; a railway ran through the lower side of the warren. The ground was rugged and weedy there, but from the sandhills themselves the views were enchanting. Long reaches of sand everywhere, Welburn running out to sea like a long narrow fork, and then the grand blue sweep of Blackscar Bay.

The tide was coming in ; there was a delicious cool lapping of waves. As they covered the rocks the line of foam circled and broke with an endless slow surging. The sunset was over now, the sands looked gray and silent, all sorts of silvery pale lights stirred across the purple shadow of the water, one or two stars trembled out of a long cloud, the air was buoyant with salt spray,

Lights sprang out one by one from the distant town; the great building on the sand, which Rotha found out afterwards was the Convalescent Hospital, grew brilliant in a moment; they were lighting the lamps on the sea-wall too. All sorts of creeping shadows came over the barren sands. The air was chilly now. Rotha shivered and stood up, and then gave a weary little sigh as she went stumbling up and down in the warren, now climbing up some yielding sand-wall, and now sinking ankle-deep in a treacherous bank. She was fairly tired when she had reached the little bridge, but her restlessness had worked itself off a little.

She stopped for a moment at the gate, and then the fancy seized her that she would stroll round and look at the church; she could see it was lighted up still. She felt very forlorn wandering round her new home; but anything was better than those twilight rooms, she thought. She was glad to feel that she was getting so tired: no worn-out child would sleep sounder than she would now. The choir had been practising in the church. As she went in at the lich-gate two or three village lads came out; one had his surplice on his arm, and, as she stood aside to let them pass, a tall man came striding out from the porch. He had a loose wide-awake, very broad in the brim; even in the dark Rotha noticed the brown irregular face and the gleaming teeth. The boy with the surplice on his arm seemed waiting for him, for they went on together. Both looked hard at her as they went by.

The organist was still playing; all the lights had been extinguished but one; there was a sweet perfume of lilies as Rotha timidly pushed open the swing doors. One or two gentlemen were in the organ-loft. Rotha could hear their voices speaking in a subdued way as she crept behind a pillar. What a strange new experience it seemed to her!—almost like a dream: the empty church, the roll and swell of the organ, now pealing through the aisles and now dying away, the dim light, the sweet scent, the blurred outline of painted windows, the shadows lurking among the slender arches. The void and ache of her own heart suddenly stilled into peace. Rotha never knew how it was that she was kneeling there with the tears streaming through her fingers; she knew of no conscious prayer that rose to her lips; but something of the hard bitter strain was lifted off her, the misery and un-reality seemed lightened.

When the organ ceased she looked up for the first time, and then rose hurriedly to her feet. They were coming down the aisle now. Rotha crept still further into the shade of her pillar, but they were talking still in under tones and did not see her. One was a large man, with curly hair and wide open gray eyes, and the other—Rotha trembled strangely as he passed—the other was Robert Ord.

The organist had come out now, humming to himself; in another moment the last light would be extinguished. She could hear them talking in the porch still; her courage was fast failing her, but there was no help for it. Both looked round in surprise as she came towards them. The elder gentleman, whom she knew to be the clergyman, held open the door and looked kindly at her as she passed. It might have been impulse or mere desperation, but at that moment she moved her eyes and looked full at Robert Ord with a grave slow inclination of the head; she never saw whether he returned the salutation or not. Her heart was throbbing almost to suffocation as she descended the steps. As she passed out of the churchyard she knew they were following her; she had an odd sort of feeling, as she turned in at her own gateway, that they were still watching her through the darkness. The lights were shining at the Vicarage as she passed. Through the open windows she could hear boys' voices; a deeper voice kept chiming in with a laugh. A woman's shadow moved to and fro across an upper window. Two dusky figures turned in at the gate. Rotha looked up at the starlit sky; as she went down the gravel-path she could hear Meg singing as she walked up and down trying to calm herself.

When she went in the lamp had been lighted, a couch stood invitingly near, the curtains were undrawn, and the crisp evening air stole through the open window. Meg gave a welcoming smile as she closed the piano.

"Where have you been, Rotha? Why, my poor child, how white and weary you look!" she said as she came forward.

"White and weary, indeed!" Rotha gave one of her wistful smiles as she looked up in Meg's face. "Sit down by me, Meg. How bright and homelike it all looks. I have been very weak and wicked, while you have been singing like an angel; but it did me good—that and the music in church."

"In church, Rotha?"

"Yes, I have been in church, and on the shore, and everywhere; but I think I liked the music best. As I came out in the porch I saw him, and he saw me. What a handsome man he is, Meg! if only he were not so ungentle."

"Whom do you mean?" asked Meg anxiously, for there was a strange shining in Rotha's eyes.

"Who? why, Robert Ord, to be sure—my Nemesis, as I call him. I think I have seen them all now, only no one knew me but he. Meg, wasn't it strange, almost beautiful, after what has passed, that we should meet first there?"

"Do you mean that you met in the church, dear?"

"Yes, and then in the porch. I turned round and looked at him. I felt I had a right to be acknowledged there. I suppose you will chide me for being fanciful, but somehow I took it as a good omen. It seems to me as though it must come right now."

"I quite understand you, dear."

"Do you, Meg?"

"Yes, fully and entirely." And then Rotha, with the same strange shining in her eyes, had bidden her good-night and gone up to bed.

"Who was that young lady in black who gave you so marked a recognition?" asked the Vicar curiously, when he had locked the door and overtaken his brother in the churchyard.

"Oh, you noticed that, Austin, did you?"

"Yes; I was holding open the door for her. I thought she seemed nervous; she passed me so hurriedly. Why, Robert!" suddenly struck by something peculiar in his brother's tone, "you don't mean to say that that was——"

"Our neighbour at Bryn? Indeed I do, Austin. There she is before us—just turning round by the schoolhouse. You can see her like a black shadow in the distance."

"Good heavens! and that was Miss Maturin?" ejaculated the Vicar; but his brother remained silent.

"To think of her coming to church the first evening," he began again, after a long pause, during which they had been walking on briskly. "Why, she could only have arrived at Kirkby this afternoon."

"I don't know where you got your information, Austin," observed the other drily.

"Why, I should certainly have heard it from Peter Farebrothers if she had come yesterday. I met him down in Blackscar last evening, but he never said one word about Miss Maturin being expected."

"Peter is not quite such a talker as his wife, I suppose. Well, Austin, what do you think of her now you have seen her? She is no beauty, eh?"

"I could not possibly tell in such a moment. She appeared to be in great trouble, and had evidently been crying. As far as I could see in the dim light she looked very young. I was so surprised when she turned round and bowed to you in that marked manner."

"Wasn't it cool and self-possessed? That is just what I so

dislike in those sort of women. They have such an astonishing amount of assurance." And Robert, who was in no very good mood, thought of that walk from Eglistone Abbey when Rotha had quietly declared her intention of not shunning him.

"Yes; and it was so strange, too, her coming to church the first evening of her arrival," returned the Vicar, who had been much struck by this coincidence. "Are you coming in again to us this evening, Robert?"

"Well, I don't know. I have not said good-night to Belle. Perhaps I will come in for a moment."

The Vicar paused with his hand on the gate.

"Better not say a word about it to-night. Mary has had a worrying day, and Belle does not seem very well. It will not make them sleep sounder to tell them we've seen Miss Maturin."

"That is as you think best," returned Robert, rather shortly. He had no particular wish for any gossip with Mary, but it did strike him as rather hard that he should not say a word or two about it to Belle. It did not mend matters that Belle had a sick headache, and could not come to the supper-table. He bade them all a gloomy good-night on hearing that, and went back to his desolate house. It looked very desolate to-night. As he turned in at the gate he looked across at Bryn. There were lights moving in the upper windows; there was quite a stream of radiance on the little bridge. "So it has come at last!" he muttered. "I wish I could have spoken to Belle to-night. How oddly the girl looked at me, and how pale she was! Austin was right. She looked younger than usual, or else it was the gaslight. Well, all I hope is that I am not beginning to hate her."

What made Robert Ord pause in his prayers that night—"forgive us our trespasses?" Long after the lights were out at Bryn and the Vicarage people asleep Robert Ord tossed wearily on his bed with the broken clause weaving in and out of his thoughts: "forgive us our trespasses."

# CHAPTER XII.

" There was a little stubborn dame
Whom no authority could tame,
Restive by long indulgence grown,
No will she minded but her own."
WILKIE

" ARE you going to church this evening, Rotha ? "

" Yes, Meg."

" Very well ; I will accompany you." And without any further word Mrs. Carruthers 'quickly arrayed herself in her bonnet and shawl and followed Rotha through the green door in the lane.

The day had been a strange one to both the women. It was the first day in their new life together. Rotha had come down to breakfast that morning, looking indeed grave and preoccupied, but with a certain quiet determination which had grown out of her last night's struggles. Meg, who was watching her, was secretly relieved to see her take the head of the table, instead of relinquishing it to her, as she had once threatened to do. After breakfast she had had a long housewifely conversation with Hannah Farebrothers, and had then asked Mrs. Carruthers to go over the house again with her. As they went from one room to another Rotha quietly pointed out one or two improvements that might be effected in the arrangements, and asked her opinion. Meg noticed she avoided the passage that led to Mrs. Ord's room till the last, when she had led the way to it hurriedly, saying that Mr. Tracy had wished her to go over the inventory of the plate and linen, and that she supposed that an unpleasant business had better be got over at once.

The stores of shining things, the hordes of velvet and satin and delicate old cobweb lace, were like revelations out of another world to simple Meg, who had never seen anything finer than her mother's collar of real Valenciennes. The fairy godmother in

Cinderella might have conjured up those dainty little heaps of Mechlin and point lace. There was a warm subtle fragrance of attar of roses hidden among those heaps. Rotha's slender fingers counted, adjusted, and readjusted all in perfect order. "Yes, that is very beautiful, I suppose; but I am no judge. There are the collarettes, Hannah; put them back carefully into the collar-box. I have finished the list now." And the young girl put back her hair wearily from her brow as though she had finished some troublesome business. Meg could hardly credit such sublime indifference.

They had spent the afternoon on the shore together, and after tea the bells had rung out, and Rotha had announced her intention of going to the service. Meg would not have gainsaid her for the world; but she felt terribly anxious. "What a brave spirit she must have!" she thought, as she moved down the pew to be nearer to her. Rotha looked across at her with an odd little smile, as though she read her thought. Most of the small congregation were already in the church. The churchwarden, a white-headed old man with square shoulders, lumbered across the aisle and offered her a hymn-book. The tall young man with the brown puckered face went swinging across the chancel with stray surplices on his arm; and the boy who had waited for him the previous evening came out of the vestry-door and looked hard at Rotha as he passed. Just before service commenced two ladies came in and took their places near her.

Rotha looked at them a little curiously; they were evidently sisters, and very quietly dressed. The elder lady was rather matronly, and had a sweet motherly face; and the younger one was very beautiful, but just a little worn and faded-looking. Rotha found herself watching them from time to time with unwonted interest; directly they had entered the clergyman took his place in the reading-desk. Rotha recognised him at once as the same who had held open the door for her last night. He read the service in a clear sonorous voice. Now and then there were odd breaks in it as of caught breaths, which gave it a momentary hesitation. Rotha noticed this peculiarity in a moment; to her there was something persuasive, almost pathetic in those low tender breaks. Afterwards, when he preached, she understood the suppressed power and tenderness of the man. Austin Ord often hesitated in his delivery; his language was simple and often homely; but now and then the force and evidence of the truth within him found outlet in a flood and torrent of words. Then he was eloquent; then his power made itself felt; then he stirred men's hearts, appealing to each separate individuality, winning them less by the power of argument than by the gentle ness of love.

"Our parson always seems to be preaching to himself," was the observation of a poor parishioner once ; and the homely speech goes far to explain the general tenor of the Vicar's sermons. They were more persuasive than aggressive.   The thunders of the law were seldom touched upon except in some case of notorious backsliding, and then the Vicar would be simply terrible.   Austin seldom alluded to the pit of perdition ; the brimstone and fire of the Dissenters were an offence to him.   He rarely informed his flock that they were miserable sinners except when he read the Confession ; he left every one to apply to himself "the worm, and no man" of the Psalmist.   Instead of that he was always telling his people that he loved and pitied them ; he spoke to them as though he knew so well that they must be oppressed with their own knowledge of their sin, as though he must help them to bear the sorrow of their own pitiable failures, as though the one thing to be dreaded was their lack of courage.   "Never lose heart," he would say Sunday after Sunday.   "A scrupulous sadness cannot help any one ; we may be very sorry for what is past and yet not lose our manhood over it.   We have all been spendthrifts, have all wasted our substance ; let us at least gather up the fragments that remain."

Rotha liked his voice, it gave her a comforting assurance of pleasant vigour and strength.   The tall young man, whom Rotha fully recognised as another Ord, read the Lessons ; she was sure in her own mind that he was the youngest brother, Garton ; but, all the same, he puzzled her.   She could not make him out at all. She thought of the gleaming teeth last night and the laughter through the Vicarage windows ; she could not reconcile last night's merriment with the stern ascetic face and dark closely-cropped hair.   As he went swinging backwards and forwards through the chancel with his head thrown well back, and his grand-looking shoulders squaring themselves, he reminded her of some young Knight-Templar or monkish soldier of the cross.   There was a martial stride with him ; as he sang he kept up a singular swaying of the body—an impetuous yet restrained movement ; a swarthy colour overspread his face.   By and by, as she came out, he passed her, crunching the gravel with firm footsteps, a boy hanging on either arm, and a whole troop at his rear.   Mrs. Carruthers asked, "Who was that strange young man in the ugly wideawake?" but Rotha was thinking of the Vicar's voice and of Belle Clinton's beautiful face, and so she got no answer.

Those evening services were the only breaks in Rotha's solitary

days.    One, two, and then three weeks had passed over, but still
no friendly footstep invaded the privacy of Bryn—no greeting came
to the ears of the two recluses.

For a little while Rotha hoped against hope; she thought the
Vicar must call; but as the days passed on and he made no sign,
she quietly abandoned all such hopes and began to look her position
in the face, and for fear her courage should fail before the blank
prospect of her monotonous life, she set herself daily tasks, she
took up a slow grinding of regular employment and duties which
were to fill up every hour of the day.    An idle moment was an
abomination to her—she fought her restlessness stoutly.    Meg was
almost stunned by her prodigious energy.

When her light household duties were discharged, she devoted
herself to a severe course of self-improvement.    She studied music
under Meg's tuition; she even began German.    One day she sent
in from Blackscar a bale of flannel and some remnants of coarse
woollen stuff, and, with Mrs. Carruthers' help, began to cut it into
an infinite number of garments.    She made Prue and Emma help;
her basket of ready-made linen would have done credit to Dorcas;
to see her stitching in the midst of her maids would have astonished
the most industrious matron.    While she worked she made Meg
read to her.    Rigid in her self-discipline, she was inflexible and
hard in her choice of books.    She and Meg did a vast amount of
politics and theology.    Carlyle and Ruskin were their lightest
specimens of literature.

During their hours of recreation they worked in the garden or
went down to the shore; now and then they did an afternoon's
shopping in Blackscar.    As they passed down Kirkby village
Rotha used to look longingly into the open cottage-doors: she
would have given anything to enter.    She was craving for parish
work, for intercourse with her fellow-creatures, for something that
would take her out of herself.    Such a monotonous existence
might do for Meg.    Mrs. Carruthers never wished for society, or
found their days dull; she had her piano and her books, and her
daily thoughts for Rotha's comfort; but even she would have liked
to have ministered to their poorer neighbours.    As they passed
the schoolhouse she would stop and listen to the children's singing
till Rotha would pull her impatiently on.

Rotha never dared to enter one of the cottages; she used to
look wistfully at the women as they stood in the doorway with
children clinging to their skirts.    One evening during a severe
thunderstorm she had begged for a moment's shelter in a cottage,
and the request had been most civilly granted.

Rotha sat by the fire and played with the baby, and told the elder children a story. The mother, who seemed a decent kind-hearted creature, spoke very respectfully to Miss Maturin and looked pityingly at her black dress.

"You are the lady from Bryn, are you not?" she asked when the story had come to an end.

Rotha nodded, and at that moment the door was briskly unlatched, and a lady in a gray cloak appeared on the threshold. Rotha turned crimson, for she knew it was Mrs. Ord.

"Good evening, Nancy; and how are the children?" she began, in a cheerful voice, and then as she came forward she caught sight of Rotha, and stood transfixed. "I have only brought the ticket for little Johnnie," she continued, quickly recovering herself. "Oh! there you are, Johnnie. No, my boy, no, I can't sit down; I am going on to the church now." And before Nancy could interpose a word she had closed the latch and was gone.

"Goodness sake's alive! and to think of her coming and going in such a moment as that," cried Nancy, looking downright vexed. "It is always Miss Belle that is in such a hurry, but never the Vicar's lady. Ah, they're pleasant folk at the Vicarage, and no mistake. Do you often go there, Miss Maturin?" She knew her name even.

"No, I have never been there," returned Rotha simply, but the instant she said it she felt she had lost ground. The woman was too civil to pursue her inquiry, but she was evidently taken aback. To have been at Kirkby three weeks and not to have called at the Vicarage was a thing that perplexed honest Nancy. Rotha saw the doubt and dim suspicion in the woman's face; she attempted to carry on the conversation, but she was evidently distrustful of her visitor. Rotha took advantage of a neighbour's entrance to put an end to the awkwardness. As she bade good-bye to the children, one little lad detained her to ask a question about the story. Rotha was just outside the door, speaking to the boy, when she unfortunately caught a sentence or two not intended for her ear.

"And what do you think, Mrs. Price, the Vicar's lady never gave so much as a 'good evening.' 'I have just brought the ticket for Johnnie,' she says, and 'Nancy, I can't sit down,' and then she shut the door quite quick and sharp, and then I put that there question. Wasn't it strange now?"

"Why, neighbour, I don't know," replied the other voice, evidently belonging to Mrs. Price. "Folks will talk: there's Master Farebrothers always hinting there's ill blood between the Vicarage and the big house. Maybe there is, and maybe there

isn't, but all that I say is that such as her can't be no good if
the Vicar's lady won't so much as move to her."

"Move to her, indeed; why——" But here Rotha heard no
more, for she dropped the boy's hand hurriedly and moved away.
This was what they were doing for her—making her the talk of
the village. Rotha did not know much about being sent to
Coventry, but it did strike her that she was to be pointed at and
set apart as though she had some plague-spot on her. She might
remain within her own walls or walk through the village; it was
all the same since Kirkby, in the person of its lawful representative,
had virtually excommunicated her.

Despite of her efforts to bear up bravely, her hopes were
waning fast. As she left the cottage a feeling akin to despair
seized her. Of what avail were her endurance and her patience
since only four walls were to be the witnesses of her daily struggles?
How was she to grapple with her enemies or live down this blot on
her good name since they refused to meet her in fair fight? She
would have preferred the stormiest encounter and the sternest of
rebukes to this cold barrier of distance and silence. They were
doing her no harm: they were only letting her alone—simply
ignoring her; but no course that they could have pursued, no
openly-betrayed displeasure, no cutting mark of contempt or
dislike, could have wounded her half so much. As she went home
in the dusk through the wet sandy roads a heart-breaking sense of
failure and utter hopelessness possessed her. Meg was singing a
Latin chant as she entered—"In Te Domini Speravi." The stars
were shining out, there was a gleam of yellow lamplight. Rotha
sat down on the wet doorstep, under a clump of white lilies, and
covered her face with her hands and cried like a child.

Meanwhile the Vicar's conscience was ill at ease; he was in
the position of a man whose practice was at variance with his
teaching, an element of discord was disturbing his daily peace,
conflicting duties harassed him; as he had once exclaimed, in his
dry way, "His soul was weary of his life because of this daughter
of Heth;" but not even in his soul-weariness could he refrain from
avowing himself a coward.

It was all very well for him to scoff at procrastination; how
often had he told his people that it was a weakness beneath a
reasonable man? "Never put off till to-morrow what ought to
be done to-day" had been his favourite maxim. "Delay only
complicates matters and doubles a difficulty." "Now" is the
wise man's axiom, and "presently" the fool's motto—all very
good words doubtless. And now he was himself deferring a plain
duty day by day, putting it away from him, striving to forget it

with the by and by of the most arrant coward. No wonder the Vicar's conscience was ill at ease, and that his cup had lost much of its sweetness. And now his words had come true, for he was doubling his own difficulty. The longer he delayed, the more he disliked the whole business. A peacemaker by nature and pro-fession, he was loath to stir up strife and ill-feeling with any man or woman, and in his secret heart he believed that such must be the issue of any visit on his part. In his large-hearted tolerance he had refused to give entire credence to his brother's suspicions. He had declined to criminate or to let others criminate without satisfying proof. He had rebuked Robert for his rancour. He had not refrained from accusing Mary of a want of charity. But all the time he was aware that Robert's words were prejudicing him against Miss Maturin. He had gone over them day after day and night after night till not a shadow of doubt remained in his own mind. Yes, the temptation was so evident. There was such facility and scope for any feminine manœuvres. Putting himself in her place, and looking from her point of view, he could even believe it hard for her to do otherwise. All people were not gifted with the same delicate perception of honour, the same stainless integrity. It was an error and weakness of youth, not the deep scheming of age. And yet youth could scheme too. She was poor and covetous, and covetousness was a deadly sin. But all the more he considered it his duty not to be hard on her. She had looked longingly on what was not her own, and had sought after it, and worked for it. Hundreds had done the same, and no one thought worse of them. But all the more he felt as though he must keep his womankind from such an one.

After all the Vicar was not free from the Ord feeling, only there was this difference in the brothers, that while Robert hugged and cherished his pride, Austin wrestled against it as a fierce enemy, and mourned over it as a heavy sin. No one knew better than he how often it had got the better of him and warped his judgment ; how many of his failures, known only to him and his God, were attributable to this hereditary failing. Conscious of his own short-comings, he could bear with the faults and follies of others. He knew why his heart was so unnaturally hardened against this girl, why he could not hold her blameless. He was resenting his family wrongs, his injuries in his brother's person, the Ord poverty so grimly mated with the Ord pride. Do what he would, he knew he had not really brought himself to forgive her. The mere men-tion of her name was abhorrent to him. How was he to go to her on his pastoral errand, to calmly sift evidence, and discriminate and judge ; to reprove temperately and gravely if needs be, as he had reproved greater sinners than she was ever likely to be? Would he not be rather tempted by his very sternness to break the bruised reed, and to repel rather than to allure her?

Our Vicar was perplexing himself sadly over these difficulties during these weeks that he held himself aloof from his new parishioner. But while he was summoning up his courage for a final effort, the Gordian knot was cut for him in a most unexpected way. Nettie Underwood, no uninterested observer of the Vicarage movements, had determined to give her parish priest a lesson.

During the first two or three weeks after Miss Maturin's arrival Nettie had kept herself tolerably quiet, only dropping out hints now and then as to whether cards had been left at Bryn, hints which had always been coolly quenched by the Vicar. But when a month had passed over, and the Vicarage party made no mention of their wealthy neighbour, Nettie's curiosity and indignation exceeded all bounds. She accused the Vicar and Mary too of want of charity. A very tolerant little person herself, she began to take up cudgels openly in Miss Maturin's defence, and announced her intention very speedily of befriending the stranger who had come into their coast.

Perhaps this was the more provoking in Nettie, as this line of conduct was dictated solely by curiosity and a sheer love of opposition. Nettie was not personally prepossessed with Miss Maturin. She had seen her at church once or twice, and had spoken of her contemptuously as a poor sickly-looking body, and had been much offended at her dowdiness. Had she been any one but the owner of Bryn, she would have held her up pitilessly to the sarcasm of her three-and-twenty bosom friends. But the mystery that enshrouded Bryn, the strange recluse lives of the two women, the silence of the Vicarage concerning them, and the whispers which daily became bolder and more exaggerated in the village, fired Nettie's giddy little head, and filled it with all sorts of impracticable schemes and fancies.

Nettie was of course aware that Robert Ord had been disinherited by his aunt. Kirkby and even Blackscar were generally cognisant of the main facts of the quarrel which had ended so disastrously for the three brothers. Already there had been many shrewd surmises in the village, that Miss Maturin would be looked upon pretty coldly by the Ords. They had but slightly guessed the truth, however. Such a suspicion as was darkening Robert Ord's mind was never likely to come to their knowledge. Nothing was more probable than that a coolness should at first ensue between Bryn and the Vicarage. And however much such a state of things was to be deplored in the parish, it was only human nature all over. People were talking the matter over pretty freely by this time. There were speculations afloat about how long the Vicar was likely to hold aloof from his new parishioner. "It was a pity for him to fight his brother's battles," they said. "Every one knew how Robert had brought the trouble on himself by his unyielding spirit. They would wait a little longer to see if the Vicar and his wife meant to do their duty; if not, it was certainly fitting that others should set them an example of Christian charity."

Robert Ord had little idea how his daily movements were being canvassed and censured. It must be confessed that, in spite of his handsome face and prepossessing manners, he was scarcely such a favourite with his contemporaries as his brothers. The lordly airs and proud bearing that might have become the owner of Bryn were sadly out of character in the managing clerk who lived in a shabby house on two hundred a year. People called him exclusive and unsocial; and Belle was scarcely more of a general favourite. Amongst his bitterest detractors was Nettie Underwood, who had taken an honest dislike to him from his having ridiculed certain of her airs and graces. Nettie, who accepted no reproofs except from the Vicar, was at no pains to hide her antagonism, and a most amusing feud was carried on between them.

When Nettie prepared to enter the lists in Miss Maturin's defence, she chose to believe the whole blame of the coolness lay at Robert Ord's door. The Vicar was influenced by his brother; neither he nor Mrs. Ord cared to anger him by taking notice of their neighbour. What if she, Nettie Underwood, should put an end to this unhappy state of things, and by a bold move contrive such a meeting for all parties as should restore matters to a better footing?

True, it was rather a risk. Nettie was not quite sure that such a course would be successful. The Vicar might not approve of such scheming, or Mrs. Ord might be annoyed. Nettie thought and thought over the matter till her small head ached, and she was in quite a fever of excitement before she could bring her tactics to perfection, and make up her mind that the game was worth playing.

Nettie Underwood was by nature a schemer; to plan and to manœuvre were the pleasantest excitements of her daily life. Every one knew what odd out-of-the-way things Nettie was always doing. She had curious systems, even in her charities. Her almsgiving was always conveyed anonymously. People never knew their benefactress till weeks afterwards, when Nettie's mysterious hints betrayed her. Aunt Eliza was her pet fiction. She caused it to be popularly supposed that she could do nothing without her aunt's permission. Applicants to Miss Underwood the younger were always referred to Miss Underwood the elder. That worthy lady was often perplexed by the constant appeals made to her in public. "I know nothing about it; you must go to my niece," she would say helplessly. Nettie's harum-scarum ways were a sore grief and worry to poor Aunt Eliza.

As in duty bound, Nettie confided to her aunt her little plan for breaking the ice between Bryn and the Vicarage. And as the more she thought about it the more feasible the whole scheme appeared, she grew quite eloquent over her subject; and though Miss Underwood shook her head very doubtfully, she was soon coaxed and talked into a state of negative quiescence. "You leave it all to me, auntie. I tell you I've arranged everything. We will have Miss Maturin and her dragon, Mrs. Carruthers, to tea, and ask the Vicarage party to meet them, Mr. Robert and all." And Nettie clapped her hands in mischievous delight at the thought of her daring scheme.

"Shall you tell the Vicar, my dear, that Miss Maturin is coming?" asked Miss Underwood anxiously.

"Gracious, aunt!" returned the girl, opening her eyes. "How can you ask such an absurd question? Why, there would be no good in asking them at all in that case. No, no; you leave it to me. I will go down to Bryn to-morrow and make a ceremonious call, and when I am quite sure of Miss Maturin I will go over to the Vicarage."

"But suppose the Vicar should be displeased at your officiousness, Nettie?" remonstrated Miss Underwood. "Remember you are only a young person, my dear. You see, we don't know the rights of the case. Mr. Ord may have some very good reason for not hurrying on an intimacy. If, as you say, the ice must be broken by a third party, wouldn't it be better for Mrs. Blake or Miss Brookes, as the leading ladies in this parish, to undertake the business? I hear Mrs. Blake is most anxious to call at Bryn."

"The Underwoods are every bit as good as the Blakes, Aunt Eliza," said Nettie, tossing her head, "though she is the widow of the colonel, and goodness knows what besides. And as for Miss Brookes and her Roman nose, and her broad hemstitched handkerchiefs with cotton lace on them, I have no patience with her and her airs; and all because she's first cousin to a baronet, who beat his wife and died from drinking. I haven't a Roman nose, thank heaven! nor had a gouty old colonel for a husband; but if I don't hold my own against two such women, my name's not Nettie Underwood. And as for your trying to dissuade me from a clear Christian duty, and one for which the Vicar will thank me—why," finished Nettie, losing breath and connectedness together—" why, I didn't think it of you."

" Well, well, my dear, don't go and put yourself out."

" But I am putting myself out, and one ought to put oneself out to do one's duty. You are like the Levite, aunt, 'who passed by on the other side.' I hope I've not read my Bible for nothing, Aunt Eliza—and such a beautiful copy of it too as you have given me! And when I see the clergyman of a parish neglecting his duty, and making his family neglect it too, and when I see an innocent girl slighted and put upon just because an ill-tempered old lady chooses to leave her her money, I think it's time for the members of that parish to testify their displeasure; and I won't sleep another night upon it. I will just go over this instant to Bryn." And Nettie rose decidedly, having reasoned herself into a belief that her scheme had not a single flaw in it.

The visitors' bell at Bryn had grown quite rusty with disuse. As its hollow clang sounded through the house Rotha and Mrs. Carruthers started. Rotha was the first to recover herself. " I suppose it is the Vicar come at last," she said, with a little colour and dignity. But her hands trembled as she shook the threads from her dress. Both were therefore disappointed when the door opened, and a little lady, with bright eyes and colour, and dressed in fresh crisp muslins entered the room.

" I see you don't know who I am," said Nettie winningly, as she held out her hand with the utmost frankness. " I am Nettie Underwood, who lives in the little corner house, next door to the sexton's, and opposite the lich-gate. Aunt Eliza would have come with me, but she is cutting out for the clothing club; and as we are neighbours, and that sort of thing, I thought I might just come over without ceremony."

Nettie had introduced herself with perfect ease, and with a fluency that rather astonished Rotha. It was something pleasant, after their long seclusion, to have this bright chatty little creature owning herself for their neighbour and making friendly overtures. Rotha a little relaxed from her gravity as she strove to answer Nettie's numerous questions; during the next half-hour she felt as though she were being put through her catechism, only the answers were far more difficult. " What is your name, N. or M. ?" Rotha found herself dreamily answering " that it was a fine day; that she liked Kirkby; that the rabbit-warren was delightful, and Bryn a most pleasant house; that no one had called upon her, and that she was not disappointed, having never expected otherwise; that the sermon on Sunday was a very good one; and that, above all

9

things, she admired the Vicar's preaching. And at this part of the conversation she turned round and began hurriedly to question Nettie as to whether there were much distress in the parish. Nettie tried to bring the conversation back to the Vicar's family, but Miss Maturin became suddenly reserved; her artful questioning was of no avail. Rotha listened, but seemed absent and preoccupied. She had resumed her work, too, most industriously. Nettie fancied that she was much interested in the few details that she dropped for her benefit concerning them, but she made no observation, and seemed rather relieved than otherwise when Nettie turned the subject by abruptly introducing the object of her visit. "Aunt Eliza and she had set their hearts on making her acquaintance. Yorkshire people were never ceremonious. And would she and Mrs. Carruthers just come over to-morrow, in a quiet homely way?—they were only plain folk," and so on.

Miss Maturin coloured and hesitated; she would have given worlds to refuse the invitation. On the whole, she was rather disposed to like Nettie Underwood: she thought her a most winning little person—she was so original and piquante, and then her good-natured frankness was so taking. She was quite prepared therefore to reciprocate her advances in a general way, but Rotha was rather shy and reserved; even taking tea with Nettie and her aunt seemed a formidable thing after the quiet life they had been leading.

"Supposing other guests—the Vicarage people, perhaps—may be there?" She hinted as much as she stammered out a civil refusal.

"Oh, of course, quite by ourselves: Aunt Eliza cannot bear parties," was Nettie's evasive answer. By and by, when she had gained her point, and had left Rotha much fluttered at the prospect of this sudden gaiety, she felt rather ashamed of her little fiction.

"I shall have to tell her it was an after-thought," said wicked Nettie to herself as she knocked at the door of the Vicarage. "'In for a penny, in for a pound.' I hope fibs are not very sinful. We are told that we mustn't do evil that good may come. One can't do everything that is in Aunt Eliza's Bible. I suppose it is a fib not to call myself Eliza Ann. I wish there were some punishment invented for every person who gave an ugly name to a child. Eliza Ann, indeed!" And then Nettie dressed her face in smiles as she walked into Mrs. Ord's presence.

Nettie did not find the second part of her business so difficult as the first. Nettie Underwood's little tea-parties were no novelty to the Vicarage folks; many pleasant evenings had been spent in the little house next door to the sexton's, and in truth Aunt Eliza was somewhat of a favourite at the Vicarage.

"Yes, they would come," Mrs. Ord answered graciously. "She could answer for Austin and Garton, and even Belle made no objection; and, if Belle came, of course Robert would accompany her; yes, to-morrow would suit them very well, as the boys were all going to a friend's to spend the evening."

Nettie did not stay long when she had got her answer: she was afraid the Vicar might come in and gainsay his wife's words. To tell the truth, she was a little nervous. She had played her cards well, the cause was a good one—she was more than ever convinced of that; she was rather inclined to look upon herself in the light of a heroine; there was a pleasant spice of novelty and excitement about the whole affair. But still the idea of the Vicar coming in just now made her a little nervous.

Her spirits rose perceptibly when she found herself in her own little drawing-room.

"Well, my dear?" inquired Aunt Eliza, rather anxiously.

"Well, aunt, they are all coming to-morrow, and so we must make the best of it. It is a pity you did not come with me to Miss Maturin's, for I am sure you would have been charmed: she is just one of your and Mrs. Blake's sort—goody-good, and that sort of thing, you know. She and the dragon—what a hideous woman that Mrs. Carruthers is! and Miss Maturin's no beauty— were cobbling a lot of old serge and flannel; there was a clothes-basketful, and they had Macaulay's *Essays* open on the table—isn't she an estimable young woman, aunt?—and they both looked as dowdy and dreary as a couple of Quakeresses. I had to talk hard to keep my spirits up all the time."

"And she's no beauty, you say?" inquired Miss Underwood, who, in spite of her beard and her loud manly voice, had a great fondness for good looks.

"A beauty? Good gracious, no, aunt! She has smooth hair and a nice figure and white hands, I believe, and people would call her ladylike; but she has the palest face I ever saw—quite sickly-looking, and any one could see she has been a companion. There's no style about her, and she was so quiet and inanimate." And here Nettie groaned, and threw herself down on the sofa with a querulous petition to Aunt Eliza to go and see after the tea.

# CHAPTER XIII.

"'Thy heart can feel, but will not move ;
Thy soul, though soft, will never shake."
LORD BYRON.

THAT night Nettie slept the sleep of the just, and woke in a bustle. Straws will show which way the wind is. Long before breakfast was over in the small corner house by the sexton's, the entire household, consisting of Aunt Eliza, two feminine domestics, and a very fat spaniel who went by the name of Lumber, were made fully aware that the young mistress was not perfectly easy in her mind, and that something rather out of the common was to happen to them this evening. Nettie—who would not have owned for worlds that she was nervous, but who felt nevertheless like some miniature Guy Fawkes, who had entered into a conspiracy to blow up somebody, which would end probably in her being blown up herself—Nettie was in a fuss and bustle from morning to night.

Rather an indolent housekeeper, and in fact ruling vicariously, Aunt Eliza being both head and hands, Nettie on this occasion floundered helplessly in buttery and china cupboard, whisking things into their wrong receptacles, and rustling in her voluminous skirts into all sorts of improbable places. She nearly drove Sarah, a stout Lancashire wench, frantic by standing over her to watch the compounding of certain sponge-cakes and fancy biscuits ordered for her guests' delectation. She got a pestle and mortar and set to work herself, rolling up her sleeves above her white elbows and enveloping herself in a floury apron. Sarah would have gladly dispensed with her help ; she beat up the eggs into a thin froth, her pounded sugar was lumpy, she could not keep her hands off a certain stewpan where peaches were simmering ; when extra heat was required she would keep opening the oven-doors in her interest to look after the spiced bread. Half an hour after that she was harassing Aunt Eliza and Catherine in the china cupboard. She broke one of her favourite violet-and-gold cups ; that calmed her for a little while, and then she went off to her flower-vases, but even these did not satisfy her. A little basket of bright-coloured leaves that she had arranged for the centre of the table turned out a failure. Fussy work is seldom successful work, as Nettie was finding to her cost.

As for Aunt Eliza, she could hardly call her soul her own. Nettie's tea-parties were always trials of patience to that much-enduring woman. Her niece's orders were so apt to be contradictory. But to-day her powers of endurance were severely tested : she had to loop and unloop the curtains a dozen times for Nettie's inspection ; her arrangement of chairs and table was declared too stiff and then too negligent ; the card-basket was first to be produced and then hidden in obscurity ; books and engravings were declared stereotype and formal, and peremptorily interdicted, and yet the drawing-room table was finally strewn with them. Aunt Eliza sat down on the sofa and fanned herself with the feather-broom and duster by turns while her niece talked and argued the matter.

Long before the proper time arrived Nettie coaxed her aunt to go up and dress. Miss Underwood, in her innocence, was for putting on a certain well-preserved black silk which she called her second best company dress, and was judged good enough for all home occasions. To her sore perplexity Nettie turned up her nose at this respectable garment, and insisted on a violet chêne, which she had lately and mysteriously presented to her aunt wrapped in a soft white lace shawl. Now, to poor Aunt Eliza's manifest discomfiture, both shawl and dress were to be worn.

"But, my dear, my best silk dress for visiting, and just because the Vicar and his wife and this young lady are coming ! Supposing I get it spotted at tea-time ? Catherine is so careless, and——"

"Now, Aunt Eliza," said positive Nettie, "what is the good of your talking as though you had only one gown in the world ? When it is shabby you shall have another—that's all. And mind you pin your collar straight, and don't rumple your cap-strings. You know you can make yourself look nice if you like." And Nettie, who in her secret heart believed that Aunt Eliza was a very handsome woman in spite of her brown front, patted her aunt coaxingly with her little fat hands, and finally turned her out of the room.

When Miss Underwood returned in her robes of majesty, with her best and glossiest front, and with a certain pleasant consciousness of a French silk which stood alone with richness, she was a little disappointed to find her niece had donned a simple everyday dress. Nettie sometimes affected simplicity and childishness.

Perhaps she knew the blue ribbons matched her eyes, and that the white dress set off those pink cheeks of hers. She was in quite a flutter of spirits by this time.

"Now, Aunt Eliza," she began, as she flitted round her relation, settling her brooch and putting in all the crooked pin-points— Aunt Eliza's pins were always crooked—"I will tell you what I have been thinking about. Mrs. Ord and Belle are sure to come first; they always do. Now, I don't want to spoil the fun by going out to receive Miss Maturin, and to send a servant after her will be so formal. So, Aunt Eliza, when you hear the bell, you must just go to the top of the stairs, and so break the ice a little."

"Wouldn't Catherine do better, my dear?" ventured Miss Underwood, who felt instinctively that she and her dress ought to be in the sofa-corner, for even Aunt Eliza could be dignified sometimes.

"Now, aunt, how can you be so silly," returned Netty crossly, "when I have just said a servant would be so formal? I thought this was going to be your evening. I'm sure I said as much to Miss Maturin. I laid a stress on your wanting to make acquaintance with her, I know; and now, when I've contrived a little pleasure for you, and you looking so beautiful, too, in your new dress," continued artful Nettie, "you are going to be disagreeable and spoil it all."

Aunt Eliza was a big woman, but she was not proof against such flattery. She gave Nettie one of her loud kisses as she sat fondling Lumber rather sulkily, and promised to do her best by their visitor.

Nettie was right in one of her surmises. Mrs. Ord and Belle did arrive first; Mary came in, looking very bright and cheerful, with her work in her hand, but Belle looked unusually ill. Both established themselves very cosily at Miss Underwood's work-table. Mary made a laughing apology about the size and quantity of her work.

"Fancy work only makes me restless," she said, in answer to a satirical observation of Nettie's. "I always think it waste of time, only fit for fine ladies or for the Nettie Underwoods of society," she finished slyly. "Belle does a little sometimes; she likes all the ornamental parts—the braiding, etc. I sometimes make believe that darning is my fancy work: I have to do such quantities of it."

"Why did you not bring your darning to-night, Mrs. Ord?" said Nettie, who was not more than half pleased at such specimens of industry in her own drawing-room. And then the Vicar came in and began to play with his wife's reels of cotton as he talked to Nettie.

"Garton will be here directly," he observed presently; "he is only waiting for Robert."

"Mr. Robert is coming, then !" exclaimed Nettie joyfully, who had been rather uncertain till this moment whether her adversary had decided to lower his weapons on this occasion.

"Oh yes ! he is coming," returned the Vicar, as he glanced with an amused smile at Belle. And Nettie, who was rather quick at such things, took it into her wise little head that there had been some words on the subject ; and she was sure of it when Robert entered a few minutes afterwards with his brother.

Robert was in one of his difficult moods ; he had been very wrathful when he had heard of Nettie's tea-party, and with Belle for accepting the invitation. He did not like Nettie Underwood, as she well knew ; he thought her a forward presuming little person ; but, when Belle was for staying at home and letting Mary go without her, he was just as displeased. Why should she be moping at home alone ? People were always accusing her of reserve and exclusiveness. He wished her to mix more with other girls, and rub off some of her shyness. Go ! Of course he would go. Wasn't it his privilege to escort her everywhere ? Poor Belle could not tell him that such unwilling gallantry was valueless in her eyes ; but she made up her mind that her evening would be spoilt, and spoilt it was.

Robert knew he had been disagreeable and contrary, and when he entered the little drawing-room he was in that stage of penitence which is rather aggressively sulky. He thought Belle must know he felt sorry ; but as there was no evidence of such sorrow in his face, Belle did not know it, and felt that he grudged her her little pleasures. She had been rather inclined to think the tea-party would be rather amusing, but if Robert were going to be stiff and silent he would spoil every one's pleasure. Poor Belle ! she need not have troubled herself, for it was not ordained that Robert should be the wet blanket of the evening. Nettie changed colour when the ominous bell was heard. She talked fast and nervously to Garton when Aunt Eliza rose to leave the room. After all, Aunt Eliza's task was the easier.

Miss Underwood was accustomed to look at everything from her niece's point of view. She remembered Nettie's disparaging words regarding their visitor, and was therefore agreeably disappointed and not a little surprised at the favourable impression made on her own mind by the young stranger.

Miss Maturin turned round with a winning smile as the elder lady advanced ; her little overtures of help were acknowledged by the young girl in a very sweet low voice. Miss Underwood stood by admiringly as Rotha smoothed the coil of dark brown hair, which showed the small head to such advantage; she thought the clinging black dress set off the tall slender figure to perfection, and could not understand Nettie's accusation of dowdiness. They were quite friendly by the time they came downstairs, Miss Underwood's voice travelling before them as usual.

"You never told us you had a visitor, Nettie," said Mary, putting down her work with an air of mild surprise. The Vicar stopped in the midst of a ludicrous anecdote that he was narrating, and shot a sharp suspicious glance at the door.

"No, I—I——" It was an after-thought, she was going to add, but she was spared the additional fib by the entrance of Miss Maturin. There had been quite a buzz of voices round Mary's little work-table, but at this unlooked-for apparition a dead silence fell on the whole party. Nettie's quick nervous voice broke upon it quite abruptly as she went through the necessary introductions.

"How dreadfully late you are, Miss Maturin! I hoped you would not have been so ceremonious—we are all friends here. Mrs. Ord, Miss Clinton, Miss Maturin, the Vicar, Mr. Robert I think you know already"—and so on. Considering all things, Nettie did it pretty well.

Rotha bowed gravely as she acknowledged each introduction, and then for a moment her dark eyes glanced reproachfully at her young hostess. "You told me that you would be quite alone, Miss Underwood?" she said in a low voice, but which was perfectly audible to every one in the room. In spite of its gentleness it testified to some displeasure.

Nettie coloured and hesitated; she was sure her little scheme was discovered now—it would never do to tell any more fibs about it. "After-thoughts and surprises are sometimes pleasant," she said rather saucily. "We Yorkshire folk are rather famed for our hospitality. We are often given to entertain angels unaware." Nettie knew that the Vicar was apt to rebuke her for irreverent quotation, and she rather hoped he would do so now—anything would be better than that stiff silence. But the Vicar was determined to hold his peace till a more fitting opportunity.

"Oh Nettie!" said Mary, much shocked; and then she too relapsed into dumbness. Rotha flushed up crimson as she glanced round the circle once or twice rather pleadingly. She was vexed and indignant for them as well as herself. She saw what a trap had been set for them all, and felt humiliated in her own eyes. She turned a little away from Nettie after that flippant answer of hers, and addressed herself to Miss Underwood.

It was no use endeavouring to secure harmonious relations at present—they must fit into their places by and by. Nettie was inclined to take the whole matter rather coolly now. Miss Maturin's dignity made her cross; every one felt awkward and annoyed, and tried to get rid of this feeling by talking as fast as possible; the circle broke up into twos—a discord of duets jarred everywhere. Garton fenced himself up in a corner with Lumber and tried to teach him tricks. Robert came over to Belle's side and talked sulkily in her ear. Rotha, dropping out of the conversation now carried on between Mrs. Carruthers and Miss Underwood, heard fragments and snatches of the whole.

"Trust!—paid for! Look at him, Bob; how well he balances my shilling! Miss Nettie, your dog is a paragon of talent. Come, Lumber, sit up again."

"I don't think the new curate will do at all, my dear: that stammer seems inveterate, and is very disagreeable; the old people complain sadly of him."

"What a pity! And he seems such a good earnest young man, Austin."

"Yes, it is lamentable how all good earnest young men with impediments in their speech think themselves especially fitted for the Church. In my opinion even the slightly-halt and maimed ought to be debarred from the service of the sanctuary; incompleteness or imperfection there ought not to be tolerated. George Greenhithe is a fine fellow, but to my mind he has mistaken his vocation."

"We can't get the mothers to work, my dear," came in Miss Underwood's deep bass; "some of them have never been taught even to put in a patch."

"You might have classes for the elder women," returned Mrs. Carruthers timidly.

"Yes, and waste all our firing and gas. Bless you! we can't get the mothers to attend. Some are laundresses or charwomen; they go out at seven in the morning, and never get home till eight in the evening. 'How am I to mend my children's clothes now?' said one only the other day; 'why, it's eight or sometimes nine before I get back, and by the time I've cleared up the place a little, and washed out a few things, and got my master's supper, I'm just clean ready to drop.' And so they are. What those poor creatures have to go through, some of them! And that's why good ready-made linen, that they can buy cheaply with a few pence, is such a help to them. We are making striped shirts for the men now."

"Oh! do let me help Miss Underwood," exclaimed Rotha eagerly. "Mrs. Carruthers and I do a great deal of that sort of work."

"Aunt Eliza, ain't we ever going to have tea?" broke in Nettie's fretful voice at this juncture; and Aunt Eliza dropped her knitting-needles in some confusion as she started up in obedience to her niece's summons.

There then ensued another awkward pause. "Will you take my aunt downstairs, Mr. Ord?" said Nettie decidedly; "and, Mr. Robert, please give your arm to Miss Maturin. The rest of us can pair ourselves." And she laughed over her shoulder as she took possession of Mrs. Ord. But Mary had not her pleasant smile ready for her.

Belle looked after her lover anxiously as she saw him cross the room on his unwelcome errand; it made him still more angry to see how simply and naturally Rotha accepted his attention—somehow she was always compelling him to admire her dignity.

But, in spite of Rotha's ease and Nettie's talkativeness, it was not a sociable meal. Full justice was not done to the dainty provisions; Aunt Eliza's excellent Souchong had lost its flavour; every one missed the Vicar's merry speeches and droll jokes: Austin was very grave—a sure sign that he was displeased; he talked parochial matters with Miss Underwood, quite ignoring his favourite Nettie. Garton sat between Belle and Mary, and kept up a low-toned conversation with them. Mary tried to include Mrs. Carruthers once or twice, but Meg was shy, and gave blunt abrupt answers. The jarring elements were not to be reconciled.

Robert talked across the table to them at intervals; now and then he addressed some stereotyped remark to his next-door neighbour: "He hoped she had enjoyed her visit to London?" "No," she answered frankly, "she had been in no mood for enjoyment, but they had made her very comfortable. She had liked Mr. Tracy's wife and daughters very much."

"Rather old-fashioned," Robert surmised, with a slight sneer.

"Oh, old-fashioned, of course. But she liked such old-world ways; it was rather refreshing after so many foolish novelties."

Robert tried to be politely interested, but the failure was evident. Rotha bent over her plate in relieved silence till the next remark was forthcoming.

"Did she like Kirkby?" Rotha gave a quick startled flush, and then an odd sort of courage came to her.

"I like Kirkby sands and sea, Mr. Ord," she answered quietly, "better than I like Kirkby welcome." And at that moment, by a strange coincidence, her eyes met the Vicar's. Somehow that look of honest reproach struck the ground from the Vicar's feet. He was glad that the sudden ringing out of the church-bell gave him an excuse for withdrawing.

"Why, you are not going to the service, Mr. Ord?" cried Nettie in genuine dismay, as she saw him rise. "It is Mr. Green-hithe's week. Besides, it is too cruel to break up our evening like this."

"I will look in again after church and fetch Mary," was the uncompromising answer; and Nettie's heart sank most unpleasantly as she marshalled her little party upstairs. Garton had his sacristan's duty to perform, and accompanied his brother. Nettie did not like to confess that she had failed, but she felt terribly cross. She left her remaining guests to do what they would, while she seated herself at the piano and ran off a valse, which jarred sadly with the bells. Nettie always played valses when she was out of temper. Aunt Eliza smoothed her silk dress nervously, and left off talking to Mrs. Carruthers when she heard the flourish of the keys. Robert hummed the tunes softly as he turned over the big scrap-book and album on the centre table. Mary and Belle were snugly at their work again. Rotha, lacing and interlacing her long fingers on her lap, suddenly took heart of grace and approached them.

"Do let me help you," she said rather hurriedly, and taking up some work of Mrs. Ord's that lay on the table. "I do so like braiding, and I am so tired of doing nothing. May I take this pinafore and try?" And she looked so pleadingly at Mrs. Ord that Mary could not refuse her. "Thank you; then I will take this to begin on. No, do not disturb yourself," as Mary made room for her on the sofa, "I shall see better by the centre lamp;" and she carried off her work and began to sew contentedly.

Robert looked across at her now and then as he turned over the big folio: the lamplight streamed full on her—on her brown hair and long eyelashes and pale face. It was an interesting face, after all, he thought, only too long and thin, but the mouth was very sweet. Those covert glances made him both moody and confused. What was there about this girl, so seemingly gentle, he thought, that turned him to gall and bitterness? Do what he would, he could not make her look conscious or ashamed; there she sat, a stranger and alien amongst them, knowing and owning herself as such, and quietly acquiescing in such knowledge. The very dignity of her meekness tried him sorely; no blame could be attached to the modest reserve in which she had chosen to entrench herself. Hypocritical or real, he felt instinctively that the impression made upon his brother's mind must be a favourable one, and his brow grew blacker at the thought. How was he to prevent himself from hating her? Aunt Eliza's voice struck in most opportunely now.

"Nettie, my dear, Mrs. Carruthers is good enough to say that she will sing to us."

Nettie's waltzing fingers broke over the keys with a final flourish and quaver. "What! Do you sing, Mrs. Carruthers? How delightful!"

"Yes, but only sacred music," answered Meg gravely; and the clear brown light came into her eyes. "Of late years I have cared for little else."

The Vicar's wife looked up with an approving smile.

"I think we all enjoy sacred music better than anything," said Mary, looking very much like her husband as she spoke. Meg's stoop and eye-glasses were forgotten now: a thrill of suppressed excitement passed through the circle as the grand deep voice filled the little room. Belle put down her work, and her eyes filled with tears, and even Robert looked moved and surprised. The Vicar, coming in, took his place at his wife's side noiselessly; only Rotha sat and worked on, seemingly unimpressed.

"Do not leave off; pray—pray give us something more," cried Nettie, delighted.

Meg received their praises as simply as they were given. She sang everything they asked her without stint or limitation. When Garton became urgent with her to repeat a favourite passage, she complied with perfect good-humour and precision. There was quite a circle round the piano presently: even Belle joined it. The Vicar drummed with his fingers delightedly as he listened; now and then he left off to watch Rotha sitting so patiently aloof.

The chiming of the church-clock interrupted them all.

"It is very late. I must go now," said Rotha, as she came up again to the little work-table. "I wish I could have finished the braiding for you, Mrs. Ord." Mary thanked her rather formally. "Good-night," continued Rotha, quite ignoring the eulogism passed on the beauty of her work. Then the Vicar rose and held out his hand.

"Good-night, Miss Maturin. To-morrow I shall do myself the honour of calling at Bryn; that is, if you are not otherwise engaged."

Rotha gave him one of her queer wistful looks, and then something seemed to rise up and choke her, and she turned away.

"Shall you be at home?" he continued, watching her keenly.

"I shall always be at home to my clergyman, I hope," was the low-toned answer. Perhaps it came to our Vicar in the light of a reproach, for he drew back instantly.

Rotha included all her other adieux in one grave comprehensive bow, and only Garton followed his brother's example and shook hands. She hardly spoke at all till she wished Nettie good-bye, and then there was no resentment in her smile and shake of the hand.

"It has been a horrid evening, I am afraid," said Nettie, with a dismal shrug of her shoulders.

"No, you must not say that. You meant it kindly, I am sure. But it was very unfortunate. You must never ask me again with them—never!" cried the girl, with a sudden pang in her voice that struck Nettie. "I don't think they wish it. It is very strange, but no one seems to care to know me." They were standing outside the door in the moonlight when Rotha said this. The sadness of the words sobered Nettie instantly.

"Yes, indeed, Miss Maturin, they do. I care to know you, and Aunt Eliza too; every one will when they have once broken the ice. In a small place like this there are always difficulties. People get into cliques and sets, and no one knows at first who belongs to which. It is so confusing."

"I fancy Meg and I will make our own clique," answered Rotha, smiling very sadly.

"Oh! that's stuff and nonsense," returned Nettie, with a droll little laugh. "Why there's Mrs. Blake dying to get you into her set, and that's the tip-top of Kirkbý society—*la crême de la crême*, you know, only it's rather heavy. I like my set the best. You should come to one of my 'tea-kettle gossips,' as I call them when I have the pick of my twenty-three friends. I don't think you would go away with such a grave face as you have to-night."

"Oh, Miss Underwood! I did my best; I did, indeed," began Rotha, pleading. "But I was so taken by surprise, and——"

"Oh, you mean about them!" returned Nettie, nodding in the direction of the drawing-room window. "Yes, yes, I understand. Of course they were very stiff and disagreeable—Mr. Robert especially. But you take my advice," she continued, linking her arm good-humouredly in Rotha's as they walked down the little footpath together. "Just let him have his ill-humour out. He's prejudiced—that's what he is. He can't bear to see any one enjoying the goods that he thinks ought to belong to himself. Bless you, I know all about it! And so he's gone and put everything in a wrong light, and made them all stiff and uncomfortable together. Of course they won't thaw all at once. It's very unfortunate, as you say," continued Nettie, with breathless candour, "all the more that I have put my foot into it. But if there's one thing I hate it is meanness, and it is dreadfully mean."

"Miss Nettie, I am waiting to say good-night," said a voice behind them, and there was the Vicar striding down the path.

Rotha released herself from Nettie's arm in some confusion.

Had he heard—was it possible that he could have heard the last speech? Nettie was wondering the same as she put out a pettish hand to him.

"What, are you going already? It is impossible to be in two places at once. You might have waited till I came back," and Nettie's voice was full of outraged dignity.

"I left a message with your aunt," he replied coolly. "Mary and Belle are upstairs still. I am hurrying home to write an important letter. Miss Maturin, you are without an escort; we are going the same way. I will walk with you to your door."

"No, indeed, Mr. Ord," returned Rotha hastily. "I have Mrs. Carruthers with me." But the Vicar was determined. Nettie bade them good-bye with some confusion and then pouted, because the Vicar only lifted his hat to her as he went out. As she stood leaning against the little gate and watched the three long shadows in the moonlight she thought of Rotha's sad words—"It is very strange, but no one cares to know me." Perhaps Mr. Ord had repented of his coldness by this time, and had taken this opportunity of making friends. He often had odd ways of doing things, Nettie thought. But for once Nettie Underwood's surmises were wrong; for all the way the Vicar only spoke to Mrs. Carruthers about church music; and when they parted at the door Rotha had not once opened her lips, except to say good-night.

"Are you very tired, dearest?" asked Mrs. Carruthers, as she lingered on the threshold of Rotha's room when they had retired for the night.

"No," said Rotha very quietly, as she gave her cheek passively to her friend. "I am so glad that you have had such a pleasant evening, and that they admired your singing so much, Meg." And then she closed the door, still smiling, and Mrs. Carruthers went away.

The smile was still on her face when she reached the dressing-table. But stretching out her hand to the glass for some purpose or other, she suddenly saw with surprise that she was quite white to her lips, and tried to sit down before the gathering faintness should overpower her. "I am glad she is gone. I am glad she did not see me like this," she said feebly, as she struggled with the languor that oppressed her. "I suppose the strain was too great, or I made myself out braver than I was."

Braver than she was? Ah, One alone knew where the frail girlish heart found all its strength and power of patience! Long after the Vicarage people were asleep, and Meg was calling on Jack's name in her dreams, Rotha was praying her nightly prayer over and over again with streaming eyes—"Lead me in a plain path, O God, because of my enemies!"

# CHAPTER XIV.

## THE VICAR GOES TO BRYN.

" Upon her face there was the tint of grief,
  The settled shadow of an inward strife,
  And an unquiet drooping of the eye,
  As if its lid were charged with unshed tears."—BYRON.

" *Duke.* What's her history?
  *Viola.* A blank, my lord."—SHAKSPEARE.

THE Vicar was in no very enviable frame of mind the following afternoon as he went up the sandy road towards Bryn. It was bad enough to be inwardly conscious of failure, and to know that his practice had not exactly tallied with his precepts. But that he should have been taught this lesson by a chit like Nettie was humiliating, to say the least of it. On his return home the previous evening he had said very little to his wife about Miss Maturin, but had expressed himself as being very wrathful with Nettie.

"I hope you will be very severe with her, Austin," Mary had remarked. "I consider that she has put an affront upon us all, and especially on Robert."

"I am beginning to doubt my ability to fight all Robert's battles," returned the Vicar, with a sigh. "But you need not be afraid of my leniency with Nettie; if I do rebuke her, it will be in no very measured terms, I assure you. But I hardly know whether it will not be wiser to leave her alone altogether."

"I think she ought to be lectured for her meddling," Mary had answered, and then the subject had dropped. After that she had tried to say a word or two that might induce Austin to speak of their next-door neighbour, but her hints were disregarded; the Vicar could not be persuaded to open his lips on the events of the evening.

As he crossed the bridge and rang at the bell he had not yet made up his mind what plan he should pursue during the coming interview; on the whole he thought it would be better to let circumstances guide him. If Mrs. Carruthers were there he would confine himself to mere commonplaces, and watch Miss Maturin closely as he talked. But if she were alone, well! he hardly knew what he should do—he almost thought perfect frankness would be the best. He little thought that Miss Maturin had taken the matter into her own hands, that she had chosen to be alone, and had sent Mrs. Carruthers into Blackscar on some pretext, that she might be free from all interruption.

The Vicar had wondered in which room he would be received. He rather thought there would be some little state in the mode of his reception. But here he was wrong. The drawing-room door indeed stood open; he could see the marble pillars, and the black-and-gold Chinese cabinet, and the long slants of sunlight through the French windows, as he passed, but he was not invited to enter. The rosy-cheeked maidservant ushered him instead into a sunny little room which he remembered to have been his aunt's breakfast-parlour, where Miss Maturin was alone.

She laid aside her work to receive him, but took it up again immediately. Some women feel less nervous when they have their needle in their hands. Rotha Maturin was one of these: she must always be turning those restless fingers of hers to account. As the Vicar sat down he could not fail to note the pleasantness of the surroundings, the little refined womanly touches which make a room so characteristic of its owner: the freshly-filled flower-vases, the few well-chosen books, the basket heaped up with useful work, a half-finished illumination beautifully designed; outside the lilies, and the lawn with its beds of creamy tea-roses and geraniums; a pair of doves cooed from some hidden recess, and a small black kitten was chasing the fantail pigeons.

"You see I have kept my promise," said the Vicar, turning to Rotha with a scrutinising smile. As he spoke he noticed the smoothness of her hair and the swift movements of her thin white hands; there was a womanly propriety about her whole person that pleased him better than mere beauty, her very gravity seemed fitting to him.

"I have expected you for a long time," she replied; "perhaps it was my ignorance, but I thought a clergyman always visited all the members of his congregation." She spoke quite simply and without any intention of reproach, but the Vicar looked slightly perturbed.

"It is rather difficult in these free churches for a clergyman to know all his parishioners," he returned hesitatingly. "I have given offence more than once from this cause. One lady left my church because I had never been near her. I found out afterwards that she had been a constant attendant for more than six months. These mistakes will occur, but I am only mentioning this casually. Of course I have been aware for some time that you are a member of my congregation."

"Yes, Mr. Ord, and I have fully understood why you have deviated from your ordinary rule with regard to me."

"Indeed, Miss Maturin."

"Of course I felt how difficult it must be for you to come here."

"Do you mean on my aunt's account?" And the Vicar looked at her very keenly as he asked this question. But Rotha raised her eyes to his without flinching.

"No, Mr. Ord; I do not mean that. I do not think that you would shrink from coming to Bryn from a sense of painful associations. Men are braver than women in everything. I think, nay I am sure, that you have avoided it from a far different reason."

She was coming to the point now; how pale she was, and her voice was beginning to tremble; but in his heart the Vicar thought she had the better courage of the two. He hardly knew what to make of such valour.

"Of course I knew why you have refrained from coming to see me," she continued, and her voice was very sad. Then the Vicar drew his chair a little closer.

"Miss Maturin, do you mind speaking out a little more plainly?" he said. "We are trenching on a painful subject, I can see. Half measures are always unsatisfactory. Would it not be better that there should be full confidence between us?"

"I think it would, Mr. Ord."

"Well, do you mind telling me in plain words why you think I have refrained from coming to Bryn?"

Then for a moment a feeling very like shame dyed her face with crimson. There was something very painful in her blush, and he could not fail to see it. For a moment it undid the favourable impression that her manner and words had hitherto made on him, and perhaps the consciousness that it would do so drove the hateful colour still more hotly to her face.

"I mean, of course, if you do not mind," he said, rather more coldly.

"Oh, Mr. Ord, how can I help minding? But still, I will tell you if you wish it. Of course it is on your brother's account that you have hitherto avoided me."

"On my brother's? Do you mean on Robert's account?"

"Yes, undoubtedly."

Then it was the Vicar's turn to hesitate.

"Well, Mr. Ord?" There was a touch of sharpness in her tone elicited by pain.

"You are right, of course," he replied in a very low voice. "But still I am far from acknowledging that I have done my duty. I ought to have come and told you the truth if needs be."

"When I first saw you I made up my mind that you would certainly do so."

"Yes, and my delay has done you harm; I can see that plainly."

"Oh, as to that, of course I am the talk of the village. How can people help suspecting things when they see even their pastor holds aloof? When you failed to come I knew then what hard things he had been saying about me, and how you had all judged and condemned me in your hearts. Is it not so?" she continued, looking at him full as keenly as he had at her.

"No, Miss Maturin, you are wrong there."

"Wrong in thinking that you have condemned me?"

"Yes; whatever the others may have done, I have refused entire credence to my brother's words till I could come and judge for myself."

"That was kind of you, Mr. Ord, and I thank you for it most heartily. I did not like to think that a clergyman could be so unjust."

"You must remember that appearances are sadly against you," he replied, a little piqued by this implied rebuke on his brother. "It is very difficult to say all that one feels to a stranger, but you must pardon me if I add that my brother is a man of strong discernment."

"And of strong prejudices too," she returned, with a faint smile. "I cannot fancy him soon parting with an idea that he has once formed. If I were not afraid of troubling you, Mr. Ord, I would ask you to listen to my defence. It would be such a relief if I might go over it once again."

"Do so, by all means," was the reply. And as the Vicar composed himself to listen, the wonderful softness of her voice and bearing filled him again with a feeling akin to admiration. If she should indeed be innocent of this grievous sin of covetousness, how nobly and well would she have borne herself under the bitterness of their accusation! He thought then that she would be a woman of no common stamp, of whom any one might be proud—worthy to bear comparison with Belle or even his own Mary; but, all the same, he felt as though he could not hold her guiltless.

So Rotha Maturin told the story of her life, and she told it well. She used few words, she made no attempt to work upon his feelings—a simple statement of facts, ungarnished, almost bare, was all she offered. When she had finished, she sat with her hands folded and her head just a little drooping, waiting for his reply. The quietness of her manner might have been taken for indifference, but the Vicar did not misunderstand it.

"Well, Mr. Ord?" she said at last, as he still sat silent, revolving her last words. Then he got up and walked about the room with his face still turned from her.

He almost wished now that she had not told him her story: it made him so full of pity for her. What an unloved hard-working youth! Was it any wonder that amid such temptations the longing for what was not hers should cleave to her? Would Robert's or his hands have been cleaner if they had been placed in the same circumstances? Good man as he was, he almost shrank from asking himself the question.

"Neither do I condemn thee." The words came to him again and again as he paced the room. Should the servant be less merciful than the Master? Was it for him to cast the first stone at this erring child because he and his were so sorely injured? The hardness of his prejudice was dying out as far as he was concerned; he could tell himself with a clear conscience that he had forgiven her. But would he be fulfilling his duty? Ought he not to refrain from his pity until she had been led to acknowledge her fault? The world might gloss it over and exonerate it, but until she had owned that she had "coveted and desired other men's goods" he ought not to throw open his hearth and home to her; until she had confessed her sin the forgiveness must be qualified.

Poor Rotha! She did not need any words to tell her of her condemnation. She sat watching the Vicar with dry hot eyes as he walked heavily to and fro. Her little story had failed then? Why was her word to be always doubted? For a moment, as she sat apart, she thought she would fling all her hated possessions away, and go out of Bryn empty-handed and with head erect; they must believe her then, she thought. But a few minutes' reflection showed her the folly of this impulse. Where was her endurance? Would it not be cowardly to fly from her troubles? Was she sure that such a reckless step would clear her in their eyes? Would it not be nobler to live it down? Ay, and she would do it, too. "God defends the innocent," she said, with an inward sob, and then the Vicar came to her side and took her hand.

"My child," he said in a low tender voice, "you do not know how earnestly I desire to be your friend." And as she lifted up her sad eyes to him in some surprise, "Yes, indeed; and no less your friend because I cannot hold you perfectly guiltless in this thing."

She tried to answer him, but she could not; her head dropped lower and lower. "Oh, my God! do not try me above what I am able to bear," came from her inmost heart, but her lips were firmly closed.

"Do not mistake us," he continued, still more earnestly, "we shall not be hard on you. My brother is prejudiced, but even he spoke most feelingly of your youth and temptation. You are not the first who has been gravely tried and has fallen."

The drooping head was raised a little.

"The shock of our disappointment is broken now," he went on. "You need not fear that we shall grudge you your possessions. All we ask you is to acknowledge that you have wronged us, by word if not by deed, and to show some sorrow for the wrong."

The head was raised higher—higher; the firm lips unclosed.

"Mr. Ord! Would you have me perjure myself?"

"My poor child! Why ask me such a question?"

"Would it not be perjuring myself if I took a lie on my lips? How can I tell you I have done this thing when I am innocent? Why will you all persist in believing what is false?"

"My dear Miss Maturin!"

"Mr. Ord," she said passionately, "we are both traversing a circle, but we shall never meet, for you are on one side and I another. Can I make you see with my eyes when my very whiteness is blackness to you? Why do you ask me to defend myself when you know—you know you will not believe my word?"

"I would believe you if you would only be candid with me in this matter."

Then she rose, drawing up her slender figure to its full height, so that he was obliged to rise also.

"Do you wish to dismiss me, Miss Maturin?"

"No, Mr. Ord; I am not quite so ungracious as that. But I owe it to my own dignity not to talk any longer on this matter."

"Do you know you are grieving me terribly?" he went on.

"I am sorry for that, Mr. Ord."

"I did so desire to be your friend, but now you are setting yourself so deliberately apart from us; how can I help you if you will not be persuaded in this thing?"

"You cannot help me," she returned hurriedly. "No one can help me who does not believe my word. Don't look so sad, Mr. Ord. I can feel how kind and good you are in spite of all this miserable misunderstanding. It will not be your doing if I am talked about and slandered by the whole village."

"I hope nothing of that kind will happen," he returned; and then Rotha briefly told him the remarks she had overheard.

"That will never do," he exclaimed, much concerned; "Mary must call on you at once. I think it would not be wise, under the circumstances, for you to come to the Vicarage—at least for the present; but no time must be lost in letting people know that Mrs. Ord has called."

Rotha hesitated for a moment, and then a great yearning for kindness and sympathy seized her.

"Yes, yes, you may send her. Do not leave me all alone here," she pleaded; and now her eyes brimmed over with tears. "You and Mrs. Ord shall say what you like to me, and I will try and bear it if you will only let me hear sometimes a kind voice from the outer world. Meg is always so sad, and it is so dreary here."

The pathetic voice, the childishness of the appeal, which came nevertheless from a woman's wrung heart, were too much for our Vicar, and he stretched out his kind hand to her.

"I will come, my child—I will come, and Mary too, never fear; and perhaps in a little while you will not be afraid to confide in us. Have you anything else to say?" he continued, for she seemed as though she were about to speak.

"Yes; I was going to ask you if you would find me some work. You don't know what it is for two women to sit here all alone and eat their hearts out. Give me something to do for those who are more wretched than I—any work—I would not refuse the meanest office—indeed I would not, Mr. Ord."

As she raised her face, flushed with its earnestness, he thought what a good face it was, and for an instant the doubt crossed him, had he—had they all been mistaken?

"You will not refuse me because of my unworthiness?" she continued, misinterpreting his silence.

"Refuse you, poor child! Who am I, after all, that I should judge of your worthiness or unworthiness? I was only considering the difficulties attendant on your proposition. Perhaps, for the present, I will not put you on our regular staff of workers; but there is an old blind woman who would be most thankful if any one would read her a chapter daily; and there is a poor girl dying of consumption, who has a drunken mother—it is a very sad case indeed. I do not know whether you would care to undertake such a painful duty?"

"Try me," was Rotha's answer. And then, with sweet

humility, "If there be any work that Mrs. Ord or you wish done, and that you think the other ladies will not like, I hope you will reserve it for me."

"Very well—then that is a bargain," he replied cheerfully, not caring to show how much he was touched. "I shall come up and see you again about these cases, and perhaps I had better take you to poor Annie myself; one can never tell what sort of reception a lady is likely to meet with from that wretched woman. I have taken you at your word, Miss Maturin; the task is no easy one, I assure you."

"I am not afraid," returned Rotha simply.

"Perhaps Mrs. Carruthers might be induced to help us with our school and clothing-club? I am afraid I am very covetous, but I must turn that magnificent voice of hers to account. I wish it were possible to make her choir-master."

"That reminds me that I have another favour to ask, Mr. Ord. You see," with a faint smile, "your kindness is making me bold. Do not, please, be angry with Miss Underwood; I am sure she meant it kindly last night."

The Vicar's face grew dark. "It was very dubious kindness then, Miss Maturin. I am greatly disposed to be very severe on the subject with Miss Nettie."

"Yes, but you will not?" she pleaded earnestly. "I know how wrong it was to you all—how very, very wrong, but I am sure she meant good to us all; miserable as I was, I could not help feeling that, and I did so hope you would forgive her."

"Well, well, we shall see about it," returned the Vicar, but his smile was a little forced, and then he bade her good-bye. It might have been the force of old habit, but he went through the glass door out on the lawn, and so to the green door in the wall. As he let himself out he glanced back, and saw Rotha standing among the lilies and watching him.

It was noticed by every one at the Vicarage that the Vicar was not himself that day: he was grave and preoccupied, and scarcely spoke to Robert when he came in to spend the evening. When the boys had gone to bed, and he and Mary were alone, he briefly related his interview with Miss Maturin, and begged her to lose no time in calling at Bryn.

"I don't think we are justified in letting a young girl be the talk of the place," he continued. "Graves will be getting hold of it, and we don't want to be slashed by his virulent tongue. I know he would do anything to spite me and Robert." Now Graves was the editor of the *Blackscar and Kirkby Herald*, a shoemaker by trade, and a Radical and Dissenter, and was much given to snarl at the heels of the so-called High Church party.

Austin's innovations, few and simple as they were, had given great offence to the Rector of Blackscar, a worthy gentleman of the old school, who clung to the black gown and the "high pulpit" as though they were the symbols of his party. A surpliced choir had recently been started at Blackscar, much to the tribulation of the elder members of his congregation, and it was a fine thing to see the Rector gallantly bringing up the procession on a choir festival in his short, well-worn, corded silk gown. The Rector had been rather averse to the surplices for some time, and had united his groans with the elder members, who thought fustian jackets and clean collars would have been more in accordance with the views of St. Paul; but the groans had been overborne by the younger portion of the congregation. A "bee" was organised by some enterprising young ladies; the surplices were duly sewn and stitched, and a large parcel deposited at the Rectory on the Saturday night. Next morning the rosy-faced country lads walked sheepishly to their places, the beheld of all beholders, looking for all the world like a flock of white geese, as one irascible old lady in the greengrocery trade suggested: "Or like the cherubim and seraphim, continually," as was remarked by one mother, whose red-headed lad was the black sheep of the whole choir from his habit of eating sour apples during the sermon.

The surplices had carried the day, but the Rector's soul was sad within him. He had always been a little high with the neighbouring clergy, especially with the Rev. Austin Ord, whose daily services had been a great offence in his eyes, but he had now become almost tyrannical; latterly he had taken up Ebenezer Graves, the editor of the *Blackscar Herald*. Ebenezer made shoes for his Reverence, and for Mrs. Price and the young ladies, and the Rector often came to his shop, ostensibly for boots, but in reality for a gossip. Mrs. Graves, who managed her husband's business, a thin bilious-looking woman with a nasal drawl, was also in high favour at the Rectory.

"A very worthy man; very worthy people, my dear," the Rector would say. "Pity they are Dissenters. Writes very good articles does Ebenezer, quite native talent. I think Blackscar ought to be proud of him: it is no use Ord snubbing him and putting him down on every occasion; the man can't help having a fluent pen, I suppose."

"Ebenezer hates Mr. Ord," put in one of the younger daughters. "I believe it is because he told him that he ought to look after his business better and make his own shoes. Fancy the author of the 'Bullfinch's Elegy' and 'The Lamb's Complaint' making shoes!"

"Yes, and he said 'The Lamb's Complaint' ought to be that it was generally too much done," put in another daughter.

"And he declared the 'Bullfinch's Elegy' reminded him of treacle and brown sugar," whereby it might be seen that Austin was apt to be a little funny at the expense of the poet shoemaker. At home he was rather more plainspoken; he called Ebenezer Graves a canting rascal, and was very indignant when Mary wanted to buy Laurie some boots there, pleading that they were cheaper than at any other shop in Blackscar. Therefore the Vicar's fear with regard to themselves and Miss Maturin was not without foundation. Letters had often appeared in the *Blackscar Herald* containing mysterious hints and surmises by an unknown correspondent very damaging to some inhabitant of Blackscar; little private family matters had even been divulged in this manner. Once or twice an injured person had been inclined to sue Ebenezer for libel, but the hints had been so obscure, and the whole couched in such mysterious language, that there was nothing of which one could take hold. "They should try a good horse-whipping," Garton had said once. "What is the use if they cannot prove the article is his?" returned the Vicar; "he would only have you up for assault and battery. There's no getting at the rascal. I remonstrated with him once in very strong language about one of my parishioners being annoyed by just such a letter. 'Why do you allow such a libellous thing to be printed in your paper?' I said to him when he had denied all knowledge of the writer. 'Why not?' was his only answer; 'it is a very good letter. People think the Correspondence Corner the most amusing in the whole paper. The man who wrote that article knew what he was about. I don't see a thing's libellous because the cap happens to fit one of your congregation. Bless you! some of these things are just make-ups, and mean nothing at all.' 'I am positive that there is meaning in this,' I replied. 'My friend feels himself much injured. You ought to induce your correspondent to retract the invidious paragraph and write an apology.' 'I don't think he'll do that,' he said, quite coolly. I declare I came out of the place in a perfect rage."

Therefore, when the Vicar mentioned Ebenezer's name on this occasion, Mary looked grave, and said at once that she would call. "I don't think you feel so badly about her now you have been to Bryn," she said, arguing rather shrewdly from her woman's judgment.

"I don't know what to think about her, Mary," returned the

Vicar, rather sadly. "I am only sure of one thing, that the whole affair is making me quite miserable. I cannot help thinking all day that we are letting ourselves be blinded by Robert's prejudice and mere circumstantial evidence. And yet, what can we do? Not Proven is not equivalent to Not Guilty. And I tell you what, Mary—faulty or not faulty, covetous or not, she is the sweetest-spoken woman I have met for a long time."

"Oh Austin!"

"Yes indeed, dear; and you must go and speak kindly to her. Whatever Robert may choose to do, it is not for us to refuse the cold water of charity. Perhaps by patience and gentleness we may win her from her reserve."

"I don't think I shall sleep all night for thinking of what I am to say to her," said Mrs. Ord ruefully.

"Come, Mary, that is not brave. Don't think about it at all; that is the best way." And with that homely counsel Mrs. Ord was fain to be content.

Procrastination was not one of Mrs. Ord's sins. She had decided to go on the morrow, and punctually at the appointed hour she set off to perform her difficult duty.

Miss Maturin had evidently expected her visit, for Mary found her alone as on the previous day.

"My husband has prepared you for my visit, I hope?" she said, when they had shaken hands and had sat down. But this time Miss Maturin had not taken up her work.

"Oh yes; he told me to expect you. I think, under the circumstances, it was very good of him to send you."

"Oh no; you must not say that."

"Oh, but it was! It was goodness itself. And it was kind of you too to come."

"Of course I should do as he wished." But Mary, when she had said this, felt as though her words had implied some reproach.

"But nevertheless it was very kind, Mrs. Ord. I don't know whether you will care to hear it from my lips, but I think I never knew any one so good as your husband."

"I was afraid you might think him hard."

"Hard? oh no! Of course it hurt me to have him saying such things of me, and refusing to believe my words, but through it all his gentleness touched me to the heart."

"Austin is always gentle," replied Mary, and her eyes looked very softly at Rotha. It was not in a wife's nature to hear such sweet praises of her husband unmoved.

"Yes; I saw that in his face. As far back as that first evening when he put open the church-door for me I longed for him to be my friend. Do you know, when he was pleading with me yesterday, I almost wished that I had done this thing—that I might confess it, I was so sure of his sympathy and forgiveness."

"Why did you not?" was on Mrs. Ord's lips, but she prudently refrained herself. She was very much startled then when Rotha answered her unspoken thought.

"You see I could not say what was not true, Mrs. Ord."

"No, of course not," returned Mary hastily, and then there was an awkward pause.

"I was so afraid that you might think us unnecessarily hard," she went on, anxious to sound this singular girl more deeply. "In your position I think I should be tempted to defend myself more boldly."

"If you were in my position," replied Rotha gently, "you would know how hard it is for a lonely stranger to do otherwise than I have done. When the first shock of it all came upon me I was at once paralysed ; then I was for giving it all up and going away, but Meg proved to me that I was wrong."

"Do you mean Mrs. Carruthers?" asked Mary, much interested.

"Yes ; she showed me how morbid and cowardly I was, and how God would take account of my stewardship ; and she told me that if I carried my cross well, it would in the end carry me ; and it is none the less a cross because it is laid upon me by a fellow-creature."

"Mrs. Carruthers must be a very good woman," returned Mary. She was inwardly wondering whether Meg believed in her friend's innocence.

"Yes, she is one of a thousand ;" and then, with a sudden impulse, she told Mrs. Ord a little of Meg's strange history. Mary listened with unfeigned sympathy : it was a safe topic, and led their thoughts into a less painful channel ; and the allotted half-hour had long ago passed before she had bethought herself of taking leave.

"Be sure you tell Mrs. Carruthers that I hope she will come to the school," she said, as she rose from her chair. "I shall be most thankful for her help."

"Not more thankful than Meg will be," returned Rotha, "she is so fond of children."

"And Austin will see you about those cases to-morrow. We are so glad to get any one who will read to poor Annie. He told me to say again that you were to send for him if you were in any special need."

"Thank you. He is very kind. Am I—am I to see you again, Mrs. Ord?" And she looked wistfully into Mary's pleasant face ; there was something so lovable and trusting in it.

Mrs. Ord hesitated.

"Never mind; of course you must ask your husband. I shall quite understand if you do not come." And there was such sweetness and sadness in her tone that Mrs. Ord's heart quite ached for her, and she bade her good-bye so kindly that the poor girl coloured with pleasure.

"Well, Mary," said the Vicar, as she came into the study and leant over him silently, "was the task a very difficult one?"

"No, not very," returned Mary absently, as her fingers strayed among his curls. "But, Austin, I do feel very unhappy."

"Unhappy, my darling!" And the Vicar put back his head that he might see her face. "Why, nothing has happened surely?"

"No, not happened; but, Austin, I do feel as though we may be wrong about this. When I sat and talked to her I almost thought that Robert could not be right."

The Vicar drew a long breath.

"There was something so thoroughly true about her face; she does not look as though she knew how to deceive; and it would be deceit if she kept telling us that she never wanted the money. Oh, Austin! suppose we are wronging her all this while?"

"I am afraid the same doubt has occurred to me," he said in a grave voice. "Once or twice yesterday I had some unpleasant twinges. It is certainly very dreadful to think that we may have been accusing an innocent girl wrongly, but appearances were so much against her; and then I never knew Robert to suspect a person unjustly before."

"It will be a comfort to think the blame will be his and not ours," returned Mary.

"Why, that would be a poor comfort, and of which I should decline to avail myself. No, no, my dear! We must not shelter our mistakes under other people's. 'Every one for himself,' in a wider sense, 'and God for us all.' I don't know how it is, Mary, that you have infected me with your fears—I suppose by giving colour and expression to my own thoughts; but I feel as though this were a thing rather to pray over than talk about." And such an anxious line came across the Vicar's forehead that Mary stooped and kissed it away.

"Dear Austin! she was so full of your goodness to her."

"Was she, Mary?" Then, in a half-whisper full of feeling, "Dear Lord! Should I not be good to one of the stray lambs Thou carriest in Thy bosom?" Then, in his natural voice, "Look there, Mary," and he pointed to a little picture of the Good Shepherd that hung over his writing-table. "Look how that foolish lamb has got entangled in that thicket, and how sorely the briers and thorns must be wounding him ; and now look how the Shepherd helps him.　He has gone down upon his knees, and with his own hands is putting aside one cruel bramble after another, calling to him fondly all the time.　One sees the foolish little face raised to bleat its answer.　By and by he will carry it on his shoulders rejoicing.　That is just how He deals with all His erring ones."

"Well ?" whispered Mary—she was kneeling by him now.

"People think I am not bitter enough in my invectives against sin, because I am so ready to put aside the briers.　But these men are more like hirelings.　It has come into our hearts to distrust this poor child ; nay, more, to be angry with her.　We accuse her of coveting our money and diverting it into a .wrong channel—is it not so ?"

"Yes, Austin."

"And we have been very bitter about it, and said all manner of harsh things, all the while knowing that we ought to be heaping coals of fire on her head.　I am far from saying still that I hold her guiltless, but, all the same, last night and to-day I have felt very sad."

"It is not our fault," whispered Mary.

"No, dear, it has not been our fault in the first instance ; but I ought to have gone to her before.　People are beginning to say things to her injury, and it may be very bad for her and for us too."

"But, Austin, what are we to do ?"

"Well, Mary, we must wait and pray ; that is all we can do for the present.　I forgive her from my heart, but for Robert's sake I cannot have her at the Vicarage.　Why, he and Belle would be up in arms !　You can go and see her now and then, just to stop people's tongues ; and be sure you let Mrs. Blake know you have been to Bryn.　They will get to understand in time that we have no wish to be intimate."

"And if she be not really what we think her ?" asked Mary, returning to the principal subject of her thoughts.

"Well, God defends the innocent—we are too liable to forget that—and in His good time He will enable her to prove it to us. Any way, my course is clear.　I must get an influence over her and induce her to repose confidence in me.　I am putting her to a severe test now by the work I have given her.　The way in which she performs that will be a great argument in her favour.　In old times, Mary, an accused person had to walk blindfold over nine ploughshares of burning iron."

"I think she walked over one last night," replied Mary, rather soberly.　And then, as the Vicar looked meaningly at his watch, she gathered up her things and went away.

# CHAPTER XV.

## THE BLACKSCAR HERALD.

" Now, hear me ; there be troubles in this world
That no man can escape, and there is one
That lieth hard and heavy on my soul,
Concerning that which is to come :
                    I say
As a man that knows what earthly troubles mean
I will not bear this one—I cannot bear
This one : I cannot bear the weight of you.

.        .        .        .        .

                    " My heart is sore for her
How long, How long ?"

                              JEAN INGELOW.

FOR six long weeks Rotha Maturin had enjoyed a seclusion as deep and almost as monotonous as Mariana in her moated grange ; and as the days had lengthened into weeks, a sort of patient heart-sickness, which amounted well-nigh to hopelessness, had crept over her, making her weary of her life.

But all at once the whole aspect of things had changed ; from the moment Nettie Underwood had wrought out her daring scheme, and brought Rotha and her detractors face to face, a faint suspicion of brighter days began to dawn slowly over Bryn.

There were signs of life about the place now ; the rusty bell began to have its proper share of work, and the servants ceased to start at its wiry clanging ; other footsteps besides Rotha's and Meg's crunched on the trim garden-paths between the lilies. Rotha's days were no longer purposeless, nor her task self-imposed ; as she went to and fro on her errands of mercy, her slow movements became brisk ; Meg would come upon her in the village, walking fast with her head erect, and her brown hair rippled with the sea-breezes ; sometimes there would be a soft colour in her face —she would nod and smile quite brightly as Meg looked across at her from the schoolhouse. One day Garton Ord had met her before the smile had quite died out, and had walked with her the whole length of the village street, and right before the Vicarage window, where Belle was sitting at her work.  He touched his hat rather mischievously as he passed ; Belle took no notice of it then or afterwards—Garton was always doing odd things. Since their evening at Miss Underwood's he had always a pleasant word for Rotha when they met, but he had never gone so far as to retrace his steps and walk with her.   Rotha tried gently to shake him off, but it was no use ; she looked up at him shyly once or twice as he went striding down the road beside her in his shabby coat, with his flapping wideawake, and his great brown hands gesticulating fiercely.

"How often has my brother been to Bryn ?  I think this feud is all nonsense ; " he went on, "Let bygones be bygones ; it struck me the other night that we were all riding full tilt against windmills —and in the dark too."

"The Vicar has been to see me twice ; he came the last time about poor Annie, and to fetch Mrs. Carruthers to the school. How long have you arrived at this conviction, Mr. Ord—about the windmills, I mean ?  I thought you were all going to break my heart between you."

Garton looked round at her with a kind smile as she said this—he was a tender-hearted fellow ; lately he had had a feeling that it was just possible that Robert had been wrong—he had seen little things now and then which had brought this feeling home to him ; he had watched her pretty narrowly that evening while he was teaching Lumber tricks in the corner, and her quiet dignity and patience had made a great impression on him.   From his seat in the choir-stall he could see her plainly, evening after evening, sitting behind her pillar ; often when the little congregation had broken up he had left her still kneeling, with her face hidden in her hands.   Garton would not tell how or when his conviction had become certainty—in the home-circle he never uttered her name ; but now, as Rotha spoke, he faced round upon her impetuously.

"Never mind about the windmills.   I suppose we shall always look in the glass darkly as long as we are here ; things must clear themselves up by degrees.   I think we have all treated you very badly, Miss Maturin, and I, for one, am heartily sorry for it ; but there, you needn't go and tell my brother that I said so."

"I am not likely to have the opportunity, thank you, Mr. Ord.   I suppose you do not know how much good you have done me, so you must forgive me being silly over it ; " and Rotha dried her eyes and smiled at him gratefully—she was flushing happily, her cheeks had a pretty pink colour in them—her hair was blowing

softly over her temples. At the gate she stopped and gave him·
her gloved hand.

" I suppose you will be at church as usual this evening ? " he
asked absently. He was wondering why Belle and Nettie had
called her so plain. Rotha took her hand away, with a little
laugh.

" Oh yes, we always go ; I am getting quite used to my
corner. There is Mrs. Carruthers waiting for me. Good-bye, Mr.
Ord," and then she left him still standing there. Meg thought
she saw tears in her eyes as Rotha ran past her indoors. All that
afternoon she could hear her moving about her room and humming
to herself in sweet little·snatches.

" Was that Mr. Garton Ord who was standing with you at
the gate ? " Meg had asked her as they sat at dinner. Rotha
looked up with a little fun and defiance in her eye.

" Yes, it was he. We walked from the school and right over
the bridge, and he has made me so happy, for he doesn't—he
doesn't believe all that odious slander. Oh, Meg, he was so kind
about it ! "

" Kind about it, was he ? " answered Meg. " Well, I thought
I knew that ugly felt hat of his ; he is the most singular young
man I ever met. I am glad one of the Ords has come to his
proper senses at last, but I wish it was the Vicar ; " and Rotha
echoed the wish with a sigh.

Bryn had no lack of callers now. Nettie Underwood and
Aunt Eliza were constant visitors, and the day after Mrs. Ord's
visit Mrs. Blake had called, and had been very kind and concilia-
tory. Nettie, who came in afterwards and found Rotha rather
dispirited by the interview, was of the opinion that all would have
gone well if only Miss Brookes had not chosen the same day for a
visit of ceremony to Bryn.

Every one at all conversant with Kirkby society knew of
course that Mrs. Blake and Miss Brookes were the leading ladies of
the place—*la crème de la crème*, as Nettie phrased it. Not to
know Mrs. Blake or Miss Brookes—and voluntarily to acknowledge
the fact—was to be lowered for once and for ever in the eyes of
the feminine portion of the Kirkby community. In all things
relating to fashion and etiquette their opinion was simply infallible.
Any stranger coming to settle in the neighbourhood found it
utterly impossible to steer through the shoals and quicksands
which engirt all such small societies without abandoning him or
herself to the able pilotage of one or the other lady. Nettie, in
spite of her envious sneers, never ventured to condemn a bonnet
that Mrs. Blake had approved. The one dressmaker at Kirkby

·was almost abject when Miss Brookes found fault with a trimming, and threatened to withdraw her custom—and yet Miss Brookes was long in paying her bill, and always omitted the odd shillings and pence.    But then if you want cream you must pay for it, as Nettie often remarked.

As is not uncommon in such cases, these ladies were very dear friends, and—to borrow another of Nettie's expressions—they generally hunted in couples.    The great difference between them was, that whereas Mrs. Blake's cream was very good cream indeed —in respect of its richness and sweetness—Miss Brookes' was slightly iced, and was touched with a slight flavour of frigidity, which rather congealed an unwary stranger.

Mrs. Blake was a little fair-haired woman, with quiet retiring manners and a soft caressing voice.    In spite of her furs and velvets, her handsome house and big footman, there was nothing very formidable about her.    She did not inspire one with a tithe of the awe which Miss Brookes always created in the mind of a stranger.    Whether it was her Roman nose or the Indian shawls which she always wore in such massive drapery—not unlike a Roman toga—the unbending lines of her tall stiff figure, or the resolute loudness of her voice, she certainly was a most imposing woman.    Nettie, who always suffered a martyrdom in her pre- sence, was of opinion that many people would have been com- municative, and as a matter of course more sociable, if " my cousin Sir Peregrine and my brother-in-law the bishop had not been dragged in at every available pause ; " but then every one knows that this was only wicked envy on Nettie's part.

Rotha would have got on very well indeed with Mrs. Blake if Miss Brookes had not been announced a minute afterwards ; as it was, she was painfully fluttered and confused.    Nettie had not come in as she expected, and Mrs. Carruthers was unfortunately out.    She had given a very warm welcome to her first visitor, whom she knew perfectly well by sight, and had already been addressed once or twice as " my dear " in return ; but at the first sight of the Indian shawl and Roman nose her shyness returned on her tenfold.

Antagonistic feelings are generally reciprocated.    Rotha knew that curiosity and not neighbourly kindness had brought Miss Brookes to Bryn.

Mrs. Blake was hoping that Rotha liked her new home—it must have been rather trying for her under the circumstances— and so on, in a gentle reassuring voice.    Rotha thanked her. Yes ; she liked it better than she ever thought she would.

" Ah, but you must be quite settled in it by this time," interposed Miss Brookes. "You forget, my dear Mrs. Blake, that Miss Maturin is far from being a new comer. You have been here two months, have you not, Miss Maturin?"

"Oh no; not quite so long as that," returned Rotha quietly.

"Oh, I thought it was longer. I was asking Mrs. Ord yesterday whether you had returned her visit. I am sure I forgot what she said in answer."

"Mrs. Ord only called on me yesterday," replied Rotha, trying to bear Miss Brookes' hard glance with composure.

"You know she told us that, Delia," observed Mrs. Blake reproachfully.

"To be sure, to be sure," responded Miss Brookes in her loudest voice; "and that is why we are here to-day, Miss Maturin. It would never have done to have anticipated the Vicar's lady, you know; in a place like this one is bound to be particular. I cannot say that the Ords have shown very good taste in their mode of proceeding. It is what my cousin Sir Peregrine would have called bad style altogether; but, all the same, Miss Maturin, we must stand by one's vicar."

"Of course!" murmured poor Rotha. Miss Brookes' steel-coloured eyes had never once been removed from her face yet.

"No one thinks that the Ords have done the right thing," murmured the lady decidedly; "but, there, they have been severely tried, poor things—that ill-tempered brother of theirs especially. The heart knows its own bitterness, Miss Maturin."

Rotha was thinking just then that her inward bitterness at that time was very great.

"Of course you feel sore yourself," she went on in a would-be sympathising voice. "Any one would in your place; but you're young, and don't know the world just yet. Mrs. Blake and I were talking about it last night over our piquet, and we are quite of opinion that the best thing for all parties would be to take no notice of past coolness, but just return the call as early as possible."

"Return the call!" exclaimed Rotha, utterly bewildered; and then a moment afterwards she turned as red as fire.

"Yes, the call at the Vicarage, my dear. Mrs. Blake and I think it cannot be made too soon. It is still quite early. Why should you not accompany us now? I have a business errand this afternoon with the Vicar."

"Oh no! Indeed I cannot. I—I am engaged. Miss Underwood is coming to me——" and here Rotha broke down utterly.

"I don't think Miss Underwood ought to stand in your way,"

11

returned Miss Brookes coldly. "She would be the first, I am sure—in spite of her frivolity—to estimate the importance of losing no time. This coolness is influencing the parish."

"My dear Delia, that will do," interposed Mrs. Blake's soft voice, "you are quite overwhelming Miss Maturin. You forget she is a comparative stranger, and perhaps cannot understand her own position. Miss Brookes means well, my dear; we want to help you over this awkwardness, if you will allow us."

"You are very kind," responded Rotha gratefully. Mrs. Blake looked pleased. Rotha's shrinking and modest manners rather prepossessed her in her favour.

"I hope you will accept our kindness, then," she continued, with a pleasant smile; "we have wasted much time already over these troublesome quibbles of etiquette. I do not mean to be formal any longer; two or three friends are coming to me to-morrow evening, Miss Maturin, and I shall be most happy to introduce you to them, if you will allow me. I will send the carriage round for you at seven o'clock."

"Oh, pray, do not—I mean—that is—I do thank you extremely, but I must not accept your kind invitation."

"Not accept Mrs. Blake's invitation? You cannot be serious, Miss Maturin."

"No, no; I cannot," returned Rotha, turning her shoulder on her tormentor, and addressing the elder lady. "I know how good it is of you to ask me, and how kindly you mean it; but it is impossible. I cannot explain myself, but indeed it is impossible for me to go into society just now."

"Go into society, my dear Miss Maturin! What a singular expression! There is no cause for such romantic seclusion, is there?" and Miss Brookes regarded the black dress critically through her eye-glass.

"I know I am expressing myself very badly," returned Rotha, with a little dignity; "but you cannot tell what it costs me to refuse Mrs. Blake's kindness."

"Then I hope you will think better of it, my dear," replied Mrs. Blake, but her tone was not quite so cordial. "Nettie told us that you were at her tea-party the other night, and I have only the Vicar and his wife and two other ladies coming. I trust you will not think us obtrusive," she continued, hesitating slightly, "when I say that I think it would be better rather to conciliate than to shun those with whom we have a coolness, but whom notwithstanding society compels us to recognise."

It was a very long speech for the gentle little widow, and directly she had finished it she rose with an apologetic air.

"We must not press the point, Delia," she said quietly, as Miss Brookes seemed about to annotate her remark. "I am sure that Miss Maturin understands that we have only spoken for her good ; we must leave her to think over it now. May I send the carriage for you to-morrow, my dear ?" She finished with a little lady-like obstinacy which showed that even soft-spoken Mrs. Blake liked her own way.

"No, thank you, dear Mrs. Blake," returned Rotha firmly. "I know it seems ungracious of me to reject your kindness ; but I have made up my mind to refuse all invitations for the present, and if you knew everything I am sure you would say I am right ;" and after that there was nothing more to say.

"Now you have gone and done it," was Nettie's first words, when Rotha, with much soreness of spirit, had made her acquainted with the result of the interview ; "and if you were Simeon Stylites himself, or what's his name on the top of the pillar, you couldn't be more shut out from Kirkby society, my dear Rotha."

It was "my dear Rotha" now, for the two girls now called each other by their Christian names. "No, you will find I am right, and you will have to do without cream for the rest of your life." But whether Nettie was right or wrong Rotha led a very active life now ; the Vicar found her plenty of work, and expressed himself as well pleased with the mode in which she discharged it. Ruskin and Carlyle were quite discarded, and Butler's *Analogy* accumulated dust on its covers. Rotha was always out now ; in the evenings, as Meg and she worked, they had all sorts of pleasing or unpleasing experiences to narrate, anecdotes of Meg's scholars, or the last bit of gossip at the clothing club ; painful incidents connected with the wretched home where Rotha's *protégée*, poor Annie, lay dying ; long histories of the several patients in the Convalescent Hospital, where she was now a constant visitor. Very often Nettie and Aunt Eliza dropped in with their work also, and then there was plenty of talk. Nettie would chatter volubly till Aunt Eliza would point to the clock warningly ; sometimes Meg would play and sing to them, or they would read the last new novel aloud. Rotha would forget all about her troubles then, and laugh her low musical laugh, to Nettie's great delight. She could hardly believe sometimes that it was the same grave sad-looking girl of whom she had spoken so slightingly.

Rotha's work suited her admirably—she had a way of meeting difficulties which hardly belonged to her age ; she was wise as well as patient, and made light of the many disagreeable incidents to which district visitors are continually liable, added to which she had an innate dignity which effectually protected her from anything like impertinence. Poor Annie almost worshipped her; the dim eyes of the dying girl learned to brighten at her approach. From the first day Rotha surrounded her with all sorts of tender ministries; her little offices were all the more touching, that they were performed so simply and unconsciously; the reading and talk almost always came last. Rotha knew how the besotted creature she called mother neglected her; she never forgot the squalid sight when she first entered the stifling garret. Now, day after day, little comforts and luxuries found their way to the invalid. The Vicar, when he called and found them together, was not slow to appreciate the change; all traces of dirt and squalor had disappeared: there was clean linen on the pallet-bed, fresh flowers and fruit on the little table, one or two simple pictures on the sloping whitewashed walls.

The improvement was still more apparent in poor Annie herself; the pale shrunken face looked as though it had been freshened with pure water, the rough unkempt hair was combed back and confined with a ribbon, and the black fevered lips had cool drinks ready for their relief. Not till the little room was all swept and garnished would Rotha give her the sweet holy lessons that were to make her nights less wearisome. When Rotha looked up from her Bible that day at the Vicar's entrance she saw a look on his face that set her heart beating with happiness. "Well, Annie," he said, taking the thin work-roughened hand in his, "it is a hard troublesome business climbing the dark mountains, is it not? But you see God gives you flecks of sunshine by the way; the fruit and flowers must be like texts to you in the night." And his eyes dwelt musingly on a crimson rose and one single white lily reposing side by side in the cracked earthenware jar.

Annie wiped the tears from her eyes. "Oh, sir, if you would only tell me how to thank Miss Maturin—the things she has done for me!—I never knew a lady like her."

"Hush, Annie, you know I like to do them."

"You must give her a text in return sometimes, Annie. I will leave one with you for to-day—'Inasmuch as ye did it unto the least of these ye did unto me;'" and as he said this there had been that look on his face, its warmth lasted Rotha all day. Rotha's other charge, old Sally, was quite a character in her way; the hours that Rotha spent in her cottage were always productive of mutual pleasure. There was a quaintness and originality about the old woman that Rotha heartily enjoyed.

Sally was a Londoner by birth, and was very proud of having been born within the sound of Bow bells. She had lived all her life in a northern manufacturing town, and yet she still mentioned

Whitechapel and Shadwell with regret. In conversation she always spoke of "them Northerners" with a bitterness of accent, as though fate had compelled her to pitch her tent among a horde of savages. Rotha first won her heart by buying her a woollen shawl that had been knitted in Chatham Place.

"It is so fine and fleecy, you see," she said, fumbling over the web with her wrinkled fingers. "Ah, London is the place for people to get their money's worth. Them Northerners make everything by steam, and charge according."

She was rather fantastic too in the matter of her blindness. It was nine-and-twenty years, she would assure Rotha, since she last saw the light of day last Michaelmas, and no offence to the Almighty, who sends cataracts and hailstones and all the plagues of Egypt for His own wise purposes, and saw fit to make her a stiff-necked and useless hulk all her days ; and thereupon she would shake her head and lament her infirmity with a gentle obstinacy of sorrow which no amount of spoken or written consolation could soothe.

"Why, Sally, how old are you ?" asked Rotha one day, when the old woman's lamentations had interrupted the course of their reading.

"Well, if I live till Easter, ma'am, which the Lord forbid, I shall be eighty-three."

"Eighty-three ! Then you are past the fourscore years of the Psalmist, Sally. Well, it is only to be patient a little longer—a very, very little bit longer it may be."

"Yes, I suppose I'll have to be dark till kingdom come," returned Sally disconsolately. "It is a long tunnel to be in nine-and-twenty years ; but it is not that that worries me ; lately it has been coming in my head that it ain't the pleasantest sort of thing to have to grope one's way into heaven—it will be kind of hard, Miss Maturin, to be standing out so long in the cold, feeling about for the door, when others are going in as spry and smart as possible."

"But, Sally, my dear woman, you are making a mistake—there will be no blindness there."

"No, not when you are once inside ; but, law bless you, I've thought it all over, and what a mighty dazzle it will be, to be sure."

"'Thine eyes shall see the King in his beauty,'" murmured Rotha, wishful to turn the old woman's whimsical thoughts to account.

Sally caught her breath for a moment. "Ay, that's grand, that is. Do you mind, Miss Maturin, reading to me one day about the New Jerusalem a'coming down, and all about the palms and the gates of pearls ?"

"Oh yes, I remember it very well, Sally, and we had a long talk about it afterwards."

"Well, I've been thinking it over. I do a power of thinking sometimes of a night, when my old bones won't let me sleep for aching, and I've thought about it till I've been pretty nigh crazed, I can tell you; and it does seem to me that I'd rather see a green field, with the wind blowing over it, and the buttercups and daisies all in a smirks of nods, than I'd see them shining streets of gold; it seems all a dazzle together—there now."

Sally's "there now" sounded argumentative, but Rotha was just then trying to control her risible muscles, and was in no mood to continue the subject; but, as she closed the book and put back her chair, she quietly remarked that our earthly and obscure light would there be purified and strengthened. "We shall be as the angels, you see, Sally."

"Ah! and the angels don't want shades, you mean. I don't care so as the scales will drop somehow from my eyes; but twenty-nine years is a long pilgrimage in the dark, and all the wrong turnings taken too. Well, if you must be going, thank you kindly," and Sally got up and dropped her best curtsey as Rotha went out of the door.

So Rotha was beginning to find that though cream was with-held from her, she had still a keen relish for such skimmed milk as came in her way; she had returned Mrs. Blake's call, and had found Nettie's words correct. Miss Brookes had been there as usual and had been simply terrible, and, in spite of Mrs. Blake's sweetness, Rotha was made to feel that she had put herself out of the pale of all Christian fellowship by refusing her friend's mediation.

"We had such a pleasant evening," Miss Brookes observed casually, "and the Vicar was most agreeable—he expressed himself as deeply regretting the cause that kept you away."

"And what cause did you assign, Miss Brookes ?" asked Rotha, somewhat proudly.

"Of course, my dear, I told him the truth; he certainly had the candour to acknowledge that he had been very slow in making the first advances; but he agreed with me that it was a great pity that such advances were not more warmly received."

"My dear Delia, I never understood Mr. Ord to say as much as that."

"No, not in exact words, my dear Mrs. Blake, but he most certainly implied it. I asked him if it were not a great pity that Miss Maturin were not there, and he distinctly assented."

"You must have misunderstood him," returned Rotha, very quietly. She was not a bit afraid of Miss Brookes to-day—she went on with the subject she had been discussing with Mrs. Blake with the utmost composure. When Miss Brookes contradicted and found fault with her, she held to her opinions with smiling tenacity; her leave-taking might have been a piece of consummate acting; she managed so admirably during the whole visit, and it was a somewhat prolonged one, that she had not given either lady an opportunity to patronise her.

But, in truth, she was beginning to show herself competent to fight her own battles; and, indeed, her courage was very great; and there is no knowing how soon she would have gained an advantage by her own prowess but for an untoward incident that shortly afterwards occurred.

It happened in this wise.

The Vicar was sitting in his wife's room one evening before tea —it had been his habit lately—little family matters had been harassing both wife and husband during the last few weeks, and the Vicar would come into the mother's room for a leisure half-hour or so and discuss them freely, without fear of comment from the boys or Belle; and, indeed, Belle had grown so sadly unsociable of late that it was almost a relief to be without her constant presence.

The Vicar was both tired and harassed this evening, and Mary had in consequence given him up her own chair, and was making his fatigue a pretext for all sort of soft manipulations and womanly fuss, though in reality she was the more tired of the two. These half-hours were very precious to her, and she looked rather disappointed therefore when she saw Robert come up the gravel-path and enter the open window.

"Here is Robert; how early he is. I suppose he has come to tea," she said, with a spice of regret in her voice; for Robert's visits lately had been rather depressing than otherwise.

Robert did not look as though he had heard her remark; he gave her a brief nod by way of good evening as he entered, and then unfolding a newspaper that he had in his hand, placed it before his brother without a word, and then walked slowly away to the window.

The Vicar looked rather surprised, but took up the article without remark; but Mary, who was struck dumb by the mystery of the proceeding, was quietly reading it over her husband's shoulder. Robert looked round at them once, and then began to whistle.

"What does it mean?" she exclaimed. "Oh, Austin, what a

dreadful shame !"    The Vicar lifted his hand with an injunction
to silence ; he was reading it over slowly and ponderously, almost
spelling the words, as Mary thought in her impatience.    Robert
had resumed his whistling before he put it away from him, with a
look of grief that went to his wife's heart.

"Well, Austin, what do you think of Ebenezer now ?"    The
Vicar stretched out his strong right arm with a sufficiently eloquent
gesture.

Robert nodded with grim approval.    "Horse-whipping, eh ?
Well, he deserves it richly, the rascal !    How dare he use his
scurrilous pen at our expense, and just now too, when we cannot
give him the lie !"    The Vicar shook his head sadly.

"I always feared this ; I was always afraid of it," he said in
a deeply-pained voice.    "Poor unhappy girl, she has fallen into
the hands of Philistines indeed."    And he began to pace the room
with the utmost agitation.    Robert, as he watched him, grew a
little mystified.

It was a copy of the *Blackscar Herald* that he had put before
his brother, and it was dated two days ago ; the offending article
had met his eye in looking over the correspondence corner, where
choice little bits of fashionable scandal were often served up hot,
and peppered to suit certain palates among the weaker sex.

The Vicar recognised the slander and venom of Ebenezer
Graves' pen in a moment, in spite of the sobriquet he had chosen
to assume.

"That truth is stranger than fiction," it began, "is a somewhat worn-out and hackneyed phrase ; but all the more we are
tempted to make use of it in discussing certain curious circumstances
which have recently come to our knowledge, and which, in point
of interest, certainly reduce the Hon. Miss Blank's affair, which
we have lately been noticing, to a very second-rate place indeed ;
all the more that these circumstances are connected intimately
with certain well-known and highly-respected residents of our little
watering-place.

"The facts—for that they are facts we have ample means of
proving—are these, and we may suggest in passing that they
would form capital material for any three-volume sensational
novel : A certain clergyman intimately connected with the so-
called High Church movement, but which, by the bye, we would
gladly stigmatise by another name, has made himself somewhat
singular by holding aloof from an influential parishioner who has
recently come as a stranger into our neighbourhood.    Now, without
stirring up any vexed question about the house-to-house visitation,
of which this reverend gentleman is a somewhat loud advocate, it

does seem rather worthy of note that a person of such wealth and influence should be suffered to take up her residence in a strange parish ; to be utterly ignored—we might almost say insulted—by the Vicar of that parish ; but the cause has recently leaked out. There is a sad secret at the bottom.

" The new comer is looked upon not only as an interloper, but as a usurper ; Blackscar and Kirkby are not unacquainted with the facts of a certain unhappy family quarrel, in which an eccentric lady disinherited all her rightful heirs in favour of a young dependent.

" It has been whispered lately—indeed we have heard it from more than one source—that things have not been quite shipshape and above-board, and that the family of the aforesaid reverend gentleman have very good cause for holding themselves aloof. Old ladies in their rightful senses do not endow penniless dependents with all their property. The family complain, and very justly, that they were not permitted to hold any communication with the deceased lady, that their letters were returned unopened, and that they were kept too long in ignorance of her final illness. The facts speak for themselves, and we are compelled in justice to avow that the family have shown great magnanimity in keeping so long silent on the subject. We can only, in conclusion, hope that report as usual has slightly exaggerated the matter ; and that, at all events, the breach which threatens a scandal in the parish will be healed by some compromise—coals of fire not being fashionable in the nineteenth century."

" The fellow ought to have his impertinence rammed down his throat," began Robert, when his brother had taken two or three turns across the room without speaking : then the Vicar had again stretched out that sinewy right hand of his.

" Oh, Austin, what will she do ?" exclaimed Mary, with the tears in her eyes—the whole thing seemed so terrible ; then the Vicar faced solemnly round on her.

" What did I always tell you, Mary ? Didn't I say that fellow Graves would be up to mischief ? Granted he is a foul tongued villain, whom have we to blame but ourselves ?"

" Ourselves, Austin ?"

" Yes, ourselves. Have we not put it into that man's power to injure her ? have we not caused her to be talked about ? What can be more injurious than for a young woman's actions to be canvassed as hers have been canvassed ? Of course people will believe the worst of her. I am almost ashamed to think now what a paltry part we have been acting."

Robert frowned.

"I confess I do not understand you."

"Perhaps not. That is because you will not be convinced. In your heart you are just as bitter as ever against Miss Maturin. You have chosen to lay this sin to her charge, and you would have her expiate it to the last dregs. But I tell you plainly, once for all, that such is not my opinion."

"Do you mean that you have acquitted her?" asked his brother, with a sneer.

The Vicar hesitated.

"Acquitted her? Well, no; perhaps I can hardly say that. Sometimes I have been tempted lately to believe her innocent; and then again the whole thing sounds so plausible when I am away from her. I cannot think how the doubt has arisen. It is a miserable affair altogether."

"Do you think we shall make it any better by talking about it?"

"Humph, that depends how we discuss it. Look here, Robert, I have told you that I differ with you in opinion, and yet that I am not quite prepared to hold Miss Maturin innocent; but, all the same, I have made up my mind what I shall do."

"And what is that, if I dare ask?"

"I shall have her here."

"Here! in this house? Have you lost your senses, Austin?"

"No, Robert, I am in sober earnest;" and the Vicar made himself very big as he stood on the rug. "The fact is I am sick of these half-measures. We must do one thing or the other. I have said over and over again that I decline to criminate this poor girl on mere circumstantial evidence, and yet all the while I am allowing myself to treat her as though she were guilty."

"But what if this be the truth?" and Robert laid his hand musingly on the paper.

"It is not the truth," almost shouted the Vicar. "It is a base fabrication of lies. Have we ever accused her in our sober senses of keeping back our letters? When we were most hard against her did we not acknowledge that there were extenuating circumstances in her favour? Supposing that she were guilty, are we to condemn her without mercy because an unjust will has rendered all restitution impossible? Do I not see clearly how severely she is expiating her fault? No, I have made up my mind; she may have done wrong—though, for my part, I begin to doubt it—but we have no right to inflict so frightful a penalty."

"It is only what she deserves," muttered Robert sullenly.

"Perhaps so; but for Heaven's sake don't let us be eternally climbing into the judgment seat. We are too interested to be fair judges. I have tried to adopt a medium course, but this fellow Graves has made all such medium policy unavailable. By this time the scandal will be half over Blackscar—it will not be enough for Mary and me to call at Bryn. We must disarm suspicion by making her welcome here. Mary, I am sure you agree with me."

"I don't know how it will answer, Austin," returned his wife, with a doubtful glance at Robert's face, which was just now looking very dark.

"My dear, it must answer," replied the Vicar decidedly. "Robert will have the good sense to see that I must act conscientiously in my own house. I am very sorry that I can no longer espouse his quarrel, but a clergyman is more fettered in these matters than a layman."

"You need not trouble to apologise to me, Austin," returned Robert, biting his lip, and his brow was very black indeed. "I should be sorry to interfere with any one's conscience. Of course, Mary, you will understand that Austin is virtually forbidding me his house; for he can scarcely expect me to meet Miss Maturin here on terms of intimacy."

"Intimacy? No; but I suppose you can treat anybody who visits here with civility," retorted the Vicar, who was becoming slightly warm in his turn.

"Allow me to say that I am the best judge of that myself," returned Robert haughtily. "I hope you will explain all this to Belle, Mary; it will surely make her dependent position more tolerable to know what sort of companion Austin is selecting for her."

"Mary will do no such thing. While Belle is under my roof she must certainly meet those with whom my wife and I see fit to associate; and I think it would be wiser of you, Robert, and more in accordance with charity, not to incense her any further against Miss Maturin; she endorses all your opinions."

"Belle and I quite understand our own affairs, Austin."

"My dear Bob, why need you be so touchy?" and here the Vicar laid his hand on his brother's shoulder. "Mary and I have both enough to bear without having to fight you and Belle, separately and collectively. Take my advice; just think over the matter coolly and dispassionately, and leave Belle for once to me."

"On the contrary, Austin, I am going up to her now. Belle has no relish for any more of Mary's lectures; Mary misunderstands her so."

"Poor girl, I wonder who does understand her—she herself least of all. I wish you would spare her feelings a little more than you do, Robert. I suppose you are going now to make her happier by telling her I have forbidden you the house."

"That is exactly what I am going to do."

"Pshaw! what nonsense."

"Austin, don't let him go," exclaimed Mary; "Belle is far from well to-day, and I will not have her agitated. There," as Robert went out, shutting the door after him, "now we shall have a miserable evening."

"Well, Mary, and how was I to prevent it? Never mind, let him go and do his worst—a wilful man must have his way. He is in one of his perverse moods, and Belle must manage him as best she can. I am not going to take the trouble to reason with him when he is like this. Heigho! what a trying world it is. Leave them alone upstairs, and give the children their tea. I am going out now."

"Not without your tea, surely, dear Austin, and you are so dead tired."

"Nothing to what I shall be when I come home," and the Vicar nodded with quiet good-humour as he took up his hat and went out

# CHAPTER XVI.

' The small, fair face within the darks of hair
I used to liken, when I saw her first,
To a point of moonlit water down a well :
The low brow, the frank space between the eyes,
Which always had the brown pathetic look
Of a dumb creature who had been beaten once
And never since was easy with the world.
Ah, ah—now I remember perfectly
These eyes, to-day,—however large they seemed,
As if some patient, passionate despair
Like a coal dropt—and forgot our tapestry,
Which slowly burns a widening circle out,
Had burnt them larger, larger.'          *Aurora Leigh.*

" He would have saved me utterly, it seemed,
He stood and looked so."                  *Ibid.*

MRS. ORD obeyed her husband's orders with a heavy heart; she knew that the Vicar valued his cup of tea above everything; that he placed it, indeed, among the good things of this life which he would be very unwilling to forego; neither was he always careful to moderate his desires in this respect. She had known him to discuss six cups of this fragrant beverage with the utmost cheerfulness and with unabated relish, and to consider himself aggrieved if withheld from the seventh; and yet now he had gone out faint and tired, utterly refusing all such refreshment, and leaving her in ignorance of his movement.

Upstairs all was sufficiently quiet—neither Belle nor Robert made their appearance. As Mrs. Ord dispensed the few homely viands to the hungry lads, she was straining her ears painfully to detect the faintest sound; it was no good pretending at last to disguise her anxiety. She drank a cup of tea standing, and then charging the boys to keep quiet until Garton should come in, she made some excuse and hurried away.

Scarcely twenty minutes had elapsed since Robert had left

them, closing the door somewhat loudly ; but Mary became aware (as she entered the drawing-room) that he had made good use of his time notwithstanding.    Belle's face always had a strange capacity for looking miserable on the shortest possible notice, but to Mary's knowledge it had never looked so utterly woebegone as on this occasion.

"Mary," she said, almost before her sister was within the room, and her voice sounded quite sharp with misery—"Mary, come here.    Is this true, that Austin has forbidden Robert the house?"

"No, Belle, it is not true."

"Ah! but, all the same, he is making it impossible for him to come here.    It is just as though he were shutting the door against him with his own hand.    Mary, I don't want to say anything specially unkind about Austin, but if he carry out what he threatens we can no longer be friends."

"You and I, do you mean?"

"No, I am talking about Austin ; but of course you take his part, so it will amount to the same thing.    Mary," she continued excitedly, as her sister put on an unusually severe look, "you must tell him—you must tell Austin—from me that if he do this thing he will not only injure Robert, but he will drive me from under the shelter of his roof."

"That is what she keeps saying," observed Robert ; who, to do him justice, was already beginning to repent of his hasty expressions of wrath.    He had never seen Belle so fairly roused before, except once ; and, to tell the truth, the sight did not please him.

"This is your work, I suppose," retorted Mary, turning upon him still more severely.    "I do not know whether it be part of your plan to set Belle against Austin, but I shall certainly take my husband's side.    I wonder you are not ashamed to act so treacherous a part in your brother's house.    Things have come indeed to a cruel pass when, after all his kindness, Belle can refuse to live with him ;" and Mary looked very stern as she thought of her own and her husband's wrongs.

"I don't think Belle ought to be blamed because my brother makes her position intolerable to her," returned Robert indignantly. "A bare crust and freedom would be better than such a state of servitude.    How is she to go on living here when I am not allowed to come to the house?"

"Robert, I must say that I think you ought to be ashamed of yourself."

"Thank you, Mary."

" How can you make Belle believe such a falsehood as that! just because Austin's duty as a clergyman will not allow him any longer to stand by and see this poor girl oppressed. Keep away from the house, if you will; but it will be your own pride that is shutting you out. As for Belle, if she choose to set herself against the man who has been such a brother to her all these years, and who could ill afford to share his bread with her, she is not the girl I thought her."

"I cannot help it, Mary," returned Belle, who was beginning to show symptoms of strong hysterical excitement. "It is no use your turning round and saying hard things against Robert, because he has his faults like other men."

"Oh dear! oh dear!" sighed Mrs. Ord.

But Belle again interrupted her—" He has declared to me that nothing will induce him to meet Miss Maturin here; and I cannot say that I think he is wrong. Austin ought never to have thought such a thing possible; and if he do not come here, where am I to see him? We might as well give each other up if we are to be separated."

"Now, Belle, I thought you promised that you would never say such a thing again," began Robert reproachfully; but Mary's sternness again interposed.

"If Belle's love for you, Robert, is to lead her to do wrong, I cannot say that I, for one, should be grieved at such a separation. I don't see—I never have seen—that her engagement has brought her any happiness. The fact is," she continued firmly, "you do not study her enough. When she wants soothing, you excite her; you try her patience with your ill-humours. When she is at her brightest, you depress her; and yet you have no sympathy with her little moods. In spite of your goodness, Robert, there is something selfish in your love; and whether Belle is angry or not, I will tell you the truth."

"You hear what is Mary's opinion of me, Belle?"

"Then, again, if you had any generosity you would not seek to stir up strife between her and Austin. Do you think Austin will ever let her quit his roof till you have given her shelter under yours? You talk about her dependent position as though women with brothers and lovers are ever independent, while all the time your pride is making her bread so bitter to her, she can hardly endure to swallow it."

"Mary, I declare I will not listen to any more of this. Austin and Belle may settle it between them as they will; but I vow I will not enter the Vicarage walls again until—until——" But whatever vow Robert was imprudently taking upon himself in his anger was to remain a mystery for ever, for at that moment Belle astonished them both by going, for the first time in her life, into a downright fit of hysterics.

It was a very silly affair altogether; but it was the wisest thing that Belle ever did, for it brought Robert to his senses in a moment, when Mary's wrathful eloquence could prevail nothing.

Granted that the scene was most humiliating and distressing, still the whole thing was a novelty to Robert, and could not fail to impress him with the heinousness and cruelty of his own conduct. That Belle, grave, quiet, sensible Belle, should be one minute in fits of mad laughter and the next convulsed with sobs; that she should be clenching and unclenching her little hands in a way that would be ludicrous if it were not so terrible; that she should turn so persistently from him and bury her pale face in the sofa-cushions when he tried to take her in his arms, with all manner of endearing speeches,—were things frightful to contemplate. Mary, who was but little less alarmed, pushed him away without the least compunction.

"You should never treat hysterics like that, Robert," she observed, with a little feminine contempt; "leave her to me, if you please. Belle, if you are not quiet directly I shall send for Austin!" And then she applied one remedy after another, with hands that would tremble in spite of her best efforts.

But Robert, who was very determined, was not to be pushed away for more than a moment. The poor fellow was cunning enough to detect the trembling. He took the sal volatile into his own hands, and turned that strong will of his to great account. Notwithstanding his provocations, Mary was constrained to admire him.

Belle had the grace to be thoroughly ashamed of herself when the fit of weakness was over. She sat up among the sofa-cushions very sad and silent, leaning her aching head on her hand, but saying very little about her illness. Her fair hair had come unloosened in the struggle, and lay damp and soft on her forehead, and as Mary stooped to smooth it back she was struck with the painful delicacy of her sister's look. Robert noticed it too, and for the first time a chill feeling almost of fear crossed him.

"Belle, dear, you are quite sure you are better now?" he asked anxiously.

"Oh yes, much better," and Belle closed her eyes wearily.

"Well, you have given us a terrible fright, but it is over now. You must not think any more of what I said," he continued hesitatingly.

"How do you mean?" she asked faintly; "what am I not to remember?"

"Well, all my ill temper against Austin. When a man is provoked he often says more than he means; you should not have been so ready to take me at my word, you silly child."

Belle's hand closed suddenly round his wrist.

"Do you mean that you will come here after all, Robert?"

"Of course I shall come here. How can I help it when you are taking it to heart like this? I did not think you had so much feeling, Belle," he continued mischievously, but Belle was too much in earnest to perceive the tender raillery.

"But Miss Maturin will be at the Vicarage sometimes," she continued, and Robert was quick to detect the pain in her voice.

"Never mind, Belle, I suppose I must bear it; after all, she has done mischief enough already without setting us four by the ears. I only hope Mary is ashamed of her crossness." Mrs. Ord shook her head smilingly, but she dealt him a comfortable little pat on the shoulder, and Robert put back his handsome head, and laughed at her, and so peace was declared.

And after that Mary and Belle made it up between them. Mary got on her knees before her sister, and said all sorts of comforting little things, and coaxed and scolded her in a breath, and Belle lay and looked at her with her great beautiful eyes, and said little, and they were all very foolish and very happy.

Meanwhile the Vicar, forgetful of his inner man, had taken up his worn felt hat and sallied out faint and tired; his errand was an important one. The Vicar was no ascetic. In spite of his goodness he was not one lightly to forego any of his creature comforts, and the renunciation of his cup of tea had gone hardly with him. As he halted a moment on the door-mat he told himself that it was a triumph of mind over matter; but the latter would take its revenge in an aching head on the morrow. As he walked down the garden-path it was a pity Robert could not see him, he looked so big. At the little gate he met Garton, to whom he told his errand at once; he was going to Ebenezer Graves.

Garton stared when he heard that. I would not advise you to have anything more to do with him, Austin," he observed, and thereupon the Vicar received a piece of intelligence that filled him with amazement. Robert had only just returned from a most exciting interview with the recreant editor of the *Blackscar Herald*.

"Do you mean that Robert has really been pitching into this fellow Graves?" ejaculated the Vicar in an excess of astonishment.

"Pitching into him; I believe you," returned Garton, rubbing his hands in great enjoyment, and rocking to and fro against the little gate. "I never saw a man so cowed and crestfallen in my life. Robert made me go with him in case he should be tempted

12

to do violence to the fellow; Bob had got his spirit up, I can tell you."

"But why did he not tell me he had been to the man?" retorted the Vicar in sore perplexity. "Here he has left me abruptly, will not listen to a word of reason, and talks about turning himself out of my house, and all the time the foolish fellow had not the courage to confess that he had taken up cudgels himself in Miss Maturin's defence—Robert, too, of all men."

"Oh, that is just Bob's way; he is so terribly hard, you know. He would go and do the right thing just for the sake of doing it, and make himself so disagreeable all the time that there's no bearing with him. I suppose you said or did something to offend him."

"I told him I should have Miss Maturin at the Vicarage."

"Ah, that was quite enough, no doubt; he would turn round and tell you that you had shut the door in his face. Poor old Bob, he will never bring himself to forgive her."

"But, Gar, why should he enter the list at all on the girl's behalf? He had much better have left the business to me."

"So I told him when he explained the matter to me; but he chose to be obstinate over it. 'Austin has enough work of his own to do,' he said. 'Ebenezer gives him plenty of kicks and side flings already. No, no; you'll see how I'll manage the scoundrel.' And, true enough, he did give it him; the rascal quite shook in his shoes."

"Yes, but how could Robert refute the attack, believing in it all the time, as he does?" asked the Vicar perplexedly.

"Oh, as to that, I could see he was very careful not to compromise himself. Ebenezer could not nail him to a single point.

"'How dare you bring all these slanderous charges against a lady?' he repeated over and over again. Graves had his wife in at last as a sort of protection. 'You will bear witness, Jemima, that he attacked me first,' he said, almost whimpering; 'and you have no right to bully me, Mr. Ord. How was I to know that our correspondent had said anything damaging to the lady? Reports of that kind are often erroneous.'

"'Very well, Mr. Graves, you may take your own choice,' said Robert, quite quietly. 'You may either make your correspondent retract the article with an apology next week, or I will have you up for libel. My brother and I are quite determined to put a stop to this sort of persecution; so unless you want your paper to be ruined you had better get rid of this bad habit of yours of inventing scandalous stories about people. Do you understand me, Mr. Graves?'

"'I will see what I can do,' muttered the fellow, quite sullenly, and Robert came away.    I don't know how he managed it, but he actually got through the whole affair without compromising himself. Bob is awfully clever."

" He is awfully good too, if he would but let people find it out for themselves," returned the Vicar; "and here I have been accusing him of want of generosity; I suppose it was my blunt assertion put him out.    Well, I will finish my work.    Go in for the lads, Gar;" and the Vicar unlatched the gate and walked thoughtfully down the road.    This unlooked-for generosity on Robert's part was making his cause a little difficult, but he was not one to be easily moved from his purpose, and so he went on to Bryn.

He had planned his visit none too early, and had a shrewd suspicion of how he would find matters.    Mrs. Carruthers, as she met him in the hall on her way to church, looked grave enough to verify *these* suspicions.

" I am so glad you are come, Mr. Ord," she said, warmly welcoming him.    " I can't think what is the matter with Miss Maturin to-day; she has scarcely spoken or eaten for hours, and she will not answer a single inquiry as to whether she be ill. I was almost unwilling to go to church to-night, but I thought she would rather be alone.    Will you go to her?" she added.    The Vicar nodded.    Mrs. Carruthers pushed open the door of the little sitting-room, and Mr. Ord entered unannounced.    As usual the room was filled with evening sunshine; it slanted full on the pretty tea-table, from whence they had just risen; but Rotha still sat in her place with her empty plate before her.    When the Vicar first saw her she had her two arms on the table; her shoulders had a weary stoop in them, and her face was hidden in her hands. The sound of the opening door evidently startled her; when she saw who it was she rose at once to her feet and remained standing.

" I suppose you knew that I should come to you," he said gently, as he took the unoffered hand and pressed it in his.

Then she shook her head.    " No, Mr. Ord, I never expected to see you here again ;" and as she turned from him he saw that the newspaper lay half-hidden under her plate.

" You thought I should not come to you in your trouble ?" he repeated reproachfully; " you were wrong, you see.    I hope you do not think I am less your friend because you are just now so sorely in need of one."

Her only answer was to turn hurriedly from him and burst into tears ; covering her face with her hands, and pressing him to leave her, she wept as though her heart were broken.    Only once before had Rotha so wept.    Good Christian as he was, his thoughts were very bitter against Ebenezer as he heard her sobs.

"My dear Miss Maturin, hush! poor child, poor child! it has gone very heavily with you, I fear."

Gone very heavily with her! Could he guess, as she sat hiding her face from him in her misery, the utter hopelessness that had crept over her during the last few hours—the crushing pressure—the outraged pride—the whole helplessness of a woman knowing her own innocence, yet powerless to defend it. A few months ago the cruelty of the thing would have gone hardly with her—but now—now, when a little promise of brighter days had come, it was unbearable.

She had taught herself to regard the man who was near her as her friend—as one tolerant enough to help her in spite of her supposed sin. She had spoken of his goodness as though it had been a joy to her; her work had been very pleasant under his eyes: as she had gone about it she had told herself that one day he would do her justice and believe in her; she remembered Garton's honest bluntness of avowal, and then her bliss had been very great. But now of what avail were all these things since Blackscar and Kirkby would believe in her guilt? Would it be possible any longer that they should defend her?

No, he could not be her friend; but for all that she must tell him what it had come into her heart to do. Just now his sympathy was keeping him silent. By and by he would ask her some question that would make it easy for her to tell him that she had made up her mind to go away; for her burden was too heavy for her.

"Miss Maturin," he said at length, "can you not understand that this is very bitter to me as well as to you?" And as she shook her head mournfully, "Indeed it is; when I read that paper I felt cut to the heart—it seemed to me so wantonly cruel."

She turned her face to him at that. "Mr. Ord, it has been my deathblow."

"Hush! you must not say that."

"Ah! but it has," and here she struggled ineffectually with her emotion; "it has been the deathblow to all my hopes. You will never know now how I have planned and worked, and all I meant to do. Everything would have come right, I know, if they had let me stay here a little longer."

"Stay here! at Bryn, do you mean?"

"Yes, it is my own, is it not? No one has the right to drive me away, have they? And I was beginning to love it so in spite of all; if I could only have stopped on here and worked as I was working I am sure people would have grown to believe in me. I have so prayed to be allowed to live it down."

" You will live it down if you will only be brave over this."

"I shall not try," she replied, turning very white. "In the heat of the day my strength has failed. I am going away from here, Mr. Ord."

" I rather dreaded to hear you say so," was the answer ; " but perhaps it is only natural. How long do you intend to remain away ?"

Rotha looked up at him rather puzzled. "If I go away, of course I shall never return," she replied simply. "I am very sorry, for Meg's sake ; poor Meg, she was just beginning to feel happy here. It is hard for her to go back to her old drudgery ; but there is no help for it."

" Do you mean, Miss Maturin, that you seriously contemplate leaving Kirkby—utterly and entirely, I mean ?"

" What can I do ?" she answered bitterly ; and there was a passionate ring in her voice no one had ever heard before. " How can I live on here when the very poor about my gate will look upon me as little better than a thief ? Can I go about the streets protesting my innocence when people are pointing their fingers at me as one who has defrauded the injured of their rights ? Will they believe me if I cry shame on them for the baseness of their falsehood ? Mr. Ord, you know—you must know, that it is not possible for me to do otherwise than I am doing."

" Nevertheless I intend that you shall not leave us."

" Who is to prevent me, Mr. Ord ?"

" Who is to prevent you ? Why I, if it lies in my power— common sense—your own conscience—the dictates of prudence and generosity—nay more, your very self-respect."

" They will be all as nothing in this case. Do you think I should sacrifice Meg if it were possible to remain—that I should renounce all hope and plans for the future ? Mr. Ord, your argument will not shake me ; I am determined to bear all this no longer."

He gave her a pitying look before he resumed his speech ; he could see now how wrung and galled her spirit was within her. A difficult piece of work lay before him, but its toughness did not daunt him ; he was not the less patient with her now that trouble was making her reckless.

" You know, of course, that the conditions of the will oblige you to live at Bryn ?" he continued after a pause ; " pardon me if I remind you of what you know already—the clause is a binding one, I believe."

" I have no intention to set it aside," she returned, with a little scorn. " I know in leaving Bryn that I shall leave it a beggar,

but anything will be better than these gilded chains; poverty cannot degrade me, though at first it will be hard to bear. We must
go back to our teaching, Meg and I. Poor Meg, it is very sad for
her, certainly."

"I should think it sadder for you."

"No, I am younger, and in spite of my sorrow I am not quite
so hopeless. I shall go away from here, and in a few years perhaps
I shall forget my troubles. When I next come," she added, with
a bitter smile, "your Convalescent Home will have got its new
wing, and the Almshouses will have been built."

"You mean that, in case of your refusal to live at Bryn, the
money is to revert to the original purpose—at least to the purpose my aunt proposed to herself after she had disinherited her
lawful heir."

"Yes, Mr. Ord; the Almshouses were much in her thoughts.
I cannot think what induced her to give them up, unless indeed it
were natural caprice."

"Very likely," returned the Vicar quietly. "Well; so it is
your intention, Miss Maturin, to let the property go out of your
hands and to resume your old drudgery of teaching,—in short, to
use your own expression, to leave Bryn a beggar?"

"That is my intention, certainly."

"Have you any idea that by doing so you will at all alter the
present state of feelings towards you?"

"No," she faltered; "I have no hope at all of that kind."

"Perhaps you are not aware that it may rather injure you than
otherwise; some people are so unjust that they may hold it rather
a corroboration of their suspicions than otherwise."

He touched her there—he saw her wince. "I cannot help it,"
she answered despairingly. "I have tried what I can do to remove
it, but it is all no use; people must think of me as they will—it
will be all over some day."

"Yes, if we be not weary of well-doing; have you forgotten
that?"

"I have forgotten everything, I think," she answered in a tired
voice, putting back her hair from her face—such a worn young face
it looked. "Mr. Ord, when I think of Meg—poor Meg—I hate
myself for being such a coward; but the sin is with them who are
driving me to desperation."

"That is true in one sense, but we may not rid ourselves of
the responsibility of our own actions; if you carry out this intention, you will cause suffering to many."

"You mean that poor Annie will miss me. I am afraid she
will, but it will be only for a little time; what hurts me most is

that the hospital will claim all the money, and I have been saving it all so carefully for him."

For him—the words had escaped her almost unconsciously. As soon as she had spoken them she shrunk back in uncontrollable confusion, and covered her face with her hands. "Oh, Mr. Ord," she exclaimed, "what have I said! I never meant any of you to know this."

He had scarcely understood her meaning at first, but now a certain quick brightness came into his eyes as he leant forward— he almost held his breath in the intensity of his surprise and suspense.

"Do you mean that you are saving it for Robert? Don't be afraid to trust me," he continued pleadingly; "you hardly know how important this all is—on my honour, as a gentleman and a clergyman, I will not betray your confidence."

She looked at him a little comforted.

"You will not even tell your wife?"

"No, no; this shall be solely a matter between you and me— your words shall be as though they had not been spoken. Did I understand you to say that you had been keeping the money for him?"

"Yes," she returned, still hesitating; "all of it that I could honestly spare from my necessities. Meg and I are used to live simply, you know; there is no sacrifice in the case—none. I know that I cannot make restitution in my lifetime, but, all the same, it makes me happier to think that it is all being saved up for him."

"But, my dear Miss Maturin, you are much younger than Robert. Women on an average live longer than men."

"Yes, happy women do, no doubt. I should be sorry to believe that in my case; but at least his children will have the benefit. The idea surprises you, perhaps," she continued, with a faint smile; "it did Mr. Tracy; but it was the only thing that gave me any comfort. It may be possible for some people to enjoy themselves at the expense of others, but this is not my nature."

"I most thoroughly believe you: in giving up your property, therefore, you are making this noble intention of yours, with regard to my brother, null and void. Never mind, the Convalescent Hospital will reap the benefit."

"Oh!" she said reproachfully. "Why do you remind me of that? Are you going to make it as impossible for me to go as it is to remain?"

"I hope, indeed, that I shall succeed in making it impossible."

"But why—why be so cruel?"

"Because Kirkby, and Kirkby Vicarage especially, cannot afford to part with you, Miss Maturin—because they shall not part with you until they have acknowledged themselves to be in the wrong. Do not misunderstand me, and think I am saying this on account of what you have told me about my brother. In my own mind I think Robert will never derive any good from your money, or any one else's. No; I say this solely because I believe in you, and think you are an injured woman."

Before he had finished speaking she had risen to her feet, and was confronting him.

"Mr. Ord, say that again," she panted.

"What am I to say again?" he asked, taking her two hands, and still holding her before him. As he looked at her something like a mist passed before his own eyes.

"What you said just now—that you believed in me," she replied, hardly able to get out the words in her agitation, and trembling all over.

"Very well; I will repeat my words. I said that I believe in you, and I do. I believe that we have wronged you utterly and bitterly, and that you have never done this thing of which we accused you."

"Thank God!" was all she said; but, oh, the sparkling brightness of her face, and then a little astonishment mingled with her joy!

"Well," he said, smiling, "are you disposed to forgive me? I confess I hardly like to ask your pardon."

Then, in her sweet humility, she put that by.

"But, Mr. Ord, I cannot understand it. Surely you did not come here this evening to tell me this?" and her eyes dwelt for a moment on the offending *Herald*.

"You mean that you cannot understand my sudden conversion. Well, I will tell you the truth. Just before I came here my brother asked if I were prepared to acquit you, and I told him 'No.' At the time I certainly meant what I said."

"Ah!"

"I knew how I should find you. When I came into your presence just now, and saw you bowed down with grief—my doubts were still heavy on my mind—they were there; but, to be candid with you, they were certainly lessened."

"How so?" she asked timidly.

"Well, I had overcome my prejudice. Perhaps I should be right in saying that I was no longer disposed to be hardened against you. I had been proving you lately. I could not reconcile the fact that came before my eyes with Robert's suspicions, and every day I found it more difficult to doubt Annie's patient nurse and comforter. Do you understand me ?"

"Yes," she returned humbly; "but I am afraid I was only working for your praise then."

"It may be so; but it struck me you were laborious and self-denying. I knew you to be patient. When you talked to me, in your grief, about going away—and giving up everything—it was impossible not to believe you were in earnest. It is true I hinted that others might attribute such conduct to far different motives; but, in my own mind, then I began to see you were innocent."

"Is that all ?"

"No; it is not all. I supposed you managed to convince me by your own words. There, will that do ?" he added, smiling.

Somehow he found it difficult to explain to her how his doubts really had been set at rest. How could he tell her that it had been those few unconscious words of hers that had carried conviction straight to his mind ?

"I am saving it all so carefully for him." Could he ever forget the tenderly mournful intonation of her voice as she said that, and the shrinking confession that had followed her words ? "I never meant any of you to know this," she said to him in her distress; and then, when he had drawn her on with his promise of secrecy, what did he hear ?—that she was living simply, only supplying her necessities in fact, that an abundance should be laid up for him, for the man who had wronged her, and for his children after him—and this was the woman whose pure generous heart they were crushing to the dust. He wished now that he had not given her his word—that it were possible that others might share his knowledge—it would make his defence of her so much less difficult; but when he hinted at this wish she reminded him of his promise with a decision against which there was no appeal.

"I could not stay here and look any of them in the face," she said in a frightened voice, when he suggested it. At that he smiled a little.

"You are thinking better of your intended exodus then, Miss Maturin—you are not leaving Bryn now ?"

"Of course I am not leaving it," she returned with energy. "When you said you would prevent me, how could I know what means you would take ? Do you think I would ever go away from Kirkby now that I have a friend here who believes in me ?" She might have added "two friends" when she thought of Garton. but a little consciousness kept her silent.

"Ah, so my argument has been successful, after all? By the bye, Miss Maturin, I have something to tell you, only all this has put it out of my head till now—do you know who has been taking up the cudgels in your defence?" and he glanced meaningly at the obnoxious paper.

She shook her head. "How can I know?"

"Well, I will tell you; it was Robert. Garton told me all about it, and I was very nearly as surprised as you are. Robert seems to have done his work well; Garton says the fellow fairly shook in his shoes. He has consented to write some sort of apology. I hardly know whether he will go so far as to retract entirely; so you see things are not quite so hopeless as you made them out half an hour ago."

"No, indeed; but oh, Mr. Ord, how good of your brother, when all the time he believes—at least, he suspects—this of me; and I was going to wrong him so by going away."

"Ah! true; that would have argued badly for his prospects," returned the Vicar, with a twinkle in his eye, as he thought of Rotha's full-grown heir; but Rotha was too much occupied with her own thoughts.

"I always said he was just in spite of his hardness," she said at last. "Thank you, Mr. Ord; I am glad you have told me, it will make it easier for me to bear things in the future. It does not seem to me that I shall mind what people think now."

"But, all the same, I am afraid that your troubles are not yet over. I hope you have not forgotten Mrs. Blake and Miss Brookes."

"Ah, Miss Brookes is the worst—I am terribly afraid of that woman. No, I have not forgotten them; but I feel even as though I have a panacea for all ills."

"And what is that?"

"That you believe in me," she said touchingly; and somehow the Vicar had no answer ready.

"I was going to ask you if you would do me a favour," he said presently, in his usual manner. "I want your assistance in a little matter that I have to settle in the village. Do you think you are too tired to come with me?"

"Too tired! oh no," she returned, with alacrity; but he hesitated a little when he saw her face.

"Are you sure you are not? Well, perhaps it will be better to have it over. Put on your bonnet then while I stroll out in the garden for a breath of air."

# CHAPTER XVII.

## MRS. ORD HEARS ARTY HIS PRAYERS.

> " I know her ! the worst thought she has
> Is whiter even than her pretty hand !
> She must prove true ; for, brother, where two fight
> The stronger wins, and truth and love are strength."—TENNYSON.

ROTHA had acceded to the Vicar's request with alacrity. She was far too happy to feel any surprise at it being preferred—she was not even curious on the subject. She bathed her swollen eyes, and was very careful about the adjustment of her bonnet-strings ; she even caught herself smiling at the rather forlorn-looking image in the glass.

" I wonder what people will say to my red eyes," she thought. "I declare I look as pale as a ghost ;" and a vision of Belle's beautiful face rose before her as she ran downstairs. Prue looked up in surprise when her mistress passed her; the light footstep scarcely touched the ground, she thought. The Vicar was standing in the doorway leading into the lane.

" You have not been long," he said, with an approving smile, and then they walked down the road together.

Rotha felt as though she could hardly keep her feet in order ; she felt extremely happy, and yet in an odd sort of dream too. Her tears had made her weak ; she felt a little dazed,—that he should believe in her ! She wished all Kirkby could have seen her walking beside him, her friend ; she gave him wistful glances now and then, inexpressively touching. Somehow that brief walk was stereotyped in her memory for ever. Years after she could see it all : the sunset sky all gilded with amethyst and crimson, the west a perfect flood of yellow glory ; just below the horizon the clear blue outline of the Leatham hills ; in the foreground the church, with its weather-worn lich-gate ; a stone cross, with a wreath of withered immortelles ; some children swinging on a rusty chain. Down the white sandy road comes the Vicar, slow and ponderous. What a grand-looking man, Rotha thinks, as she looks up at him. He has crisp curly hair, with open gray eyes and massive shoulders. His footsteps go thud, thud, beside Rotha's springy ones. He carries his felt hat in his hand as they come near the church. They can hear music through the open door—"Oh, Paradise! oh, Paradise!" Rotha's pulse gives a little thrill as she hears it. "Where loyal hearts and true, stand ever in the light."

"Amen!" she whispered.

The Vicar had gone over to speak to the verger. He came back presently, and they retrace their steps. "All rapture, through and through;" he is humming it from where they left off. The clouds are all crimson and gold now; the air has a soft crispness in it.

"Where are we going?" asks Rotha, a little bewildered.

They had been walking up and down just to listen to the hymn, and now he has unlocked another door in the wall.

"'Open, Sesame.' Do you not like wandering in a strange garden of an evening, Miss Maturin? It always reminds me of a German Mährchen. Do you admire my fuchsias?"

They are walking down a gravel-path; two ducks come waddling over the grass to Rotha's feet; a little white kitten, up in an apple tree, grins at her like a gargoyle as they pass. There are beds of scarlet geraniums and mignonette; a westeria trails clusters of gray grapes over a low bow-window; a passion-flower climbs over the porch. A sleepy voice sounds querulously from the upper regions.

"Where am I? Why do you bring me here?" cries Rotha in an uncertain voice.

She is more in a dream than ever; the Vicar puts her hand on his arm with a smile.

"I will tell you by and by," he answers, stopping to gather a great creamy rose, and slipping it between her fingers. "At present we have to go upstairs. Don't be frightened, it will be over soon;" and he draws her across the threshold.

Rotha gives herself up for lost now—they are stumbling up a dark staircase; more roses like the one she has in her hand came peeping through a little lattice-window all festooned with greenery. The sleepy voice they heard in the upper regions has descended, and is blowing through a tin trumpet.

"Be quiet, Arty, you rogue; come and make friends with this lady." And Rotha bends down to an invisible curly head.

"Mother, the lady has kissed my curls," shouts Arty, turning short round into an open door; "she has, indeed, and I won't let Uncle Robert cut them off. Will you play 'Gefoozalem,' Uncle Robert?"

" What lady ? Hush ! " says his mother, "you are disturbing your aunt. Why, Austin!" and then Mary rises in confusion. In the sudden stillness Rotha can hear the ripple of the water behind the sand-hills. Coming out of the light and glory, the room seems full of dusk corners—a black dress comes out of one; a tall dark man bows to her from a distance; there is a mass of white drapery glimmering somewhere. Rotha is conscious that she is crushing her rose between her fingers—the carpet is strewn with pale creamy leaves—one flutters on to Arty's curls; the Vicar has her hand still firmly on his arm; she feels she is white to the lips.

" Mary, I have brought Miss Maturin to see you ; make her very welcome, my dear ; " and, as he delivers himself of his little speech, he lifts his boy in his arms and smothers him with kisses, and Mary takes Rotha's hand.

The Vicar has retreated to the rug, and is eyeing the white drapery rather doubtfully. " Why, Belle, child, are you ill ? " he asks kindly.

" Hush ! Austin," says Mary again, and she drops Rotha's hand and comes up to the sofa a little anxiously. " Yes, Belle has been ill, but she is better now," and she whispers something into her sister's ear ; but Belle colours and looks at Robert.

" Will you not sit down, Miss Maturin ? I think we can find you a chair." A tall figure passes between her and the light— the waves are rippling up louder than ever now—they seem surging over the sand-hills.

" Thank you," says Rotha. There is only a bare flower-stalk between her fingers now; the blue convolvuli on the carpets seem twining into knots and festoons. " Are there such things as blue convolvuli ? " thinks Rotha, with a little wonder. There is a curious lump in her throat; her temples are throbbing with sharp pain, and her eyes are aching and swollen.

Robert had brought her a chair—and now he has gone off somewhere. She can hear him whistling softly at a far-off window; he has taken no notice of Mary's whisper, and Belle still colours and hesitates.

" It will be too late in another minute," says Mary, with a patient sigh ; and then Belle gets up and crosses the room—a cold hand holds Rotha's for a moment, and the Vicar, with a pleased smile, presses his boy to him.

" What lots of kisses you are giving me to-night, father," says Arty, a little ruefully.

" There are two more to give to your Aunt Belle," says Austin, with a laugh, as he releases him; and Arty blows an ode to freedom through his tin trumpet.

" Do you think the walls of Jericho will soon blow down ? You are Jericho, Aunt Belle, and I am going to walk seven times round you.   Where are the palm trees, Uncle Bob ?"

" Hush, Arty, that is not a proper game," said his mother, quite shocked.   " Austin, will you ring the bell, please ?   It is time for Arty to go to bed; Deb will hear him say his prayers to-night."

" Am I to pray for the lady too ?" says Arty, rubbing his curls sleepily.   As he blows a last refrain he is a little unsteady—his head nods drowsily on Deb's shoulder.

" Do you know I have had no tea to-night, Mary," says the Vicar, rather solemnly.   " Why should. Deb hear him say his prayers? he will only gabble them.   Let Miss Maturin go upstairs and take off her bonnet, my dear, and then we will have some tea together in your room."

" Oh, Austin, I am so sorry I did not think of it before," she says remorsefully.   As she goes out of the room she is a little mystified—why should not Deb hear Arty his prayers ?   Austin has never before objected to that godly handmaiden.   She makes a little excuse to Rotha as they go up the dark stairs.   " Mother's rooms are always untidy," she observes, as she picks up a broken drum and a whole file of soldiers off the floor ; the soldiers are oscillating on their zigzag parade; as Mary picks them up they drop off by twos and threes.

" Let me help you," says Rotha, with a little laugh—and in another moment she is down on the carpet ; in the dim light she can see faint patches and stains everywhere—some marbles crunch under her feet and roll under the bed.   By and by Arty comes in with bare rosy feet and startles them.

" Miss Maturin, I am quite ashamed.   Arty, come here and say your prayers."

" Why should I not play at my Jericho game, mother ?" says Arty, as he huddles up his feet in his mother's dress.   " Deb's cross, and I wouldn't have said my prayers to her."

" Shut your eyes, Arty ; do you think the child-Christ will be beside your bed to-night if you talk like that ?" says Mary's cooing voice.

A hushed feeling comes over Rotha as she sits down by the open window.   By and by, when Deb is making the tea, and Arty is prattling after his prayers, she begins to have a dim consciousness why the Vicar has sent her upstairs.

" I think my room has the best view in the house," says Mrs. Ord cheerfully, as she tucks away her son under her arm.   Arty is going in for a cuddle to-night.   " I often sit up here of an evening when I am not at church."

"Yes, it is very beautiful," returns Rotha. Somehow her hot eyes will keep filling with tears as she looks over the dark sea and at the distant lights. The mother and boy opposite seemed framed with a dim halo—it is all so peaceful and still; a young moon trembles on the verge of the sea, and one or two stars show like sparks of gold against a long cloud. There are two figures moving up and down among the sand-hills; a woman's cloak flutters far out at the margin of the waves—the lights come flickering up upon the sea-wall. "There is Meg taking her solitary stroll," thinks Rotha; and then Mrs. Ord's voice breaks in a little plaintively:

"Yes, when one looks at a scene like that, one is ashamed of being discontented."

"Are you ever discontented?" asked Rotha curiously. Mary laughed, and then dimpled consciously in the twilight, and then laughed again.

"I wish Austin had heard you ask that. Do you know I was small enough to feel ashamed when he told me to bring you upstairs. I was afraid you would think everything so poor and shabby, and Arty's toys did look so bad," finished Mary. She scolded herself afterwards for her confession, but she was a woman who missed sadly the beauty and fitness of things. She always said that one of the joys of heaven to her would be that there would be nothing worn out or broken there; "and breakages are so trying to the temper," she would add naïvely.

Rotha looked round the room when Mrs. Ord gave vent to this womanish speech; and then she told Mary plainly that "she thought it the most delicious old room she had ever seen; she liked the motherly arrangements—Arty's high chair, and the big chintz couch, and the round table with its litter of boxes and puzzles."

"Yes, but you cannot think how faded all the curtains are," returned Mrs. Ord disconsolately; "and I have darned them till I don't think they will bear another wash; I have had them fifteen years. And as to the carpet—— Well, with great boys how can you expect carpets to wear properly?"

"Carpets won't last for ever," returned Rotha sententiously. She had a dim idea that the Vicar had not sent them upstairs to talk about carpets, but it was very nice all the same. "I think this is a dear room," she continued, with a little burst, "and I would not mind a bit about its shabbiness," and then Arty was sent away, and the two women became more confidential.

"I suppose tea is ready now," Mary had observed, suddenly rising; then Rotha had put her hand on her dress very timidly to detain her.

"Please do not go just yet, Mrs. Ord, I want you to know how good your husband has been to me." Then Mary sat down again directly.

"I am very glad to hear it," she returned, with a little effort. She too had felt, as she held forth on carpets, that her eloquence had been a failure ; but, ignorant as she was of the result of her husband's mission, it was hardly possible for her to become animated on any other subject. "I am very glad he has been good to you. I think there is no one like Austin for helping when one is in trouble," finished Mary, with innocent tautology. She was always ready to expatiate for any length of time on the cardinal virtues of her husband.

"No one like him. Well, no. I suppose a drowning wretch believes in the goodness of the man who saves him. When I think of your husband, there seems no limit to my gratitude. Do you know what he has done for me, Mrs. Ord ?"

"No, my dear, will you tell me ?"

"I will, if I can get the words out ; but when I think of his nobleness, my heart seems ready to burst. If I had not been a woman I think I should have fallen at his feet when he told me he believed in me."

"Did Austin tell you that ?"

"He told me that, Mrs. Ord. I was standing up on my feet, and he took my two hands, and I could see there were tears in his eyes. 'I told you that I did believe you, and I do,' he said, and his voice seemed almost divine to me. 'I think we have wronged you utterly and entirely, and that you have not done this thing of which we accused you ;' and then it was that I could have fallen at his feet in my joy ; but I only said, 'Thank God !'"

"You did right," returned Mary seriously; "but now do you mind telling me a little more of what passed between you and Austin ? I want to know what it was that induced him to change his opinion so quickly."

"You shall hear everything," returned Rotha, and she related the conversation that had taken place between her and the Vicar. Mary listened breathlessly as Rotha spoke of the bitter fit of recklessness that had come over her, and of the course she had been prompted to take in her despair. She wiped her eyes once or twice as Rotha spoke of that dreary exodus ; but all at once there was a flaw and gap in the narrative. Austin's words were repeated where there seemed no solidity of foundation for them ; the speech that had wrought the Vicar's conversion had no place in Rotha's record. Mary felt the discrepancy, and said so.

"It was something that I said by mistake, dear Mrs. Ord, that I never meant any one to hear ; it is quite between him and me, you know," she continued, hesitating. "One sometimes says things to one's clergyman."

"Yes, of course."

"Not that I had ever meant to tell him," she went on quickly, with the truth that seemed inherent in her; "it was quite a mistake—quite, though I cannot be sorry for it now. When I said it I had no idea how it would influence him."

"Was it then that he said those words?"

"Yes, then, or almost directly afterwards. When I think of it I am puzzled to comprehend how it all happened; it was such a simple thing that I said, and it seemed such a clear duty, I can hardly understand now why he magnified it."

"And it is quite between you and him; no one else must know it?"

"No; no one. Dear Mrs. Ord, you are not angry with me?"

"Why should I be angry with you? You could not have a better confidant than Austin; you are quite safe there. I am only sorry—that is, it seems a pity—that people should not know what cleared you in his eyes."

"It does not seem to me a pity at all. For the matter of that, what have people to do with him or me either?"

"I think we should always be desirous to prove our own innocence," returned Mary gently, as though rebuking Rotha's pride.

"Ah! and have I not been? Dear Mrs. Ord, you must not be vexed with me; but, indeed, I cannot let any one know this;" and Rotha crimsoned up to the roots of her hair in the twilight as she thought of her impulsive words. "It would put me in a false position, and make me so terribly conscious; and, after all, people might misunderstand me, and look upon it in quite a different light to what he does."

"Very well, then, we will say no more about it," returned Mary, but she felt a little natural regret as she said so, being only a woman, and curious, as most of her sex are; in reality, she was dying to know those few words that had wrought Austin's conversion. "Of course I am of my husband's opinion," she continued, with a soft laugh, and then she stooped down in the darkness and kissed Rotha.

But for the kiss Rotha would have been slow to understand her words; even now she hesitated. "What does that mean?" she asked; "does it mean that you too believe in me?"

"Of course I believe in you, if Austin does. Austin cannot be wrong," returned the weak woman. She was perfectly abject on this subject. To her her husband was something short of a demi-god; her faith in his goodness and cleverness was so simply

13

transparent that her brothers-in-law would laugh at her fond credulity. " Mary will never go in for the rights of women," Garton would say. " When Austin holds up his little finger she dare not say she has a soul of her own."

Mary did not mind their laughing one bit—the clauses in the marriage service were always terribly real things to her. She loved and honoured and obeyed the big homely priest with an excess and perfectness of reverence that was almost touching. It was not enough that she gave him her beauty and youth, and a daily and hourly self-sacrifice ; it was not enough that she made home sunshine for him and his boys ; but she adopted his opinions in a way that would have incurred the scorn of any strong-minded woman of sound judgment. When Austin was for daily services, and had announced the fact in the family circle, Mary was full of enthusiasm on the subject, though the day before she had privately informed Belle that she thought them terrible interruptions to work. She would tie on her bonnet with the utmost cheerfulness and trudge off with her boys beside her if she were ever so tired and busy. The face that was dearer to the Vicar now than in its young beauty would always beam on him brightly from morning till night. No wonder, when the Vicar read that lesson out of Proverbs about the woman "whose price is above rubies," that his voice would tremble, and he should think of that other woman " whose clothing was not of silk and purple," for whose sake he had given up a goodly inheritance, but who, he thanked God, was his patient helpmeet and his joy for ever.

Meanwhile the Vicar was doing his own special work down-stairs ; he had got rid of the two women by a pretext that had been sufficiently transparent to the one, though Mary's tender conscience had remained sore for some time after his reproof as to Arty's prayers : since the daily services Deb had often had occasion to hear them ; her grievance over that and the carpet had quite ruffled her spirits for the time being.

But the Vicar had chuckled to himself as he closed the door after them. It was a favourite theory with him that nature had intended him for a diplomatist, and that in consequence Government had lost a good deal in his being ordained a priest ; but as the Vicar's notions of diplomacy mainly consisted in maintaining his own opinions and having his own way, and making every one else like his way too, it was the most clumsy conceit possible. The fact was, he could not employ *finesse* at all—he hardly understood the word ; he would take a raging bull by the horns, or would go among any number of the same noisy cattle as likely as not, with his colours pinned ostentatiously in front, and would not be one whit daunted by their bellowing ; but in truth he was too honest for a diplomatist, he hated shams too inveterately, and was too ready to maintain that black was not white to insure him much political success. In the pulpit he was like a lamb, but an argument on some subjects—say Messrs. Bright and Mill, the Fenians, or Disestablishment—and he would be transformed into a roaring lion, and the Vicar's roar could be a very loud one indeed.

He had a notion that he would employ a little *finesse* on the present occasion, and so he walked up to his brother.

"Well, Robert, I have done a tolerable bit of work this evening. In my opinion things are pretty much now as they ought to be."

"That means you have got your own way, I suppose ?" returned Robert, who was in no very enviable mood, and whose words were in consequence rather brusque than pleasant.

"Exactly," agreed his brother, with perfect good humour.

"And lost no time about it either," observed Robert shortly.

"Oh, as to that, I hate procrastination. When a thing's to be done it ought to be done quickly," returned the Vicar, feeling rather guilty as he uttered this truism, and wishing that he had put it in practice two months ago. He did not like to look back on the slow torture of those days and weeks.

"I have no doubt Miss Maturin is extremely obliged to you, Austin."

"Well, as to that, she is rather grateful certainly, poor thing. By the bye, Robert, I hope you have thought better of your threat, and that your evenings at the Vicarage are not yet numbered."

It was very clumsy of the Vicar ; he might have known that a man of Robert's calibre could not bear that sort of good-humoured bullying—he would not have stood it for a moment. In fact he was growing decidedly cross—stiffening up for a breeze certainly—only Belle, who was lying very quiet, slipped a stealthy hand in his, and a very soft persuasive little hand it was, if she had only known it.

"I think I should have kept my word but for Belle," he replied, a little less sulkily.

"Oh, Belle was the mediator, was she ?"

"I don't think you would have admired her style of mediation," observed Robert, with grim humour. "Of course when a woman gets up a scene, and makes a fuss in real earnest, she can turn any man round her finger ; " and Robert, as he said this, looked as though he rather enjoyed his subjugation. The Vicar was greatly amused ; it was a new thing to hear that Belle could turn Robert round her little finger—he felt rather inclined to pursue the subject; but Belle looked so anxious and so uncomfortable that he went off on another track instantly.

"Well, now that matter is settled, I want to speak to you about something else. Why did you not tell me you had been to that fellow Graves? I had it all second-hand from Garton."

Robert bit his lip and looked a little annoyed.

"I did not see any good in telling you, Austin."

"Why not? I should have gone to the man myself if it had not been for Garton. Gar gave me an account of the whole affair verbatim."

Robert was silent. He particularly disliked being reminded of his good deeds. He was a man who would have followed literally the Divine exhortation "not to let his left hand know what his right hand doeth." He had not a grain of sympathy with the Pharisee of the present day; he would have hidden such things, if needs be, from the wife of his bosom; and, in truth, his acts of kindness were by no means rare. Women, in general, understood this reticence. He never shirked a duty, however difficult, if he had taught himself that it was a duty; but, all the time, he would make himself so disagreeable over it that, as Garton said, there was no bearing with him. He was quite on the *qui vive* to be disagreeable now.

"I must say that I think it was very noble of you."

"Pshaw! what nonsense, Austin."

"Very noble, indeed, considering the light in which you regard the whole affair. I don't think anything has pleased me so much for a long time. Belle has a right to be proud of you to-night."

Again Robert pished and pshawed.

"What a fuss you make about nothing," he observed brusquely; but, in spite of himself, he could not fail to be touched by his brother's honest praises.

"I think we shall get an apology out of him," he said presently; and his voice had lost its gruffness.

"He will not retract entirely, then?"

"Oh, as to that, I don't think we ought to expect it. I, for one, should hardly wish that," he added, with the truthfulness which seemed as inherent in him as it was in Rotha. There was a certain obstinacy of truth about both that would always come to the surface, even though it were to their own injury. "You see I could not conscientiously press for it."

"That is why it would have been better to have left it to me; not but what I should have found it quite as difficult as you did a few hours ago. Now of course it is different."

" How is it different?"

" Well, then I had my doubts in common with you; now I am satisfied that we have all of us been wrong."

" You believe in her innocence !"

" I would stake my life on it. My dear Robert, you have never made a greater mistake than you have committed there."

Robert looked at his brother and then walked away without saying a word; but, as he got to the door, he felt as though he had received a blow. He was a good man. He had done a generous thing that day, and he had done it well according to his light; but his brother's words were as gall and bitterness to him; and yet, at the same time, so strange are the workings of the human heart, the first faint doubt came to chill and harass him. Was it possible that they were all right and he wrong? Was not the suspicion bred merely of his own envy? But he stifled the feeling instantly; right or wrong—innocent or guilty—he knew he hated her, and he hated himself no less for his meanness of anger. He had got to the door when he remembered Belle, and came back to say good-night to her.

" My dear Bob, don't go away like this."

" We shall do no good by any further talking, Austin."

" There I am quite of your opinion. I suppose we must agree to differ a little longer."

" I shall certainly take the liberty to differ."

" Well, so shall I; but we need not quarrel over it. Life is too short for quarrels; give me your hand, dear old boy," and as Robert gave it to him and felt Austin's cordial grasp, the evil spirit seemed to pass out from him, and the old brotherly love took its place.

" Greater is he that ruleth his spirit than he that taketh a city "—the words kept haunting him as he turned the key in his door and went into his solitary ill-lighted room. He said them aloud once to get rid of them; but by and by, when he went up to his cheerless bedchamber, others seemed to replace them in his brain. They had chanted them last Sunday, he remembered, " How good and pleasant it is, brethren, to dwell together in unity."

" I don't believe there's such another good fellow as Austin in the whole world," he said, as he laid his head on his pillow. " I wonder what makes me such a bear to him?" and then, as he fell into a doze, he woke up with a start, for the sweet low refrain seemed floating close to his pillow—" Behold how good and pleasant it is, brethren, to dwell together in unity."

# CHAPTER XVIII.

> " What thou bidd'st
> Unargued I obey ; so God ordains ;
> God is thy law ; thou mine : to know no more
> Is woman's happiest knowledge and her praise."
>
> MILTON.

Two things happened that night, and both were fraught with con-sequences—Robert Ord had a terrible dream, and the Vicar proposed another tea-party.

Robert dreamt that he was in a place between two seas, and that the waves came lapping up slowly to his feet; and that the place was all barren and desolate, and full of shivering night-winds, while now and then a strange solemn music seemed to come from the stars and curdle his blood. And a voice said, "Look and see ;" and a whole chorus of whispering voices answered, "Look and see." And he thought that he was standing on a bank of gold and silver shells, and they were all breaking and crunching under his feet, so that there seemed no foothold for him. But as he stumbled among the shining heaps he saw a white dress floating down a narrow channel between two mountains ; and as it passed him he could see it was Belle, lying with her hands crossed on her bosom and her dead face turned up to the stars.

He thought that in his horror he plunged into the current and tried to catch her by her golden hair. He could feel distinctly the icy waters closing round his ankles and creeping above his knees ; and then it seemed darker and colder, and the stars went out, and a great hollow moaning of wind filled the cavern of the mountains, which seemed peopled with dark gibbering shapes ; and one of the shapes said—" Doré can paint the Inferno better than he can paint Paradise—he is of the earth earthy. The man is not born yet who can paint the seven palaces of the Infinite." And another shape said, " Are mysteries in the hands of madmen ? The earth is peopled with madmen ; there is one yonder trying to catch a

freed soul by the dripping of golden hair." And they all said,
"Look and see." And a sound of mocking laughter filled the air.
And the water came bubbling into his teeth, and he set them hard,
and said—

"This is the intermediate state, and I am the only living
man, and yonder is my dead love; but all the shadows of the
shadowy land itself shall not prevent my laying my head on her
breast."

And as he spoke his hands seemed full of damp straggling hair,
and it seemed to get about his face and neck, and choke him with
its wet coils; but he put it by, and stooped over her, and tried to
kiss her lips, and started away with a cry, for from the dead face
there were Rotha Maturin's living eyes looking reproachfully at
him with an awful smile in them.

And the cry woke him, and he saw it was the gray light of
morning, and got up and looked over the sand-hills to the dim
seaward line of froth and spray, and at the dim white roads, and
at the yellow flare of a distant lamp; and then he struck a light
and tried to read, but he could not get rid of the ghastly vision;
so when the day had fairly broken he dressed himself and went
out, and walked away into the country for miles, and brought back
ferns and wood-flowers, dripping with dew, and sent them to Belle,
who lay and looked at them all that day.

Meanwhile the Vicar had proposed another tea-party; and if a
thunderbolt had descended to her very feet Mrs. Ord could not
have looked more astonished.

"When did we give our last tea-party, Mary?" he said to her
that night, when she had returned from her usual pilgrimage to
Belle and the boys. Mary had her candle in her hand, and she
looked a little surprised as she prepared to extinguish it.

"I think it was about three weeks ago, Austin."

"Ah, that is short notice, certainly, but I don't see how we
can help ourselves. Well, we must give another, that is all." And
then it was that Mrs. Ord had sat down with that annihilated look
upon her face.

Now tea-parties were much thought about in Kirkby and
Blackscar; they were, in fact, the only dissipation in which the
inhabitants of the place greatly indulged; dinners were not much
in vogue—they were voted extravagant and a bore—and only the
very gay portion of the community gave dances; a few of the
parvenus, or here and there a naturalised stranger, would send out
cards of invitation for a dinner *à la Russe;* and there would be
cold soup and warm champagne, and lukewarm coffee to follow,
handed round by hired greengrocers in disguise; but the attempt

was rather coldly looked upon—the parvenus were called preten-
tious, and the naturalised stranger rather snubbed in consequence.
Mrs. Blake had certainly given several of a very superior description in the colonel's time, but since his death it had been understood that she had retired from the world as far as dinner-parties
were concerned; and Miss Brookes' poverty and single blessedness
accounted for her singular animadversions on the same subject.
People were not slow to understand that the leading ladies of the
place set their faces against them, and so it came to pass that tea
and muffins was the only form of refreshment that could be genteelly
offered to one's guests. As a matter of course every one, from the
greatest to the least, gave tea-parties; Kirkby, especially, fairly
steamed with them; in the season—which, by the way, lasted
from September to May—there was a perfect round of these festive
gatherings. But this was not all; there was as much fashion and
etiquette in the Kirkby tea-parties as in any Belgravian assembly;
it was quite amusing for a stranger to go the round of a season
and note the diversity of these entertainments.

There was Mrs. Stephen Knowles' kettledrums. Mrs. Knowles
was one of the naturalised strangers who would not be convinced
that dinners *à la Russe* were devices of the Evil One to entrap
unwary sinners to the much drinking of lukewarm champagne.
Mrs. Stephen Knowles was a little woman, but she waged a big
war—she would dine late, and she would put dahlias and nuts and
oranges in the place of vegetables, and the dingy greengrocer in
the white cotton gloves always cut up the joint at the side-table.
But after a time it did not do. Mrs. Stephen Knowles soon found
that people did not respond readily to her invitations; there were
gaps at her table—her choicest guests deserted her at the last
minute; and so it came about that she and her husband dined in
solitary grandeur, and Mrs. Knowles gave kettledrums, and the
greengrocer in the white cotton gloves handed about greasy muffins
at an early hour in the afternoon.

Then there were the Lancashire teas at the Traverses'; the
Traverses were Lancashire people, and always promoted eating and
drinking on a heavy style; people always lunched very early when
they came to the Traverses', that they might do justice to the
salmon and the cold game. The diversity of bread-stuff used to
create envy in the bosoms of more than one Kirkby housekeeper;
people did not mind the hot bread and cakes—every one made
cakes—but the fruit tarts were felt to be an eyesore; somebody
had heard Miss Brookes say that fruit tarts were vulgar. Mrs.
Travers used to lament loudly that no one did justice to her
daughter's pastry except the Vicar, who always partook of the

neglected dish and frequently asked for more ; but then the Vicar always would do as he liked.

Next to the Traverses came Nettie's "tea-kettle gossips," which were chiefly conspicuous for sweetmeats and scandal. Very snug little entertainments these, and very much in request ; and then there were Miss Brookes' evenings, to which people went once or twice in the winter, as a sort of duty—for about the same reason that induce other and more fashionable people to go to Court.

People did not enjoy these evenings, but they always went as a matter of course. Miss Brookes never regaled her guests with anything but the thinnest bread-and-butter and the plainest seed-cake. She thought eating and drinking vulgar, and said so openly at the Traverses' when she sent up her plate for more game, and there was not much conversation either ; the whist-table was the prevailing feature of the evening. Directly tea was over there was a general stir and shaking of silk and satin skirts—the genteel and frosty atmosphere thawed a little—the young people were set down to Pope Joan in one corner, while the elders shuffled and cut for partners, and played long whist for love with the utmost perseverance till the entrance of Miss Brookes' little maid with sandwiches and ginger wine warned them it was time to disperse.

But the tea-parties that were most greatly loved were those given at Mrs. Blake's and the Vicarage ; for a long time there was great indecision as to which should have the palm, but latterly people had decided in favour of the Vicarage. The parties at Oakmead, Mrs. Blake's house, were very nice—there could be only one opinion as to that ; it was very nice, for instance, to sit in a room with ruby velvet curtains, with a blazing fire, and an extravagant number of wax candles—Mrs. Stephen Knowles had once counted four-and-twenty. And it was very pleasant to drink one's tea out of real Dresden china ; the tea-table at Oakmead was the prettiest sight possible ; Mrs. Blake always presided over it herself in the good old-fashioned way, and the coachman and footman handed round the tea and coffee, and the gentlemen helped them. There was nothing stiff, in spite of the grandeur ; there were plenty of nice things, and people were expected to do justice to them. Sometimes cards would follow, but oftener there were games that should include the young people, who never felt in the way at Mrs. Blake's. When the Vicar was there it was understood that music was to be the order of the evening, and the young ones sang duets and glees, in their fresh young voices, under their hostess' gentle patronage. Sometimes she would prepare little surprises for them of hothouse fruit in the conservatory. There were all sorts of cosy nooks and corners about the long drawing-room. that made the young people very sociable. One or two very happy little understandings had grown out of these evenings, which gave rise to a report that Mrs. Blake was a match-maker.

But notwithstanding all these attractions the Vicarage carried off the palm : there was a hearty genial atmosphere there that people recognised and appreciated ; and then the Vicar was the perfection of a host.

Every one who came felt that he or she was separately and individually welcome, and that their comfort and entertainment were matters of importance in the eyes of the Vicar and his wife : no one was left out in the cold for a moment : shy new comers were entertained in corners by Mrs. Ord, and challenged and brought into notice by the Vicar ; young persons with a pet talent felt themselves of importance, and were ready to clear their throats or take off their gloves at the shortest notice ; silent people were paired off with talkative people. No one was neglected ; and, though cards were strictly forbidden, certainly no one found the time heavy on their hands. And then everything was so well ordered. Mary had the knack of making her rooms cosy—she liked plenty of light, though there were no wax candles. She and Belle were always busy days before concocting all manner of simple and inexpensive delicacies. Belle would dress the table with flowers and lights and evergreens. She had wonderfully skilful fingers, and would go quietly in and out, ordering things, while her sister sat talking among her guests ; Garton was very useful too in keeping the boys in order, and Robert, though he was generally quiet, looked very distinguished as he went about among the ladies saying civil things, and holding his head very high.

A tea-party at the Vicarage was therefore considered the most important event of the season, the only regret being that they were so few and far between. But both the Vicar and his wife had decided that they were expensive luxuries. Mary, with all her economy and management, found it very hard to make ends meet ; even candles and muffins cost something—the family would go without some trifling comforts for days after one of these simple feasts. She was beginning to be a little ashamed too of her one well-preserved silk dress. The Vicar had bought her a pretty cheap muslin, and in a fit of generosity she had made it over to Belle, alleging as an excuse, when Austin reproached her, that Belle had a lover, and was ten times worse off for dress than she. Belle had made up the dress herself, and had worn it to Robert's great delight, and he had bought her some ribbons to match. Belle had looked lovely, but the Vicar shook his head, and had been heard to mutter that there was more to be had of the same pattern; and now if they had another tea-party he would carry out this terrible threat.

Mrs. Ord was thinking of this when she sat with the extinguished look on her face.

"And, Mary, of course, I shall get you that dress."

"Oh, Austin, what nonsense!"

"What! is it not pretty enough? I declare I thought the pattern was lovely; you and Belle ought always to wear blue."

"The idea of comparing me to Belle—an old married woman like me."

"An old married fiddlestick——" But here we will not repeat all the Vicar said; there are some men so blind as to admire their own wives even after fifteen years, and the praises were just as sweet to Mary as when she first heard them; she would blush as brightly over them as ever she did then.

"But my dove-coloured silk is as good as ever," she pleaded. Oh Mary, Mary, how could you come out with such a fib, with the grease-spots in the front breadth that Mrs. Blake's maid with all her efforts could not remove? "At least—that is, it is quite presentable."

"I don't know that, my dear. I thought Belle said something about its being scanty, and you have worn it twice over everywhere. People must have new dresses sometimes," persisted the Vicar, knowing all the time that his best coat was getting sadly frayed at the edges and decidedly shiny at the elbows.

"But if we cannot afford it, love," reminded his wife gently— she knew all about the frayed edges, and would have gone in rags cheerfully if only Austin were well dressed. She had turned over the coat only the day before yesterday and noticed the shininess, and then he wanted those shirts so sadly. "I will have the dress in the spring if I want it, Austin," she continued. "Besides, I cannot wear blue just now."

"There was one with violet," he returned decidedly; "it was almost prettier than the blue, and perhaps you would not like to be the same as Belle. I shall go to Alison's to-morrow and order it," finished the Vicar, who was apt to be a little dictatorial on the subject of his wife's dress. Then Mary sighed, for she knew that her rash generosity had availed nothing.

"But, Austin, is it absolutely necessary that we should give another tea-party?" she asked, after a pause; for it just occurred to her that she had as yet said no word as to her husband's astounding proposition. But the Vicar, who had been waiting for some such word, answered her, with considerable briskness:

"Well, yes, Mary; I think I may say that it is absolutely necessary—at least, it appears so to me."

"But, Austin——"

"Well, my dear?"

"People will wonder so."

"Never mind that."

"And then I am so sure that we cannot afford it. How are the boys to have their new boots? and there is winter coming, and that heavy coal-bill not settled yet." Then, at the mention of the coal-bill, the Vicar did look somewhat grave.

"My dear wife, I am very sorry to worry you."

"Oh Austin!" with a deprecating blush.

"But I don't see how I can help myself. If you only knew how uncomfortably sore my conscience is about all this business. I have thought it over, and it seems so right that we should do this thing, even though we should have to pinch a little afterwards, Mary."

Mary assented rather doubtfully.

"Besides, I don't see that we need make it such an extravagant affair. Come, dear; don't you think you and Belle could contrive to entertain our friends at a very trifling expense?"

"Perhaps we might, if only——" and then Mary stammered and hesitated, and finally added, under her breath, "if only he would dispense with the dress."

She could have bitten her tongue before she had said the words, when she saw the grieved look on his face, and heard the tone in which he said, "Oh Mary, Mary!" She had her arms round his neck in a moment, so great was her penitence.

"Husband, I never meant to hurt you by refusing your gift."

"Nay, Mary, it is not that—why, what nonsense, love;" but for a moment he seemed to find it difficult to explain himself. "I suppose my pride needs this humbling; but to think I cannot lay out a few poor shillings on my wife's dress!" She heard him catch his breath quickly, and then he went on in his usual voice: "Do you think I don't see how the boys want their boots? I was lying awake for hours last night thinking of them and the coal-bill, Mary. Well, dearest, I was a poor man when you married me, but I never thought that the time would come when I could not afford my wife a gown."

Mary kept her arms still round his neck, but without a word. She was a woman who had the rare gift of knowing when to speak and when to be silent; these moments of depression were very unusual with the Vicar, whose sweet temper and almost childlike faith enabled him to rise above daily trials which would have crushed or subdued weaker men. He used to say that he was a poor priest who could not bear poverty uncomplainingly. One of his quaint sayings was that poverty was handed down with Apostolic succession, and that the poorer the priest the more was he in accordance with the primitive custom of the early Church, "whose ministers worked with their hands." "Grand hands," he would say, "that could sew the rough canvas of a tent, lay lightly on the sick with healing touch and dispense the bread of life. Now, when the poor wretches crowd about us for alms, and we can truly say, 'silver and gold have we none,' no halting cripple springs into renewed life and vigour at our touch ; and yet such as we have—our daily life, our strength, the labour of our brains, the fervour of our prayers, the purity and weakness of our efforts, the patient endurance of our infirmities, 'such as we have we give unto you.'"

It was a charity sermon for the Convalescent Home, and he had ended his discourse with some such words as these. Many of the patients had heard him ; and some remember to this day the long wistful look of tenderness that accompanied his words, and how he stretched out his hands over them as though to evoke the Healer. . Nor was it the sick only who shared his sympathy—he was one who had learnt by experience the black woes of poverty, and who owned that Christ's poor ought to be ranked among the "noble army of martyrs."

"We think too much of the stake and the faggot, and the cleansing-fire, and the white robes washed in blood," he said once, "and all the while Christ's poor—the little ones and the old, and the women—the women, Mary—are all out in the cold—stumbling on in the darkness ; from dreary morning to hopeless night, working and toiling, not for comforts, but that they may keep their wretched body and still more wretched soul together, and no one tells them that they are martyrs." And when he had spoken like this, he would push away his cup or plate, and go down to the school, and gather all the little ones around him and tell them of the Child who lay one winter's night in a manger, and who, when a man, wrought out His Divine ministries, and lived and died the World's Wonder, having nowhere to lay His head."

Mary had often been strengthened by her husband's teaching ; but now and then he would tell her, still in the quaint phraseology which was at times habitual to him, that his "manna-pot was empty and all its sweetness gone ;" and she would understand that things had gone heavily with him, and that for the time her Samson was shorn of his strength. "The Philistines are upon me to-day, Mary," he would say, when the evidences of his poverty were unusually crushing. "I must leave off writing sermons just now, and let you and the boys preach to me." And he would come in and sit silently in her room, or let the boys coax him to join in their games, till the bitter mood was over, and he could assure her, with the sweet brave smile which always made her lip tremble, that her " Richard was himself again."

She drew her hand now across his forehead, with a touch as though she would smooth out the deep wrinkles, but she knew better than to speak to him—this woman, who was so wise and tender in her love. Another time she would talk to him cheerfully, and tell him, as she had told him many times, that she wore her old stuff gown as proudly for his sake as she would have worn silks and jewels if he had given them her, and another time he would believe her ; but just now she knew his heart was wounded past its usual patience at the thought that he must deny this trifling gift to the woman he loved ; and yet that he would deny himself and her she had not a doubt. So she only stood beside him quietly smoothing out the furrows with her soft hands.

" Very well, Mary," he said at last, and speaking as though he were very tired, " it shall be as you wish. We will make as little fuss as possible over this tea-party, and you shall do without the dress." And Mary's thanks were as gratefully spoken as though he had endowed her with some costly gift.

For the next few days Kirkby was in a state of unusual excitement, which the news of a second tea-party at the Vicarage was not at all calculated to allay. On the receipt of the invitation Mrs. Stephen Knowles had put on her bonnet and stepped across to her dear friend Mrs. Travers, where, in spite of the earliness of the hour, a choice clique, composed of the Misses O'Brien, the Montague Thompsons, and Nettie Underwood were already assembled, all discussing the two absorbing topics of the day—the extraordinary letter in the *Blackscar Herald,* and the little less extraordinary invitation to the Vicarage.

The first of these topics had already been discussed, the chief speaker being Miss Matilda O'Brien, an elderly young lady, of the class Albert Smith has immortalised as the " Prancers," and whose remarks were always more or less acid. Miss O'Brien had been holding forth on this occasion till her temper had become decidedly acerbated, chiefly owing to Nettie throwing in a contumacious " Fudge," after the manner of the renowned Mr. Burchell, sometimes elongated into the feminine and somewhat striking interjection, " Fiddle-de-dee."

" Fiddle-de-dee, Mattie," repeated Nettie rather loudly, at this juncture ; " you may say what you like, but I am not going to believe all that trash."

"I do hope you are wrong, Mat," suggested her sister humbly. Kitty O'Brien was a poor sickly cripple, very young and weak, and was generally understood to be snubbed by her elder sister.

"It is no good giving your opinion, Kitty," returned Miss Mattie sharply, "every one knows you always differ from me on principle. I say again, it is a very strange proceeding of the Vicar's, asking all the leading ladies of his congregation to meet so soon again at his house. Mark my words, girls, we shall hear the rights of the matter that evening."

"Do you really think so, Miss Mattie?" asked Mrs. Stephen Knowles eagerly, untying her bonnet-strings, with the notion evidently that they were like ideas, and were all the better for being loosened. Mrs. Knowles' bonnet-strings were always more or less in a state of crumple.

"Think it, Mrs. Knowles? I am sure of it; it is no good, Nettie, saying fudge and nonsense. Of course the Vicar would not leave an influential parishioner unvisited if it were not for some wise purpose, and he has asked us to tea just as a sort of pretence to get us all together and warn us against having anything to do with Bryn and Miss Maturin; and I for one must say that I never liked the look of her. Those pale down-looking women never have much good in'them."

"Oh, and you begged and prayed me to take you to Bryn!" exclaimed Nettie. "You ought to be ashamed of yourself, Mattie." And Nettie, who had remained staunch to her new friend in spite of the animadversions of her clique, grew so very scornful and personal in her remarks that by general consent the subject was abruptly changed, to be resumed on the earliest opportunity. Indeed it would not be too much to say that during the few days that still intervened before the evening in question the one half of the female population of Kirkby was for ever putting on its bonnet to call on the other half with any morsel or crumb of gossip that could be gleaned on the subject.

Of course many curious facts leaked out. Two figures, one very much resembling Garton Ord, who in his cassock and round hat looked not unlike one of the wooden Shems in Noah's Ark, had been seen in the twilight walking in the direction of Bryn; but as the Miss Travers who vouched for the truth of the incident was shortsighted, and was supposed, indeed, to be blind of one eye, no one attached much importance to her story; but a greater excitement ensued when her sister Amy declared that from the top window of their house she had seen Miss Maturin distinctly walking in the rabbit-warren with the Vicar.

"Depend upon it, my dear, he was giving her ghostly counsel

and advice," said Mattie O'Brien in a tone that made every one jump—it was so suggestive. Kitty looked up with her sharp bright eyes, but said nothing.

In point of fact the lame girl knew more about it than they supposed. In her halting way she knew a good deal of the movements of other people. Walking down the sea-wall she had met the party coming up from the sands. The Vicar had his four boys with him; and Miss Maturin held Arty by the hand. She might have added that Rotha had rosy cheeks, and was laughing merrily; but of late Kitty had never added her yea and nay to the village gossip. Perhaps she had found it useless to differ from her sister; or perhaps she had grown indifferent to the trivialities of her daily life; or it might be that the sharp bright eyes had learnt to look higher—since Kitty had known the sad truth that her halting footsteps would soon cease altogether, and that she must lay aside her crutches soon at the entrance of the dark valley.

Kitty and the Vicar were great friends, and he nodded brightly enough to her when they met that evening.

"Father says that Kitty O'Brien will soon sit at the 'Gate Beautiful,'" said Arty, in a tone loud enough to reach the lame girl.

"Hush! Arty; oh, Arty, hush!" cried Rotha, as she looked wistfully after the little shrunken figure.

Kitty gave a brisk little nod all to herself when they had gone out of sight, but there were tears in her eyes too.

"'They shall mount up with wings like eagles:' ah, that is what he said last Sunday; and then when he spoke of the 'Gate Beautiful' he looked at me. Well, the sooner it is over the better. It is just the dip and the first touch of the cold water that is so bad; but I shall ask him to keep near me and hold my hand. I daresay it is only a childish fancy—Mat would laugh at it—but I think I could die more easily if he would hold my hand."

Long before some very sad events that changed the aspect of this story took place, poor little Kitty O'Brien had her wish.

"When it grows dark still hold my hand and say the 'Lighten our darkness' out loud, please," she said to him; and the Vicar, who understood the feeble childishness of the petition, assented, and held the little hand in his as the dying girl went out through the cold and darkness and into the light beyond. Somehow, after that, he always used that collect for light by other death-beds.

And the short-sighted Miss Travers had been right, after all. Garton Ord had met Rotha at the lich-gate one evening after service, and had walked with her to her own door, and this time Rotha had not been shy with him.

"I wish I had been at the Vicarage the other evening," he

had begun, in his usual abrupt fashion—Robert always found fault with his abruptness—"I think it was a capital idea, Austin bringing you in like that, without fuss or ceremony. It must have made you feel at home directly."

"I won't say that," returned Rotha, smiling, "but it made me very happy."

Somehow, since that evening that they had talked about windmills, she had felt very grateful and friendly to the poor fellow, who seemed in everybody's way, and who yet had no place of his own. She seemed to understand by a sort of dim instinct that he was not one whom the world had surrounded by a visible halo of success, but she liked him very much in spite of that; and had he not been the first to own her innocence?

"It was so honest of him to tell me that he differed from his brother," she thought, when she recalled the conversation; and so her heart was very soft to him.

"There is no need for me to tell you how good your brother is," she continued after that expression as to happiness; "I only wish I did not feel so overwhelmingly grateful."

"I don't believe there's such another fellow as Austin," burst out honest Gar enthusiastically, and unconsciously echoing Robert's words.

"No, indeed; but then you are all so good."

"All?—not Robert, I suppose?"

"Why not Robert?" asked Rotha innocently, repeating the name; "I hope you don't think I exclude him because he is still a little hard to me. His hardness is certainly a misfortune, but then think how I have wronged him."

"Wronged him, my dear Miss Maturin?" and Garton faced round on her in the dark road with the utmost astonishment.

"Innocently, of course," she returned, colouring deeply; "and his unfortunate prejudice has undoubtedly caused me great unhappiness; but I don't mean to fret about it any more. I am sure it will all come right."

"I wish there were more like you," returned Garton, striking his hands together, and squaring his shoulders. "I would give something for a little of your charity, Miss Maturin. Robert tries my temper more than any one."

"That is because you do not understand each other," she answered in a quiet old-fashioned way, as though she were older than the young man before her, who was trying to time his impetuous strides to her even footsteps; "of course I don't know much, but, from the little I have seen, I should think you must be like flint and steel to each other."

14

"Robert must be the steel, then, ha! ha!" laughed Garton. "I wish he could hear you say that. Polished and cool, that's just what he is. Miss Maturin, you are a keen observer."

"I hope you don't think me impertinent," said Rotha, as she echoed the laugh—Garton's boyish "ha! ha!" was so very infectious. She could see the brown face and the white teeth gleaming in the dim light. Up in the sky the stars were coming out by twos and threes. How many nights ago was it since she sat looking at the reflections of the stars in the waters, and hearing Arty say his prayers—how many? What did it matter—what did anything matter since she was so very, very happy?

# CHAPTER XIX.

## THE VICAR'S ATONEMENT.

" Page.—Madam, there is a lady in your hall
    Who begs to be admitted to your presence.
Lady.—Is it one of our invited friends ?
Page.—No ; far unlike to them.   A stranger.
Lady.—How looks her countenance ?
Page.—So queenly, so commanding, and so noble,
    I shrunk at first in awe ; but when she smiled
    Methought I could have compass'd sea and land,
    To do her bidding."

BAILLIE.

WHILE Kirkby thought and spoke of little else but the tea-party
at the Vicarage, Rotha looked forward to the eventful evening with
mingled feelings of pleasure and pain : on the whole the pain predominated.   There were times when an absolute dread took
possession of her, when she thought of the ordeal that awaited
her.   There was nothing for it but to turn her attention resolutely
to other things, and to do her daily work so thoroughly and heartily
as to leave no time for cowardly reflections.

Rotha despised half measures.   She was very intolerant of
herself and other people in such matters.   She was aware that she
drove her chariot-wheels heavily just now, but she drove on for
all that.   On the night before the party she went to bed quaking
in every limb, and cried herself to sleep, as a means of keeping up
her courage ; and in the morning she woke up with a firm belief
that she was pre-ordained to martyrdom.   She carried this conviction in her face to the breakfast-table.

Some hours after, when she had stitched a collar of a surplice
upside down, and had tried to translate a piece of crabbed German,
and had not made sense out of a single sentence, she came down
ready dressed for the evening, and asked Meg, with a lurking
smile, whether she would do.

Meg, who was very short-sighted, put up her eye-glasses and
looked her over—to use idyllic language, much as "careful robins

eye the delver's toil"—and then dropped them again with a dissatisfied look. Rotha looked wofully pale, and wore her old black silk.

"Not a flower—not a trinket," grumbled Meg.

Rotha stood up very slim and straight under the reproof. "Not the vestige of an ornament," went on Mrs. Carruthers discontentedly.

"Criminals ought not to be decked out with ornaments when they are brought before the bar," returned Rotha gravely; "it is true victims were garlanded for sacrifice under the old dispensation, but not the new dispensation victim of the Old Bailey."

"My dear, what a ghastly joke"—and Meg dropped her eyeglasses and then picked them up with a frightened air—Rotha was decidedly odd to-day. "You forget this is to be the evening of your triumph."

"Meg, do you recollect the story of Haman?"

Mrs. Carruthers shook her head—her wits were wool-gathering to-night. Rotha laughed good-humouredly as she smoothed Meg's sandy hair and tucked in a loose end. Meg wore her hair in thin ropes and braids, and in truth its colour was not unlike tow.

"For shame, Meg, do you ever read your Bible—I mean the story of Haman, the son of Hammedatha the Agagite?"

"My dear Rotha, are you sure you are well?"

"You mean I am rather odd; don't be afraid to mention the word. If you are nervous, never mind Haman for the present, though I confess my thoughts are still running on Mordecai the Jew. My mention of the Old Bailey offended you; I know nothing at all about the Old Bailey, but, all the same, I did feel such a criminal as I dressed myself."

"Rotha, if you would but be sensible."

"Impossible, Meg; just think of the twelve jurymen—jury-women, I mean—who are to sit on my case presently, and the grim leading counsel at their head; it does not matter a bit just now that the judge—my judge—has acquitted me, he'll have to take his notes all the same; and you ask me after that to take pride in dressing myself."

"I think, if I were you, I should wear the symbol of my innocence," remarked Meg obscurely. The speech was somewhat metaphorical, and had reference to a certain white dress which was laid out mysteriously in Rotha's room; it had been ordered for this evening, but at the last moment she had chosen to indulge this grim fancy.

"Presently—by and by," replied Rotha, who understood the metaphor perfectly; "not while waiting for the verdict though.

Wouldn't the twelve jurymen—jurywomen, I mean—be astonished if I were suddenly to pop up during tea and say, 'Not guilty, my Lord,' and the other learned gentleman knows it? How the Vicar and the leading counsel would stare!"—and Rotha, who had worked herself gradually into this rash humour, and was as tired as heart could wish, laughed over this wretched little farce of hers till Meg scolded and reasoned her into gravity.

She was as grave and inanimate as the seven sleepers when she entered the Vicarage drawing-room. She had stipulated some days ago that she was to be the first visitor, so only the family were assembled.

It was odd that the Vicar should also notice her dearth of ornament. Rotha's appearance must have been rather striking in its simplicity. She had put back her hair from her face too—always a hazardous experiment with thin faces: before she had been five minutes in the room he had taken out a handful of ferns and late scarlet geranium and had desired Mary to pin them in her dress.

"Flowers for girls, and jewels for married women, and both for the mistress of Bryn," remarked the Vicar oracularly, from his favourite platform the rug; and, despite his whimsical smile, Rotha read a rebuke in his eyes—whether from that or the flowers she had no lack of colour now; she understood that he also would have had her dressed as though for a triumph.

Robert, who was holding some silk for Belle, looked up at his brother's speech, and what he saw greatly surprised him; yes, it was true—she had no ornament, not even a ring, nothing but a silver brooch, which she might have picked up anywhere for a few shillings. Was this artifice—was she studying effect? No, he could not but acknowledge to himself that this might possibly be an evidence of good taste. What would have been his feelings if she had come there decked with the Ord jewels?

How well he remembered them! He could go over the whole list in his mind now. How often, as a boy, he had stood by Aunt Charlotte's dressing-table, turning out the casket with rough boyish hand, half-disdaining and half-admiring the glittering baubles. What wonderful emerald and diamond rings she had worn on her fingers; and there was the pearl necklace, which she used to tell him should be his wife's on her wedding-day, "providing I approve of her, Robbie dear," she would add, "and I hope she will have a pretty white neck to set off the pearls." And then she would go on to tell him that she would lend her her favourite set of rubies on the day when she went to Court, "for a lady ought always to pay that homage to her Sovereign," and, added Aunt Charlotte, "I shall see that your wife is not remiss in her duty as an Englishwoman."

"If I have a wife, and she goes to Court," remarked Master Bob stoutly, "I hope she won't wear those dirty yellow lace flounces that you did, Aunt Charlotte, and I think those red stones hideous."

"That's because you are such a very, very little boy," answered his aunt; but she had looked rather affronted, nevertheless; what a sad scapegrace he had been, to be sure. He recollected very well her coming into his room one night with those same red stones shining in her gray hair, half hidden under the rare old lace, and she wore more on her throat and arms. He must have been ill, he thought, and feverish, for he called her a hag and Medusa, and pushed her away, screaming that he could see the red tongues of the snakes in her hair, and she had pulled them out, crying that she was a miserable old woman, and that her boy did not know her —that her Robbie, her darling, was dying. He was stabbing himself with these memories, and growing very stern over them, when a singular interruption occurred. Belle left off winding the silk in some displeasure. Mary had asked her and Rotha Maturin to go downstairs and arrange the flowers for the tea-table—a finishing task that Belle had always been accustomed to do alone.

Belle could hardly believe her ears, but Rotha rose at once— as usual her quick instinct comprehended the little ruse. She gave the Vicar a pleased look as he opened the door for her; and Belle, with a bad grace, had to follow.

So far as sociability was concerned, the plan did not answer at all. Rotha soon discovered that Belle was one who liked a monopoly even of labour, so she soon gave up her arrangement of vases and dishes, and watched Belle's nimble fingers instead.

And she found out three things.

She noticed first that, though Belle had never looked more beautiful than on this evening, there was a strange wanness and shadow over her beauty which was quite indescribable; secondly, that as she moved about she kept her hand to her side, as though in habitual pain—she did it very quietly, as though to avoid notice, but the movement spoke volumes; thirdly, putting two and two together—the wanness and the pain—she took it into her head that what seemed sullenness was in reality repressed suffering; and so she arrived at the conclusion that, in spite of her evenness and repellent manners, Belle Clinton was at heart a loving woman.

And she noticed something else; she had detected two or three times a sad wistfulness in Belle's large dark eyes whenever she fixed them on her lover's face; and as she went downstairs she said this singular thing to herself—"Belle Clinton's love for Robert Ord is a suffering, and she knows it; there is no happiness in her face;" and then, "Robert Ord is a very noble lover, he has given freely everything he held most precious, except his heart; and he thinks he has given that, but he is wrong."

There are strange surprises in life—quick revelations. A stranger will at times grasp a mystery of years; sudden flashes reveal a chasm. This girl, who had never loved, never tasted the sweet-bitter experience of womanhood, who had led such a strangely repressed existence, realised in a moment the twofold suffering of Belle Clinton's life.

And, being a keen observer, she read the mystery two ways, but it was but a sudden lightning flash that made the rift in the clouds. By and by, as the clouds broke, she read it all clearly enough.

It was dreary work standing by and doing nothing. Belle was unusually taciturn; her position thoroughly displeased her. She was angry with Mary and Austin for making her a party to the ruse; she answered only in monosyllables to Rotha's admiring ejaculations. Girls seldom found Belle Clinton communicative. Rotha offered once to relieve her of a heavy vase. "Do let me carry it; it is easy to see you have a pain in your side," she said.

"Oh, that is nothing; I'm used to it," was the indifferent reply, but the observation evidently annoyed her.

"Pain is not a pleasant companion," returned Rotha cheerfully; "you are not very strong, Mrs. Ord says. She tells me that you work too much."

"Oh, Mary is always croaking. Don't you think it better to wear out than rust out, Miss Maturin?"

"When a life depends upon us, I think it is best to do neither," observed Rotha simply. She would speak the truth that was in her, even to this singular girl. Belle looked up in astonishment at the earnest tone. "It seems to me that people are often working when they had better be playing, and so they miss the salt and the sunshine of life. It is not every one who has learnt to play properly."

Belle did not answer, but Rotha fancied she heard a sigh, and then Garton and the four boys came in, and Rotha's brief penance was over.

Rotha was a great boy-lover, and she had long desired to make acquaintance with the curly-headed denizens of the Vicarage. She had been much struck by Guy's handsome face, and even loose-limbed Rufus had come in for a share of her admiration; but Laurie had taken her fancy most; she had singled him out from the rest of the choir before she knew who he was, and had spoken of him to Meg as "the little king;" the sobriquet had been suggested by the boy's sleepy grace of movement, and a certain proud carriage of the head as he walked up to his place in the choir stalls.

The boys know Rotha pretty well by this time. They were very sociable well-mannered lads, Guy especially, and so in five minutes they were all quite at their ease, and "the little king" was retailing an anecdote with great gusto.

"Who is that dark-complexioned boy who is so often with you of an evening?" asked Rotha, when Laurie had, with much absence of mind, left his anecdote to be finished by his elder brothers. Garton and the boys exchanged glances at Rotha's question, and Garton laughed guiltily.

"Do you like boys, Miss Maturin?" asked Garton as he administered a warning shake to Guy.

"Indeed I do," returned Rotha warmly; "but the boy I am asking about does not seem to me to be a gentleman's son—he is a bright-eyed intelligent lad, in a rough coat like a sailor's."

"That's Garton's Shadow," called out Guy, closing with his uncle in rather a summary manner—"we've nicknamed him Gar's Shadow, for short. He is a regular David, is that fellow. Come on now, if you want to argue," he continued, doubling up his fist in a tempting manner; but Garton manacled him in a moment.

"Peace, my son! we must have no sparring in a lady's presence. Miss Maturin, if these lads will be quiet, I will answer your question. The boy's name is Reuben Armstrong, and he is the best and the most unhappy boy in the parish. Now, Rufus, we don't want any of your remarks."

"Garton is afraid we're going to peach. Don't be nervous, my dear boy," remarked Guy soothingly, and Rufus grumbled out:

"Oh, we're nobody; don't take any notice of us. We haven't got a drunken father who beats us and throws us out of window —oh no!" And a sudden chorus of "Oh noes," uttered ironically by the other boys, brought Aunt Belle on the tapis, with a stern admonition to be quiet.

"Boys, do behave yourselves. Garton, you don't keep them a bit in order; what will Miss Maturin think?"

Miss Maturin evidently thought it good fun enough. For the time being she had forgotten all about the twelve jurywomen, who were unshawling at that moment in Mrs. Ord's room. Arty was on her lap examining the workings of her watch. "And, do you know, it was a silver watch like Garton's," Guy informed his father afterwards; and "the little king's" fair head was very close to her shoulder, and so she looked very happy. Garton, lounging against the mantelpiece in his shabby coat, caught himself wondering again why the women thought Rotha Maturin so plain. "They couldn't have seen that pretty dimple when she laughs," he said to himself. "I like her face ever so much better than Belle's—Belle never laughs."

Belle moved away again when she had made her protest. The lads' merriment generally wearied her.

"Don't put yourself out, Aunt Belle," Guy had remarked patronisingly; "Rufus and I will keep him in order. Is there any other information that you want respecting 'the Shadow,' Miss Maturin?"

"He is rather a substantial shadow," laughed Rotha. "He is a broad-shouldered, thick-set lad enough. No, Guy, I won't ask any more questions, as it seems a sore subject."

"The boys are jealous," interposed Garton.

Another scornful chorus, culminating in "Oh yes" and "are we?" which reaches Mother Mary's ear, and causes her to say that the boys are enjoying themselves somewhere, and would Austin go and look after them.

"By and by," remarks the Vicar. "Mrs. Blake and Miss Brookes are not yet arrived, and the moment for the *coup d'œil* has not yet come."

"Uncle Gar saved Reuben's life," observed Laurie, absently deserting his brother's side and going over to the enemy. "Reuben was out among the rocks, and got out of his depth, and cramp came on; and Uncle Gar jumped in in his long coat, just as he is, and brought him out."

"That's enough—shut up, Laurie;" but Laurie chose to prose on in his gentle way.

"It was awfully deep; and the water got into Uncle Gar's clothes; and he could hardly drag Reuben, he was so heavy. Aunt Belle saw it all from the shore; didn't you, Aunt Belle?"

"Yes, Laurie," returned Belle, with a shiver, "and I never expected to see either of them again."

"Yes; and she said Reuben looked like death when Uncle Gar carried him in; and we've called him 'the Shadow' ever since, haven't we, Rufus?"

"Laurie, if you say another word I will double your Latin Delectus to-morrow."

"No, no—he has told it so prettily," pleaded Rotha, looking up respectfully to the hero of Laurie's tale. "What a brave thing! No wonder the boy is fond of you, when you have saved his life."

"He has no one else to love," replied Garton, with a sudden reddening over his sunburnt face at Rotha's praise; and then the Vicar came in.

He looked rather amused at the little group.

"Arty, you rogue, you are up to mischief, as usual. Come, Miss Maturin, you and Belle have done your work well, and I am going to take you upstairs."

Rotha rose without a word. It was a positive fact she shut her eyes when the Vicar opened the drawing-room door, though she opened them again directly. She said afterwards that it was the longest room she had ever walked up in her life; and that she was sure that for the moment the twelve or thirteen ladies were quadrupled in her eyes. Meg told her, when they talked the little scene over, that when she entered the room she looked so white that she was afraid she was going to faint, but that her bearing was grand almost to haughtiness.

"You have no idea of the majestic way you bowed to Miss Brookes, and you looked so tall—oh, ever so much taller, Rotha."

Rotha had no conception of the way she looked. All manner of introductions were going on; there was a general stir and movement. The Misses Travers were rustling their new blue dresses in quite a deafening manner; Mrs. Stephen Knowles' garnet-coloured satin came into most unbecoming juxtaposition with Miss O'Brien's canary silk. In the midst of the turmoil Nettie rushed forward and kissed her, and tore a yard and a half of her muslin flounce in making room for Aunt Eliza. In the little sympathising hubbub that ensued Rotha found herself in a seat by Mrs. Ord, with the Vicar whispering something into her ear.

"You are a brave woman," said the voice, "and our little *coup d'œil* is over."

Rotha drew a long breath, as though she had come out of some deep water, and then she was herself again.

She could look round quietly now. She was quite fenced in by her friends. The Vicar still kept his position at the back of her chair, and Aunt Eliza was on the other side. Nettie, as she pinned up her dilapidated flounce, talked across to her with studied cheerfulness.

"Somebody else besides Nettie Underwood likes surprises," she said, with a meaning look at the Vicar.

The Vicar laughed, and glanced merrily over the discomfited heads of ladies, whispering among themselves, and glancing askance at the unexpected guest; but Miss Brookes disdained whispers.

"Some people like anything theatrical," she observed in rather a loud key.

"Mary, I believe Miss Brookes is dying for her tea. Robert, my dear fellow, make yourself useful among the ladies—there are no gentlemen to-night, you know. Miss Maturin, allow me to take you down." It was really very cunning of the Vicar, as his wife told him afterwards, for Miss Brookes was bent on making herself disagreeable.

Rotha felt quite at her ease sitting between the Vicar and Garton, with Aunt Eliza's kind face opposite. It was perfectly evident now to all the ladies that the obnoxious Miss Maturin was the Vicar's most favoured guest of the evening. Had he not caused her to take precedence of Mrs. Colonel Blake, a privilege never before accorded to any unmarried lady? and had he not placed her in the seat of honour at his right hand? and did not Garton Ord stretch out a long arm everywhere to secure if possible a Benjamin's mess of such good things as the table furnished? Certainly, if the Vicar had wished to create a sensation by this novel surprise which he had prepared for them, most clearly he need not be disappointed, for a more crestfallen and disconsolate set of women could not be seen anywhere; nevertheless, as the Vicar looked at Miss Brookes, he was not quite at ease in his mind.

He had told himself that this tea-party would achieve a perfect success, and that there would be no need for him to say a single word; he would contrive it so that the fact of their reconciliation with Rotha Maturin should be patent to all eyes. He had hoped so at least, for his own and Rotha's sake, seeing that the saying of such words could not be pleasant; but what if Miss Brookes should compel him to abandon this silence? The thought made him a little anxious in spite of himself.

Mary, at her end of the table, was not a whit happier in her mind; before five minutes were over she was quite sure that Miss Brookes was bent upon making herself most thoroughly disagreeable. From the moment the Vicar had entered with Miss Maturin on his arm, that good lady had arrived at an alarming state of rigidity; so extremely angular had she become that her lace shawl could not retain its position at all, but kept slipping from her shoulders, and had to be held on by the elbows in a most graceless fashion. In vain had Mrs. Ord tried to engage her in conversation; Miss Brookes' steely glances would rove to the other end of the table, where Rotha sat looking very quiet and happy under the Vicar's wing.

"Hem," coughed Miss Brookes, rather more loudly than was consistent with a baronet's first cousin; Mary in an agony telegraphed signals of distress to Robert, who either could not or would not understand them.

"Hem," again coughed Miss Brookes, and this time Rotha did unfortunately look up, and was nailed at once by one of the steely glances.

"Did you speak to me?" asked Rotha timidly, and changing colour. She did not much like raising her voice, even now, before the twelve jurywomen; a dim suspicion came across her that the deep waters were not passed yet.

"I was trying to attract your attention certainly," returned Miss Brookes, coolly dropping her eye-glass, and once more trying to arrange her shawl round her shoulders. "One needs a speaking-trumpet across such a long table. I was only going to observe that you have very soon changed your mind."

"Miss Maturin is not a Quaker," remarked the Vicar, promptly coming to the rescue. "I thought ladies were always allowed to change their mind."

"Not without good reason, Vicar," returned Miss Brookes sharply. She always addressed the Vicar somewhat familiarly, and just now she resented his interference. "Young people will have whims and fancies sometimes, but it is possible to carry them too far, as in this instance."

"In what instance? Suppose we change the subject, Miss Brookes."

"Miss Brookes means when I refused Mrs. Blake's invitation," returned Rotha, colouring deeply. "I am very sorry to appear so rude."

"Appearances are deceitful sometimes," moralised the Vicar. He did not like the course the conversation had taken, but it was too late to check it.

"Appearances were certainly not in Miss Maturin's favour in this instance," remarked Miss Brookes, with a scornful laugh that chilled Rotha. "My dear, when you used that singular expression to Mrs. Colonel Blake the other day—you remember the expression, Catharine, that Miss Maturin used—that you could not go into society, we hardly expected to meet you here this evening."

"I daresay not, Miss Brookes."

"No, indeed; and it was just after Nettie Underwood's tea-party, too, that Mrs. Colonel Blake asked you."

"Yes, I was so very, very sorry to have to refuse," began poor Rotha, "but—but"—but the Vicar again came to her relief. "But circumstances over which she had no control prevented her from availing herself of the pleasure, et cetera, et cetera. Never mind excuses, Miss Maturin, they are mischievous things; if Mrs. Blake will give me the favour of five minutes' conversation after tea, I'll undertake to set you right with her, and the next time she asks us both to Fairmeads we will go. I'll promise her that."

The shawl had slipped down again, and Miss Brookes gave her head a displeased toss. The Vicar had tackled her successfully this time; but that she was meditating an assault in a fresh place was evident; and the Vicar groaned inwardly as he passed up his cup to be replenished.

No; there was no help for it, he must perform his penance thoroughly; so he made a face at Arty, who had found his way to Miss Maturin's lap, and in another moment he was on his feet.

"Ladies and Gentlemen,—I ought to say ladies, as the gentlemen are limited this evening to my brothers and my four worshipful sons,—I know it is not the fashion to christen a Kirkby tea-party— except, perhaps, a select few—such as Mrs. Stephen Knowles, for example, who is fashionable, and gives kettledrums, and Miss Nettie Underwood, who has delightful tea-kettle gossips; but still it is not an ordinary custom. Now, if I were inclined to christen this particular tea-party, do you know what I should call it?"

A pause, a subdued rustling among the younger jurywomen, and then Arty shouts out, "Call it the 'Old Ladies' Feast,' father," and is promptly suppressed by Garton—so promptly, indeed, that he chokes, and has to be patted on the back. The Vicar waits a minute till Mary's maternal alarms for her youngest-born subside, and then he begins afresh—he is warming to his work. Rotha looks up at him anxiously.

"No, Arty, my boy, I would not call it the 'Old Ladies' Feast,' because there are no old ladies here. When you have lived a little longer, Arty, you will know that ladies never grow old. If I were to christen my tea-party, I should give it a better name than that —I should call it 'The Vicar's Atonement.'"

Great excitement in the jury-box—Miss Brookes dropped her shawl for the ninth time, and looks across at Robert, who is frowning at his plate; Belle is playing with the trinkets of her watch-chain; Rotha leans back in her chair, so that Garton's broad shoulders may shield her from notice—she has not a vestige of colour; perhaps Garton understands the movement, for he keeps his arms still on the table. As for the Vicar, he has what Guy called "his grand preaching look" on his face, and is waxing very big—he had made up his mind to the work, and is quite warm now.

"Yes, I should call it 'The Vicar's Atonement.' Why, you dear people, you have no idea what a culprit I have felt for this last week. Isn't it next Sunday that I shall have to preach my sermon on charity? Sunday next, isn't it, Gar? Well, I'll not shirk it; it is not my way to shirk anything, and I hope you will all listen to me most attentively. But remember this, that I shall be preaching every word to myself, as well as to you. If I did not think that, I should just take the thirteenth chapter of Corinthians and read it all through without another word."

"Oh, Mr. Ord!" interrupted one young jurywoman bashfully —Amy Travers by name—a silly young thing of nine-and-twenty.

"Who was that who spoke? Yes, indeed, Miss Travers; and I daresay the consciences of a great many amongst us will not be quite free on that occasion. I daresay there has been plenty of silly things said in many drawing-rooms this week. About that wretched letter in the *Blackscar Herald,* for example; I daresay you've said a few things yourself, Miss Amy, that you would not have cared for Miss Maturin and me to have heard—eh, ladies?" (Unmistakable confusion in the jury-box; the leading counsel frowns more darkly over his plate, and Miss Brookes watches him.) The Vicar has his eye on both, but he does not look once at Rotha, shrinking under cover of Garton's broad shoulder, but Garton still keeps his arm on the table.

"Bless you, we know all about it," continues the Vicar, "and that makes me feel so guilty. Mary there will tell you how sore I have been. I feel it was such a shabby thing of us allowing this coolness to spring up just because poor old Aunt Charlotte chose to treat Robert so badly; but as Miss Maturin has forgiven us, I need say nothing more about that, except to express our grief for the sad mischief to which our coolness has led; that, I confess, has given me great uneasiness."

"Who wrote the letter, Vicar?" The question was in Miss Brookes' sharp voice.

"My dear Miss Brookes, I have no desire to know the writer, but Graves has to bear the odium, of course. I daresay you ladies have agreed by this time that it was a most infamous letter—and you were right. I can tell you Robert made short work of the whole business" (oh, cunning, cunning Vicar!). "The fellow shook in his shoes, Garton tells me; so I hope next week there will be some sort of apology."

At the mention of Robert's name, the jurymen to a man—or rather to a woman—come over, except Miss Brookes, who still slips her shawl and looks at Robert. Robert sees her looking at him, fights a bitter battle with his pride, and half succeeds; his brow clears a little, and he looks up pale and resolute.

"Oh, Robert Ord," thinks Rotha, "there is something noble about you in spite of all;" for he looks straight at the Vicar, and says:

"There will certainly be an apology, Austin; I insisted on it."

Miss Brookes draws on her shawl well now, and hugs herself well up in it: she is vanquished.

The Vicar nods pleasantly at his brother, and goes on:

"So you know now, dear ladies, why I call this 'The Vicar's

Atonement.' I want to atone for my want of charity to this poor child;" and he lays his hand lightly on Rotha's, keeping it there in his fatherly way; "and I want you all to help me to make up to her for all the pain and annoyance to which she has been subjected during her brief sojourn amongst us, and to promise her that she shall be better treated for the future." And then he releases Rotha's hand and sits down.

In truth he has done his work well.

During the lull that follows the Vicar's words you might hear a pin drop. Garton has moved his arm at last, and is rubbing it gently as though it is cramped. Rotha has raised her eyes to the Vicar with a look that only he can understand, for it speaks of undying gratitude. There is a brief silence, but when they all rise from the table Mrs. Blake—gentlest of women—comes round to Rotha and kisses her; and after that it is only a repetition of the Vicar's queer illustration of sheep jumping through a gap in the hedge.

Yes, the verdict was "Not Guilty, my Lord." Rotha might have worn her white dress after all, but nobody could think the black one unbecoming now the sweet pale face is suffused with blushes of happiness. Even Belle roused a little out of her apathy to wonder if it were possible that Robert—her Robert—could be wrong.

To Rotha the rest of the evening was simply a triumph, swelled by Meg's glorious singing. When it was over she walked home with Garton in the starlight, saying little snatches of the "Te Deum" to herself.

"What did you mean by the story of 'Haman,' Rotha?" asked Meg, in her slow ponderous way, as they were about to retire for the night. She had been puzzling over it several times that evening.

Rotha had the grace to look a little ashamed of herself, and then she burst out laughing.

"Oh, Meg! the idea of remembering my silly speech."

"But you looked as though you meant it, Rotha."

Rotha grew rather grave.

"Well, perhaps I did; but, all the same, I don't want to explain myself, it seems so ungrateful after all this happiness; it is the one thorn in the handful of roses—the death's-head at the Egyptian feast; and, after all, Haman the son of Hammedatha the Agagite was a terrible heathen to say such a thing."

"What thing?"

But Rotha would not tell her.

# CHAPTER XX.

> " Murmur not ! whatever ill
> Cometh, am I not thy friend
> (In false times the firmer still)
> Without changing, without end ?
> Ah ! if one true friend be thine
> Dare not to repine !"          BARRY CORNWALL.

AND so a little sunshine had come into Rotha's life.

And the stigma and stain of a grievous suspicion was removed.

" Not Guilty, my Lord."

" Not Proven," still echoed one dissentient voice ; for, alas !
the baseless fancy which Envy had engendered in Robert Ord's
brain still lurked there in dusky corners, and came to light in
slow brooding moments of pain ; only with this difference—that
he dare no longer avow his suspicion openly.

And why ?

He had grown to be ashamed of it.

Nay, more ; since the night of the Vicar's declaration a little
doubt had crept in ; he still maintained to himself that he was
right, but he had begun to argue on the matter. Argument pre-
supposes doubt, assurance needs no reasoning. Robert began to
assert his right to this ill-founded dislike, but his pride ceased to
uphold him ; it was the first evidence of weakness.

The conflict had begun in earnest now ; henceforth there would
be no peace for Robert Ord. The better part of his nature was at
fault, his inner integrity was disturbed ; the man was bred for
nobler uses than to expend all this waste of passionate resentment
against one poor woman, whose only fault was in being the unwilling instrument of a most unworthy revenge.

Sometimes in the dead of night he would start up and ask
himself, could he be wrong ; was it all a mistake—a morbid
fancy ? He had heard that dwelling on a single thought creates
monomania ; had his brain become diseased with brooding over

his wrongs? Latterly he had had stings of conscience, little quivering goads of remorse, which had moved him to generous impulses; but he always grew harder afterwards. Ever since his championship in the case of Ebenezer Graves his antagonism had become even more intense; all the more that in their outward relations he could find no fault with her. Rotha's instinct detected all this; in her quaint way she had spoken of it as "the one thorn in the handful of roses;" but she never would allow even to herself how much power it had to wound. She could afford to wait now, she said, and it was in her nature to be patient; and certainly she showed wonderful tact and discrimination.

Since the night of her triumph, as Meg called it, she had been a daily visitor to the Vicarage—the Vicar and his wife wished it—and already a very strong friendship had sprung up between her and Mrs. Ord. Mary, who had no friend but her husband, felt a great comfort in this little interchange of womanly feeling; Belle had long ceased to be her confidante, and there were many things with which she preferred not to trouble Austin; and Rotha was a useful and sympathising listener, and had such old-fashioned simple ways.

So Rotha came every morning to the "mother's room." But for helping Mary she would have been very idle just now. Poor Annie's suffering life was ended, and Rotha had many spare hours in consequence. The Vicar, when she had applied to him for work, had flatly refused to employ her. "You have worked enough for two women already," he said, very wisely; "you must learn to play a little now. Your visits to old Sally and the Convalescent Hospital will employ you quite sufficiently;" and Rotha, though she chose to argue the matter, felt he was right. And, after all, there was no fear of her being idle: the Vicar always found her with her thimble on in Mary's room. "I wish Nettie Underwood could see you," he would say sometimes, when he came in of a morning and found Rotha stitching away with a heap of white drapery in her lap. Rotha would look up and smile; these visits of the Vicar were the most sunshiny parts of the day. He had begun to treat her to the same gentle raillery with which he treated Mary and Belle. How the girl's cheeks used to flush over those innocent jokes—what a tender earnest vein of feeling ran under all the raillery—what a great loving heart, she thought. Her eyes would glisten for hours after one of these sallies. "I am so happy that I am almost afraid of my own happiness," she would say to Mary sometimes. Mrs. Ord would be touched by the simple expression of feeling; the child-like element of Rotha's nature came very plainly to the surface just now. I think

15.

Mary, being a very simple woman herself, liked her all the better for it.

Rotha was devoted to Mary, but it would not be too much to say that she half-worshipped the Vicar. She told Mary once that she thought he was faultless, and Mary quite agreed with her—they both thoroughly believed the little fiction. They would sit and plot for hours against his peace, as the Vicar quickly discovered: Mary, who had never had a secret from her husband, quaked daily over some scheme of Rotha's devising; they would sit smiling in his face all the time they were stitching those beautiful linen shirts and cambric handkerchiefs, whereof the stuff had been surreptitiously conveyed into the house. Unfortunately for them, the Vicar knew fine linen and cambric when he saw them, though he chose at times to disguise his knowledge. He chose to shut his eyes now.

"You women are always working," he would say sometimes. "I hope you are not running up too long a bill at Alison's, Mary." And then he would take up the linen softly, as though its touch were pleasant to him. He was a man to whom no purple and fine linen would have come amiss. Mary would quake more than ever when she saw him do this.

But if the Vicar's eyes were opened, he had no mind to protest just now, and so for a little while Rotha had her way.

Shirt-making is very pleasant work to those who like it. Rotha soon came every morning, and stayed for hours in Mary's room, but Belle seldom joined them; as a rule, she preferred taking her portion of work upstairs; she always complained there was no light in the "mother's room," but somehow Belle did very little of any work just now. Rotha was not the only one who noticed her flagging strength.

Sometimes Garton or one of the lads would drop in. Rotha was a great favourite with all the "five boys," as Mary called them; but for that she would have had small opportunity for seeing them, for it began to be an understood thing that she never came of an evening without a special invitation from the Vicar, and out of consideration for Robert these invitations were very rare.

But sometimes he would ask her, and then Rotha would come at once. It was not a part of her plan to avoid Robert Ord; Robert was always very civil when they met; if visitors were present, outsiders to the Vicarage, he would make a point of accosting her with studied politeness, but otherwise he would keep much to himself.

The only singularity about their intercourse was that he never shook hands with her since the day that they had parted at the King's Head, Barnard Castle; he never once offered his hand; there seemed to be a tacit understanding that no hand-clasp should pass between them till the day that Robert Ord should come to her and acknowledge that he had done her this wrong.

That day was far enough off now, Rotha thought sometimes : as she watched him and saw the sweet gravity of his ways with Belle—he was more lover-like than usual just now—she could hardly suppress a patient sigh. "It is so dreadful to be so disliked," thought poor Rotha. At such times she would feel sad in spite of her happiness, but nothing could exceed her gentleness with him and Belle—poor Belle, who was growing more wayward than ever with her increased suffering.

But she had a stanch friend in Garton, and soon afterwards she was able to render him a great service.

Since Laurie's account of his daring exploit, which Belle had corroborated, he had risen greatly in her estimation. Women are not slow to appreciate natural prowess; she began to look upon Garton rather in the light of a hero, and was disposed to think in consequence that he was somewhat unfairly treated, and that if every one had his dues Garton Ord would be occupying a very different sphere; but she saw, or thought that she saw, that Robert and even the Vicar held another opinion. Mary, too, when Rotha spoke on the subject, would always shake her head and say Garton wanted ballast.

"He is nearly three-and-twenty, and he does not even earn bread and cheese for himself," Mary would add; and then Rotha would be silent.

"Do they expect him to dig for it?" she sometimes said to herself indignantly. "How can a man learn half a dozen trades at once? I understood he was to be a clergyman." She thought Garton very hard worked indeed, though she would have been puzzled to specify the exact nature of his employment. From her window at Bryn she could see him working in his own or the Vicar's garden as though his livelihood depended on it. She was always meeting him in the village or on the shore surrounded by boys, and never without a ponderous volume under his arm. When she went into church there he was striding up and down the aisles in his long cassock, or swinging round odd corners to look after stray choir-boys. When service was over he would stand bareheaded by the lich-gate, keeping order and marshalling the unruly lads; ten minutes later she would see him through the schoolhouse-window, leading the singing or drilling raw recruits into practice—and doing it all too in a brisk, energetic, cheerful way that was very pleasant to see. Rotha could not understand that remark about ballast at all ; so she was very kind to the young man when they met, and in a simple transparent way patronised and made much of him.

And one night she made acquaintance with Gar's Shadow.

It happened in this wise.

Rotha had been down to the Convalescent Hospital after service one evening, to see a patient who had met with a severe accident ; she had been unexpectedly detained, and it was quite late by the time she had finished her errand.

It was a wild night, and as Rotha left the safe shelter of the building she could hardly keep her footing ; it was very dark, and the wind howled and rushed at her round corners like a mad thing —bonneting and buffeting her at every turn ; the sea seemed lashing itself sullenly to make a night of it. Little eddies of sand swirled round Rotha, stinging her face and neck like crowds of sharp midges ; the lights on the sea-wall wavered before her, and a damp mist of rain seemed to wet her to the skin. "If I could only get round the next corner," thought Rotha, fighting for her breath manfully, "I should be all right." The next minute she was taken off her feet, and drifted right on to a dark object, over which she stumbled, and only saved herself from falling by being brought up against an opposite wall.

"Oh dear ! I hope I have not hurt anybody," said Rotha breathlessly ; for the object had moved slightly, and in the darkness was looming gradually into the figure of a boy,—of a boy lying, or rather crouching, in a doorway, with his head hidden in his hands.

The boy lifted up his head, and seemed to listen through the whirlwind, as Rotha panted out the inquiry.

"It is a dreadful night," she continued, shivering. "Don't you think it rather foolish to be sitting on a wet door-step in such a gale as this ?"

"I would as lief be here as anywhere," muttered the boy disconsolately, and then they turned their faces to the wall. "It always tears round this corner like this," he observed indifferently, "sometimes I have been half blinded by the sand—there are drifts of it to-night."

Rotha wiped her eyes ruefully ; they were smarting by this time. Down below there was a faint flickering of street lamps, and some little pools shining under them. Something in the boy's attitude or voice seemed to strike her, and she stooped over and touched his shoulder.

"My poor boy, and you are so wet ! But I cannot see your face. Is it Reuben Armstrong ?"

He started up as though ashamed of the recognition.

"Yes, I am Reuben; but don't tell him—don't let him know, I mean, that you saw me like this."

"Of whom are you speaking, Reuben?"

"Of Mr. Garton. He would be so sorry; it would vex him, I know, to hear father has turned me out again on such a night."

"Turned you out of doors, do you mean?" exclaimed Rotha, horrified. The wind was whistling so loudly she was obliged almost to shout her words.

The boy nodded, and then drew himself up against the wall in a patient sort of way, as though he were used to it. Rotha fancied his voice sounded as though he had been crying, but it was impossible to see anything clearly. Poor Reuben! She was as wet and tired as she could be; but she could not leave him like this.

"But, Reuben, this is dreadful. I never heard anything so shocking in my life. Let me knock at the door and persuade your father to let you in." In such an emergency it seemed to her the only thing she could do, but the boy's frightened voice stayed her.

"It is no use—it is no use, indeed," he continued; "he has been having too much down at the Green Dragon, and he is sure to turn his hand against mother or me when that's the case. I don't care so that it is not mother. I think I had as lief be here as inside to-night." But Reuben could not keep his teeth from chattering as he spoke.

"But why not go down to Mr. Garton?" persisted Rotha; "surely he or the Vicar would give you shelter for the night?"

"They have done it often enough already," returned the boy sadly; "but I cannot bear to put them out so. Mr. Garton has often gone without his own dinner when father has locked up the food from us. I think I should have starved once but for him"— and now Rotha could see the tears glistening in his eyes—"he took me into his own bed one night when father had kicked me out into the street. But I would not let him know for the world to-night."

"But why not? You will die of cold by the morning," pleaded Rotha. But she was spared further speech by the stealthy opening of the door behind them. Through the crack Rotha could see a thin haggard-looking woman trying to shield a rushlight from the draught of air. In another moment a gust of wind extinguished it.

"Is that you, mother?" whispered Reuben, putting his face to the crack.

"Whist, lad! Oh, Rube, Rube, he is rumbling out curses to himself now on his bed."

"Has he struck you, mother? You speak faint like."

"Nay, nought to speak of; it's thee I'm thinking of, lad; thou'lt starve of cold out yonder. Slip through into the kitchen, and I'll make thee up a bed on settle."

"Mother, I dursn't."

"Come, lad, and I'll give thee summat to eat; thou art pined with hunger—thy stomach must be quite pinched like. Come, Rube !"

"No, no, I dursn't; he would kill me !"—and Rotha could hear he was sobbing bitterly now—"he said he would break every bone in my body. Shut the door, mother, and say good-night; it is not so very cold out here."

But Rotha came close.

"He says right. Shut the door, Mrs. Armstrong. He shall go home with me. Come, Reuben, I am getting wet through," and she put out a soft hand in the darkness and drew the boy on. "There, good-night, and God help you, you poor woman."

Reuben tried to thank her as they battled through the storm, but she would not let him speak.

"I could not leave the poor Shadow on the door-step," she thought to herself. She was quite in a pleasant glow and bustle when she arrived at Bryn, and would not let Meg be anxious at her wet appearance for a minute. "Just stir up the fire, and tell Prue to mull some wine directly," she said, as she ran off to change her dripping garments. In five minutes she reappeared with all sorts of comforts for Reuben. The boy's dejection cleared a little as he felt himself invigorated by the warmth and cheerfulness. When he had done justice to the good supper provided for him Rotha took him up to his room. "To-morrow, when you are rested, we must have a long talk together," she said, as she left him.

She sat over her fire a long time that night, and scarcely looked up when Meg bade her good-night.

"I think I see my way clear," she said aloud, as she shook herself from her musing. "They say man's importunities are God's opportunities; and one of these days I shall have to give an account of my stewardship. I never felt glad that I was rich before this."

Rotha had her talk with Reuben the next morning; and, in spite of the boy's reluctance to implicate his wretched parent, she managed to glean sufficient facts to assure her that the poor lad was habitually ill used; for Armstrong was, at the best of times, a hard churlish sort of man; but in his drunken fits he was so savage that his wife and boy often suffered severely from his violence. His elder sons had run away to sea when mere boys, unable to endure his intolerable temper. And, but for his poor broken-down mother and Mr. Garton, Reuben confessed he would long ago have followed their example.

"It is Mr. Garton keeps me most," finished Reuben. "It is no good my staying any longer with mother, it only makes things worse. She will interfere and take my part when he threatens me. I don't think he would touch her but for that; and it does make my blood boil to see him lay his heavy hand on her."

"But why does Mr. Garton keep you from running away, Reuben?" asked Rotha, rather curiously.

The boy coloured and looked down.

"He does not keep me," he said at length, hesitating, "I keep myself. I don't feel as though I can leave him when he wants me so."

"Wants you so!" repeated Rotha in a little surprise.

"Yes," returned the boy in a low voice, "but I should not like him to hear me say it; but I know he has a hard life, and that people don't understand him. He tells me sometimes that he would feel so lonely without me. I have always been so much with him since he saved my life. You know all about that, don't you?" he continued, raising his eyes to Rotha. Her kindness was fast thawing his reserve.

"Yes, I know all about it," returned Rotha musingly; and at that minute Garton entered the room. He had been down to the cottage to see Reuben, and had heard from the boy's mother what had happened.

Rotha shook hands with him rather shyly, but he had no eyes for any one but his favourite.

"Oh, Rube, Rube!" he said, as the boy sprang to meet him; and Rotha could see there were tears in his eyes. "To think of your being turned out on such a night as that, and never to come to me in your trouble! But for Miss Maturin's kindness, what would have become of you?"

"I did not want you to know anything about it," pleaded the boy.

"He was afraid of disturbing your brother," added Rotha; but Garton only shook his head sorrowfully, and said again, "Oh, Rube, Rube!"

Rotha never liked him so well as when he stood there, with his arm round the boy's neck, and the muscles of his strong face working with agitation.

She went out of the room softly by and by, thinking they would like to be alone; when she came back Reuben had evidently been crying.

"Reuben says he will be late for school, Miss Maturin; he is only waiting to say good-bye to you, and thank you for your kindness."

Rotha made believe not to notice the red eyes. She shook the boy's hand heartily, and said, "But I shall expect you back to dinner, Reuben, remember that; we have not finished our talk yet. Mr. Ord, if you are in no hurry, I should like to say a word to you."

Garton muttered something about the boy's lessons, but sat down again nevertheless; he looked tired and dispirited, and opened the conversation very gloomily.

"Isn't it a shame to ill-use a boy like that, Miss Maturin? I feel sometimes, when I go down to the cottage, I can hardly keep my hands off such a brute. I tell Austin the fellow must be bound over to keep the peace."

"Something must be done for the lad at once," returned Rotha with decision; "I could not sleep another night and feel that such a thing was likely to happen again."

"If I could only have the power to shelter him," groaned Garton, rocking himself to and fro, "but I am no good to any one. I often wonder if Rube and I were born under an unlucky star, for there seems no place for us anywhere."

"I wish I could help you," returned Rotha timidly; "I think I can, as regards the boy. I don't see the use of money, unless it be to do other people good; I was thinking last night that if you and Mr. Ord agreed, I would remove Reuben entirely from his wretched home and put him at some good school. Of course I will only act in the matter entirely by your advice."

Rotha spoke very diffidently, as though she were asking instead of conferring a favour. Garton looked at her for a moment as though he could scarcely believe his own ears.

"Do you mean it?" he gasped at length.

"Yes, but I think we ought to consult the Vicar; there is the Grammar School, and if he goes to that we might board him in some nice family. I suppose his father would not object."

Garton's answer was conclusive.

"Let us go to Austin at once," he said, picking up his felt hat and twisting it out of all shape in his sinewy hand. "Miss Maturin, you are an angel;" and Rotha laughed and reddened as she ran off to put on her bonnet.

The Vicar was in his study writing his sermon, but he put away his papers very good-humouredly when he saw them.

"Why have you left those few sheep in the wilderness?" he said to Garton, rather reproachfully; "the boys have been waiting for you an hour."

"They must wait a little longer," replied Gar carelessly, as he rested himself on the Vicar's little writing-table. "Miss Maturin and I want to consult you about something."

And Rotha opened her little business. She was rather bashful at first; she thought it must look odd, her taking such notice of Garton's *protégé*, but her pity gave her courage.

"Do you not think it a good plan?" she finished; "the Grammar School will cost very little, and Mr. Garton says he knows of a nice respectable family who would be too glad to board him."

"If Robert were not such a misanthrope, we might take him in ourselves," grumbled Garton.

The Vicar gave him a quick disapproving glance.

"Oh no, that would not do; it would not be fair to Robert to ask it; you are rather too Quixotic in your friendship, Gar. Well, you want my sanction to the scheme, do you?" he added, turning to Rotha.

"Yes, if you will give it," she returned, feeling rather damped. Reuben was right, and not even the faultless Vicar thoroughly appreciated his younger brother. Rotha, who was very enthusiastic, did not think him in the least Quixotic. She took the term quite as a reproach. "Well, the plan is a good plan," continued the Vicar, "and I can see no objection to it. Garton has been a little foolish about the boy, as Robert and I have often told him; he has given him a smattering of learning, and placed him in a false position. A thoroughly good education will remedy this evil; and if, as you say, we can remove the poor boy from his father's influence, it will be the making of him, no doubt; the lad's a good lad, I believe, though Garton has done his best to spoil him."

"Have you finished your sermon, Austin?" asked Gar sulkily. "I know my fondness for the boy is little short of high treason."

"No, Gar, no; it is a very venial offence, after all; but I don't wonder my boys get jealous. There's Guy, now, would do anything for his uncle," he continued, turning to Miss Maturin, "and he's always threatening to pummel Reuben. I believe Garton's influence over boys is almost magical; it is a good thing he is not likely to afford such an expensive luxury as a wife."

Garton rocked himself and laughed; but Rotha asked why very innocently.

"Because, unless she were as inveterate a boy lover as himself, she would be wretched. How would you like to see your husband, Miss Maturin, always going about with a troop of village lads tramping at his heels, or clumping with hobnailed boots over your best carpets? No, Gar's cut out for an old bachelor. If he had lived a few centuries ago, he would have been a monk; wouldn't you, Gar ?"

"I think they had the best of it," assented Garton; but Rotha, who had rather coloured over the Vicar's speech, turned the conversation to Reuben; and Garton, becoming very matter-of-fact all of a sudden, it was arranged that he and the Vicar should go down at once to Joe Armstrong's and settle the matter.

Reuben came back to dinner, and was strictly charged by Rotha to return to Bryn the moment afternoon school was over. The Vicar had found no difficulty in arranging things. Joe Armstrong was soon made ashamed of his last night's violence; he was a selfish worthless coward, and was glad to be rid of such an incumbrance as Reuben; perhaps the boy's steady patience aggravated him.

"The lad's nought to me," he kept saying, "a lazy good-for-nothing chap, who won't work, and cares for nought but book-learning and psalm-singing; the gentlefolks have turned his head already, and the best they can do is to finish their job."

"Miss Maturin undertakes to give the boy a good education, and to article him to some useful trade," exclaimed the Vicar, "and she will be responsible till then for his charge and main-tenance, only stipulating that you renounce all control over him."

"The lad's nought to me," returned the man sullenly, "a young artful viper;" but the Vicar cut short the list of vitupera-tion. On the threshold he lingered a moment to exchange a few kindly words with the poor mother. "You have a sad cough, Mrs. Armstrong," he said; "is that why we never see you at church?"

She shook her head, and motioned with her lips to her husband.

"Joe, is this true, that you keep your wife from coming to church?" demanded the Vicar sternly.

The man rose with an oath and took the pipe from his lips. "What's it to you, parson, if I do?—a canting, hypocritical, pack of rubbish."

"It is a great deal to me, Joe Armstrong," retorted the Vicar; "and I do not choose to see one of my flock absent Sunday after Sunday. What, do you not know there are six days on which to work—that you live, and make your wife live, like a heathen; nay, worse than a heathen—an infidel?"

"Oh, if parson's going to jaw, we had better have that door shut, missus. I don't want folk to think we patronise street preach-ing." The woman looked distressed at her husband's insolence.

"Don't mind him, your Reverence," she whispered; "he ain't slept it off yet. Oh, Joe, Joe, how can you go for to outrage his Reverence?"

"You shut up, missus," was the rough rejoinder, "and leave me to mind my own business. If parson don't like my words, he needn't listen to 'em. I want no cluttering round here. I ain't a going to be converted, I can tell you."

The Vicar turned his mild eyes on him; there was something very solemn in their light.

"Perhaps not, Joe Armstrong, but remember there's a hell for you, and such as you, for whom the Saviour has died in vain;" and then, as the man slunk away, awed in spite of himself, he took the woman's rough hardened hand in his.

"Good-bye, Harriet, my wife shall bring you up some stuff for your cough. One of these days I hope you will learn to fear God, in spite of your husband; you must try and come to church sometimes when he will let you, for it is the only place, the only place on earth, Harriet, where the weary are at rest."

Garton made Rotha shudder when he related this interview; in this one day they had made a great start towards intimacy. Garton had taken her to the Grammar School, and had introduced her to Mr. Dentry, the head-master, and after that they had gone round to the house where Garton intended that Reuben should live.

Rotha commended his choice afterwards; she thought he had shown a vast amount of common sense in the whole business. Mrs. Summerson was a widow, with small means, very gentle, and prepossessing in appearance and manners, and had boys of her own who went to the Grammar School, and were members of the choir; and Reuben was already good friends with them.

Rotha, who had led to the subject very delicately, soon found that she was conferring a benefit, and that Mrs. Summerson would gladly board the boy. The only difficulty lay in coming to terms; neither of the three understood business in the least, and Rotha was disposed to be too liberal, so they were obliged to have recourse to the Vicar again, who settled the matter in five minutes.

It was quite dark when they got back to Bryn, and Reuben was there before them. Garton had been invited to tea in honour of the occasion, and by Rotha's orders Meg had prepared quite a festive little feast.

On their way home Garton suggested that they should break the thing gently to the boy. "I never saw any one so sensitive," he remarked, and to this Rotha agreed.

"I think you had better do it yourself," she said. "I am such a stranger to him." She had had fits of shyness all day, and one was strong on her just now.

But she afterwards asked Garton wherein the preparation consisted, for directly he caught sight of his favourite he forgot all his wise precautions; he just put his hands on the boy's shoulders and said :

"Reuben, this young lady has adopted you; she is going to take you away from your wretched home and put you at a good school, where you can learn like a man. Hold up your head, and thank her, boy; and, Rube, Rube, God bless you!—but I am so happy."

It might have been the sudden break in Garton's voice, but Reuben showed no intention of holding up his head; on the contrary, it drooped lower and lower; while Garton, recovering himself, expatiated on the bright future that lay before them, till at last the boy raised his eyes, full of intense joy and gratitude, to his young benefactress, and then, overwhelmed by his conflicting feeling, threw himself on the breast of the best friend his desolate childhood had ever known, and burst into a passion of tears.

# CHAPTER XXI.

## TYLER AND TYLER.

"Her sweet humour
That was as easy, as calm, as peaceful,
All her affections, like the dews on roses,
Fair as the flowers themselves, as sweet and gentle."
BEAUMONT AND FLETCHER.

"As free her alms—as diligent her cures;
As loud her praises, and as warm her prayers.
Yet was she not profuse; but fear'd to waste,
And wisely managed that the stock might last;
That all might be supplied, and she not grieve,
When crowds appear'd, she had not to relieve,
Which to prevent, she still increased her store,
Laid up and spared, that she might give the more."
DRYDEN.

THE fogs and mists of November had set in now. Others, besides Belle, shivered at the strong north wind that rattled at the old-fashioned window-frames at the Vicarage, or whistled so shrilly round the chimney-stacks. The boys no longer ran races on the shore or climbed the sand-hills of the rabbit-warren. There was a sombre line of seaweed now, over which the surf bubbled and frothed; the sea and sky vied with each other in grayness; the breakers, as they rolled sullenly in, brought shivers of broken rafts and splinters of wood. People shuddered at the tell-tale fragments; rumours of wrecks were heard everywhere. One night, over at Welburn, the signal-gun was fired, and rockets were sent off; a schooner had put in too close to land, and had gone to pieces on the low black rocks that lay bedded in the froth and slime. Next day the poor people went down in shoals to grope in the surf for floating firewood and washes of grimy coal.

Belle used to watch the line of little carts coming up from the shore; sturdy brown-faced women, with browner babies in their arms, walking with plodding step beside their donkey's head. Belle had seen these same women working in the harvest-field among the reapers. Next spring they would be turning the hot swathes of hay underneath a burning sun. How she envied these strong-limbed daughters of labour; this girl, whose iron will was ever battling so fiercely with her failing strength! As she sat and watched them, her face would be full of a dumb misery; how long should she be able to hide from them or from herself her conviction that things were not well with her?

For a little time she strove, but with partial success. Mary's affectionate eyes could not be blinded to the fact that her sister seemed more ailing than usual. She had taken cold; the bitter weather tried her; the season was more than usually inclement, she thought. Rotha, to whom she confided her anxieties, said that in her opinion it was more debility than anything; she noticed that Belle's sickly appetite rebelled at the plain fare of the Vicarage table. "She does not eat enough to keep up her strength," she concluded; "I remember I once heard Mrs. Ord say that bark and port wine were a specific in such cases. She always said it was a good old-fashioned remedy."

Mary sighed. She could not tell Rotha that wine was a forbidden luxury at the Vicarage, and that it was not in her power to provide the delicacies that would tempt Belle's capricious palate. She changed the subject as soon as possible; but the heaviness of her heart was plainly legible in her face. Rotha, who had learnt to read her tolerably well by this time, was quite willing that the subject should be changed. She had made up her mind what she would do. By and by Mary was taken into her confidence, and from that time they plotted and carried out their little schemes together.

Belle was to be coaxed to eat, that was the first thing. Every day choice poultry or game made its appearance on the Vicarage table. Mary would avow it openly at first as a present from Bryn, and the Vicar would thank Rotha for it when they met; but after a time this recognition of her gifts were, by mutual consent, tacitly unacknowledged. Belle seemed to enjoy it more when left in ignorance of the giver. Every now and then Rotha would send over hothouse fruits and all manner of soups, jellies, and dainty creams. It was reward enough for her to hear that Belle had done justice to them. Mary would come with a happy face to say how Belle had enjoyed such and such a thing; "and the port wine was really strengthening her," she added—for one day, when the Vicar was out, Mary and Rotha cleared out the lumber from the disused cellar, and the choicest contents of one of the bins at Bryn found their way on the Vicarage shelves. Mary threw her dusty arms round Rotha when they had finished that little job. Garton, who

had been packing up the bottles for them—rare old bottles, defiled
with cobwebs and sawdust—called out to them mischievously that
Austin was coming. Rotha shut the door hastily, and they all
stood listening in the darkness, till Mary thought of the black-hole
at Calcutta and grew nervous. They were all whitewashed and
covered with sawdust when they came out. How Rotha laughed !

The Vicar said nothing when Mary filled Belle's glass at dinner.
He had seen certain cut-glass goblets stained with that same ruby
fluid ; he knew exactly from what bin Rotha had taken it. No
wine like that, he thought, to put new life into a languid frame.
He rather marvelled at the indifference with which Belle drank it.

Belle took it, as she took all Rotha's gifts, with indifference
amounting to dislike ; if she dared she would have refused them.
Robert, when he heard of them, strove hard to conceal his displeasure. Belle guessed at this feeling on her lover's part, and it made
Rotha's kindness intolerable to her. Rotha was over bold once.

One afternoon, when Belle had a headache, and was lying shivering on the couch, Mary had brought down an old rug to cover her
sister, and Belle had drawn it discontentedly over her, complaining
of its roughness ; and, as Rotha looked at her, she thought how
strangely out of keeping the dingy covering was with the fair face
that rested so fretfully against it. When she went home that
night Meg was surprised to hear her rummaging in the big wardrobe in Mrs. Ord's room. Next 'afternoon, when Belle lay down,
she found herself in a nest of costly Cashmere shawls, with a sweet
spicy smell lingering in their soft borders ; surprise kept her silent,
and then she averted her flushed face with a word of thanks. She
lay warm and hidden all the afternoon ; but the next day the
shawls were sent back with a pencilled line of excuse in Mary's
hand, and the old worn rug was in its place again.

Rotha felt herself repulsed, and no wonder ; but she solaced
herself with Mary's delighted gratitude. She was diverting her
bounty into another channel now.

What friends those two women had become ! Mary was too
genuinely humble to withstand Rotha's generosity very long. It
began to be an understood thing between them that Rotha was no
longer to be deprived of the happiness of sharing her good things
with those she loved. She would thank Mary with touching
fervour for giving her such happiness, but both agreed that it
must be kept from the Vicar, at least for the present. How they
did scheme to deceive him ! Rotha was the braver by far ; but
Mary, whose conscience was for ever accusing her, blundered sadly.
The Vicar laughed in his sleeve at her clumsiness.

What a day that was at Thornborough when they went to

buy flannels. Mary, who had never transacted such an extensive marketing in her life, would not hear of buying flannels anywhere else—they must go to the good old-fashioned drapery establishment of Tyler and Tyler. How the man who served them must have smiled at the eager woman! Mary's hands trembled as they fingered bale after bale of flannel; the sweet face was all flushed and smiling under the shabby bonnet; Rotha's dimples were soon in full play.

"While we are here you had better help me choose my new silk dress," Rotha said to her; "and then there is the carpet and curtains for your bedroom; you know you have promised we are to look at them to-day."

"Yes, but how are we to put the carpet down without his noticing it?" returned Mary helplessly. She was still fingering the gray flannel with a love of delight; she could get shirts for Robert and Garton out of all that quantity. Did Rotha guess that, when she ordered all these extra yards, poor Garton's wardrobe was so sadly dilapidated? She was still thinking of the shirts when she followed Rotha dreamily into the next department. She was still absent when Rotha asked her opinion—the shimmer of the silks dazzled her; she held on to a silvery gray much as she had done to the flannel.

"Gray won't suit me at all," said Rotha impatiently, "I am too pale; I like that rich prune best, and look how that lovely changing blue would suit Belle."

Mary looked as she was bid—she assented to everything; her hands wandered over the shining heaps, but she was a little confused. She did not in the least guess why Rotha got her so quickly out of the silk department, or why she was left alone to stare so long at a green mossy carpet. Her thoughts would keep wandering to the white and gray flannels, and the blue serge for Arty's suit. In her own mind she was opening a certain brown paper parcel. Should she cut the string, or would her fingers untie it? Out they came —four pairs of strong boyish boots. She could almost smell the new leather. How they would stamp up to their seats in the choir-stalls, Guy especially. Guy had been so ashamed of his old boots; and then there was something else.

"Well, have you fixed upon that carpet," interrupted Rotha, coming suddenly behind her, "green is such a good wearing colour, and those curtains will match so nicely?"

Mary started almost as though she had in reality dropped the boots; the green moss might have been in its native dell for her. "I think it lovely, but far, far too good for the purpose; this is Kidderminster, a felt would do nicely," she said in a little flutter.

" We will have it !" Rotha had answered decidedly. "There, I think we have done; let everything be sent to Bryn as soon as possible."

She was a little pompous as she gave her orders; but for her stuff dress and close plain bonnet she might have been a young princess. She took Mary's arm and walked out of the shop very slim and straight; Mary looked quite an ordinary woman beside her. It was just this about Rotha—this certain nameless grace— that had abashed Robert Ord once or twice.

She burst out laughing when they were in the street.

"Ought people to pay for their purchases before they are sent home?" she asked. "I thought the man stared a little when I offered to write out that cheque. How droll it seems writing cheques. I wanted to laugh dreadfully all the time. I think I shall always deal at Tyler and Tyler's, it is so pleasant to have the two masters bowing you out of the shop in that way."

" They don't often have such liberal customers," replied Mary.

She was in the open air, but she still felt a little dizzy. Tyler and Tyler's dark warehouse always appeared to her after this like Aladdin's Palace. Rotha might have been a benevolent geni conjuring up shining heaps of marvellous silks and stuffs. How the carpets had unrolled themselves at her bidding! There was no such thing as gray flannel in the *Arabian Nights,* but Mary's thoughts still clung about the dun-coloured bale; she had some difficulty in rousing herself.

"I don't know what we shall do about the carpet," she said in a voice between crying and laughing. "Rotha, I feel as though I shall never dare to wish for anything more; you seem to guess my very thoughts, just like a fairy godmother."

"Never mind about the carpet, we must wait our opportunity, I suppose; and I won't be a fairy godmother, because they generally turn cross in the end. You must come over to Bryn and cut up all that flannel, and then I will ask Nettie and Aunt Eliza; and Meg and Prue and I will help you, and we'll have a regular 'bee,' and Mr. Garton shall come and read to us."

And so Rotha chatted on; she had still hold of Mary's arm— they were wading through the wet slushy street. The sky was grayer than ever, and a thick atmosphere of fog and smoke seemed to swallow up the dingy buildings. People turned round to look at Rotha's happy face; some one brushing past her hastily, stood still in astonishment.

Rotha flushed up suddenly when she saw Robert's look. They were lighting up the gas now. As he stood under one of the lamps

Robert's handsome face looked more haggard and thoughtful than she had ever seen it.

"You here, at this hour, Miss Maturin! I thought I must have been mistaken until I saw Mary." Mary gave a nervous laugh.

"We do not often honour Thornborough with our presence, do we, Robert?"

"Mrs. Ord and I have been shopping," put in Rotha. "I daresay you saw us come out of Tyler and Tyler's just now; Mrs. Ord has been helping me choose a new silk dress." Rotha spoke up steadily, but she still looked a little confused. This expedition to Thornborough was to have been a little secret; Robert was the last person whom the two women would have selected for their confidant.

"It is rather late in the afternoon for shopping; you could hardly distinguish between the different shades, I should think," shrugging his shoulders slightly.

"I wanted to judge of them by candlelight," returned Rotha demurely. "We must not keep Mrs. Ord standing in this fog any longer; we are going to the station now." She dropped a little curtsey as she drew Mary's arm again through hers—the dimples were rebellious now; she did not dare to lift up her eyes.

"Women are all alike," muttered Robert cynically, as he pulled up the collar of his coat and strode down a side street, where a flaming gaslight or two made darkness visible. "A new dress transports them into the seventh heaven; how happy she looked, to be sure!" He was almost inclined to resent Rotha's happiness as personal, and to think very poorly of her in consequence; but he could not forget it. Once or twice, as he went hither and thither in the deepening gloom, or shut himself up in his lonely counting-house, he found himself recalling a bright girlish face, in a close plain bonnet, with brown hair lying softly over the temples, and sweet unsteady lips, ready every moment to break into laughter. "How rosy and well she looks! It couldn't have been all that dress made her so happy. She holds herself as straight as a young fir tree. I suppose, if I admired tall women, I should admire her;" and then Robert stirred the gaseous coals till they fell into a blaze, and wondered what it was in Rotha's face that allured and yet repelled him; and then he remembered how he saw her first, standing in her black gown under the low apple trees, with a lace kerchief tied over her brown hair. Rotha was a little subdued after that encounter; Robert always seemed to have the power to chill her somewhat. Mary, on the contrary, chirped all the way home like a cricket; she burst into her husband's study in quite an excited way.

" There's a parcel come for you," said the Vicar, who was very busy—too busy to notice her absence, Mary thought. "Where have you been so long, my dear ?"

" Rotha had some things to get in Thornborough," said Mary, getting behind his chair. " If you are busy, Austin, I will not disturb you by talking. Rotha will be in to tea by and by." She gave his shoulder a triumphant little pat as she passed him ; she knew well what the parcel contained. If only they had not creased it. She ran upstairs like a young girl. Austin leant back in his chair, and smiled as he heard her. " What plot are they hatching now ?" he muttered to himself as he went on with his " loaves and fishes." It struck them both as very odd he should preach that sermon the following Sunday. Mrs. Ord went up to her room, and then she locked the door. She did not dare trust herself to open the parcel till she had done that ; how carefully she unfolded it from its wrapper, and shook it out ! There it was, cut out of finest cloth, soft and glossy as satin. Superfine—it must have been ultra-superfine. How grand her Austin would look in it ; no frayed edges, no shinings of the elbows now. She took out the old coat and laid it aside tenderly to be repaired, and then she hung up the new one in its place. She was a simple woman, hardly wise enough for this generation perhaps ; but, as she shook out the glossy folds, she suddenly wrapped her face in it and cried for very joy.

It must have been about a week after that Rotha noticed one morning that the Vicar was not quite himself. Mary, too, seemed unusually worried, though she tried to evade Rotha's inquiries.

Rotha, who was as persevering as she was keen, set herself to discover the reason of this sudden gloom, and she succeeded so well that Mrs. Ord, though with evident reluctance, admitted that her husband was in temporary embarrassment, and that he had had some almost sleepless nights in consequence.

When Rotha had discovered this she was determined to know more, and by and by, by a little quiet perseverance, she managed to elicit the facts of the case.

The Vicar had ordered in a large supply of coals for the winter's consumption, but, by some inconceivable oversight, a blunder on his or Garton's part, it was just discovered that they already owed a bill dating from the Christmas before. The Vicar, who was very careful to pay his bills quarterly, was in the utmost consternation, and had told Mr. Browning, the coal-merchant, that he had no means of paying such a large sum in full, but that he must meet it by instalments. The result had been a great deal of unpleasantness. Mr. Browning had said a great many uncivil things, and

Robert had been much ashamed of the whole transaction. Since then the Vicar's pillow had been set with thorns, and, though he had striven hard to bear himself with his wonted patience, the effort had been manifestly too hard for him.

"No wonder he looks ill," finished Mrs. Ord, "for I am sure he had no sleep last night or the night before; and, though he bears all Robert's aggravation like a lamb, I can see how it frets him. Sometimes, when I go into the study without his hearing me, I find him sitting with his head in his hand, doing nothing; and though it is Thursday, and he has to preach twice next Sunday, he has not touched one of his sermons."

"What does Mr. Robert say?" inquired Rotha sternly.

Mrs. Ord's pitiful eyes and the thought of the Vicar's misery were too much for her compassionate nature. She had come this morning full of another surprise she had planned for Mary. Mary would not care a bit about the gray dress now.

She put her question rather anxiously.

"Robert always says that Austin is so careless about his papers," returned Mrs. Ord; "that he tears them up too quickly, or throws them in the waste-paper basket, and that he must have torn up Browning's bill, and the bill delivered that came afterwards; but that's such nonsense. What's the use of Robert telling him that when the thing's done? If Austin is a little quick in his movements, he makes fewer mistakes than most men."

Rotha smiled a little; when would Mary Ord believe that her husband had been to blame!

In spite of the Vicar's faultlessness she was inclined to think that he might be a little too quick sometimes.

"I do feel as though it were so mean of me to be telling you this," continued Mrs. Ord.

Then Rotha looked up rather troubled.

"I hope you do not repent your confidence?" she said gravely.

"Repent it! No, not in that way. You don't know what a comfort it is to tell you all my worries; but, all the same, I feel as though it were mean of me."

"And you will let me do this thing for you?" pleaded Rotha almost in a whisper.

"What? pay all that money?" returned Mrs. Ord, quite shocked, with vehemence. "Rotha, promise me that you will not frighten me by proposing such a thing again," and Mrs. Ord looked almost desperate. Then, as a matter of course, Rotha got on her knees beside her friend; it seemed impossible to her that this business should be transacted at arm's length.

"Mrs. Ord, I thought you had begun to love me," she said in a hurt voice.

Then Mary, who was very soft-hearted, took the girl in her arms and said all manner of nice affectionate things; but Rotha did not look satisfied.

"If you loved me you would not refuse me such a little thing as that," she kept saying.

"If it were only a little thing, Rotha!"

"Well, is it not to me? Have I not heaps and heaps of money lying unused in the bank? and is not Mr. Tracy always worrying me about investments? Why shouldn't I choose my own investments, I should like to know?" and Rotha grew a little pompous over her words; she thought she had put it rather neatly.

"But, if I cannot take it, dear?" said Mary, gently stroking back the hair from Rotha's hot face.

"Why should you not take it? Would you not take it from Belle, if she offered it? What have I done that I should be treated so differently from her?"

"Belle is my own sister," returned Mrs. Ord, hardly able to refrain from a smile over Rotha's petulance.

"Well, and am I not your friend? your slave of the lamp, if you will? and does it not make me happier than a queen to share my good things with those I love? Mrs. Ord, I did not think you could have been so proud with me!"

Then Mrs. Ord stroked her hair, sorely troubled.

"I don't think it is pride," she said at last; "if it were, I should get over it, for Austin's sake. Oh, Rotha!" she said, suddenly breaking out into unwonted agitation, "it goes to my heart to refuse you. But why will you persist in heaping all these coals of fire on our heads?"

"I suppose because I love you so," murmured Rotha, speaking rather inaudibly. Every moment her heart was more set on this thing. Mary's objections had no chance against her eloquence; when reasoning failed she tried coaxing. No woman knew how to coax better than Rotha. It ended at last by Mrs. Ord having a good cry on her shoulder, and saying a great many incoherent things; and then Rotha tied on her bonnet in a great bustle, and, after promising to be back in an inconceivably short time, gave Mrs. Ord another reassuring kiss and set off.

It does not take long to transact a little business like that. Rotha had paid a visit to the Blackscar Bank, and had received the money with her own hands, and was back long before Mary had believed it possible. After that there was another little talk, and then Deb was called, and, with many hints as to precaution and safety, the precious money was confided to her care, and she was strictly charged to bring back the receipted bills to her mistress. Everything would have gone on well if only Arty had not clamoured for a walk. Mary, who never refused the little fellow anything, could see nothing unreasonable in such a request, so Master Arty was put in full walking trim, and the two sallied forth together, while Rotha and Mary sat down to their interrupted work.

Now it so happened that the Vicar was walking slowly down the Kirkby road when he felt himself suddenly clasped by the knee, and there was Arty, looking very red-cheeked and blowsy, with his white comforter dangling behind, and his straw hat set rakishly over one ear, and a filial grin of delight on his face.

"I've caught you, father," panted Arty. "Ah, ha! and Deb's ever such a way behind."

"Have Deb and you been having a walk?" observed the Vicar, taking his little son's hand as they retraced their steps. "What have you done to your trumpet, Arty? it is squeezed out of all shape."

"Deb says the music is all dead, father," returned Arty mournfully; "I used it as a hammer at the coal-house. We haven't been a nice walk at all, father; we have been up a lane all coals. and into a nasty yard, and a little man just like my Jack-in-the-box talked to Deb for ever so long."

"Oh, Master Arthur!" said Deb, who had overheard the last words.

"Has your mistress been sending you to Browning's again?" interrupted the Vicar in some surprise; but Arty's chattering was not to be silenced.

"Yes, father; and the dirty little man like Jack-in-the-box looked so pleased, and patted my head; he had such dirty fingers. I heard him ask Deb to give his compliments to you—are compliments good to eat, father?"

"Hush, Arty; be quiet a moment, my little man. Is that what he has sent to your mistress in return?" he continued, holding out his hand for the rather formidable-looking envelope. "Poor Mary," he thought; "she has been trying to get him to agree to a compromise," and he sighed the dull heavy sigh that Mary had heard so often.

"Yes, sir; that's the receipt," answered Deb. "Master Arthur and I had to wait ever so long because Mr. Browning hadn't the proper stamp. He said he was very sorry to have to put this pressure on you, sir, only things were so bad this winter. You will find the receipt all right, sir," she continued, as her master looked first at her and then at the paper as though stupefied; and at that he tore it open. Yes—there it was; a genuine receipt, stamp and all. For a moment he was utterly bewildered, and then the truth flashed on him.

"Was any one with your mistress just now when she sent you?" he asked.

"Yes, sir, Miss Maturin."

But Arty broke in again breathlessly:

"Yes, and mamma had red eyes, and Deb said she had been crying—didn't you, Deb?"

"Now, Master Arthur, what a chatterbox you do get, to be sure," returned Deb, turning scarlet. "I'm sure your ma looked quite cheered-like when she gave me the money. Look how you are twisting your comforter, Master Arthur; you're all of a strangle," and Deb confusedly busied herself in putting him tidy.

The Vicar, who had listened to them both in a sort of maze, put his hand on the boy's head fondly and turned back with him to the house.

"Never mind about the receipt, Deb; I will give it to your mistress myself," he said, as he let himself in with his latch-key. But he did not go straight to his wife's presence; instead of that he went to his study and closed the door.

We need not follow him there. What if his inborn enemy is strong within him, and he has to fight a battle with his pride? Is he less an Ord or more than mortal because he is enrolled among the ranks of them who serve? What if his gratitude is for the moment blotted out—and the thought is bitter within him that he must take these things again and again from this girl's hand—are his needs the less? Leave him alone. Presently he will take out his paper, and, like Hezekiah, spread it before the Lord, and then will he aver that with the good man these words are true—

"He shall deliver thee out of six troubles; yea, in seven there shall no evil befall thee."

# CHAPTER XXII.

## THE LITTLE SISTER.

' Yet in herself she dwelleth not,
    Although no home were half so fair ;
    No simplest duty is forgot ;
    Life hath no dim and lowly spot
    That doth not in her sunshine share."
                                        LOWELL.

" Fair ladies ! you drop manna in the way of starved people."
                                        SHAKSPEARE.

ROTHA was humming over her work ; it was a habit of hers when anything particularly pleased her. Mary compared it one day to the low twitter of a little bird ; but the Vicar, who had overheard her, and was not quite so poetical, would have it that it was something between a very loud purr and a whole hive of honey-bees.

"Do you always purr when you are pleased ?" he asked once ; but Rotha never could break herself off the habit. It was louder than ever this morning.

She had told Mrs. Ord all about the gray dress, and they had made a pilgrimage up to her room, whither Rotha had had it surreptitiously conveyed.

"And you chose this when I was looking at the carpet ?" repeated Mary for the third time.

"Yes ; and I was longing so to get that lovely blue for your sister, but I dare not—after—you know what I mean," finished Rotha hurriedly.

Of course Mrs. Ord knew what she meant ; she could not forget, nor Rotha either, how the soft nest of Cashmere shawls had been disturbed.

"It would be a pity to go to such expense, and then for her not to wear it," she said gravely. She had exhausted a whole string of superlatives over the dress—its wonderful sheen and richness, and the splendour of its trimmings.

" I have never had such a dress as that since I was married," she said as they went downstairs again. " I remember how my poor mother decided that I must have two good silk gowns in my wedding outfit. No wonder Austin thinks the dove-coloured one rather old-fashioned; do you know it has been turned twice?"

" I never noticed it was shabby," returned Rotha; " but then you look so nice in everything. I am so glad Miss Evans has finished it so soon. You will be able to wear it at Mrs. Blake's to-morrow."

" I ought to save it for your party, Rotha," said Mary, with a smile.

Somehow the beautiful dress failed to awake the enthusiasm that her husband's coat had done. She was thinking of that and the coal-bill all the time she was fingering the real lace edging. But Rotha would not hear of any postponement. She was to wear it first at Oakmead, and then at Miss Brookes', and Bryn should come third on the list. For Rotha was being rather universally fêted just now; Kirkby and Blackscar vied with each other in doing homage to the young heiress. People were full of compunction at this time, and wondered at their own blindness.

The news of the Vicar's speech had spread far and wide. Rotha was almost overwhelmed by the number of pressing invitations. The winter season had just begun, and prodigious feats were undertaken in the shape of tea-parties. Mrs. Stephen Knowles and Mrs. Travers had excelled themselves, and Nettie Underwood and the Ollivers rapidly followed suit. The Vicar and his wife had been present on all these occasions; and Rotha had overheard certain remarks on Mrs. Ord's dove-coloured gown which had made her feel very hot and angry.

It had been decided by Rotha's friends that there must be a return party given at Bryn. Mary had undertaken the management of the whole affair, and Rotha had already sent out the invitations. The gray dress was intended partly for this occasion, when Rotha played her part of hostess to perfection, and the party was the greatest success of the season.

But neither Belle Clinton nor Robert Ord was among the guests; but people did not wonder at that—they knew Belle Clinton was too ill.

They had drifted on to the subject of the party now, but Mary was rather absent, and wondered why Deb had not made her appearance. " It is only a very little way, and she has been gone nearly an hour," she said presently, breaking in upon Rotha's humming, and then the Vicar came in.

Rotha did not know why, but her heart began to beat rather

quickly when she saw him.   He looked very pale, paler than she
had ever seen him, a thing always very noticeable in a florid man.
But it was not the paleness that disturbed her; she knew the
sleepless nights would account for that; it was a certain expression in his face which she had never remarked before—a likeness
to Robert.   She had never noticed the marked similarity between
the two brothers until now.   It brought to her mind suddenly
something that Mary once said, "that Austin had never been a
favourite with his aunt on account of his quick temper; but that
was the family complaint," Mary had added, laughing.

Could she have been right?   Was it possible that the Vicar, as
a young man, had had his share of the family inheritance—pride
and a domineering temper?   Garton was fiery, she knew; she had
noticed how, at a sneer from Robert, the blood would rush over his
face, and he would bite his lip to keep down the angry word; but
she had never seen the Vicar moved from his gentleness.   Now, as
he sat opposite to her, there was a weariness and sternness of look
about him that she failed to comprehend.   How did she know that
he had fought a battle with himself and had conquered?   His eyes
looked very gently at her for all that.

"Always at work," he said, stretching out his hand to her
across the table.   "I suppose I am not to know for whom all that
beautiful stitching is intended."

"Not just yet," returned Rotha, blushing; and then he took a
paper from his breast-pocket and pushed it across to Mary.   "Here
is your receipt, my dear; I think you will find it right," he observed, very quietly.   Rotha looked up at Mary's exclamation; the
two women exchanged guilty glances full of dismay.   What did it
mean—could he have met Deb?   Mary, who had undertaken to
break the whole matter to her husband that night, felt very confused by Rotha's presence, and was rather at her wit's end for an
answer.

"I met Deb, and she said you would find it right," continued
the Vicar calmly; he was regarding the women's agitation with
the utmost sangfroid; he saw that Rotha had risen as though to
leave the room, and had then sat down again.   "What pluck she
has; she is determined to brave it out," he thought.   He was quite
pitiless to Mary, who was fumbling over the papers, and making
believe to treat it as a matter of course.   "Don't you think you
ought to look if it be quite correct?" he persisted.   "It was a large
sum of money to entrust to a servant."

"Oh, Deb has been with us so many years," returned Mary
hurriedly; "where—where did you meet her, Austin?"   She was
not in the least prepared for such an emergency.   If only Rotha

were not present, she thought she could have been quite eloquent;
but Rotha had sat down again, and the eloquence was not forthcoming ; the bale of gray flannel was upon her conscience, and then
there was that carpet rolled up at Bryn.　Mary almost wished for
the moment that she had never seen the inside of Tyler and Tyler's.
But, though the Vicar knew all about it, he was not disposed to
help her; perhaps he meant to punish her a little first for her
secrecy.　He answered her question in the gravest possible way.

"I met Deb near the Grammar School.　By the bye, how does
your young *protégé* get on, Miss Maturin ?　Arty was with her ;
the young gentleman does not seem to have enjoyed his walk at all ;
he would have it that a sort of Jack-in-the-box with dirty hands
had patted him on the head in Mr. Browning's office.　Is your
receipt all right, my dear ?"

"Oh yes, Austin," answered Mary, rather pettishly—that is to
say, pettishly for her.

She began to understand that she was to be tormented for her
sins ; how she longed to make a clean breast of it all !　Austin's
questions were like pins and needles, but, all the same, the eloquence
would not be forthcoming.

"What's the matter, Mary ?　Surely I may ask a question
about Browning's bill ?" and now a little twinkle did come into
the Vicar's eyes, but he looked grave enough the next minute.
"How long have you made Miss' Maturin your banker, my dear ?"

Then Rotha started and changed colour again ; she began to
wish now that she had left the room.　Was he really angry ?　He
had never once looked at her.

Then Mary broke down altogether, and her eyes were very
piteous indeed.

"Oh, Austin, I could not help it ; she would do it," she exclaimed.　She was deserting her friend very treacherously, but the
Vicar would not let her finish.

"Answer for yourself, Mary ; am I right in supposing that you
drew this money from Miss Maturin ?"　But Mary would not
answer calmly.

"I couldn't help it, Austin ; I could not indeed ; she would
make me tell her what was troubling me.　I think she noticed
how worried you looked, dear, and then there was nothing for it
but that she would pay the whole bill.　I did not like taking it at
all, Austin ; but, indeed, I could not refuse her."

"That is because you are so soft-hearted, Mary.　It never
occurred to you, I suppose, that you might tell your husband before
you took upon yourself to pay his bills ?"

"Yes, it did," returned Mary, who was nearly broken-hearted

at this unexpected reproach ; she really believed that Austin was angry with her for her want of confidence.   " I wanted to tell you directly, dear ; but she was so afraid you would refuse to take it."

Now all this was very dreadful to Rotha, and this time she looked at the door so earnestly that the Vicar interpreted her thoughts at once.

" No; don't go, Miss Maturin.   I have something to say to you both."

" If you will only hear me first," pleaded Mary.

" But I will not ; I mean to punish you for your silence. Who ever would have believed you could have been such a little traitor !" But there was a sorrowful vein running through the Vicar's jest that robbed the words of their sweetness.   Rotha was almost sure now that she had pained him ; tears sprang to her eyes at the mere thought.

" I will not ask you again, as I did just now, for whom you are putting in all those delicate stitches," he said, laying his hand again on her work.   " It may be that I am not so blind as I appear.   Shall I tell you a few things that have come under my notice ?"

" No, no; please do not," she pleaded, lifting her eyes to him for the first time, but his look soon sent her to her work again.   She knew now why naughty children never could stand the Vicar's eyes.

" Last Sunday the boys showed me their new boots, and Laurie, who was very communicative, told me that he and his brother had gray flannel shirts, the same as Bob Travers', that we admired so, Mary.   There was a hint also of a new suit for Arty."

Mary gave a little gasp of surprise, but Rotha worked on harder than ever ; her cheeks were flaming.

" But that is not all.   The other evening, in the twilight, I took out my old coat for Mary to repair—she is a neat hand at binding—but when I got to the light I found that my old coat was transformed into a new one.   I was slightly surprised, I confess, but I hung it up again, feeling that some benevolent fairy had been at work—the same fairy, I supposed, who had put the wadded dressing-gown across my arm-chair, and who, I found, had visited Arty with big brown parcels containing toys, sweetmeats, and other heterogeneous articles dear to childhood.   Arty is not one to keep a secret, mind you ; he does not take after his mother in that," darting a look at poor Mary.   Oh, if only Rotha could hold up her head !   " And then Arty is such a listener.   I had no idea before that there was so much truth in the proverb, that ' Little pitchers have great ears ;' but he's a tremendous fellow at listening.   Some- times he comes to me and tells me his dreams ; though, by the bye, he will have it they are true. He had a wonderful dream the other night of a grand new carpet, like the softest moss, which he declared was for mammie's room, and curtains with real flowers running over them; but that was nothing to the funny dream when he saw Uncle Gar and Mammie and Miss Maturin all covered with whitewash, with their arms full of cobwebs and bottles. And the worst of it all is the rogue evidently believed it to be true."

"'I call Miss Maturin "Santa Claus," father,' he said once, 'because she rains sugar-plums on my pillow. Last night I woke up and found a big drum—and'—what is the matter, Mary?" For Mary, that mildest and softest of criminals, had crept up to his side quite abashed.

"Oh, Austin! how could you—how could you?" was all she said. Then the Vicar took down the little hand from his shoulder and drew her towards him.

"Nay, Mary, I should rather say, how could you?" he demanded still gravely.

Then Rotha, whose cheeks had hung out every possible sign of distress over the Vicar's speech, could bear it no longer.

"Oh, Mr. Ord, I cannot believe that you are really angry with me!" she exclaimed; "but if you would listen to me a moment." And as she spoke she came a little nearer to him and looked appealingly in his face.

"Well," he said, turning towards her, "it seems I must put both of you on your defence. Mary's silence has pleaded guilty, am I to say the same of you?"

"Yes, if you like," she answered gently; "I shall not deny your charges. I suppose Arty's dreams were all true."

"Well!" he reiterated for the second time, and then again that appealing look came into her eyes; she looked like a child scarcely penitent, yet longing to be forgiven.

"If I have offended you," she began again, and then paused— "if I have offended you, I am very sorry. But no, I will not believe that I have; it was all so beautiful, and we were so happy, that everything cannot be spoiled for us like that."

"No, indeed," ejaculated Mary. She began to understand dimly the workings of her husband's mind; but Rotha again interrupted her.

"Mr. Ord, supposing you had a sister," and then she stopped, —"a little sister, and she had all the good things of this world given to her, and you were left out in the cold; and supposing" —hesitating again—"all these good things had come to her by a dreadful mistake, which, when she thought of it—which she did continually—always made her feel very unhappy;" aud here for a moment Rotha's voice grew troubled.

"Well, my child?" said the Vicar encouragingly.

And she went on. "And suppose, in her unhappiness—the little sister's, I mean—God put a thought into her heart, which took away all her pain, and made her feel quite warm and comforted, and supposing," coming a little nearer, and touching him softly on the arm, "she—this little sister, I mean—came to you"—"Came to me!" repeated the Vicar, as she hesitated again. "Yes; and, speaking in her reverence and love, told you of this beautiful thought that grew in her heart day by day, and prayed you not to despise her little gifts because they made her so very, very happy; and supposing that the little sister"—coming still closer, and clasping her hands together—"begged you, out of your great tender heart, never to hurt her again as you have hurt her just now, but, if she has made a mistake, put it all down to her ignorance; but to be sure that she will never offend so again." And as she bent her face over the kind hand that was stretched out to her she felt a light touch on her hair that calmed and hushed her in a moment.

"God bless the little sister," finished the Vicar solemnly. "Ay, and she shall be blessed; child, I will not have you cry like that; it is you who have been breaking my heart all this time with your love and gifts."

He talked to them presently when Rotha was a little calmer, and, drawing his wife very tenderly to his side, he told them both the bitter battle he had fought with his pride, and how his heart had been very soft towards them all the time Mary had believed he had been reproaching her with want of confidence.

"My own Mary, do you think I have not blessed the little sister over and over again for making your dear face grow so much brighter day by day?"

"You see your name will stick to you, Rotha," he said presently, calling her for the first time by her Christian name. "Whatever you may be to Mary, to me you will always be 'the little sister;' I hope that you like your new title?"

"My 'little sister' brought gifts," returned Rotha meaningly, but blushing a little over her words.

"And so may this little sister, but not too often; she may carry them now and then to her great big brother out in the cold, though it is not nearly so cold as she supposes it to be," and he looked fondly at the dear woman whose love had shed such sunshine over his life. "There are others far more cold and dreary than we are, Mary."

"Ah! true, there is poor Belle," said the happier sister.

"Yes, poor Belle," echoed Rotha, and the Vicar added rather sadly, "Yes, and poor Robert."

And after that Rotha went home.

These were golden days with Rotha. "The little sister," as the Vicar often called her, was never for many hours absent from the Vicarage; she and Mary were still hard at their work, and there seemed at present no end to their labour. Garton or the Vicar would come and read to them sometimes, but Belle persevered in her unsociable habits.

"I do wish you would come and sit with us downstairs," Rotha said one day when she and Belle were together for a minute; "it feels almost as though I were separating you from your sister"—which was partly true, as her constant presence had afforded Belle an excuse for her taciturnity.

"Why should I come?" Belle had answered. "I don't think that either you or Mary can want me." She was in a sick sullen humour this afternoon; but Rotha, who saw she was suffering, was very patient to her.

"I am quite sure that we both want you, Miss Clinton," but Belle did not answer; poor soul, she was growing more warped and diseased day by day.

"Why can we not be friends?" continued Rotha yearningly; "your sister loves me and the Vicar also—you are the only one in the house who has not a kind word for me; dear Miss Clinton, it does seem almost too hard sometimes." Then Belle turned upon her proudly; she could not bear even a word of reproach from this girl, and yet she knew it to be true.

"What do you expect?" she said harshly; "am I so happy that I can forget the past? Why do you taunt me with my coldness?"

"I taunt you, Miss Clinton?"

"Yes, you and Mary too. What is my own sister to me now when you have come between us? Once I could tell Mary nearly everything and be sure of her sympathy; but now even she and Austin are changed to me."

"Is this my doing, Miss Clinton?"

"Is it not?" was the unjust answer. "Look at Robert; is he the same man when you are by? I tell you this—you are blighting my life and his, and yet you come to me and ask me to be friends."

"I do," returned Rotha; "in spite of your hard words I ask it still. Am I to blame for your lover's bitter injustice? You are not yourself this afternoon, or you would not speak like this." She did not truly realise the truth of her words till she saw Belle's colour change to ashy white as she tried to answer her. In another moment the generous-hearted girl was by her side.

"You are faint—you are in pain," she said. "No, you must not speak; lean on me a moment. Good Heavens, to think of any one enduring this pain, and hiding it from every one!"

Belle clutched her sleeve nervously.

"Mary—don't tell Mary," she whispered through her white lips. "I will do anything you like, but don't tell Mary."

She was quite passive now. When Rotha placed her on the couch and covered her up, she let her bring her wine and chafe her cold hands almost as though she were grateful for it. And certainly no sisterly hands could have more gently put back the damp hair from her brow; as she did so, tears no efforts could repress gathered to her eyes.

The painful spasm was over, and then Belle looked wonderingly at her.

"Are you crying for me or for yourself?" she said, more gently than she had yet spoken.

"For you," answered Rotha, dashing the tears away half-ashamed. "I cannot bear to see you suffer so; it makes me wish that I could take your place for a little while."

"You are a strange girl after all my hard speeches—thank you," and Belle closed her eyes wearily.

"May I stay with you?" asked Rotha wistfully. "I can see the pain is better, but still I do not like to leave you." And Belle, who seemed sinking into slumber, signified her assent.

She woke towards evening, and found Rotha still watching her.

"Have you been here all this time?" she asked curiously.

Rotha nodded.

"Your sister came up, and I told her you had not been well. I made light of it, as you wished, and she has gone out now. She told me to bring you a cup of tea when you woke." And Rotha, who had been stirring the fire into a cheerful blaze, busied herself over a small tea-equipage in a brisk cosy manner that was very pleasant.

Belle said nothing as she drank the tea; she looked very pale and weary still; but every now and then her dark eyes looked across at Rotha rather wistfully.

Rotha caught one of these glances and asked if she wanted anything.

"No, nothing—only I wish you would not be so kind; it

makes me feel your words are true, and that I have been too hard to you."

"No; I will not let you say that."

"I think you were right, and I was not quite myself. I think I get half-crazed sometimes with misery. I ought not to have reproached you with Robert's bitter speeches."

"But if you believed them?" said Rotha timidly.

"Well, sometimes I think I do. One can't help one's thoughts, and it is not like him to be so prejudiced; and then again there are times when I half fancy he is wrong. I think the doubt and struggle make me seem so hard to you; often and often I do not know what to think."

"Don't think about it at all;" then with a touching inflection of voice, "only let me love you and do something for you."

"It seems so dreadful," she continued, after a pause, "to see you so unhappy, and to know that but for me he would have the right to shield and protect you. You said just now that I have blighted both your lives, and, God knows, I feel you are right."

"I ought not to have said that," returned Belle remorsefully; but Rotha, still with the same touching sadness, answered her:

"Why should you not say it? I think I can bear your reproaches better than your silence. I do not feel that I shall ever be afraid of you again. Yes, I have spoiled your life; dislike to me is changing his nature—do you think I cannot see that? I am made the minister of this unholy revenge, and, in spite of my happiness, I shall bear the bitterness of it to my dying day."

How mournful the voice; how sadly the mild eyes looked out at the faint streaks of the wintry sunset, at the unchanging grayness of the sea, at the bleak barrenness of the waste of sands! How the thin soft hands grasped each other in a set patience like an act of prayer! Belle, lying back on her couch, watched her—sorely troubled. Her own thoughts were a mystery to her, but from that time her conviction of Rotha's innocence grew to be a certainty.

"Only let me love you!"—the words came back to her as she lay that night tossing on her sleepless pillow. "Only let me love you"—how meekly she had said it! Could she of all people afford to throw away such love?

There was silence between them for some time, and then Belle, looking very sick and sorrowful, stretched out her hands to Rotha.

"Can you forgive me my hardness?" she said, almost in a whisper, and Rotha's only answer was to stoop down and kiss her brow.

# CHAPTER XXIII.

"She has an eye that can speak
Though her tongue were silent."
AARON HILL.

"Sometimes when hard need has pressed me
To bow down where I despise,
I have read stern words of counsel
In those sad reproachful eyes."
ADELAIDE ANNE PROCTOR.

MEANWHILE the shirt-making progressed most satisfactorily; but, alas, Belle was not among the workers.

Ever since the day of her hysterical attack a gradual, and at first scarcely perceptible change had come over her; the strange wanness and shadow that Rotha had noticed became more marked; day by day she grew thinner and paler; the pain in the side was almost constant now. Rotha sometimes met her on the stairs labouring as though for breath. Now and then Mary started and changed colour at the sound of her sister's hard dry cough. She and the Vicar were growing seriously uneasy; but still Belle, rigid in her waywardness, would have it that nothing ailed her.

"I am only so tired—so very tired," she would say when Mary with tears in her eyes implored her to spare herself. "I think I took cold that night at church. I shall have to give up evening service this bitter weather, that is all."

Poor Belle! Evening service was not the only thing she gave up. One by one her duties were laid aside; Rotha had her district now; she never went among her poor people.

"When the spring comes I must take up my work again," she said to Rotha. But she never told her that the day before she had tried to creep to the nearest cottage and had failed.

She was more alone than ever now. Working made the pain in her side worse, and after a time she found it impossible to conceal her sufferings. She would lie for hours on the little square

couch in the drawing-room, looking out vacantly at the blue tops
of the Leatham hills ; but she never cared for Mary or Rotha to
keep her company.    The morbid reserve that seemed inherent in
her nature grew upon her with indulgence.    She never seemed to
talk much to any one but Robert.

"It only makes me cough," she said fretfully, when Mary's
affectionate reproaches were unusually urgent.    "I am so tired, and
I want to be quiet and get rested for the evening."

"But you are always tired, Belle !" Mary would reply.    "It
seems to me you are more tired every day.    I wish Robert could
see you now; he would not think that Austin and I were making
a fuss about nothing."

Belle shivered slightly at the mention of Robert.

By what superhuman exertions she continued to blind him was
known best to herself.    He was the only one who was ignorant of
the real state of the case.    Mary, with all her efforts, failed to
enlighten him.

"Belle has never been strong," he would say, "and this cold
she has caught hangs about her and keeps her weak ;" and he would
go about his daily work quite cheerfully.    "She will be better
when this damp raw weather is over," he would think as he went
to and fro through the slushy streets.    He always believed Belle's
version of herself.

"She was better," she would assure him, "much better, only
she was so tired, and her cough was still troublesome."    He knew
nothing about those long mornings and afternoons on the couch.
She had always a bright colour of an evening.    No matter how
ill she had been that day, she would creep down from her room to
meet him, looking lovelier than ever.

"Mary tells me you have been worse to-day," he would say
sometimes, looking at her anxiously; but she always contrived to
evade his inquiries.    As she sat talking to him he would wonder at
the brilliancy of her beauty.    How was he to know that her eyes
were bright with repressed fever, and that it was only his presence
that stimulated her to such exertion?    How was he to know?
She was never pale or silent with him.

She was always so ready with her excuses too.    "Where is
your opal ring?" he asked her once, rather reproachfully, and she
had returned him an evasive answer ; she never told him the ring
had dropped so repeatedly from her wasted hand that she feared to
lose it.    Soon after she borrowed a certain old-fashioned keeper
that Mary wore on her little finger ; the next day the opals shone
in their accustomed place.

With her strong will she was blinding herself and him ; she

would go upstairs to her own room when her lover had said good-night, carefully closing the door behind her; but if any one had seen her holding on with her frail strength to the balustrade and coughing at every step! The Vicarage walls were unhappily thick. Belle never spoke of the slow torture of those long wakeful nights, of the restlessness and burning fever that consumed her, and so no one knew why nature took its revenge in added prostration in the morning. Mary declared that anxiety about her sister was aging her. One day she came down half crying to the Vicar to avow her belief that Belle was using rouge to deceive her lover. Rotha, who was doing some copying work in the study, quite started at the idea.

"She was as white as that cloth, quite ghastly ten minutes ago," reiterated Mary; "and I gave her some sal volatile, but when Robert came in just now she begged me quite in a flurry to go down to him, and when she came into the room a few minutes afterwards her cheeks had a fixed red in them, quite a spot of colour, just as though they were painted. You know yourself, Austin, Belle never had a high colour."

"No, Mary, you were the blooming one," returned the Vicar lightly. "Do you remember when I used to compare you to a pink apple-blossom?" and then as she persisted in her uneasy suspicion he grew serious, and muttered something about "hectic" and "fever." By and by he told Mary that he was determined to speak very firmly to Belle, and insist on her seeing a doctor.

Rotha was obliged to leave early that evening, but the next morning she learnt from Mrs. Ord that the Vicar's firmness had been unavailing. Belle seemed to have a rooted antipathy to the very idea. "Austin had been very stern," Mary added, "and Belle had been hysterical." Next day the doctor had come to the house by the Vicar's express orders, and Belle had locked herself up in her room, and had refused to see him, and the Vicar was very angry.

Robert was angry too. He thought it very childish of Belle; but he added in the same breath that in his opinion Mary and Austin were teasing her unnecessarily. "If she were really ill she would be only too glad to see a doctor," he said. "Why not leave her alone a little? It is this dreary weather that tries her. I really thought she looked much better last evening till Austin upset her; he had no right to issue his commands like that."

Mary, as she heard him, could have wrung her hands over his blindness and her sister's obstinacy. In her eyes it was little short of suicidal; but Rotha, though she would not have hinted at it for worlds, had a dim suspicion of the real state of the case. She was sure that Belle's refusal to see a doctor of her brother-in-law's providing was based upon far different motives, and that she knew more about herself than any one guessed.

One raw November day she had come upon Belle within a stone's throw of the Blackscar Infirmary, and Belle had a little white parcel in her hand very much resembling a bottle of medicine. Rotha had not seemed to notice, however; but shortly after she had questioned one of the nurses whom she knew, and had learnt that Miss Clinton often visited the Infirmary, and that to her knowledge she was more than once closeted a long time with Mr. Greenock, the house-surgeon, so that it was very probable she was on the list of out-patients.

Rotha would have given worlds to have shared this knowledge with her friends, but on reflection she dared not; her quick intuition had instantly divined that there was a twofold motive for this secrecy. Doubtless, in the first instance, Belle's unselfish generosity had induced her to take this step, fearing that her brother-in-law would incur serious expense by her constant ill health; the other motive, too, it was not difficult to guess.

Rotha was sure that Belle was uneasy about herself; at times there had been a haggardness and despondency about her for which there would seem no adequate reason. Rotha noticed she never spoke of the future. There seemed no buoyancy of hope in her life when Robert talked of the summer and of the pleasant holiday he hoped to have, and how he meant to take her and Mary for a week to ramble among the glens of Burnley-upon-Sea. Burnley-upon-Sea, where the cows walked over the sands at evening, and the long green woods stretched dimly down to the shore. Belle would turn away her head to hide the tears in her eyes; she would choke something down as she tried to return a cheerful answer.

" Do sing something lively," she would say of an evening when Mrs. Carruthers sat down to play one of her glorious symphonies; a terrible weariness would be on her when Meg sung some of her old favourites—"Eve's Lament" or "Angels ever bright and fair"—but no one could get Meg to lay aside her sacred music now. Rotha would take her place sometimes and sing old-fashioned ballads in her fresh young voice; it came somewhat flatly after Meg's grand music, to be sure. " It is rather like hearing the twittering of birds after service," the Vicar would say in his droll way, but I think they all loved the girl's voice. Belle would ask faintly for " Auld Robin Gray" or " My Mother bids me bind my hair;" the last she was never tired of hearing. "Those are not very gay songs, Bella darling," Robert would say with a smile; he rather preferred Meg's selections. Rotha would go back to the

music-stool again and again ; she knew why Meg's anthems jarred
on the sick nerves.   What if no chord of Belle's nature thrilled in
unison with their sublime lessons of faith and resignation, still
clinging as she was with a breaking heart to the objects of her
earthly love ?

"Will any one sing ?"   It grew a habit with her to say this,
and so it came to pass that Rotha no longer needed the Vicar's
invitation ; and even Robert looked to her presence of an evening
as a necessary ingredient to Belle's pleasure—Belle, who, since the
day of their reconciliation, had never again repelled her advances.

Rotha was able to watch her very closely therefore, and this
was the result of her watching.   She was convinced that up to a
certain point Belle knew the truth about herself, and that she was
bent on concealing her knowledge for some purpose of her own.
Rotha shuddered at the thought of those dreary pilgrimages to the
Infirmary ; she used to wonder how Belle got there.   Mr. Greenock
had the reputation of being a very clever man, but, as he said himself, he was no alarmist.   It was just possible, therefore, he might
confirm Belle in her blindness, and that she might scarcely know
the extent of her danger.   But if this were not so, and Belle really
understood the grave nature of her symptoms, she might possibly
be deriving great benefit from the proper remedies, which the
surgeon's skill would be sure to devise.

To betray this secret of Belle's seemed to Rotha perfectly useless.   She knew her quite well enough by this time to be sure that
such interference on her part would never be forgiven.   Not that
such a motive alone would have influenced her ; but she knew
that if she told Mrs. Ord, Mary would at once inform the Vicar and
Robert.   Every one would be up in arms ; Mr. Greenock would be
consulted ; the real nature of the mysterious malady would certainly be known ; but the result would be such a fit of angry
obstinacy on Belle's part that it would be doubtful where the
mischief would end.   No, no ; she must let things take their course
a little longer ; if matters grew worse, she might take upon herself
to speak.

Rotha's intention was good, but it was the reasoning of inexperience.   She was ignorant of the nature of Belle's disease ; it never
occurred to her that contact with the sharp northern breezes was
as injurious to her physical frame as the secret strain on her spirits
was to her mental frame.   It might be that the doctor's skill
would be brought to bear in vain on the overwrought mind and
body, reacting on each other so lamentably.   If Rotha had spoken
out, doubtless the result would have been exactly as she prophesied,
and there would have been much bitter work to go through with

Belle, but it would have answered better in the end ; a great deal
of precious time would not have been lost, and Robert Ord would
have been spared the heavy remorse that was to embitter his life
for so long.

But, if Rotha made this mistake, she was nobly to atone for it ;
her secret uneasiness and a few words that Mrs. Ord had dropped
in her trouble led her to form all sorts of impracticable and generous projects for Belle's relief ; till at last, one of these appearing
rather more tangible and worthy of trial than the others, it was
determined to put it to the proof without delay.

" If things are allowed to go on like this," Mrs. Ord had said
to her, " I shall not have a sister long ; Belle will go into a
decline."

And it was during the long sorrowful conversation that followed
these words that Rotha proposed that change of scene and a
milder climate should be tried for Belle.

" If I can only get your brother-in-law's consent," finished
Rotha, " the thing can be done without delay. She will not
listen to such a plan from us, I know, but a word from him will
do it."

" Yes ; if he will only say the word," sighed Mary.

" He will if you put it before him properly ; could not the
Vicar speak to him, dear Mrs. Ord ?  He might tell him that we
would go wherever he thought best—the Isle of Wight, or Devonshire, or even the south of France, and if you liked Laurie might
go with us too ;" for just now Mary chose to believe that Laurie
was delicate.

" Oh, Rotha, how good you are !" said the mother gratefully ;
and then there was an instant's silence, during which Mary turned
over the project in her mind ; in her eyes it seemed without a
single flaw.

" But I shall never dare to speak to Robert," she said, shaking
her head mournfully.  " I have no influence over him now.  The
time was when he would listen to a word from ' Mother Mary,' as
he called me ; that was when Belle and he were first engaged, and
I used to think him the dearest fellow in the world ; but now—
oh, Rotha, I never saw a man so altered ;" and Mary looked so
sad and so unlike herself that Rotha hastened to console her.

" Never mind about speaking to him," she said ; " perhaps it
would be better for me to do the whole thing myself ; a stranger
can sometimes put a thing more strongly, and I think he is too
just to let his personal dislike interfere with Belle's good."

" But supposing he does not consider it for her good ?" interrupted Mary ; she was very despondent about the whole affair,

"He is as blind now as a man in his proper senses can be, and he is just as likely to throw cold water on your generous offer as not. Talk of pride—the proudest Ord that ever lived could not hold a candle to him."

"Never mind, I will try," returned Rotha bravely; she was very frightened at the thought of the task she had undertaken, but she would not hear of cold water for a moment. "I suppose I would as soon take a bull by the horns," she finished, with an attempt at a smile; "but I mean to carry it through."

Rotha spoke of her plan very quietly in discussing it with Mrs. Ord, but it was the greatest sacrifice she had made in her life. Kirkby was just now especially dear to her, and the thought of leaving it, perhaps for months, was very bitter; it was simply banishment from all she loved, and that was not all,—the charge she contemplated was in itself somewhat overwhelming; how was she to nurse a person of Belle's unhappy disposition? and yet she would be responsible for such nursing. Belle was at all times difficult to manage, and Rotha had very honest doubts as to her own powers of management.

"Perhaps, when we are alone together, she might be more sociable and allow me to do things for her," she said to herself as she pondered over these difficulties; "but anyhow I am the only one who can go with her. I wish I were more fit for such a responsibility."

Poor generous-hearted Rotha—but it was just these things which tested the girl's nobleness—the basis of her whole nature was self-sacrifice.

The woman who, if she had had the power, would most certainly have had the magnanimity to beggar herself for her enemies would assuredly not scruple at any personal self-denial that might benefit her friends. To see a duty clearly and to try and perform it was a natural sequence with Rotha. It was this singleness of aim, this great-heartedness—if there be such a word—that first won the Vicar's respect for her. He told Mary one day that she was at once the weakest and the strongest woman he had ever seen.

It had come into her heart to return good for evil in her dealings with Robert Ord, and no amount of ill usage upon his part could move her from her purpose. Robert Ord's pride literally shrank from the scorching of her coals of fire; her gentleness was pitiless cruelty to him. It was this recognition of her strength for good that brought out all his latent obstinacy. It grew to be a neck-and-neck race between them; but as the stars of heaven fought against Sisera, so circumstances fought against Robert Ord and forced him to succumb at last to a woman's hand—when his will was divided against itself, and the man sat down in his weakness and gloried in it.

Rotha said nothing about her regrets to Mary. A little shrinking consciousness kept her silent on that point; but she put the whole scheme in such a bright light that Mrs. Ord was quite cheered. The only difficulty was in the impossibility of Rotha ever finding an opportunity for a private talk with Robert. He never came to the Vicarage till tea was over, and then he went straight into the drawing-room, where they were all assembled. Rotha could neither seek him at his own house nor ask him to Bryn.

"I am sure I don't know how we are to manage it," said Mrs. Ord helplessly, "unless you are to waylay him in the passage;" but Rotha had a better plan than that. She knew he came home from Thornborough on Saturday at an early hour in the afternoon, and she resolved to go and meet him.

"I think the sea-wall would be a better place of rendezvous than the draughty passage," she said, trying to look very brave; but she felt rather like a mouse trying on a lion's skin—it was such a gigantic purpose, and then the skin was such a tough one.

How she hated the very thought of Saturday; but she was not going to flinch for all that. Every time Belle coughed she felt convinced her plan was a wise one.

"She wants sunshine and change of air," she thought. "It is so dreadfully bleak up here."

At the appointed hour she was pacing up and down the sea-wall like a sentinel on duty, and looking not very unlike a mouse —with plenty of soft fur outside and many inward shivers within. She had a fresh shiver every time she saw a tall man in the distance, and then she chafed and grew hot because he was late. She knew that he always came home by the way of the sea-wall. She had kept a strict look-out, but yet she feared she had missed him. No; there he was, in his brown overcoat, looking straight before him, as he always did, as though he were challenging some distant object.

Of course he stopped to accost her, and of course Rotha stopped too; the time had gone by when he would pass her with a slight bow; since then there had been much surface intercourse between them, and Robert was always extremely civil—he was very civil now, exceedingly so.

"It is rather a cold afternoon for a walk," he remarked, with a smile. Rotha, when she was more than usually provoked, always said Robert had a special smile for her. When asked to describe it, she would turn round and demand "if you had seen an icicle trying to thaw—and failing?" she would add when particularly severe. This frosty smile was a matter of course, but that he should add that she looked pale and tired was rather surprising—it almost took her breath away.

"I suppose I am somewhat tired," she returned hurriedly; "I have been waiting for you such a long time." It was his turn now to look astonished.

"Waiting for me! Is anything the matter?" as a sudden thought turned him chill.

"Anything the matter—no, not more than usual. It is only a slight favour that I am going to ask you. Do you mind returning by the sands, there are so many people about here?" She spoke in a quick nervous manner, as she often did to him, but her movement left him no choice. When a lady tells a gentleman that there are so many people about, he may be sure she has something very important for his private ear; and therefore, much as he disliked having business with Miss Maturin, he could do no less than assist her civilly down the sandy bank and wait for her to explain herself; he could not well remonstrate in words, whatever he might do in manner.

"Don't you find this soft sand very unpleasant?" he remarked in a voice that told Rotha very plainly that he did. He had promised Belle an afternoon's reading, and he had brought a book by her favourite author, and this lengthened detour by the sea did not please him at all; but Rotha pointed to a crisp line lying apparently right out to sea. "The sand is quite hard and firm out there, and the tide is going out. I never walk in these sandy ruts if I can help it," and she began to walk very quickly and decidedly towards a range of salt-water pools with rugged stepping stones thrown in here and there. Robert Ord, as he followed her, felt compelled to admire the agility with which she sprang over the slippery rocks. "Now we are on *terra firma*, and I can talk," she said as they gained the slip of sand. They were on a long island now; the waves came lapping in with a little splash and gurgle; a gray line of sea closed in everywhere; the sky overhead had a faint red light in it. In the west a great crimson sun hung like a ball of fire; a rough wind swept over the surface of the sluggish pools; black drifts of seaweed lay everywhere. Rotha, walking very swiftly, turned her face to him and began:

"I daresay you think it very strange of me to waylay you like this; I never can do things as other people do, however much I try." Then Robert essayed another frosty smile—a gentleman cannot always say the truth to a lady; nevertheless, he thought it very strange indeed.

"I had no other opportunity of speaking to you alone, and every day is so important, and then one cannot ask such a favour as that in a moment."

"I thought you said it was a slight one," he retorted. He could not resist the pleasure of taking up her words, though he knew it made her nervous—it made her nervous now.

"I suppose it is a great one, after all," she returned very humbly; "for I am going to ask you to entrust something very precious to me, Mr. Ord—we are all growing so very anxious about Belle."

Now, if he had not flurried her so, Rotha would hardly have constructed her sentence in that way; one cannot pick and choose one's words in a flurry. Of course he took umbrage at her calling Miss Clinton Belle, and still more at her using the pronoun "we." "She seems determined to make herself one of the family," was his inward comment. "I wonder if she thinks we are all as blind as he is;" which enigmatical thought must be unriddled by and by.

"About Belle!" he repeated, elongating every letter till it seemed a separate syllable, "anxious about B-e-l-l-e!"

Rotha, who felt she had compromised herself in some way, went on hurriedly, "Is it possible, Mr. Ord, that you do not see how really ill she is? I know she tries to conceal her sufferings from you, but indeed you must not allow yourself to be so blinded." Her tone was very earnest, almost solemn, but Robert interrupted her angrily:

"Blinded! That is just what Mary says; how one woman will use another woman's words! If you listen to all Mary's exaggerations you will have enough to do, Miss Maturin. I suppose she has asked you to come and tell me this; but I warn you that I am not easily frightened."

"I can see that you consider it a liberty," returned Rotha in a low voice. "You are always so ready to misunderstand me. Mrs. Ord has not sent me; I have come of my own accord, because I thought that a stranger"—laying an emphasis on the word —"might more easily open your eyes."

"You mean cure my blindness?" returned Robert sarcastically.

"Yes; if you prefer that term," and then she hesitated for a moment, as though at a loss how to proceed. "You are making my task a very difficult one for me, but I expected that. I knew you would resent my interference; but I have begun to love Miss Clinton very dearly, and I have grown to be so very, very sorry for her that I could no longer keep silence."

"Belle ought to be very much obliged," began Robert in the same sarcastic tone; but Rotha stopped him.

"Belle understands me now. She will know I mean kindly. Mr. Ord, please do me this favour. Try to forget that it is I who am speaking to you, and listen to me, if it be only for her sake. I do fear—I begin to fear greatly, that she is more ill than you believe her to be."

"There I differ from you," he returned decidedly. "Miss Maturin, I put it to your good sense; if Belle were as ill as you make out, would she refuse to see a doctor ?"

Rotha paused. What would he say if he knew that Belle was an out-patient of the Blackscar Infirmary ?

"I don't think your criterion is a good one," she replied at last. "Miss Clinton is one who would endure a martyrdom rather than own her sufferings. I have heard of certain animals who always hide away from their kind when they are wounded. I think Miss Clinton would do the same."

"She is not a woman who complains if her finger aches," returned Robert sharply. Rotha sighed at his evident incredulity.

"No; she never complains. You are right there. It is only we who have watched her know that she has sleepless nights ; that she eats next to nothing ; that the pain in her side is at times intolerable ; and that she can get no rest by night and day, from her harassing cough. Mr. Ord, you say you are not easily frightened ; I think you would be if you saw how ghastly she looks sometimes."

"Mary has contrived to frighten you, that is certain," he returned somewhat impatiently. "Poor Belle ! I don't think she would thank you for exaggerating all her little symptoms to me, Miss Maturin. I am sure you mean it kindly ; but you do not know Belle as well as I do. She has never been strong."

"Never, Mr. Ord !"

"No, not for many years. I suppose circumstances have somewhat tried her ; but she never lost her spirits so completely till this summer. To add to her depression she has a bad feverish cold. I think that is about the long and short of it."

Rotha shook her head.

"You have not accounted for the pain in her side, Mr. Ord."

"She has had that for years," he returned eagerly. "It is only rather worse lately. You talk of her sleepless nights and loss of appetite ; Belle never was a good sleeper, she is nervous too, and her close confinement to the house these few last weeks has destroyed her appetite. Her malady is a bad feverish cold, you may depend upon it."

"Cannot you induce her to see a doctor?" pleaded Rotha. Like Mary, she could have wrung her hands over his blindness.

"By and by," was the somewhat evasive answer.

Then, in despair, Rotha tried upon another tack.

"I think Blackscar does not suit her," she said presently; "these northern winds are so piercing." And Rotha gave a little shiver.

"That is because you are not acclimatised," was the response. "Belle has lived here more than half her life. She likes a bracing atmosphere; I have often heard her say so."

"People do not know what is best for them," said Rotha quickly. "One may get uneasy even about a feverish cold. I will not beat about the bush any more, Mr. Ord, for it seems that we can never agree. I am not very old, and I do not understand nursing; but, nevertheless, I am going to ask you to trust Miss Clinton to me for a little while."

"To you!" he repeated in a tone of displeased astonishment.

"Yes; to me. I wanted Mrs. Ord to tell you all about our plans, and she would not; she thought I ought to speak to you myself. We would go anywhere you wished, Mr. Ord—to Ventnor or Torquay, or to the south of France; it does not matter where, so that you will let her go. I promise you I would care for her; I would indeed, as though she wére my own sister."

"This is a very extraordinary proposal," muttered Robert, and then he walked on in displeased silence. Would she never understand that he loathed her gifts and her kindness? He knew all about Tyler and Tyler's now. She was going to surfeit them with her patronage—them, the Ords! It would not be too much to say that the coal-bill literally suffocated him; and now she wanted to extend her patronage to him and Belle. Belle's ill health was to make his life a burthen to him; she would take her to the south of France, anywhere—to Madeira, perhaps, or Mentone. What was money and time to her?

"Well?" said Rotha wearily. She had only been a short half-hour with him, but her face was utterly changed, the freshness and dimples all faded—she looked, as she felt, sick at heart; they had passed the chain of pools now and were toiling up the sandy ruts by the rabbit-warren. "Well?" she reiterated, and then he forced himself to speak.

"I cannot say that I quite approve of your plan," he returned coldly; "but, all the same, I feel I ought to thank you."

"Why do you not approve of it?" she inquired; then again he was silent.

"Is it because you are afraid to trust Miss Clinton to my care —that you are unwilling to part with her? Mr. Ord, I did not think you could be so selfish."

That stung him in a moment.

"You have no right to say that," he returned angrily. "I am not thinking of myself. Miss Clinton may go if she please."

"Do you think she will go against your wishes?"

"You must take your chance of that," he replied coldly; "I shall certainly not argue against my conscience. I do not believe Miss Clinton to be as ill as you and Mary make out. I suppose I have my own opinion, and my opinion is that her disease is partly mental. I don't think a prolonged absence from those she loves best, and the society of strangers"—again a stress on the word— "will conduce materially to her well-being; but I have no objection to her trying it."

"You have every objection, you mean," exclaimed Rotha indignantly; she could not quite keep her temper—never had he been so provoking. "Why do you not say at once that none of your belongings shall ever be entrusted to my care? Why not speak out plainly and tell me this?"

"Because I cannot be so churlish to a lady. Miss Maturin, why will you always force me to say unpleasant things? You know that nothing will induce me to accept a favour at your hands; but, as you choose to accuse me of selfishness, I shall certainly not stand in Belle's light; she may go with you if she like."

"Do you think she will go without a word from you? One word will do it, remember; she trusts me now. Mr. Ord, you have made me so angry that I do not know how to entreat you; yet for Belle's sake I would entreat you, if I could, to say that word."

"You may spare your entreaties," he replied, still more coldly; "for I shall certainly not persuade her. How do I know whether such a course will be for her good? Miss Maturin, I cannot help it if you and Mary will misunderstand my motives."

"I understand you," she repeated sadly. "I feel as though I have known you for a hundred years, and that in all those hundred years you had never said a kind word to me, as you never will— as I feel you never will."

"Another home truth," he replied bitterly. Her reproach seemed to sting him with sudden pain; his brow grew darker as they went toiling up among the sand-hills of the warren; now and then Rotha stumbled wearily over the grassy ruts.

"How tired I am!" she said suddenly, with a tremble of the lip like a child; "but then you always tire me so."

"I am sorry to hear it," he replied coldly. "Pray allow me to offer you my arm," and he extended it as he spoke, but he was not prepared for the fire that flashed from her eyes.

"I would rather walk till I dropped—till I died," she returned, "than take your arm."

Her face was crimson with shame when she had said it; she was hot and cold all over; that she should be betrayed into passion with him, that she should have spoken to one of them in that way! Oh, if she could only throw her arms round Mary's neck and confess her sin; she was so miserable, so very miserable. Robert had made her no answer; he had dropped his arm and was walking a little way apart. What would she have said if she had known that he liked her all the better for the speech? It was as though an angry dove had suddenly flown into his face and startled him. It was her unchanging gentleness that had always goaded him so; it made him feel so desperately in the wrong. Yes; he was sure he liked her the better for her petulance. When he next spoke his voice was quite gentle.

"I think you have had your say," he returned, with a smile that was not at all frosty; "supposing, as you are tired, that we go home, it is getting quite dark now."

Then Rotha turned her hot face to him very humbly.

"I think I should ask you to forgive me, if there were any hope of your doing so," she said, with the sweet dignity that belonged to her.

"There is nothing to forgive," he returned quietly; "I like you all the better for your speech; I deserved it for provoking you. You and I never can get on together, Miss Maturin; we are always making each other sore; but I had no right to be so savage with you just now."

He wanted to hear her speak again, but she only gave him an odd wistful look full of yearning pain. Why was it that, with all her happiness, she longed so intensely for this man to be her friend? And he—did he really hate her as much as he thought he did? Was this bitter antagonism, this strife of words, bred only out of his hatred and his pride?

He wanted her to speak again, and yet he carped at her every word; in one short half-hour he had run the gauntlet of his passion; he was even more fiercely weary than she.

"I will mention your plan to Belle when I get home," he said, trying to rouse her from her apathy.

Her white face and weary bearing seemed to reproach him more every moment; that cursed temper of his—why could he not keep his sarcastic tongue within bounds? That very patronage that irritated him so was meant kindly. She looked so footsore and tired that if he dared he would have offered his arm again. Once he did put out his hand to save her from a deep rut, but she shook off his touch almost unconsciously.

"Perhaps Belle had better give her answer herself," he continued still more gently, as he noticed the movement.

"No," answered Rotha, looking hopelessly across the long dim waste that lay before her; "there is no need for any talk between her and me. I have promised Mrs. Ord to come up this evening, and then you can tell me yourself." The plan had lost all its interest to her now.

There was very little more talk between them, and at the gates of Bryn they parted. Rotha told Meg she was tired to death, and shortly afterwards went up to her own room, and Robert went to the Vicarage and sat down beside Belle, but he did not at once open his book.

"I have something to tell you first," he said, and then and there he told her of Rotha's plan.

"How kind—how very kind!" murmured Belle, and a faint colour came to her faded cheek—a touch of the old lovely colour; this new thoughtfulness on Rotha's part filled her with astonishment and gratitude. As Robert talked, a feeling of hopefulness crept into her heart—might it really be that the disease could be arrested? She had heard of wonderful cures at Mentone; it was a long way certainly, but if he wished it. Rotha was right when she told Robert Ord that one word from him would do it.

Robert had repeated Rotha's words very correctly, and no one could have found fault with his manner, although it might have been slightly deficient in warmth. He put before Belle all the advantages and disadvantages of the scheme as he saw them himself; this thing was practicable and worthy of consideration, but another would not do for a moment.

"Now, I must leave you to decide for yourself," he said; and Belle, waking up from a rose-coloured dream, missed a certain enthusiasm in his voice.

"But what do you wish, Robert?" she asked, looking full at him. "Of course I shall not go without your consent."

"You have my consent, certainly," he returned, but his manner was decidedly cold.

"And your approval, I suppose? I mean that you wish me to go."

"Nay, Belle, that is putting it too strongly, my dear. Of course I cannot be enthusiastic at the thought of our being separated perhaps for months, but if you think it will be of benefit to your health, I am very willing for you to try it, and doubtless Miss Maturin will take good care of you ; but it is a long way."

His voice was very affectionate, but Belle understood him in a moment.

"He does not care about accepting such a favour from her," she thought ; "but she is kind, very kind. You are right," she said aloud, "it is a long way ; and—no, no—I cannot go !" Her eyes grew feverish, and for a moment she held his hand convulsively between her own.

"But, Belle !" he remonstrated.

"No, no ; I have decided. I can see you do not wish it in your heart. I never meant to go away from you—never, Bertie. Don't let us talk of it any more, dear ; now read to me a little because my head aches so."

He could not refuse her, and so he opened the book; but, as he read, the sentences were meaningless to him. Do what he would, he could not feel easy with himself. She had told him that one word from him would do it, and he knew what she meant; but he also knew that no such word had been spoken. All the time he had been conscious that his manner betrayed him, and that his words lacked enthusiasm. What if the time should come when not one word, but a hundred, would hardly suffice to get her from his side ? What if he must loose her clinging arms with his own hands and pray her, for her dear love, to leave him ?

What are the shadows that darken Robert Ord's face as he sits reading by the firelight ? They are not caused by the story he reads, pathetic as it is. No—he is down on the shore again. There are the gray salt pools stretching into watery chains, with their tangle of slimy seaweed. Far out to sea the black rocks lie unhidden and bedded in slime. Faint creeping shadows haunt the sand-hills ; their green tops look rugged and bare ; a rough wind rushes to meet them as they plough their way through the coarse vegetation. A slim tall figure by his side goes swiftly on. What does he hear ?

"I would rather walk till I dropped—till I died—than take your arm."

Were those the words she used ? How her eyes flashed with brown fire ! He could see her tremble as she said it.

"Robert, how tired your voice sounds to-night !" says Belle tenderly.

Yes, he is tired ; there is a terrible ache at his heart, which he cannot understand. By and by, when Belle speaks again to him, he closes his book and sits beside her moodily. What's this weight that has suddenly fallen upon him ?

18

"I feel as though I have known you for a hundred years, and that in all those hundred years you have never spoken a kind word to me."

With what pitiless sweetness the voice breaks in upon him! Oh, darkening shadows of the coming years, how does Robert Ord read them? Listen to a word of his said as he sat alone in a strange homestead in a foreign city:

"Oh, fool, fool that I have been! Do men gather grapes of thistles? She is right; I have 'sown the wind, to reap the whirlwind,' and have richly deserved my harvest."

# CHAPTER XXIV.

" The two walk till the purple dieth
  And short dry grass under foot is brown ;
  But one little streak at a distance lieth
  Green, like a ribbon—to prank the down.

" Over the grass we stepped unto it,
  And God knoweth how blithe we were !
  Never a voice to bid us eschew it :
  Hey the green ribbon that showed so fair.

" Tinkle, tinkle, sweetly it sung to us,
  Light was our talk as of faëry bells—
  Faëry wedding bells, faintly rung to us,
  Down in their fortunate parallels.

" Hand in hand, while the sun peered over,
  We lapped the grass on that youngling spring ;
  Swept back its rushes, smoothed its clover,
  And said, ' let us follow it westering.' "

                                    JEAN INGELOW.

ROTHA never spoke to any one about her conversation with Robert
Ord.

"I have tried my best, but of course I have failed," was all the
explanation she ventured to Mrs. Ord ; but the hurt colour had
risen to her face, and she looked so troubled that Mary, with great
delicacy, forbore to question her.

Something jarred sadly just now in Rotha's sweet nature ; since
that afternoon on the sands—nearly a week—she had never voluntarily mentioned Robert's name.   It was apparent even to others
that she shunned him ; she could not bear to acknowledge even to
herself that he had wounded her past her usual patience, and in
her heart she tried to forgive him, but it had been very hard.   It
was therefore a strong proof of her magnanimity and the tenacity
of her will that she was set more than ever on doing him good in
spite of himself, and such was the fixity of her purpose that the
man, with all his pride and obstinacy, had no chance against her.

Experience was teaching her some useful lessons, however. He would accept no favour at her hands—that was what he had told her; well, and was she not to blame? She had been too blunt hitherto in her offers of help; a little subtlety of stratagem might be advisable in raising such a heavy weight. It might not be possible to be both lever and fulcrum at one and the same time, but at least might it not be within her power to set other agents at work? Rotha's girlish wits were hard at work again, and it was not long before the opportunity she sought presented itself.

Just about this time Rotha received another invitation to Mrs. Stephen Knowles', to one of her far-famed dinners *à la Russe;* and Mrs. Stephen Knowles, whose soul delighted to honour the young heiress, intended to gather an assembly of the choicest spirits that Blackscar and its neighbourhood could afford, and it was to be a very grand affair indeed.

Rotha, who was much oppressed by the magnitude of the proceedings, being, in spite of her little pomposities, the humblest creature possible, was in great trepidation, and said a great many naughty things to Mrs. Ord about Kirkby and Blackscar, and Mrs. Stephen Knowles in particular, killing the fatted calf in her behalf; at which Mrs. Ord laughed and scolded in a breath.

"If the fatted calf has been killed, it must be eaten," Mrs. Ord affirmed with emphasis, and therefore Rotha must have a new dress; for Mary was always lecturing her friend on the duty of keeping up an appearance suitable to her station, and Rotha, who knew that Mary only acted as the Vicar's mouthpiece, and who remembered his rebuke as to the lack of ornament on the night of the tea-party, had consented to lay aside much of her enforced simplicity.

On this occasion a pink dress was the result of Mary's eloquence —actually a pink dress. But even then Rotha had refused to deck her pretty white neck and arms with the Ord jewels. " I shall wear flowers," was her sole answer to her friend's rebuke. " I feel already something like the ugly duckling transformed into the swan in this gaudy dress; I don't believe I am Rotha Maturin at all. I am almost glad, after all, that you and the Vicar will not be there to see me." But Rotha, as she uttered this little bit of girlish silliness, was glad that she looked so young and fair in the pink dress, and went off quite happily when Meg and Mary had admired her to their heart's content; and it was certain that no one at Mrs. Stephen Knowles' missed the lack of jewels.

Most of the guests were strangers to Rotha. The only name she recognised, with the exception of one or two of her Blackscar neighbours, was Mr. Ramsay of Stretton.

Rotha knew all about Mr. Ramsay of Stretton. The wealthy ironmaster was a man of great repute in the neighbourhood; but it was not the thought of his vast capital that filled her with such interest. She knew it was Emma Ramsay who had been Belle's unsuccessful rival, and how Robert Ord had refused to barter his love for any fabulous number of thousands. "Noble fellow!" thought Rotha, with a sudden warm impulse; but nevertheless she felt a little surprise when she saw Emma. There was no accounting for tastes certainly, and perhaps at that time Belle Clinton had been very beautiful, and not at all faded; but she thought Emma the brightest-looking girl she had ever seen.

Yes, Emma Ramsay was there—Lady Tregarthen she was now; for the ironmaster, disappointed in his first choice of a son-in-law, had married his sole remaining child to a young Welsh baronet, Sir Edgar Tregarthen, a young man, very sturdy as to pedigree and very small of person, but a well-meaning young fellow on the main.

Rotha fraternised with Lady Tregarthen after dinner. Emma was a very pretty little matron now, thoroughly content with herself, and disposed to think her Edgar the very impersonification of all that a man ought to be. She took a fancy to Rotha, and made her promise to come over to Stretton, where she was now staying with her father, and Mr. Ramsay afterwards endorsed his daughter's invitation. Rotha liked them both very much indeed; but she liked the father best. She admired the ironmaster's strong hard-featured face; his manners were a little uncultivated perhaps, but there was a downright sterling honesty about the man that captivated Rotha. He had sat beside her at dinner, and then, and afterwards, he had been much disposed to talk about the Ords; he seemed especially interested in what she told him about Robert Ord.

" He is a good fellow—I believe a thoroughly good fellow," he said, returning to the subject, when he had brought his cup of tea to the sofa, where Lady Tregarthen and she sat chatting; "but he is a man who will stand in his own light all his life, foolish fellow. He might have been driving in his own carriage by this time if he had consented to listen to any one's advice but his own." Lady Tregarthen, who had been talking volubly up to this moment, looked up at her father a little reproachfully as he said this, and, whether intentionally or not, rose to join her husband, who was at that minute talking to his hostess; but Mr. Ramsay did not seem to notice his daughter's slight hauteur, he only slipped into the vacant seat beside Rotha and went on with the same subject.

" He was handsome enough then to have married any one,"

he continued, as though pursuing a train of thought—"a fine manly fellow, every inch of him; half the girls were in love with him, I believe. And then he had such brains; they would have been a capital to any other man. He was just fit to be the head of a large concern, as he would have been if he and Emma—— By the bye, Miss Maturin, did you tell me he was managing clerk to Broughton and Clayton?"

"Yes, Broughton and Clayton of Thornborough," replied Rotha. "It is a miserable prospect for him and Miss Clinton; for I believe he only has a salary of a little over two hundred a year, and they have been engaged for nearly five years already." And Rotha sighed as she thought of Robert Ord's haggard looks and Belle's faded beauty.

Mr. Ramsay gave a grunt of displeasure.

"Serve him right. What business had he to be so headstrong, and turn his aunt against him, as he did? She was a termagant, I grant you, but he was her match. Good heavens, Robert Ord a managing clerk at Broughton and Clayton's—a trumpery concern like that! And Broughton has two sons coming into the business, I hear. That was another of his obstinate tricks, taking a situation in that way instead of waiting for his friends to help him."

"It is not easy to help Mr. Ord," began Rotha sorrowfully; but at that moment Mrs. Stephen Knowles had come up and scolded Mr. Ramsay for his monopoly of Miss Maturin. And after that there was no opportunity of renewing the conversation; but at parting Mr. Ramsay shook hands with her very cordially, and begged her to come and see his daughter at Stretton.

"It is only a drive of six or seven miles if you take the Leatham road; and you are obliged to air your horses, you know. By the bye, is poor old Sphinx alive still—the bay mare, I mean?"

"Mrs. Ord's carriage and horses were disposed of after her death. If I come to Stretton it will be by train, Mr. Ramsay," returned Rotha quietly.

"Well, come any way, so that you come," was the good-natured rejoinder; but Rotha saw that he was a little surprised nevertheless.

That night, as she sat alone over her fire reviewing the events of the evening, she thought much of her conversation with Mr. Ramsay, and of the strange interest he had evinced in Robert Ord.

"He has a powerful influence, if he could only be induced to exert it in his favour," she said to herself; and there and then she determined to go over to Stretton and plead Robert Ord's cause with the man whose daughter he had refused to marry.

"Sir Edgar Tregarthen is a much better match than Robert

Ord," thought Rotha, who scarcely knew how the ironmaster had coveted Robert Ord's brains. "I daresay he was a little sore about it at first; but by this time he must have forgiven him— he looks so good-natured, and so does Lady Tregarthen." And she thought for a moment that she would make Lady Tregarthen her confidante.

Rotha slept upon her resolve, and a few days afterwards she went over to Stretton.

Mr. Ramsay and his daughter received her warmly, and she had a very pleasant visit.

"I have listened to all you have told me," Mr. Ramsay said to her at parting, "and I promise you that I will think over it. It is easy to see you are on his side—all women are—but I tell you this, that if it had not been for his confounded obstinacy he might have been in my dead boy's place by this time : he was so like poor Bob, too ; but there, it is no use fretting over spilt milk. He has treated me very badly, but a man will have the choosing of his own wife after all."

"And you will think over it," repeated Rotha timidly.

"Yes, I will," he returned decidedly ; "I promise you as much as that. But I am not the man to do things in a hurry, any more than I do them by halves ; it is against my principles. I must turn the thing well over in my mind first."

He considered a moment, and then went on :

"What sort of berth do you think will suit Robert Ord— another place as manager in a larger concern, say at five hundred a year ? Carter's not dead yet, but he might be superannuated ; or the same post, with a still larger salary, in the house of a connection of ours—Fullagrave and Barton's, who have a large branch house in America. Fullagrave writes us that they are in great want of a man who is honest, and long-headed as well ; his Yankee manager has turned out a failure."

"I think he would rather stay in England, for Miss Clinton's sake," returned Rotha thoughtfully.

"Humph ! that comes of being tied to a sickly girl. In that case we cannot do so much for him ; Carter may object to being superannuated. Well, I'll think the matter over. I suppose, though you are a woman, you can keep a quiet tongue in your head, eh ?" turning on her with good-humoured brusqueness. Rotha laughingly assured him that she could.

"Well, well, you look dependable ; and he is not to know who has done him this good turn—very right, very proper, I understand. Now, good-bye, if you must go. I'll undertake that Emma shall not forget you," and the worthy ironmaster shook hands with her till her wrist was nearly dislocated. She was too happy to heed the pain, however; all the way home she assured herself that her mission was successful, and that, after all, Belle would get better, and would be married perhaps in the early spring.

Rotha was thinking about her visit to Stretton and about all manner of pleasant things one day when she was in an odd mood for dreaming.

Rotha was sitting on the root of a tree in one of the glens of Burnley-upon-Sea—the wild glen, as it was called; she and Garton and Reuben were doing an afternoon's gipsying on their own account, very much to the astonishment and scandal of Blackscar and Kirkby, if they had known it, and somewhat to Mrs. Carruthers' surprise.

Rotha was very simple for her age in some things, in spite of her wise old-fashioned ways, and Garton was just as ridiculously inexperienced. Meg often called them a couple of children; and, as far as freshness and originality of idea and a certain chivalry of thought were concerned, they were undoubtedly an excellent match.

For they were both fond of ridiculing the world's fashions, and they both retained an implicit belief in the goodness of human nature, which was almost pathetic to older and wiser people.

Garton's creed was, that man was made in the image of God, and that therefore there must be a certain amount of goodness in every man, if you only knew where to find it. Rotha held the same creed, with a private reservation of her own; for she thought the Divine Image must be entirely blotted out in such men as Joe Armstrong and Jack Carruthers.

She told Garton horrible anecdotes of this latter *bête noir*. I believe she regarded him as a sort of fiend incarnate. She drew such touching pictures of Meg's love and gentleness that Garton ever afterwards regarded that ungainly woman with the utmost reverence. Both the young people always treated her as though a visible halo surrounded her pale sand-coloured hair. Reuben, who was at a tender age of boyhood, and of course believed in all heroines, from Jael, the wife of Heber the Kenite, down to Grace Darling and Florence Nightingale, was rather disappointed that a heroine like Mrs. Carruthers should be short-sighted and use eye-glasses.

Rotha was Reuben Armstrong's heroine, and she knew it. The boy, though he still remained faithful to his old allegiance, contrived to combine with it a great deal of honest devotion to Rotha; in his half-holidays he was often up at the house of his young benefactress with Garton, who had begun to go in and out of Bryn very much as his inclination prompted him. Rotha, it is true, never invited them in so many words, but she would welcome them very kindly. She used to brighten up at these unexpected visits; it gave her a curious feeling of pleasure to see Garton Ord making himself at home in that house.

Garton often made Rotha his confidante. The poor fellow would blunder out all his troubles to her in these morning visits to Bryn. He would come up with a message from Mary and stop for hours. Meg was not always present during these interviews. Poor Garton never knew what real womanly sympathy meant till he knew Rotha. Mary was always very kind and sisterly with him; but there had been a flavour about her kindliness which seemed to hint perpetually at that want of ballast on his part. Garton always took her advice very dutifully; to do him justice, he was well aware of his shortcomings, but he liked Rotha's sympathy best.

Rotha was always ready to listen; she took him under her simple patronage in a way that would have astonished the Vicar if he had known it. Garton told her about all that sad illness of his that had preceded his examination, and how he had failed to pass in consequence; he told her, too, with a touch of compunction in his voice, how his brothers had been straining every nerve to procure the means of giving him another chance, and how little hope there seemed to be of their meeting the necessary expenses.

"I ought to have gone up to the last examination," he said to her one day; "but I am afraid I should have wanted an awful lot of coaching. Austin does the best for me that he can under the circumstances, but he has his boys and the parish; he is too hard-worked as it is."

"What will you do?" Rotha asked him on that occasion, with much sympathy; and Garton had told her that he was fast losing all hope of ever entering the Church, and that matters were now becoming serious. Austin's income, he was sure, was barely sufficient for his own family, burdened as he was with the maintenance of his sister-in-law, and he felt that he could no longer live at Robert's expense; it was therefore a mooted question whether he should accept a stool in the office of Mr. Slithers, the attorney at Thornborough, with a small but increasing salary, or whether he should emigrate to New Zealand.

Rotha did not like the idea of New Zealand at all, and said so frankly, but she saw that Garton himself rather inclined to the latter proposition, which had been Robert's idea.

"A stool in that close dark office for seven or eight hours a day—how long do attorneys' clerks work, I wonder?—would kill me," he said impetuously. "I suppose I am as fond of good things as other men, but I would rather live on dry bread, with plenty of fresh air and freedom, than fare as Dives did, and be cooped up in Mr. Slithers' office; why, it would kill me!" And as he squared his shoulders and threw out his strong chest there had been a look upon his face which had compelled her to believe him.

Oh, how Rotha sighed as she thought of that surplus sum lying idle at the bank, which caused such an endless correspondence between her and Mr. Tracy! Mr. Tracy was always worrying her to have it invested in some Consolidated Ironworks Company, which was just now offering large profits to the shareholders; but Rotha begged him not to hurry about it, as she thought she had heard of a better investment than the Consolidated Ironworks Company, about which she would inform him presently. I don't know whether she called it "the Ord Fund," but some of it certainly went in the coal-bill, and in that cheque at Tyler and Tyler's.

Rotha could not see her way clearly to help Garton at all. An unmarried young lady, however rich and sympathising she may be, cannot offer to pay the college expenses of a penniless young man. Rotha could not very well offer her purse to Garton, neither could she plead his cause with the Vicar as she did in Reuben's case; but, all the same, she was very sorry for him.

Garton and Reuben were going over to Burnley-upon-Sea, and they asked Rotha to join them. It was the beginning of December now, and it was their intention to spy out the fatness of the Burnley woods with regard to mistletoe and scarlet berries, that they might make a descent on these spoils at a future time, before the young rustics laid ruthless hands on them. Rotha, who had often heard of Burnley but had never seen it, agreed without a moment's hesitation. Something was said as to Guy and Rufus joining the party, but at the last moment it was found that the Vicar had carried them off. Rotha had often been out with the boys before, either with the Vicar or with Garton. Guy and Rufus, and now Reuben, had been anxious to show her all their favourite haunts. She and Mrs. Carruthers often joined their shore-parties; but to-day Meg had been tired, and Rotha proposed leaving her behind. If Mrs. Carruthers had her doubts of the propriety of the proceeding, she did not give utterance to them. She was rather too simple-minded for a chaperone; and then Rotha looked so happy. She wore a red cloak; they wore red cloaks then—"Colleen Bawn," they called them—fussy little cloaks done up with rosettes, and a new gipsy hat besides; and then she would carry the luncheon-basket, which she had provided in case they should get hungry.

"I am sorry Guy is not coming," she said, as she nodded a good-bye to Meg, "for I have put in some of his favourite cheese-cakes."

She chatted away gaily to Reuben as they walked to the station. Mattie O'Brien met them coming along; she looked full at Rotha, at the scarlet cloak and the gipsy hat and the fresh girlish face under it—for Rotha was proving that even a pale complexion can look fresh sometimes—and afterwards she looked at Garton.

"What was Miss Mattie staring at?" asked Rotha merrily, when she had passed.

Garton looked at her with a little blending of fun and admiration in his eyes.

"I suppose she was comparing you to a robin redbreast in her own mind, Miss Maturin; what do you call those cloaks, 'Colleen Bawn'? I am glad you have left off those close Quaker bonnets; they make you look like a female Methuselah."

"Did Methuselah ever walk with Shem?" asked Rotha roguishly. "How I confuse the ages of those old antediluvians—those giants of long days!" She had told Garton once how much he resembled the wooden Shems of her childhood, when Noah's ark had been her one Sunday game; "though what there was particularly pious in playing with diminutive elephants and tigers and Brobdingnagian cocks and hens," she continued on that occasion, "passes my comprehension; it only served to confuse my young mind with the relative sizes of things; for a long time I believed an ichneumon to be far larger than a hippopotamus."

"What a droll child you must have been!" Garton replied. He didn't mind a bit being compared to Shem when he strolled down to the schoolhouse in his cassock, not half so much as Rotha did when he quizzed her little black bonnet.

"I never thought you noticed ladies or their dress," she said, with a little natural pique.

"No more I do generally; but I like a cosy and comfortable thing like that," pointing to the red cloak, and Rotha felt glad her Colleen Bawn was admired.

Rotha was much pleased with Burnley-upon-Sea; she thought it a little gem among watering-places. They had a turn on the pier, and Garton told her how the cows walked over the sands at evening, and they looked at the blue sea, all flecked with sunshine to-day, and the white cliffs, and the deep green ravine, over which they presently walked on their way to the beautiful gardens which are laid out in the glen.

"The glen is partly cultivated, you see," said Garton as Rotha wondered and admired to her heart's content. "In the season the bands play, and people sit about on the grass with their work and books, or go down to the spring to drink chalybeate water; it is a perfect paradise for nurses and children."

Rotha thought it must be a perfect paradise for other people too in the summer; even now, in its wintry aspect, with its leafless trees, it looked very pleasant. She would stop at the gardener's ground to inspect the flowers; she filled her luncheon-basket with hothouse flowers on her way home. By the gardener's house is a turnstile or gate which leads to the wild ravine or glen; here is nature's cultivation, aided but little by the hand of man; a long walk winds through the glen for nearly a mile; benches and rustic seats are placed at intervals for the weary pleasure-seekers. The walk ascends slightly, and then bends downwards; on either hand are nut-copses and blackberry-thickets, dear to boy and girl-hood; everywhere ferns and bracken spread their gigantic fronds; down below a tiny rivulet or stream splashes a hidden way among the trees. Rotha longs to see it in summer; the winding walks and steep descent are slippery with fallen leaves and miry clay; in the drier parts they crisp the brown bracken stalks under their feet; the dead leaves lie in rotting heaps everywhere, but it has a wintry beauty of its own nevertheless. By and by Rotha grows tired; they have been scrambling up and down the steep sides of the glen, wading ankle-deep in leaf-mould—the sweet decaying smell is everywhere; now and then the black earth gets slippery, and Garton's strong arm is in great request; sometimes he has to put back the sharp brambles for the red cloak to escape unscathed; now and then a low hanging bough obstructs their progress. Rotha, who is very fleet and sure-footed, laughs at every difficulty. The birds fly out from the thicket at the sound of Garton's answering laugh. Reuben whistles like a blackbird himself as he trudges after them with the luncheon-basket. They find out a dry sunny nook presently, looking down into the dell, and Garton praises the cheesecakes, and they are very happy.

A pair of children truly, to listen to their talk; Garton makes believe that some water Reuben has just fetched for them is from a well-known wishing-well of fairy repute, and each one has been challenged to propound his or her wishes.

Reuben states his, nothing loath; his ambition is eminently boyish, and refuses to soar high; he thinks to be top of the upper fifth and to be elected a member of the football club must be little short of heaven—he does not say so exactly, but you can divine it in the brightness of his eyes.

"Happy Rube," says Rotha. She gets a little thoughtful at this juncture, and refuses to say exactly what she wishes.

"I don't think there is much left for you to desire, Miss Maturin," says Garton, with the least possible approach to a sigh; "you can afford to set the fairies at defiance. It is only such unlucky beggars as I who ought to long for the old wishing-wells back again. I remember when I was a boy I used to believe in them—we Northerners are rather great at superstition, I can tell you."

"You have not told us your wish yet," said Rotha timidly. Garton, who had been pelting Reuben with dead leaves all the time he had been talking, stretched himself lazily and looked up at the blue sky.

"What is the good of wishing anything?" he said, very disconsolately. "Haven't I often told you that I was born under an unlucky star? It is to be hoped there is a place for me above, for I seem to be in every one's way down here."

"Oh, Mr. Garton!" says Rotha, much shocked. Reuben, evidently accustomed to such like expressions from his friend, goes on pelting him; Garton puckers up his forehead, rocks himself, and finally brightens up.

"I will tell you what I should like. If I were to choose my place in the world, I would live all my life at Kirkby, and I would be Austin's curate."

"You would be your brother's curate!" exclaimed Rotha. She was astonished, and perhaps a little disappointed, though she hardly knew why. She could not understand a young man being so moderate in his ambition; Garton's simple unworldliness was almost a fault in her eyes. She thought he ought to desire to be a rector, or at least a vicar. Who ever heard of wishing to be a curate? Mary was right. She was afraid he wanted ballast.

"Yes, I should like to be with Austin," he returned in answer to her exclamation; "he and I would pull on very well together. I should want more than he could give me, though. I confess I should like to live on more than bread and cheese all my life."

"I expect very little would content you," observed Rotha, wishful to draw him out.

"Well, I don't know. I should not consider myself, for instance, 'passing rich on forty pounds a year.' No, no; poverty is a cross-grained jade, and I should like to shake hands with her and part for ever. A man with a healthy appetite may live on bread and cheese, but a little meat is good for him sometimes for all that," and Garton rocked himself, and looked so wise that Rotha stared at him.

"Bread and cheese?" she repeated. "What nonsense you are talking!"

"I don't think you know the taste of bread and cheese as well as I do," returned Garton solemnly; "and when you do take it, it is not with the rind on. Bless you! we often build up our castles together, don't we, Rube? Rube is to live with me, Miss Maturin, and if I can manage it, little Johnnie Forbes, the lame boy, besides. And we are to have a cottage just a stone's throw from the church, with a garden all round it, and a bow-window to my study, looking towards the sea; and Rube is to have beehives and poultry, and I'm to have a big telescope and a dog; and we are to bribe Deb to come and keep house for us. When Rube builds the castle, he always puts in 'and plenty of marmalade for breakfast.'"

"For shame, Mr. Garton!" says Reuben, with a very red face; but it is a very favourite castle, and he chuckles over it nevertheless. Rotha looks at them both a little wistfully. What a pity, she thinks, that so simple an ambition cannot be gratified. She goes off in a dream presently, but Reuben wakes her up.

"You might have had the cottage over and over again by this time," says the boy reproachfully, but his eyes are full of mischief. Garton bursts out laughing; Rotha looks at them for an explanation.

"The bow-window wouldn't look on the sea, though," says Rube provokingly, dodging behind a tree to escape Garton's missile; "but it is quite within a stone's throw of the church; and you know what Mr. Robert and the Vicar said."

"Does he mean Nettie Underwood's house?" exclaimed Rotha in surprise, and then again Garton burst out laughing. He was a little vague in his explanation, but Rotha afterwards discovered that Reuben's joke was not without some foundation. Not many months ago Nettie Underwood had laid rather violent siege to the young sacristan—waylaying him on his way to and from the church, and otherwise making his life a burthen to him.

Garton had always been indifferent to Nettie, but now she decidedly bored him. He turned sulky, and would not have anything to say to her when she came to the Vicarage, bristling with gay-coloured ribbons, and armed at all points for conquest. As far as he was concerned, Nettie might take her pink cheeks and bright eyes elsewhere; he told Robert so when that young gentleman counselled him to a more prudent course. "What should I do with a girl like that, who chatters from morning till night, and has three-and-twenty bosom friends?" said poor Garton, shrugging his shoulders. Nettie's little vanities and follies provoked and perplexed him. "If I marry at all, my wife shall be a lady," he continued, with a dignity never seen before in Garton

Ord, "and not a girl who is ashamed of her own Christian name, and who laughs and talks so loud in the church-porch that the churchwarden had to reprove her; and that's what she and Miss O'Brien did last Sunday, Robert."

"Nonsense!" returned Robert sharply; "your wife a lady, indeed. You may think yourself lucky if you ever get one at all, Gar. After all, beggars ought not to be choosers; and a good little girl like that, with six hundred a year of her own, will not go long without having plenty of admirers."

"Let her have them," answered Garton stoically. "If I am a beggar, I won't sell my beggar's right of freedom for six hundred a year—not if I have to take Nettie Underwood with it." And he made this resolve so very potent to the young lady herself that Nettie took the hint and ceased her blandishments; but whether Garton's plain face had really captivated her fancy or not, she certainly turned a little sore on the subject, and was understood to be very cutting and distant to the young manhood of Kirkby and Blackscar in consequence. Since then she had been distinctly heard to declare to about fifteen or sixteen of her most intimate friends that it was her intention to live and die Nettie Underwood unless she could meet with a gray-haired widower of about forty-five years of age, of independent means, with a soul for poetry, and who would not object to Aunt Eliza.

Rotha had not understood Reuben's joke in the least, but she did not forget it; she was a little silent over the sparring-match that followed the lad's mischief. By and by, when they propose walking to the head of the glen, she pleads a little fatigue still, and begs them to leave her. "It is so warm and sheltered here, and this old trunk makes such a comfortable arm-chair," she says in the childish way that Garton already finds so irresistible. Somehow, he leaves her very unwillingly; the sunny motes flit before her eyes as she watches them disappear between the slender tree-boles—Garton has his arm round the boy's neck as usual. "What a young David for such a Jonathan!" thinks Rotha, and she falls into a dream again. She is thinking of all the foolish things they have been telling her—the bow-windowed study, the big telescope, the garden, and the beehives.

Rotha is nearly two-and-twenty now, but she has never really been in love; she has led a life too much repressed, too prematurely old for that.

In the fairy stories the prince comes to the rescue of the princess shut up in her brazen tower, guarded by all manner of hideous dragons. What delicious old stories those are!—older and bigger children read them again and again. One can fancy the stripling wielding his enchanted sword till the noxious reptiles lie dead at his feet: the little princess peeps through the keyhole. What a golden-haired blue-eyed hero he is, she thinks. Presently, when the brazen doors roll back on their well-oiled hinges, she will run into his arms all smiles and tears. There is no shyness or nonsense of that sort in fairy tales. The princess follows the prince through the world if he holds up his finger to beckon her. "Will you marry me?" he says, taking off his cap with the ostrich feathers, or his golden helmet, whichever it is. "Yes, that indeed I will," returns the princess, "I am so tired of spinning;" and then he gives her his hand. Ah! there is the white palfrey, ready saddled and bridled, and now they are off; the wicked fairy godmother shakes her crutch after them, but she has no power now. Poof, away, true love for ever! Of course they marry and live happily ever after, in the good old-fashioned way.

Nobody comes to the poor little princess at Miss Binks', as she sits in the back parlour hearing the younger children strum their eternal scales and exercises. Little fragments of dreams mix with the cracked chords, the wintry fire burns blackly, the room is full of shadows. C minor, C major; you must not put the pedal down; keep your wrist a little more elevated, Miss Carson, please.

Rotha is back in her dream again. Through the dim arcades of her fancy comes the prince—always the prince. Sometimes he is on horseback, sometimes on foot. He has blue eyes and yellow hair; he is tall and black-bearded. Sometimes he has a brown moustache, like the stranger who was at church yesterday. He comes up to her and holds out his hand; he tells her a different story every time. He is a wandering artist, a German student, a nobleman in disguise. He has servants and carriages and horses; or he has a cottage covered with perennial roses. Of course it is the same refrain. They are conjugating the same old verb to· gether: "I love, thou lovest, he loves."

"I can't see to play any more," says Miss Carson, yawning drearily, and Molly brings in the candles.

Molly has her dreams too as she blackleads her kitchen stove. The young ladies at Miss Binks' confide to Molly that they are in love with the slim-waisted young drawing-master, who has flaxen hair and pink eyes, and is supposed to be in a consumption. One of them, Miss Roper, thinks she will never get over it.

"Lor-a-mussy, Miss Belinda!" says Molly, smearing the black-lead from her face, "when you are older you will know the differ-ence between a white-headed little stick like that and a man. You should see my Jem."

"Do you remember little Em'ly's idea of a gentleman's dress

in *David Copperfield?* 'The sky-blue coat with the diamond buttons, the nankeen trousers, the red velvet waistcoat, and the cocked hat,' and David Copperfield's youthful fear that the cocked hat would hardly be considered appropriate!"

Molly's prince had a wide mouth and a turn-up nose and sleek shining hair. On Sunday, when he came courting, he wore a plush waistcoat and a blue neckerchief with white spots as big as half-crowns. How Molly gloried in that neckerchief! It is impossible to say whether she or the pupil-governess, Miss Maturin, despised the slim-waisted drawing-master the most.

Rotha had her dreams too in the dreary London house where she lived so long. As she read more they grew brighter and more alluring. She would extemporise all sorts of marvellous stories for herself as she sat gazing at the red-hot coals, when Mrs. Ord was having her nap in the twilight.

The fire burns very brightly; Rotha's cheeks glow with the heat as she shapes out an ideal future for herself. Does she see the woods of Burnley-upon-Sea, I wonder? Does she see herself sitting in her red cloak on the mossy tree trunk? Who is this coming through the dim vistas between the leafless trees? If a prince, a sorry one indeed: a tall figure, broad shouldered and deep chested; a prince, in a shabby coat, who has seldom worn gloves in his life, with a brown strong-featured face, with dark closely-cropped hair, with white gleaming teeth. A prince who swings his arms and laughs loudly; "a prince who looks like a boyish ascetic—half monkish, half kingly."

"You look like a picture, Miss Maturin," says Garton Ord as he comes up behind her. "What a pity I am not an artist. Rube will have it you only want the wolf to look like a grown-up Red Riding Hood; those saplings behind you make a sort of frame."

"It is getting cold now," says Rotha. "I thought you were never coming." Her cheeks have a pretty colour in them as she rises sedately.

Down they go through the deepening twilight. The woods are all gray now.

"We shall be late for the train," says Garton, looking at his silver watch. "I am afraid we shall have to run for it."

He holds out his hand to Rotha—that is what the prince always does in the fairy tale, you know. Rotha hesitates a moment before she takes it. I suppose it must have looked rather absurd—a tall gentleman and a tall lady running hand-in-hand.

"Oh, I am out of breath," says Rotha presently.

"Never mind, there are the lights of the station," pleaded Garton, "just one effort more."

19

" Have you had a pleasant day ? " asks Meg as she comes out to meet them.

" Yes, very pleasant," answered Rotha, with a shy look at Garton ; " but we nearly lost our train, though."

" Miss Maturin has been studying the picturesque all day. It is a pity we never met a soul," says Garton mischievously.

" How do you know that I had not plenty of company when you left me ? " returns Rotha, with a smile.    " Either I fell asleep and dreamt a little while, or else the woods of Burnley-upon-Sea are haunted."

" You looked rather as though you had been dreaming," says stupid Gar.

# CHAPTER XXV.

" M.—They make this thought too plain,
They wound me—Oh, they cut me to the heart !
When have I said to any one of them,
I am a blind and desolate man ?

. . . . . . .

F.—Never, my brother—no
You never have !
M.—What could she think of me
If I forgot myself so far ? or what
Could she reply ? "

JEAN INGELOW.

NEITHER Garton nor Rotha was likely to forget that day in the Burnley Woods ; very serious consequences will sometimes result from comparatively simple causes, and " Be sure your sin will find you out " is an adage that will hold good to the end of time, be the sin ever so venial.

Rotha had no idea that her pleasant ramble afforded food for a dozen gossiping tongues. Blackscar had got hold of the whole affair from beginning to end, and was making the most of it, after its usual amiable fashion ; and, quite in contradistinction to that wholesome proverb that " Rolling stones gather no moss," the Burnley story grew and flourished to a fabulous extent.

Miss Mattie O'Brien had met the little party on their way to the station ; quite by chance Miss Mattie mentioned this fact to a choice committee of ladies at that time sitting in the Travers' drawing-room, and Rotha's red cloak and gipsy hat were discussed with a zest and enjoyment of which the other sex can form no adequate idea. It was rather singular, therefore, that Miss O'Brien should repeat the same story at Mrs. Stephen Knowles' and at Nettie Underwood's ; the most inveterate story-teller is apt to grow weary of repetition—memory becomes treacherous, a little judicious touching up here and there becomes absolutely necessary and heightens the interest. Mystery is always acceptable ; a word

will sometimes imply so much.   The last person who heard this
titbit of scandal was a deaf lady, Mrs. Effingham, the widow of a
half-pay officer.   The whole story was shouted through her ear-
trumpet, and she ever afterwards firmly believed that Garton Ord
and Rotha were engaged.

Some of these reports reached Robert Ord's ears.   Young Jack
Effingham often went by the same train to Thornborough.   One
day he formally congratulated Robert on his brother's brilliant
prospects ; Robert was first incredulous, and treated the whole
thing as a joke—probably a hoax on Jack's part, and then he
waxed wroth.   Belle told him she had heard the same thing from
Mrs. Effingham and Amy Travers ; she could not understand what
had given rise to such a report, neither could Robert ; but, all the
same, he determined to give his young brother a hint.

Robert never took any pains to disguise his contempt for
Garton.   Garton's thriftless ways and want of success were very
sore points with him ; he could not understand a sturdy young
fellow, with such thews and sinews as Garton's, being content to
eat another man's bread.   He had no patience with what he chose
to consider his morbid views ; he had many angry arguments with
Austin on the subject.   The Vicar, who was keenly alive to the
young man's faults, was yet very tender over this intense longing
of his to enter the Church, and was always inculcating patience on
Robert.

" I know it is very hard for you to have this burden," he said
once ; " but we must be careful not to press him too closely.   I
fear indeed that he must resign all hope of entering the Church ;
it is more application than ability that is lacking ; but what a
faithful priest he would have made !   Let us give him a little time
to get over the disappointment, and then you can speak to him
about Mr. Slithers ; but I think, after all, the New Zealand
scheme would suit him best."

The Vicar had made the foregoing speech at the time that he
was so sorely pressed about the coal-bill, and since then Robert
had spoken very seriously to Garton about the emigration plan,
which Garton had taken in very bad part ; and there had been
some ill blood between the brothers in consequence.   Garton had
promised to think over it, however, which he did every hour of the
day, but as yet he had arrived at no determination ; and Robert
was just getting impatient again when Jack Effingham's unfortunate speech, and the absurd reports that were at present rife in
Blackscar, made him more than ever desirous of Garton's obtaining
some useful post at a distance.   To do Robert justice, he took a
very unprejudiced view of the matter, and was far more inclined to

blame Garton than Rotha. "Gar has no right to be always up at Bryn," he said to himself as he left his office one evening; "of course people will talk about it. It is all thoughtlessness, for he can't be such a fool as to think she would have him. Besides, I don't believe Gar cares for her a rap; why couldn't he have married Nettie and settled down like a sensible man? Why, I am sure the girl was half in love with him; women have droll tastes sometimes. I'll speak to him to-night; he has no right to allow Miss Maturin to be talked about like this. In spite of his stupidity Gar is a gentleman, and I can touch his pride there;" and Robert buttoned up his coat and looked very resolute as he jumped into the Blackscar train.

About an hour after this the brothers were sitting over their comfortless meal in a nondescript sort of apartment upstairs which went by the name of the study.

The dining-room, where Garton ate his solitary dinners, was a dismal room on the ground-floor, as damp and almost as cheerful as a vault. Belle never entered it without coughing; the damp came through the walls in dark unsightly patches—the few articles of furniture were more for use than ornament. The carpet would have blushed over its patches if it had any colour left; traces of Garton's muddy boots left indelible marks here and there; no fire ever burnt in the rusty grate. While Garton ate his dinner he would open the door that led into the kitchen for warmth and company. The kitchen was the only bright place in the house—a long low room, with a beam across, from which an occasional side of bacon or a York ham dangled in company with strings of onions and bunches of sweet herbs. The small latticed windows were laced across with vine-leaves, and the door opened on to the lawn. Garton liked to dangle his long legs from the spotless table and talk to old Sarah as she shelled peas or sliced beans by the hearth. Sometimes on a cold winter's day he would eat his dinner there by preference. Sarah and he were great friends; she spent hours, with her iron-rimmed spectacles on, darning his dilapidated socks. But for her care and providence he would often have had a scanty meal; he would deny himself proper food sometimes to leave the joint presentable for Robert. Garton had a healthy appetite, and used to make up with bread and cheese. Sarah always baked a pie-crust cake, or some such simple delicacy, on these occasions. When the old woman fell ill Garton's attentions were almost filial. In the winter she suffered much from rheumatism; Garton would black his and Robert's boots, or fetch water from the pump, and do many a menial office to relieve the faithful old servant. Perhaps the highest praise that Garton Ord ever won was spoken by old Sarah. "He mayn't be clever, your reverence," she said once in her droll way, "and nought but a blind fool 'ud call him handsome, but when it comes to our taking our places at the Supper up above it is the young master, God bless him, that will be called to the upper chamber." And the Vicar, who heard these words, drew his hand before his eyes and said, "God grant it, Sarah."

The study, as it was called, was a tolerably comfortable apartment immediately over the dining-room; and, in spite of its shabbiness, had a cosy well-used air about it.

The hangings were faded, it was true, but there was plenty of light; the old brown-stained book-shelves fairly groaned with books. Robert was a great reader, and would go without a meal to purchase a book; the old arm-chairs were capital places for a lounge. In winter the kettle sang merrily on the old-fashioned black hob, and a bright fire was necessary for the making of toast. Garton, who was housekeeper, butler, and gardener in one, always made extensive preparations for his brother's comfort. In the evening he would begin his proceedings by clearing the table for the tea-tray —a very simple process, which consisted of pitching a dozen books into a corner with a well-directed aim; this having tested his muscles, he hustled the black cat off Robert's particular chair, and, turning up his coat-sleeves, proceeded to make toast. Amongst his other accomplishments, Garton considered himself great at making tea. It was the drollest sight in the world to see him presiding over the tea-tray with the gravity of a judge; it always excited Mrs. Ord's risibility. He would peer into the teapot a dozen times, with the fragrant steam curling round his nostrils, while he tenderly stirred up the brown liquid; he would describe all sorts of mysterious circles with the teapot as he filled the cup —"to be shaken before taken" was a standing joke in the family; he never talked at such moments, but his forehead would be a mass of wrinkles. He had a knack of carving a bare bone of mutton, too, and of making a little go a long way. Robert knew nothing about the bread-and-cheese dinners, but he often praised old Sarah's economy, and wondered at Garton's appetite: the pile of toast would disappear in a twinkling; Robert would look up from his book with a joke at his brother's expense. Garton shared all his choicest morsels with old Cinders, the black cat. Cinders would sit for hours on the arm of his chair, purring softly if he touched her. Garton would drink his last cup of tea without milk that Cinders might have her saucerful.

Robert rarely made more than one or two remarks during the course of tea; he liked his book better than Garton's conversation;

they seldom agreed on the same point, and wrangling is apt to be tiresome. On this occasion, however, Robert seemed inclined to depart from his usual rule ; for, as he passed his cup to be refilled, he asked Garton, with some appearance of interest, what he had been doing all day.

Garton, who was peering into the depths of the teapot, oscillated it gently from side to side before he answered.

"Doing? oh, much as usual; it was Wednesday morning, and we had Litany, and a funeral; and I dug up the new onion-bed before dinner, and cut up some more firewood; and afterwards Rube and I went up to Bryn and took the ladies down to the shore. It was such a glorious afternoon. I have only just got back; they asked Rube to stay to tea." Garton might have added, with perfect truth, that he had been much aggrieved that the invitation had not been extended to him. But Rotha, who had been a little shy with him ever since the day in the Burnley Woods, had prudently refrained from such asking, as Mrs. Carruthers would be away.

This was the opportunity that Robert wanted ; he had decided to give his brother this hint, and he had determined also on two things—he would speak very plainly to Garton, so that there should be no misunderstanding of his meaning ; and he would take care to preserve his good temper, that Garton should have no excuse for any sullenness. He commenced the conversation therefore very good-humouredly.

"Gar, my dear fellow, I hope you will not take it amiss, but I want to say a word or two to you on that subject." Garton, who was giving Cinders her tea, looked up rather surprised.

"About Rube, do you mean?"

"No, about Miss Maturin, and I hope you will not mind my speaking very plainly; but you have no idea how people are talking."

"Why shouldn't people talk?" returned Gar stupidly. He had not the faintest suspicion of his brother's meaning. Robert looked disposed to be annoyed for a moment, but he repressed his impatience and went on :

"No man—no gentleman, I mean—is justified in allowing a woman to be talked about as people are talking about Miss Maturin. Do you know what Jack Effingham had the impudence to say the other day?"

"Not I ; Jack is impudent enough for anything," returned Gar indifferently.

"Jack is a keen observer, and a man of the world in spite of his youth ; which is more than I can say of you," returned Robert, exasperated by Garton's unconsciousness; "and of course, when he congratulated me on my brother's brilliant prospects in life, and Mrs. Effingham and Amy Travers said much the same sort of thing to Belle, they must have had some ground for their speech."

"What did Jack mean?" asked Garton, now thoroughly bewildered; but he grew a little hot nevertheless. Robert was driving at something certainly.

"Why, he only repeated what other people are saying—his mother and Amy Travers, for example—that you and Miss Maturin are on the eve of an engagement."

What made Garton turn so suddenly pale? Did the arrow shoot home?

"Oh, Bob, they never said that surely!"

"Indeed they did, Gar. I can vouch for it that Jack believed it too; he was quite crestfallen when I pooh-poohed it. I had some difficulty in persuading him that such an idea had never entered your head."

"How dare people tell such lies?" interrupted Garton warmly.

"They think they are speaking the truth. Don't get hot about it, my dear boy, but let us think how we are to put a stop to the scandal. I don't mind telling you the whole thing touches my pride very closely; that one of the Ords should be accused of fortune-hunting; that a beggar—forgive my speaking plainly, Gar—should be courting an heiress, and she Miss Maturin! No; it cannot be borne for a moment. Don't you see for yourself now how wrong you have been?"

The unusual paleness still overspread Garton's face; it was easy to see the unexpected accusation sorely troubled and bewildered him; but at his brother's last words he raised his head indignantly.

"Wrong! I am always wrong, but I don't exactly know how. Come, out with it, Bob. I can see you think I have been to blame."

"You have assuredly been to blame, Garton."

"What! You dare to insinuate that this has been the reason of my visits to Bryn?" And Gar's dark eyes flashed with a look never seen in them before. Robert liked this display of pride in his young brother; it showed some degree of manliness. His next words were spoken most kindly.

"Hush! sit down, Gar—what is the use of losing your temper? Of course I don't accuse you of such meanness—are you not an Ord?"

"If you had meant it——" returned Gar more calmly, as he reseated himself.

" Well, what then ?" interrupted Robert, with a laugh ; for Garton did not seem inclined to finish his sentence.

" Oh, nothing ; but I wouldn't have broken bread with you after such an insult—that is all. I may be a beggar—thank you for reminding me of the fact—but I am not an unprincipled one. I was always under the impression that I was a gentleman."

" So you are, Gar, every inch of one," returned Robert, anxious to soothe his brother's hurt pride ; he never respected Garton more than during this little ebullition of natural resentment. It was not Robert's words, but some strong undercurrent of feeling that made Garton so sore.

" If I blame you," went on Robert, " it is for want of thought and due consideration of what is owing to a woman ; you are so unlike other men, and have led so strange a life, that I hardly know how to make you see this ; but I can only repeat that you have quite forgotten your position with regard to Miss Maturin. May I speak more plainly ?"

" I think you are sufficiently plain, Robert."

" All the same, I cannot allow you to misunderstand my meaning, Gar. I am eight years older than you, and have eight more years' experience—that ought to go for something ; and I tell you this, that no one but an accepted lover ought to be doing what you are doing."

" Does friendship go for nothing, then ? I think you forget that Miss Maturin and I have been friends from the first. Austin and Mary know that I visit at Bryn ; they have never found fault with me."

" Neither should I if you were prudent in respect to those visits. I don't think either Austin or Mary knows how often you are at Bryn—of those daily visits, daily walks, and long excursions. Do you think Blackscar and Kirkby don't draw the only natural conclusion from all this ? Of course people's tongues are loud on the subject. Jack had a good foundation for believing that you and Miss Maturin were engaged."

A hot flush passed across Garton's swarthy face ; there was a tight pain at his heart that nearly suffocated him. Were all these pleasant visits, these delightful rambles, to be given up ? His voice was changed and husky when he next spoke. Robert thought his manner very strange.

" I am afraid you are right, Bob ; I have been very thoughtless." He kept his face averted from his brother, and went on, " I forgot that people are fond of meddling in our business. I thought an Ord would be above such a suspicion, but I see they have misjudged me. I think Miss Maturin would be grieved if she knew of what I was accused."

"Every one would not consider you a fortune-hunter," returned Robert in a tone so meaning that Garton stared at him in surprise. "They might think—I am only supposing a case, you know—but they might think, Miss Maturin being young and not so bad looking —at least it would be a more natural conclusion—that—that you, in fact, had fallen in love with her." And Robert, who had strong suspicions during the last few minutes that his brother was not quite so indifferent as he had at first imagined, looked steadily at Garton ; but Garton met his eyes almost fiercely.

"Well, what then ?" he replied, clenching his hand rather unnecessarily.

"Only—only that you would escape with a scorching, that is all. Don't go into a passion, Gar ; I am only guessing at other people's thoughts."

"Or retailing your own—which ?" replied Garton in the same fiery tone. "Look here, Robert ; you mean well, I believe. You think you are pulling me out of the fire, eh ? and you want to do me a good turn. But you are not doing it in the pleasantest sort of way. You are insinuating that I am a fool, and that I have been a fool all along. So I have, but an innocent one. I have thought it no wrong to indulge a harmless friendship—only a friendship, Robert. Miss Maturin has been very good to me "— his voice trembled a moment—" and it is my nature to be grateful for kindness. If the world chooses to misunderstand it, it is more of a fool than I."

"My dear fellow, no one but you can afford to set its opinion at naught. Depend upon it, 'in the multitude of counsellors there is wisdom ;' one cannot dispense with its rules."

"I have never meant to dispense with them, Robert. If I did not follow your advice now I know what I know, I should be more of a knave than a fool. In future you will not have need to complain of my frequent visits to Bryn."

Robert looked pleased. He really had his brother's welfare at heart.

"That's right, old fellow, you have taken my advice very sensibly, and it is first-rate of you." But Garton did not respond very cordially.

"Yes, it is all right. I suppose I ought to thank you for making me so uncomfortable, but I will tell you the honest truth. I would snap my fingers at Blackscar and its old women's tales if it were not for the fear that it might do her harm, and that per- haps in time she might get to believe it. No, I couldn't stand that. Besides, there is the danger of scorching, you know." And Garton laughed a hard bitter laugh, that had more pain than merriment in its sound, and which made Robert look at him again; and then he got up and put his hand on his shoulder.

"Gar, old fellow, I have not quite finished my advice."

"Haven't you, Bob?"

"No, the hardest part remains; don't think me cruel, lad. I only speak for your good. But do think once again of the emigration business."

"I knew that was coming, Robert." His face was paler than ever, and he set his teeth hard.

"Gar, dear boy, I swear I only mean it for your good; you are wasting—rusting here. Better go away."

"Why?" asked Garton moodily; but Robert drew his arm round his neck as though they were boys again; and then he stooped down to the dark cropped head and whispered something very low in his ear.

What made Garton suddenly look up and wring his brother's hand?

"Too late! God bless you, Robert. Yes, I will go anywhere —anywhere; but she shall never know why—never, never!"

# CHAPTER XXVI.

## IN THE DARK.

" No backward path ; ah, no returning,
　　No second crossing that ripples flow :
' Come to me now, for the west is burning ;
　　Come, ere it darkens : ah, no ! ah, no ! '

" Then cries of pain, and arms outstretching—
　　The beck grows wider, and swift and deep—
Passionate words as of one beseeching—
　　The loud beck drowns them : we walk and weep.

" Farther—farther : I see it—I know it—
　　My eyes brim over, it melts away :
Only my heart to my heart shall show it,
　　As I walk desolate day by day."

　　　　　　　　　　　　　　JEAN INGELOW.

ROBERT rather congratulated himself on having done a good stroke of business that night ; he had struck when the iron was hot. He drew a long breath of relief when his brother had left the room.

"I have brought him to his senses about the emigration plan. Thank heaven, that bit of troublesome business is over for good and all," he ejaculated devoutly. "Poor old Gar !" he continued, with a pang of natural sympathy ; "who would have imagined that he would have been so bitten ?"

And he thought with some degree of bitterness of the hand that had dealt this fresh blow. His heart was full of pity as he heard Garton's restless footsteps overhead. He lay and listened to them far into the night ; a touch of compunction haunted him as those weary footsteps passed to and fro. He was glad to remember now that his words had been wise and temperate ; considering all things, he had rebuked Garton's thoughtlessness very mildly ; the poor fellow's hot denials and reproaches, his indignant refutations, his irate defence, had been far from displeasing to the elder brother,

"I did not think he had so much in him," he said to himself over and over again.

Robert's sympathy was very real; but he had no conception of the fierce misery that was making the night a long torment to Garton. The incessant movement, the long restless strides, the hasty stumbles in the darkness, when the candle had guttered to its feeble end, were so many proofs of the intolerable feelings of the young man, who took no heed of the cold and darkness—groping from end to end of the narrow room in a blind helpless way.

Sometimes he stood, with folded arms, looking blankly through the darkness, or rocking himself in his old accustomed manner. A little glimmer of light from a street lamp cut into the darkness and showed him like a swaying gray shadow on the wall. A dull surging broke the silence. Under the lamp there was a stretch of white shining road; a barrier of darkness seemed to close it in. As he stood and looked out at it a dull hopeless gloom seemed to settle round his heart and rob him of all courage.

He wondered now how it had come about. Robert's shrewdness had brought this sudden revelation of his own feelings home to him. He was racking his memory to discover when it was that he first loved her; but his mind was too confused, his pain too real, to follow out any given clue of reasoning. He had called his love friendship, and under this disguise had tasted of her sympathy and found it very sweet. He had blundered out all his troubles to her with an eagerness that should have revealed his own feelings. No other woman had ever seemed so sweet and gracious to him. And now all this pleasantness of intercourse must be broken up. She was the light of his eyes and the desire of his heart—ah, he knew this now. The one woman whom he could and would have dared to love, despite his beggary, but who was never to know—never, never—that he had so dared to love her.

He wondered with a sort of terror how he should bid her good-bye. A sudden anguish filled him as he thought of her youth and graciousness. What a simple kindly friendship had existed between them! On his side he had always been very loyal, but with a sturdy independence of opinion which she had found amusing. What nonsense he had talked to her, and how patient she had always been with him! She had never been weary of his discontent and moodiness. Her eyes would shine with a tender pity as he blurted out his grievances. She always seemed pleased to see him, no matter how troublesome he had been. She would meet him half a dozen times a day with the same shy bright smile; a kind hand would be put out frankly to him. Sometimes she would indulge in a little joke at his expense, but the joke never hurt him.

He thought of that day in the Burnley Woods, and the wonder

with which she had regarded his simple castle-building. She had been a little disappointed with his lack of ambition, he thought, and no marvel. How paltry it all looked now—the little cottage with the bow-window, Reuben, Johnnie Forbes, the lame boy, with Deb to keep house. Ah, what a different castle he would build now! A dull misery of longing took possession of him as he cherished the bitter-sweet fancy—a little room all sunshine, gleaming white lilies outside, a tall slim girl with a plaintive face, with sweet frank eyes.

"Oh, my God!" cried the poor fellow in his anguish. "And I must never tell her that I shall love her to my dying day."

It was the hour of his weakness. By and by a certain strength of acquiescence came to him—he struggled no longer; in a word, he accepted his fate.

One by one he put away his hopes from him. One by one he looked the bitter conditions in the face; his love was hopeless—unrequited; he must give that up—he must renounce all hopes of entering the Church. He had given his word that he would go anywhere; he would keep his promise. There should be no delay, no looking back, no undue dallying with regret. The stern asceticism of Garton's nature came to his assistance here. As soon as possible he would leave Blackscar and England. The sacrifice might be a cruel one, inasmuch as it involved all he held most dear, but at least it should be complete.

He did not tell himself that he should not dare to trust himself often in Rotha's presence, but, all the same, he knew that such was the case. A few bitter drops, of which even his manhood was not ashamed, were wrung from his eyes when he thought of his boy-friend Reuben, who would fret after him sorely. The thought was a bitter one, but he put it away from him as soon as possible.

"He has a friend in her—he belongs to her now," he repeated, with a vague pleasure in this mutual property, and a fresh dimness crossed his eyes as he thought how Reuben would never allow her to forget him.

There was much painful work in store for him. It was nearly morning now, and he was terribly jaded, almost worn out; but with that unselfishness which was part of his nature he resisted the temptation to seek his bed, but lay down for an hour in his clothes that he might not over-sleep himself, and so that old Sarah, who was very ailing, might find the fire lighted as usual.

He went through his self-imposed tasks as sturdily as ever. He smiled bitterly once or twice as he blacked his own and his brother's boots. "What would she say if she saw me do this?" he thought, with an odd mixture of pride and pain. "Fancy a

hewer of wood and a drawer of water daring to love the mistress
of Bryn !" He looked up and nodded to his brother as he came
whistling through the courtyard with his arms full of faggots.
The whistle was very sweet and shrill, but Garton's eyes had
purple rings round them, and the dark face was as pale as a girl's.

"Good morning, Robert," he said, with an attempt at cheerfulness. "Sarah has the rheumatism very badly this morning; I
hope you are not in a hurry for breakfast."

"Pretty fair; I suppose I shall catch the usual train," returned
Robert carelessly. "Sally would do very well if you did not
spoil her so. I'll be bound you were up at six chopping that
wood; and I don't think we, either of us, had too much sleep last
night. I might have had a dozen men overhead, to judge by the
tramping."

"Did I disturb you? I am sorry," answered Gar. "I always
walk a mile or two if I am restless. If you are waiting for breakfast I may as well put on my coat, for I want to speak to you."
He broke into whistling again as he followed his brother upstairs.

"What a fine fellow he is, after all," thought Robert. He was
full of pity at the sight of the dark rings—Garton's pale face and
puckered forehead haunted him through the day; once or twice
he had twinges of remorse. How he had undervalued him! A
hundred instances of the poor boy's goodness of heart rushed to
his mind; he had nursed him in that long illness of his; and he
remembered how Garton lay for hours parched with thirst rather
than wake him, when he knew he was overtired; he had broken
down under the strain of that watching, and then Garton had
nursed him in his turn; he recalled Garton's clumsy attempts,
his odd mistakes, the patient way in which he set himself to
retrieve his queer blunders. Those strong brown hands had been
as gentle as a woman's. It made Robert's heart very soft to
remember these things; it struck him all at once how he would
miss Garton, and how empty his daily life would be without him.
He looked up when Garton's whistle ceased.

"Did you say you wanted to speak to me, Gar?"

"Yes, but begin your breakfast, please, or you will lose your
train. Of course, I want to speak to you. I did not waste much
time in sleep last night, as it happens, so I went over everything
in my own mind; and I want you to know that, as far as I am
concerned, it is all settled."

"What is settled?"

"That I will go to New Zealand—Timbuctoo—wherever it
is; and the sooner the better. I will go for my outfit to-morrow
if you like."

"It won't be much of an outfit, I am afraid," returned Robert ruefully, "but I have a few pounds at your disposal, to which you are heartily welcome. And you have really made up your mind, Gar?"

"Yes, Bob."

"My dear boy, you are doing very right, and I honour you for it, old fellow; you are just the sort of man to get on over there. I should not wonder if you come back with no end of money."

"I don't much think I shall come back, Robert."

"No, not for some years—eight or ten, perhaps. It's a bit of a wrench, Gar—I know that; but anything is better than this rusting life down here. It will make a man of you—it will, indeed."

A faint smile came to Garton's lips. Robert was kind, very kind; but how could he know—how could any one know—that death would rather have been preferable to him than this lifelong separation from those he loved? Come back! He would never come back. Reuben might come out to him by and by; but Blackscar, and Kirkby, and Bryn he should never see again! A profound sadness seized on the unfortunate young man as these thoughts occurred to him. Robert cleared his throat once or twice as he looked at him.

"You must not lose heart over it, Gar."

"I don't see that it matters what I lose; it will be all the same a hundred years hence. I suppose you and Austin will write sometimes; I shall tell Miss Maturin "—a new strange falter over the word—"to send Reuben out to me. I forget if you said it was to be New Zealand, Robert?"

"Well, Mathias has offered you a free passage there; so, unless you prefer Canada or Melbourne——"

"All places are the same to me," interrupted Garton indifferently—"out of England, I mean. Oh yes, of course, New Zealand will be the best. What made Mathias offer me a free passage, I wonder? Have I ever heard of him before? I forget all about it."

"I was of great service to Mathias once. It does not matter, so I need not refresh your memory," returned Robert hurriedly. It was his way to ignore any good deed he had done. "A man is always grateful to the person who happens to help him, but few men make so much fuss over it. He heard me talking about this emigration business, and then he offered me that free passage for you."

"I thought you were too proud to accept such a favour, Robert?"

"One must swallow one's pride sometimes—I am learning that.

And then I have done Mathias more than one good turn. It was a great many years ago, when we were young fellows. In short, he owes me money."

"Ah! that is a very different affair."

"Anyhow, it would not do to lose such a chance; and then Mathias has an influential friend or two over there, to whom he will give you letters of introduction. The whole thing speaks for itself—it does indeed."

"I am quite of your opinion, Robert, that it will be the best possible thing for me to do—under the circumstances, I mean."

"I am so glad you agree with me, Gar."

"Of course I felt you were right, Austin and you, from the first; but now it is doubly my duty. Whatever happens, remember you have nothing with which to reproach yourself."

"I hope not," returned Robert, somewhat bewildered at the solemnity of this address. Garton's face was haggard with want of sleep, and his eyes were dim, with no lustre in them; and then there was that sternness of repressed feeling in his voice. Was he cruel in thus driving him away? But when he thought of the allurements of Bryn his heart hardened itself.

"There is nothing like putting a good face on a thing, Gar, and keeping up your courage," he began in a cheery tone; but Garton again solemnly interrupted him.

"You will tell Austin what I say. I don't care to go into the matter again with any one—least of all with him." And Garton's lip trembled as he thought how he had hoped to work under that kindly rule. "The decision was for me, and I have made it; and there is no one to blame, but only circumstances. As far as I am concerned, as I said before, I am ready to get my outfit to-morrow. Shall I go up with you to Thornborough to-day and do it?"

"Gently, gently, my dear fellow; we have not spoken to Austin or Mathias. There is plenty of time, plenty. You need not get into a fever about it." He was more bewildered than ever by the young man's sternness and vehemence.

"Things have gone worse with him than I imagined," he said, as he put a stop to the conversation by rising from the table.

Garton eyed him wistfully as he went out.

"I suppose he will miss me when he finds things are not quite so comfortable," said the poor boy sadly as he took down his cassock from the peg.

Old Widow Larkins was cleaning the church when he went in. He nearly stumbled over her pail as he went swinging down the aisle. He had plenty of work to do there that day. There were a village wedding and two funerals, and later on a baptism. Some strangers to the place commented afterwards on the strange dark young man who seemed to do everything for everybody. When the people had all gone away he locked the door on the inside and went up and knelt down alone before the flower-decked altar. He was only a young man, very faulty and not over wise, not much more than the hewer of wood and the drawer of water to which he had likened himself. But, as he knelt there, Garton Ord prayed the noblest prayer but one that ever was prayed—" Oh Lord, I am oppressed; undertake for me!" And he prayed it thrice with a patient sigh, as though his heart were broken. Was his manhood less strong when he invoked another and a higher Strength? Surely such men as Garton Ord are the little ones of the Kingdom?

Rotha could not understand what had become of her friend. She had not seen him for three whole days, and she was as restless and uneasy as a woman could be. He had gone down to the shore with her and the boys on the afternoon in question, and she had brought in Reuben and Guy to tea, not extending the invitation to Guy's uncle as Mrs. Carruthers would be out. She had noticed, or fancied she noticed, a shade of disappointment on Garton's face at the omission, and he had lingered more than a moment at the gate, as though unwilling to break up the little party. Was he hurt? Did he think her stiff and inhospitable? There had been a look of reproach in his eyes as he had turned away, as though she had been guilty of some breach of friendship. This had been on the Monday evening, and the next day she had a cold and did not care to stir from the fireside. As it happened, none of the Vicarage party made their appearance, not even Guy or Laurie, her most frequent visitors. Garton, too, kept himself completely aloof; Meg saw him at church in the evening, but, being short-sighted, could give Rotha no information of his looks; and he had only bowed to Meg from a distance instead of coming forward as usual to shake hands.

Rotha thought this very queer, but she did not say so. The evening was a dull one, and she went to bed early and dreamt all night that she and Garton had a quarrel. The next day it was no better. Rotha's cold was still troublesome, and the weather was unusually inclement. Rotha, who was an unwilling prisoner, grew slightly ruffled in spirits towards evening. To add to her discomfort Mary came in on her way to church, and was very sympathising on the subject of Rotha's cold, and slightly mysterious on every other subject. Rotha, with unusual querulousness, wanted to know what they were all doing with themselves.

"I feel as though I have been dead and buried these two days," said the girl, with a little fretfulness. She wanted Mary to give up church and stay and talk to her.

"Doing good is better than saying your prayers, don't you think so?" said Rotha, with a droll inflection of voice. She liked to shock Mrs. Ord sometimes. Mary was always so good and serious.

"Oh, my dear, no," said the earnest woman. "We must do one without leaving the other undone. And then when one is so worried——"

"Are you worried?" cried Rotha affectionately. "Is that the reason why you have all left me to myself so long? I did not think you would have treated me so badly unless something were the matter."

"But, my dear——"

"Of course something is the matter. Don't you tell me all your worries? When persons have something on their minds they had better always talk it out," said Rotha, with a little decision. "Saying one's prayers is all very well, of course; but a friend's help and sympathy are not to be slighted."

"I never slight yours. Oh, my dear, what a dreadful notion! One may be worried on other people's account," finished Mary, with a sigh. She had sighed several times very distinctly. "And, after all, talking will not do any good in this case."

"I have no wish to interfere in other people's business," said Rotha stiffly. "You have always treated me so as one of the family, that I have grown to consider myself as one of you—that is all." Rotha was more than ruffled, she was positively aggrieved now; the tears stood in her eyes. She was certain now that something was the matter—something probably in which Robert or Garton was concerned, and which she (the little sister) was not to know. She drew herself back from Mrs. Ord's caressing arm with a little dignity.

"The bell is stopping now. Don't you think you had better go?" she said presently. She had her face averted when Mary stooped and kissed her. She took all her friend's affectionate exhortations as to her cold with perfect coolness. "You are feverish—a bad cold always makes one feverish," said Mary, with a placid sigh. "You must take care of yourself, and we shall see you about in a few days." Rotha shed a few tears when she was left alone. A positive sense of injury took possession of her. She had only been a prisoner two days, and already something had taken place at the Vicarage which she was not to know, and then it was so strange of Garton. She determined nothing should keep her indoors on the morrow, but when she awoke the next morning she was forced to reconsider her resolution. A damp drizzle of mist and rain threw a metaphorical wet blanket over everything, her cold was still obstinate, and it would be little short of madness to stir from the fireside.

Rotha thought it the longest morning she had ever spent in her life. Mrs. Carruthers was induced to agree with her too. Rotha was a trifle contrary; she would not open her lips or be interested in anything. Meg was quite relieved when it was time to go down to the schools. When she had gone, Rotha drew her chair to the fire and was miserable to her heart's content. The whole world was against her, and the weather too. What was this thing they were keeping from her? Rotha had not long to ask herself that question, for just then, to her surprise, the door-bell rang and Reuben Armstrong came in.

It was not a half-holiday, but he had come up to Bryn with a message. As he gave it—standing cap in hand, as though in haste to be gone—she noticed the boy's eyes were red and swollen, and his face was flushed with crying.

"Why, Rube," she said reproachfully, "you have not got into any trouble with Mr. Dentry, surely?"

Reuben shook his head and looked rather indignant at the supposition.

"Your father has not been near you?" But again the boy shook his head.

"What is the matter, then?" she continued impatiently. "Rube, you must tell me; you look as though you have made yourself ill with crying."

Reuben's eyes brimmed over.

"Don't you know? Haven't they told you?" he began eagerly.

"No one has told me anything," returned Rotha, with a touch of the old soreness; "there is some mystery—I am quite aware of that; but no one has thought it worth while to tell me anything."

"And you don't know that they are sending him away?"

"Sending whom—do you mean Mr. Garton?" Something sharp seemed to shoot through Rotha's heart then. She caught her breath once or twice. "Why don't you speak out plainly, Reuben? I think you are under some mistake. If this were true, don't you think they would have told me themselves?" said the girl, with a little natural impatience.

"Perhaps Mr. Garton told them not. Oh, Miss Maturin, he is so unhappy; he could hardly speak to me last night when he told me about it. I think, I do think, they will break his heart between them."

"Reuben, you are very wrong," said Rotha rebukingly; her

face was very pale, and she spoke hurriedly. "My dear boy, I don't think you know what you are saying. Why should they send him away?"

"Of course, it is his own doing; he is too noble to eat another man's bread—don't I know that?—but, all the same, they have driven him to it. He is never to be a clergyman—never; and he is going away to the very end of the world."

"Oh, Rube, God forbid!" and a hot flush of pain came to Rotha's cheek. "We must not let him go, Rube. You are right; it will break his heart. Why did you not come to me last night and tell me this?"

"I thought you knew," returned Reuben mournfully. "It is no use; they will not let you do anything, Miss Maturin—it is all as good as settled. One of Mr. Robert's friends is to give him a free passage to New Zealand, and he is going to Thornborough to-morrow to get his outfit."

"Without telling me!" exclaimed Rotha. She was indignant, even in the midst of her trouble, but Reuben was too miserable to heed her.

"It·is all Mr. Robert's doing—every bit; he will try to prevent my going out to him, I suppose, but I will go if I work my way for it; in a few years I shall be a man." He cheered up for a moment at the thought, and then in an instant broke down again. "He saved my life," said the boy. "I can't bear to see him go away. Oh, what shall I do? what shall I do?" And Reuben laid his head down on the table in a perfect agony of crying.

Rotha could not have cried for worlds: her eyes were hot and dry, and her throat ached; her pain almost bewildered her. He was going away—her friend and companion, clumsy honest Gar. No more pleasant morning visits; no loitering on the shore; no more happy excursions to Burnley and Leatham Woods; no lingerings under the lich-gate to look at the stars; no tall form striding up and down the dim aisles; the dark face missing from the choir-stall. Rotha thinks stonily of these things; through it all she hears Reuben sobbing with a sort of impatience, "What shall I do? what shall I do?"

Rotha goes up to him and gives the lad a little shake.

"Reuben, leave off crying. Can you give a message from me to Mr. Garton?"

The boy nods his head. Rotha's hand is very cold, and it lies like lead on his shoulder. A dim hope creeps into his heart; perhaps, after all, she may do something.

Rotha clears her voice; it is scarcely so sweet as usual, but it is wonderfully steady.

"I shall be at church this evening, Rube. When the service is over, tell Mr. Garton that I shall be waiting in the porch to speak to him. Whether it be wet or fine, remember, I shall be there."

"Is that all?"

"Yes, that is all. The little sister may have lost her power, but she will try what she can do, for all that. You are a good boy, Reuben—a faithful friend; you deserve his love. There, go. I shall rely on you, Rube, mind you don't fail me." And then, somewhat to Reuben's surprise, she bends down and touches the boy's forehead with her lips.

# CHAPTER XXVII.

> " 'Silence !' he exclaimed,
> A woman's pity sometimes makes her mad—
> A man's distraction must not cheat his soul
> To take advantage of it.   Yet 'tis hard.
> Farewell. . . .
>       But I love you.' . . ."
>
> *Aurora Leigh.*

ROTHA had quite made up her mind what to do.

As soon as Reuben had gone she went to the window and took a calm survey of the weather outside.   The prospect was not very promising.   The damp drizzle had ceased, but a gray sea-fog was creeping over the sands.   A raw mistiness pervaded everything; it was scarcely an evening for an invalid to stir abroad.   Nevertheless Rotha felt no doubt of the prudence of her undertaking.

She communicated her intention to Mrs. Carruthers with admirable sangfroid.   She only shrugged her shoulders with pretty petulance at that excellent woman's dismay.   Meg's remonstrances fell on deaf ears.

"When one has a duty to perform, one must fulfil it at all risks," she repeated, with a little dignity.   She nodded at Meg with wide-open anxious eyes.   Two bright spots of colour were in her cheeks.   There was repressed impatience in her every movement.   She scarcely listened when Meg pleaded a sick headache as an excuse for not accompanying her.

"You had better go to bed early," Rotha said to her.   "You ought to speak to some doctor about these headaches."   She was not indifferent to her friend's sufferings; she was simply self-absorbed.   She sat in a fever of excitement while Meg sipped her tea; an intolerable mixture of pain and pity filled her heart to overflowing.   "What is the good of making friends if one must lose them ?" she thought.

Meg, on her part, was sorely bewildered by the girl's impatience and wilfulness. A dim suspicion of the cause kept her in sympathising silence. She sat with throbbing head while Rotha roamed hither and thither in her gray dress. "It must come to her, as it must come to all of us," she thought, and a pitiful feeling came over her as she remembered her own miserable past, a longing to take the girl in her arms and shelter her from all possible trouble and disappointment. She was a little indignant at the way things had gone. "She has seen no one else, and she does not know her own heart," thought Meg sadly. The young man's peculiarities repelled and annoyed her. In common with many other people she was inclined to undervalue Garton Ord.

Meg, in her wise experience, thought that she saw how Rotha's possible future was shaping itself, and was rather inclined to be angry at the sorry result. She thought Rotha, with her sweetness and cleverness, might marry any one. The young people's pretence at friendship did not blind her in the least. "They will go on talking and laughing till they find they are necessary to each other, and then one or other of them will wake up." She did not know that the waking had already come to poor Garton, and that he was finding it very bitter. She was thinking rather of Rotha's restlessness these three days, of her unusual pettishness and caprice. Rotha's wide-open eyes, shining with impatience, her glowing cheeks, and hot hands were so many signs to the watchful woman of the reality and truth of her surmises.

Rotha, on her side, knew nothing of her friend's suspicions. She was a little chagrined at her scant sympathy, that was all. She went up and kissed her, almost penitently, before she left the house.

"You must go to bed before I return," she said, with some remorse. "I would rather have the headache than the heartache," she thought as she struggled through the damp fog.

She went to her usual seat behind the pillar and knelt down for a long time. It could hardly be said that she prayed, for her prayer was in some such fashion as follows, for she said over and over again, only in different words :—

"If Garton Ord refuse to take my advice, what shall I do? and if he refuse to accept my help, what shall I do? And then he is my friend, my very own friend, and I cannot let him go away;" and once, "God forbid!" very energetically. I do not know whether Rotha added an "Amen" to these clauses, but it certainly struck her with some degree of shame that there had not been much reverence in her petitions. She sat and looked towards the chancel very humbly at this point of her reflections.

"I ought not to have been here to-night," she said, with a sigh at her own shortcomings; "I am as bad as those who bought merchandise or sold doves." And as these salutary thoughts prevailed, she chose the longest hymn she could find in her book and read it three times over without taking in a word of its sense. And why? Merely because a tall dark figure had brushed past her as it went down the aisle to the vestry, and she had looked up and seen Garton Ord's face, looking sad and pale and worn, as she had never seen it before.

And after that it was all no use.

Rotha stood up in her place or knelt; she listened attentively; she sang with her usual heartiness, but the strain on her mind was terrible. She could not keep her attention from wandering; chill doubts haunted her; she was afraid of herself and him. Was she right in seeking a confidence which had been withheld from her? And then the remembrance of the poor boy's worn face drove all hesitation from her mind, and after that she had a strange fancy.

They were singing that beautiful hymn, "Thy will be done." Rotha was singing it too with tears in her eyes. She was looking at the altar and the lilies; the dim white globes seemed blossoming from the frescoes; the tall painted windows were full of blurred outline and shadow. Reuben was crying quietly behind his book.

> "If Thou shalt call me to resign
> What most I prize—it ne'er was mine."

Was it fancy, or did Garton suddenly look towards the dark corner where Rotha was singing? But when she turned her head again he was standing with his face to the lilies, and his lips pressed tightly together as though in pain.

Rotha heard a sigh behind her, which she knew came from Mary. She was quite aware that Mrs. Ord had come in late and was sitting a little to her left; but, when service was over, she did not once turn her head. She sat in her place steadily, while Mary stood up and fidgeted with her wraps. By and by she had an instinct that her friend was waiting for her in the porch, but she took no heed. Mrs. Ord was not quite easy in her mind as she went down the churchyard alone. She remembered Rotha's petulance and soreness of the previous evening, and was a little exercised in her mind in consequence.

Rotha sat still and waited, not very patiently it must be owned. She saw Garton go into the chancel with the wrappers for the altar, and a moment afterwards Reuben followed him. He was giving him her message. She could see him start and turn quickly to the boy. He seemed hesitating, but it was full three minutes before Reuben was dismissed with an assenting word. Reuben came down and stood beside Rotha for a little while in her dark corner.

"Wasn't it a beautiful hymn?" he whispered. "He was angry with me because I couldn't sing it. He sang every bit, down to the last verse, and then he broke down himself."

"We ought not to think of our own worries in church," said Rotha dogmatically. She was a little pale and cold sitting in that dark corner. Her conscience misgave her as she thought of the strange merchandise she had brought in that evening. The sellers of doves were nothing to her. She was every bit as bad as Reuben. Reuben answered her very prettily.

"If we don't bring our burdens, how are we to lay them down? That is what the Vicar says. How can I help being sorry for him, loving him so dearly as I do, and seeing him so unhappy? Oh, Miss Maturin, he looks so bad, almost as though he were going to be ill."

"There, that will do," said Rotha. She pushed the boy from her with hot feverish hands, though she was so cold.

Something shining fell on Reuben's sleeve at that moment.

"You must hurry home. Mrs. Summerson does not like you to be late," she said as she rose hastily. Her gown blew about her feet as she went out into the porch. The sea-fog had cleared off, and one or two stars trembled above the blackness. The wind was blowing the sand up among the graves. The white crosses and tombstones gleamed in the dim haze. Rotha coughed and drew her cloak round her as she drew back into the church, nearly stumbling over some one as she did so.

"I beg your pardon," said Garton, with a nervous laugh; "I thought you heard me, but I suppose the wind was too boisterous."

Rotha scarcely answered as he put open the door for her. The little surprise had agitated her. She went on, leaving Garton to follow. She scarcely took any notice when the young man came up with her, panting and breathless; in reality a new sort of shyness kept her lips closed.

"I had to lock up the church," he said. "Had you forgotten that when you walked so fast? I hardly thought I should have overtaken you before you reached Bryn."

"I forgot about the keys," returned Rotha apologetically; "one cannot help hurrying in such a wind."

"It was not fit for you to have come to church," he replied decidedly. "Mary has told us what a cold you have. You were coughing dreadfully through the service."

"It was nothing," returned Rotha indifferently. The mention

of her cold reminded her of the old soreness. He knew of her indisposition then, and had never cared to inquire after her. When it pleased him he could come three or four times in the course of one day, but now this sad trouble of his was turning even him against her. She held herself aloof as this thought crossed her ; her voice went out to him rather tremulously in the darkness.

"I thought you had forgotten me. You have all been too busy these three days to think much of any one but yourselves," exclaimed the girl in a hurt voice. "Mrs. Ord came to me and was dreadfully mysterious. I suppose I was foolish to mind it. Of course I have no right to be considered."

"You have every right, you mean, Miss Maturin. Why should you say such a thing?" Garton spoke vehemently, but his tone was hardly as steady as usual.

"I suppose Mrs. Ord was told not to confide in me," continued Rotha plaintively. "When Reuben came in this afternoon he burst out crying, and told me everything. I liked Reuben's red eyes better than Mrs. Ord's mystery."

"I told Mary to say nothing about it," continued Gar. "I wished—that is, I thought it better——"

But Rotha broke in upon his stammering.

"You thought it better that I should not know. Why did you not give Reuben your orders too? Mary and the Vicar tell the little sister everything. Perhaps you would rather not come in to-night, Mr. Garton? Meg is not very well. I suppose you meant to have come and wished me good-bye before you sailed?"

Rotha quickened her steps, with secret exasperation and impatience. Her voice trembled as she delivered herself of this cutting speech. Tears sprang to her eyes in the darkness.

"May I not come in? Why are you so angry with me to-night?" asked Garton humbly. The poor fellow knew nothing about women ; he could not understand the girl's soreness and hurt feelings. He followed her up the gravel-path with his head drooping ; he was utterly dejected and miserable. Rotha gave a little stamp with her foot as she choked back her tears. Her cheeks were burning again.

"He does not care for me ; nobody cares for me," she thought.

She went straight into the parlour and laid aside her hat. She refused Garton's help rather impatiently when he wanted to relieve her of her damp cloak. She hated herself for her pettishness all the time, but she could not help it.

As for Garton, he had betaken himself to the fireside after his repulse. He held on to the mantelpiece tightly as he looked down into the red gleaming coals, his head resting on his arm. He did not alter his attitude nor move when Rotha swept past him rather impetuously in her gray dress, though he started slightly on hearing himself addressed.

"Will you not sit down?" she said, still more impatiently, as though goaded on by his dejection. "Three days ago I don't think you needed to be invited to take a seat."

He lifted his head from the mantelpiece at this.

"Why do you say such things to me?" he said, almost fiercely; then, dropping his voice, very sadly, "You must not; I cannot bear it."

Rotha was electrified by the sudden change of manner. Her colour rose, and she said more gently:

"I am afraid I was cross. I did not mean to be, but one cannot help being vexed by such seeming unkindness."

"What unkindness? I don't understand you. Do you mean that any of us have treated you badly?" he demanded, so vehemently that Rotha was frightened. "Pshaw! what a fool I am, as though Robert's persecution were not enough to turn you against us."

"I did not mean that," returned Rotha, quite shocked. "Hush! what nonsense. Haven't I forgiven him? Do I not forgive him every day of my life? Mr. Garton, you ought to know me better than that."

"Well, what then?" replied Garton gloomily. "Do we know any one? Are we sure even of ourselves? If you mean that I have acted unkindly in keeping all this miserable business a few hours from you, and in making Mary hold her tongue about it, you have a very poor idea of my motives in doing so."

"I confess I was hurt. I thought we were such friends," returned Rotha in a voice that was perilously sweet. Had she any idea how she was torturing him? He had drawn his chair to the fire, and was bending over it with his hands propped heavily against his knees; his forehead was puckered up with pain. As he spoke he scarcely raised his eyes above the gray hem of her dress. Was there a glamour before his sight? As she sat there in the radius of the fire-light an ineffable majesty seemed to surround the young girl. Her youth and sweetness abashed him. He had always seen beauties in her which no one else had seen, and now a sickness and impotence of longing seized upon him when he remembered that all this beauty and grace was not for him.

As he sat there with his moody glance bent on the fire, he knew every trick of her countenance, every fold of her dress and wave of her hair. In the long dreary years that were to follow, how he would remember this evening, when he listened to her innocent reproaches with the wind soughing among the garden trees, and the dull lapping of the distant waves on the shore !

"I thought we were such friends," repeated Rotha softly. "Why did you not come and tell me this yourself? Did you not know how sorry I should be for you?"

"Yes, I knew," returned the poor fellow, with a groan. He could have put out his hands and prayed her to refrain from torturing him so. What good was it to him for her to recall their innocent friendship, who had loved her and would dare to love her to his latest breath? He looked upon her with sad deprecating eyes.

"Yes, we have been friends; but we shall be so no longer. What happy days Rube and I have had here; and then that time in the Burnley woods ! Well, it's all over now—over and gone, as the children say. I shall leave Reuben as my legacy to you. I wonder if you will thank me."

"Don't," cried Rotha, stung into sudden pain. "Mr. Garton, I hardly know you to-night; you are so unlike yourself, so sad and stern. I am almost afraid of you."

"Afraid of me?" Garton gave her one of his sudden brilliant smiles for answer, but it soon died away. Another of those frank innocent glances would unman him, he felt. He must guard himself; he must be very careful. In another half-hour it would be time for him to take his leave; he breathed more freely when he remembered this.

"Reuben will fret sadly after me," he continued, with a sigh; "the lad is terribly constant. I believe the foolish fellow will break his heart over it."

"He will be right," returned Rotha; "I mean"—colouring up —"you have been such a good friend to him. Mr. Garton, will you tell me once for all why you are going?"

"Why?" repeated Garton, somewhat embarrassed; he had roused from his apathy now, and was looking at her in some confusion. "I suppose because Robert cannot afford to send me to college, or to maintain me any longer in idleness."

"Yes, I know; but is that your only reason?" added Rotha impatiently.

She was watching the young man with keen wide-open eyes; the evidence of his confusion was clear enough to her. Poor Gar, he was clumsy enough to betray himself at any moment; and then the girl was the cooler of the two. He was more embarrassed than ever as he answered her.

"It was the reason why the New Zealand scheme was first started," he stammered. "I have told you all that over and over again. I knew it was right that I should go, but I could never make up my mind; and lately Robert has been pressing me."

"Mr. Garton, do you remember that text about the plough and the looking back?"

"Yes, I do," he returned, with an emphasis that startled her, "and, God helping, I mean to act upon it."

This was not what Rotha meant.

"I don't know in what way you are contriving to twist my meaning," she said, rather bewildered. "I meant, of course, is it right for you to renounce the desire and fixed purpose of your life to be ordained?"

What made Garton suddenly pass his hand before his eyes?

"I would rather be a door-keeper in the house of my God." How often he had chanted those words in the daily services, and what fulness of meaning had they not borne to him! Had he not desired with pure hands to serve in the sanctuary? Very slowly and reverently he answered her, "Yes, it is right."

"But why?" persisted Rotha.

"Because it has been plainly shown me that my work and place are elsewhere. I have hoped against hope. I have waited till I am heart-sick. Miss Maturin, do not let us talk any more about this."

"But I must talk about it. How am I to help you and keep silence? Mr. Garton, if this be your only reason you need never go to New Zealand; I will make it all right with the Vicar."

"You, Miss Maturin!"

"Yes, I. Do you think that I am not to be allowed to earn my title of friend; you forget I am 'the little sister.' Mary— Mrs. Ord, I mean—calls me her Aladdin's lamp, and her Fortunatus' cap, and all sorts of pleasant titles. We were talking about wishing-wells in Burnley woods the other day, Mr. Garton. I will not promise to conjure up the little cottage with the bow-window, and the telescope, and big dog; but I think I can manage about the college."

"You! what do you mean?" demanded Garton huskily. A dark flush rose to his face; his hands worked nervously. Was she going to help him; was she—— Ah! but it was hard, terribly hard.

"It does not matter what I mean," returned Rotha, with a low musical laugh, but she coloured too as she spoke. "The Vicar and I will settle it all between us. Do you remember how we managed about Rube? Mr. Robert need not know."

"Do you mean that you propose to pay my college expenses, and that you are going up to the Vicarage to tell Austin so?"

"There is no reason to put it in such plain words," faltered Rotha; "and, after all, you are to know nothing about it—the Vicar and I will settle it. You are not too proud to take such a little thing from me?" she continued winningly, as she stretched out her hand to him—the little soft thin hand whose touch he knew so well. The poor boy trembled all over as he took it.

"You will not refuse such a little thing to your friend?" she continued pleadingly. Then he shook his head.

"I could refuse you nothing, Miss Maturin. Do you think I could be proud with you? It is not that. No; don't stop me, you know I must go away."

"But why?" she persisted, pitiless in her sweetness, and her eyes looked so softly at him.

Garton burst into something like a groan, and then he threw her hand away from him with a violence that hurt her.

"You ask me that,—you—you—when you must know how people are talking! Do you think I can stay here," he continued passionately, "and be accused of such things, when perhaps it may end in your believing them?"

"What things? Who is talking?—about you and me, do you mean?" A dim perception of his meaning began to dawn on her. "Look how you have hurt me," she said piteously, in the childish way that was so irresistible to him; "are you angry with me because people choose to say foolish things of us?"

"But if you come to believe them," he repeated hoarsely. "Forgive me, Rotha; I am half mad to-night. I would rather die than harm a hair of your head. If I am a beggar," cried poor Gar, "I am a gentleman, and *noblesse oblige.*"

"Sit down and tell me what you mean, and why you call me Rotha to-night, Mr. Garton?" She laid her hand on his sleeve with a soft persistence that compelled him to yield to her. Rotha was very pale now, but she was the calmer of the two. To tell the truth, she forgot herself at the sight of his excessive agitation, which puzzled and frightened her at the same time. "What are people saying about us, and why do you so assure me that you are a gentleman?"

"I beg your pardon," said Garton vehemently; "if I have offended you, it is for the first time. No man can bid good-bye to the woman he loves and measure his words; if I say 'good-bye, and God bless you, Rotha,' you need not be angry with me, you will only be Rotha in my prayers."

The woman he loved—he—Garton—her Garton. Rotha was deadly white now, and then she turned crimson to her finger-ends; but he could not see her face, it was so averted from him; at his next words it drooped lower and lower. Had she dreamed this ? Could it indeed be true ? What was the meaning of that strange new happiness that set her heart beating so wildly ? Not for worlds—not for worlds could she have spoken then.

"Forgive me," said Gar—he had risen again to his feet, and was regarding her mournfully—"you know now why I stayed away. I ought not to have come here to-night, and you have tried me so, beyond my strength even. They thought I was a fortune-hunter, and that I dared to aspire to an heiress. They little knew me. If we never meet again after to-night—and we never shall with my consent—look up in my face and tell me, Rotha, that you never suspected me of such meanness."

She looked up quickly to the honest face above her, and then drooped her head lower than ever.

"Never—never !" she faltered ; "how dare they say so ?"

"What does it matter ?" he continued, cheered by her manifest sympathy ; "what does anything matter so that you think well of me ? I can go more happily now."

"Why should you go ?" faltered Rotha. How pale her face was !

"Hush, you must not tempt me ; how can you, knowing what you know now ? Of course I must go away ; how can I bear to live on here, and see you every day, and know," and his voice trembled, "and know you are not for me ?" He paused, and then went on, "You must not be sorry now I have told you this. I could not help it. I could not indeed. God bless you, dear, for your noble thought, as I shall bid God bless you in my prayers when I am far away."

The little hand trembled out to him again from the folds of the gray dress ; there were tears in the bright kind eyes ; the sweet face was covered with blushes.

"Don't go, Garton ; I want you." And then in a voice of intense feeling, "I was a poor girl, without a friend but Meg in the world, till all these good things came to me ; but what are they worth—what is anything worth—unless I may share them with those I love ?"

Could he mistake those brave tender words ? The strong man trembled like a child when he heard them.

"Rotha, do you mean me ?" he whispered ; and Rotha, looking up with a smile and a blush said, "Yes."

# CHAPTER XXVIII.

## A LOVE IDYLL.

" Moon of the summer night !
  Far down yon western steep
Sink, sink in silver light !
  She sleeps, my lady sleeps !
    Sleeps !

" Dreams of the summer night
  Tell her her lover keeps
Watch while in slumbers light !
  She sleeps, my lady sleeps !
    Sleeps ! "                    LONGFELLOW.

AND after that neither of them knew exactly what had happened.
The prince had come to Rotha—the prince in the shabby coat;
but this time it was the princess who had held out her little hand
to him.

"Don't go, Garton; I want you."

"Do you know what you have said, Rotha?" asked Garton;
"do you understand what your words imply?"

"Oh, hush! yes, I know," returned Rotha hurriedly.

She sat in her place a little shy and frightened. She cast odd
wistful looks at Garton, who was standing beside her with a face
transfigured with joy. The poor fellow would have liked to have
knelt down and kissed the hem of her garment for very reverence
and gratitude; he would have burst into some fond worshipping
phrase if he had known how; but Rotha understood him. She
thought his silence very eloquent; the chiming of a church-bell
jarred on them like a discord, startling Rotha by the lateness of
the hour.

"How late it is! You must go now," said the girl softly.

She took away her hand with a little decision. She looked up
at him with bright impatient eyes as though bidding him to
leave her.

"If I go now I may come again to-morrow, may I not?" said

21

Garton, lingering. "I shall wake up and think it is only a dream, I know. Are you sure that you really meant it?" persisted the foolish fellow. "What am I to tell my brothers, Rotha? Of course Robert must know if I am not to go away."

"Tell them what you will," returned Rotha, blushing; "I suppose they will understand that you were unhappy, and that I would not let you go." She grew rather hot over her lover's incredulity. "Of course I meant it when I said I wanted you," she said, a little tremulously; she was dazed, and his impatience bewildered her.

"Come, Garton, you must go now."

She put out a soft hand again, and half led, half drew the excited young man to the door. She let him out herself into the wind and storm. It might have rained showers of roses on them both. A shy good-night followed him through the darkness. Garton, turning round in the garden-path, saw her still standing, with flowing dress and hair, on the doorstep, with the silver lamp in her hand. The radiant figure haunted him all night long.

Rotha went up to Meg when she had let out Garton. Meg was not asleep when she entered. The elder woman knew at once by the girl's kisses and silence that something had happened. She drew her into her arms without a word, and let her cry softly to herself. Rotha shed a few tears of wonder, and happiness, and excitement on Meg's shoulder. The strain and flurry of the last few hours had worn her out. This natural outlet to her pent-up feelings soothed and relieved her. By and by she sat up and told her friend all.

Meg was not much surprised; she lay and listened with a throbbing head to the shy recital. How strange and yet how familiar it all sounded! A hot quiver of pain darted through Meg's temples as she thought how she had known it all. Meg lost herself once in the midst of the girl's eager talk; the pine logs fell asunder, sending out a shower of sparkling fragments. A cricket came out and chirped upon the hearth; the room was full of a clear ruddy light. Meg is back again in the shabby parlour of Chatham Place. There she is, a tall ungainly figure, with faded pinks in her belt. She is playing on the cracked old piano; the cool evening air comes through the wire blinds; the room is filled with warm spicy smells; there is a bowl of dull red carnations. "Encore, encore!" cries somebody from a distance. "Play that again, Maggie," says a sweet old voice. A wrinkled hand beats time softly. "Ay, do Madge, it is my favourite." A tall figure blocks up the light. Handsome Jack Carruthers is standing behind her; a dark intent face leans down to hers. Are those her tears splashing on the ivory keys? "Ay Jack, for better, for worse; nay, for worse, worse only." Meg wakes up with a start and shiver, and a dull shadow seems creeping over the room.

"Do you love him? Are you sure you are happy? He is very good, but not good enough for my darling," says Meg, when Rotha had finished.

"Good! I wish I were half as good as he is," thought Rotha, when she went up to her room. She was a little disappointed at Mrs. Carruthers' reception of her news. Meg had said very little, but she had kissed Rotha and wept over her.

"It is too late to ask my advice now," Meg had said very solemnly, "and perhaps, after all, I should not have cared to give it. You have accepted Garton Ord's love, and I pray that he may be worthy of my darling's choice, but I would have her be very sure of herself and of him too."

Rotha had gone upstairs with these words ringing in her ears. In spite of her happiness they had a little sobered her. It was clear that Meg had been thinking of her own unhappy choice. To her such a subject must always be more or less invested with gloom. Nevertheless the words had been said, and Rotha had felt herself somewhat sobered by them.

"Do you love him? Are you sure you are happy?" Meg had asked her anxiously, and then she had averred it as her conviction that he was hardly worthy of her friend's love. Doubtless it was rather chilling to the girl's enthusiasm; she sat down a little troubled as she pondered over Meg's words.

"Was she sure?" Of course she was. Rotha repelled the doubt indignantly. Was he not the best, the noblest, the dearest? Her breast heaved, her eyes filled with tears, as a hundred recollections of the young man's goodness crossed her mind. Rotha was right when she felt that she loved him dearly. Nevertheless Meg was right too. Mrs. Carruthers had grasped the truth instinctively when she told herself that Rotha's affection for Garton Ord was more a sentiment than a passion, and that the imagination had as much to do with it as the heart.

Propinquity has much to do with such cases. One remembers the quaint old name that Shakspeare has given to the pansy— "and maidens call it Love in Idlenesse." How many a girl and boy fancy has grown out of summer's wanderings and the *dolce far niente* of holiday-time—youth, spring-time, and love joining hand in hand! In after years things are different. Damon is not for ever piping to his Chloe; a little honey may refresh the eyes, but too much sweetness may cloy a man's palate for all that. Adam, as he delves in the sweat of his brow, is not always thinking of his

future Eve.   One who has lately gone from us, and who gave his
all of earthly love to one woman, as child and girl and wedded
wife, once said, "Love is the business, but not the sole business of
a man's life."

Rotha had always had a pleasant liking for Garton ; his society
had become a sort of necessity to her.   Those three days of his
absence had seemed a break in her life ; he had fallen out of her
daily existence, and Rotha had been restless.   Garton was away
from her, unhappy and miserable, and all the sweetness had gone
out of everything in consequence.

And after that it had all come so suddenly on her, "and maidens
called it Love in Idlenesse," or, as Meg would have said, love in
pity or out of pity.   When Rotha questioned her heart in the
presence of Garton its answer appeared conclusive.   She put out
her hand to him with a great throb of pity and love, with genuine
blushes, with a little burst of honest frankness.   She would make
him happy; it must all come right, she thought.   Poor Gar's
passionate protestations awoke responsive thrills.

Rotha was in a great measure blind to Garton's failings.   The
faults that provoked others were to her but the errors of circumstance.   In some degree he was glorified in her eyes.   The stern
or ascetic side of Garton's nature, which Mrs. Carruthers found so
grievous, was simply admirable to the young girl, who would have
gone through fire and water for those she loved.   She looked at
Garton through the glamour of her own imagination.   She invested
him with a hundred imaginary attributes.   Garton, with all his
clumsy honestness and his tender heart, would have fallen far short
of this standard, for no one knew his own faults better than Gar.

As she thought about it now, Meg's doubts ceased to harass
her.   "He will owe everything to me.   I shall make up to him
for all his disappointments and his wasted life," she said to herself.
" I need not fear that he does not love me for myself now.   How
noble of him to go away without asking for anything, and now he
will have it all—have it all."

When Burnley Woods are green with summer sap, when the
red leaves of autumn flame deep in windy hollows, or when the
winter snows lie crisp and untrodden in the bosky dells, how will
Rotha remember that she has promised to be Garton Ord's wife ?

# CHAPTER XXIX.

## BETWIXT AND BETWEEN.

'' En avant—en avant ! not doubting, nor fearing,
 Though clouds gather round thee, obscuring the sun,
Yet turn not away from the duties before thee,
 Give each thy whole strength as they come ' one by one.'

'' Steadfast and strong, though the path should be lonely—
 Never look back though thy heart seem to yearn
To linger awhile with the beautiful day-dreams
 That come with their brightness to tempt us to turn.

'' Sweet the reward when the labour is ended,
 To feel that each day thou hast faithfully striven ;
It may be that soon the great Master will call thee
 To render account for the life He has given.''

HELEN MARION BURNSIDE.

As for Garton, he went home through the wind and rain as though he were treading on air. He came back once and put his lips to the stone where the silver lamp had been gleaming. He murmured a thousand blessings as he looked up at the curtained window, where the firelight was still playing on the blind. He imagined her still sitting there in her gray dress, with downcast eyes, thinking of him. He would have lingered there, Heaven knows how long, in the rain and darkness, keeping watch and ward over that hallowed threshold, but for Rotha's little Skye terrier Fidgets, who flew barking at him round a corner. He quitted the dim garden-walks with reluctance. Rotha would have wondered if she had seen him pacing up and down underneath the soaking evergreens. Garton would have paced on there quite happily for hours, entirely oblivious of his outer man, but for Fidgets' annoying attentions. The dog positively refused to recognise his friend. He growled at Garton's wet overcoat, till Garton gave up the contest and retired.

He performed a few more acts of worship, however, in the front of the house, leaning on the gate which Rotha and he had so often entered. Was Rotha or he the happier now ? '' Oh, God bless her for all her dear love and goodness to me !'' cried Gar, lifting his hat in his youthful chivalry. How many more delirious things he would have said and done are doubtful, but Fidgets found him out again and came grumbling through an aperture in the wall. Jock and Jasper from the Vicarage joined in the duet inside, and all the village dogs took up the chorus, while Garton, baffled by the canine music, took himself and his raptures to the sea-wall, till he felt sober enough to go back to Robert.

The study looked very cosy when Garton entered. The fire was blazing, the lamp freshly trimmed, and the Vicar sat in the arm-chair which Garton usually occupied opposite to Robert, with Cinders comfortably curled up on his knee. Garton could hear their voices as he climbed up the dark staircase. The cheerful light almost dazzled him coming in from the gloom outside.

Robert broke off directly at Garton's entrance. His face looked flushed and excited, his eyes sparkling, his whole appearance and manner changed. The Vicar also looked beaming. The two confronted him with some curiosity. Garton, with his radiant face, his wet coat and muddy boots, presented a strange appearance to his two brothers. Austin put his hand on his wet shoulder rather anxiously, and Robert exclaimed in surprise :

"Why, where have you been, Gar? It is nearly eleven o'clock; and, my dear fellow, just look at your boots."

"Yes, I know," returned Garton, not looking at them, however, and shaking himself like a water-spaniel. "I have been with a friend a part of the evening, and since then I have been taking a walk by myself on the sea-wall."

He did not add that his friend had been Rotha, and if Robert had any suspicion as to the cause of his radiant looks he did not say so.

Austin was the next to speak.

"Making the most of your liberty, eh? Now I'll be bound your friend was Rube Armstrong, and that you were both making a night of it up at Bryn. Here have Robert and I been wearing out our patience waiting for you. Mary has sent in once to know when I was coming, but I would not go till Robert had told you the news."

"What news? It ought to be pleasant to judge by Bob's face," replied Gar dreamily. He wondered with a sort of pride if they could guess how little their news could affect him. It was something to see Robert look happy, however. "Is Belle better?" he asked, with a consciousness that this news must be about her.

"Better. No, I cannot say that she is," replied the Vicar, becoming a little grave at the question. "Mary will have it that she gets gradually worse."

" Oh, Mary is always croaking," interrupted Robert hastily.

" It is natural that she should be anxious about her only sister," returned the Vicar mildly. " I cannot bear to see her worry herself so; it is making her quite thin. You know you were getting anxious yourself, Robert."

" Yes, but this will make all the difference; it will put a stop to the unsettled state of things; and then the change of climate, you know."

" You think, then, of arranging it before May?" inquired the Vicar significantly.

Robert nodded and then looked at Garton.

" We have not told him your news yet. Look here, Gar; we are talking in hieroglyphics, old fellow. What should you say if you had not to go to New Zealand after all?"

Gar stared at him stupidly. Not to go? Of course he was not going now; but how did they know? Robert took up his brother's parable rather impatiently.

" That is not the way to begin, Austin. Gar will never understand us like that. Listen to me, Gar. You recollect Aunt Charlotte's oldest friend, Mr. Ramsay of Stretton?"

" Remember him? Of course I do. Emma Ramsay was a pretty girl, too," he added mischievously for his brother's benefit, and, for a wonder, Robert did not resent the joke.

" Well, she is Emma Tregarthen now—Lady Tregarthen, I should say; and is prettier than she ever was, only rather stout. Well, what should you say, Garton, at Mr. Ramsay sending for me early this morning in quite a friendly way and telling me that he had accidentally heard that I was managing clerk at Broughton and Clayton's, and not getting on so well as I ought in the world, and then making me the most brilliant offer you ever imagined?"

" I should say he was a jolly old fellow and no end of a brick," cried Garton rapturously. " Is he going to take you into the works at Stretton? Bravo, Bob! The star of the Ords is rising now," and, boyish as ever, he clapped his brother gaily on the shoulder.

" No nonsense, Gar; you have not heard me out. He can't take me in at Stretton, though I see he wants me, because Carter refuses to be superannuated, and very sensible too of Carter. By the bye, he told me, Austin, that he had always hoped to see me at the head of that concern, in poor Bob Ramsay's place, but of course the fates would not have it," moralised Robert, looking very handsome and sentimental, as behoves a man who had had to choose between two beautiful girls.

" That was when he hoped you would be his son in-law," returned the Vicar, smiling. "It is getting late, my dear fellow, and you are leaving Garton a long time in the dark."

"Not in the dark now," answered Gar, with a happy laugh, but of course his brother misunderstood him.

"What do you guess?" asked Robert in surprise. "I was utterly taken aback when Mr. Ramsay told me that, knowing how my abilities were thrown away, he had taken the liberty to recom- mend me to the house of Fullagrave and Barton, old correspondents of his, who had applied to him for a well-qualified English manager."

"An American house!" exclaimed Garton, opening his eyes.

"Yes, I should have preferred England, if only for Belle's sake. Of course I know she will be willing to accompany me," he con- tinued, with a smile; "still it is hard parting her and Mary. It is all arranged; Mr. Ramsay has the power to arm me with full credentials. I have given Broughton and Clayton three months' notice. My salary is to be six or seven hundred a year, and I trust, before two months are out, Belle will be well enough to marry me. Mr. Ramsay says there can be no objection to my taking a wife out, as we are to have a house rent free on the premises. So Belle will be quite a rich woman," finished Robert; but his voice was a little husky as he thought how late, how very late, all these good things had come to them. More than once the fear had crossed his mind that evening that Belle was hardly fit for the new duties she was to take on herself.

"Have you told her?" asked Gar excitedly. "My dear Bob, I heartily congratulate you." He was a little absent now and then; he wondered when a break in his brother's talk would allow him to bring out his news. It was glorious to think that Belle and Robert were at last to be married, and there could be but one opinion at Robert's good fortune; but he must be forgiven a little natural egotism if he wished that Robert would not be quite so prolix.

"No, I have not told Belle yet; Mary begged me to say nothing to-night. Garton, you don't look half surprised enough, and you don't ask me why you are not to go to New Zealand."

"No," returned Garton, trying to suppress his impatience; "I forgot all about that part of it, Robert."

"Well, I am coming to it now. Mr. Ramsay did not send for me this morning only to tell me this news, but because he thought I should be a likely person to assist him in a sudden difficulty; he has no sons, as you know, and his staff, though efficient, is some- what small, and he wants a trustworthy person with a fair amount of brains to discharge rather a delicate commission for him."

"Well!" ejaculated Garton. Robert was decidedly prosy in

his happiness; these particulars were not at all interesting to Garton; he began to think of Rotha standing out in the dark with a silver lamp in her hand; he could hear the sweet good-night echoing among the trees; he shifted his place and moved restlessly, somewhat to Austin's amusement, as Robert went on with his explanations.

"You see he is rather in a fix just now, as the Yankees say; he has just heard from very reliable sources that the Vera Cruz mines in South America are not yielding profits to the shareholders; that, in fact, there are rumours of immense losses. Mr. Ramsay is not one of the directors, but he has dabbled very largely in shares; and the person he has appointed to watch his interests over there has not quite come up to the mark. Some of the most influential shareholders have been selling out, a panic has been the result, and the directors want to hush it up; in fact, Mr. Ramsay cannot satisfy himself whether there be serious cause for alarm or not;—do you follow me?"

"Of course I do," returned Garton impatiently; he could not understand what Robert was driving at, or why these lengthy particulars should be interesting to him. The Vicar, who was watching him, exchanged a droll smile with Robert.

"It does not strike you as particularly interesting, does it? Well, it will soon; don't be in a hurry, Gar; it is coming presently. Well, Mr. Ramsay would go over himself, but he is not as young as he was, and he dreads the voyage; but he asked me if I knew of any one tolerably trusty who would go over there, and who would watch the whole thing for him and keep his eyes and ears open. The process, as Mr. Ramsay explained it, is very simple. His principal business would be to seek out a certain retired Spanish merchant, of whom Mr. Ramsay has lost sight for many years; this Don Gomez would give you—I mean the person in question—every reliable information that was to be had. You see it is very simple. The only thing is, there's not a moment to be lost; Mr. Ramsay wants immediate action."

It was evident Garton was getting very restive; he understood now at what Robert was aiming; he would have to bring out his news in a very different way than he intended; this long business talk was intolerable.

"Well, Gar," continued Robert good-humouredly, "I suppose you know what I am after now? Mr. Ramsay offered very handsome terms, and I owed him a good turn for what he had done for me. Of course I told him that my brother would be the person. Aren't you glad it is South America and not New Zealand, Gar?"

"You told him I would go!" burst out Gar. "How dare

you ?—I beg your pardon—what right had you to say such a thing without my leave, Robert ?"

"Tut! lad, don't lose your temper.   Austin, just look at him. Do you think I would have answered for you if I had not been sure of your consent?   Have you not been breaking your heart days enough over the New Zealand scheme? and didn't you tell me that you would go anywhere, to Timbuctoo if I liked?"

"Circumstances alter cases," returned Garton; his muscles were quivering, his whole frame seemed strung up to the contest, he looked every inch an Ord.   "I hope you have not given your word, Robert; for I do not mean to go to New Zealand or South America either."

"Hear him," returned Robert in calm exasperation; "did you ever see any one so provoking in your life, Austin?"

"I thought you would have been overjoyed, Gar," said the Vicar reprovingly.   "Robert thought he was doing the best for you; he knew how you hated the thought of leaving England. The whole thing would not occupy you more than five or six months; it would simply be a pleasant change, and Mr. Ramsay held out the hope to Robert that if you pleased him in the way you discharged your commission he would take you into his works at Stretton."

"And," put in Robert, with an uneasy glance at Garton, "I would not have given my word to Mr. Ramsay if I had had a doubt of your approval; but there was not a moment to be lost— not a moment, Garton.   He wants you to start by the *Phœnix* next Wednesday."

"And what did you say, Robert?" asked Garton, trying to keep himself still.

"I told him you would go," returned Robert steadily.   "Why, Gar, what's the matter with you?"

"Oh, good heavens! give me patience," cried poor Gar. "Robert, you were wrong, very wrong, to pledge your word to Mr. Ramsay.   How am I to go now?   Indeed I cannot.   Miss Maturin and I are engaged!"

A dead silence followed Garton's hasty words.   If a thunderbolt had fallen between the three they could scarcely have appeared more astonished; the Vicar especially could hardly believe his ears.

"Engaged!   You and Rotha!" he gasped out; but Robert interrupted him.

"Do you intend to tell us that you have had the meanness to propose to her?" he almost thundered.   But perhaps it is not well to repeat the words of a man when he is angry; forbearance and a tolerant estimate of other men's motives were not among Robert Ord's virtues. The Vicar too was at first scarcely less displeased. Neither could rid himself of the impression that Garton had taken an ungenerous advantage of the young heiress.

"Go on," said Garton, with a little scorn; "I shall not defend myself."

He folded his arms and listened with pale face and fiery eyes to Robert's brief cutting speeches. The Vicar looked disturbed, as well he might, at the high words that raged between the brothers. Oh, the Ord temper! Garton had his share of it, without doubt.

"Hush! that will do, Robert," said Austin in an authoritative manner.

His great calm voice seemed to have an instantaneous effect on the excited young men. He put his hand on Robert's shoulder as he spoke.

"I don't think we ought to be so hard on him, Bobus," using unconsciously the name that belonged to their boyhood. "Let us rather hear what the lad has to say for himself."

"He ought to have gone away like a man without saying anything," returned Robert bitterly; "he told me he would."

"I never said that I would go away without bidding her good-bye," replied the other vehemently. "Would you have me slink off like a thief or a coward? Was it my fault that I loved her," burst out Gar, "when every one in my place must have done the same?"

"No, no," broke in the compassionate Vicar. He began to estimate the force of Garton's temptation. He held out his hand to the poor boy kindly.

"We've been too hard on you, Gar. Tell us how it all happened, lad."

That touch of real sympathy beat down all Garton's stubbornness in a moment. His eyes glistened. The sullen look passed out of his face.

"I will tell you, Austin," he said eagerly; "but I will have nothing to do with any of his questions. If Robert chooses to insult me, he may take the consequences. I never went near Bryn at all till she sent for me."

"Sent for you!" echoed the Vicar in surprise.

Robert looked up then with gloomy eyes, but said nothing.

"Yes; she sent me a message by Rube. She had heard all about my going away, and wanted to prevent it; you, who know so much about her generosity, Austin, can guess what she offered me. She was pressing it on me as innocently as though she were my sister, and I got up and flung her hand away. I don't think I quite knew what I was about, Austin, and then it all came out."

"Hush! don't say any more. Yes, I understand." He turned his back on Garton, and began to walk up and down the room as though somewhat agitated; understand—of course he did—he could see it all clearly. The frank offer of assistance and the abrupt refusal, the girl's innocent reproaches and the poor fellow's sudden burst of anguish; he could fancy the sternness with which Garton flung away the little hand and rose to depart. Perhaps she saw his look of despair, and——

"Yes, yes, I see how it was," muttered the Vicar. He turned back and put his hands on Garton's shoulders, and looked up in the young man's face with kind wistful eyes.

"Do you think you are worthy of her, Gar? Oh, Gar, you are both so young for your age; are you sure that you know your own minds?"

Garton was silent a moment, and an expression almost of sadness crossed his face. "I shall try my best, Austin, you may depend on that; but how can I ever hope to come up to her?"

The Vicar smiled a little sadly; he seemed about to speak and then checked himself.

"You were going to say something, Austin?"

"Yes, but I was afraid I might hurt you; the fact is the world will judge you somewhat harshly in this, Garton; it will say, and justly too I think, that a man has no right to owe everything to his wife."

"That is what I say," muttered Robert. Garton looked from one to the other rather doubtfully.

"Perhaps it might not do in some cases," he said at last, very slowly. "Of course I should prefer it otherwise—any man would; but I shall not be such a fool as to let my pride stand in the way. I think it would be cowardly after what she said," and the dark face worked, and softened as he remembered Rotha's words—"I was but a poor girl, Garton, without a friend but Meg in the world, till all these good things came to me; but what are they worth—what is anything worth—unless I may share them with those I love?" She had said this to him in her sweet humility; would he ever forget those words? He knew what she meant; with womanly generosity she was stripping herself of all adventitious distinctions; her wealth was to be apart from herself, a mere adjunct of circumstances. In these few words she would have him know that in her sight they were more than equals.

Rotha's unworldly nature was likely to be a great comfort to Garton; it gave him strength now to repel his brother's forcible argument; it was not well in some cases, perhaps, but to be daunted by such a bugbear as this would be unmanly, he told himself; but Austin's words were, nevertheless, very grievous to him.

He stood with a clouded face while Austin looked at his watch and exclaimed abruptly at the lateness of the hour.

"If you are going in next door I shall come with you," he said with some decision, when the Vicar seemed preparing for departure. Austin sighed wearily, but offered no objection to the lad's impatience; the conversation would keep, he thought, till to-morrow, but Garton was evidently not of his opinion. Robert watched them out with gloomy eyes; he sighed bitterly once or twice when he was left alone.

"Who would have thought the boy would have had such good taste?" he said, half aloud, as he dragged his chair nearer to the fire and stirred the decaying embers together. "Pshaw! if she be what they make out, how could such a woman care for him?" he continued disdainfully. He struck the logs heavily with his boots —a shower of bright sparks flew hither and thither. "Gar has no pride," he muttered, leaning his elbows on his knees and staring at the flame. "If I had loved her ever so, I would have gone away without saying one word to her, if she looked at me for ever with her soft pitiful eyes; eyes—I never saw any woman's like them, they talk to you almost like a dumb animal's;" he shaded his with his hand and looked steadily into the lurid cavern before him. What face was that that seemed to start up suddenly before him? Not Belle's, certainly; there is no halo of pale golden hair, no gray eyes brimful of unspoken fondness. This is a sweet tired face, with brown hair blowing softly over the temples, the lips quiver sadly, the eyes are full of passionate brown fire. "I would rather walk till I dropped—till I died— before I touched your arm;" he wonders with a groan when these bitter words will cease to haunt him. Well, Garton has a strong arm, and she will lean on that—on that—a strange smile wreathes his pale lips as he follows out this thought—"Oh, Robert, Robert Ord, the time will soon come when you will wish that you had never been born than that you should see such a sight as that."

One can imagine what sort of kind brotherly counsel the Vicar gave when the study door had closed on him and Garton, and how he forgot his weariness, and patiently listened to the young man's eager outpourings. Garton got more than a glimpse of the great loving heart then; he listened with tender reverence when Austin touched gently on his failings and pointed out the path of duty that lay before him.

" You must go away, that you may be worthy of her," he said, not heeding how Garton winced at his words.   " You must work bravely for her and yourself too before you can enjoy your reward. When you come back you will be in a far different position, Garton, from what you now occupy.   Then you will have earned something towards your college expenses; your career will be open to you, and the good things will not come into empty hands as they do now."

" Enough, I will go," said the young man ; he held out his hand to his brother, and the Vicar was almost startled at his paleness.   " I hope you will not have reason to repent of your advice, Austin," he added with a wistful smile, touching in its sadness ; " but it shall never be said that I shirked my duty."

He went back into the next house and walked up straight to Robert, who was still sitting, brooding over the embers, with his elbows on his knees.

" Well," said Robert, not looking up at him, however, " you and Austin have found plenty to talk about."

" You are right," returned Garton sadly.   All the brightness had gone out of his face; he looked weary and dull.   " Robert, you meant it for the best, and I will not say any longer that you were wrong.   I will go by the *Phœnix* on Wednesday."   Robert looked up quickly, and then in a moment all his sullenness melted, and his whole heart yearned over his brother.

" God bless you, lad, you have lifted a weight off my mind.   I did give my word ; and, Gar, I really thought I was doing it for your good."

" Don't let's say another word about it, Bob.   I've got to do it, and that's all."

" Yes ; but I must say something.   Look here, dear boy, I did not mean half of all those hard things I have been saying."

" Did you not, Robert ?"

" No, of course not ; but I felt for the moment as though you had disgraced us all."

" I shall never do anything to disgrace you," returned Garton quietly.   " How can I when she cares for me ?   I am glad you have told me this, Bobus.   It makes it easier for me to go away. If I never come back"—his voice faltered—" you will try to think the best of me, will you not, dear old Bobus ?"   And before his brother could answer he dashed his hand across his eyes and hurriedly left the room.

# CHAPTER XXX.

A WOMAN'S REASON :—"I LOVE HIM BECAUSE I LOVE HIM."

> " Dear soul, not so !
> That time doth keep for us some happy years,
> That God hath portion'd out our smiles and tears,
> Thou knowest and I know.
>
> " Therefore I bear
> This winter-tide as bravely as I may,
> Patiently waiting for the bright spring day,
> That cometh with thee, Dear."
>
> ARNOLD.

THE bright beams of a December sun awoke Rotha the next morning, and a pleasant conviction that things were not quite as they were yesterday, and that something very wonderful had befallen her, was the first sensation that stole upon her.

How different everything was from yesterday !

Then she had wakened to a sense of weariness and discomfort, a cold sea-fog had enveloped everything ; Meg had come shivering into her room, bringing a gust of raw dampness with her. But to-day, when Rotha opened her eyes, all was glitter and light : a fresh wind swept over the lawn, stirring the shining rainpools ; the drops were still glistening on the evergreens, a robin chirped busily in the ivy. Out beyond in the morning sun lay the chain of low grass hillocks, long stretches of yellow sands, and then the blue curve of the bay—Welburn sloping in the distance like a breadth of dun-coloured cloud. Everywhere, as far as the eye could reach, were salt-ponds, trails of black seaweed, purple rocks uncovered in the sun, and masses of hummocky sand. Rotha looked almost as bright as the morning itself as she sat opposite Meg at the sunny breakfast-table ; upstairs Prue and Catherine were singing over their work ; the open windows and clanging doors bore witness to the fresh sea-breezes. Hannah Farebrothers, in her snowy sunbonnet, was pulling cabbages in the kitchen-garden. Peter came in at the green door on the lawn with Jock and Jasper barking at his heels; Fidgets flew down the lawn, his every hair bristling, to repel the intruders; and Garton's black cat, Cinders, who was taking a constitutional on her neighbour's wall, stepped gingerly among the broken bottles, looking down at them all in sooty disdain.

"What a beautiful day! Oh, how happy I am!" thought Rotha as, breakfast over, she stood by the open glass door feeding the robins; she broke off to wave a smiling good-bye to Meg, who went down the garden with her music-books under her arm.

"I am going to the organ first, and then to the school," Meg had said to her. Rotha looked after her with curious wistful eyes. "How strange it must feel to have lived one's life and to have been disappointed with it!" thought the girl sadly. "Meg cares only for her children and her music; she has no world of her own at all; she only lives in other people's lives—in mine and in little Stacy Maurice's, for example. I fancy, by the way she talks about her, that Stacy is her favourite. She spends her whole life in doing good and praying for that good-for-nothing husband of hers; and yet, I suppose, when she married him she expected to be happy as I am," moralised Rotha, with the unconscious superiority of one who feels that her own life will be so different.

She was rather absent when Hannah came in with a budget of domestic news. She gave all sorts of contradictory orders to the astonished woman, and then laughed and scolded herself in a breath. While Hannah talked about the miller and the price of flour, and the reasons why the last batch of bread had been so slack-baked, and how Prue's grandmother would find them in new-laid eggs all the year round at a cheaper rate than Gammer Stokes would, Rotha was wondering when Garton would be round, and how he would look, and what she would say to him, and whether he had told the Vicar—which latter point was speedily settled for her by the entrance of the Vicar himself.

Rotha had not expected him, and his visit took her quite by surprise, and for once in her life she felt decidedly nervous; she coloured and stood quite still by the window till he came up to her.

"Well, Rotha?" he said. He waited till Mrs. Farebrothers had curtsied and withdrew, and then he held out his two hands to the girl almost fondly. How pretty she looked as she stood there before him with downcast eyes, with her dark lashes sweeping her cheek! The gray dress and soft blue ribbons seemed to lend her colour.

"Is it really so, my child?" he said earnestly. "Have you quite made up your mind?" And Rotha's happy blush was sufficient answer.

What a long talk they had walking up and down the sunny old garden! How wisely, and with what gentleness he talked to her! Rotha lost her shyness now as she listened to him.

He told her in grave uncompromising words how the world would look upon her choice. "If she wished to marry Garton," he said, "and had made up her mind that it was for her happiness, it was not for them to interfere. But he would have her consider the thing in all its bearings, and not gloss over its difficulties."

He touched very tenderly too on Garton's failings, taking care to do justice to his nobler qualities. "He is very humble-minded —singularly so," the Vicar added, "and his faith is almost child-like. He will love you dearly, Rotha," he continued; "it is in his nature to be faithful." And then he hinted more than once at that want of ballast which was Garton's most serious defect.

"Gar is such a lovable fellow, and is so full of grand impulses," he said regretfully; "but, Rotha, I am half afraid that you are cleverer than he; a woman ought not to be cleverer than her husband."

"Goodness is better than cleverness," returned Rotha, blushing. She clave with a faith that was almost touching to her belief in Garton's goodness, and then she added naïvely, "I do not like to be called clever."

"Goodness is not everything," returned the Vicar gravely. "In marrying, a woman ought to be able to look up to her husband —to lean on him, so to speak. Do you think you could depend on Garton? that you could go to him for advice in all your difficulties and troubles? Be assured, the happiest woman in the world needs such help daily. And then if he could not give it, think, Rotha, how grievous it would be to be disappointed in him after all."

"I shall not be disappointed. He is sure to be good to me," replied the girl innocently. "I suppose, as he is not much older, that we shall help each other; and then we can always come to you for advice, as I do now," she added timidly.

"When you have a husband you will go to him. Mary tells me everything." He smiled a little over the girl's refreshing *naïveté*, though it made him rather grave inwardly. He was afraid, as Mrs. Carruthers was, that Rotha was a little misled by her imagination in her estimate of Garton's character.

Rotha in reality was a good deal puzzled by the Vicar's questions; his solemnity disturbed her. The sun was shining; the birds were twittering around her. She was happy; the world was beautiful.

"Oh, why will everybody be so grave about it? Was no one

ever engaged before?" thought Rotha indignantly. "What does it matter, if he be not clever, if I love him?" She put on a provoking little face as she turned to the Vicar. "I shall tell Garton that I shall always come to you for advice," she said, nodding at him. She had taken her handkerchief in her old way and had tied it gipsy-like over her brown hair. Her eyes were full of shy happiness.

"Well, well," he said, smiling; "if it must be so, it must be, I suppose. If I were Gar, I would not have you with such a proviso." He patted her hand thoughtfully, and then relapsed into gravity.

"Yes, it was a good thing," he said, "for both their sakes, that Garton was going away; it would test the reality of their affection for each other, and would make a man of Gar by teaching him to depend on his own resources; he would come back worthier of her than he was now."

Rotha looked up in some alarm at this.

"Going away—Garton going away!" she said. And just then the Vicar espied Garton himself coming through the trees to meet them.

Another time Rotha would have been rather bashful at thus meeting her lover for the first time under the Vicar's eye; but consternation at this sudden piece of news overbore this feeling, and as Garton came up to them—rather sheepishly, it must be confessed, at the sight of his brother—she put out her hand to him with a little impatience at his delay.

"What is this?" she said, rather peremptorily. "What does it all mean? The Vicar says you are going away." She looked up at him with wide-open eyes full of distress, with a fall of the lip like a child's; she actually believed that Garton was going to New Zealand, after all.

Garton took the little hand tenderly; he looked from one to the other rather doubtfully. The Vicar was grieved to see how worn and haggard Garton's face still was: strong agitation, sleeplessness, and the alternation from despair to sudden joy, and now the reluctance with which he viewed his enforced absence for so many months, made sad ravages in the young man's appearance; the radiant look of last night had almost disappeared.

"What have you told her, Austin?" he said, addressing his brother. "Robert has detained me, Rotha; I meant to have told you myself." He held her hand in a grip that was almost painful.

"Don't—you are hurting me; you are always hurting me, Garton," said the girl in a droll voice.

After the Vicar had left them she showed the red mark to Garton, who looked grave over it.

"My great hands are enough to crush those little fingers," he said, stroking them remorsefully. "What a little hand you have, Rotha—such a small thin hand!"

"Never mind, it is not a pretty one," returned Rotha hastily, drawing it away. "Garton, am I to understand that you are going to New Zealand, after all?"

"To New Zealand!" laughed Gar. "No; not unless you have a fancy for going there too. I can't say that I have any desire just now to pitch my tent among wigwams."

"Are there wigwams in New Zealand? How funny!" exclaimed Rotha. "I thought by the Vicar's laughing that I must be wrong, after all; but he certainly said that you were going away; and when—and where?" demanded Rotha, somewhat puzzled.

"Rotha, dear, I will tell you. Yes, I am going away," he returned in a troubled voice. He began to explain to her as well as he could how it had all come about, but at the first mention of Robert's name she stopped him.

"Robert thinks it necessary! What right has he to interfere between you and me? If he hates me, is that any reason why he should send you away?" she exclaimed indignantly.

"Hush, dear; no one sends me away. I am going because it is right for me to go," returned Gar, with a touch of sturdy independence. "Sweet heart"—the young man used the word in its Saxon sense, which rendered it infinitely touching—"sweet heart, do you think I should be worthy of you if I shirked my duty?"

"No," returned Rotha in a choked voice; "if you wish to leave me, you must do so, I suppose."

"If I wish to leave you? Oh, Rotha, how can you say such things," burst out the poor fellow, "when you know I worship the ground you walk on?" How eloquent he could be—this great clumsy Garton! "Don't make it too hard for me," pleaded Gar; "it is bad enough to have to go away without leaving you sorry and caring for it."

"Would you have me not care? How cold it is out here!" shivered the girl. Her kerchief had become untied and her brown hair blew softly over her neck; the pretty colour had faded out of her cheeks; she looked pale and wistful.

"Perhaps we had better go in. I thought that red cloak would have kept you warm," he returned; "but these winds are so treacherous." He followed her through the open glass doors; the robins were still chattering and twittering in the ivy. Rotha said nothing as Garton placed her favourite chair by the fire and brought her a footstool; she sat with the red cloak dropping off from her shoulders and her hands folded wearily in her lap. Garton stood and watched her with that strange new heartache of his till he saw the tears in her eyes, and then he could bear it no longer; he was standing beside her "mountains high," as she phrased it in her droll way, but now he suddenly got on one knee and put his arm around her. "Don't, Rotha; don't, my dear girl," he said—"just as though he had been used to comfort me every day of my life," Rotha said afterwards.

What were they after all but boy and girl in spite of their years? No one but Rotha would have thought much of Garton's eloquence or of his clumsy attempts to cheer her, and yet she was as honestly comforted by it all as though he had used the most persuasive arguments.

They got up a figurative tableau of Millais' "Huguenots" after that, which was very striking and characteristic in its way. Rotha was for tying the white scarf round her lover's arm, but Garton would not hear of it for a moment. Perhaps in her secret heart she was only trying him—very young women like to test their power sometimes; it did not offend Rotha one bit that he preferred his independence and his duty. Garton's firmness and loyalty to his brothers satisfied that duty-loving nature of hers. "How can they say he wants ballast?" she thought indignantly, as she remembered the Vicar's grave warning.

She said something of this to Garton afterwards when their little scene had been enacted; they were sitting now side by side, like sensible people, and Rotha looked as grave as a judge.

"I should not have cared for you half so much, after all, if you had not been firm in this," she said to him. She looked at the young man with sweet serious eyes, in which there was more approval than pain. Garton, in spite of his heavy heart, thrilled at her praise.

"I thought you would feel so; I was certain of it," he replied in a low voice.

"And you must not go and talk about it as though it were six years," continued Rotha cheerfully, who did nothing by halves, and was determined now to think the best of it. She was getting quite brave and matter-of-fact over it all; but such is the perversity of human nature that Garton, though he came out so strong in the character of consoler, relapsed dismally at this juncture.

"I don't know about years; I think it will be an eternity to me," he rejoined lugubriously. "It does seem so hard just when we were going to be so happy, and Wednesday will be here in no time."

"Why, it is Friday now. Oh," gasped Rotha—a sudden cold water damped her resolution and chilled it thoroughly— "Wednesday, how dreadfully near! Could they not spare us another day?"

"It would not do; besides, what is the good of prolonging one's misery? Of course every hour is worth its weight in gold," returned Gar somewhat contradictorily, feeling all at once like a condemned criminal waiting for a reprieve.

"No; it would not do," returned Rotha decisively; "we had better make the most of our time and not spoil the little that remains to us. Perhaps it will be better for us both when you are once gone; six months is not such a long time after all, and then, you know, I shall expect plenty of letters."

"I am not a good hand at that, I am afraid," said Gar, with a rueful smile. "Robert is the letter-writer of the family. After all, Rotha, I am afraid that you will find out that you are cleverer than I."

The Vicar's very words. Another dash of cold water to Rotha.

"Never mind if I am," she returned impatiently. "I do not think that sort of thing has anything to do with us two. You can write and tell me, I suppose, what you do on board ship, and what friends you make, and all that; and I daresay you will contrive a short message or two to Rube," she added mischievously.

"Oh, I daresay I shall manáge as much as that, and perhaps a little more. I can tell you, for instance——"

But it is useless repeating all Gar's words. Love-making was a novelty to him as well as to Rotha, and most likely he said and did a hundred extravagant things. Robert's cool quiet style would not have suited Gar's passionate nature at all.

Rotha thought it all very beautiful; and then they set themselves to plan out the few days that remained to them. The Vicar had made Garton promise that he would bring Rotha round to the Vicarage in the course of the morning, and he further stipulated that she should remain there the rest of the day. This they both considered charming. The next morning Garton was under an engagement to accompany Robert to Stretton, where he was to talk over business and receive final orders from Mr. Ramsay. Robert was to stay at Stretton over Sunday, but Garton promised to take an early train that he might spend at least an hour or two at Bryn. "This day was as good as lost," Garton observed regretfully; but Rotha consoled him by telling him that they would be together all Sunday, and that he was to bring Rube up to tea. Likewise she yielded to his entreaties that Meg and she should do a morning's shopping in Thornborough on Monday, where Garton would be most of the day getting together necessaries for his voyage. Robert had agreed to do the greater share of the business, and was hard at work already in Garton's service, as, indeed, were Mary and old Sarah; and, though they did not know it, he was at that very moment planning how he could stint himself to lay out a few more pounds on his brother's poor outfit.

"Yes; but we shall have to be back pretty early," observed Rotha, who was very brisk and businesslike over these details; "you have not forgotten the party at the Rudelsheims'?"

Now the Rudelsheims were among the naturalised strangers appertaining to Blackscar and its environs. They were worthy folk of German extraction, and were rather favourites with the Vicarage people; but they followed Mrs. Stephen Knowles' example in setting at defiance all Blackscar tradition, and in utterly abhorring the very name of tea-parties.

The tide of popular disfavour had indeed been too strong for that latter lady, who had succumbed so far as to tolerate kettle-drums and to allow tea and thin bread-and-butter to be handed round at an unwholesome hour of the afternoon; but Mrs. Rudelsheim, or Madame Rudelsheim, as she dearly loved to be called, would have nothing to say to such weak sophistries. She took every opportunity of laughing at Mrs. Stephen Knowles' "slop dawdles," as she called them.

"When I entertain my friends, I will entertain them properly," she would say. "Dancing is good for young people, and I do not see why they should not have it." And, in accordance with this peremptory benevolence, the Rudelsheims issued invitations for a party.

Rotha was going, but not Mary. Mrs. Ord had scruples about dancing—theoretical, but not practical ones; but the Vicar had promised to look in during the evening, and Aunt Eliza had engaged to chaperone both Rotha and Nettie. Robert had an invitation, and so had Garton, and Rotha was extorting from the latter a reluctant promise to be there.

He was not in the mood for dancing, he said; and then there were other objections. Madame Rudelsheim's parties were rather grand affairs—at least in Gar's eyes. He could not tell Rotha very well that his dress-coat was so shabby that he was ashamed of it; neither could he explain that even gloves and boots were a consideration to him. Gar never felt his poverty quite so bitterly as he did at this moment. If Rotha had been as poor as himself he would have confessed his difficulties without hesitation; but their hours together were numbered, and she had alleged all sorts of pretty arguments why he should be there, and Gar felt that in this point he was compelled to yield.

"And the next day—what shall we do on the next day?" exclaimed Rotha when this was settled. She looked just a little grave and tearful when Garton told her what they should do.

"It will be my last day," said Gar sadly, "and I must spend it with you and Rube; there will be packing and all manner of things to settle, I suppose, but I think we could manage to go over for a few hours to Burnley, you and I and Rube. I think that was the happiest day I ever spent in my life, and I want to see the dear old spot once more."

"Yes; we will go," returned Rotha dreamily; what strange fancies she had had in those dim old woods! She thought it was very nice of Garton to propose it. By this time it was growing late, and Rotha reminded him that Mary would be expecting them.

It was later still when they got to the Vicarage, for Meg came in, and that detained them. Garton looked sheepish again when Mrs. Carruthers shook hands with him and wished him joy; but he did not look so when, a few minutes afterwards, Rotha and he walked down to the Vicarage. Mary was expecting them, and met her friend with open arms. "Oh, my dear, Gar is not good enough for you," said the affectionate creature in a voice between laughing and crying. "I don't care a bit for your hearing me," she continued, nodding at Garton, who was standing by looking shame-faced and happy; "if you love her you will not mind being told how good she is. Rotha, how shall we manage to make enough of you, and to think of it being Garton after all?" finished Mary, who was still in a highly-strung pitch of excitement, and had kept up a variation of this one particular sentence ever since the news had been told her.

Belle came down presently, while Mary and Rotha were still talking. Both of them absolutely started at her ghastly looks. She went up and kissed Rotha with some show of kindness, but without any attempt at congratulation, and then went and sat silently in her place.

Only once Rotha attempted to speak to her; once when Garton, who had been lingering by her chair all the afternoon, had been summoned by the Vicar to come down and speak to a choir-boy who was in disgrace, and Mary, who had a secret liking for the culprit, had followed him. When they had gone out Rotha crossed the room and knelt down beside her.

"Dear Belle," she whispered, "will you not wish me happiness? Every one has but you." She repented the speech the moment she had said it when she saw the reproachful look with which she answered her.

"Oh, Rotha, how can you? Do I look as though I could wish any one happiness? No, I don't mean that; I do wish it you, dear, none the less that you have everything, and that my heart is broken; and, before Rotha could say a word, the unhappy girl had thrown her arms round Rotha's neck in a burst of bitter weeping.

# CHAPTER XXXI

## IN HOC SPERO.

"Through my happy tears there look'd in mino
    A face as sweet as morning violets;
    A face alight with love ineffable,
    The starry heart hid wonder trembling through."
                                                    MASSEY.

                    "To his eye
    There was but one beloved face on earth,
    And that was shining on him; he had look'd
    Upon it till it could not pass away;
    He had no breath, no being, but in hers.
    She was his voice; he did not speak to her,
    But trembled on her words; she was his sigh,
    For his eye follow'd hers, and saw with hers,
    Which colour'd all his objects;—he had ceased
    To live within himself; she was his life,
    The ocean to the river of his thoughts,
    Which terminated all; upon a tone,
    A touch of hers, his blood would ebb and flow,
    And his cheek change tempestuously."          BYRON.

BELLE's fit of agitation lasted so long that Rotha was frightened.
In vain she caressed her, in vain she implored her, with a hundred
endearing expressions, to tell her what had occurred to distress her.
Belle would say nothing, and absolutely refused to be comforted. She
had a paroxysm of coughing presently, and then she allowed Rotha to
assist her to her own room and do many little womanly offices for
her.  She lay quite still, with heaving breast and closed eyes, while
Rotha loosened her hair and freshened her burning face.  But, when
she had finished, Belle put out her hand to her and said hoarsely:
"Do not mind me ; go now.   Garton will be wanting you."
"But I should like to stay with you," returned Rotha pityingly.
But Belle shook her head.
"I would rather be alone ; you know I must be alone some-
times.   I shall like to think of you all being happy downstairs.
You are too good to me, Rotha.   I do not deserve it, and I never
think of any one but him."

She looked up with quivering lips when Rotha kissed her.

"Do not tell any one; do not let Mary know that I have been so silly. She would not understand. I shall be punished for it, for I shall not be able to come downstairs and see him to-night."

And a bitter sigh echoed her words as Rotha closed the door.

Rotha had no intention of obeying Belle by keeping her counsel. She found Mary alone when she returned to the drawing-room, and at once told her what had occurred, taking blame on herself for her inconsiderate words. Mrs. Ord, who looked very distressed over the whole recital, relieved her at once by throwing quite another light on the matter.

She told Rotha that Robert had been in that morning, quite contrary to his usual custom, and, finding Belle and her together, had told Belle in her presence about Garton's engagement and his own appointment.

"Robert had behaved beautifully," Mrs. Ord added, "and had broken the double news very gently to Belle, who had, on the whole, seemed to have taken it very quietly. He put everything in a clear concise way, dwelt a little on the benefits of the large salary, and the comfortable house that awaited them; and then asked her in a quiet straightforward way whether she thought she could get ready for him towards the end of February, or if she would prefer waiting till a few days before they sailed, 'unless, indeed,' he remarked with a smile, 'you are unwilling to leave Mary and come with me so far.'"

He went on a little more after this, and then pressed gently for her answer. Neither of them could see Belle's face, for she had kept her hand over her eyes all the time he had talked. Once or twice she had shivered slightly, but for the most part she seemed keeping herself still by force. When he had finished she had uncovered her eyes and looked at them so strangely that neither of them could understand it; and there had been a strained worn look about her face that had gone to her sister's heart.

"You know I am not well enough. I don't think I shall ever be well enough to be married," she had said to them; and then calling her sister to her, "Mary, tell him I cannot. Does he not know what is the matter with me?"

"I don't think any one knows what is the matter with you, Belle," he returned, but Mary saw a flushed uneasy look come into his face. Belle caught her breath with a little sob of impatient pain as he went on. No, she was not well; he knew that, he repeated, but she must give him her word to see a doctor without delay; and Belle, in a tone of reckless misery, promised that she would; and then she had surprised them both by fixing on Mr. Greenock, the Infirmary doctor. She would not hear of the family practitioner, Dr. Chapman.

"Very well, then, it shall be Greenock." Robert had returned, and, as far as he knew, he was quite as clever as the Blackscar practitioner. And then he begged her smilingly to compose herself, and to leave all other arrangements to him and Mary.

"And what did Belle say?" interrupted Rotha breathlessly at this point. She had turned red and pale over Mary's narration. She knew now why Belle had shrunk from the look of her happy face. "Oh, Mrs. Ord," she cried, "I am so afraid that Belle thinks herself very ill, and that it is preying on her mind."

"That is what I think," returned Mary, drying her eyes. "I have told Austin so over and over again. Oh, Rotha, suppose this is the beginning of decline; she looks so like poor Aunt Isabel, who had disease of the lungs and died quite young. And then to think that Robert would not let you take her away."

"He does not understand," returned Rotha in a low voice. "But I am afraid now a milder climate ought to have been tried long ago. I do not see myself how she is to be fit for a long sea voyage. But Mr. Greenock will tell you. Did she say anything more before she left you?"

"No; Austin came in, and she let us kiss her, but at the first word of congratulation she stopped us. Robert wanted her to go and lie down—he is very gentle and considerate with her now—and she went away directly. But I heard her tell Austin first that she had promised to see Mr. Greenock, and that he would tell us what she had tried so often lately to tell us, only she could not. And as she said this she turned so white that Austin put his arm round her, thinking she felt faint. But it was not faintness, Rotha, it was misery. She knows she is worse than we think."

"Why not send for Mr. Greenock at once?" interrupted Rotha hastily; but Mary shook her head. It was hard to see Mrs. Ord's fair face so troubled and worn.

"No; it will not do to hurry it. We know Belle too well for that. She has promised to see him on Tuesday, and Robert will not be back from Stretton till then. Tuesday will be Garton's last evening too, and Wednesday will be Christmas Eve. Oh, Rotha, what a Christmas this will be for us all, if Mr. Greenock says that Robert will have to go alone!"

"He cannot leave her surely?" interrupted Rotha.

"He must. What can he do? He will have thrown up his situation too. If she be not well enough to accompany him, the engagement will have to be broken off altogether, and that will kill her. Oh, Rotha," continued Mrs. Ord remorsefully, "I did not mean to have said all this to-day. I was trying to forget it when you and Garton came in. Ah, my dear, my dear, you must not cry to-day of all days, just when we all meant to be so happy too."

"I cannot help it," returned Rotha, struggling with her tears. "It seems so dreadful for her, and then for him not to see it." She broke off suddenly as Garton re-entered the room, and after that nothing more was said between them.

This conversation damped the rest of the evening to Rotha. Garton, though he sat near her and talked to her, missed the old merry smiles. Rotha was grave and abstracted, almost sad. Mary was upstairs with her sister most of the time, and the Vicar was busy. Robert never made his appearance at all. Just before she went away she stole for a moment into Belle's room to wish her good-night; but Belle seemed weary, and hardly spoke to her, and with a heavy heart she crept away. The next day things were hardly more cheerful at the Vicarage; Robert and Garton had gone to Stretton; Belle had relapsed into one of her taciturn moods; and Mary, after a few attempts, hardly made an effort to be cheerful. She was very sympathetic, however, and had a long confidential talk with Rotha about her own prospects. And in the afternoon the Vicar, seeing how things were, put aside his own business and took them and the four boys for a country ramble, which lasted so long that Garton had already made his appearance at Bryn and was harassing the soul of Mrs. Carruthers by his restlessness and repeated expressions of wonder as to what had become of Rotha.

The walk had done its work thoroughly, and Rotha came in by and by just as Garton loved to see her, with her brown hair ruffled and her bright face freshened with the wind. She had brought them all in, in triumph with her, and Mary laughed and looked like her old self as she helped Mrs. Carruthers to make arrangements for so large a party. Rotha let her do it; she stood talking to Garton in a low voice till she was summoned to her place at the head of the table.

These sort of impromptu gatherings were Rotha's delight. She had sent off Guy to fetch Reuben, and when he returned with the lad her pleasure was complete. Garton indeed would have preferred having Rotha to himself — love-making and tender speeches were hardly possible before the lads. But Rotha, in her unselfishness, never thought of such a thing; she was quite content to beam at Garton at intervals across the boys' rosy faces. She talked more to the Vicar than to him; it made her shy to encounter several pairs of round curious eyes every time she addressed him. Rufus and Laurie were always telegraphing their astonishment to each other, and Arty's audible remarks made her desperate ; she wished Garton would not break off his conversation every minute to catch her faintest words ; he did all sorts of things, this clumsy lover of hers, that confused and put her out of countenance. The Vicar could not help admiring the graceful tact with which she checked and kept him in order. After tea, when Mary had stolen away to look after Belle, she taught the boys games, and made them happy in a dozen ways. She played and sang to them, and joined in some of their favourite glees ; but, through it all, she was always conscious that Garton was near her or following her about with wistful eyes.

She went into the long drawing-room once, in the moonlight, to put away some music, and there she was startled by seeing him standing between the pillars like a black shadow. "Oh, Garton," she said, "I did not know you were following me. How you startled me !" And then, as he did not answer, she went up to him and touched him on the arm.

"Come, Garton, the boys are going. I think the Vicar wants you."

"Let him want me," returned Garton, detaining her. "Rotha, do you know that you have hardly spoken to me this evening ? I have been almost jealous of those boys—Rube especially."

"Rube, your favourite ? Oh, for shame !"

"My dear, I suppose it is only natural. I have so few hours left to me, and they will see you day after day." He held her fast for a moment, as though under some strange agitation. "Rotha, put your little hand here a moment," and he held it firmly to his heart. "Do you know, dear, it aches so to-night that I can hardly bear it ?"

She looked up in his face, almost frightened. Was it fancy, or did the moonlight make him look so pale ?

"My dear Garton—my poor boy !"

He smiled at that.

"I cannot help it, dear ; it is a sort of feeling—a presentiment, I suppose. People are always talking about those sort of things, and perhaps it has come to me. I cannot get it out of my mind that it would be better for us both if I were not going away."

"Oh, Garton !"

"There, perhaps I ought not to have said that. These things are always in God's hands, and I am doing my duty. You remember what you said about putting 'the hand to the plough'? There must be no looking back in one's work, eh, Rotha ?"

"No ; but I do not know how I am to let you go," said Rotha remorsefully, feeling that she had not made enough of him. She heard the boys tramping out of the front door, but for once she had forgotten her duties as hostess. "Oh, Gar, if you talk like this I shall never be able to let you go."

"Yes, you will," he returned, with that wonderful new gentleness which had come to him in the last few days, and which reminded her of the Vicar. "I do not fear you, Rotha. You are the bravest girl I have ever seen. You would let me go if you knew that I should never come back to you."

"Dear Garton, do you think I would be so hard-hearted?"

"It would not be hard-heartedness, Rotha; but perhaps I shall never make you understand, any more than you would if I told you that I loved you a hundred times more than you loved me."

"No, indeed," returned Rotha, rather indignant at this admission.

"Nevertheless it would be the truth," he returned quietly. "I have watched you so much these two days, and I know you so well, dear—don't misunderstand me," he continued, with a touch of his old vehemence, as Rotha tried to draw away her hand, "I am not complaining—why should I? It could not be otherwise. The time may come—I do not say it will, Rotha—when you will give me all that is in you to give; but it will not come to me just yet. Hush! Is that Austin calling?"

"He is only speaking to Mrs. Carruthers. Garton, what makes you talk so strangely to-night? Have I done anything to hurt you?"

"Hurt me, my darling?" But she need not have asked the question, for his answer fully satisfied her.

"What a grand room this is, Rotha!" he said presently, when they were still standing gazing out on the moonlighted lawn. "You look too young to be the mistress of this great house; and to think that it all belongs to you!"

"Do you mind it?" she returned softly. "I am keeping it all for you and your brother."

"For me!" He absolutely started. A sudden film came before his eyes; he had not realised before that all these good things were to come to him.

"Yes; but we must not forget Robert," said Rotha, following out the unspoken thought.

"Do you mean you and I? No, we will not forget him. You must not think me strange or ungrateful, Rotha; but it almost oppresses me to think that I may possibly share all this some day; it does not seem right or true. I wonder," he paused, looking round him with strange unseeing eyes; and then he stooped and kissed her softly once or twice.

What was that dull pain beating at his heart—that shadow that darkened his face with subtle trouble, and which haunts him even now? What though he never dwell here, in the presence of the woman he loves? "In thy Father's house there are many mansions" for thee and such as thee, Garton Ord.

The next day was Sunday. It was one of those soft wintry days which seemed snatched from the early spring. The robins chirped busily in the ivy; here and there a snowdrop peeped out from the ground. The sea was all in a glitter again, with a maze of deep blue shadow. Rotha, in soft blue dress, looked perfectly in unison with the day itself, as Garton thought, as he came through the lich-gate to join her after service.

Rotha long afterwards looked back on that day as one of the most peaceful she had ever spent. Garton had lost that feverish restlessness which had somehow oppressed her in spite of herself. He was a little quieter than she had ever known him, but full of thoughtfulness for her and Reuben. Reuben came up to Bryn by Rotha's express desire, and the three spent the afternoon together in the old way.

But once, when Garton and she were left alone together, he said suddenly:

"I have been thinking, Rotha, that I should like to leave you a little keepsake, and I have nothing in the world but my mother's keeper. It is very old-fashioned, and hardly worthy of your acceptance; but I should like you to wear it, dear, when I am away." And Rotha changed colour very prettily as he slipped the quaint old ring on her finger.

Nothing more was said for a few minutes, and then Rotha asked Garton if he did not like the old German custom of exchanging rings at a betrothal.

"There is a ring upstairs among your aunt's treasures that I should like you to wear for my sake," she said quickly; and before Garton could answer her she had left the room, and shortly after returned with the little case in her hand. She blushed a little as she held it out to him. "Look here, Garton; this ring always reminded me of you somehow, and you must wear it as a kind of talisman to preserve you from danger. When you are lonely and home-sick you can look at it and think of me."

"But it is too beautiful. Oh, Rotha, how can you?—and after my poor old keeper too!" he returned in a broken voice.

Garton was right as to its beauty, for the ring was of a singular design, and almost unique of its kind. In the centre was a recumbent cross formed of tiny rose diamonds set round with blue enamel, and graven on the broad gold band itself were the words, *In hoc spero* ("In this I hope").

Garton kissed the glittering cross reverently as Rotha put it on, and there were tears in his eyes as he thanked her. "*In hoc spero,*" Rotha heard him whisper, once or twice. "I wish all crosses were as light to carry as this;" and once, very solemnly, "Dear, you are right, and the cross is the only talisman."

The next morning Garton was under an appointment to meet his brother at Thornborough; and, according to promise, Rotha and Meg set out also for a day's shopping. Rotha was in hopes that Mary would accompany her, but at the last minute the Vicar came round to say that Mrs. Ord was unwilling to leave her sister. This damped the expedition a little; but, as Rotha had a great deal of business to transact, she started reluctantly without her. She got through all her commissions before Garton was at liberty to come in search of her. As they walked through the smoky streets or looked in at the shop-windows for the trifling gifts that Garton proposed to buy for Mary and the boys, they met Robert once or twice, evidently bent on more important errands of his own; but he barely noticed the little party beyond lifting his hat to the ladies, and Rotha was certain that he was anxious to avoid coming into direct contact with them.

When he had passed, however, Garton had plenty to say in his brother's praise. He told her that Robert was stinting himself that he might procure comforts for his journey; Robert had been with him to the different shops and ordered things almost lavishly; he had attempted to remonstrate with him once or twice, but Robert only answered that he meant to do his best for him.

"I don't think I have ever had so many things in my life before," finished Garton, who knew nothing about the handsome travelling dressing-case and writing-case with his initials stamped in silver on the Russian leather. Mary knew all about it, and so did the Vicar; but Rotha's desire was that they should be slipped into the bottom of the box, and only be brought to light as a pleasant surprise on the voyage.

Rotha went into the Vicarage on their return and found Mary already marking some of Garton's new things. A heavy travelling-trunk blocked up the passage; Garton pointed it out rather sadly as they went through the hall. "Forty-eight hours more and I shall be on my way," he observed, with a sigh, which Rotha was only too ready to echo.

It was arranged that Garton was to come up to Bryn and wait for Rotha, while the carriage went to fetch Aunt Eliza and Nettie; but Rotha, who had put off dressing for the party till an unconscionably late hour, was not nearly ready when he arrived; and to beguile his impatience he sent up all sorts of messages by Mrs. Carruthers, to Prue's and Catherine's great amusement.

Meg gave ludicrous accounts of Garton pacing up and down like a Polar bear; his hair was just a quarter of an inch long, Meg protested; and she was sure that Madame Rudelsheim would take him for an escaped convict. "And he has holes in his gloves already through fidgeting them, Rotha; and he looks such a giant in his dress-coat." Rotha burst out laughing at the flattering picture.

"There, give me my fan and gloves, you ridiculous woman," laughed Rotha. "I must go down now and ask if I shall do."

She went rustling into the room in her pink dress—her white neck and arms showing through the folds of some flimsy scarf. She burst into the presence of the astonished Garton radiant and smiling. Wonderful pearls gleamed on her neck. She wore glittering armlets and serpents with brilliant heads. She stood tapping the ground before him with her satin slipper.

"Shall I do, Garton?" she said. "I have put on some of the old jewels in your honour to-night." She laughed at the awe and reverence with which the young man seemed to regard her. A hot flush crossed Garton's face as he answered. Rotha sparkling with jewels seemed different from the Rotha in the gray dress and blue ribbons. He could not make her understand this, but in his humility he seemed to be suddenly removed miles away from her. What could there be in common between such as he and the radiant girl before him?

Garton did not say all this—he would not have known how to speak, but he looked at her with grave wistful eyes.

"How will you do? Don't ask me. I do not know you to-night, Rotha. Are those Aunt Charlotte's pearls you have on?" He glanced anxiously at her hand to see if the old keeper was there, but it was half hidden under a glittering diamond hoop.

"Do not you like me to wear them? Are you not pleased?" asked Rotha. She felt disappointed and half ready to cry. She was a thorough woman, and wanted her lover to admire her. She wished Garton would not stand looking at her with such big solemn eyes. Perhaps he thought that a future clergyman's wife had no business to wear jewels. She moved her bracelet up and down her arm so restlessly that it unsnapped, and Garton had to come to the rescue with bungling fingers. He looked at her in a queer uncertain way when his clumsy hands had achieved the clasp.

"I was half afraid that I should be kept at arm's length this evening. I cannot believe that you belong to me to-night, dear," he said wistfully. It was this humility, this self-distrust, that was Garton's great stumbling-block in Rotha's eyes; another time

23

she would have waxed a little impatient over it, but now it only pained her. She drew back from him with tears in her eyes; in a moment she felt both chilled and wounded. After what she had done for him—how could he—how could he!

Rotha was too gentle to retaliate, but Garton felt the silent reproach instinctively; in another moment he was beside her.

"Oh, Rotha, I did not mean that. How could you misunderstand me? Sweet heart, dear heart, how can you be what you are and not be deserving of my reverence?"

But Rotha's answer was right womanly.

"I would rather be loved, Garton."

"Well, and are you not?" But the rest of his reply must have been tolerably satisfactory to Rotha, to judge by the happy blush and smile with which she answered him.

Madame Rudelsheim's handsome rooms were in a blaze of light, and dancing had long commenced when Rotha and her party entered. To Rotha it was a dazzling spectacle; she leaned on Garton's arm, a little confused and giddy: the whirling couples, the lights, the music, the gay dresses, the small knots of chaperones and wallflowers nodding like well-preserved exotics against the wall, the conservatory with its compound lights, a blending of Chinese lanterns and moonlight, were like the shifting of a kaleidoscope to Rotha, whose sole notion of a party was derived from the breaking-up at Miss Binks', where the young ladies were all dressed in a uniform of white muslin, and dancing was carried on to the limited hour of eleven.

"How beautiful it all is! Don't you like parties?" asked Rotha, with little gasps of admiration. Her eyes sparkled, her cheeks glowed; how pleasant it was to be there, among all those people, leaning on his arm! She moved away from him a little reluctantly when her partner, Mr. Effingham, came to claim her. As for Garton, he might have been in earnest, he glared at him so; Gar could not dance. He went off rather sulkily with Rotha's flowers in his hand. He stood by Aunt Eliza's side, rearing himself against the wall in a thoroughly English-like bad humour; the poor flowers rather suffered for it. Rotha came up for them and her fan presently—rather to Mr. Effingham's surprise. He half believed Jack's account was true, after all. Gar gave them without a word; as far as that went, he was quite content to fetch and carry for her all the evening. He had her scarf, a scented gauzy thing, hanging conspicuously over his arm; nay, under other circumstances he would have been quite happy to have stood in a corner all the evening and watched her—his lady of delight; but he could not help feeling hurt and sulky when one gay partner after another whirled her away. Rotha was much sought after, and it was only natural, but perhaps it was trying for Garton. Mr. Effingham in particular became abhorrent to him—probably because he was the handsomest man in the room, and danced often with Rotha. Gar longed to go after him and tell him that she belonged to him. Before the evening was half over the impulse was strong upon him to make his claims known to the whole room; he leant against the wall hour after hour buttoning and unbuttoning his huge gloves, or pulling the fronds of maidenhair out of Rotha's bouquet. He stood like a stony young giant when Rotha innocently brought up her partners to him, and frowned heavily over the graceful badinage as though every joke were treason to his love. I think, after a little while, Aunt Eliza would have gladly dispensed with his close attendance—he trampled on her rich silk dress and answered all her cheerful remarks with monosyllables. He burst into a gruff laugh when Aunt Eliza feared that he was not enjoying himself, and then checked himself with a twinge of remorse.

"No; I am not, but she is," he said in a tone that told Aunt Eliza everything. "Does not she look beautiful?—just fit for this sort of thing," he burst out after a moment. "Of course every one admires her—no one else in the room can compare with her; and then how gracefully she dances!"

"Why don't you take her in to supper?" said Aunt Eliza, nodding at him till her brown front got slightly disarranged. "Of course I see how it is: you should not let Mr. Effingham monopolise her. He is handsome, but he is no good—more whiskers than brains; there's Nettie there won't say a word to him."

"He—I hate him—that is—— Confound his impertinence! there he is making up to her again. I beg your pardon, Miss Underwood, but there are some things a fellow can't stand." And with these obscure remarks Garton threaded his wrathful way through the dancers to where Rotha sat fanning herself, with the obnoxious Mr. Effingham leaning over her.

Garton almost pushed against him as he held out his hand to her.

"Come," he said, "they are going down to supper now, and I want to get you a good place."

"Miss Maturin has accepted my escort, I believe," lisped young Effingham, with a twirl of his moustache, and with what he intended to be a fascinating smile.

"I beg your pardon, Effingham," retorted Gar, "Miss Maturin is engaged to me for this. You promised, you remember?" with a change of tone so meaning and tender that it was not lost on the watchful rival. Rotha coloured a little as she answered :

"Yes, I remember; but I thought you had forgotten me. You seemed so engrossed with Aunt Eliza. You see you must excuse me, Mr. Effingham, but I shall be ready for our next dance."

"That is if Mr. Ord will allow us. I had no idea that I was interfering with a monopoly," he returned, with a perceptible sneer. It was lost on Garton, however, as he hurried Rotha away.

"How often have you been dancing with that fellow?" inquired Garton hastily. "I hate him! None of the Effinghams are any good, I can tell you."

"Hush! he is behind us—he will hear you. He dances very nicely—that is all I know. Don't let us talk about him. I am so glad to get back to you." And Rotha looked so honest and so genuinely happy as she said this that Garton was instantly mollified, and all his sulkiness vanished under the magic of her smiles.

That hour was the one oasis of the evening to Gar, the rest was a splendid blank; and he roused himself to such purpose, and was so devoted and attentive, that it was sufficiently patent to every one at their end of the table how things stood between them. Nothing is perfect in this world, and there is always a cause for discontent to leak out. Such is the contradictoriness of human nature, and female human nature in particular, that Rotha wished that his manner to her had not been quite so *empressé*, and that he would not look at her so often. How she hated herself for this feeling afterwards! but it made her a little quiet at the time— perhaps because she was aware that Mr. Effingham still watched them from a distance. How glad she was that there was no room for him at their table!

He came up by and by to claim her for the Lancers. Rotha, who was drawing on her gloves, was very cool and dignified all of a sudden, but she rose without a word.

"Do put on your scarf; it is so cold and draughty in the passages," said Garton, following her. Rotha bit her lip with something like vexation at this unwelcome pertinacity.

"No, no, I don't want it; give it to Aunt Eliza to hold if you are tired of it," she said impatiently. How she wished afterwards she had spared him this rebuff!

He went off sadly enough after that. As he passed through the hall there was a sudden loud ring at the door-bell, and a moment afterwards he was shivering in a draught of cold night-air.

" I suppose a carriage has arrived for some one ; I wish it were ours," muttered Gar disconsolately ; and half in curiosity he turned back to question the waiter, the very green-grocer in disguise who was at all the Blackscar parties, and who rejoiced in the mellifluous appellation of Gubbins.

"Gubbins, was that the carriage from Bryn ?"

" Carriage, sir ? no, sir ! I was just coming to find you, sir. Your brother, sir "—motioning to a small apartment where hats and coats had been multiplying and dividing all the evening under the care of a large-headed youth in a suit of tight livery—"your brother, sir, wanted you fetched immediately."

"All right, Gubbins, that will do. It is I, Garton. Come in here, my dear fellow ; I want to speak to you." And Robert, taking hold of Garton's arm, gently led him into the little room and shut the door.

# CHAPTER XXXII.

## "GOOD-BYE, GAR."

" Glitters the dew and shines the river,
 Up comes the lily and dries her bell ;
But two are walking apart for ever,
 And wave their hands for a mute farewell.

.    .    .    .    .    .

" And yet I know, past all doubting, truly—
 A knowledge greater than grief can dim—
Know, as he loved, he will love me truly—
 Yea, better—e'en better than I love him.

" And as I walk by the vast calm river,
 The awful river so dread to see,
I say, 'Thy breadth and thy depth for ever
 Are bridged by his thoughts that cross to me.'"

JEAN INGELOW.

MEANWHILE Rotha went through the Lancers somewhat languidly, and for once Mr. Effingham's gay chatter fell unheeded
on his partner's ear. Rotha was absent, a little *distraite*—she
was wondering what had become of Garton, and why he had not
followed her into the room. Aunt Eliza was still in her old
corner, talking in a loud voice to a very sulky young wallflower,
who gave her small cool answers in return. Nettie was carrying
on a violent flirtation with a stout bald-headed widower, old
enough to be her father and the happy parent of nine children ;
and Mat O'Brien, in an audible voice, was telling Mrs. Stephen
Knowles that the thing was as good as settled. How flat, stale,
and unprofitable these sort of affairs were, after all ! Everybody
was enjoying themselves, it was true—except the chaperones, who
were just getting drowsy. Rotha began to be a little tired of it
all. The lights were not quite so bright, the flowers were faded,
the music had degenerated into a mere jig. Mr. Effingham's talk
was tedious. Rotha looked wistfully across to the empty corner,
but no impatient young giant blocked it up, no dark eyes followed

her up and down the room; no wonder her dancing was spiritless and that her unlucky partner got short answers.

"I wonder where he is? How I wish this dance were over! I am afraid that he has not enjoyed the evening as much as I have," thought Rotha, with an undefinable feeling of remorse as she remembered that she might have given up at least one dance to stay with him; and then she resolved mentally that Mr. Effingham should not again tempt her. She had been angry with him ever since his speech as to Garton's monopoly; and then Garton did not seem to like him.

"It is your turn now; ladies to the centre," observed her partner. "It is a bore, you know, and all that sort of thing"— and he shrugs his shoulders slightly and walks to his place, looking handsome and used up. "Ah, there's our monopolising friend," he continues presently, with a cool well-bred stare, which Rotha immediately resents; but she looks up very eagerly notwithstanding.

Yes, he was right; there was Garton making his way towards them, pushing through the dancers with a pale determined face. Rotha's flowers are all to pieces now, strewn hither and thither as his strong shoulders part the crowd.

"I don't congratulate you on your choice of a bouquet-holder, Miss Maturin," says Mr. Effingham, caressing his whiskers to hide a smile. "Ladies to the centre again, if you please."

Garton makes a hasty stride and lays his hand on her arm, her dress.

"Rotha, I want you."

"Presently," she says, with a smile; and she goes up and makes strange fluttering movements with three other ladies. Garton watches the grave profound salaams with a mixture of contempt and impatience. "Hands across!" Rotha is back in her place again, and now the gentlemen perform mysterious evolutions and turn their backs disdainfully on each other.

"Oh, Rotha, do leave all this nonsense. I want you," says Gar, trying to speak steadily. His face is very pale indeed by this time; he looks like one who has received a shock.

"How can I come in the middle of a dance? Is anything the matter? Has our carriage come? How strange you look, Garton!"

"There is nothing the matter; at least I shall have to go home alone if you will not come. I am wanted directly," says Gar in an agitated manner.

"I don't know what you mean. Of course I will come if you want me," returned Rotha, quite bewildered. "I am afraid something is the matter, Mr. Effingham, and I must go home. There is Annie Johnson without a partner. Shall I tell Aunt Eliza we are going, Garton?"

"No; leave her alone, she will only be in our way. We can send back the carriage with a message presently. I am so sorry to disturb you, dear, but it could not be helped." And Gar looks at her with such sad eyes that Rotha feels quite frightened.

"But what is it? and why must we go home?" she inquires, pressing his arm. The music sounds softly in the distance. There is a sweet overpowering smell from a daphne near. The Chinese lanterns have burnt out in the conservatory, and the moonlight pours in unchecked. She detains Garton by the door, but he draws her on.

"Hush! I can't tell you here, they are all coming in. I don't think I quite understand how it is myself, though he has been telling me. I only know that I am to leave you directly." Then, with a sudden burst of despair, "Oh, what shall I do without you, Rotha, my darling?"

"Leave me directly?" cries Rotha, with a start. Her hand tightens insensibly on his arm. "Oh, my dear boy, do tell me plainly what you mean."

"Hush! there's Robert. It means that I am going now, this morning, and not to-morrow evening, as we thought. Ask Bob to explain it; it is more than I can." And Gar's face worked with agitation.

Rotha gave a little exclamation when she saw Robert, but he did not hear it. He looked a little moved from his usual calmness when he saw her coming in on Garton's arm. Undefinable feelings of remorse chilled him; a nameless pain smote upon his heart as he marked her clinging gesture. How young and fair she looked in her evening dress! Jewels, too! He always knew how well she would look in jewels. How milky-white the pearls were against her soft neck! but the clear eyes looked up at him sorely troubled. He saw quicker than Garton, too, that she was trembling. He came up to her with what Mary called "his good look on his face."

"This is a sad business. I am so sorry for you and Garton. It is all the fault of those telegraph clerks that the mistake has occurred. Do sit down;" for she was trembling more than ever at his kindness. "Garton, my dear fellow," with a touch of impatience at his brother's dilatoriness, "why do you not give Miss Maturin a chair?"

"Thank you. I am very silly; but——"

"But Gar was too sudden. Yes, I understand; that was

always his fault, dear old boy." He sent Garton off with prompt
thoughtfulness for Rotha's wraps, and then poured out some wine
and brought it to her, putting it to her lips himself. Tears came
to Rotha's eyes at this. She was a little giddy and stunned at
the quick transition of events. She was tired, too ; and this was
the first kindly office he had ever rendered her. Of course Robert
misunderstood her emotion, but he was not the less kind.

When Garton brought the furred cloak he took it from him
and wrapped her in it himself. In trying to fasten it his hand
accidentally touched hers, and with a sudden kindly impulse he
took it for a moment in his as though to detain her. Did she
remember, even at that moment, that it was the first time their
hands had ever met ?

" There is no hurry—at least not until you are ready. Was I
right in thinking you would come with us to the Vicarage ?"

" Do they expect me ?" asked Rotha.

" Yes, Mary does ; and so does Austin, I believe. If you are
really ready there is no time to be lost." And Rotha rose immediately.

" How soon must he go ?" she said presently, when they were
in the carriage. Garton's hand had already felt for hers in the
darkness, but he had not trusted himself to speak, and Robert's
sympathy kept him silent.

" In little more than an hour," he replied. " You know we
have to go to Stretton first, and then he is to take the six o'clock
train to London ; of course I shall go with him and see him on
board. They expect to drop anchor about four."

" But why—what is the reason of all this hurry ?" persisted
Rotha, with dry lips. She leant back in the carriage, too confused
and giddy to follow the explanation that Robert gave her. She
never understood more than that it had been a mistake in a tele-
graphic message as to the time the vessel was to leave the docks,
and that it had been rectified too late. Robert had arrived from
Stretton a little before midnight, and had found the Vicar and his
wife up. Mary was hard at work at some of Garton's things, and
he had stayed to explain matters and put everything in train
before he set off to find Garton. By these means very little time
had been lost, for Garton was so bewildered by this sudden parting
with Rotha that his arrangements were hardly to be depended on.

Yet, even though their very minutes were numbered, he could
not bring himself to speak to her ; but the convulsive pressure of
the hand he held spoke volumes. Once, somewhat alarmed at his
continued silence, Rotha put up her other hand and touched his
face in the darkness, and then she felt something very like a tear

on his cheek. "My poor boy—my own poor boy!" she whispered. But Garton only said, "Hush! don't be too kind to me to-night—I cannot bear it; it will unman me." And then kissed the caressing hand humbly as though to atone for his words.

It seemed a long drive to all three before they were set down at the Vicarage. The Vicar was in the dining-room awaiting them; a bright fire burned cheerily; breakfast was already laid on the table, and Deb came up with the steaming coffee-pot soon afterwards. Short as was the interval that had elapsed since Robert had left them, Mary and Deb had already got through half the packing, and Garton's presence was urgently required for its completion.

"We have brought Miss Maturin," said Robert, leading her in. "I thought you would take care of her, Austin, while Gar and I finish going through the papers. I will bring him back as soon as possible," he added gently as he placed Rotha by the fire. Tired and sick as she felt, she could not help giving him a grateful look; its sweetness lingered long with him through the wretched time that followed. He could not fail to remember afterwards that she had acquitted him of blame.

Rotha sat quietly by the fire after the brothers had left the room. Gar had given her one long wistful look as he went out. Highly as the Vicar esteemed her, he never fully realised her gentleness and unselfishness till this moment. Robert's kindness had roused her from the bewildered state into which Garton's agitation had thrown her, and she was now quite collected and full of thought for them all.

"Do not mind me," she said to the Vicar as he hovered near her anxiously. "We shall have plenty of time to think of ourselves and our own loss afterwards. Do go to Garton. I am sure he wants all the help you can give him." And, as he quitted her reluctantly, she followed him and begged him to be sure and tell Mary to put her presents just inside the trunk that he might see them the moment he opened it.

When she was left alone she cast about in her own mind how she might comfort him. She would hardly have a minute to exchange a word with him perhaps; and then the others would be with them. And yet she longed to say some such word of comfort to him.

There was a little worn Testament which she always carried about with her, and which had belonged to her mother, and her name and her mother's name had been written in it. After a moment's hesitation she thought that would do, and sat down with trembling fingers to pencil a few words on the title-page. The effort made the tears spring to her eyes, but she wiped them courageously away. " It will never do for him to see that I have been crying," she thought; but, notwithstanding the resolution, one or two drops blurred the handwriting. Garton afterwards read these few tender words, the noblest farewell that any lover could pen :—" The Lord watch between me and thee when we are absent one from another. —Your faithful friend, ROTHA MATURIN." How many Mizpahs are set up between loving hearts in this earthly wilderness !

After that she sat herself down again with the book on her lap and patiently awaited their return. Robert came in first and began arranging and sorting some papers. He looked up a little surprised when Rotha rose suddenly from her seat and offered to help him. " No, no; you are too tired," he began, but at her reiterated request he gave way. She stood beside him, following his directions with a quiet intelligence that won his good opinion. She never asked after Garton or seemed the least impatient till he returned. Robert gave her more than one curious look of mingled admiration and pity when she was too much engaged to notice it. The white fur cloak, the starry flowers in her hair, and the un- gloved hands sparkling with rings, all came under his notice ; but, most of all, the wistful young face with its quiet air of sadness and its patient droop of the head.

The Vicar came in next, and then Garton in his dark tweed travelling suit, and afterwards Mary, who came round and kissed Rotha without a word, and then began pouring out the coffee. Mary looked as though she had been crying, and there were dark lines under the pretty eyes, but she spoke with her old cheerfulness now and then. The rest gathered round the table and made some pretence at a meal, as though to set Garton an example ; but he told them he had already supped, and only wanted a cup of coffee. Rotha made him break bread, however, and then he sat for a long time with his hand drawn silently over his eyes. He started up presently from his place as though he had forgotten something.

" Rube ; I have not wished my poor Rube good-bye."

" There is no time now," returned Robert ; " besides, the whole house is asleep."

" Yes, I know ;" and Garton sat down again with a heavy sigh. " No one thought of rousing him, I suppose ? and now it is too late. Poor Rube," he went on in an agitated voice, "how un- happy he will be to wake up to-morrow and find me gone !"

" No, no ; nonsense, Gar," said Robert, with a touch of kind peremptoriness ; but Rotha stopped him. She put her hand gently on the young man's arm.

" You can trust him to me, Garton, can you not ? I will go to him to-morrow myself, and if he frets I will take him home. You know he belongs to me now as well as to you."

"Trust him to her?" Rotha might well treasure the smile with which he answered her; the rugged brown face worked and softened with conflicting feelings. "Come, Mary, I am ready to go up and wish Belle and the boys good-bye."

"Go, my dear fellow; we have only seven minutes," called out Robert, and Gar nodded in answer. Rotha had slipped the little Testament into his hand as they sat at the table. He had a choked sort of feeling that his good-bye would be as mute as hers when it came to the point. He hardly understood himself what the bitter ache at his heart meant, but it almost suffocated him.

Arty was fast asleep in his cot, and murmured drowsily in answer to his uncle's kiss. He had all the contents of his Noah's Ark littered on the coverlet, and the elephant and a cassowary reposed on his pillow. Gar leant over the little fellow fondly. The other boys had been roused at the last moment by Deb, and sat shivering and miserable on the respective edges of their beds, especially Laurie, who began to cry. Garton kissed them and bade God bless them one after another, and sent his dear love to Rube; and then he went to Belle, who was waiting up for him.

Belle had never got on very well with Garton, and Mary was surprised to see how much she seemed affected at saying good-bye to him. She turned quite pale as he leant over to kiss her.

"Good-bye, dear Belle; get well soon, and marry Robert." And Belle folded her arms round his neck just as though he had been her brother.

"Good-bye, dear old Gar. Forgive me for having been so often cross with you. I never meant to be so, dear. I always loved you, Gar."

"And I you, dear. There—there is Robert calling me, and I must go to Rotha. Don't come down with me, Mary; better not, better not. "Oh, Mary!"—and he leant against the half-closed door with whitening face—"I feel as though I shall never come home again, and as though this were good-bye for ever."

"Gar! Gar! don't let Belle hear you, my dear boy. This is very, very wrong." And Mary put her hand tenderly on the dark closely-cropped hair.

"I can't help it. Hark! is that Austin's voice? Good-bye, dear sister; take care of her for my sake."

"You have only two minutes, Garton. Robert is having the luggage put on the fly. Go to Rotha, my dear boy." And the Vicar put his hand on his shoulder and led him gently in.

"Not good-bye," said Rotha, putting her soft hand over his

mouth as though to silence him; "not good-bye. I like farewell so much better."

"Farewell, then," returned Garton, taking her in his arms; "farewell, and God bless you. If I kiss this dear face for the last time, His will be done."

"My own Garton," murmured the girl, putting back her head that she might look at him,—"my own Garton, you do not fear to go now, do you? You would not have it otherwise?"

"No; not otherwise," he repeated; and the mournful steadfastness of his look haunted her long afterwards; it reminded her much of a martyr's look,—"not otherwise, while I have this talisman." He held up his ring that she might see the glittering cross. "*In hoc spero.* Beloved, that must be our motto;" and before she could answer he closed her fair face suddenly between his hands. For a brief moment she heard the beating of his heart and his whispered "God bless you!" Another minute his hand was within the Vicar's grasp; and then he was gone.

# CHAPTER XXXIII.

"How sweet is woman's love, is woman's care !
  When struck and shatter'd in a stormy hour
  We droop forlorn ! and man, with stoic air,
  Neglects, or roughly aids ; then robed in power,
  Then nature's angel seeks the mourner's bower.
  How blest her smile that gives the soul repose,
  How blest her voice, that, like the genial shower
  Pour'd on the desert, gladdens as it flows,
  And cheers the smiling heart and conquers woes."
  
                                        GALLY KNIGHT.

THE next day was a blank as far as Rotha was concerned.

It was daybreak before the Vicar had taken her home; and then she had dragged herself wearily to her bed, too tired and dispirited with the evening's strain to do more than fall asleep with Garton's name on her lips. She woke late the following morning, and opened her eyes on a wet cheerless prospect, on dripping trees, sea-fog, and all the depressing accompaniments of a hopelessly rainy day. Her head ached too, and she felt stiff and jaded with the unaccustomed exercise of the previous evening. She would have liked to have been where she was another hour or two, reviving the bitter-sweet memories of last night, their happy evening together, the unlooked-for interruption, and Garton's fond farewell. But, mindful of her self-imposed task, she roused herself with a strong effort and went out in search of Reuben.

It was already so late that she met him coming out of the Grammar School with a troop of boys at his heels, and conveyed him off to Bryn, where she kept him the whole afternoon. She had a little trouble with him at first, as Garton predicted. Reuben burst into a flood of indignant tears when he learnt that his friend had really gone. "He ought to have come and wished me good-bye," sobbed the boy. "I didn't think it of him; he might have thrown a little gravel against my window, as he did once, and then I should have understood in an instant. It was cruel of him to forget me when I never forget him; and perhaps I shall not see him again for such a long time," finished Rube, to whom six months seemed an interminable period, and South America the very end of the world.

"He didn't forget you, dear. Have I not given you his messages? You must not be so hard on him, Rube." Perhaps the task of comforting Reuben was the best thing that could have happened to Rotha. Gar's shadow was next to having Gar himself.

She kept the boy with her most of the evening, and only sent him away because her head ached so that she could hardly bear it. It gave her an excuse for dismissing Meg too. In spite of her pain she felt it would be a relief to be allowed to sit quietly and speak to no one. She was glad that Mary sent round a kind little note instead of coming herself, for she began to feel so wretched that even her friend's society would have been irksome.

Rotha was almost surprised to find how she missed Garton. She had been very brave all day, and had succeeded wonderfully in comforting Reuben, and she had even astonished Meg with her cheerfulness. But towards evening the effort had been manifest; even while she sat and talked to Rube about his studies, a curious sick longing took possession of her—vague feelings of remorse for her neglect last night—a yearning to see him again and hear his voice. Not till he had really gone did Rotha discover how much she loved him, and what a blank his absence would leave in her daily life.

Six months—only six or seven months! Rotha scolded herself, and cried shame on her foolish cowardice; but the pain was none the less real while it lasted. She was spent, too, with physical exertion; and, though she hardly remembered it just now, her heart was very heavy about Belle: undefinable fears haunted her dreams; she had cried herself to sleep like a child, but even in sleep an uneasy pain pervaded her slumbers—all sorts of misty images chased each other across her brain. Garton's sad face seemed always before her; he seemed asking her for some help that she could not give. Once she had a terrible dream, but she could not remember it when she woke. Some haunting terror seemed upon her, and she woke with a stifled scream to find Meg bending over her, and watching her uneasy sleep. That soothed her; and afterwards she fell into a dreamless slumber, and woke more refreshed this time to find Mrs. Ord by her bedside.

Robert had returned from London late the previous night, and had begged Mary of his own accord to go round to Rotha in the morning and give her the latest news of Garton — a fresh instance of his new thoughtfulness for her, which made the colour come into Rotha's pale face.

Robert had seen Garton fairly on board, and had left him tolerably comfortable. Mr. Ramsay had accompanied them to London, and had expressed himself as much pleased with Garton's appearance and bearing. Gar seemed to have plucked up more heart about the whole affair, Robert added, and had entrusted him with loads of messages for them all; and among them a precious little scrap for Rotha, evidently pencilled on the leaf of his pocket-book while Robert was still on deck, and thrust, half-crumpled, into his hand at the last moment.

How strange it was for Rotha to read that queer cramped handwriting for the first time when Mary had gone! She took it out of the folds of her dress, where it lay hidden, and read it over and over again. If only Garton could have seen the way in which she kissed it—though she did not know then that that crumpled paper would be one of her greatest treasures.

"My own Rotha," it began, "how many hours have we been parted! and I have been thinking of you every minute since then. I do not think you knew how full my heart was when I bade you good-bye this morning—farewell, I mean, you like that word better, you said; but perhaps I had better not speak of that now.

"I want to tell you that I have just read your parting message to me. I found it on the title-page of the little Testament, under-neath your mother's name. Oh, how I should have loved her, Rotha, if I had known her!

"Dear little book! all marked and underlined. I shall carry it next my heart till, God grant it so, we meet. Robert is waiting —they are going to drop anchor — the pilot has just come on board. God bless you, my darling! Yours, in every sense of the word, GARTON."

These few words from Garton made Rotha almost happy. She felt ashamed of the inactive misery of last night. "If Garton were here, he would tell me that I ought not to neglect my work," she said to herself, and, more because she thought it would please him than even from a sense of duty, she went down to the church with Reuben to help with the decorations.

It was rather dreary work in spite of her efforts—the church always brought Garton so vividly before her; she found herself starting at every footstep in the momentary notion that it was his. On all sides she heard whispered lamentations and regrets among the ladies concerning the absence of the young sacristan. The Vicar was there and did his best to help and direct the workers;

but Garton's taste and ready good humour were not easily to be replaced; he had always been the universal referee on these occasions, and it gave Rotha a heavy pang to see Reuben filling the flower-vases for the altar—a work that had always been his delight. She heard Nettie and Aunt Eliza talking in sympathising whispers about his lonely Christmas on board, and how he would miss the services; and her eyes filled with tears as she twined long trails of holly and shining evergreens over the chancel-screen.

The Vicar noticed her dejected look, and wanted her to leave her work to be finished by Nettie and come home with him; but Rotha quietly refused—it was not her way to shirk any duty, however painful, and she had Garton's work to do as well as her own. So she had a cup of tea at Nettie's and stayed on till everything was finished, and then joined in the eve service.

She was glad afterwards that she had done so, for it soothed and refreshed her, in spite of the pain it was to her to see the boys walk up to their places in the choir-stalls without Garton at their head. How sorely she missed the dark earnest face, and the clear deep voice that had always led the singing! The lessons were read by a stranger; and after the service was over no tall figure went swinging to and fro across the chancel to extinguish the lights and cover up the altar. Reuben performed these offices very sadly and slowly, as though his heart for once were not in the work.

Two things had struck Rotha during the service—the Vicar was not in his place, a very unusual thing on Christmas Eve; and the prayers of the congregation were requested for one travelling by sea; and after they had risen from their knees that beautiful hymn for those at sea had been sung. It was evident that some of the Vicarage people had intended to be there; but, when Rotha had summoned courage to look round, no one was in the Vicarage pew.

This puzzled her and made her rather anxious, and she was not the less so when she found Rufus waiting for her outside the church with a note from Mary.

"I have been all the way up to Bryn," exclaimed the boy, "because father understood that you were not going to remain to the service; and Mrs. Carruthers sent me down to wait for you here. I have been waiting for more than half an hour. I thought they would never have finished that last hymn."

"Why were you not in the choir, Rufus? Yes; was it not beautiful—so soothing, too? How pleased he would be to know we had sung it!" And, without waiting for the boy's answer, she

24

carried the note down to the lich-gate and read it by the light of the street-lamp.

"Dear Rotha," it said, "please come to us. Mr. Greenock has been here, and we have had a terrible scene with Belle. She knows now what is the matter with her; but it has broken her down utterly to have her fears verified, and I dare not leave her. Austin has been obliged to stay at home to tell Robert. He is in a dreadful state, and no wonder. Do come to me at once."

"I ought to have had this note an hour ago," exclaimed Rotha; and, without waiting for Rufus to follow her, she set off for the Vicarage at a run that brought the boy panting after her. "Don't knock," he cried, "I have the key; and it would disturb Aunt Belle. I will go and fetch mother." And, almost before Rotha could grope her way through the dark hall, Mary had come to her side silently, and, taking her hand, brought her into her own room and closed the door softly.

"Oh, Mrs. Ord, I am so sorry," began Rotha; "did Rufus tell you I was at church?"

"Hush! yes, I know. I have been wanting you; but it could not be helped, and she is quiet now. Oh, Rotha, what a day this has been!" And Mary began to cry, but in a subdued patient sort of way that went to Rotha's heart.

"Dear Mrs. Ord, and you are so tired!" said the girl in a sympathising voice, at which Mary leant her head against her shoulder and cried more than ever. It was some time before she could recover herself to speak plainly.

"I didn't mean to do this," she said at last in answer to Rotha's silent kisses; "but I think it has done me good. Oh, Rotha, I hope I am not rebellious, and I have Austin and the boys. But still she is my only sister." And the tears coursed more swiftly down Mrs. Ord's face as her grief resolved itself into words.

"Perhaps it is better so. Oh, my dear, to think of her going day after day to that Infirmary without letting us know how ill she was—and all to spare Austin! I cannot bear to think of it. And then for them to say that all this strain and anxiety has been killing her!"

"Who are they? Dear Mrs. Ord, would it not ease you to tell me everything plainly out? Is it Mr. Greenock who has been telling you all this?"

"Yes, Mr. Greenock and Dr. Chapman. Mr. Greenock wished a consultation when he found how things were, and then they told Austin, and he fetched me.. They say one of her lungs is quite gone, and that she is in a very precarious state. Mr. Greenock said he could not understand how any one could have suffered so much and have done what she has done; and he declared if it had gone on—this concealment and strain, I suppose he meant—that she could not have lasted three months."

"But I don't understand. Is it as you fear—is it"—decline, Rotha was going to add, but she hesitated. Mary shook her head mournfully.

"That is what I cannot find out—neither of them would speak plainly. Mr. Greenock did not say much, but I could see he dreaded the worst. He would not exactly say that she was in a decline, but he owned that he feared it. Dr. Chapman took a milder view of the case. Both of them agreed that a warm climate should be tried without delay. But I noticed that, though Dr. Chapman spoke hopefully of Torquay now and Mentone next winter, and added his conviction that by these means a partial if not a complete cure might be effected, Mr. Greenock only looked grave; and it struck me afterwards that he had recommended it as a last chance, and that he knew it could only prolong her life for a few months; and I can see that Austin fears it too."

"But, Mrs. Ord, would not it be cruel to remove her if they know it is of no use?"

"That is what Austin said. He wanted Mr. Greenock to give us leave to keep her with us; but both he and Dr. Chapman agreed that the March winds would kill her. They want her to go to Torquay in about two or three weeks' time, but she must not undertake the journey this weather in the state she is in. One thing, we are not to allow her to break off her engagement—at least not yet, or we shall take away her last chance. But, oh, Rotha, I know they think that she will never be well enough to marry him."

Rotha sighed heavily. "I am afraid not; but they are right, and it would kill her at once. Oh, Mrs. Ord, how dreadful it will be for him when he knows it!"

"Hush! don't speak so loud—he knows it now. Austin has been with him all the evening. We have had hard work with him to get him to believe it; he fights against it so. I don't think he gives up all hope yet, though he knows he must go without her. He turned round quite fiercely on Austin when he said something about the engagement having to be given up. He declares he will come over in six months' time and marry her. Oh, Rotha, it is plain to see that he is half beside himself with remorse; it is more that than grief that is troubling him."

Rotha leaned her head on her hand; she hardly knew what to say. "He ought to have sent her with me," she returned slowly at length; "he knows that himself now. Mrs. Ord, I don't quite know what to do, but I think I should like to go to him. He might listen to me now. Hark! what is that?" she continued, turning very pale. Everything startled her just now, but it was only the dining-room door opening and the Vicar calling softly across the hall for Mary.

Mrs. Ord went at once, and Rotha followed her; the Vicar held out his hand to her with a little surprise when he saw her. "Robert has been asking for you," he said. "I did not know you were here; I thought Rufus came in alone."

"I was at church, but I came directly afterwards. Did you say"—turning paler than ever—"that he was asking for me?"

The Vicar nodded. "He is in there; he has been asking for you two or three times this evening. He wished me to tell you when you came in that he wanted to speak to you alone."

Rotha looked bewildered, as well she might—wanting to see her, and alone!

Robert was leaning against the mantelpiece with his back towards her; but he started at her entrance and raised his head, and then, after a moment's hesitation, held out his hand. It was not taken for an instant; perhaps Rotha hardly perceived it, but a bitter smile wreathed his thin lips at what he imagined was her pride.

"You need not to have hesitated," he said sharply—the sharpness of pain, not anger. "I meant to have told you—but never mind, it will keep; the thing is, that I have sent for you. I suppose I ought to thank you first for your kindness in coming to me. Some women would not have acted as you have, but I confess I am in no mood for mere courtesy to-night."

"Neither am I," returned Rotha quietly. His harsh words, his pale face only inspired her with pity. With an involuntary movement she went up a little closer and looked at him with straightforward honest eyes. "You are in trouble, and you have sent for me," she said softly; "and now what can I do for you?"

"Stop," he said hoarsely. "I don't want pity—least of all from you. Pity her if you will. Good heavens, to think how she loves me, and that I, blind fool that I am, have as good as murdered her!"

"Mr. Ord!" She is constrained to cry out his name, his violence is so terrible to her; and then, with a sudden pitiful impulse, she goes nearer and lays her hand on his arm.

"Have you sent for me to tell me this?"

"Yes, to tell you this—this, and anything else you like. Oh, you may humble me at your pleasure. I am a proud man if you will, but this is your hour of triumph. I would rather have you triumph over me than pity me. Why do you look at me like this, Miss Maturin? Do you think I am mad to-night?"

"I think you are," she returned softly. "God help you! Mad with pain and disappointment and remorse, you are cruel to yourself, cruel to me, to Belle, to everybody. Was it your fault that you were so blindfolded that you could not see the truth?"

"Yes," he returned, with a dogged sort of honesty; "it was my fault, I would not allow myself to be convinced. Is your memory so bad that you have forgotten our conversation down on the sands?"

She drooped her head sadly; she could not help it. Why should he recall those bitter moments? Humiliated—ah, and had she not been humiliated then!

"Well, I see you remember," he continued, watching her; "you tried to convince me then. You would have saved her for me if I had only permitted it; and I let her fade before my eyes, brute that I was, rather than owe her preservation to you. No, do not stop me; if I did not know my motives then, I do now."

"No, no," she cried, putting out her hand to stop him. "Don't talk so—you must not talk so; it was this terrible prejudice against me that hardened you. I came between you and your happiness, and made you mad."

"More shame to me!" he retorted. But she put out her hand again to stop him.

"Ah, you are more cruel to yourself than you have been to me," she exclaimed. "If you mean that you have sinned against me, have I not forgiven it long ago? Mr. Ord, you have sent for me, but it is not Miss Maturin who has come to you now—it is the little sister, Gar's future wife, who prays you to be reconciled to her."

Her hands went out to him tremblingly as she uttered his name; she had forgotten everything at the sight of his terrible grief. If he had wronged her she did not remember it now. "Gar's brother! Poor Robert," he thinks he hears her say so softly. As he turns away and folds his arms over his breast something that would have been tears in other men glistened now in Robert Ord's eyes. Another moment and her hand rests on his outstretched palm.

"Forgive me if you can," he begins in a broken voice; but she stops him.

"Hush! I understand you. There is no need to say anything more."

"There is every need, you mean. Do you think I shall spare

myself? You told me that I must never come and offer you my hand till I would own that I had wronged you. I own it now."

" I know it—I can see it. Please spare yourself this."

" Spare myself!" he repeated scornfully. " Oh, I have been so good to you—you may well ask me to do this. Because I envied you your possessions I must look upon your every act and word with a jaundiced eye. I must even sacrifice my poor Belle to my unnatural rancour. Oh, you were right when you said you would rather die than touch my hand."

"I am touching it now; it feels like the hand of a friend. Mr. Ord, these things are all passed and over. I have forgiven them long ago. Why will you recall them ?"

" To do you a tardy justice," he replied vehemently. " Because, God knows, I have done you a bitter wrong ; because you were as innocent as a little child, and I was cruel to you."

" Not cruel—only hard, and hardest of all to yourself. You were wrong to your better judgment, and now the scales have fallen from your eyes. Indeed it is all forgiven. You know me now, and you know I am your friend."

" My friend !" he muttered, " my friend !" A strange softness crept over his face, and then he turned it away and leant heavily against the mantelpiece; but at that moment something hard and bitter passed out of Robert Ord's heart for ever.

By and by she knew why he had sent for her—not to tell her this, as he reiterates again and again, but to beg her on his knees, if needs be, to take Belle away. It is her last chance—her only chance, he affirms sadly. And Rotha slowly and seriously grants the request. She cannot tell him what she has told Mary, that she believes it has come too late.

Mary came down presently to tell Robert that Belle was asking for him. " She is growing restless again and wonders what has become of you, dear. She knows now that Austin has told you everything."

Robert turned very pale.

. " I did not mean to have seen her to-night," he said. " I am half afraid of what I may say. I think you had better come up with me, Mary." And Rotha was left alone.

She might have been alone about twenty minutes when she heard Mary calling her, and went up at once.

" Belle wants to bid you good-night," began Mary cheerfully as Rotha entered ; but Belle's feeble voice interrupted her.

" No, not good-night. I want to speak to you, Rotha. Please come here." And Belle raised herself from Robert's arm and held out her hot hands to Rotha. How beautiful she looked with that hectic flush on her wasted cheek and her eyes burning with fever !

"Dear Rotha, come here. Tell him—Mary will not—that it is all no use, and that he must not send me away. Tell him it will kill me."

"It will kill you to remain here, Belle. Mr. Greenock and Dr. Chapman both said so."

"That is what he keeps saying. Oh, Rotha, ask him not. He knows that he is going in less than three months, and yet he wants us to be parted. It is not enough that I am never to be his wife, but he will not even let me see the last of him." And Belle flung herself down on the couch again as though her last hope were taken from her.

"For your own good—only for your good, Belle; it is your last chance. You know they said so."

"But they did not think so," she returned in a voice of despair. "Rotha, does he think that I shall care to live when I am never to be his wife ? Tell him to ask me anything but this."

"I cannot," he returned in a low voice. "Dear Belle, why will you persist in speaking as though there were no hope ? Did not Dr. Chapman say that a winter or two at Mentone would set you up ? Go with Miss Maturin in a fortnight's time, and I will come down to Devonshire to wish you good-bye."

"Good-bye !" she returned in a bewildered voice ; "it is not you who have to say good-bye surely ?"

"Yes, for a little while ; but it will not be long, I will promise you. Only do as the doctors tell you, and in six months or a year's time I will come over myself and take you home with me."

"Take me home ! Only hear him," she returned in a faint voice. "He is deceiving himself still. Dear Robert, why will you not understand that we must give it all up ? I am your poor friend, dear, but I shall never be anything more to you."

"Dear Belle, do not refuse him ; he means it for your good," exclaimed Rotha. "Look at him ; you are breaking his heart." For, overcome by her words, Robert had covered his face with his hands. In another moment Belle had flung her thin arms round his neck. Never to her dying day did Rotha forget the look of despairing love on her face.

"Oh, Robert, don't ; anything but that. Dear Bertie, put down your hands, and let me see your face. Do you really mean that you wish me to go ?"

"Yes, really and truly ; for my sake—for the sake of your own love." He looked at her eagerly, almost hopefully ; but there was no answering gleam in Belle's eyes.

" For your sake ? yes, I understand. Kiss me, Bertie. I will go. No, not that name—that is what I used to call you ; it must be Robert now."

" I like the old name and the old ways best, Bella."

" Do you, Bertie ? Ah, there it is again. Are we alone, or is Rotha there ?"

" I am here," said Rotha, coming gently to her side. " I am waiting to say good-night, Belle."

" Good-night," returned Belle dreamily. " I thought I was alone with Robert, and that I was, oh, so tired ! You will have to carry me upstairs to-night, Bertie. Where is Mary ?" But, before her sister could be summoned to the room, Belle, exhausted by her emotions, had fainted away.

# CHAPTER XXXIV.

## UNDER THE ROD.

" To us,
The fools of habit, sweeter seems

To rest beneath the clover sod,
  That takes the sunshine and the rains,
  Or where the kneeling hamlet drains
The chalice of the grapes of God ;

Than if with thee the roaring wells
  Should gulf him fathom-deep in brine ;
  And hands so often clasp'd in mine,
Should toss with tangle and with shells."
                                    *In Memoriam.*

It was the saddest Christmas Dáy that the inhabitants of the
Vicarage had ever known.   Uncle Gar's absence was loudly
lamented by the boys, who could imagine no holiday without
their favourite playfellow and adviser, while it was felt as a very
real loss by the other members of the family.   Mary especially
missed the bright unflagging spirits and helpful good-nature which
had gone so far to make Gar's influence with the lads ; she had
always called him her eldest boy, and had been very motherly and
watchful over him, claiming a right to lecture him on all his shortcomings, to which Gar had submitted with a tolerable amount of
patience.   But even Garton's absence sunk into comparative insig-
nificance beside the fact of Belle's failing health, and it was quite
sufficient to note the Vicar's grave looks and Mary's troubled face
to see how heavily this new blow had fallen on them.

If Belle had lacked somewhat in gentleness and warmth to
those with whom she lived ; if she had been self-absorbed, reticent,
and failing in that large influence that might have been hers, it
was all forgotten now ; and nothing was remembered of her but
her sorrow, her passionate devotion to Robert, and the fortitude
with which she had borne her ill health ; or, if this were not suffi-

cient to win their forbearance, was she not Mary's only sister—the sister whom she had loved, and with whom she had borne through her own happy married life, and whom Austin had cherished for her sake with more than a brother's patience?

And as it was with them, so it was with the boys. No need to hush their noisy footsteps and merry voices now, as the lads crept about the house bating their very breath for fear Aunt Belle should be disturbed. Aunt Belle, who had never won their boyish confidence, who had never tried to win it, on whose knee they had rarely clambered since their babyhood, and whom they had always held in an awe and reverence which their mother with her open arms and ready kisses had never inspired.

It was strange to see the lads waiting upon her; Guy especially, who was in reality her favourite, was very helpful and zealous in her service. It must have given Belle many a pang to remember how little she had interested herself in Mary's boys—their very affection was a reproach to her. Arty one day got into her lap and put his arms round her neck. "Dear Aunt Belle," said the affectionate little fellow, "why don't you get well when we all love you so? It makes mammy so unhappy."

"I don't think you can love me much, Arty," replied Belle, fixing her hollow eyes mournfully on the child. "I have not done much for you; I have been very selfish and wicked, Arty." And then, before the boy could answer, she pressed him to her closer than she had ever done before and burst into tears.

Mary, who was working at the other end of the room, hurried across and lifted her boy off his aunt's lap.

"Oh, Arty," she exclaimed reproachfully, "you must not tire poor Aunt Belle so." But Belle, struggling vainly with her emotion, said, "No, it is not that, dear Mary; let him stay—it is not Arty that tires me, it is only"—drawing her sister's face down to hers and kissing it remorsefully—"it is only because it makes me so unhappy, Mary, to think how little I have done for you and your boys."

Poor Belle! Always self-tormented and self-absorbed, worn to a shadow by consuming sadness, shedding bitter tears over a useless past, and fighting against the doom she feels is irrevocable —baffled, weary, and unconvinced—so did she drag on her heavy days. Willingly, right willingly, would Austin have ministered to her sick heart and soul, but Belle shrank from his loving counsel. "Ask Austin not to come and read to me," she said more than once to her sister; "it looks so as though I were dying. If I grow worse I will send for him." And the Vicar, albeit with a heavy heart, forbore out of consideration for her morbid fancies.

"It seems wrong, but what can I do?" he said once to Rotha; "her mind is harassing her body, and both are alike sick, poor soul! but she will have none of my healing." But Rotha only murmured quietly, "Leave her alone, Mr. Ord. Belle is like no one else; she is fighting it out with herself. By and by her weakness will overcome her, and she will cling to your every word as eagerly as she now repels them; but just now she only remembers that she is unhappy."

Rotha's unspoken sympathy, so intense and so delicately manifested, did much to win Belle's wayward confidence. Her soft voice and quiet ways were very pleasant to the sick girl, whose shattered nerves could bear so little; she felt Rotha's presence a rest, and grew more than reconciled to her sister's brief absences from her room if Rotha could take her place. In many ways she suited her better than Mary. Mary, oppressed with many cares, had lost much of her wonted cheerfulness; faint streaks of gray were plainly discernible in the mother's pretty hair, her smiling face had grown worn and anxious-looking; it was not always easy for her to conceal her uneasiness when Belle coughed or looked more than usually ill; and Belle, who disliked to be pitied, would turn impatiently from her questions and caresses. She would have deceived them all still, and cheated herself too, if it had been possible.

But Rotha's face, grave only with reflected sadness, grew daily more necessary to her; she would watch for her coming every morning, and brighten perceptibly at the sound of her footsteps. She could always bear her to talk to her when Mary's voice fretted her into a fever; and her reading was a real refreshment during the long twilight, when she lay and waited for Robert.

Rotha did not always go home at these times. Robert always looked for her, and expected her to be there. Since the day of their reconciliation, when he had owned and acknowledged her as a friend, Rotha had no reason to complain of his manner to her. As far as she was concerned he was an altered man.

He never met her now without a kind smile and a hearty grasp of the hand; if she stayed late at the Vicarage, however tired and jaded he was, he would always walk up with her to her own door.

Others besides Rotha noticed the almost deferential reverence with which he addressed her; it seemed as though he were always trying to make amends for his past injustice to her. The Vicar openly congratulated her on this happy condition of things, but Rotha just now was a little silent over the whole matter. If the truth must be told, she felt somewhat oppressed by it all; in her humility it was almost painful to feel herself so watched and considered.

She was somewhat perplexed too at his sudden change of opinion, but at her first timid questioning on the subject Robert had stoutly denied that it was sudden.

"I had my doubts a long time before I would own to them," he said to her, with the rare honesty which had first won her esteem for him; "but I think it was that talk down on the sands that first shook my faith in my own judgment. I would not give in at the time—but it somehow conquered me; and then your giving everything to Gar : that did not look like covetousness— did it?"

"I wish he would come back!" sighed Rotha, touched by this reference to her lover; "how many days is it since he went away —hardly a week yet, Mr. Robert?"—turning to him half seriously, half playfully—"you had as much right to come up to Bryn and steal some of my property as to send away Gar."

She was afraid she had hurt him, for he did not answer. But a moment afterwards she saw his eyes fixed on her with a strange indefinable expression.

"Send him away? Yes, you are right. I am afraid it was my doing. Evil for good—not good for evil. Miss Maturin, I wish I could have gone in his stead! Yes, I wish to heaven I could have gone in his stead!"

"And left Belle? Oh, for shame, Mr. Robert!"

"Yes, and left Belle. What is Belle to me, or I to her now? Shall we ever be man and wife? Oh, my poor girl! How little I knew when I gave up everything for her sake that we should ever come to this! Miss Maturin," turning on her abruptly, "do you believe in long engagements?—I do not."

"I don't know," faltered Rotha. "I think it is a great test; it was so in Jacob's case. Seven years is a long time, Mr. Ord."

"Why will people always quote Jacob as an example?" returned Robert impatiently. "An exception is nothing to the rule. Did Rachel's beauty fade, I wonder? Did Jacob eat out his heart with that long waiting? Do you think it well that all freshness should wear off? Do Belle and I love each other the better for knowing each other's faults and learning painful lessons of forbearance for half a dozen years? Does not the heart grow old too sometimes?"

"No," replied Rotha indignantly. "If that be your man's sophistry I repel it entirely. 'Many waters cannot quench love,' we read, and many years ought not to exhaust it. Belle may try you, Mr. Ord—you see I am speaking plainly—but she never loved you better than she loves you now."

"I do not deserve it," he returned in an agitated voice. " I feel you are right—women always are. Never mind if I meant what I said just now. Heaven knows I would cut off my right hand if I could make amends to her for what she has gone through for my sake ; and if she may only be spared to me for a few years I will guarantee that I will make her happier, poor child, than she has ever been before."

"I am sure of it," replied Rotha, and then the subject dropped. But she never forgot his words : they convinced her that her suspicions were true—that Robert Ord's remorse was greater than his love ; that, however noble and faithful he had been in his allegiance to his betrothed, the engagement had been a hasty one ; and that in spite of his warm affection Belle was not loved, never had been loved, with the whole strength and passion of his nature.

Rotha hardly knew whether she resented this for Belle's sake ; but it was certain that this instinctive perception of his lukewarmness kept her a little aloof from Robert, and caused her to redouble her tenderness and pity to Belle ; for she now watched jealously for every symptom of coldness on his part, but could not find the slightest fault with his manner. Never since the days of his early love, when her beauty and her too evident affection for himself had tempted him from his prudence, had he been so gentle, so devoted ; and less keen eyes than Rotha's would have judged that his was the deeper affection of the two.

But alas ! alas ! though in his remorse and pity he would have cut off his right hand to have been allowed to call her his wife, her face was not the dearest to him, neither was her name the oftenest on his lips. But those who saw his altered looks and marvelled at his sorrow never guessed Robert Ord's secret, and least of all she who had exercised so baneful an influence over his life.

Did he know it ?

Ay, and battled with the sore temptation as only a good man can battle, crushing and stamping out the unholy thing with his strong proud will till he believed he had trodden it under foot.

Was it his fault that his oppression had begotten this ; that out of his hatred and her exceeding patience had sprung the mad infatuation which was to make him gray before his time and embitter so many of his future years ; when his memory could recall to him nothing but the tears he had caused her to shed, and the hopes that through his means had been broken ; when the knowledge of her forgiveness and sisterly affection were no consolation to him, and he fed on the ashes of his unhappy passion ?

Did he love or did he hate her ? It was long since Robert Ord had asked himself that question. The little stab that her reproachful words had given him that day when they had walked side by side on the sands had first awakened him to the sense of his danger. How her face had haunted him !—it haunted him still ; but not till the hour when he heard that she was to be his brother's wife—when he saw her clinging to Gar's arm—thinking of Gar, sorrowing for Gar—not till then did he know· that Belle's dying beauty was nothing to him compared to Rotha's wistful eyes and the sweet pale face which was henceforth to be his torment and his delight.

Oh, inexplicable workings of human nature, entangled and involved and interwoven with all manner of devious threads ! Was it Rotha's womanly instincts or the mere prompting of her generous love for Gar which made her shrink more from Robert in his strange new amity than ever she had done in the days of his bitter warfare ? ·

It was almost a week since Garton had left—a long week, as it seemed to Rotha, sitting so patiently in Belle's sick room day after day.

Rotha flagged a little in the heavy atmosphere, as was natural, but she never complained of its dullness. It seemed a dreary exchange for the free happy life of the last few months, when Mary and she sang and laughed over their work, and Garton and the boys came and teased them out of all propriety ; how she missed their boating excursions and their happy rambles, and the grand teas which Meg prepared to surprise them on their return ! Now hour after hour she sat listening to the faint click of her own and Mary's needles, broken now and then by low-voiced conversation while Belle dozed. Here was daily suffering to be witnessed—suffering borne patiently indeed, but without the cheerfulness of real submission. Here was the languid body and unquiet mind acting and reacting lamentably on each other—suffering which Rotha strove to lighten, but without success. Still it was something that Belle liked to have her, though it did seem a little hard for Mary that Rotha's were the only absences ever noticed. Not that Mary's unselfishness ever wasted a sigh on this ; she would sigh a little sadly over this new infatuation of Belle's, but only remonstrated when her exactions were likely to be injurious to Rotha.

"Has not Rotha come yet ? How long she is !" was often

the querulous complaint of a morning. Rotha would come up presently with all sorts of pretty excuses for her delay, in the shape of tiny baskets embedded with moss, with rare hothouse flowers or choice fruit daintily nestled in the greenery. Sometimes it would be a picture, or a new book, or a portfolio of engravings from Bryn—all sorts of little surprises to cheat the invalid's new day into brightness. It was a sign of changed feelings on Belle's part that the Cashmere shawls were in their old place. One day she made some sort of mention of them in a shamefaced way, and the next afternoon she woke up to find them covering her. Belle drew them over her face and shed a few silent tears underneath their soft folds. It was so like Rotha's magnanimity.

One afternoon Rotha had left her somewhat unexpectedly, in obedience to a summons from Meg. Mrs. Carruthers wanted her up at Bryn on some domestic business. Belle was a great deal better, and she could leave her comfortably, especially as Guy promised to be on guard when his mother was not there. It was a lovely afternoon, and even these few steps were a refreshment to Rotha, and so was her quiet talk with Meg.

She had promised to be back again as soon as possible, but by the time her letters were written and tea was over it was getting late—almost time for Robert to be back from Thornborough, and then she would no longer be wanted. She said something of this to Meg as she put on her hat.

"I shall just say ' good-night ''to Belle and see she is comfortable, and then I shall come away. You shall not have another lonely evening, Meg, if I can help it. We will have one of our regular home-evenings—music and a little reading. How delicious it will be !" And Rotha ran off with one of her sunny smiles.

It was moonlight, and the sea looked just as she loved to see it—all black shadow, save for one broad pathway of silver ripples. Down by the bridge lay a stretch of shining sands. The whole scene, so full of fixed shadow and gleaming light, the white road, the dark wintry sky, sown here and there with stars, seemed full of a new beauty to her, and a sense of her unworthiness and littleness suddenly smote upon her as she remembered the pleasant lines that had been appointed to her, and how from "If needs be " she had learnt to say, "It is well."

"God is very good," said the girl softly to herself, "and I am, oh, so happy !" And as she looked over the moonlight haze she thought of Garton, sailing farther and farther from her, but without any mournfulness. "What is, is right," she thought.

It was about the time when the family were generally gathered round the tea-table—the most sociable hour of the day, as the

mother called it—but, to Rotha's surprise, the meal remained
untasted on the table, and only Laurie and Arty were in the room
—Arty sitting disconsolately on Laurie's knee with his finger in
his mouth, and his small round eyes fixed on the cake ; both were
rather incoherent in their answers to Rotha's questions. Arty
opined that somebody was cross, Deb was for one, and they weren't
going to have any tea at all, at all.

"Do be quiet, Arty," interrupted Laurie, giving him a shake ;
"here I have been telling you Jack the Giant-Killer for the last
half-hour and it is all no use."

"I don't want Jack Anybody. I want my tea," returned
Arty, beginning to whimper. "If nobody's cross, why can't we
have some, Laurie ?"

"Where is every one ?" asked Rotha, bewildered by the
children's disconsolate condition, so unlike the mother's ordinary
care. Arty's hair was rough and his collar tumbled, and Laurie's
hands were covered with ink.

"Where's everybody ?" repeated Laurie slowly. He always
meditated over his words. "Oh, I don't know. Guy's up with
Aunt Belle, and Rufus has gone to the telegraph office, and mother
is shut up with father in the study, and Uncle Robert is there too,
and—do be quiet, Arty ! Deb has just been in, and is going to
bring us our tea ; and it is so dull all alone," finished Laurie,
running his blackened fingers through Arty's hair, at which Arty,
being cross enough already, fairly roared.

Rotha could learn nothing from Laurie's drawled-out sentences,
so she betook herself to Belle's room, but Belle had fallen asleep,
and at first sight she thought Guy was asleep too, for he was
curled up on the easy-chair with his head on his arms, but he
started at her light footstep and held up his hand.

"Hush ! Aunt Belle is asleep, and mother says we must be
very careful not to wake her ; she had such a bad night." And
Guy, having delivered his message, seemed inclined to put down
his head again, but Rotha knelt down and put her lips close to
his ear.

"What's become of the mother, Guy ? Is she busy ? Why,
Guy, you have been crying."

"Oh, hush !" implored the boy. He sat up quite straight
now, and looked very frightened. "If you wake her what am I
to do, and mother not here ? Don't ask me any questions," he
continued, with quivering lips, and trying hard not to burst out
crying. "I must not tell you anything; they told me I must
not."

"Not tell me ? Is anything the matter ? Oh, Guy, if you

love me don't keep me in suspense. There is not anything the matter, is there, dear ? You have only tried to frighten me."

" I haven't," returned Guy indignantly. " I wouldn't be so wicked. Oh, dear Rotha, do go downstairs ; I can't bear it," cried the boy, trying to swallow his sobs,—" I can't bear it, when we all love you so, to see you looking at me like this."

" Oh, Guy, don't." The lad's rosy face was quite pale now, but it was not so white as Rotha's as she rose stiffly from her knees. Why does she put her hand to her side as though she had been struck there ? why do her thoughts fly to Garton instantly ? " That it may please Thee to preserve all that travel by land or by water." " We beseech Thee to hear us, good Lord." Why do these clauses rise unbidden to her mind as she leans for a moment over the sobbing child ? Guy, who never cried—who, his mother said, had never cried since his babyhood—and Guy loved Garton ; she remembers that.

" Do go down, Rotha ; they are all in the study," groans out poor Guy. Rotha makes a gesture of assent and goes slowly down, not hurriedly, but dragging one foot heavily after another, as though they were suddenly weighted with lead. When she had got there she paused in the dark hall and said two things to her-self—or rather the two things got themselves spoken unconsciously in her mind. " Whatever happens, God is good, and I must remember that. And if anything be wrong with Gar—my Gar—I would like to lie down and die before life is a long misery to me." But she never knew she spoke thus within herself ; she had a notion instead that she was standing for nearly half an hour try-ing to turn the handle of the study-door with her nerveless hand, and listening to Mary's low sobbing inside, and yet five minutes had hardly elapsed since she had left Guy.

If she had gone in quite unprepared she would have known at once that something had happened. The Vicar was sitting in his usual place at his writing-table, just opposite the picture of the Good Shepherd, with his head bowed down on his hands, and Mary was kneeling beside him with her arms round his neck, and Robert—but Rotha saw nothing beyond the Vicar's motionless figure and Mary's tear-stained face.

" Oh, Austin, here is Rotha ! Why, my dear, my dear, who has sent you in here just now ?"

" Nobody sent me. I came of my own accord." How strangely her voice sounds ! Her lips have become suddenly dry ; her strength fails, and she leans heavily on Mary's shoulder to support herself. There is a deep-drawn sigh behind her, and then some one, she fancies it is Robert, places her silently in a chair.

25

"Mary, I was not prepared for this. Robert—Mary, what shall we do? I am becoming weak with all this suddenness. I must have time." Was that the Vicar's tone, so broken, so irritable? Who was it that said Garton was his favourite brother, his pupil, his—— No matter, the strongest man will give way under a sudden shock.

"Some one must tell her, Mary; this is a woman's work," says Robert, still from the background. Through it all Rotha fancies his voice comes from a distance—miles away—muffled—sepulchral. She shudders away from it.

"Yes, Austin, I will tell her; dear husband, dear husband, as though I would not spare you this ten times over." When did Mary Ord consider herself when Austin was in trouble? But, with a sudden terror, Rotha puts out her hands as though to ward off her approach; she would stop up her ears if she could, she knows it all; why need they trouble her with words? But Mary, pressing the cold hands to her bosom, falters out "that she loves her, she loves her, and that she must be very patient, for their heavenly Father had afflicted them all. Do not look at Austin, my dear, do not look at my husband, he is not himself just now, he cannot help us. Look at Robert, Rotha darling; he is so brave and thoughtful for us all." But Rotha, moving her dry lips, shakes her head and fixes her eyes still on Mary.

"When our dear boy left us only a week ago——"

"Only a week ago!" repeated Rotha; then suddenly, "Oh Gar, Gar!"

"When our poor boy, our dear Gar, sailed last Tuesday night, Heaven knows how little we expected such bitter tidings, how much need there would be for our prayers—'That it may please Thee to preserve all that travel by land or by water.' 'We beseech Thee to hear us, good Lord.'"—The two little hands locked together on Mary's bosom struggle hard to be free.—"'We beseech Thee, we beseech Thee, good Lord.'"

"Oh, Mary, the cruel sea, the cruel hungry sea! Oh Gar, Gar!"

"Robert, what shall we do? She guesses, but she does not hear me. She looks blind and deaf—stupefied almost, poor darling!" But Rotha only repeats again and again slowly, "Oh Gar, Gar!"

"When our poor Gar," began Mary again, this time very slowly,—"when our poor Gar left us never to return again——"

"Never to return again!" repeated Rotha, and then stopped suddenly with a low moan.

"He little thought what would happen so near home. They

were fog-bound, Rotha; and on Sunday night," said Mary, speak-ing as though to a little child, "when they were quite near home, and all but the helmsman were asleep, a great vessel ran on to them and sank the ship, and they were all—oh, pitiful God!—all lost but a few men and two or three women."

"And Gar was not among them—speak louder, Mary, louder; the waves seem to drown your voice! The waves! Oh, my poor boy, my poor boy!"

In the many mansions she knows it now—no need to tell her more. Somebody behind her says, "That will do. Open the door, Austin, and give her air." Cold fragrant waters splash on her forehead. She has a notion that Mary has taken her in her arms and is crying softly over her. The Vicar's massive figure seems to block up her vision, but he does not say much. She tries to tell him that she is not faint, that he must not be so sorry for her, because it is his loss too; but breaks down at her first word and hides her head in Mary's bosom.

"The Lord gave, and the Lord hath taken away," said the Vicar solemnly. His voice reaches Rotha. She can hear him, oh, so clearly! "Dear wife, I have been very weak. I ought not to have left this to you. It is not poor Gar, it is happy Gar now, and she will think so by and by." And as he lays his hands on her head pitifully, yet in silent blessing, Rotha suddenly looks up at him with wild eyes and prays him to take her home.

But it is not the Vicar—it is Robert who takes her; but she hardly knows it, for she is looking up at the starlit sky, where her saint is—her lover, her Garton. She has no idea of the strong arm that is supporting her all the way, or of the looks of anguish that he casts on her pale uplifted face. She scarcely knows what he says as she totters into Meg's arms, but she wonders with a dreary wonder why Meg cries so. Mary cried too, and Guy; but she has no tears, only a hot choking pain. By and by, when she lies down on her little white bed, and Meg extinguishes the light and leaves her, by her own desire, to the friendly darkness, Rotha turns her face to the wall with an exceeding bitter cry, "Oh Gar, Gar, I loved you so! Come back to me, Gar!"

# CHAPTER XXXV.

" I hold it true, whate'er befall ;
    I feel it, when I sorrow most ;
    'Tis better to have loved and lost
Than never to have loved at all."

*In Memoriam.*

' Oh ! blest be thine unbroken light !
    That watch'd me as a seraph's eye,
And stood between me and the night
    For ever shining sweetly nigh.

" And when the cloud upon us came,
    Which strove to blacken o'er thy ray
Then purer spread thy gentle flame,
    And dash'd the blackness all away."

BYRON.

NEVER till she had lost him did Rotha know what Garton had been to her, and how their brief engagement and the loss of his great love would influence and sadden her life. For a little while she seemed utterly broken.

It was not that she rebelled against his cruel fate—cut off in such an awful way in the midst of his youth ; it was not that she failed in meekness and submission, or complained that her lot was unduly hard. She was far too humbly and sincerely a Christian for that. It was only that the spring of her energy and life seemed broken by the suddenness of the shock, and that for a little time she seemed so crushed that it was difficult to rouse her.

All the next day she lay on the couch in her own room, with her face hidden from the light, as she had hidden it on the previous night ; just ill enough to be soothed by Meg's attentions, but neither asking for nor needing sympathy, and keeping perfect silence in the midst of her grief.

But, as hour after hour passed on, Heaven only knew the bitterness of that girlish heart as the tide of recollection swept over it, recalling Gar's tenderness and sad farewell. Once, towards even-

ing, when the tide was rising, the low surging of the waves seemed
to break the stillness of the room. Meg never knew why she
suddenly buried her face in the cushions and tried to stifle her
sobs. Many and many a night for long afterwards she dreaded to
go to sleep for fear that sound should mingle with her thoughts,
and so the awful scene be reproduced in her dreams. Often she
started in affright, thinking she heard the crash of the broken
timbers, the angry rush of the water, the despairing cries of drowning men, and amongst them one dark figure, steadfast, yet with
the look of mortal agony on his young face, calling on his God as
he went down into his yawning grave.

Oh, no marvel if she brooded silently over her trouble, and
shrunk from the least mention of any of the facts; not for many
a long week did she learn any of the distressing details, though
she must have known that the papers were full of them, and that
the country was ringing from end to end with news of the sad
disaster. Meg put them all carefully aside in case she should ask
for them, but she never did; by and by she heard all the particulars from another quarter, when she was better fitted to bear it.

From the moment they brought Rube to her they ceased to
be seriously uneasy, for at the sight of her favourite the white
strain on Rotha's face relaxed; and though she wept bitterly, anything was better than the numbness and apathy of the last few
hours, and tears, as they knew, would ease the overburdened heart.

Rotha was more herself when she had seen Rube: the boy's
sorrow seemed to arouse her to the conviction that others were
suffering as well as herself. She did not try to comfort the poor
child—that would have been impossible; but she stroked his
curly head as he knelt beside her, and whispered to him that he
was her boy now, and she would love him—oh ! so dearly—for
Gar's sake. And then she called to Meg faintly to take him away,
for he would make himself ill with crying and she could do nothing
to help him.

But the next day she had him again, and the next day after
that; and Meg found that she would do anything that Rube asked
her, and that she seemed always more restless and unhappy when
the boy was away. After his second visit she roused herself to
inquire after her friends at the Vicarage, and found that, to her
surprise, Robert had been every morning and evening to inquire
after her.

He looked very ill, Meg added, and he had told her that the
Vicar had been far from well too. Mrs. Ord had sent all sorts of
affectionate messages to Rotha ; but she had not come round herself, as Belle was fretting so sadly that she could not leave her.

Rotha was greatly disturbed when she heard this.   She felt as
though it were selfish for her to be sitting alone and feeding on her
grief while Mary had her own and her husband's trouble to bear,
and was worn out besides with attending on her sister.   She
thought how Gar would have acted in her place, and wept and
prayed that she might have strength to do what he would have
done.

She tried, and not ineffectually, to make some sort of beginning
that same evening, and sent Meg round, laden with good things,
and with a little pencilled line to Belle, in which she told her that
she had not forgotten her, that she was thinking of them all from
morning to night, that she sent them her dear love, and that she
would come round very soon, when she felt she could help and not
distress them.

It so happened that as Meg left the house, charged with Rotha's
commissions, she met the Vicar coming slowly towards Bryn, bound
on much the same errand as herself.   Meg turned back and let him
in with her own key, so that he went in, as he wished it, quietly
and unannounced.   Rotha was sitting by the fire in her black dress,
looking white and weak, as though she had had an illness, but
trying to interest herself in some work Meg had wished her to do.
She started up when she saw the Vicar; her composure visibly left
her, and she trembled violently.   But he sat down beside her with
his old kind smile—a little graver, perhaps—and questioned her so
tenderly about her health, and what she had been doing with herself, that her agitation soon subsided, and she found herself talking
to him, soothed in spite of herself by his calmness and sympathy.

And yet the Vicar looked worn and ill, and there were dark
lines under his eyes which betokened sleeplessness and pain.   He
looked like a man who had battled through some great sorrow and
had attained peace.   He could think now for others besides himself, and very tenderly and skilfully he set about performing the
work which he had in hand—which was not only Rotha's consolation, as she found out afterwards.

But just now he seemed to have no thought but for her, and
indeed the weary young face smote him with strange feelings of
compassion.

"I have been thinking of you so often, Rotha," he said.   "I
have thought of the little sister as one whom He hath loved and
chastened, and who will always be dearer to us than ever now,
because Gar loved her."

Ah! she has not heard the name since, and her tears fall fast.

"Do you remember what I said that night about our dear boy—
that he was not poor Gar, but happy Gar now? Ah! Rotha, think

of it literally, not figuratively, 'drawn out of many waters,' and so brought into the haven where he would be."

"I know," she returned ; "but so young, and to die so terrible a death !"

"Is it terrible, I wonder?" mused the Vicar. "They mount up to the heavens, they go down again to the depths, it may be their soul is melted because of trouble. Let us hope that bitter baptism, that weary chrism, were less terrible than our imagination paints them. Oh, Rotha, never forget 'man's extremity is God's opportunity.' What if the angel of healing went down with him into the troubled waters? Are not the darkness and the light both alike to him?"

"He was fit to die," said the girl, weeping ; "none more so—I know it."

"He would not like to hear us say so, and yet we may console ourselves that 'this our brother rests in sure and certain hope.' When I speak of Garton I always think of some trusty young soldier of the Cross. If any one loved his Lord, he did. It seemed to me," continued the Vicar solemnly, "at least in my poor human judgment, as though he always strove to follow the advice of the Wise Man, 'Let thy garment be always white, and thy head lack no ointment.' He was not worldly wise, Rotha, hardly as clever as most men ; but it may be that of such is the kingdom of heaven."

Rotha still wept, but more silently. These praises of her lost love were like a sweet solemn dirge. "Oh, if we could only be like him !" she murmured out of a full heart.

"Yes, indeed," returned the Vicar ; "he has taught me many a lesson, has my poor boy, when he only thought he was learning from me. Once, when he was a very little child, Rotha, a mere infant at his mother's knee, he asked if he might not pray to die young; and only a few years ago he told me that he always missed out that clause in the Litany, 'From sudden death, good Lord, deliver us.' I had some difficulty in persuading him that it merely meant 'sudden unprepared death.' Oh Rotha, when I think of his hidden life among us, a life so different from other men's, I feel sure that the Lord's mark was on him."

"I always said he was good," faltered Rotha. "When all were against me, he was kind to me. Even that dreadful evening at Nettie's he came up to me and wished me good-night. Do you think I shall ever forget it? He was my best friend, the kindest, the truest, and he loved me. Oh Mr. Ord, what shall I do, what shall I do?"

He waited quietly until the pent-up feelings had had their vent, and then he took her hand and told her—what she knew already, and yet what it was always good to hear—how the sinless One had wept beside an open grave, and how since then the tears of all mourners had been hallowed. He told her that she was right to weep for Garton, for a nobler and a braver heart had never gone to its rest. And then when he had said this he asked her to listen to him, for he wanted to tell her about some one who was more unhappy than she, and when she looked at him inquiringly he told her that it was Robert.

"Robert!" repeated Rotha doubtfully. She was a little confused as to the Vicar's meaning. "Robert more unhappy than she?" Her sad face seemed to add "impossible."

"Yes, Robert; my brother, Rotha. When I saw him just now I was almost shocked at his appearance. He looked as though he had gone without food or rest for days; his eyes were bloodshot, his face quite haggard, and his hand felt almost as weak as yours. I could hardly speak to him, he startled me so."

"But why?" asked Rotha, quite bewildered. She began to feel rather frightened at the Vicar's description. "Surely it could not be Gar's loss only? I did not know he loved him so," she said, with quivering lips. "I thought he could not understand him; that he made him impatient?"

"Perhaps so," returned the Vicar; "but, Rotha, do not your very words give the clue to Robert's misery? If he felt he had always been kind and patient to the poor boy, do you think his grief would be so unbearable? You know the tenacity with which Robert clings to one idea. Well, he has got it into his head that it is all his fault that this has happened—that, but for him, Gar would never have gone away. He tells me that you said so, and he says that he never means to see you again."

"What!" exclaimed Rotha, sorely troubled, "not see me—Robert! Mr. Ord, surely you misunderstood him, he could not have said that?"

"He not only said it, but I am afraid he meant it," replied Austin. "He says he has injured you past all hope of forgiveness, and that you will not care to see his face again. He was terribly vehement over it. You know Robert's way. What with this hopeless engagement of his and Gar's death, and all his morbid feeling, I am afraid he will torment himself into a fever. He looks ripe for anything to-night, and, Rotha, we can hardly bear any more trouble just now. My dear child, where are you going?"

"I am going to Robert, of course. Come, Mr. Ord."

"But now, at this late hour of the evening?"

"Why not? There is no time to be lost. Did you not mean me to go and see him?"

"Yes, certainly, when you are stronger. I only hoped you would volunteer, but not to-night. You are not fit; and it is so cold and damp outside, snowing hard too."

"Do you think the snow ought to prevent my going to Gar's brother? Oh, Mr. Ord, how can you think such a thing? Would not Gar have gone?" And the Vicar, secretly overjoyed at this unlooked-for success, offered no further objections.

It was a bitter night. The wind had subsided, but the air was full of the driving snow. The roads were already covered with it, and Rotha shivered and clung closer to the Vicar's arm, for it seemed to her excited fancy as though the whole place was one great winding-sheet, and she was being pelted by frozen tears. She had no idea she was so weak till she stood at the Vicarage gate with trembling limbs waiting for him to go in.

"Not there!" exclaimed the Vicar. "Robert is in his own house. He never stops long with us of an evening now." And, opening the door, he looked back and beckoned her to follow.

Rotha was a little staggered when she found it was Robert's house that she was to enter, but she took courage when she remembered it had been Garton's home too. She followed the Vicar through the dark hall and up the narrow staircase, wondering how she was to account for her intrusion, but perfectly convinced she was doing the right thing all the same. She waited while the Vicar tapped at the study-door, and followed him closely when the impatient "Come in" gave them á right to enter.

"I have brought a friend to see you, Robert," began the Vicar cheerfully. "Rotha heard you were far from well, and she wished to accompany me and judge for herself. Well, my dear fellow, what's the matter?"

"Miss Maturin here—in this house!" burst out Robert. But Rotha stepped forward and laid her hand lightly on his shoulder.

"Yes, I have come to see you, Robert," speaking his Christian name for the first time so naturally. "I could not bear to think that Gar's brother was ill, and I might do him good, and yet keep away. I am very weak. May I sit down?" she said softly, taking the seat next him.

Ah! there was no need to question the Vicar's account when she saw his face.

He had been sitting, or rather crouching, over the fire when they had entered, and had hardly raised his head till Rotha's name was mentioned; a more desolate figure, amid more desolate surroundings, it was scarcely possible to see. The fire had burnt low, and was merely a mass of reddened embers; a candle guttered on the table by the side of a smoky reading-lamp, and a solitary meal, untempting and untouched, was spread amidst a mass of books, inkstands, and heterogeneous rubbish. Cinders lay curled up on Garton's empty chair, and beside her was his old felt hat, still left as he had last flung it down. How tenderly the Vicar took it up, and lifted the favourite cat on his knee!

"Don't touch it," said Robert savagely; "he left it there." He had made no sort of response to Rotha's friendly pressure—unless the weary stare he gave her may be called one; only, when she took that seat beside him, he turned away his face with a sort of groan. If this had come to him, if her reproachful face were to haunt him, let him die, for what good was his life to him?

"Will you speak to me? I am not very well, and I have come to see you. Dear Mr. Ord, ask him not to turn from me when I am so sorry for him—so very sorry for him."

"Do not waste your sorrow upon me," returned Robert hoarsely, addressing her for the first time. "Austin, why did you bring her when you knew that I never intended to see her again? Have I not darkened her life sufficiently without bringing her here?"

"He did not bring me; I came of my own accord," returned Rotha, trying bravely to restrain her tears. "I heard that you were ill and unhappy, and tormenting yourself; and I said, 'If Gar's brother wants me, he will never send for me; I must go and tell him that it is all right—that it will never be wrong again between him and me.'"

"Rotha, are you mad? Do you hear her, Austin? Right between her and me, when she knows that but for me that poor boy would never have gone away—would be happy now—yes, happy, and sitting where you are!"

"God would have it otherwise," replied the weeping girl. "Do not make it too hard for me to say, 'His will be done.' I will not blame you—no, not for worlds; because you had pledged your word, and thought it right for him to go. Could you know that he would never come back again—that we should see his face no more?"

"If I thought you could forgive me——" he began; but she interrupted him.

"There is nothing to forgive—nothing," she said hurriedly. "To think I could cherish bitterness against his brother when he loved me so dearly, and wanted me to be his wife! Oh, put away these terrible fancies; they are not worthy of you. Dear Mr. Ord, tell him that I will love him and be his sister if he will only let me."

But the Vicar, making her a sign, moved quietly away; he thought it well that, for a moment at least, he should leave him to her woman's tenderness. It was well he did so, for he had scarcely left the room a minute before Robert, overwhelmed by his conflicting emotions, and worn out by sleeplessness, broke into those convulsive tearless sobs which are so terrible to hear—a man's agony finding sudden vent, but giving no relief, and tearing his frame to pieces with useless throes.

Rotha lost her courage when she heard those terrible sobs.

"Do not; I cannot bear it. You are hurting me. Do not make me sorry that I came. Oh Gar, Gar, if you were only here to help me! What would you say to see him like this?"

"Have I frightened you, Rotha? Give me your hand a moment—there, it will pass directly. Oh, forgive me! I know you do—I feel you do; but if you knew what I have suffered! There, say something more to me; call me Robert again; it may exorcise the demon within me."

"Poor Robert! There—you are better now. You were ill; you could not help it. You have not slept for nights, perhaps, and that has shattered your nerves."

"I think I prayed not to sleep," he returned, shuddering. "Have you not seen it all, Rotha? I have, over and over again. I dare not shut my eyes, for fear that poor boy's face should haunt me. Last night I saw him clearly: he had his hands clasped on his breast, and his dead eyes seemed to look me through and through."

"Hush!" said the girl, trembling; "it was only a dream. When I see him I always fancy there is a halo round his head."

"I cannot get his voice out of my ears. How long ago is it? hardly a fortnight, since he said, 'Good-bye, Robert; I hope you will not miss me much. Take care of yourself.'"

"Are you doing as he said?" returned Rotha gently; "the Vicar tells me that you eat nothing. I can see you have not tasted anything this evening. No wonder your nerves are unstrung if you neglect yourself like this."

"What does that matter? What good am I to any one? Oh, if these three months were but over, and I could get away somewhere—anywhere, out of this place."

His agitation began to return, but she laid her hand on his arm and called him brother softly, and then put aside her cloak, and told the Vicar, when he came back, that she was not going to leave him just yet; and begged him to help her to put things a little comfortable for him.

Did she guess what she was doing for him when she laid aside her own trouble and weakness to minister to the stricken man who a little while ago had been her greatest enemy? Years after-

wards he told her that she had saved him from brain fever, for
sleeplessness and want of food, and the morbid dwelling on one
diseased idea, had driven him well-nigh mad. " A few hours more,
another night of that terrible solitude, would have done for me,"
he said; and Rotha, as she recalled the fierce fire of his eyes and
the strangeness of his manner, felt within herself that he was
right.

Some one besides Robert blessed Rotha as she moved softly
about the comfortless room. In a little while she had coaxed the
sullen embers into a cheerful blaze, the smoky lamp was re-trimmed,
and the little black kettle sang merrily on the hob, the cricket
came out with a premonitory chirp, and Cinders, rousing herself
in the belief that something was going on, jumped uninvited on
Robert's knee and purred loudly as she whisked her tail in his face.

The Vicar knew how to be useful, and had the table cleared in
a trice. Old Sarah toddled up with more tempting-looking viands;
and then he and Rotha sat down to break bread at Robert's table.

When had Robert ever failed in his duty as host before? But
he failed now. He let Rotha bring his cup to him, and, though he
loathed the very sight of food, he ate and drank to please her.
The Vicar told Mary afterwards that he almost shuddered at the
haggardness and beauty of Robert's face; and that, as Rotha sat
beside him in her black dress, she looked, but for her uncovered
hair, like a young sister of mercy.

Rotha did not say much till tea was over. She began to look
somewhat spent, and the Vicar told Robert that he must take her
away; but before she left she told him that she should be at the
Vicarage to-morrow, and that she hoped he would be there. And
then she whispered to him a few words, that he must never hurt
her so again, for that it was all right between them—that she
prayed for him every night, and pitied him from her heart.

Later on, just as Robert was beginning to relapse into his
dreary brooding, and the cricket had gone in, and the fire had
begun to burn very low, the door opened, and a round boyish face,
very sleepy, and no longer rosy, thrust itself into the room.

" Please, Uncle Robert, it's nearly eleven ! aren't you going to
bed ? There's such a jolly fire in your room, and mother's mulled
some wine, and it's all so comfortable. Do come and see."

" A fire in my room ! Am I ill ? Good gracious, Guy, whatever brings you here at this time of night ? Go home, lad, and go
to bed, do."

" I am not going to bed till you do," maintained Guy sturdily.
" I've come to keep you company, Uncle Robert, and to see that
your fire does not go out, and that you have proper food to eat,

and that Cinders does not drink up all the cream. Holloa, Cinders, come here."

"But, Guy," remonstrated his uncle feebly, but cheered unconsciously by the lad's sleepy face, "this is all nonsense. I am not ill—at least, not very. Who sent you to me?"

"Who sent me? Oh, father and Rotha. I was asleep when they came in; but it was so jolly getting up. I heard Rotha tell him that you must not be left alone to feed on your own thoughts. Mother came in, and got all comfortable; but she is gone now. Come along to bed, Uncle Bob, there's a good fellow; for I am awfully sleepy, and I won't budge an inch till you do."

Rotha knew what she was about when she persuaded the Vicar to wake up Guy, for the boy dearly loved his uncle, and for his sake would be ready to sacrifice anything. He sat on the bed and chatted till the mulled wine, and the warmth, and the company had made Robert drowsy. Half a dozen times in the night he turned out of his warm bed, roused by Robert's restless mutterings :

"Is that you, Gar? I didn't mean it, Gar. I wouldn't have sent you away for worlds."

"No, of course not. Go to sleep, Uncle Bob; it's only Guy."

"Only Guy! My dear lad, are you sure of it? I thought it was Gar; give me your hand, boy—there." And Robert, turning over on his side, and muttering still, would fall into another short moaning sleep, and so on, until with the dawning day he slept soundly for a few hours.

# CHAPTER XXXVI.

" I watch the clouds flit over the moon
 And wonder if it can be,
That her tremulous eye looks tenderly down
 On those graves in the deep lone sea.

" Are they safe from thy furious blast, O Wind,
 In the haven where they would be :
Hast thou wafted them on to the stormless shore,
 Where there shall be 'no more sea?'

" Was their prayer on their lips when the Master's voice
 Rang over the deep that day,
And the gallant ship with its freight of souls
 Sailed into the 'far away?'"
                                          HELEN MARION BURNSIDE

" Hold it up before me, Father, Father !
 Hold it up before my closing eyes ;
Dimly o'er my sight the death mists gather,
 And my way looks lonely through the skies.
   Loose the silver cord,
   'In hoc spero,' Lord,
 Only this can lend me wings to rise."          *Ibid.*

ROTHA had not failed in her errand of mercy, and although at one time Robert had been very near it, he was saved from an attack of brain fever.

But for some time his nerves seemed completely shattered. He could make no pretence at cheerfulness now as he sat by Belle's side ; nay, more, he could hardly rouse himself sufficiently to talk to her. He was ill himself—irritable and restless. The whole atmosphere of the place was oppressive to him ; and, seeing how things were with him, he was almost feverishly anxious that there should be no unnecessary delay in the Torquay plans, and that Belle should be removed as soon as possible from the saddening influences that surrounded her.

Rotha was of the same opinion—Rotha, who had long ago

taken up her old duties at the Vicarage, and was fulfilling them as heartily and unselfishly as ever.

Save that she was graver and paler, that her words were few, and her smiles sweeter and sadder than of old, no one would have guessed that she had gone through a great trouble. Even Mary marvelled at her sometimes, and wondered what Austin meant by saying that Rotha was growing older. Perhaps the Vicar knew that the brief summer beauty of freshness and colour had died out of the girl's face, never to return. It was a careworn young face now, too grave by half, when she came in wearily of an evening, and there was no need to force her cheerfulness any longer. Too grave, oh ! far, far too sorrowful, when she crept to her window in the winter's night to look up at the stars and wonder what Gar was doing; and to tell him, as though she felt him very near her, that she was doing all she could for Robert and for them all; but that she was so tired, so very, very tired.

Nobly as she had worked for them all, she had never so denied herself, so forgotten everything but their interest, as she had done now. It was almost heroic, the way in which she put aside her own grief to bear with Belle, to cheer Belle in what seemed to the others a tedious convalescence ; for she was better now, wonderfully better, as Robert said, and the doctors had given permission for her to be removed at once. The weather had become unusually mild ; there was no time to be lost, and Rotha, acting by her friend's advice, had sent Meg, with little more than a day's delay, off to Torquay to secure the most commodious lodgings that could be found, so that everything might be ready for an immediate start, while Mary, with many secret tears, set about the preparations for her sister's journey.

It was decided between Robert and the Vicar that the leave-takings were to be made as brief as possible—the doctors had laid a great stress on that ; anything like agitation or excitement was to be warded off as much as possible, and, after many consultations, it was arranged that Belle was not to know of it till the day before that appointed to start. It was no use prolonging her misery, and she had promised him to go whenever he wanted her, as Robert very justly remarked ; and as soon as Rotha could tell him that her arrangements were completed, he would break it to Belle as quietly as possible.

So one morning Rotha came round to the Vicarage very early. There was no time to talk it over, for Robert had to leave by the next train to Thornborough, but he promised to be back in time to tell Belle that same afternoon.

It so happened that Belle was unusually well and cheerful that day; she had coughed very little, and walked up and down the room frequently on Guy's arm without seeming tired. Poor Mary —who knew she was so soon to lose her—hardly dared to come near her all day for fear her tell-tale face should betray her, and yet could hardly bear her out of her sight a moment.

"She looks so pretty and so good, and she has got her old lovely smile," cried poor Mary, coming as usual for consolation to her husband; "and she has actually laughed once at something Guy said. Oh, Austin, it does seem so hard that I cannot go with her!"

"My darling Mary, you know Rotha has offered you over and over again to go."

"Yes, I know; but how could I leave you and the boys? I could not do it, Austin; and then there is Robert looking so ill, and Deb laid by, and Arty, and the parish!" And Mary put down her tired head on the Vicar's shoulder as though it were her only resting-place. It was well she did not see the look of pain that crossed her husband's face as he drew her tenderly within the shelter of his strong arm and comforted her.

Robert came in presently, tired and harassed, and went up to Belle; he was with her alone for a long time, and then came down looking pale and utterly spent.

"Thank heaven, that is over!" he said to Mary; "I do not think you will have any difficulty with her now. I have tried to be as gentle as I could with her, but I was obliged to be very firm too. But I am afraid it goes very hardly with her, poor girl."

Mary was afraid so too when she saw Belle. Belle was lying quite still—so motionless, indeed, that Mary fancied she was asleep till she saw a tear rolling down the white sunken cheek and stooped to kiss it away, and then Belle opened her eyes.

"Is that you, Mary?" she cried; and then she suddenly stretched out her arms to her sister. "Oh, Mary, he is going to separate us; he is going to send me away, and I shall never see your dear face again!"

But Mrs. Ord could not answer her, and for a little time the sisters mingled their tears together.

"You must get well and come back to me, Belle; I shall want you so much—oh, so much, my pet," cried poor Mary, kissing Belle's fair hair, her hands—even her dress. "I cannot bear to think you are going so far from me, and that Rotha will do everything for you and not I."

Belle shook her head, and then began stroking Mary's face half dreamily.

"Do you remember, when we were little children together,

Mary, when we slept in the great sloping attic that looked out on the apple trees, and how I, the younger and weaker little sister, would never go to sleep till you had put your arm round me and said, 'Good-night, God bless you, Belle'? Do you remember it, Mary?"

"Remember it, darling! too well, too well; but why do you ask?" sobbed Mary, melted by this tender recollection.

"Because I was thinking—don't cry, Mary; I can't bear to see you cry—I was thinking how, when that comes, I should like you to put your arm round me and say that over again. It would make it feel less terrible, and more like going to sleep if you will only say 'Good-night, God bless you, Belle!' as you did then." And drawing Mary's face down on the pillow, she told her not to fret; for she did not mean to make her unhappy, for if God heard her prayers she would surely come back, if only to lay her head once more on that faithful breast.

A more beautiful morning had rarely dawned than that on which Belle took her sorrowful departure from Blackscar. Robert was to go with her to the station, and Guy had also pleaded to be allowed to accompany his uncle; but the rest of the boys and Austin and Mary came no farther than the Vicarage gate. Mary had hardly slept all night, and her red and swollen eyes bore witness to the tears she had shed. It went to the Vicar's heart to see how the sisters clung to each other at the last moment.

"Good-bye, Mary; one more kiss, Mary. Good-bye—good-bye, my darling sister."

"Dear Mary, let her go. Robert is waiting to lift her into the carriage."

"You hear what Austin says, Belle, darling; you must go now. Good-bye, my precious, and God Almighty bless you."

And Robert, gently disengaging Belle from her sister's arms, lifted her into the carriage and placed her by Rotha's side.

But even then, while Austin was giving her his brotherly farewell and blessing, Belle leant across him and held out her arms again to her weeping sister.

"One more kiss, Mary darling—one more kiss, my own Mary," and hung about her neck till Austin gently, but firmly, put his arm round his wife and drew her away.

She scarcely spoke a word after that till Robert took leave of her in the railway carriage; but she was as white as death and trembling all over when he took her in his arms.

"It is not good-bye, Belle, you know. I am coming very soon."

"Yes, yes; the sooner the better, Bertie; but it will be good-bye then." And, as he stooped over and kissed her with some emotion, she only looked at him with strange wistful eyes. "It will be good-bye then, Bertie, will it not?"

It was a long desolate journey, and scarcely less so to Rotha than Belle, and a heavy responsibility to the young nurse; and it was a greater relief than she could have imagined to see Meg's friendly face awaiting them at the station: it seemed to give a home-look to the strange surroundings, and even Belle, though sadly exhausted, smiled faintly when she saw Mrs. Carruthers, and held out her hand with a feeble welcome.

Rotha wrote a tolerable account to Mary the next day; she said, of course Belle was suffering from the reaction of excitement and unusual exertion, but that in other ways she seemed much the same; and a few days after that she was able to give even a better report. Belle had recovered from the fatigue of her journey and was able to sit up and look about her a little. They liked what they could see of Torquay, though of course Belle had not yet gone out; but they had very pleasant apartments, in the house of a widow lady. The rooms were all on the first floor, and opened into each other, and Belle's sitting-room was especially pleasant, as it looked over a lovely old garden, with a patch of sunny road beyond, planted with rows of trees. Rotha said the place where their house was situated was called "Torquay within the Hills," and she described the air as perfectly delicious. Mary had been guided in her choice by the advice of Dr. Vivian, who had recommended this locality as singularly adapted to all pulmonary complaints.

Dr. Vivian had been to call on Belle once or twice, and Rotha told Mary that he seemed to understand Belle's complaint thoroughly; he had spoken most cheerfully to his patient, and had recommended them a great many pleasant walks and drives. Belle was to see Bishopstowe, and Babbicombe Bay, and Warren Hill, and Daddy Hole Common. She was to go out every fine morning and see all the objects of interest in Torquay. Rotha wrote amusing accounts of the trawling with long nets in Torbay, the walks they had in the Torwood Road, and their visit to the quaint little fishing-town of Brixham. Belle had a little pony-carriage, Rotha added, and was greatly interested by the novelty of everything around her.

Mary used to read those letters to the Vicar with tears in her eyes. "Do you think she will get better, Austin? I have heard of people living for years and years with only one lung; and perhaps the other is not so much diseased as Mr. Greenock thought." But the Vicar only shook his head; he noticed how Rotha's letters were filled with descriptions of scenery, and how little she said about Belle herself. The doctor's visits were touched on very lightly; she always spoke of Belle as being happier or brighter, but never once said that she was really better. One day the Vicar shut himself up in his study and wrote a long letter to Rotha, which she answered by return of post. But he never showed either the letter or the answer to Mary; but for a long time afterwards he was very grave, and went about as though he had something heavy in his thoughts.

Robert was in London just then on business connected with his firm, and it so happened that something very strange befell him there, of which Rotha was to hear shortly. One day, when they had been about three weeks at Torquay, and Rotha, in spite of the doctor's prognostications, was beginning to cheat herself into the belief that Belle was better, she was sitting in her own room, while Belle was having her noonday rest, when a large official-looking document in Robert's handwriting and the postmark London was put into her hands.

She had not an idea what it contained, and was opening it listlessly enough, when she caught sight of a never-to-be-forgotten cramped handwriting, and a moment afterwards something lay sparkling at her feet. With a low cry she snatched it from the ground, and sank back half fainting into her seat.

What is it that she devours with such hungry tears and kisses —which she presses alternately to her bosom and her lips?

There is the ring that she placed on Garton's finger, with the diamond cross that he kissed so reverentially, and the words "*In hoc spero*" traced round on the blue enamel; and there on her lap lies the "message from the sea."

Not for a long time—not until she has read it over and over through her blinding tears, not until she has found Robert's note and mastered its contents, is the bewildering mystery cleared up; not until Meg has come to her aid and read it slowly and patiently again and again can she understand how it has come to her—out of the very shadow and blackness of death.

And yet how clearly Robert explained it all!

"I am sending you something very precious," he wrote. "Heaven grant you may receive it safely. I am sending the very letter he was writing to you just before the terrible concussion took place—the very ink was wet, you can see, as he thrust it hurriedly into his bosom; you can tell that by the half-obliterated words at the end.

"How he gave the ring and letter with his last dying love, you must read in another man's words; I have taken it down myself from his lips, just as he told it me, and remember he was the very man who saw our Gar die. Another time, when we meet, perhaps I will tell you by what strange chance I lighted on him in this great city; and how, in a lonely coffee-house under the shadow of the mighty dome of St. Paul's, I heard word for word, as you have it here, how our poor Gar perished like the hero he was."

Will she ever weary of the sweet perusal? She spreads the crumpled paper out again—blotted, half defaced with ink, and in some parts scarcely legible. She reads once and yet once again her " message from the sea."

" My darling Rotha," it began, " I am sitting down in my cabin to write to you by the light of a very smoky lamp; the rest of the passengers are just thinking of retiring to rest, and only the watch is on deck. Just now I went up to see what chance there was of our beating down the Channel to-morrow—for you will be surprised to hear that, though it is Sunday, we are only now anchored off Dungeness—but the pilot tells me that the wind is still ahead. We have had ill luck enough already to begin with : to think we are still here on anchorage, and it is Sunday evening.

" But I have not sat down to complain, but just to let you know how things are going. I told you once that I was a bad hand at a letter, and I am afraid you will agree with me, for I do not think I have made much of a beginning, though I mean to send a little more than a message to Rube.

" It is not more than five days since I said good-bye, but I feel as heavy-hearted as though it were five months. I know now what people mean by home-sickness, for I am just sickening for the sight of one dear face that is all the world to me. It is not always easy for a man to express what he feels. I have tried over and over again to tell you how much I loved you, but I never could ; and now I think that I shall die before you know what you are to me.

" That is a strange sentence, and I do not know why I have written it; but it is Sunday evening, and my heart is just as heavy as lead. I cannot help feeling as though some great gulf lies between us. It may be because I have never been far away from home before that I am so low and miserable.

" I have been thinking of you so much, my darling. I do not think you are ever out of my mind for a single minute. You do not know what a man's love is when he gives it all to one woman, as I have given it to you. I have often said to myself, ' She will never understand it, but if God grant that I ever make her my wife I think she will feel it then.'

" Do you remember, sweet heart, my telling you that I was not clever, and how indignantly you assured me that such a thing should never be mentioned in connection with you and me? I have blessed you for those words over and over again; and yet, all the same, I am rejoiced to think that you are cleverer and better and wiser than I. Do you think I would have it otherwise? Only put your little hand in mine, Rotha—the little soft hand whose touch I remember still—and I think I can follow those dear feet wherever they climb.

"Do you remember, too, my telling you that your love was not to be compared to mine, and that perhaps some day you might give me all you have in you to give? Not for worlds would I have even that otherwise; how could you misunderstand me so? The very thought of the treasures that yet are unwon only nerves me to yet stronger efforts. How could you, being what you are, Rotha, give all at once to such a one as I? No; dearly as you love me, you could not give me all. One day you shall tell me your thoughts, and I will try and understand them, and then perhaps I shall be able to tell you what I mean.

"There is a little deaf-and-dumb boy on board, Rotha, that somehow reminds me of you. I suppose the eyes of most mutes are eloquent, but I have never seen any like this boy's. They are brown and soft, and have strange appealing looks in them, like a dumb animal's in pain.

"You know my fancy for boys. This one has taken my fancy strongly. He is such an afflicted little creature, and without parents, and he and his mulatto nurse are bound like myself for Buenos Ayres; on such a long journey we are sure to become well acquainted" (Ah, Gar! on such a long journey; ay, along the Valley of the Shadow of Death).

"He takes to me already. You must tell Rube not to be jealous. Dear old Rube! he must not have a boyish rival in my heart. To-day he sat beside me on the poop for hours, holding the lapel of my coat, and looking quite contented. Tell Rube his name is David; but he will not be like the first David to me— who was, as one may say, the captive of my own bow and spear, for I suppose, humanly speaking, I saved his life. Dear lad! he has rewarded me for it over and over again.

"And tell him, with my love, that I hope he has forgiven me for not bidding him good-bye, and tell him to remember me in his prayers every night. There's a word, too, I might say to my torments, Guy and Rufus, but it is getting late, and I suppose I must turn in.

"I shall finish this to-morrow; but now God bless you, my own dear love—and——" Then came some blurred unintelligible words, and then Death wrote Finis.

Oh, how the girl wept and smiled over her treasure, and then, hiding it in her bosom, read in Robert's handwriting, traced boldly on the thin foreign paper, the sad particulars of Garton's death !

And this is what it said, taken down from the lips of the sailor, Richard Martin :—

" I was seaman on that unfortunate *Phœnix*, sir, and have served under Captain Murray for, I should say, nigh upon five years, and, though I say it, a finer captain never commanded a finer vessel.

" Well, the vessel that we left off Dungeness, with nothing but the masts standing up out of the water, left the London Docks about nine o'clock on Wednesday morning, bound for Buenos Ayres, and with, I should say, about three hundred souls on board, some of them belonging to a gang of navvies that were going out to work some contract, the rest of them saloon passengers and the crew.

" But you don't want to put down a lot of sailor's yarn ; but just to tell that lady about the unfortunate man who put the letter and the ring in my hands when we had climbed up upon the pile of boats and were holding on together for dear life. Yes, sir, I quite understand you , and I hope you'll cut me short if I spin it out ; for, as sure as my name's Richard Martin, I'll tell that poor young lady all I know.

" I recollect his coming on board with you, sir, for I was just hauling that coil of rope when he stepped across the gangway—a tall dark sort of a chap, with the cut of a parson about him, but a fine figure of a man too.

" He was a civil sort of person—none of your fine gentlemen, who won't give a word to a rough seaman. He used always to say ' Good morning, mate,' and sometimes he would stop and have a bit of chat with me ; it seemed to cheer him up, for at other times he looked so down-hearted that I often said to myself ' that young man has left his sweetheart,' for I kind of know how a man will carry on when he leaves a woman behind him.

" I remember, too, that I got it into my head that he was going to be a parson. I thought so when he reproved two of my chums for swearing. I recollect him sitting down and talking to them in a simple hearty sort of way, and how when Joe Greene—he who had a widowed mother—slunk away fairly ashamed of himself he followed him and shook hands with him, and told him that he would be a fine fellow if he would break himself of that evil habit. That's Joe Greene, sir, that you saw alongside of me in the bar, and a more sobered chap I never set eyes on ; as he should be, when he was saved out of all those poor drowning wretches.

" There was a deaf-and-dumb child on board, under charge of

a mulatto nurse, going out to some relations who lived in Buenos
Ayres ; and it was odd what a curious fancy that afflicted little
creature seemed to take to that young gentleman.  Joe Greene
was pointing them both out to me that same day—it was Sunday,
I remember—'That's a simple sort of chap, Martin,' he says, 'to
let that child sit alongside of him for hours like that.'  I remember his saying that now, though I made no sort of observation at
the time.

"But I am taking up your time, you will say, and I have not
told you how it came about that we were lying at anchor so snugly
on Sunday evening, when we had left the London Docks early on
Wednesday morning.

"Well, we ran down to Gravesend all right ; and then we found
the wind dead against us, and had to lay by till Friday.  On
Friday we had middling weather, but the wind was still rising, so
we towed down the Channel ; but the pilot passing word, we cast
anchor off Dungeness.

"Here we were snug enough, and, the watch being set, the rest
of us turned in to our hammocks, and I for one was soon fast
asleep.

"Well, sir, all at once I was wakened by an awful crash, just as
though it were the Day of Judgment, and every rock that was on
the earth was rent to pieces ; and immediately afterwards I heard
the captain sing out, 'All hands to the boats.'

"Well, sir, I heard it afterwards from one of my mates, who
saw it all from first to last, a great lubberly steamer had cut the
*Phœnix* asunder amidships, and there was a big hole in the ship's
quarter, which was letting in the English Channel on us.

"It is all in the papers, and you don't want me to go over it
again ; but I wish to say that nothing that the papers can say will
give you an idea of the horrors of the scene.  When I rushed up
on deck it wasn't only the women who came swarming up the
ladders shrieking fit to tear your heart to pieces, it was the men
too, half-maddened by mortal terror, who crowded round the boats
fighting for their very lives.

"Well, sir, you've read it all ; you know how that vessel
sheered off regardless of our cries ; how the cannon would not go
off, and we sent up rockets for no manner of good ; and you
know how our captain stood by the boats and tried to save the
women.

"Bless your life, sir, I did what I could, but it was like fighting with savages, and in the dark too : the wrong people got into
the boats and could not be made to leave them ; the men, the
navvies especially, were like mad, and wouldn't obey orders.  I

could see we were doomed, and the captain, he says to me, 'Martin, save yourself—you've got a wife and seven children ashore, but my place is here.' I wish the papers had said a little more about the captain, for if any one ever died at his post our captain did.

"Well, Joe Greene and I were struggling at the boats between the main and mizzen masts, but bless your heart it was no manner of use, for we couldn't move them, and up comes that young gentleman you say was your brother, sir. 'The ship's going down very fast,' says he, and, seeing nothing for it, we three jumped on to the pile of boats.

"Joe Greene, he splutters out, 'I wish some one would tell my poor old mother I was thinking of her now;' and the gentleman, he says, holding out his hand, 'Martin,' he says, 'if you live to get on shore, and I hope with all my heart that you will, will you send this letter and this ring to the young lady? You'll see the direction written inside;' but lor, sir, there was no direction at all. 'And tell her,' says he, with a sort of sob, 'that the thought of her is making me strong to die, and that even at this minute I am thinking of her and bidding God bless her with my latest breath.'

"And I said, 'All right, mate, but hold on if you're a man, and we may be picked up after all;' for he was a plucky sort of chap, and did not seem to be holding on at all.

"Well, sir, he might have been saved like the rest of us, and that's the hardest part I am coming to, but that negro woman I told you of began howling and screaming, as indeed most of the other poor creatures were, and begging us to save the child. So the gentleman, he says, 'I can't stand this, Martin; give me a hand, my good fellow, I must go and fetch the child;' and I said, 'Not for worlds, mate. Don't leave these ere boats.' But he did not hear me, and just swung himself down, and I saw him lift the boy in his arms and try to get back to us.

"You'll excuse me a moment, sir, but it makes even a rough seaman feel soft to think of a brave man caught in the net like that. 'Joe Greene,' he screamed out, and then I saw the sea rise to the level of the poop, and then the white foam seemed to sweep him away, with the child still clinging round his neck; and I can't help thinking, sir, that somehow that little child will just lead him by the hand into the kingdom of heaven.

"You don't want to know any more; or how Joe Greene and I got hold of some rigging, and how we were picked off it by the lugger *Betsy Jane;* or how I got up to London and saw you, sir, in this same coffee-house. But I hope you'll tell that young lady that I've done my best by her, as sure as my name is Richard Martin."

A postscript by Robert added, "I have seen Joe Greene, and he has confirmed Martin's account; but I think it needs no comment on my part, save to say that to our brave Gar the words may surely be applied, 'Inasmuch as ye did it even unto one of the least of these my brethren, ye have done it unto me.' And once more, 'And a little child shall lead them.'"

# CHAPTER XXXVII.

## ON THE DARK MOUNTAINS

"For me, my heart that erst did go,
    Most like a tired child at a show
    That sees through tears the mummers leap,
Would now its wearied vision close,
    Would childlike on his love repose
    Who giveth His belovëd sleep.

"And friends, dear friends, when it shall be,
    That this low breath is gone from me,
    And round my bier ye come to weep,
Let one, most loving of you all,
    Say, 'Not a tear o'er her must fall,
    He giveth His belovëd sleep.'"

E. B. BROWNING

THREE weeks passed very quietly and smoothly with Rotha and her charge. Belle had grown more reconciled to her banishment, and seemed to take interest in her new surroundings. The delicious balmy air, the pleasant drives, could not fail to soothe the poor invalid after her long and tedious confinement to the four walls of the Vicarage. There she had been afraid to pass even from one room to the other; but here the sunshine and soft air tempted her to many a short stroll on Rotha's supporting arm, while the very sight of the wild flowers, which even at this season of the year nestled in sheltered hollows, the long green lanes, the enchanting views, were sources of enjoyment to the weary eyes from which they had been so long debarred.

True, her spirits were still variable, and there were times when the old sullen depression seemed to return with tenfold power, but these moods were rare. In general she was very patient, deeply grateful for any little attentions on Rotha's part, and touched sometimes almost to emotion with the unfailing kindness with which Meg and she nursed her.

But as it is with the flame of a candle as it gutters to its close before the feeble spark is extinguished, so was it with the treacherous disease to which Belle was slowly succumbing. From the first Dr. Vivian had held out no definite hopes of recovery, though he had once declared that Belle's youth and constitution were in her favour; but since his second visit he had never repeated this. He had spoken very cheerfully to his patient, and even to Rotha, but it had struck the latter that his cheerfulness was forced, and that he kept his real opinion to himself; and very soon she was strengthened in this conviction, when she was sure that he looked upon Belle's case as entirely hopeless, and that his skill was merely directed to soothe and alleviate the few short weeks or months that still remained to her. It was very difficult to realise this sometimes when she looked at Belle. Never had Belle looked more lovely than now, when her cheeks were glowing with diseased colour, and her eyes brilliant with the fever that was wasting her so imperceptibly. But this condition of things could not last.

On the day after Rotha had received her precious letter a sudden and alarming change was apparent in the sick girl. All at once there was a decay of the vital powers; the deep tight cough returned with increased violence, and emaciation set in; exertion became impossible; every moment brought on the laboured breath, the rapid pant; a fainting-fit of long duration added to her nurse's anxiety. In a day or two Meg was obliged to lift her in her strong arms from her bed to her couch in the adjoining room; at night her restlessness and suffering were so great that one or other remained in close attendance by her side. After three or four days of suspense and watching, Dr. Vivian told Rotha that every symptom of the most rapid decline had set in, and that it was impossible to say how long or how short a time she might linger.

Under these circumstances Rotha wrote off to the Vicar and implored him to send Mary at once to her dying sister, and to communicate the bitter tidings to Robert; but great was her consternation at receiving the Vicar's reply. In it he told her—and with what grief she might imagine for herself—that his dear wife was ill with an attack of pleurisy. She had caught cold one bitter day in going about her district, and had neglected to take proper precautions, and fretting about her sister had retarded her recovery. She had been confined to her bed some days when he wrote, but they had neither of them let Rotha know for fear of adding to her anxiety. Under these circumstances he had decided in keeping from Mary the knowledge of her sister's dangerous condition, at least for the present. He told Rotha, to her further grief, that Robert had been despatched to Glasgow on important business, which would detain him for the next four or five days, and that unless there were any immediate danger it would be extremely difficult to recall him ; but he charged Rotha to telegraph if any alarming change should take place.

"It seems as though in becoming one of us," he concluded, "you have come into a larger share of trouble than of joy ; we are walking among the shadows now, Rotha, or it may be in the very fire of the furnace, and that seven times heated. Ah, well for us, my child, if amid its exceeding fierceness we may discern the form of One who walked before us in the fiery way, and know it as the form of the Son of God."

The Vicar's letters, always so wise and tender, were Rotha's great comforts, and just now she needed something especially bracing to nerve her to the bitter duty that lay before her—that of acquainting Belle with her hopeless condition.

She was only waiting for an opportunity, but it came soon.

"Does Dr. Vivian say I am better, Rotha ?" asked Belle one day when the doctor had just been paying his morning visit.

"Why do you ask, dear Belle ?" returned Rotha, quickly averting her face from the invalid.

"Because I think I feel so," replied the sick girl. "I have not coughed half so much this morning, and the pain has left me. You do not answer, Rotha ; you do not look at me. Does he—does he think me worse ?" And Belle raised herself on her elbow and looked at Rotha anxiously.

"He does not think you better," returned Rotha in a low voice.

"Not better !—that means worse, of course. Come here, Rotha. Has Dr. Vivian said anything—anything that I ought to know ? Oh, Rotha," with a sort of despair as she saw her face, "it is not that—it is not dying, is it ?" And, as Rotha knelt down and folded her silently in her arms, she repeated in a frightened voice, "Do not tell me—I cannot bear it—that I have got to die yet."

"Dear Belle, try and say 'His will be done ;' it is the only thing that can make it easy."

"I cannot," repeated Belle in a choked voice, "I cannot—it would be a falsehood to say it. What have I done that it should all be made so hard for me ? Just as I was beginning to hope too that I was getting better, and it was only those dreadful winds that were killing me."

"I thought you knew it," returned Rotha gently. "You seemed as though you did when you said good-bye to them all."

"Knew it ! Of course I always knew it. Did I not always say I was doomed ? But it does not make it easier when it comes. I wanted a little longer time to get used to the idea—to— Oh,

Rotha, it is not the knowing of it—that was long ago; it is the terror, the awfulness of approaching dissolution—the—the—oh, I cannot talk of it." And, overwhelmed by her emotion, the unhappy girl clasped her wasted arms round Rotha and held her fast.

"Oh, Belle, this is dreadful! Heavenly Father, what am I to say to her? Help me to comfort her," prayed Rotha, with streaming eyes. Then aloud, "Oh, if the Vicar were only here—if you would see a clergyman!" But Belle shook her head.

"It would be no use, Rotha; it is not that. I suppose I have gone to church oftener than most people. You forget I have lived in a clergyman's house many years, and that Austin has often talked to me, but I never would open my heart to any of them, it is not in me. You may send any one you choose, but you must not ask me to confide in a stranger." And Rotha, knowing her strange wayward nature, dared not press the point.

"If Robert were only here," began Belle presently, in calmer tones, "I think he would do me good. No clergyman could be better than Robert; you have no idea how beautifully he talks. Oh, Rotha, there it is—the sin and the stumbling-block. I have made Robert my idol, and now God is punishing me for it."

"'Whom the Lord loveth He chasteneth,'" returned Rotha, using unconsciously the Vicar's words.

"Whom He loveth, yes; but is it not idolatry all through the Bible that He condemns? Listen to me, Rotha. You shall hear what I have never told any one before—not even him. For six years—it is nearly six, is it not, since he first saw me at the Vicarage?—all that time I have never had a thought apart from him—never once—never once."

"Dear Belle, you could not help it, I suppose."

"No, I could not help it; you would have said so if you had seen him then. You can hardly judge now, he is so different, and he has shown you nothing but his faults. But if you had seen him as I have, admired, beloved, sunny-hearted and radiant with happiness, I think you would not recognise my Bertie in the careworn Robert you know."

"I can believe it; there are traces of it still. I think you will bear me witness that I have always done justice to his nobler qualities."

"Ah, he was always noble, but he is not what he was—poor Robert!—when he gave it all up for me—for me"—and for a moment a mournful smile passed over the sunken face—"when he told me he would rather have me than all his aunt's riches. But my beauty faded, Rotha, and he grew warped and weary, and then he began to misunderstand me and doubt my love ; and at last it was all doubt and wretchedness."

"My poor girl ! But hush, this is doing you harm." For the hard heavy pants interrupted her every word. But Belle persisted.

"Let me, I cannot often talk, and anything is better than thinking—even this," as the distressing cough rung its hollow knell. "I sometimes think I am not so much to blame after all ; for if he had let me do what I wished—earn my own living, I mean —I should not have lived all those years dwelling on one idea, and growing morbid over my very love ; and then I began to be afraid I should tire him."

"Belle, dear, it is all over now."

"Ah, it was all over for me a long time ago—what I have gone through since I knew first that I should never be his wife, never make him happy—that I was doomed—doomed——" And Belle covered her face with her hands and wept bitterly.

It was a terrible trial to Rotha, and one which the girl with her lifelong habits of submission and her simple faith could hardly understand. "Oh, Belle ! it is not like that—it is like going home," she said presently, when Belle, exhausted but unconvinced, had required comparative calmness ; "when the Master calls, Belle, it is hard the children are not ready."

"I am not ready," returned Belle, with a shiver. "From a child I have dreaded death—and I dread it now. Oh, Rotha, what can you say to comfort me when you know you would not be in my place for worlds ? "

It was the first time that she had seen Rotha break down, but she broke down utterly now. "Oh, would I not ? Gar ! would I not ? Oh, the pain and trouble of life," she moaned ; " the pain, and the loss, and the trouble." And for a little while she could only hide her face in Belle's pillow.

This was the beginning of many a sad hour, and many a terrible conflict, before the tormenting spirit had been cast out, and Belle lay upon her bed, white and weary, worn to a shadow, but peaceful as a little child ; and it came to her in this wise.

One night when she was unusually restless, and her few words only testified to the sore disquietude of her mind, Rotha sat down by her side and read to her the last two chapters of Revelations, thinking the glowing descriptions of the city with its golden streets and gates of pearl might soothe the tortured imagination of the poor sufferer ; but Belle only listened with contracted brow, and, when Rotha had finished, she said :

"It does me no good—it makes me worse. All the time you

have been reading I have been thinking of the shining streets, and the white-robed multitude that no man can number walking up and down them. But I don't see myself there, Rotha." She paused, and then, impeded by her broken breath, went on : " That is all glory, but unattainable glory, it seems to me. There are the river and the dark mountains to pass first—and oh," panted the dying girl, "why have the greatest saints prayed so earnestly for the gift of final perseverance if there be no conflict, no terrible struggle at the last ?"

" Oh, Belle," cried Rotha, with a pity that amounted almost to agony, "what is the meaning of faith if we cannot trust Him then ?" For it seemed to her as though Belle's stern and mystical religion had become strongly imbued with the gloomy notions of the Calvinists. " These doubts and terrors are infirmities, not sins ; nay, did not even He, the Sinless One, in His human nature, shrink from the mysterious hour of His dissolution ?" And then, turning to another page, she read the story of Gethsemane, and how, under the gray olive trees, the God-Man wrestled in the bloody sweat of His most bitter passion ; how He drank even to the dregs all the concentrated pain and terror that humanity could feel. " The cup that my Father hath given me, shall I not drink it ?" Then she closed the sacred volume and laid it aside.

But long after Belle had fallen, into an uneasy slumber did Rotha, on her bended knees, pray that the dark hour might cease, and the weary heart find its true rest. Never had she prayed so passionately, so urgently ; and, when she rose at last from her knees, it was with the peaceful assurance that she would be heard and answered.

Belle slept at intervals through the night, but nothing passed between them till the following afternoon. Belle was very quiet, and unusually silent, but every now and then her eyes rested on Rotha with a strange wistful expression, and when Meg left them together once she beckoned her to come close.

" Closer, dear Rotha. I am very weak to-day, and I think the end is not so very far off. Rotha, I want to ask you something. Were you praying for me last night ?"

Rotha pressed her hand, but did not answer.

" I knew you were, dear—I felt it. Ah, Rotha, it is all gone."

" What is gone, dear Belle ?"

" The fear of death, the trouble and the misery. I can see clearly—oh, so clearly !—and I know now that He is good. It came to me in a dream—nay, a vision rather. You do not mind my speaking so slowly and painfully, do you, dear? But I want to tell you what I saw when you were praying for me last night."

"Dear Belle, I am listening."

"I think I must have been asleep, for I woke and saw you kneeling by the bed; the candle was shining full on your hair, and I remember I tried to put out my hand and touch it, like this. And then all at once I fainted, or seemed to faint, and when I came to myself I was standing in a narrow place shut in by rocks, and before me was a deep sullen river, black and full of hideous shadows, and lapping to my very feet; and all on the other side was hidden by a gray cloud, luminous as though the light were shining through it—like a wall of mist, only clearer. And I thought that I was obliged to cross the river, and that I was standing on the brink crying and wringing my hands, and shuddering in the icy blast that seemed to sweep over the waters; and all behind me were dark mountains and rocks that seemed to shut out the very sky, and a horror of great darkness fell upon me.

"And as I stood weeping there, the cloud suddenly became more luminous, and a voice behind it said, 'When thou passest through the waters I will be with thee, and through the rivers, they shall not overflow thee.' And I seemed to answer the voice, 'But what if the sullen waters sweep me away, within sight of the luminous cloud?' And it said again, 'Fear not, for I am with thee. I have holden thee by the right hand: thou art mine.' And suddenly the scales seemed to fall from my eyes, and I could see that multitudes besides myself were crossing the river every minute, but that nearly every one had a small raft in the form of a cross. And immediately I seemed to hear the words, 'Therefore do men commit their lives unto a small piece of wood, and passing through the rough sea on a frail vessel, are saved.' And as I listened I found myself launched on the small bark with the others; and immediately the winds seemed to subside, and the waves ceased their roaring, and the light grew stronger and clearer, and my little raft floated nearer to the far-off shore. And out of the cloud I seemed to hear voices like the sound of many waters, and this is what they said :—'He maketh the storm a calm, so that the waves thereof are still. Then are they glad, because they be quiet; and so He bringeth them to their desired haven.' And immediately I awoke."

"Oh, Belle, what a beautiful dream!" intervened Rotha. But Belle, looking up and pressing her wasted hands reverently together, said:

"No, not a dream; but true—all true. I know now that

'His grace is sufficient, that His strength is made perfect in weakness.'"

A few hours after this Robert was returning to his house, jaded from a long hurried journey, when he found the following telegram awaiting him—

"Sinking fast. Come at once. No time to lose if you wish to see her alive."

Half an hour afterwards he was travelling as fast as steam would carry him to Devonshire.

"Rotha, do you think he will be here in time?" murmured the dying girl. And Rotha stooped over and wiped the clammy brow. Those who were standing round her knew that it was the beginning of the end.

"I hope so. I pray to heaven that it may be so, dear Belle."

"I should like to see him again," returned Belle faintly. The breathing was growing more laboured every moment, and the sharpened face was gray with approaching death.

"I do not want to die till he comes, if it be His will. Read that once again, dear Rotha." And Rotha, struggling for calmness, repeated again Keble's glorious Evening Hymn—or Hymn for the Dying, as it might be called—"Abide with me"—

> "Hold Thou Thy cross before my closing eyes,
>   Shine through the mist, and guide me through the skies."

"Rotha, I can hear a step. Open the door, quick!" Ah, she has heard it. Faithful to the last, she hears Robert's footstep, and knows it to be his. As he enters the room and falls down on his knees beside her couch, she nestles into his arms with a low cry of content—"Oh, Bertie, Bertie, I shall die happy now!"

"My darling Belle—my poor girl—my own, own Belle!"

"Dear Bertie, you must not grieve like this. It is better so. I am so tired, and He is giving me rest—rest—rest." The laboured breath became more difficult, the words fainter and more broken. "Where is Rotha? I have bidden her good-bye, and blessed her long ago; but now it is getting dark.

> 'Hold Thou Thy cross before my closing eyes—
>   The cross——'"

Her eyes were fast glazing now. He puts his ear to her lips that he may catch the last dying sounds. What is it that she says?

"It is growing late, Mary—cold too. Put your arm closer round me. There, good-night. God bless you, dear! Who says Bertie is here?" And as he held her closer, and called her by her name, those who were near saw that she tried to kiss him with

27

her dying lips, and failed. One moment, and Rotha gently lifted her from his arms and laid her down.

"And I heard a voice say, Blessed are the dead which die in the Lord. Yea, saith the Spirit, for they shall rest from their labours."

It was over—the brief life, the weary restlessness, the suffering; those who loved her best said, weeping, it was better so, for the feverishness and the weariness were over, and she rested at last, and rested well.

They took the poor remains back to Kirkby; that was Rotha's doing, for they knew it was the spot where she would most love to lie.

"If it be possible, let me be taken back," she had said to Rotha some hours before the fatal change came on, "and let them carry me under the old lich-gate, where I have often walked with him." And on Rotha making her a solemn promise that her wish should be fulfilled in this, she pressed her hand gratefully, and went on:

"I have always wished to be there when my time came. There is a corner by the west door where I have often stood of an evening looking over at the distant furnaces, and listening to the waves rippling low down on the shore. You will know the place; it is where Ned Blake was buried, the boy who was my favourite Sunday scholar, and who was drowned last year; it feels so high and breezy up there, and the wind sweeps so freshly over the graves, and it is just by the little path where the choir-boys go to and fro. And, Rotha, if you and the lads ever come to visit me there, don't forget to pull the nettles off Ned's grave, for I've always kept it tidy, and his poor mother is blind."

"Dear Belle, it shall be done. Is there any other wish that you have concerning that—that——" But Rotha, greatly moved, could not go on.

"No, none. All the rest must be as you and Robert like, only let it be green like the humbler graves round it, and, if Robert would not mind, just my name and 'Jesu, mercy' underneath it. Don't let them put any grand text, nothing but that, or 'Resurgam;' they put 'Resurgam' over our father's grave."

Rotha gave her word that it should be so; and when all was over she wrote to the Vicar. And so they took her back, and one wild March morning, when the dust was whirling down the white roads, and the wind swept the long grasses of the churchyard, and the gray clouds scudded over the sunless skies, the Vicar went down bareheaded to the gate, and under the old lich-gate they carried her, and laid her close to the dead boy's grave, and under the shadow of the west door.

And in time the green grass grew over it, and the sun shone down, and the dews and rains of heaven swept sadly over it, and the swallows that built their nests under the church eaves twittered and chirped endlessly about it ; and there, in process of time, was placed a fair marble cross at the head, with but few words graven upon it :—

"ISABEL FELICIA CLINTON,

Died February 29, 186—

Aged 25.

JESU, MERCY."

But the cross had not yet been erected, and the sods were hardly green, when Robert Ord went up to Bryn to wish Rotha good-bye. She was sitting alone in the sunny parlour, and put down her work hastily, as though she suspected his errand.

"You are going ? you have come to say good-bye ?" she said, looking in his pale face anxiously. He had been walking up and down for hours trying to school himself to calmness, and yet he could hardly meet her eyes as he answered her.

"Yes, it is good-bye now, and for long enough, Heaven knows. I suppose it will be four or five years at least before I get a chance of seeing any of you again."

"So long as that ? Oh, Robert !"

"Yes, unless——" He stopped, and then completed his sentence recklessly enough—"Unless I am dead and buried, I ought to say."

She sighed heavily, then put her hand in his, as a sister might have done.

"Poor Robert ! and going alone too. It seems hard, very hard, and yet it is better than staying behind and missing it all daily," she finished in the patient tired voice that was habitual to her now.

His heart smote him for his selfishness. Had she not suffered too ? How white her young face had grown ! how thin, how anxious-looking ! Some joy had passed out of her life, some hope that would never be renewed. A painful consciousness that this was so, that she would be very faithful to Gar, seized upon him as he looked at her. How could he ever ask her to come to him and comfort him for the loss of Belle if this shadow of her dead love were to be for ever between them ? Even now, when he had come to wish her good-bye, that look of pain on her face was not for him, it was for Gar—always Gar.

"You will write to me sometimes, Rotha ?—you will not forget me ?"

"Forget my brother!" answered the girl reproachfully. Oh, how often she called him that now! How innocently she clung to the conviction that Gar's brother must be hers too—that the name must be as soothing to him as it was to her!

He turned pale at that, even to his lips. Ah, the sods were not green over Belle's grave, and yet the mad infatuation for the living was blending with his sorrow for the dead. Rotha—his sister—impossible! His face was stern enough, but he had schooled himself to patience—he bore even that.

"No; I knew you would not. I ought to know your kindness of heart by this time, Rotha. When I ask you to write to me, remember that I shall be interested in anything, everything that you do."

"It is good of you to say so——" she replied gratefully. But he interrupted her.

"Never mind how trivial it is—it will be sure to please me. Sometimes you may tell me about my godson, Guy, he has grown very dear to me lately, and about Rube—poor Rube!—and then there is Mary; I do not like to go away and leave her looking as she does."

"She will be better soon," returned Rotha hurriedly. "You know we are all going away, and for her sake principally."

"Have you any idea where?"

"Yes; the Vicar and I have been talking it over. It is to be Lucerne or Zermatt, and the boys, even Arty, are to go with us. You know who is going to take the Vicar's duty for a couple of months?"

"The clergyman who came to poor Belle at the last."

"Yes, Mr. Hillyer; he has resigned his curacy, and is waiting for another. We shall be away quite two months, all June and July, and we are going to Filey for a few weeks first."

"I am glad to hear it, for your sake as well as hers. You look pale and worn, almost as though you had been ill yourself."

She smiled at that, as though the subject did not interest her.

"You must take care of yourself, for—for all our sakes."

"It is nothing," she replied in a low voice; "only my nerves are out of order, and I cannot sleep—that is the excuse I am obliged to make to Mary to get her away. She has only agreed to go because she thinks I need a change."

"Poor Mary! she never likes to leave Austin; Belle would have been just like her. Oh, Rotha, no other woman will ever love me as she did."

Rotha shook her head; she thought so too. And then her eyes fell on the glittering cross which she wore now night and day on the same finger on which he had placed his mother's old keeper. Some one would have loved her as well, if he had lived, as ever Belle had loved Robert—faithful even in death, blessing her with his last dying breath.

"Well, I must go now," exclaimed Robert hurriedly, as though the action moved him ; "there is nothing more to say, and I have all my packing to do."

"Nothing ; but God bless you, and grant you a safe voyage," said Rotha, rising ; but now the tears were in her eyes. She was thinking of what had befallen his brother ; she was sorry—yes, she was sorry even for him.

"If I do not say anything it is because I cannot," he said, pressing her hands hard. "The only thing I dare say is, God love you and bless you for all you have done for me and mine."

"And you too, dear Robert." And then she put up her face and kissed him, and called him brother once more. And he went.

But that night, an hour before he was to start by the night mail to Liverpool, he left his brother and Mary, and went secretly and alone to the churchyard.

It was quite dark now ; the wind was still abroad, and howled drearily round the church, and the rain splashed sullenly on the tombstones, or dripped silently into tiny pools. But Robert, as he stood bare-headed and with folded arms, heeded it not, for the fierce fever and pain that burnt in his veins.

But once, as he stooped and plucked a few blades of grass from the grave and hid them in his breast, a sudden overwhelming sense of his loneliness came over him. "Good-bye, Belle," he cried, pressing his lips to the dripping sod, and stretching out his arms over it in the darkness. "Good-bye, my darling. Never woman loved as you would have loved me." Then whispering low, as though he would hide his secret in her very grave, "You know it now, dear, do you not ? But you are not angry with me ? Oh, Belle, to think that my heart is broken with all this, and that you are not here to comfort me !"

Three-quarters of an hour after this Robert had bidden good-bye to Kirkby and Blackscar, and had taken his place by the night mail for Liverpool.

# CHAPTER XXXVIII.

## THE CHILDREN'S HOME.

" I pray you hear my song of a nest,
    For it is not long :—
You shall never light in a summer quest,
    The bushes among—
Shall never light on a prouder sitter,
    A fairer nestful, nor ever know
A softer sound than their tender twitter,
    That wind-like did come and go."
JEAN INGELOW.

"A maid of fullest heart she was,
    Her spirit's lovely flame
Nor dazzled nor surprised, because
    It always burned the same.
And in the heavenward path she trod,
    Fair was the wife fore-shown ;
A Mary in the house of God,
    A Martha in her own."
PATMORE.

THERE are pauses in life, strange pauses, every now and then.

The tide of human circumstance sometimes flows sluggishly and sometimes swiftly. There is a turn, a slight ebbing or flowing ; uncovered rocks glisten in the sun ; there are coloured sparkles, light frothings ; the foam and bubbles burst in the sunlight ; snow-white sails gleam on the horizon. The children build up their sand-castles, and deck them proudly with sea-weed and shells. In the evening the golden tide silvers and breaks into dark blue shadows —how fair it is, how grand ! In the morning the children rise early and go down to the shore to seek their treasures, but, alas ! everything is changed : a sullen wind sweeps over the sands, the sea is all gray, the sky hangs low, the waves break into foaming heaps, terrible rolling avalanches of gray froth ; the gulls fly inland ; there are rumours of wrecks ; the fishermen's wives grope wearily to and fro. So it is with the tide of life ; so does it ebb and flow in calm and storm. Now and then there is a break of summer monotony—changeless, unvarying, almost colourless; the tints are pallid—all grays or misty blues.

And then comes a long waiting, as the children wait for some ship that never comes after all. And just as, weary of play, and weary of constructing battlements of sand for the waves to demolish, they watch for the dim white sail which flutters for a moment on the horizon, so do their elders sit afar off, listening, sometimes for months, sometimes for years, and waiting for what the tide shall bring them.

Such a pause had come to Rotha—a break, when the strange tide of events that for the last ten months had swept her on so hurriedly from one transition to another had at length rolled away, leaving her bruised and battered indeed, but with much soundness in her; when months and even years sped on in a calm unvarying round of duty not unmixed with pleasure; when Time, that great healer, did its salutary work, and Garton became but a beautiful memory, a link onward and heavenward.

Five years, five whole years, and Rotha is Rotha Maturin still.

Brief must be the record of these years, during which Rotha strove more and more in her honest woman's endeavour to follow out the Divine precept, "Whatsoever thy hand findeth to do, do it with thy might;" when she took up new work and found it rich with blessings; when "full measure meted out was pressed into her bosom," and she reaped her woman's harvest of pure unselfish joys.

Five years, five long years, and the Vicar looks proudly round at his growing lads, Guy—almost a man now—and Rufus, half a head taller than himself; and the mother's hair is quite gray, but her face is sweeter in its chastened gravity than it has ever been before; and Robert is working still, uncomplaining, but sad, in his far-off home; and the swallows fly down on the marble cross, and the daisies grow up among the grass on the dead boy's grave and on Belle's; and in the church, just opposite to where Rotha sits, is a noble painted window, with the Man of Sorrows bearing His cross along the bitter way; and under it is written :—

"In memory of
GARTON ORD,
Who died December 29, 186—
Aged 23.
IN HOC SPERO."

It was soon after the anniversary of his death that something very unexpected befell Rotha. Mr. Effingham made her an offer.

He had come up very boldly to Bryn to prefer his request, and bore himself in a way sufficiently manly; but Rotha shrank back, feeling herself wounded, she hardly knew why.

"I never gave you any encouragement—any right to speak to me like this, Mr. Effingham," she said, turning pale and trembling at this strange story of love. Her tone was repellent, almost indignant.

"I never said that you did," he returned sullenly; "but when a man loves a girl I think he has a right to tell her so."

Poor George Effingham! He had a heart somewhere in spite of his shallowness, and, to do him justice, he was smitten by the woman as well as the heiress. Rotha relented at the sight of his crestfallen looks. He had not much to say for himself; but he was tolerably honest, and then there were tears of positive disappointment in the poor fellow's eyes. Her next words were more gentle.

"Perhaps I ought to thank you, Mr. Effingham. Many girls would feel themselves honoured by what you have told me. If I have been impatient or ungrateful, you must forgive me; it is not my fault that I cannot forget him," continued the girl, bursting into tears. "I don't think that I shall ever be able to listen to any one after Gar."

But, as he turned to go, she held out her hand to him with a little contrition for her hardness.

"You must not be hurt or angry because I cannot forget my trouble. I do not want to be any one's wife now that poor Gar is gone. I do not mean to marry—never—never," cried the girl, with a flush. "But I hope I shall be your friend always," smiling in the face of the discomfited young man. "There, go, Mr. Effingham, and God bless you!"

Rotha kept her word, for Nettie did not marry the widower after all; but fifteen months afterwards she married George Effingham, and made him the best little wife possible. George told his wife everything, like a man. But he was hardly prepared for the confidence she gave him in return; he found that Nettie had loved Gar really and truly, and that many of her reckless and fantastic ways had grown out of her disappointment.

She never told Rotha, though Rotha guessed it; but they all three became excellent friends. Nettie gave up fifteen out of her three-and-twenty bosom friends when she married, and consoled herself instead with her babies. But if any one had asked who was the most notable housekeeper and the most domesticated little matron in the whole of Blackscar, they would tell you that it was Mrs. Effingham.

This was the first little episode that disturbed Rotha's monotony; but by and by there was another, when a great work grew out of a little speech of the Vicar's.

Rotha was still insisting on being Lady Bountiful at the Vicarage; but at last the Vicar—that most enduring of men—became restive, and told her that it would not do at all; on which occasion he addressed her in the following words :—

"It will not do, Rotha, and I really mean it. And now I am quite determined that we shall come to an understanding with one another, for this sort of thing must not go on."

"What sort of thing, Mr. Ord?"

"Now, Rotha, I can tell by that quiet curl of the lip that you are going to be troublesome; but I beg to inform you that I am quite serious."

"So am I—painfully so, I assure you. Now, Mr. Ord, what sort of thing?"

"Do you want me to publish a list of your iniquities? You are growing too barefaced a sinner for me to deal with. Never mind. I will serve you up a *resumé*, hot and strong. First, there was taking Mary away to Filey—a piece of generous forethought that prevented a relapse after Belle's death; then there were the travelling expenses to Zermatt, and maintaining an establishment there for two months, when Mary and the boys and Reuben were your visitors."

"And you would not be. Oh, do you think I have ever forgiven you that?"

"Forgiven, forsooth! because I had a little bit of manly independence left. I like that. But that was nothing to my feelings when I got home. The Vicarage papered and painted from garret to basement—my servants bribed and made accessories to the plot—new carpets and curtains all over the house—fresh chintz in the drawing-room—a new easy-chair in the mother's room—a new-fangled writing-table and a lot of oak furniture in the study! When I think of it now," finished the Vicar, passing his hand over his face to conceal his smile, "I almost wonder that I can have anything to do with such a criminal."

"Now, Mr. Ord, we have heard this almost twenty times. You forget that I heard you tell Nettie the other day that it did your heart good to see dear Mary's face light up at the sight of her renovated house. I am sure you never liked any writing-table so well as this."

"Bless her!" very nearly said the Vicar, but he checked himself in time and went on sternly with the list.

"I don't think perhaps I ought to mention the marble cross and the memorial window in the same category?"

"No—oh no," faltered Rotha, with quivering lip, and the Vicar, clearing his throat several times, went on in the same serio-comic manner.

"But I do not think that a clergyman's wife ought to dress as Mary does. I do not understand it myself, of course," continued the Vicar, somewhat puzzled; "and, except that her dresses are black and shiny, I do not know much about it. But I do not think Mrs. Stephen Knowles ought to say, as she does, that Mrs. Ord wears the most expensive stuffs that are to be got. I heard her say so myself the other day." But to his surprise, Rotha, after vainly trying to answer him in the same vein, suddenly burst into tears. "Nay, my dear child, I am only in jest. What is this ?"

"I did not mean—I tried not. But, Mr. Ord, you must let me do this for Mary; you don't know how I love to do it, and I never had a sister. And now she is everything to me, and I want to feel that I am a sister to her in Belle's place."

"Dear Rotha, you are a better sister to her than ever Belle has been."

"No—no—don't say so ; almost her last words were for Mary; and, if it were true, she would never think so."

"My faithful-hearted Mary, no—nothing could ever shake her belief in Belle's goodness and affection to herself. Dear Rotha, we are ending our conversation rather sadly. Don't fear for one moment that I shall ever call you to account for what you do for her. Be sisters in heart and deed if you will, but, Rotha, you have done enough for us now—let it rest here."

Rotha was silent for a moment, and then she said very gravely, "Do you really wish it ?"

"Yes," he returned, without hesitation; "my circumstances are better now, since the burden of poor Belle's maintenance is withdrawn, and I have no longer to help Robert in supporting Gar. Robert is quite rich too, and he talked in his last letter of having his godson sent out to him."

"No, no," interrupted Rotha hastily; "let it be Rufus—Rufe has no taste for learning, and Guy has. I will accede to all your conditions if you will only let me provide for Guy."

The Vicar shook his head doubtfully, but Rotha laid her hand on his arm persuasively and went on :

"He is more than sixteen now, and is getting a great fellow—too big to be idle, and be a burden to his father. In another year or two my boy"—Rotha always called Reuben her adopted son—"is going to Oxford. I am glad and thankful the dear boy is anxious to be a clergyman. Let Guy, Robert's godson, go with him; and let me feel," whispered Rotha, laying her cheek against the kind hand, "as though this were my monument to Gar; and that the two boys he loved so fondly may become faithful priests, as he would have been if he had been spared." And, deeply touched, the Vicar, after a little hesitation, granted her request for his eldest born.

It was some words of his dropped shortly afterwards that gave Rotha the idea which she was so ready to carry out.

She was complaining to him that, in spite of her lavish gifts, her money seemed to accumulate rather than otherwise.

"We want so little, Meg and I, and we prefer to live simply," added Rotha. "And there seems so little chance of its finding its way, after all, into Robert's hands, or his children's either; for I fancy, after what has happened, that he will not marry any more than I shall."

"And it is my opinion that both will marry; but all in good time," prophesied the Vicar, who was the only one who had a glimmering of Robert's secret.

Rotha looked surprised and a little hurt, for it was only six months since she had refused George Effingham; and Mary, her sole confidante, knew she had refused him, and Mary told everything to her husband. After such a proof of faithfulness to Garton's memory, she scarcely liked to be told that it was possible, nay, very probable, that she would marry after all; and Robert, too, who had cared for one woman for five years.

The Vicar saw the girl's hot flush, but he took no notice. His knowledge of the world told him that Rotha would think very differently presently. "If I were you, I would seek some interest or object in which you might invest your surplus money. I don't know whether you have ever thought of such a thing, or whether it would exactly suit your views, but the surgeon of the Cottage Hospital at Thornborough told me that he wished it were possible to have a small branch establishment at Blackscar, or even Kirkby, that some of the convalescent children might have a month or two of pure sea air before returning to the wretched alleys and dens where they lived."

Rotha almost clapped her hands when she heard the Vicar's words. "The very thing!" she exclaimed; "the very thing that Meg has been longing for—work among children, and I think," she added, with a quaint sadness, "that it will just suit me too."

And so it came about that the "Children's Home," as it was called, was established in Kirkby.

Rotha and Meg thought over the matter deeply before they matured their plans and laid them before the Vicar. Meg was even more enthusiastic than Rotha, although Rotha threw herself heart and soul into the undertaking.

By the Vicar's advice it was only begun on a small scale at first. Two or three of the whitewashed cottages adjoining the Vicarage were taken and thrown into one, and furnished in the simplest manner. A young woman, whose sad history had brought her under Rotha's notice, was to be the nurse in charge, and an orphan, who had been trained under Mrs. Ord's own eye, would be sufficient for the cooking and cleaning. The "Little Sister," as she now began to style herself, was to be head matron and house-keeper, with Meg under her.

Perhaps the happiest hours that Rotha had ever spent since Garton's death were in fitting up and arranging her Children's Home. Mary found her often singing over her work as she sewed carpets or stitched blinds—nothing seemed to come amiss to her nimble fingers. The boys, Reuben and Guy especially—her two devoted knights, as the Vicar dubbed them—worked hard in their leisure hours. The three gardens had been thrown into one, and made a tolerably large enclosure. Guy and Reuben laid down the new grass sods, and planted the privet-hedge to shut out the palings; while Laurie and even Arty were never weary of rolling the fresh gravel. And Rufus, who was no mean carpenter, put up shelves, fitted up the cupboards with pegs, knocked his head valiantly against the low cottage ceiling in hanging the clean dimity curtains, and was the most good-natured aide-de-camp to the two women that could be found.

His last duty was to put up the huge board over the entrance, on which Reuben had been bestowing infinite care, and paint on it "The Children's Home." It was put up at the High Street entrance, facing the church, and deeply affected Rotha when she went down to the bottom of the garden with the boys to read it.

"How big it is!—I can read it from here," said Arty, con-templating it with feelings of awe.

"It really looks like a beginning, Meg," whispered Rotha; and Meg, always chary of words, dropped her eye-glass with a satisfied nod.

The next day was a perfect fête to the young workers, for the Vicar and his wife and the new curate, Mr. Tregarthen, a distant relation of Sir Edgar's, were to come on a tour of inspection; and Nettie and Aunt Eliza were to be of the party; and in the after-noon the first patient, a crippled boy afflicted with abscesses, was to come over from Thornborough.

Rotha had come very early in the morning; but, early as it was, Rufus and Laurie had rolled the paths freshly and watered the grass, while Reuben was nailing up the last beautiful illuminated text that Rotha had finished late last night, just fronting the entrance—" Suffer the little children to come unto Me, for of such is the kingdom of heaven." Every room and nearly every cot was furnished with the same illuminated texts, all appropriate to the sick and suffering little ones who were to be received under that roof.

The visitors arrived punctually at the appointed hour, and the boys formed already a sort of guard of honour to receive them; but neither the Vicar nor Mary could forbear a smile when they saw the little sister. Rotha and Meg had arranged that, for convenience sake as well as decorum, they would wear a simple uniform of gray during their working hours at the Home; and Rotha wore a little cap over her bright hair, which suited her infinitely better than it did Meg; for, if possible, Mrs. Carruthers looked more gauche than usual in the homely gray dress and linen collar and cuffs that looked so natty on Rotha, who came bustling up with her keys dangling from her trim waistband to receive her friends.

"Peace be to this house !" said the Vicar, taking off his broad-brimmed hat; but one cannot repeat the whole of that solemn beautiful blessing, which thrilled those who heard it. And then, stepping over the threshold, he spoke a few forcible words on that text—" I was a stranger, and ye took me in : naked, and ye clothed me. I was sick, and ye visited me ;" and then, kneeling down, he invoked a blessing on the house and the work that was to be that day undertaken for the glory of God, and for the relief of His suffering children. "And oh," prayed the Vicar, "may He who took the little ones in His gracious arms and blessed them, enter with us this day, and stretch out His hands in blessing over this house ! May He strengthen the heart and hands of this ministering woman, that it may be said of her and of all who follow her in this work, in that day of days, ' She hath done what she could.' "

There was a brief silence, hushed and full of feeling. "And now," said the Vicar, rising, and giving his hand to Rotha, "We are ready to follow you, and to see and admire all that is to be seen. And first, what room are we in ?"

"They are all written up over the doors," returned Rotha in a low voice ; for she was somewhat overcome by the solemnity of the Vicar's address.

"This is called the ' The Mother's Room,' " interrupted Rube eagerly, who had kept as near to his adopted mother as possible.

"I want to feel as though I am their mother," returned Rotha bashfully, "and as though they were all my children for the time being. It will help me to be more patient and loving with them than I might otherwise be. This is where I shall write and keep my accounts, and receive visitors, and where Meg will sit too. I shall always be here from ten to one on every day in the week, and Meg from two to five in the afternoon. One or other of us will always be here."

"I see you mean to work it thoroughly," returned the Vicar, smiling. "A very good arrangement; don't you think so, Tregarthen?" And then he looked round approvingly on the snug cottage parlour, with its cool summer matting and white curtains, and the fresh flowers on the little round table, and a beautiful engraving of "Christ Blessing Little Children" over the mantelpiece. The illumination for this room was Rotha's favourite one— "Whatsoever thy hand findeth to do, do it with thy might." And on the table, as though willing to put the precept into practice, was a visitors' book, in which the Vicar wrote the first entry, and a newly-lined account-book, with a formidable array of pens bristling in a very large inkstand.

From this room they proceeded to the kitchen, where they were received by the smiling orphan, clad in a new print dress of alarming stiffness, over which she wore a snow-white bib-apron. "Come, show your cupboards, Emma," said the Vicar. And the girl, curtseying and rosy with pleasure, showed the shelves, with their rows of shining pewter and china mugs ; while Caroline, the nurse, a pleasant-looking young woman, slightly marked with the smallpox, led them into the storeroom, where Rotha's linen-press was, and where she was to keep her stores of groceries and jams and the simple medicines and salves that they were likely to need.

Leading out of this was the long low room where the children were to dine or have their lessons, and where they could also play on rainy days. There was no furniture but one long table and a few chairs and stools ; but several beautiful prints, all sacred subjects, hung on the walls ; and Mary noticed there were flowers tastefully arranged in this room, while a canary sang shrilly in a green cage, and a fine tabby cat and kittens reposed in a cushioned basket.

"Carrying out your theories, Rotha?" said her friend, with a smile.

"Yes," returned Rotha softly. "I cannot imagine children without pets and flowers ; to me it seems a part of their education. My children will delight in those kittens. If you open those cupboards, Nettie, you will find them full of picture-books and toys. You see the school-books are all bound neatly for use."

"I don't believe you have forgotten a single thing," cried Nettie, with a sigh, half admiring, half envious. "Just look at those little work-boxes for the girls, Mr. Tregarthen, and the patterns of wool-work for the boys. Why, Rotha, you could have done nothing else for months."

"You forget I have had Meg to help me; that is Meg's department," returned Rotha, blushing; and then they went up to the dormitories. They were only four neat little rooms, with three or four beds or cots apiece, all fitted up with the same pretty summer matting, and with white dimity curtains, blowing in the fresh sea-breeze; over every bed was a picture, and a text underneath; and a white plaster angel on a bracket in every room seemed to keep guard over the little sufferers.

"Oh, Austin, is it not lovely?" whispered Mary, with tears in her eyes. "If only our darling Belle had been here to see it."

"She sees it now, perhaps," he returned; "and our Gar too." And Rotha, catching the words, looked out on the sunny waves, and thought how he would have liked it.

Rotha was greatly tired by all the excitement; she had worked early and late too, and, when all her visitors except Reuben had departed, she merely stayed to welcome her little patient—a perfect "Tiny Tim" of a child, rejoicing in the extraordinary name of "Shirtle Pearl;" and, leaving Még to undress him and lay him in his little cot, she went slowly home, leaving Reuben to have tea at the Vicarage with Guy, who was now his great chum.

When she got home she found a letter awaiting her from Robert, for they had kept up a steady correspondence now for more than two years. Robert wrote extremely well, and one of his long letters was always a treat to Rotha. She had just written him a full account of her plans for her Children's Home, and doubtless this was in answer; so, asking Prue to bring her a cup of tea in her own room, she sat down by the open window to enjoy that and her letter together.

But the tea cooled, and Rotha's cheek grew white before she had read many lines; but long before she had finished it her face was burning, and, as it dropped from her hands, she put her head down on the window-sill and cried long and bitterly. But all she said was, "Poor Robert! poor Robert!" And then, "Oh, Gar, what would you say? Oh, Gar, never—never!" and kissed the gold keeper that guarded the glittering cross.

And yet it was more than two years since she had lost him— and it had been but a nine days' wonder after all—and Robert had written a letter such as few women could have resisted, and had shown her his heart with such a depth of passionate love in it that she might well weep and wring her hands, knowing that it was in vain.

What it had cost him to write it! and yet every line was tinged with hopelessness akin to despair. It was as though he knew that he tried his fate in vain, and still could not resist the attempt.

"What you will say, or what you will think, I dare not pause to ask myself, or I should never send this; but something within me forces me to speak, and demands to be heard. If I cannot wring an answer from you now, perhaps the coming years may do something for me; not that I can afford to wait, God knows, for I am growing old and gray before my time with all this misery, but because I love you so, Rotha, with every fibre of my being, with every thought of my heart, as I have never—dear Belle, sweet saint, you know it now—loved or could love any other woman."

Well may she tremble and cover up her face with her hands, and cry out that it must be a mistake—Robert! Gar's brother!—and then calm herself with saying the dear name over and over again. Does she feel now, as she must have done, that Gar was but a boy compared to this man? She reads on, page after page. Ah! he does not spare himself. She can hardly bear to read the generous self-accusing—the many acts of his past cruelty which he brings back to her recollection; it was as though he strove to humiliate himself even in her sight. Never, he tells her, has he forgiven himself—never is her face, so sweet and reproachful, absent from his mind for one moment; and then he speaks of the long atonement, of the dreary evenings when he and his remorse are brought face to face, and how little by little he feels himself purified by suffering, and more worthy to address her.

"Not that my pride would even now tell you this," he finished, "if I did not know that I might any day command an independent position in England. But, Rotha, unless I grow weak—which I may, Heaven knows, seeing to what I have come—I have almost sworn that nothing but you can ever recall me; but speak that word, Rotha, and I come.

"Yours, through and through, however you may scorn my love—Robert Ord."

Ah, well may she make herself nearly ill with weeping, and creep to her bed that her faithful Meg may not guess the cause of her grief. Not for days—days during which her white weary looks move the Vicar and his wife to compassion, not unmixed with curiosity—does she write her answer. "She is in trouble," she tells them; but begs them earnestly not to ask her why, and then goes and sits among her children till her sweet face grows calm and serene again. But that is not until she has written to him, not until she has penned a few lines with many tears, in which she tells him that she loves him dearly, dearly; that she will pray for him, and think of him day and night, but that she cannot forget Gar. No, she cannot, she cannot! And then bids God bless him for his faithful friend and sister—ROTHA.

# CHAPTER XXXIX.

## THE BROKEN CLAUSE.

"Come, lest this heart should, cold and cast away,
    Die ere the guest adored she entertain ;
Lest eyes which never saw Thine earthly day,
    Should miss thy heavenly reign.

"Come weary-eyed from seeking in the night,
    Thy wanderers strayed upon the pathless wold,
Who wounded, dying, cry to Thee for light,
    And cannot find their fold."
                    JEAN INGELOW.

BUT another episode occurred shortly which disturbed Rotha not a little, and which for a short time broke up the tranquillity of Bryn.

It was about four or five months after the Children's Home had been established. So far the trial had been a success. Nine children had been received as patients, and Rotha was now at work in earnest.

Every one who saw it—and visitors were numerous during the first few weeks—said that the home was admirably managed, as indeed it was.

Rotha was there every morning, and never left till Meg took her place. Rotha's part was to give out stores, write orders for the tradesmen, keep the accounts, and receive visitors. She also looked after Caroline and saw that the dormitories were kept tidy and ventilated.

Meg's duties were different; she presided over the children's meals, gave short lessons to those who were well enough to receive them, taught the little girls work, and sang hymns with them, and when the weather was fine took them down to the shore, where she might be seen any lovely afternoon among the sand-hills with a crippled baby in her arms, pushing Shirtle Pearl's perambulator before her, and surrounded by a crew of sickly or limping little ones. This was Meg's own work, and she dearly loved it.

Of course Rotha's time was greatly taken up, and an afternoon or an evening at the Vicarage became a rare treat. In general it was understood that Meg and she were to have their evenings free, and to spend them together in the old way, but often Meg stopped till the little ones were safely tucked up in their dormitories, and Shirtle had left off moaning himself to sleep. Meg used to sing the Evening Hymn with the children, and then come out through the sweet summer air to meet Rotha going to or from church. Rotha used to smile, but she never reproached Meg for her delay. She knew that Meg began to centre all her happiness within those cottage walls. The children loved Meg almost more than they did Rotha. She told them quaint stories when they sat among the sand-hills, and she could carry two or three together in her strong arms when they were tired. When the children were sick they always asked Meg to come and sing to them. Meg could sing them " Ye faire one with ye goldene locks" as well as she could " The Three Kings" and the Manger songs. Rotha, returning for her afternoon, would peep in sometimes into the refectory, as it was called, and find Meg sitting on the floor with the children swarming round her, telling the story of "Henny Penny," or "Goody Two Shoes," or the "Little Tiny, Tiny Woman"—kittens and children and Meg, and sometimes Rotha's little gray skye Fidgets, all in a chaotic mass together. The youngest child there, a mere baby, would clap her hands and say "Meg" if asked whom she loved, though she always finished with "Meg, and little mother too, and Meg loves Annie."

It would have been no wonder if Rotha grew absorbed in her sweet work; but she did not forget the duties that her position entailed, and, though she told all her friends frankly that she had no time for either paying or receiving mere calls of ceremony, she still accepted invitations for a quiet evening, and now and then dispensed hospitality by throwing open her pretty rooms and making all her friends heartily welcome.

These evenings were much sought after, for Rotha was an admirable hostess under Mrs. Ord's chaperonage, and among her most frequent visitors were Lady Tregarthen and Mr. Ramsay, who were both liberal subscribers to the Home.

Rotha had taken the Vicar's advice, and received all voluntary donations and subscriptions, and after the first year it was found necessary to form a ladies' committee, when Rotha was unanimously elected as secretary and treasurer, and in a little while another cottage was added, and then another, as the applications became more numerous, until at last Rotha acceded to Mr. Ramsay's generous proposition to unite with her in building new and more spacious premises; and when this was done, which was not for some years after this story closes, Meg was elected as resident lady-superintendent, and spent the last years of a long and useful life among the children whom she so dearly loved.

One cloudy afternoon late in October Meg had occasion to go into Blackscar on some business connected with the Home. Rotha, remaining on duty during her absence, was sitting writing in the mother's room, with baby Annie fast asleep at her feet, when there was a quick light tap at the door, and the Vicar entered.

"I thought Mrs. Carruthers was here, Rotha," he said rather anxiously. "Is she up at Bryn then?"

"No, she has just gone into Blackscar, and I do not expect her back till nearly five. Why, did you want her?" she asked, struck by something grave in the Vicar's tone.

In reply he went to the door and shut it carefully, and then, taking a seat, stirred the fire thoughtfully and warmed his hands over it, for the afternoons were growing decidedly chilly.

"Do you think you could find her?" he asked after a pause, during which Rotha's curiosity had been strongly roused by his unusual gravity.

"Well, I am not quite sure that I can. She has gone to the infirmary, and to the bank, and to several shops. Is anything the matter, Mr. Ord?"

"There is no time to be lost," continued the Vicar musingly, and rubbing his hands slowly over each other. "The Rector said so, and I suppose he knew. Rotha, who do you think is lying ill, apparently dying, only two or three miles from here?"

Rotha looked at him earnestly for a moment, and then the truth flashed on her.

"Do you mean Jack Carruthers, poor Meg's husband?" and the Vicar nodded.

"I have just come from the Rector's, Rotha. I hurried on here thinking I could find her before I took the train to Thornborough. You know I have to preach a charity sermon at St. Luke's?"

"Well!" exclaimed Rotha breathlessly.

"I must tell you what he said. But you must find Mrs. Carruthers, for there is no time to be lost. Mr. Hodgson sent for me directly he found out the truth.

"Early this morning he was sent for by the landlady of the 'Pig and Whistle,' a little public-house on the Leatham road, just before you turn off by the path that leads to the Leatham woods. I daresay you have often passed it; there is an old stone drinking-trough placed under a very fine elm tree, with a small green before it, always full of geese."

"Yes, yes," returned Rotha eagerly; "I went in once with Meg to ask my way."

"Well, the landlady is a very tidy body, and she told Mr. Hodgson when he got there that she was greatly troubled about a poor man who had come in for a night's lodging about ten days ago, and had lain there ever since, growing from bad to worse, till at last the doctor said that he had not many hours to live, and she thought she had better fetch a clergyman to him. She described him when he came in as very emaciated and miserable looking, almost as though he had been half-starved, with a driven hunted look in his eyes, as though he was not quite in his right mind; and she described to the Rector his moaning and restless picking at the clothes as a sign that the end was not far off."

"Oh, my poor Meg!" sighed Rotha; but the Vicar went on.

"I must tell you exactly what happened, and then leave it in your hands. Mr. Hodgson went up, of course, and found the poor creature just as she described, and a more forlorn object the Rector said he had never seen. He had evidently once been a fine-looking man, the Rector said, but a more hollow wasted face he had never seen, rendered more intensely death-like by the ragged black whiskers and beard, and eyes unnaturally large. He seemed pleased to see Mr. Hodgson, and told him scraps of his history as well as he could. He had been a sheep-farmer in Australia, and had afterwards gone to the diggings; had then lost all, and worked his way home again; and in some drunken fray had broken a blood-vessel, and had lain in a hospital for months at the point of death. He gave his name as Jack Carruthers, and told Mr. Hodgson that he had a wife living, he supposed, near London; that he had made some attempts to find her, but had never succeeded. But his description of her to Mr. Hodgson so exactly resembled our Mrs. Carruthers, whom he had met several times at my house, that, without saying anything to the poor fellow, he brought back a scrap of his handwriting with him and sent for me at once."

"There can be no doubt that it is her husband, I suppose," interrupted Rotha at this point.

"None, I think; but of course she will recognise his handwriting. Now, Rotha, I can do nothing more in the business myself, and I must leave it, as I said before, in your hands. Will you undertake to find Mrs. Carruthers for me, for I am afraid, from the Rector's account, that this is the poor fellow's last night on earth? Mr. Hodgson has promised to go again to-morrow in case he should be alive. But he could make very little impression on him. All the time he was praying he was moaning out to 'Madge' —I suppose that was his wife—to come to him."

"I will go at once," returned Rotha, lifting up the sleeping child in her arms.

"And I will wait and go with you as far as the station," observed the Vicar. And in another five minutes Rotha and he had left the house together.

The bank was already closed, but Rotha went to the infirmary and to several of the principal shops before she found Meg in the chemist's dark little back parlour waiting till sundry prescriptions had been made up. Rotha made some excuse to the druggist and took her out, and then, linking her arm in hers, led the way down one of the side streets which led to old Blackscar church and to the Leatham road.

It was a cloudy afternoon, and already it was growing dusk, and one or two drops, forerunners of a wet evening, splashed down on Rotha's mantle.

"Meg, darling, can you bear a shock? Will you promise me not to be too much upset at what I am going to tell you?" began Rotha very tenderly, all the more as she felt the sudden close grip of her arm.

"Something is the matter! You have heard of Jack! He is dead!" exclaimed Meg in a wild pitiful sort of way, as she caught sight of Rotha's grave face.

"No; not so bad as that. Meg, dear, look at this writing; is it his?" She need not have asked when she saw Meg kissing it and crying over it.

"My own Jack's handwriting! Oh, Rotha, for pity's sake tell me where you have got it. Is he alive? Can I go to him?"

"We are going to him, and I trust to Heaven that we may find him alive. But he is very ill, Meg—desperately so; dying, they say." And then as they hurried on, regardless of the fast pattering drops, she told Meg all that she had heard from the Vicar, and begged her to prepare herself and be calm for Jack's sake, as well as her own, for he was very ill, so very ill, and so on.

Meg made no answer but to wring her hands and walk on faster; once she broke out into bitter weeping when she heard he had asked for "Madge."

"He never called me anything but that when he was in a good humour," she said. "Oh, Jack, Jack, just to hear you call me that once more," and then quickened her pace till Rotha could hardly keep up with her. It was a wet evening and still early, and there were few loungers around the door of the 'Pig and Whistle'; and they took very little notice of the two ladies, who, they supposed, wished to take shelter from the approaching storm.

"It is going to be a dirty night, ladies," said one who looked like the ostler.

Rotha said, "Yes, a very unpleasant evening," and pushed past into the little dark entry, where a bright glow shone from the bar, in which a rosy-faced landlady was sitting alone at a little round table drinking tea.

Even under these painful circumstances Rotha noticed how cosy it looked, and what a bright fire it was, before the landlady started up at the sight of the two ladies, and came bustling up.

"You have a Mr. Carruthers here," began Rotha with difficulty, and in an instant a shade came over the woman's pleasant face.

"Dear, dear; yes, the poor creature! The Rector has sent you, has he?" glancing curiously at Rotha's dress and Meg's agitated face.

Rotha said "Yes" impatiently, and begged that they might be shown up at once; but Meg put her hurriedly aside.

"I am his wife, good woman—his wife—do you hear? For pity's sake take me to him at once."

"Dear sakes alive," muttered the rosy landlady; "who would have thought his wife was here, poor creature? The Madge, no doubt, he's calling after. Bet's with him now. Bet's a famous nurse, and was with him all last night. Bet's nursed two brothers and a sister, and saw a winding-sheet in the candle last night," gasped out the garrulous landlady as she toiled before them up the steep crooked staircase. "One landing more. He asked for our worst room, having little money; and he's got it, sure enough. Stoop your heads as you go in, ladies, for the ceiling is rarely low; and there is a deep step, you might break your necks leading down to the room."

"Hush, he's partly asleep," said Bet, a strong-featured, red-armed wench, coming forward. "It's been 'Madge, Madge' off and on all the afternoon till I'm that moidered I'm half crazed."

"It is the gentleman's wife, Bet," said the landlady, wiping her eyes on her apron as Meg, with a sort of sob, kneels down beside the narrow truckle-bed; and Rotha, half awed, half dizzy, looks round the comfortless garret with its lean-to roof, and its carpetless floor, and the creaking bedstead with the blue-striped counterpane. Bet puts her arms akimbo and says, "Lor heart's alive, missis, and to think of that!" and breaks into a hysterical chuckle. The rain pours down against the crazy window, the sign flaps madly outside, the fire splutters up with a faint gurgle, and the candle gutters low in the socket. Meg, kneeling with her arms extended over the bed, kisses a pale hand lying motionless on the coverlet; and the uneasy sleeper stirs and moans restlessly, "Madge, Madge!"

"Hear him," says Bet; "he says nought else."

Meg, turning her white face to Rotha, repeats softly, "Hear him?" And whispers to herself, "Thank God!"

Rotha clears the room after that, and sets the guttering candle aside and lights another; and then, replenishing the tiny fire, closes the door and comes again to the bed.

"He looks very ill, Meg," she whispers. Meg, laying the skeleton hand against her cheek, points to the wasted arm and shakes her head.

"Not long for this world, are you, Jack? Oh Jack! Jack!" she repeats in a heartrending voice, "will you not wake up once more and speak to your wife?" And, as though the suppressed agony of her tones had power to rouse him, he opened his eyes wildly and rolled them from side to side.

"Whose voice was that?" he muttered hoarsely; "it is like hers when the dead boy was carried out. Don't haunt me, Madge; don't haunt me!"

"Oh, Jack, your own Madge—never, never!"

The restless picking of the clothes recommenced.

"Who said it was my fault, and that she might have died too?" he raved more loudly. "Somebody pointed out the black bruise on her neck. Who struck her? Not I. 'Don't strike me, Jack, when I love you so,' she said, a curse on her white reproachful face. No, Madge, I did not mean that. Come here, my girl. The boy died and the mother too, but I did not murder them. All the legions of hell are trying to put it on me. But I won't say I did it, I won't!" and the voice fell into indistinct muttering.

"Jack! do you not know me, dear Jack?"

"Know you—too well," he muttered. "You are Madge Browning—tall Madge Browning—old miser Browning's daughter—ugly as sin. Who said that? Nonsense. I've brought you some carnations. Dark reds for Madge's faded colours. Don't wear white, it does not suit you. Say it aloud. Louder still. I can't hear you—love, honour, and cherish. Whom? Browning's daughter? Ah, ah, no! Nonsense. Kiss me, Madge. I'm a drunken brute, but I never meant to hurt you."

"He does not know me. Oh, Jack, one word, only one word!"

"Hush! she is playing her music—grand, grand! The 'Dead March in Saul.' No, not that. Do you hear? Ah, terrible,

terrible !" Again the indistinct mutterings, again he dozed, then woke more conscious as Meg was putting something to his lips.

" Who is this ? Not Madge—Madge herself ! "

" Yes, your own Madge, dear ; your faithful loving wife. Drink some more, dear Jack."

The hollow eyes stared over the rim of the china vessel, and then he pushed it aside.

" No more. I can't swallow. Is it really you, Madge, and not a dream ?"

" Really and truly. Thank God you know me at last ! "

" I don't know you," he repeated, half frightened. " My Madge had no gray hair, and her face was not white like yours."

" That was seven years ago, Jack."

" Seven years ago ? ay ; that's a long time, surely." He seemed wandering again, but she roused him.

" Say something to me before you go to sleep, Jack," she said, supporting the poor dying head on her arm. " Say ' God bless you, Madge,' once—only once ! "

" God bless you, Madge ! That is a prayer, isn't it ? I haven't said my prayers for seven years ; never, I think, since I was a child." He looked up in her face as though a glimmering of the terrible truth reached him even in his semi-consciousness. " I haven't said my prayers, and I am going to die."

" Say them now. Oh, Jack, fold your hands in mine and say one prayer for mercy !" He shook his head feebly.

" I don't know any. Teach me, Madge." And he let her hold his hands, and tried to say the words after her.

" ' I will arise and go to my Father. To my Father.' What next, Madge ? ' And will say unto Him, Father, I have sinned against heaven, and before—before——' " The broken clause was never finished, for he dropped his face, muttering still, upon her bosom. Two hours afterwards he slept away, unconscious still, and Meg fell weeping upon Rotha's neck, and suffered her to lead her from the room.

# CHAPTER XL

### FIVE YEARS AFTERWARDS.

> " Her letters too,
> Tho' far between, and coming fitfully
> Like broken music, written as she found
> Or made occasion, being strictly watch'd,
> Charm'd him thro' every labyrinth till he saw
> An end, a hope, a light breaking upon him."
>
> TENNYSON.

> " Yes it was love, if thoughts of tenderness
> Tried in temptation, strengthen'd by distress,
> Unmov'd by absence, firm in every clime,
> And yet, oh, more than all ! untired by time."
>
> BYRON.

Two more years passed on, summer and winter, seed-time and harvest, since Meg closed the eyes of her poor prodigal, and took up the fresh burthen of her grief and her widowhood together.

At first the shock seemed to have stunned her, and then she wept till her poor half-blind eyes could weep no more. It was sad to witness that terrible waste of love and sorrow; she grew worn and gray—thin almost to a shadow; a sick loathing of all her duties came upon her; she shrank even from her children, and for a little while cared to do nothing but to sit by Jack's grave and to brood silently over her trouble. But the dark hour passed and the pale face grew placid again under the widow's cap; and strangers, as they lingered in the churchyard in the summer evenings, often paused to hear the wonderful rich pealing of the organ, and stealing into the empty church in the twilight, saw Meg sitting alone with upturned face in the moonlight and playing fragments of strange requiem masses. Was it Jack's requiem she was playing ? Hark ! it breaks into a low monotonous chant. The moonbeams play on the chancel pavement. The perfume of fresh lilies, dim white globes with golden hearts, bound up with scented sheaves, pervades the air ; a voice tender, tremulous, breaks into deep rich tones—" I will arise and go to my Father——"

Ah! Jack's dying prayer. The broken sentence unfinished and suggestive. The strangers steal away. Meg comes out, a black shadowy figure, and pauses for a moment by a white tombstone whereon is the name "Jack Carruthers," and underneath it that noble clause from the Creed—"I believe in the forgiveness of sins."

"Where have you been to-night, dear Meg?" And Meg, with the solemn light still shining in her eyes, would often answer:

"Half-way to Paradise and back. And the music seemed like angels' wings, and carried me away till the chords jarred. And then I went to Jack's grave and wished him good-night." And Meg would turn the wedding-ring round and round on her thin finger with a happy smile. And Rotha would know that that strange communion had strengthened and refreshed her, and that for many a day Meg would be bright, almost joyous.

But the anniversary of Jack's death had come round twice, and it was now more than five years since Robert had come up to Bryn to wish Rotha good-bye. More than five years, for then the rough March winds had been blowing, and now the soft May breezes swept refreshingly over the blue summer sea, and the primroses and the cowslips had long ago made golden hollows in the Burnley glens and Leatham woods, and the children went out in the fields to make daisy-chains, and to hunt in the hedges for brier-roses and bunches of pink and white May blossoms. And Meg had taken all her nurslings to drink fresh new milk at a farm, and to see the young calves and lambs and the brood of yellow ducklings at Gammer Stokes', and Rotha was up at the Vicarage helping Mary to arrange her plans for the Sunday school treat.

"Austin has decided that it must be Burnley-upon-Sea this time," began Mary, as Rotha entered the room. Mary was sitting on her low chair by the open window watching Arty playing on the lawn with his father. They were attempting a game of cricket, with Jock and Jasper as long-stops, and the root of an old tree for a stump. And, to enhance the glory of the game, Arty had already scored more than the Vicar. Arty had taken to a jacket and trousers now, and looked very boyish in his turned-down collar and blue ribbon. And Laurie, who was lying on the grass lazily watching them with his broad-brimmed straw hat tilted over his eyes, was now a tall thin stripling of fifteen, with a fair effeminate face, that had grown strangely like poor Belle's, and which bid fair to be almost as beautiful. In fact, Laurie's beauty and his laziness, his sweet voice and his lovable indolent ways, often made Mary and the Vicar anxious about their boy's future—Mary on account of his delicacy, and the Vicar for fear that his talents should outstrip his energy. But they need not have feared if they could have known the future. For the seeds of self-sacrifice and self-renunciation were somewhere hidden in Laurie's sweet nature, and came to light nobly at a fitting time ; for, having been trained by his own desire for the priesthood, he was one of the few who, on the great day of intercession for the missions, consecrated his fresh young life to the arduous work of a missionary ; and among the names of those who were reckoned as the first-fruits of that mighty prayer which pulsed through the length and breadth of England was the name of Laurence Garton Ord.

And the mother who gave up the flower of her flock to this noble work, and the fair young creature who had promised to follow his fortunes as soon as he can make a home for her in that foreign clime, will long remember the day when Laurie, coming out from the Church "ruddy and beautiful" as a young David, walked silently home beside them, and then, putting his arm round his mother, told them that he had dedicated himself to a distant ministry, and asked his father's blessing on his undertaking.

But on this May afternoon in question Laurie was nothing but a fair-haired stripling, graceful and lazy enough indeed to justify Rotha's name, still applied to him, of "the little king." Rufus, loose-limbed and freckled still, but handsome enough in his mother's eyes, had joined his uncle long ago in New York, and was doing well. "As sturdy and independent and Rufus-like as ever," wrote Robert. While Guy and Reuben, fine young men now—Guy nearly twenty-one—were two young undergraduates at Queen's. Reuben was a reading man, and hoped to take high honours, but Guy had joined the boating set ; they were still chums and inseparable, but Reuben, the younger and steadier, kept Guy straight, aud pulled him up every now and then when his fun and inexhaustible spirit were likely to get him into mischief. Both of them wrote to Rotha dutifully, and called her "the little mother," but Rube's letters are the more affectionate and frequent. Five years have passed very lightly over Rotha Maturin. She is seven-and-twenty now, but she hardly looks it ; she is a little thin and pale, slightly grave perhaps, but the sweet face is as calm and good as ever, and she looks a mere girl this afternoon in her fresh summer muslin, with her smooth brown hair and a breast-knot of lilies of the valley. There is a pretty dimple still when she speaks, and the large eyes grow bright and dark in a moment; it is only in repose that a vague air of sadness still lingers—a quiet curve or two, an added thoughtfulness on the brow, which would tell a keen observer that Rotha Maturin has not been exempt from her woman's lot of love and suffering.

" Austin says it must be Burnley-upon-Sea, after all," repeated Mary.

" I am sorry for it," replied Rotha quietly; and then the Vicar threw down his bat and came across the lawn to shake hands with Rotha.

Five years have made less havoc with the Vicar than with any one else; he is not thinner, of course, and he continues to mourn over his superfluous weight, which he has sometimes been heard to declare is worse than even St. Paul's thorn in the flesh, but the kind benignant face is as kind as ever, and the wide-open gray eyes are quite as keen, but the crisp curls are slightly tinged with gray; but Guy says his father is as young as ever, and Mary declares that Austin will never grow old, and the Vicar tells his wife privately that he is afraid that he is a boy still in his heart, for he likes a game as much as Arty does, only Arty runs faster and gets longer innings.

" Well, Mary, have you told Rotha the news?"

" No, dear; I've been leaving it to you," returned his wife, smiling. " He has been dying to tell you himself, Rotha, and so I would not spoil his pleasure."

" Oh! I know Nettie has another boy. I met Mr. Effingham, and he told me all about it. Aunt Eliza is so disappointed—she wanted a girl this time; she had quite made up her mind for a little Eliza, but Nettie and her husband both like sons best."

" ' My son's my son till he gets him a wife;' Mary is always saying that ever since Guy danced six times with Laura Tregarthen. Poor Mary! she does not understand calf-love; she thinks at twenty boys ought to think of nothing but their mother."

" Now, Austin, I call that too bad. Laura was a little flirt, or she would never have gone on so with Guy; and I do say, and say so still, that Lady Tregarthen has very frivolous young sisters-in-law, and if Guy is to marry I hope he will not choose such a giddy little thing as Laura for his wife."

" My dear, Guy will fall in love possibly with a dozen Lauras before he hits upon the right one; boys always do, and handsome ones like Guy especially; but here we are talking about Nettie and Guy, and quarrelling as usual, and Rotha has not heard the news yet."

" I can guess it is good news though, by the way you are rubbing your hands," said Rotha merrily.

" Ha, ha," laughed the Vicar, "so it is—so it is. Capital news—first-rate news—old Bobus is coming home."

" Robert coming home!" returned Rotha, feeling suddenly rather giddy. She felt a quick flush rise to her face, and turning her back for a moment on them both, went to the table and busied herself in finding some work. "When is he coming?" she said from a safe distance.

"When? Oh, he may be here any day; the letter has been detained, and ought to have reached us a week ago. He was on his way then. I will tell you all about it if you will leave that work alone and come here. I thought the news would have interested you."

"Oh, Mr. Ord!" returned Rotha, dismayed at this implied imputation of indifference. "Of course I am glad he is coming home—poor Robert!" but her voice was not very steady, and her face was growing hotter than ever under the Vicar's keen eyes. What would she have said if she had known that Robert in his despair had made his brother his confidant, and that Austin was looking at her and wondering whether Robert had really any chance, and whether he had been wrong in advising him to come home and try what three more years had done for him, and was speculating whether the sudden burning of Rotha's face meant only confusion or pleasure.

He was to remain in doubt on this point, for Rotha now regained her self-possession.

"Is he bringing Rufus with him, or will he come alone?" she asked presently.

"Oh no. Rufe is doing too well where he is, and Robert says that a year or two more of that work will be of great service to him; and that, though he is so young—barely eighteen—he is already a valuable assistant; he means to have him over by and by when an opening presents itself. Do you know, Rotha, I always guessed Mr. Ramsay would send for Robert when that accident disabled him. Poor man! he will never be able to go down to the work again."

"And is Robert to be manager there?" asked Rotha, not lifting her eyes.

"Yes; manager and partner too, I believe. He is to have double the salary he now receives, to begin with. The firm are very loath to part with him; but Robert says that he hardly feels justified in throwing away such a chance, and especially to refuse Mr. Ramsay after what he has done for him. Don't you think he is right?"

"Quite right," returned Rotha quickly; "only he said nothing to me about all this in his last letter, so I cannot help feeling a little surprised. I suppose he has made up his mind rather suddenly."

"Yes; he tells me that he had no idea when he last wrote.

By the bye, that explains a rather misty paragraph. He says—let me see, what is it he really does say?—oh ! here it is—' I am afraid Rotha, for one, will think me somewhat inconsistent after what I once said to her, but I think you can explain my reasons for acting on this sudden impulse, and why I cannot feel justified in refusing so kind a friend and benefactor as Mr. Ramsay. A man may sometimes alter his mind without being open to the imputation of weakness.' There, perhaps you can interpret that mysterious clause better than Mary and I can." But Rotha said nothing, and coloured so exceedingly that the Vicar rather abruptly changed the subject, and Mary, after a few warm expressions of pleasure at the thought of seeing dear Robert again, and wondering how he would look, and when he would arrive, and telling Rotha that Deb and she had been beautifying and arranging the spare room that very morning for his reception, in case he should come any day, took up the subject of the school-treat again, and assured Rotha for the third time that the Vicar and Mr. Tregarthen had already fixed on Burnley-upon-Sea. "You see we have exhausted all the places. We were at Nab Scar last year, and at Finnock's Hollow the summer before, and Burnley is so near, and the children can go by train, and it is so much less fatiguing for the teachers than jolting over those country roads in open carts ; so if you do not mind, dear—being your treat—Austin thinks he could save you expense and trouble that way, for the season is not far enough advanced to go a long distance, and the gardener's wife at the head of the glen could boil our kettles for us, and it would not be far to carry the hampers ; you know Austin can always get license for us."

Rotha was silent for a moment. It was more than five years ago now since Garton and Reuben and she had spent the day there, but she had only been there once since, and then quite alone. It was summer then, and she had walked where they had walked, and sat in the same place where she had sat, and dreamt of the fairy prince, and then lifted up her eyes to see Garton striding through the dim woodland aisles. She had taken a mournful pleasure in thus following his footprints, and in thinking what he had said and how he had looked, and it had seemed as though the very place were sacred to her ; it would jar on her sadly to see it again surrounded by merry and shouting children ; but she now banished this thought as selfish, and quietly told Mary that, if the Vicar wished it, there was nothing more to be said, and then, in her usual self-forgetful way, tried to throw herself into her friends' plans, and to calculate the number of buns and the pounds of seed and plum cake that would be wanted, but she had never found it such hard work to keep her attention on anything —she made a mistake in her addition twice, and Mary, with placid surprise, put her right.

She was undecided too, till the last minute, whether Meg should not go in her place; but on Mrs. Ord objecting to this, on the ground that it was Rotha's treat, and that she need not do anything to tire herself, that the children would amuse themselves, and that there was nothing but to give them their tea and marshal them to the train, she reluctantly consented; and then scolded herself again for her selfishness, and told Mary that she was getting old and lazy,·but of course she would go, and that perhaps Meg would be glad to be spared the fatigue; and, when this was settled, she rose to take her leave.

"But, Rotha dear, Mrs. Carruthers is out, and Austin fully expects that you are going to stay to tea," pleaded Mrs. Ord, "and we have not half discussed dear Robert's coming home." But Rotha would not be persuaded; she had some work to do for her children, she said, and should rather enjoy a quiet evening. She felt stupid and tired, and her head ached a little, and, if Mary did not mind, she would come round in the morning and arrange everything for Thursday, and she thought, after all, the Vicar had been right in fixing on Burnley.

If Rotha had any work to do she certainly did not do it that evening. Meg found her sitting at her window looking out at the sunset, as though she had been doing little else for hours.

It would be difficult to describe Rotha's exact feelings when she heard of the news of Robert's speedy arrival; but from the moment the words "he may come any day" had been spoken, a curious mixture of confusion, terror, and excitement had thrown her into such a whirl of conflicting emotions that she hardly realised herself what his coming home would be to her.

Three years had passed since she had answered that passionate letter of Robert's, and the correspondence which had been carried on between them had been in a measure somewhat constrained on both sides. Robert's letters especially had been brief and rather forced; and though he had never referred to his disappointment since then, even in the most distant manner, it was in a way brought home to Rotha in every word. Robert never spoke of himself now, never even answered her friendly questions as to his health and prospects. His letters related mainly to Rotha and her affairs, every trifle to which she had alluded was canvassed and magnified; but the unrestrained outpourings of the writer's heart seemed kept in check and forced back by a strong hand; only a tenderer phrase than usual sometimes conveyed to her that the writer himself was unchanged, patient but hopeless, and perhaps no eloquence could have touched Rotha's heart more deeply than those letters—so brief, yet so suggestive; so thoughtful for her, so forgetful of himself.

Once he had been ill, but Rotha never heard of it till long afterwards. He had met with an accident, and inflammation and fever had set in, and Austin told her one day very gravely that his life had been despaired of for days, and his recovery was chiefly owing to the watchful nursing of his landlady and her daughter.

Rotha wrote a reproachful letter to Robert after that, a letter full of sisterly affection and tenderness; but he wrote back in a little surprise, thanking her for her kindness. "I should not have thought that you would have cared so much whether I lived or died," it said. "I never fancy that I am much good to any one, or to myself either. I sometimes think that my life has been a failure, and that it would be better to go to one's long rest than to labour without hope in the heat of the day. When the labourer is weary he can go home. I have no home—not a soul belonging to me but Austin; the only woman who loved me lies under the grass sod. Sometimes I wonder why God permits such loneliness, such desolate hearths, such broken 'denied lives.' Forgive me, Rotha, I am weak still from recent illness, or I should not write like this. Just now, Rachel, my faithful nurse, brought me some nourishment, and told me I was getting faint, and must be more careful of myself. I will not tell you how I thanked her,—I was very ungrateful, and she went away with her eyes full of tears. Rachel is a good creature. She thinks I ought to put a higher value on my life. She little knows—— There, I will not finish that sentence. Good-night, Rotha. Thank you for your goodness to me, dear—I was going to write 'Sister,' but I have sworn never to call you by that name; I will substitute 'Friend.'—There; it is cold enough, it makes me shiver, but many a man might think himself rich with such a one; but not when he is sick and solitary—growing old, but still far enough off his end—as I am, Rotha. Adieu. ROBERT."

That was the last letter Rotha had received, nearly three months ago, and now he was coming home. She showed no one that letter, but put it away with mingled feelings of pleasure and pain. It was hardly in woman's nature not to be touched and made proud by this passionate fidelity—this patient hopelessness. For the first time she lost sight of Garton's love, to wonder upon the length and breadth of this man's affection, that could survive distance and time and disappointment, that could refuse to be satisfied with the crumbs of her comfort. "Could Garton have loved me better?" she thought, as though for the first time she realised Robert's feelings in all their intensity, and a little fear and trembling seized her. She thought, "What if he should ever renew his suit? Would her purpose remain as unflinching and steadfast as it had done three years ago? Would Garton wish it? Would Belle?" But at this point she always broke off, shrinking from her own thoughts, trembling and blushing even in the darkness, and, folding her hands, would pray that He who had guided her through her troubled youth, and had brought her feet out on these pleasant places, would lead her still through the shadows of the future in a plain path; but not now, because of her enemies.

These petitions always calmed her, but to-night they failed. The mere recollection of the words "coming any day" threw her into a state of distressing restlessness and excitement, a longing to go away somewhere, to fly from some inevitable fate which seemed to come upon her. She resolved to avoid the Vicarage, to shut herself up in the fortress of Bryn, to live at the "Home," to do anything, in short, to put off the evil day of their meeting; and yet, such was her inconsistency, she longed to be somewhere that she might see him without his being aware of her presence. "Just to see him, and to be sure that it is Robert, and that he is well and safe, and to go away where he could not find me, or ever say what he said to me in those letters."

These were some of Rotha's thoughts; but it would be difficult to describe half of them. The leading idea seemed to be terror at what Robert might say to her, and yet in her secret heart she rejoiced at the knowledge that he was still unchanged. She fell asleep trying to recollect the contents of his last letter, and awoke depressed and restless, and passed a most unsatisfactory day, and, as often happened, everything jarred with her mood: the children were troublesome, and Caroline had a raging toothache and was obliged to go down to the Infirmary; Meg was called off in the middle of the afternoon by the Vicar, and Rotha had to take her place just as she was most longing for quiet.

The children had got through their stage of fractiousness by this time, and were playing at Nebuchadnezzar and the burning fiery furnace. The game struck Rotha as slightly profane, but she was languid, and lacked energy to interfere. It struck her as rather droll, however, that Shirtle Pearl, who was still there, should enact the part of Nebuchadnezzar and the Golden Image as well, and she got once or twice slightly confused over it; and she could not understand for a long time why the youngest boy there should be playing the Jew's harp industriously in the corner, till he told Shirtle crossly that he wasn't going to play Dulcimers for ever, and that he thought it a stupid game, which woke her up in earnest; and after she had reprimanded Shirtle gravely, and had taken the refractory Dulcimer on her lap, she told them a story, and then made them sing the hymns Meg had taught them, and told them softly about the Child Christ, who had come to their beds when they were little and weak, with His arms full of tiny crosses, and had laid one down by the side of each child, bidding them carry them bravely for His sake.

"And what sort of cross did the Child Christ leave you, Shirtle?" asked Rotha.

"I think it was a knobbly one, mother," returned Shirtle promptly, for Shirtle was an orphan, a mere waif and stray cast upon Thornborough streets, and Rotha had classed him among her adopted children. "A wery knobbly one, bursting out with abysses and such like."

"I should think being almost dark is worser than abysses," put in Sallie, a diminutive child with a patient sickly face and a shade over her eyes. "Shirtle can learn to spell, and cast up, and read pretty picture books, though his bones is so sore that he cries sometimes."

"But Sallie can pick up shells and dig on the sand, and feel the sweet sea-breeze—can she not?" returned Rotha, putting her hand tenderly on the cropped head, for she knew that by and by it would be quite dark, and not almost, with Sallie. "And what did the Child Christ say to little Sallie when he laid on her this heavy cross?"

"Carry it, and it will carry you," returned the child in her shrill little voice.

"Yes; and, heavy as it is, it is not so heavy as His—we must remember that. And when do we lay down our crosses, children?"

"Never" returned one, and "When we die" responded others; and one small boy opined, "When their backs ached or they were tired;" but he was a cripple and a hunchback, and spoke feelingly, and every one knew that poor Teddy was breaking down under the weight of his.

"Oh, Teddie, I wish we could!" said Rotha, with a compassionate glance at the deformed boy. "I wish we could lay them down, Teddie, sometimes, you and Sallie and I—when we are so tired, and our hearts and arms are so sore with the weight!" And, in that fanciful imagery so dear to children, she told them they must lie down in their narrow beds with their crosses beside them to the last—they and their crosses under the shadow of one mighty one; and how they must carry them right up to the Golden Gate itself, and there, laying them down for ever, should receive tiny jewelled crowns; and where their crosses had fallen should spring up roses, white and red, and lilies fairer than any they had seen, and the Child Christ should lead them into the City—cripples, and blind, and suffering no longer. "Now children, sing the hymn Meg taught you last Sunday," and the children united their weak quavering voices and sang "We are but little children weak," but the Dulcimer had gone fast asleep, and Teddie came and laid his heavy head against Rotha's dress.

## WON AT LAST.

'Some one came and rested there beside me,
　　Speaking words I never thought would bless
Such a loveless life ; I longed to hide me,
　　Feasting lonely on my happiness.
　　　　But the voice I heard
　　　　Pleaded for a word,
　　Till I gave my whispered answer, 'Yes.'

"Yes ; that little word so calmly spoken
　　Changed all life for me, my own, my own !
All the cold gray spell I saw upbroken,
　　All the twilight days seemed past and gone,
　　　　And how warm and bright
　　　　In the ruddy light
　　Pleasant June days of the future shone !

"So we wandered through the gate together,
　　Hand in hand, upon our future way,
Leaving shade and cold behind for ever,
　　Out to where the red sun's westering ray
　　　　Gave a promise fair
　　　　Of such beauty rare
　　For the dawning of another day."
　　　　　　　　　HELEN MARION BURNSIDE.

THE Sunday school treat was fixed for the following day, and when the children were safe in their dormitories Rotha meant to go round to the Vicarage to make the final arrangements with Mrs. Ord.

It was a lovely evening, and the setting sun streamed into the long low room where Rotha sat among the little ones; the children had broken down in the middle of the hymn, and Rotha's sweet voice took up the refrain and hummed it softly with a sort of weird accompaniment from Teddie; the rest crooned out a dolorous chorus of "We don't know it, mother," when the garden gate suddenly clicked. Fidgets, who was fast asleep, got up and limped to the door on three legs and began a furious barking,

every hair bristling with excitement.   Firm footsteps crunched up
the garden-path, voices were heard in the little passages, the door
of the mother's room opened and closed quickly.

"Run and tell the Vicar I am here, Joe," said Rotha, breaking off her humming ; "and, children, do not forget to get up and
curtsey to him."

"May we come in, little sister?" said the Vicar's cheerful
voice over Joe's head.   "Do not let the children disturb themselves ; they look far too comfortable.   No, do not come in just
yet," he continued to somebody in the background.   "Guess what
visitor I have brought to see you, Rotha?"

"That is not hardly fair," returned a well-remembered voice ;
"let me introduce myself, Austin."   A firm hand puts the Vicar
aside—a dark figure blocks up the entry, a tall man, gray-haired,
with a worn handsome face.   Rotha stands up, white and
trembling, with the sleeping boy still in her arms—it is Robert !

"Rotha, are you surprised to see me?   I did not mean to
startle you like this."

Her only disengaged hand is taken and pressed kindly, and
then Robert replaces her in her seat.   She has not spoken one
word of welcome—not one, except that low uttered "Robert !"
—but her heart is beating so that she can hardly breathe.

"That is not a very warm greeting after five years' absence,"
says the Vicar mischievously ; and Robert, gravely as before, just
touches her cheek with his lips, and says quietly that Austin
has brought him in to see the little sister in the midst of her
children, and that he is glad to see her looking so strong and
well, and so on.   All spoken in the same calm kind manner, as
though the blood that swept over Rotha's pale face did not stir
every pulse within him at the thought that he had the power to
stir her thus, that those burning blushes and quivering lips could
not mean only that he had taken her unawares.

"I hope you do not mind my bringing him in like this?
Robert was so anxious to see you," said the Vicar, trying to put
a stop to this painful embarrassment.   "You are so completely
one of us, you know, Rotha ; and Mary said she was sure you
would be pleased to see him."

"I am very pleased," returned Rotha, finding her voice with
difficulty.   "When did you come?" lifting her eyes timidly to
Robert, who was leaning against the mantelpiece watching her.

"Only an hour ago ; I got off the dust of my journey, and
talked to Mary and Austin a little, and then Mary proposed our
coming round to fetch you.   How well dear Mary looks, to be
sure ! and as pretty as ever ; only her hair is so gray—not so gray

as mine though." And he tossed it carelessly from his forehead as he spoke. "Do you not think me very changed, Rotha?"

"Very much changed. You look as though you had been very ill," she returned softly. She was regaining her calmness at the sight of his, but her colour still varied dangerously.

Yes, he was changed, wonderfully so; but she thought she had never seen a nobler face. His dark hair was quite iron-gray, though he was hardly more than thirty-six; and his face was thinner and paler, and the forehead deeply lined. But the hard-set curve of the lips had relaxed, and the curve round the mouth was exceedingly sweet and sorrowful; only when he smiled, which he did rarely, his smile was like Gar's.

"I was very near death," he returned, reading the unspoken sympathy in her eyes. "I suppose if I had not been with good Samaritans it would soon have been all over with me. Rachel cried when she received your present, Rotha. When I gave it to her I said it was so like the little sister that Austin talks about."

He had used the Vicar's title twice, but not as though he had appropriated it. Was it merely to put her at her ease with him, or to remind her that he had no hope? Somehow the name jarred on her for the first time.

"You do not find Rotha much altered, do you, Robert?" struck in the Vicar briskly. Rotha's eyes fell again before Robert's swift keen glance.

"No; she is not a day older.' How do you manage to preserve your youth, Rotha—you look so young? And do you always wear that little cap? Do you know, it reminds me of the day I met you first in the Castle gardens? You had a cap on then, had you not?"

"No; only a lace kerchief tied over my hair," returned Rotha, with a smile. "This is our uniform, Meg's and mine," she continued hurriedly. She knew intuitively why Robert looked so grave. Would he ever forget that day when he saw her under the low apple trees, a slim creature in her black dress? It made her speak to him in her own frank way to see that look of pain on his face. "Meg will be so glad to see you, Robert."

"Ah, to be sure. Poor Mrs. Carruthers! I was so sorry to hear about her trouble; but you told me in one of your last letters that she has been more settled ever since. How good you have been, Rotha, to write to me so often!"

"You were lonely, and I knew you would like to hear about everything," she returned, beginning to get hot again.

"You have no idea what letters she can write," he continued, turning to his brother, who had half a dozen of the children round his knee, and was talking to them in an undertone. "They used to be like a series of pictures to me, and clever pictures too. I don't think all these five years I have ever had to ask after anybody."

"We did not know you were a scribe, Rotha," returned the Vicar, laughing; "but here we are keeping Mary and tea waiting. Do you know we have orders to carry you off?"

"Indeed! But I do not think I can leave just yet; I have my working dress on, and the children are not in bed, and——"

"Perhaps not," interrupted the Vicar; "but Mrs. Carruthers is on her way to help Caroline, so that excuse has fallen through. And as for the working dress, if you want to honour Robert by a festive attire, we will willingly escort you to Bryn; but I can assure you that that gray serge is quite as becoming in our eyes as gray silk would be." A mischievous little speech which made Robert smile, and after that Rotha would have gone in gray sackcloth, if there were such a material; but as she still hesitated, though for far different reasons, Robert settled the matter by lifting the drowsy Dulcimer off her lap and, taking out his watch, told her that they would wait for her just five minutes—a piece of peremptoriness which reminded her of the old Robert Ord, and brought one of her sunny smiles back in an instant.

Rotha was in a curious state of mind all the evening; an uneasy sort of happiness, too nearly approaching nervous excitement to quite deserve that name, seemed to be the prominent feeling; it was very strange and very pleasant to have Robert back again. Now for the first time she realised how she had missed him, and what a blank his absence had made. The Vicarage had never looked so like itself for five years, and the Vicar seemed so wondrously content and so proud of Robert, and the boys hung about their uncle eager for news of Rufus, and the family tea-table had never looked more cheerful than it did to-night.

Rotha was very quiet and kept in the background all the evening, but no one seemed to notice it. For Robert and Austin had so much to say to each other, and were so busy in discussing the former's prospects, and every one had so many things to tell him and so much to hear, that no one seemed to perceive what a silent listener Rotha was; and though now and then Robert turned to her with a quiet word or smile, as though to show her presence was by no means forgotten, he never once strove to bring her into the conversation. But more than once the uneasy conviction seized her that her silence was understood and respected. And deeply as this thoughtfulness and delicacy touched her, it made her still more conscious. Now and then she started and flushed painfully as some tone or some expression of Robert's recalled Garton vividly. She had never thought the brothers alike, but a hundred times this evening some trick or turn of Robert's voice brought him before her. Now and then she could look at him unperceived, and then she was struck afresh by the great change in him; and once or twice the thought crossed her, of what noble metal the man must have been made that the fire of suffering had so purified and strengthened him.

She had been perfectly content in her quiet corner, but she was more than ever tongue-tied and embarrassed when he walked with her to her own door. A dread of being alone with him, a terror of what he might say under these circumstances, was strong within her when she went out of the Vicarage gate. But she need not have been afraid. Robert seemed bent on putting her at her ease. Nothing could exceed his quiet gentleness. He spake about the beauty of the night, and asked Rotha if she ever took long walks now. And he described an excursion Rufus and he had taken, which lasted till they had got to Bryn; and then he shook hands with her and bade her good-night, as though he had been doing so every evening for the last five years.

Rotha gave up her thoughts in despair when she reached her own room. To disentangle and arrange such a hopeless confusion of ideas was next to impossible. A sense of disappointment and regret—inconsistent regret—at Robert's calmness and brotherly kindness were the paramount feelings; it increased her admiration and respect tenfold, but it humiliated her. He had loved her for five years, and only three months ago had hinted at his despair. But now he was by far the calmer of the two, and she herself had been taken unawares, and had betrayed her embarrassment in a hundred ways. The calmer of the two! What if she had looked out that very moment and seen the lonely figure pacing up and down the sea-wall for hours?—could see him standing in the moonlight beside Belle's grave, and leaning his hot brow against the marble cross, and could hear him say, "Dearer than ever— the one face—the one woman in the world—to me. Oh, my God! to see her every day and not to win her, will be more than I can bear. I must—I will win her! Something tells me that I shall, Rotha."

The next day was that appointed for the school treat, and Rotha had promised to be round at the Vicarage as early as possible to help Mary and Aunt Eliza pack the hampers. But, early as it was, Robert had already started for Stretton, where he would probably be detained the greater part of the morning.

Rotha felt a little chill of disappointment, for she had quite made up her mind to be her old self with him to-day. It relieved her, therefore, and sent quite a glow of satisfaction to her heart, when the Vicar casually remarked to Aunt Eliza that she would certainly have her wish to see Robert gratified that very afternoon, for he had promised him faithfully to take the four o'clock train from Blackscar, and to be present at the distribution of buns; and, as he always kept his word, she might be certain that he would make his appearance at the time specified.

Rotha said nothing, but she worked with redoubled zeal, and at the appointed hour joined the phalanx of teachers and children on the Blackscar platform, looking singularly appropriate to the occasion in her pretty spring dress—a soft blue—with her white chip hat. Dress always set off Rotha, but she never looked prettier than she did to-day, as Mary remarked to the Vicar and to Aunt Eliza about half a dozen times.

There was nothing worth recording in the afternoon itself. As in most other school treats, the children were wild with pleasure, and ran all over the glens like a herd of young colts. Rotha strove once or twice, in quiet moments, to bring back the sweet and mournful associations of the place, but for once the effort was manifest. The day was so glorious, the sunshine so bright, the play of light and shade so delicious in the bosky dells and hollows, the little river ran underneath so brimming over with ripples and tiny gurgles of joy, the children's mirth was so infectious, the knots of eager rosy faces such warm vivid pictures set in the green bowery depths, that a less happy nature than Rotha's must have expanded to the cheering influences; and more than one bright thought kept her pulses beating to a tune they had not heard for many a long year, as she walked up and down the shady walks, or sat on one of the tiny lawns keeping watch and ward over the little ones. But about five o'clock, when the children were ranged in orderly files on one of the green lawns, and the Vicar was called upon to say grace, Rotha's eyes often wandered to the little white gate in the hope of seeing a tall figure advancing from the road; but tea was over and the children scattered to their games again, and still no Robert made his appearance.

Mr. Townsend, the Vicar of Burnley, had just entered the gardens, and Rotha was slightly surprised when, after a brief conversation, our Vicar walked quickly to the gate with him. She was tolerably near them, and saw that both looked rather grave and anxious, the Vicar especially; and the latter spoke almost irritably to some boys who surrounded him with entreaties to join their game.

" Run away, children, I can't attend to you now. Now, Sam, don't block up our way, please ; Mr. Townsend and I have business in the town." And he swung round one small lad who was in his path so hastily that he nearly tripped him up.

" Elliot," said Rotha, addressing a young Sunday-school teacher who had been with the Vicar most of the time, " what has Mr. Townsend been saying to make the Vicar look so grave ? "

" Haven't you heard ?" returned young Elliot eagerly. " All the teachers have been talking about it : there's been an accident to the Blackscar train—some collision, I believe ; and two or three people have been killed. Murray heard it in the town."

Rotha turned suddenly white, and then began to shiver.

" What train, Elliot ?"

" Why, the four o'clock from Blackscar—a goods train or something ran into it. There are not many people hurt—only the engine-driver and the stoker and one passenger were killed. The line will not be clear for another hour or two, and that's why the Vicar has gone up to the station."

" No, no," returned Rotha, half beside herself ; " don't you know his brother was to be in that train ? Oh, Elliot, for mercy's sake, don't say anything to Mrs. Ord. Suppose anything has happened to his brother. There, go, go ; don't you see Mr. Tregarthen is calling you ? "

" We are going to take some of the children on the pier," called out Mr. Tregarthen ; " the ladiés and the younger ones can stop behind, if they like. You know there is no possibility of getting home for another hour or two."

Rotha heard no more. She was in a high winding walk, just under the suspension bridge and near the entrance to the gardens ; and feeling giddy, and even her limbs tottering, she sat down, thankful that no one was witness to her violent agitation.

A collision, a railway accident, and he was in it—that was her first thought ; he—Robert—Garton's brother, the man who had loved her so patiently and so hopelessly for more than five years, and whom, as she knew too well by this terrible heartache, she was already beginning to love in return. Poor Rotha ! it needed this shock to reveal the real nature of her feelings for Robert. For months past—ever since his last letter—she had been fighting against her own heart, and hiding her eyes like a child from the destiny that was in store for her. This had been the secret of her trembling eagerness to escape a meeting. One word from him whose fidelity she had so severely tested might in a moment, she knew, overthrow the resolutions of years. And if she had doubted her heart even yesterday, one glance at Robert's face, with its evidence of suffering, would have undeceived her; and now—now, when he might be lost to her for ever, mortally hurt, or even dead—now did she realise for the first time that, however she might have tried to blind herself, her heart was assuredly and entirely his.

But to have another lover destroyed in such a cruel way— impossible, merciful God, impossible !'

"Why are you sitting here alone, and where are they all gone ? Good heavens, are you ill, Rotha ?"

He might have thought so by the way she uncovered her white face and looked at him, and then clung to his arm with her two hands, trembling from head to foot.

"Robert, is it really you—alive—unhurt ? Oh, Robert, Robert, what a fright you have given us ! Oh, I thought it must be too terrible to be true," cried the girl, with her eyes brimming over and her face perfectly radiant.

"What is too terrible ? Do you mean you have heard of the accident to the Blackscar train ? I galloped round as fast as Mr. Ramsay's horse would take me, that I might arrive before any one heard of the affair. I was afraid Austin would be frightened, but I hardly thought—I hardly hoped—that——"

He did not finish his sentence, but his own face worked, and he was evidently greatly moved at this frank expression of joy at his safe return. For the moment he held the little hands tightly in his, and then with a sudden impulse lifted first one and then the other to his lips.

"I did not expect such a sweet welcome, Rotha. How could you—how could you care so much, my darling ?"

But Rotha, scarlet and confounded at her own impulsive words, started away from him like a young fawn.

"Where is the Vicar, Robert? We must go and tell the Vicar; he has gone down to the station with Mr. Townsend."

"Come then," said Robert, holding out his hand, with a smile.

He had no wish to take advantage of the sweet impulse that had made her cling to him. For this evening at least he would respect the shy reticence that had grown out of her impulsiveness. He walked beside her with a proud and swelling heart, but out- wardly as calm and kind as ever ; but Rotha, who had overheard his last words, drooped her head and answered in monosyllables, and, as soon as she caught sight of the Vicar, took shelter under his wing directly.

The Vicar did not say much, but he looked from one to the other, and held out his hand to Robert with an unsteady smile.

"We have had a terrible fright, Robert, and I hear Edward

Elliot told her, and so she knew it too. I would not go through the last half-hour again for half my income. By what providential means did you manage to miss your train ?"

" Mr. Ramsay detained me, Austin ; and while I was waiting on the platform, chafing like a blind fool at the tiresome delay, we got news of the collision just outside Leatham Junction ; and, knowing what a horrible state you would be in, I went round to the mews where I had put Mr. Ramsay's bay mare, and rode her off to Burnley as hard as I could, and here I am."

" For His mercy endureth for ever," ejaculated the Vicar. " Oh, Bob, if I had been called upon to lose another brother— and you only just come home ! " And Robert, touched by his agitation, linked his arm in his brother's, and the two walked away together.

The line was pretty clear by this time, and the officials informed the Vicar that a special train would be ready in half an hour. So Rotha went down on the pier with the other teachers to marshal the children and hunt after stragglers. The work and the cool sea-breezes did her good, and she was successful in holding herself aloof from Robert during the return journey. She got into a different compartment, and as soon as they reached Blackscar she headed the first division of the children to the schoolhouse, where they were to receive a final bun each ; and Robert, who had to see after his horse, was left far enough behind.

Rotha left the other teachers at the schoolhouse and went off alone, in reality to get herself quieted for the evening, for Mrs. Ord had made her promise to come to the Vicarage to supper to talk over the events of the day. The church was always open, and it seemed to her the quietest place. It did not matter one bit that Meg was playing there ; she slipped into a dark pew by the door and listened to the solemn strains, feeling rested and soothed in spite of herself. She was so absorbed by the music and her own thoughts as well that she was quite unaware that after a time she had been followed, and that a tall dark figure had silently entered and taken up its station near her, awed and silenced by the weird music that seemed to peal out of the semi-darkness.

Rotha rose and went out after a time, and then paused as usual by Belle's grave to readjust the wreath which always hung over the cross. Yesterday Rotha had placed a fresh one made of sweet spring flowers, but already it was withered; a mournful conviction that this withered garland was a meet emblem of Belle's unfinished life and broken hopes crept over Rotha, and, as she laid her cheek to the marble cross, where only last night Robert had rested his weary head, she said more than half aloud :

" Poor Belle, how well she loved him ! But I can understand
it now. Ah, it is coming; I know it; I am sure of it, if only Gar
would have had it so !"

" What is coming, Rotha ? Why would Gar not have it so ?
Dear, I did not mean to startle you. I could not help following
you here." A hand is laid softly on her arm; the voice is very
calm and reassuring. What does she fear that she lays her cheek
only the closer to the marble cross, and clings more tightly to its
smooth stoniness ?

Only a churchyard—a white gleaming cross—the moon shining
from behind a bank of dark fleecy clouds ; only a tale of love told
over a grassy mound ; only a girl listening to it with her arms
entwined about the marble headstone ; only the tears from happy
eyes watering the dead girl's grave with dews of blessing for the
living, and a voice with a tender break in it like Gar's says :

" Just one word, Rotha—one word to tell me that you have
listened and heard ; or, if you cannot speak, put your hand in
mine and I shall understand you then."

What if her hand goes out to him in the darkness ? What if
strong arms draw her from her stony support, and gather her close
to a faithful breast ? Can she check those happy tears flowing all
the faster for his mute tenderness ? Presently, when she grows
calmer, she lifts up her face to him—that dear face which he has
learnt to read so clearly now—and asks him if he will take her
back into the church for a little while.

And as he yields, in some little surprise, the music breaks into
some grander measure, swelling triumphant down the echoing
aisles ; and then he understands that this is their betrothal,
and kneels beside her in that mute thanksgiving prayer of hers ;
and then, as the music ceases and Meg leaves the organ, Rotha
comes out of the porch hand in hand with Robert, and walks down
with him to the Vicarage.

# CHAPTER XLII.

## CONCLUSION.

"Ah, who am I, that God hath saved
  Me from the doom I did desire,
And crossed the lot myself had craved,
  To set me higher ?
What have I done that He should bow
From heaven to choose a wife for me ?
And what deserved He should endow
  My home with thee ?"          JEAN INGELOW.

. . . . "My story is told out ; the day
Draws out its shadows, time doth overtake
The morning.  That which endeth call a lay
Sang after pause—a motto in the break
Between two chapters of a tale not new
Nor joyful, but a common tale.  Adieu ! "          *Ibid.*

THEY were at supper at the Vicarage when they entered, but Mrs. Ord had hardly time for a reproachful exclamation before the Vicar, after one glance at Rotha's happy blushing face, had jumped from his seat and had fairly taken her in his arms.

"Is it so ?  God bless you, my dear child.  You have made us all very happy.  Won at last, and bravely too.  Dear old Bobus ! There, take her to Mary."

But Mary, startled and overwhelmed by what were to her such utterly unexpected tidings, could only hold Rotha in her arms and cry over her, and hope inarticulately that she would be happy, very happy.

"That she shall be, God helping me," said· Robert quietly. "Mother Mary, are you not going to wish me happiness too ?"

And, as he stooped his handsome head over her, she put back the gray waves of hair tenderly from his forehead and whispered, "Dear Robert, I am so glad, and our darling would be glad too," and then hid her face—poor Mary—on his shoulder and cried, remembering how, ten years ago, he had come to her for her sisterly congratulations.

"Dear Mary, I understand you."

It was a proof of Robert's new gentleness that he should soothe this burst of natural feeling so patiently and kindly. Rotha was looking shy and almost sad over this little scene, but Robert presently came to her side with a quiet happy smile, and Austin soon cheered up his wife, and the remainder of the evening passed like a delightful dream. Robert walked as usual with Rotha to her own door, but before they parted he said a grave word or two that somewhat upset her.

" I shall leave everything to you, Rotha; but do not let it be long before you become my wife. For five years I waited for a blessing which never came, and for five more I suffered almost hopeless, and now I feel as though many of my best years are gone ; but you must come to me soon, dear, and make me young again."

Rotha pondered over these words, and grew hot and cold over them, but for a little time nothing more was said to mar the beautiful serenity of those first few days when Robert and she were always together ; and she learnt hour by hour to appreciate still more fully the noble nature of the man who was to be her future husband, when the traces of his past faults became beauties in her eyes, and she could realise more and more that it was good to lean on the strong arm that was to be hers through life.

Rotha had respite for a little while, during which she learnt to know herself and Robert more thoroughly, days during which Meg and Mary were never weary of praising the sweet face that had grown so calm and trustful under its new happiness ; and then came a day when Mary and the Vicar came to her, and when Robert pleaded in a few manly strong words that there should be no delay, no dallying with time.

" I shall never grow younger, darling, and I think you know me well enough by this time to trust me with your happiness. I want my wife, to have her dear presence always near me, strengthening me."

And Rotha, with the look of meek love she already bore for him, slipping her little hand in his, said :

" Whenever you like, dear Robert, and the Vicar wishes," and quietly yielded the point, when they all said that it was no use waiting till the autumn, but that they thought she might be ready by the middle of August, and, when it was pressed upon her, Rotha said she thought so too.

Mary and Meg soon had their hands full of delightful business, and Rotha was quite passive in their hands. She did everything that her friends thought right. One or two of the rooms in Bryn were to be remodelled for the new master, and Meg, by her own desire, was to take up her abode in the Children's Home.

Rotha took far more interest in these arrangements than in ordering her fine new dresses. She made Robert come up to Bryn and look at his old rooms before the painters and whitewashers turned everything topsy-turvy. Robert was strangely moved at these evidences of his boyhood, and at Rotha's care in preserving them. He knew all about her full-grown heir by this time, for one day the Vicar basely betrayed her confidence in her presence. Robert went all over Bryn, from the garret to the basement, telling Rotha many anecdotes of his old life. He made her show him Aunt Charlotte's jewels, and further stipulated that the pearls were to be worn on her wedding-day; and before he left he drew her to him, and told her in grave tender tones how her generosity and magnanimity had humiliated him long years ago, and how the bitterness of his accusation had recoiled upon himself, and made his life for a long time barren; and how little he deserved to spend his future days under the shelter of that roof from which his bad temper and obstinacy had driven him, and how still less he deserved the crowning glory of her love.

"My future life shall be one long act of gratitude and atonement if I am spared," he finished, and Rotha, who knew his faithfulness and integrity, felt certain he would keep his words.

The summer, with its pleasant courting days, passed away only too quickly for Rotha. Robert spent all his leisure hours with her, either at Bryn or at the Vicarage. He had a horse of his own now, a wedding present from Mr. Ramsay, and rode to and from Stretton every morning and evening. By and by, when it was in the stable at Bryn, a beautiful bay mare made its appearance from the same munificent donor, and Robert ordered a riding-habit from London, and taught Rotha to ride, and was not at all surprised when she made a splendid horsewoman.

"My wife does everything well," was a speech very often in Robert's mouth.

But at present Rotha had neither horse nor habit, but was quite content when Robert took her out for long country walks in the sweet summer evenings. They went over to Burnley once or twice, and Rotha told Robert all the girlish fancies she had had in the dim wintry woods.

But she loved best to take him to her Children's Home, and see him gather the children round his knee and tell them stories of the New World and its wonders; and before long Rotha found she would have a true helpmeet in all her benevolent schemes. Robert's large-heartedness and his secret ways of doing good were proverbial in the family; he threw himself into Rotha's plans for the new Home with an enthusiasm which surprised her, until she

30

learnt more and more how his deep still nature loved to do good for its own sake, and thought nothing too small if it could benefit a suffering brother or sister.

"You can build the Home, if you like, next summer, Rotha," he said to her one day. "I have been looking over your accounts as you wish, and I see you have a large surplus sum at the bankers, in spite of your munificent deed of gift to Reuben and Guy; and although the expenses of your two sons' education are very great, I think we can afford it, for I am a tolerably rich man now, and Laurie is going to be my charge."

"We can do so and so"—how sweet that used to sound in Rotha's ears! Never to be alone any more, to have Robert to work with her, to direct her with his man's counsel and strengthen her hands with his praise; what a rest to the lonely girl who had fought such a fierce battle, and who had accepted her bitter stewardship so bravely! No need to keep it all for him any longer, who prized one word of love from her lips more than the wealth and comforts she could give him; no need to keep it all for him when she had given herself into that faithful keeping.

It was the evening before her marriage; it had been a busy trying day in spite of Meg's efforts to lighten her labours; and Rotha, when she came down to Robert, looked pale and harassed, a trifle moved from her serenity. And Robert, understanding how she felt, took her down on the shore that the fresh sea-breezes might blow her fatigue away, and let her stand there silently by his side undisturbed by questioning, till the tired eyes, dazzled by pomp of finery and the unreality of bridal garments, might grow rested by the calm of summer seas and evening shadows.

It was a proof of his unselfishness that he never spoke of his own exceeding happiness, or reminded her by look or word that this was the last evening that she would be Rotha Maturin. Now and then he spoke to her, but only of the scene that lay before them, till he was rewarded by seeing the ruffled brow grow calm again, and the old colour come back to the weary face.

"Dear Rotha, they ought not to have let you tire yourself like this. I shall take better care of you than that."

"They could not help it, Robert; there was so much to do, and Mr. Tracy came so late. I don't mind now. I am getting rested, I always do with you," and Rotha leant gratefully on the strong arm that loved to support her.

Presently, of her own accord, she asked him if they should walk towards the churchyard, as service was over, and it would be quite quiet now. Robert answered that it was just what he wished; but that he had feared to tire her by proposing it; and then they slowly retraced their steps.

They stood for a long time silently by the marble cross, till Robert saw the tears in Rotha's eyes, and questioned her gently.

"I ought not to have brought you here to-night, my darling."

"Why not, Robert? It is so quiet and beautiful up here; and see how the soft wind sweeps over the grass, as she said. Robert, I can't help thinking of Gar to-night."

"Oh, Rotha!" he drew her towards him sorely troubled, almost jealously; "not of Gar to-night, surely darling."

"Happily—only happily. Nay, Robert, you never thought that. I was so wishing he could see us to-night. I think he would be so glad, Robert."

"My darling, why should we doubt it? Surely the knowledge of our happiness, if they know it, will be as precious as ever to their sainted souls. But, Rotha, I am only a poor earthly lover, and earthly love is prone to jealousy and doubt. Tell me, dearest, if at this moment one shadow of regret for the past, one fear for the future, is in your heart to-night; for, as surely as we have crossed over two graves to each other, I believe that God intended each for each and none other."

Rotha looked up in his face, a little moved by his passion.

"Do you mean if I regret Gar still, Robert?"

He made an affirmative motion, but did not trust himself to speak.

She stole her hand in his. "What do you think, Robert?"

"My darling, it is for you to ánswer and not I."

It was nearly dark now, and she took up the hand she held and kissed it, as though that were the fittest expression of her love; but closing her suddenly in his arms he prayed her to tell him.

"Oh, Robert, to think you need my words still! Do you know, Gar once told me that I had not given him all that was in me to give, and now I feel he was right."

"What then, love?"

"I have given it all now!" And then, speaking with her face hidden, "God has taken Gar, and for a long time I was inconsolable, now I know it was for the best; for if he had lived I should have loved him well, no doubt, but not as I shall love you." And, as he pressed her to his heart, the anguish of that doubt died away out of Robert Ord's heart for ever.

THE END.

*F. D. & Co.*    *Printed by* R. & R. CLARK, *Edinburgh.*

*6s. Volumes.*

# BENTLEY'S
# FAVOURITE NOVELS.

## LIST FOR 1892.

# BENTLEY'S FAVOURITE NOVELS

Each work can be had separately, price 6s., of all Booksellers in
Town or Country.

---

### By ROSA N. CAREY.

*Nellie's Memories.*
*Barbara Heathcote's Trial.*
*Heriot's Choice.*
*Mary St. John.*
*Not like Other Girls.*
*Only the Governess.*
*Queenie's Whim.*
*Robert Ord's Atonement.*
*Uncle Max.*
*Wee Wifie.*
*Wooed and Married.*

### By MARY LINSKILL.

*Between the Heather and
the Northern Sea.*
*The Haven under the Hill.*
*In Exchange for a Soul.*

### By W. E. NORRIS.

*Thirlby Hall.*
*A Bachelor's Blunder.*
*Major and Minor.*
*Miss Shafto.*
*The Rogue.*

### By JANE AUSTEN.

(The only *complete* Editions of
Miss Austen's Works are Messrs.
Bentleys'.)

*Emma.*
*Lady Susan,* and
    *The Watsons.*
*Mansfield Park.*
*Northanger Abbey,* and
    *Persuasion.*
*Pride and Prejudice.*
*Sense and Sensibility.*

### By MARIE CORELLI.

*A Romance of Two Worlds.*
*Thelma.*
*Ardath.*
*Vendetta.*
*Wormwood.*

### By MAARTEN MAARTENS.

*The Sin of Joost Avelingh.*
*An Old Maid's Love.*

### By ANTHONY TROLLOPE.

*The Three Clerks.*

### By Mrs. ALEXANDER.

*The Wooing o't.*
*Her Dearest Foe.*
*Look before you Leap.*
*The Executor.*
*Which Shall it Be?*

### By HAWLEY SMART.

*Breezie Langton.*

### By Mrs. RIDDELL.

*George Geith of Fen Court.*
*Berna Boyle.*

### By Mrs. PARR.

*Adam and Eve.*
*Dorothy Fox.*

### By E. WERNER.

*Fickle Fortune.*
*No Surrender.*
*Success: and how he Won it.*
*Under a Charm.*

---

*For Continuation see over leaf.*

# BENTLEY'S FAVOURITE NOVELS—*Continued.*

Each work can be had separately, price 6s., of all Booksellers in
Town or Country.

By JESSIE FOTHERGILL.

*The 'First Violin.'*
*Aldyth.*
*Borderland.*
*Healey.*
*Kith and Kin.*
*Probation.*

By RICHARD JEFFERIES.

*The Dewy Morn.*

By HELEN MATHERS.

*Comin' thro' the Rye.*

By MARCUS CLARKE.

*For the Term of his Natural
Life.*

By Mrs. ANNIE EDWARDES.

*Ought We to Visit Her ?*
*Leah : a Woman of Fashion,*
*A Girton Girl.*

By Mrs. A. CRAVEN.

*A Sister's Story.*

By Mrs. NOTLEY.

*Olive Varcoe.*

By the Hon. L. WINGFIELD.

*Lady Grizel.*

By FRANCES M. PEARD.

*Near Neighbours.*

By Baroness TAUTPHŒUS.

*The Initials.* | *Quits !*

By RHODA BROUGHTON.

*Cometh up as a Flower.*
*Good-bye, Sweetheart !*
*Joan.* | *Nancy.*
*Not Wisely, but too Well.*
*Red as a Rose is She.*
*Second Thoughts.*
*Belinda.* | *Alas !*
*'Doctor Cupid.'*

By J. SHERIDAN LE FANU.

*Uncle Silas.*
*In a Glass Darkly.*
*The House by the Churchyard.*

By F. MONTGOMERY.

*Misunderstood.*
*Thrown Together.*
*Seaforth.*

By HECTOR MALOT.

*No Relations.*
(With Illustrations.)

By Lady G. FULLERTON.

*Ladybird.*
*Too Strange not to be True.*

By HENRY ERROLL.

*An Ugly Duckling.*

ANONYMOUS.

*The Last of the Cavaliers.*
*Sir Charles Danvers.*

LONDON

RICHARD BENTLEY & SON, NEW BURLINGTON STREET

Publishers in Ordinary to Her Majesty the Queen